A
WOMAN'S
AGE

Rachel Billington

SUMMIT BOOKS
NEW YORK

Published by *Summit Books*
A Simon & Schuster Division of Gulf & Western Corporation
Simon & Schuster Building
1230 Avenue of the Americas
New York, New York 10020

Manufactured in the United States of America

Published in Great Britain by Hamish Hamilton Ltd.

Printed and bound by Fairfield Graphics

1   2   3   4   5   6   7   8   9   10

Library of Congress Cataloging in Publication Data

Billington, Rachel.
  A woman's age.
  I.Title.
PZ4.B5985W0 1980   [PR6052.I4]   823'.9'14   79-23723
ISBN 0-671-40115-7

To Kevin

Acknowledgments

With thanks to the many women (especially my mother) who were interviewed by me about their own experiences from 1905 to 1975.

Part One

Chapter One

The Church Army's Fresh Air Homes give change and rest by sea and in country to weary and ailing MOTHERS and LITTLE ONES from the slums. The mothers pay what they can: pray HELP them. £2 gives two weeks holiday to mother and two children.
(Special Announcement) *The Times.*   6 September 1910

ANTI-SUFFRAGE LEAGUE
M.A.M. Maconachie has concluded a three weeks' campaign in seaside resorts on the East and South Coast on behalf of the National Anti–Woman Suffrage League. In spite of vigorous heckling, chiefly by Woman suffragists and occasionally by Socialists, the resolution against women suffrage was, we are informed, with one doubtful exception, carried in every case, and generally with overwhelming majorities.
The Times.   13 September 1910

Debenham & Freebody
Famous for over a Century for Taste, for Quality, for Value.
VELVETEEN FROCKS.
Velveteen is now extremely fashionable. The latest improvement in dye and finish have made it an excellent material for Frocks . . . We have in stock a large selection of Day Gowns trimmed with silk braid, cords and buttons, bodice lined silk, yoke and cuffs of oxydised net. In black, green, grey, brown and heliotrope. 98/6d.
(Advertisement) *The Times.*   21 September 1910

TO ALL WHO CALL THEMSELVES ENGLISH GENTLEMEN—ARE YOU DRILLED AND ARMED AND READY TO DEFEND YOUR COUNTRY?
(Personal column) *The Times.*   4 August 1914

My mother snatched the hat off her thick coils of dark hair and threw it triumphantly across the lawn. I watched it sail, veil fluttering, cornflowers bobbing, and forgot to watch the croquet ball.

The red ball sped across the short dry grass and cracked into the back of my plump legs. Ignoring my white lace dress, I rolled on the ground and screamed.

'I was winning!' cried my mother angrily. 'How could you, Vi! And do stop that caterwauling.' She smacked the grass with her mallet.

The stiff dark-blue figure of Nanny appeared from behind her. Over her arm she carried my white stockings and a pair of pink button shoes with rosettes. She didn't hurry. Her face wore an expression of satisfaction. She had told Lady Eleanor I was too young to be out among the gentlemen. And with bare legs. However hot, it was still September.

Two gentlemen stepped forward from a spidery grove of damson trees which fringed the lawn. The long shadows of their drainpipe legs mixed with the shadows of the trunks. I looked up.

'I'm hungry,' said my mother's brother. He was called Eddie Pemberton. They shared the same dark hair, blue eyes and straight black eyebrows.

My mother drew her eyebrows together furiously. She was never very convincing as an Edwardian lady. 'I was winning!'

'Ra-ra-rather,' agreed Eddie's friend, Henry Nettlefield. He was slight and pale and had brown curls not unlike mine. He stammered on the letter *r*.

Nanny reached me and I stopped crying. She brushed me down energetically. Now perhaps she would be allowed to whisk me back to the nursery for a bowl of soothing custard. The new copy of *Home Chat* had just arrived. She preferred the *Tatler* but it seldom survived my mother's onslaught in the drawing room.

My mother decided to comfort me. The organdie frill at the hem of her long white dress bounced over the stubby grass as she ran towards me.

'Poor darling Vi! Did it hurt dreadfully?' She clasped her arms round me. She smelled sweet, but I wasn't used to her caresses and a brooch at her bosom pressed into my forehead.

Eddie's friend came closer. It was a pretty picture. He liked children.

'No, Mama!' I struggled free. 'I'm better now.'

Mama was rejected. She looked as if she might cry.

'What a scene!' said Eddie disgustedly. 'I'm hungry.'

My father appeared from a thick wall of rhododendrons which separated this part of the garden from the house.

Mama turned her back on me. 'I was winning!' she cried.
'Tea's ready,' said my father. His dark-suited figure was hardly visible against the lustrous green leaves of the rhododendrons.

Henry Nettlefield who, for no reason at all, was always known as Nettles, picked up the red croquet ball. He weighed it in his hand. 'It must have hurt you,' he said to me kindly.

My mother glanced at him angrily. 'We can't even play a proper game of croquet in this wilderness!' she screamed. 'When was the lawn last mowed? And look at the trees.'

My father stood still in front of the shining leaves. 'It's teatime,' he repeated mildly. 'I'm sorry you had an accident.'

Nanny took my hand firmly. 'I'll take Miss Violet upstairs now.'

'Tea?' Mama advanced on my father. But before she reached him, her eye was attracted by her hat sitting on the lawn. She stopped, picked it up, straightened the veil, and pinned it back on her head. The action soothed her. She stroked her satin sash and smiled at my father. 'Have tea brought out to my rose garden.' She turned to Nanny. 'Put on Miss Violet's shoes and stockings, Fig, and bring her to join us. You might even brush her hair.' She smiled again and stood with arms outstretched until Eddie and Nettles came to escort her on either side.

'Why was Mama so cross?' Papa and I sat waiting in the rose garden. May Fig, my nanny, had gone to fetch me a coat. Mama had taken a detour to visit the stables.

'Because she's young.' He sighed and looked at the roses which fanned out round us, varying from the purest white through pink to deepest crimson. 'Your mother is very talented. She made this garden all herself. Before she came, it was part of the field.'

'She's not young. I'm young.'

'She's fifteen years younger than me.'

'You're old. When you were young you were a soldier. Nanny told me. What are you now?'

'A farmer.' My father sighed again.

On the horizon, a procession of servants bearing the tea things wound down the grassy path. I saw a white tablecloth, a silver-domed dish, a gleaming teapot, and a large chocolate cake dusted with sugar. I couldn't think why Papa looked so sad. To the right, I caught a glimpse of my mother's white dress between her two escorts. Behind the cake, I saw Nanny's hurrying figure.

I turned to Papa with my last gasp of freedom. 'Are Uncle Eddie and his friend young too?'

'Yes. And they live in London. And Mr Nettlefield has money.'

'You've got lots of money.'

5

'For a farmer. But I can't afford a house in London or a box at the opera or the things your mother had before we married. Your mother's the daughter of an earl.'

The tea arrived. And then Mama. Her cheeks were pink. She was pretending to be a horse.

'Neigh-eigh-eigh-eigh! Have you ever heard a guest neighing good evening, Nettles?'

'Not that I re-re-remember.'

'Our neigh-neigh-neigh-neighbours ride horses, think horses, talk horses.'

I watched, fascinated, as her delicate red mouth gaped and contorted. Perhaps she wanted to be an opera singer. Nanny stuffed my arms into a coat as if she wished it were a strait jacket.

'Do you know Northumberland, Mr Nettlefield?' asked my father.

My mother stopped neighing and poured out tea. She didn't appear to be listening to the polite conversation about her home and its surroundings. She tipped the elegant milk jug and dropped the sugar lumps with a pair of silver tongs. She smiled at her roses.

'The mountains are much bigger than I expected,' said Nettles.

My mother sat with her back to the mountains. They were only a few hundred yards away, tall and black and menacing. Soon the bracken at their base would turn brown and crackling.

'It's because they're called moors,' said Papa. 'My grandfather found coal further along the same ridge. That's when he built the house.' He sounded proud but looked nervously at my mother.

'I hate them,' she said, catching his eye. But she seemed more resigned than passionate. She swivelled round and waved her hand. A puff of sugar rose from a piece of cake she held. 'The shadow. Do you see the shadow? A great black line coming to eat up our sun before the day is half finished.'

'I have suggested removing our house to the other side of the moors,' said Papa, attempting a joke. My mother knew he was only speaking the truth, but that was not the point.

'Sometimes in winter, the sun never climbs over the mountain at all.'

'I think it's magnificent!' exclaimed Nettles, looking at my father. 'The house, the setting, everything. I can't think of a man I envy more!'

My mother began to tap her foot impatiently. The long white tablecloth waved. It looked as if there was a dog under the table. I would have liked a dog for a friend. I lost interest in the grown-ups.

Nanny was the nearest I had to a friend. I was the nearest she had,

6

too. In the evening when I was bathed and ready for bed, she relaxed enough to tell me about her many brothers and sisters and her hardworking mother and sick father. Sometimes she let me unplait her hair, which lay in complicated snakes all over her head. I loved to brush it gently down her back.

When she came to bed herself, I tried to wake up so I could watch her undressing under the voluminous tent of her nightdress. If she caught me, she cried out 'Peeping Tom! Peeping Tom!' and once she even giggled. She was only in her early twenties, though she seemed as ageless as the mountains to me.

On rare occasions my mother or father came up to the nursery when I was saying my prayers. They never came together. Papa had a thick, fair moustache, of which he was proud, and a stocky figure, of which he was not so proud. Since he had given up the army, he hunted regularly to keep himself fit. May Fig was in love with him. Once I heard her murmur in her sleep, 'Oh, no! Major Hesketh!' I was shocked that her unconscious should make free with his name.

Most evenings I went downstairs to say good night to my parents. But during the visit from Uncle Eddie and Nettles I hardly went down at all.

The night after they left, I was summoned to the small blue drawing room. It had been my grandmother's favourite room. The tall Venetian windows were almost completely filled with a view of the mountains. My mother stood at the side of them, staring out.

'Mama! Mama!'

'Darling!' She swung round. Although she never seemed to have any real occupation, not even needlepoint like other ladies, she was always impatient, in a hurry. She swept me over to the sofa. 'We're going to read and then we're going to play the piano and then, if you're really good, you shall have a sugared almond.'

She was playing 'The Grand Old Duke of York' when my father came in. She didn't see him and carried on playing. I marched round shouting out the words and flinging my arms in the air. I would have preferred to be a fairy, but didn't dare risk my mother's good humour.

My mother strummed and sang and glowed. A streak of sun shone on her face.

'What a happy sight!' said my father. My mother stopped playing.

'Go on! Go on!' I shouted.

'No. No.' She shut the lid of the piano, but not angrily. She leaned back with a languorous air. 'If only I had something to do.' She appealed to my father. 'If I had something worthwhile to do I wouldn't be so bored. So bored.'

My father went over to her and took her hand. He looked at her

7

admiringly. 'Consider the lilies, how they grow; they toil not, neither do they spin: And yet I say unto you that even Solomon in all his glory was not arrayed like one of these.'

My mother stood up and walked over to the windows. As she reached them, the shaft of sunlight was shut off. 'I know you love me . . .'

'Isn't it time for Vi's bed?' Papa remembered me. Although I was listening hard, I had had the sense to open the book we had been reading. I appeared engrossed.

'Like you loved your mother!' Mama wrenched back a curtain, as if to squeeze out an extra inch of light. To her joy, the faded material tore in her hands. Papa forgot me.

'Rotting! Disintegrating!' shrieked my mother. 'This whole house is a mausoleum. Is it any wonder Eddie and Nettles couldn't stand another minute of it? You talk of love, yet you lock me up in a rotting house where the only possible occupation is having babies and the only entertainment is handing out bloody carcasses of meat to smelly farm workers at Christmas.'

I began to wish Papa had not forgotten me. I listened hopefully for the martial tap of Nanny's feet coming along the corridor. My mother continued shouting. My father spoke gently. He never did raise his voice—not even to a horse.

There was a pause. A cry of delight. I looked up tentatively. Just in time to see my mother kiss my father's cheek. The tears that had been threatening receded.

My mother danced round the room. She flung her arms up as I had been doing a few moments before. 'A Chinese drawing room! Wall covering painted with parrots. Yellow watered silk . . . . Tasselled lanterns in each corner! Oh thank you, Tudor, darling!'

She burst open the Venetian windows and went joyfully to the garden. I heard Nanny's feet—now that I wanted to share in my mother's happiness.

'Mama! Mama! Where are you going?' She was running across the lawn, like a white butterfly, with her full sleeves.

'I'm going to London!' she called over her shoulder.

'Now, Miss Violet,' said Nanny, sensing another battle on her hands, 'bedtime is bedtime, and if Major Hesketh will excuse me I'll shut those windows before we catch our death.'

My mother went to London and returned, and went again. The blue drawing room was ripped apart. Instead, I visited my father in his warm, dark study. I complained to him that life was boring without my mother. 'I'm not a baby,' I said. 'But I only have Nanny to talk to.'

He looked concerned. The next day he told me that he had invited his two sisters and their six children to stay for a month over Christmas.

'They've been longing to come for years, and now Eleanor's so cheerful . . .' He stopped, thinking better of such a confidence. He didn't have anyone much to talk to either.

Priscilla, Dot, and baby Overley-Summers, and Daphne, William, and baby Brand-Snetley arrived on the first of December. Aunt Phyllis and Aunt Letty were following the next day. Nanny and I, equally terrified, hung over the banisters. First their trunks were dragged bumping and scraping up the back stairs, and then they appeared.

'I'm Priscilla. Priscilla Overley-Summers. My father's a peer in his own right. Your mother's only a lady because her father is an earl. It's called a courtesy title.'

Six children, two nannies and two nurserymaids seemed a great deal of people. I stared at Priscilla stupidly.

'I'm the cleverest,' she went on.

'Bossiest,' interrupted William.

'I am the cleverest,' repeated Priscilla calmly. 'Daphne is the prettiest. Dot is the most cheerful.'

'And the greediest,' put in William.

'And then there are the babies and William.' She flicked long, neat plaits over her shoulder and gave him a withering look of scorn. 'He's a boy.'

Their nannies were called Nanny Salmon and Nanny Whistle. My nanny was terrified they'd take over her nursery, but luckily, their energies were mostly reserved for complaining about the cold and the discomfort of the countryside.

'But we're never cold, Nanny,' I said worriedly. 'Why are they different?'

'Because they're Londoners.' Nanny drew herself up. The silver buckle of her belt, which was always the barometer of her emotions and disappeared altogether when she was sad or tired, gleamed proudly. 'They've got soft.'

'Soft,' I repeated with pleasure, glad to have the advantage in something over my cousins.

Nevertheless, the nursery fire blazed night and day, giving my nanny a red button at the top of each cheek. Or it may have been the excitement of company.

I was very excited too. I didn't remain overawed for long. I found the noise level exhilarating. We took turns riding a pony which I had been given for my birthday, and when it was very wet, which it often was, we ran wildly down corridors which I had never dared explore on my own.

Eventually we became so wild that the aunts insisted a lady came from the village to give us lessons. She was the vicar's daughter, called Miss Tiptree, and she brought with her her younger brother and sister, who wore darned stockings and such heavy boots that when they escaped home down the drive it sounded like a cavalry charge. Priscilla called them village children and said they smelled.

The Chinese drawing room was finished the week before Christmas. My mother had no more reason to go to London. She looked at my aunts with disdain. They were reliving their childhood and came back every day from the hunt flushed with health and spattered with mud. My mother lay on her newly covered sofa and read the novels of Ouida.

I overheard Nanny Whistle saying, 'Her Ladyship's a flighty one, all right,' but decided not to explore its meaning.

On Christmas Eve Mama organised a special tea party. Everyone was very cross about it, except us children and her.

'Hold still, Miss Twirlabout.' Nanny Fig tugged at my pink sash.

'I don't know. As if Christmas Day wasn't enough trouble.' Nanny Whistle pulled at Daphne's golden curls so hard that even she, who wanted to look neat and pretty, cried out protestingly.

Tea was wheeled into the drawing room on a vast trolley. The nannies left, mumbling about crumbs on the carpet and rich food before bed.

'Your mother does look beautiful,' whispered Daphne, who knew about fashion.

'She is beautiful,' I said proudly, deciding I could not return the compliment. Aunt Phyllis and Aunt Letty looked like two moorhens beside a peacock.

My mother wore a cherry-red velvet dress trimmed with navy-blue braid. Her cheeks were flushed from toasting cakes at the open fire. She thrust out the copper toasting fork at each of us in turn. 'I love picnics!' she cried. 'Tudor, encourage your sisters to more cake. I know how they adore chocolate!'

My uncles, who had arrived the night before, stood on either side of the mantelpiece. One was tall and one was short, and they both looked at my mother with the same expression of anxious admiration. They knew they were not supposed to admire her.

'Such an original way to celebrate Christ's birthday,' said Aunt Phyllis, who was short and stout. She twitched away a tassel from one of the Chinese lanterns which kept brushing across her face.

'These éclairs are spiffing!' cried William, who had smeared cream across his sailor suit. We were all very hot and beginning to feel sick.

There was the sound of footsteps in the hallway. I thought it was the nannies. Priscilla, more hopeful, cried, 'Father Christmas!' The grown-ups, who were farther from the door, hadn't heard. The door opened. 'Uncle Eddie! Nettles!' I shrieked, showing off to my cousins. They didn't know them. I ran to hug Nettles' legs. He always paid me attention. 'We didn't expect you!' I realised that a total silence had fallen around me. I became embarrassed.

'Good evening, Eddie, Mr Nettlefield,' said my father in an odd strained voice. He took a single step forward so that he was still some yards away. Eddie's outstretched hand dropped. He went red in the face. Nettles patted my head.

My mother crouched by the fire, her toasting fork upraised like a wand.

'Unfortunately,' said my father in a voice like our butler's, 'you've wasted a journey. The house is full.'

'Tudor!' Mama gave an odd birdlike screech. She rose up from the fire.

I dropped away from Nettles' legs and found that the nannies had appeared with grasping fingers.

'Bedtime, children,' cried the aunts too loudly.

'Nettles!' I cried. But the door came between us. The dramatic scene disappeared as if it had never been.

'You'll be seeing Father Christmas if you're not asleep soon, and then where will your presents be?' Nanny tucked in my bedclothes so tightly that I could not even feel the heavy wool stocking on the end of my bed.

Christmas Day took place without Uncle Eddie, Nettles, or Mama. Before we went to bed Papa gathered the house together for evening prayers. After we had sung several carols, he cleared his throat, put his head in his hands. 'We pray that those who have departed may return to the path of duty. Oh Lord, give strength to sinners . . .' The servants' corner shifted noticeably. A young housemaid giggled, and Aunt Phyllis and Aunt Letty chorused 'Amen' in extra-convinced voices.

I lay in bed. On one side I could just see my special presents placed on a special chair; on the other Nanny sat as usual, knitting needles flashing.

'Nanny, what's "departed" mean?'

'Gone away, dear.'

'Nanny, where's Mama gone?'

The knitting needles stopped abruptly. My father had only passed on a message that 'Her Ladyship has gone for a holiday.'

I watched the pointed needles quivering. Nanny had never before stopped knitting when I was lying in bed.

'The seaside!' she said abruptly. 'She's gone for a holiday to the seaside.'

I, who had never been to the seaside, was not struck by the absurdity of the idea. In December.

'The seaside! Oh, Nanny.' It seemed as magical a surrounding as my mother deserved. 'William says they're going to the seaside next year. Perhaps we could go too.'

'Yes, dear.' Nanny breathed a sigh of relief and took up her knitting again. I fell asleep almost immediately and dreamed of silver knitting needles which gradually turned into little silvery waves out of which my mother ascended. Below her waist she had neat rows of scales which were remarkably like Nanny's two-purl, two-plain.

'My mother's a mermaid!' was almost the first thing I said to my cousins when we came together the following summer in Littlehampton. They had all opened their mouths to shout down such an obvious bit of baby-wish when a vicious nudge from Nanny Whistle and a raised finger from Nanny Salmon reminded them that, on pain of no bull's-eyes ever again, they were absolutely forbidden to pronounce my evil mother's name. I rubbed home my victory.

'So you see, water is my element.'

Fantasies, encouraged by months of solitude in Kettleside, were soon dispelled by the bracing reality of Littlehampton. The waves were not silver frills but cold green breakers. My mother hated cold water. St Winifred's, the small residential hotel where we stayed, was decorated with oleographs of dying beasts and smelled of kippers, mutton, apple dumplings, dried pampas grass, and seaweed. The chairs and the mattresses were stuffed with horsehair. The only other inhabitants were decaying naval men who were too cowed to protest when on rainy days we trampled over their crossword puzzles.

My mother would not return to St Winifred's.

It was true that when the aunts paid us a three-day visit they stayed at the Grand Hotel, which was on the front and flew a flag, but by that time I'd already given up hope. I was not unhappy, because I had realised that although the seaside would not suit my mother, it suited me excellently.

Each morning we set off for the beach. The nannies settled themselves like great broody birds on the crest of the beach while we children threw off the hateful boots, scratchy stockings, and starched petticoats, and ran, screeching like gulls, to the water. We built our sand castles, collected shells and seaweed, played tag with the energy of escaped prisoners. The nannies, with the babies crawling at their skirts, were far enough away to make us feel we were alone. We only returned to them after bathing when it was considered necessary to raise the blood sugar level by eating a bagful of biscuits.

'I'm going to be a beach attendant when I grow up,' I said, languid in the sun.

'You can't. You have to be a man. A working man,' objected Priscilla aggressively.

'I'll be the first lady attendant. When people give me a penny for the deck chair, I'll say, "Thank you ever so" and tip my cap.'

'What rot you girls talk,' said William. 'I'm glad the chaps at school can't hear you.'

'Tomorrow,' said beautiful Daphne, shaking her golden hair so that sand fell out of it like stardust, 'we'll be on the train.'

'I'm hungry,' said fat Dot, tugging at the heavy wool of her bathing dress. 'Let's have a swim.'

When I returned to Kettleside, my father was very impressed by my round sunburnt face and open smile. The seaside was made an annual event.

At Kettleside my companions were Miss Tiptree and her younger brother and sister, who still came obediently to the schoolroom despite my rudeness and disdain, Nanny, my father, and Flo.

Flo was a new housemaid who looked after me for a couple of months when Nanny had to return home to care for her dying father. Flo had a magnetic personality. She came from Scotland and was nearly as tall as my father, with shoulders as broad and arms as strong. She had hair the colour of the inside of a blood orange. She felt it her Christian duty to counterbalance the severity of Nanny's routine.

'Let's have a bit of fun,' she cried after I had stood at my bedroom window and watched Nanny's departure. The tears swilled round my eyes. I wore my long white nightdress.

'I'm waiting for Papa to come up and hear my prayers.'

'A bit of fun won't do you no harm.'

Flo bunched up her skirts and danced a jig. The coarse red hair above her thick red face exploded out of its bun and bounced about like steel springs. Her huge arms, sleeves rolled to the elbow, shot up and down like pistons; her stockinged feet worked in intricate patterns on the floorboards.

My sense of being abandoned disappeared. 'Oh, how glorious!' I shrieked, hardly able to believe my eyes.

'You've seen nothing yet!' Flo, panting heavily, fell for a moment to the ground. 'Just let me get my breath back and I'll do the bagpipes for you.'

13

'The bagpipes! Scotch bagpipes?'

Blowing out her cheeks till they looked like croquet balls, she produced the most extraordinary sound, halfway between a wounded cat and a creaking door. I gaped admiringly.

A long wheezing groan indicated her running out of breath. 'Did you recognise the tune, then?'

I had to confess I hadn't, but Flo admitted cheeringly that not many did, though 'Bluebells of Scotland' was nearly as well known South as North. Besides, she was keen to get on to what was to her the grand climax of her repertoire. She stood in the middle of the room, cleared her throat, slightly hoarse after the bagpipes, and announced, 'A Medley of Harry Lauder Songs!' This meant nothing to me, but the whole event was so amazing and unexpected that I sat enraptured for ten minutes while Flo, occasionally kicking out her large feet, intoned:

Oh! It's nice to get up in the morning
But it's nicer to lie in bed . . .

At the end I clapped enthusiastically, adding a few genteel 'bravos' as further appreciation.

'Oh, Flo! Why have you never sung before?'

'In Mrs Fig's nursery? I'd be packing my box directly.' She assumed a slightly coy expression, absurd on her large features, interrupted by a sudden leap. Further questions had to be deferred, for shoes and hairpins. 'It's the Major. No telling, mind.'

I dropped innocently to my knees.

After Mama's departure my father became noticeably keener on prayers and church. He also spent more time with me. Sometimes he passed a whole morning in the schoolroom.

'God bless Papa, Nanny, the aunts, the cousins . . .'

'Shouldn't you name them?'

'It takes so long . . . Aunt Phyllis, Aunt Letty . . . Can I come to your study tomorrow? It's so interesting.'

Papa was easily diverted by flattery. 'I suppose you want to see my lantern slides.'

'Oh, yes. The ladies with wigs.' This was a series of Chinese ladies with parasols and stubby feet. Papa had not yet realised it recalled Mama's Chinese room, which had been locked up like Bluebeard's chamber after her departure. Once I had a terrible dream in which Papa's moustache had extended into a long black beard and he'd emerged from the room carrying Mama's head by the hair. As we approached her, Mama had opened her mouth and said in exquisite tones, 'How charming, my dear.' Nanny, woken by my screams of terror, had called it growing pains.

14

'After Aunt Letty?' prompted Papa.

'Flo.'

'Who?'

'Flo. She's the new housemaid. She's . . . first-rate.' This was a word learned from William. I took my father's smile as a compliment. He stopped smiling.

'I'm sure she is. But you don't put a housemaid in your prayers.'

'Why not?' I began to feel sulky. The glowing strains of Harry Lauder died from inside me. I remembered there would be no Nanny clicking her needles or rustling *Home Chat*. I began to feel sorry for myself.

'It's not that I don't like Flo . . .'

'I can't pray for anyone that matters.'

'Of course you can, darling. If you really feel so strongly, please put in Flo. I'm sure she deserves your prayers as much as any of us.'

'I can't pray for Mama!'

There was a terrifying silence during which I regretted my bravado. In fact I was no longer upset by my mother's absence, and although I always added her name to my list under my breath, I did it more out of habit than feeling.

My father stood up. I kept very still. He sat down again. He took my hand. 'Poor little Vi,' he said gently.

'Oh, no!' I protested, aggressive in my relief. He was not angry.

'Are you very lonely?'

'Oh, no!' I repeated hastily. 'Now I see the cousins at the seaside and at Christmas, and Miss Tiptree for lessons. If anything, I'm short of time to myself.'

Papa bent and kissed my forehead. Perhaps I should risk a different question.

'Papa?'

'Yes, my dear?'

'My cousins say the aunts say you'll marry again. They say men like wives and I need a mother.'

This time my father didn't react at all. His hand continued slowly stroking my forehead. 'Your aunts have our best interests at heart, but I shan't marry again.'

'I don't like Cousin Cynthia, Miss Blessop, nor the Honorable Alice Tinknell.' Half asleep, I recited the names of the various unmarried ladies whom the aunts had produced at the house. 'I very much don't like the Honorable Alice Tinknell even if her father is a lord.'

On the whole, I paid proper attention to the cousins' attitude towards class. I knew, for example, that it would be best not to encourage Flo's familiarity when they were visiting. Occasionally my attempts to imitate their superior manner went very wrong.

When they arrived in the winter of 1911 I made them accompany me to the kitchen, where a new cook was installing herself. Cooks came and went rapidly, since they didn't like taking orders from a man and thought Nanny took too much on herself.

'Welcome, Mrs Gaunt,' I announced grandly. 'I am Miss Hesketh. You will do what I say. I am your mistress. I would like a pink birthday cake with absolutely no marzipan.'

Mrs Gaunt fingered some wisps of hair on her chin. 'My mistress, are you? Well, I heard something different. I heard my mistress, Mrs Hesketh, lives on an island inhabited by wild Irish savages and that her feet are never shod and her hair never combed. My mistress indeed.' Mrs Gaunt snorted contemptuously.

'Lady Eleanor Hesketh,' I retaliated bravely, but my spirit was confused. Mama on an island? Swum to an island?

I ran from Mrs Gaunt's sneering face into the bleak winter garden. The cousins followed me calling, 'Vi! Vi! Wait for me-e-e-e!' I careered down the grassy paths, broke through the fat-leaved rhododendrons, and came out to Mama's rose garden set so neatly below the mountains.

I looked round wildly. I had expected to see only prickly stumps fanning out round the little paved centrepiece. But now there was nothing. I burst into tears.

The cousins came panting round me. 'I wish my mother lived on an island.' Priscilla tried to respect the embargo on my mother's name. She put her arm round my shoulders comfortingly.

'They've dug them all up,' I sobbed. 'Look. Just a horrid patch of brown earth.'

'What?' The cousins didn't understand.

'My mother's roses. They were so beautiful. She loved them more than anything.'

'Roses?' The cousins decided to concentrate on the island. 'I expect she looks like a nymph with bare feet and flowing locks. Perhaps we could play nymphs and shepherds?'

Daphne became enthusiastic. 'We could make paper garlands and unplait our hair.'

I stopped crying. 'Perhaps the island is that precious stone set in a silver sea.'

'And the roses,' said William in a matter-of-fact voice, 'have been sent to garland her there.'

In fact although my father had ordered the roses to be dug out and then buried, they reappeared the following summer in farm workers' back gardens all over the estate.

But now there was no memorial to my mother except the blank shuttered windows of the Chinese drawing room. Sometimes I stood in the garden and looked back at the house searching for those two blind eyes. If it was sunny, I wouldn't be able to find them and for a minute would think the shutters had been opened. But when the sun slid behind clouds or was clipped off by the mountains, I could see them again, tall and pale.

I didn't think of things like that when my cousins visited and when we went to the seaside. Nanny said with pride, 'You're so quick, you'll meet yourself coming back.' But for nine months of the year I hardly saw another child—unless you counted the schoolroom, which I didn't.

Flo was my friend, and Nanny. Her silver buckle winked with approval when I recited the whole of 'Up the Airy Mountain' by heart. She even tolerated Flo's antics enough to let her play her bagpipes behind our rendering of 'Abide with Me.' Nevertheless, I banished her from my room on my seventh birthday. 'You're far too old for a nanny,' William had said scornfully. 'And sleeping in your room, too. It's disgusting!' So Nanny moved out, taking her knitting and her whalebone corset, and I missed her very much.

Although I often argued fiercely with the cousins, I usually did what they considered right, even when it was against my own interests. They were my experts on the world outside Kettleside. However, even then at the age of seven, I did sometimes find their attitudes infuriatingly stuffy. Then I would show off, shouting all the things I knew would offend them most. 'I won't wear gloves for church! I won't! I won't!' 'I love Flo! I love her far more than any of you!' 'When I go riding, Alan' (this was the stableboy) 'calls me Vi! Once he touched my bare hand!'

The stables and the hunting field were very good places to show off, because the cousins were used only to quiet rides in Rotten Row. My father kept few horses for an ex-army hunting man, and the passing of Her Ladyship had seen the early exit of a black mare she had ridden sporadically and two tougher specimens used for pulling her carriage. There were three hunters, several old carriage horses which my father refused to swap for a car, and a couple of cart horses come up from the farm—much to the annoyance of Tigger, the head groom. Nevertheless, it was empire enough for me. There was no 'I am your mistress' here. Instead, I listened to endless lectures on the usefulness of spitting on tack and the right heat of a bran mash. Although secretly nervous of my dappled pony, who rolled his eyes under a thick shock of hair and whose tail dragged behind him like a train, I rode him valiantly. On the Boxing Day after my eighth birthday I joined the meet in front of our house. I was glad to see that Priscilla, Dot, William, and Daphne, on their borrowed ponies, looked openly anxious.

'It's because we don't know our mounts,' cried William defensively.

'No, it's not.' I was not allowing any wishy-washy excuses. 'You're frightened, that's all. I mean to be in at the kill!'

'You're just bloodthirsty,' shouted Dot.

'No, I'm not.' I kicked my pony while reining him back so that he gave a dramatic rear. 'I've just got more of the killer's instinct.'

'That's the spirit, my gel,' an old colonel, riding heavily, legs stuck forward, face dark red, congratulated me. 'We may be needing that soon.'

'Does a good soldier need it?' Papa, who had just mounted, joined us.

'What? What's that?' the colonel shouted, either not hearing or not wishing to hear. Personal reflections were hardly proper. 'You've always been a straight man in the field. Shouldn't have resigned. May get another chance.'

It seemed impossible that his words, rising above the loud country voices, the stamping of iron-shod hooves, and, farther down the drive, the baying of hounds, referred to war.

'War,' murmured Papa.

'I've got the killer's instinct,' I shouted.

'I hope not,' said Papa.

'You've always been a straight man in the field,' repeated the colonel. 'That's what counts in a charge. Head down, hard and straight as a good run between Crippling Copse and Fox Down. Think of Hillsdale Wood as the enemy. If I was a few years younger . . .'

He flapped shiny boots against his horse's flanks. For now we were on the move, lining up into a procession, pink-coated MFH at the front, old colonels and fathers next, children of the gentry fast behind and finally the *hoi polloi* riding whatever cart horse was available. It was a strange sort of cavalry, clinking and clattering away from our house. The footmen, standing in a line on the lawn with trays of empty port glasses in their hands, formed a Gilbert-and-Sullivan homeguard.

War found me at the seaside. I had gone there as usual with the cousins. The first indication of something astir in the world outside panama hats and shrimping nets was the way grown-ups constantly disappeared behind newspapers.

'I never thought people read before this summer,' said Daphne.

'It's the heat! They're shielding their faces.'

'They're reading,' insisted Daphne, and after a short exploration,

18

it was agreed the nearest four were actually in the process of reading.

'It's very hot,' said one of the babies, who wasn't a baby any more. So we all went for a swim. Only Priscilla and William could remember a hotter summer.

'Nineteen eleven,' said William.

'Nineteen ten,' said Priscilla.

I hung around the grown-ups. They sat in deck chairs, drinking tea out of thermos flasks. I could feel the excitement. Nannies and nurserymaids never got excited over things in the outside world. They were no use for information.

I saw another opportunity for showing off. I picked on ajportly moustachioed man who looked like a self-indulgent version of my father. He was deeply immersed in *The Times*. I wore a very pretty sailor dress, and although I had no opportunity to brush my hair, I was confident of making a good impression.

Placing my hands together and swaying slightly as if reciting Masefield's 'I must down to the seas again' for Miss Tiptree, I began in a sweet tone, 'I am sorry to trouble . . .'

I got no further. The gentleman, laying aside his newspaper with a flourish, bawled to his companion, a gentleman just like himself, 'It must be War!'

Jumping backwards in surprise, I clapped my hands and shouted 'Bravo!' which certainly surprised them.

'It must be war! It must be war!' I ran to the cousins, who were absorbed in a complicated game of French and English. 'It must be war!' I shouted.

'Which are you, French or English?' Priscilla's face was red, her plaits, unusual for someone normally neat, half unravelled.

'Fool! A real war. There's a real war coming *now*!' I kicked a pile of pebbles to underline my point.

'Here! That's our base.' Dot ran after a large pink stone.

'It must be war!' I shrieked.

'That's nothing new.' William sauntered over, hands in pockets. 'Anybody who goes to a decent school knows all about the Balkans.'

I allowed myself no doubts. 'No. No. You're all so ill-educated. This is nothing to do with the silly old Balkans. A new war! A holocaust! The End of the World!'

The following day, 4 August, war was duly declared amidst much rejoicing. Our rejoicing was curtailed by a summons to return home immediately. The only consolation during the return journey was the number of soldiers hanging around the station and eventually boarding the same London train. Flo and Nanny Whistle's nurserymaid became very giggly and had to be severely reprimanded.

'Poor lads,' said Flo defensively, 'they need a speck of gaiety, going out to their deaths.'

'Nonsense.' Nurse Salmon took off her bonnet and settled a baby between herself and the huge packed lunch. 'It's only troop dispositions.'

I found it all most exhilarating, and my farewell to the cousins as Nanny, Flo and I changed trains for the journey up North was not the usual sad affair. 'They might take me on as a drummer!' shrieked William happily. The grand climax was reached on our arrival at Newcastle station, where a wild contingent of Scottish soldiers marched and sang and played their bagpipes to an appreciative crowd. Flo lost all control, joined the shouting, clapping crowd, and was dragged away only after several minutes by Nanny, who was terrified of what the whirling skirts might reveal.

When we arrived at Kettleside, I was summoned to my father's study. He looked very grave, and I noticed suddenly that he no longer inclined to stoutness. He was quite thin. I looked with disapproval at his slippers, which I considered a sign of old age. He made me sit by him.

'I wanted to tell you myself, Violet dear, that I have rejoined the army.'

'Oh, Papa! Papa!'

'It is my duty.'

'But Papa, I'm pleased!'

'Oh.' There was a pause while he digested this. He had imagined I would be upset. 'At first I will be in England.'

'On troop dispositions,' I put in knowingly.

'Quite. And eventually I will go to the front. But not for some time yet—so you mustn't worry.'

'Oh, Papa, I'm so glad!'

'I've been out of the army for ten years.'

'Maybe you'll become a hero!'

Heroes became my preoccupation. But even heroes were not enough to make up for the changes that took place in the first months of the war.

Papa seldom returned home from troop dispositions, the stable was emptied of all but the very oldest cart horses and one young lad, and the house staff was reduced to the ancient butler, my enemy the cook, Flo, and Nanny. I tried to be 'patriotic' about it all, a word that was on everybody's lips. I understood that the men had gone to join the army, as befits the employees of an army man; I understood the women were 'doing War Work' at the munitions factory in Newcastle. But it was difficult to feel it personally. Miss Tiptree's departure to make wool for soldiers' socks out of the coats of pet dogs meant no more learning, except what Nanny could make out from her textbooks. The nursery fire was banned owing to a shortage of fuel. Soon the whole house became exceedingly cold, and I developed chilblains on my little toes and little fingers. My complaints met with no sympathy but the stern reminder that 'our men at the front are losing their toes and fingers and their noses with frostbite, so what cause have you to complain?' This information merely gave me terrible nightmares in which fingerless, toeless, noseless khaki-clad figures jostled me in Newcastle station.

'I wish to be patriotic,' I explained to my father, who returned for a short leave just before Christmas. 'But there seems nothing I can do.'

The next day the cousins arrived, and the following day the Very Reverend Mr Tiptree gave us all a short talk on war work. Although prayer inevitably figured high, there were also such suggestions as collecting peach stones, plum stones, and horse chestnuts—difficult, it was generally agreed, in December—and gathering wood and fir cones to take the place of coal—a more seasonable occupation.

We children, our nurses and nurserymaids, plus two new very small babies who had appeared since the summer, listened politely to this advice, but secretly were much disappointed to see the Reverend without his vestments. His singsong delivery remained, but his figure was much diminished. We thought he should volunteer for army chaplain and be a hero. I soon infected the cousins with my passion for heroes. I could do more about it now that I was no longer on my own. I invented Heroes and Cowards, which took us for long hours into the rhododendron bushes. The older babies were posted outside the dark tangled branches and instructed to watch for spies or enemy aliens. They did not like the job and often cried, bringing a shivering nurserymaid who said she wondered they all didn't catch their deaths.

'Better than bullets, you traitor!' William and I shouted.

When in February the cousins finally disappeared, carrying a whole sackful of fir cones for use in London, I remained obsessional on the subject of heroes. I set myself an essay entitled 'What Makes a Hero?' in which assets such as 'ability to fight on one hour's sleep out of twenty-four' mixed with 'a noble brow' and my own much vaunted 'killer's instinct.'

I waited impatiently for my father to be posted to the front. The call came at last in March. My father took me into his study again and said with an oddly embarrassed look, 'Well, it's come, my dear. I shall be leading off my men early next week.'

At last there could be a real hero in the family! Uncle Bertie was still on troop movements in England, and Uncle Arthur wasn't even in uniform. He sat in some office in London, and it was no good Daphne's pretending you could be a hero that way! I began to plan the letter I would write to them. 'Dear William, Daphne, Hetty and baby, Today Papa left for the front . . .'

'You don't look very sad to hear I'm going.' His tone had become almost wistful.

'I will when you actually go.' I tried to be consoling, but I was interrupted by an urgent thought. 'I can come to the station, I suppose?'

Midnight on Newcastle station. It was wartime cold. I was wrapped in a large tweed coat. I hugged Papa, who wore a double-breasted khaki overcoat so thick that I couldn't feel any living being underneath.

'I feel as if you'd gone already,' I cried.

The station was empty save for half a dozen guards, a couple of policemen, and a few other officers. Only the very long train, steaming and staring, made the imminent departure of a segment of His Majesty's army seem at all probable.

May Fig looked on. Her heart was as involved as mine. This was Major Hesketh, on whom her whole life depended, going off to the wars. She understood very well what risks were involved, how great the chance that he would not return. Lately the old butler had circulated *The Times* before stacking it down in the cellar, so she knew all about the casualty lists and the huge numbers of officers lost. She was not interested in heroes. Headlines like 'British Gallantry' were followed by 'Two Thousand Killed.'

'Keep your gloves on, child,' she scolded.

My father beat his heavily gloved hands together. Nanny had knitted them. She tightened her rabbit-fur collar above her close-buttoned coat.

I burst out, 'I do wish the soldiers would come. The train's been steaming and grunting for ages.'

'They'll have come and gone soon enough.'

It was true. Suddenly the dark corners of the station were blocked out with a great rush of khaki soldiers. They were jostling and shouting, their huge packs turning them into misshapen monsters. Blocking out the dark, they blocked out the wavering gaslights too, so that only their brass buttons and cold faces gleamed. It was a weird, frightening onslaught, which made me turn nervously to Nanny. But before it could overwhelm me I found myself swiftly lifted and placed securely on top of a large iron trolley chained to a pillar. Papa and I were face to face. A strange expression came into his eyes, Now that I was level with him, I noticed they were a strange greenish-grey colour.

'Do you ever think about your mother?' he blurted out suddenly.

22

'Oh no, never!' I replied just as quickly. This was almost true, but I wasn't sure if my blithe statement pleased or disappointed him. It was the first time my mother's name had been mentioned since that evening at prayers.

Papa pulled at his moustache in great embarrassment. 'She wasn't a bad woman, you know.'

I began to feel embarrassed too, and turning my head away from his anxious eyes, I caught a fiercely disapproving stare from Nanny. I was in grave danger of giggling. Instead, I cried out, 'Is she dead, then?'

My father took a step back and looked wildly at the train behind him. I thought he would get on without answering. Then he suddenly gave me a bear hug and a kiss, released me abruptly, and said firmly, 'No. She's quite well, very well, I believe. And although I cannot forgive her, I expect you will someday.' He gave me another hug. 'Goodbye, my dear. Goodbye, Fig. Take care of Miss Violet.' And he bounded for the train. It was as if our conversation had given him a sense of relief.

The stamping and pushing was transferring into the train. The noise increased with the crashing of doors and banging of windows as they were lowered abruptly one after another. I couldn't see my father.

'Is that him?' I cried. 'Or that one? At the end!'

Both men wore fair moustaches, both waved, for now that the the the greatcoats had departed the platform, a sediment of heavily muffled women and a few children stood in abandoned groups. 'Oh, no! The train's moving. And Nanny, listen!'

My view was obliterated by the soldiers filling every window, who had begun to sing. First it was 'Tipperary' and then, as one end of the train succeeded the other, 'Take Me Back to Dear Old Blighty.'

'It's too wonderfully sad.' Tears filled my eyes for the first time. I had lost my chance of seeing Papa.

For the next few months, March, April, May, June, 1915, I followed the war as closely as any general. I somehow got hold of *The Times* weekly 'History of the War,' which had started in August the previous year and kept its subscribers up to date on the latest events. I read *The Times* itself and followed the action on a large map pinned to the wall of my father's study, to which I had special permission for a daily visit. When his letters started arriving about a month after his departure, I was able to understand them better than most adults. They were detailed letters, sometimes, to my fury, blacked out or cut by the censor. They seemed to be written more as a record for himself than for a nine-year-old girl. Alone in that big gloomy house, I found my imagination gripped by his letters. In April, Ypres and The Salient meant more to me than any part of Northumberland. The spurs running north to south on The Salient, the Poelkapelle Ridge, the Gravenstafel Ridge, the Zonnebeke Ridge, the Frezenberg Ridge, the Bellewaarde Ridge were more vivid than the grouse moors. I knew the farm buildings, usually stoutly built, often surrounded with water, which formed strongpoints, fought for over and over again, better than the vicarage or our own farm manager's house or the cottages around it. I even understood the joke in a copy of *The Wipers Times* which he once included, parodying an advertisement with the paragraph 'For Exchange—A Salient, in good condition. Will exchange for a Pair of Pigeons, or a Canary—Apply Lonely Soldier, Hooge.'

I rejoiced in the moment when reinforcements arrived in London, motor buses still bearing the familiar advertisements for Mellin's Food. Casualty lists—out of two battalions involved in one assault, four officers lost and 284 NCOs and men—made me more exhilarated rather than less.

'Nanny!' I exulted one morning, 'the Canadians call Papa's soldiers the mad Durhams because they're so brave.' But Nanny would only infuriate me with her sighing.

'Mad is true enough. But it won't do for a funeral stone.'

Then at last I found an ally in a Belgian refugee lady who appeared as governess. She arrived with a suitably tragic lack of luggage and news of the *Lusitania*'s sinking. 'One thousand three hundred and fourteen lives lost,' she announced with energetic doom. Already she herself had lost father, two brothers, three cousins, and one uncle. What joy it was to have someone who didn't think trenches and funk holes were something to do with fox hunting. In June we traced with excitement the fighting in and near Sanctuary Wood; worried over 'the hairbrush bomb' and 'the jam-pot bomb,' which hardly sounded right for the twentieth century; laughed hysterically over the Germans' attempt to stop night patrolling. They held up boards reading, 'Northumbrians! Why don't you let us sleep?'

As summer moved slowly northwards, a delay much resented by Mademoiselle, who suffered terribly from the cold easterly winds and bleak landscape, a letter arrived announcing the arrival of the cousins. No seaside this war year, but an indefinitely extended stay. London was too difficult. Aunt Phyllis and Aunt Letty were fully occupied with the Red Cross. Shortly before they arrived at the beginning of July, Flo left. She had been ashamed of 'a great hearty girl like myself doing so little for my country,' and despite her much more obvious suitability to be a land girl, she determined to go to town and help turn out munitions. Nanny suspected the soldiers on leave were the real draw. When she left, I threw my arms round her neck and cried, 'You won't forget me!' and she gave a long-drawn-out wail like the lowest note of her bagpipe imitation. Her huge shoulders heaved like a ship.

When the nannies arrived, it turned out there was not a nursery-maid left between them. Heavy trays of old potatoes and barley bread, which was green and sticky and didn't taste like bread at all, particularly without butter, had to be carried along corridors and up endless stairs by arms that were used to no more than the smallest baby. The result was much more freedom for the elder children.

Mademoiselle, who was supposed to keep our minds alive two hours a day, discovered a Belgian relative in Edinburgh. 'Nine English children are worse than a division of Boches,' she screeched defensively.

My passion for the war diminished with the arrival of the cousins. At first I showed off my knowledge and tried to interest them in following my map. But William was scornful, quoting *The Times* as saying, 'A true view must be a wide view,' which he said meant not getting bogged down in details. Besides, he had a collection of shrapnel in London which he'd actually picked off the streets himself. A friend of his even had a piece of a Zeppelin. Daphne said self-righteously that her mother took the view that it was unpatriotic to know too much about the war. It might put people off it. Even cheerful Dot was unimpressed, saying that when they'd gone to stay in Sussex they'd been able to hear the guns all the way from France and see the planes. What were a map and letters compared with that?

In fact it happened that no letters arrived from Papa during July. Then at the beginning of August a short note arrived, written from a chateau at Hooge which was right on the front line. Reading the letter with less care than before, I nevertheless sensed the possibility of heroism. It seemed Papa was writing on the eve of a British counteroffensive.

'You have no idea,' I informed the cousins, 'of the bravery of my Papa. They have used liquid fire on him and his men, and here I quote, "but they advance yet again." We should say a special prayer.'

My important manner antagonised the elder cousins so much that they categorically refused any sort of 'silly prayers,' and in the end only the babies could be persuaded to their knees by threats of heavy punishment.

'Bully,' catcalled William, Daphne, and Dot.

'Coward!' echoed Priscilla.

I flew at them in such a rage that the babies escaped and no prayer was ever said.

25

At the end of the second week in August, the household was astonished by the sudden arrival of Aunt Phyllis in a motor. The motor, which she had somehow commandeered from Newcastle station, was called a Wolseley and had figured in an advertisement in *The Times* as the perfect 'family roadster.' We had all admired it there on our seaside holiday the previous year. For a while this motor, resplendent in scarlet and blue paint with a yellow stripe and huge black mudguards—shockingly contrary to the spirit of wartime minginess—dominated the extraordinary fact of Aunt Phyllis' arriving unannounced and unattended. Eventually we noticed what an unusual appearance she presented.

'Mama, why do you look like a witch all in black?'

She was wearing a black silk coat with dull silver buttons and a drooping waistband, black button shoes, black net gloves, and a circular black motoring hat covered with a heavy black veil.

'You look like a beekeeper.'

'Children! Children!' My aunt lifted her veil and began to recover from the fumes and noise and dust and bumping of her long journey. She took a step or two forward and rubbed her dark-circled eyes. We must have looked quite wild, almost unrecognisable, for she seemed at a loss to pick out the child she wanted. 'Now, now. Children inside, Nannies! I shall go to the blue bedroom, where I require a cup of tea and a digestive biscuit.' She looked around with new determination. 'Nurse Fig, follow me.'

The confusion in the nursery was most enjoyable. Nanny Salmon and Nanny Whistle supervised in a rising hubbub a total change of clothes, even for the babies, who screamed and kicked in protest. I had more luck. Being temporarily without my proper controller, I refused to do more than retie my hair ribbon and brush the most tangled curls off my forehead.

So when dear Nanny returned, quite pale and so shaky she clung to a chair, she discovered me executing a series of wild pirouettes in the middle of the room, egged on by a spruced-up Priscilla.

'Goodness. Goodness!' May Fig decided to sit on the chair. 'Goodness!' She looked at me despairingly. 'Oh, dear. Dear. Poor child.'

I spun round, faster and faster.

Playing for time, she drew the two other nannies out into the passage. My pirouettes faltered. I could hear the whisper, whisper outside the door. I crept forward.

'Poor little orphan child.'

'Not strictly orphan.'

'Well, you can't say she's got a mother.'

Aunt Phyllis had removed her topcoat. She sat on a small armchair and patted a stool by her side. 'Come, my dear niece.'

I hated this gloomy formality. It was all her fault, gloomy old witch. 'I know,' I shouted. 'You don't need to tell me. Papa is killed. I know all about it.'

Aunt Phyllis looked satisfactorily surprised and cross.

'I dreamt it last night,' I continued aggressively, a triumph over the carrier of the news seeming halfway to a triumph over the news itself. 'He was consumed in liquid flames near a huge château. He was leading his men in a great victorious assault. It's all quite clear to me. The name I see is Hooge.'

Aunt Phyllis, who didn't know about my war knowledge, was amazed. She smoothed her black silk lap irritably.

'I'd be most grateful for the telegram telling you of the news. After all, it does concern me most.' I paused, and suddenly the emotional strain was too much. My voice became childlike and whining. 'I'm awfully hungry, Aunt Phyllis. I would love one of those nice biscuits.'

My father was dead. Mourning, which Aunt Phyllis ordained in a manner we considered quite Victorian, overwhelmed grief. The boys were issued with black armbands sewn by the nannies with shiny black cotton, and we girls wore dark dresses and black ribbons. Our adventurous games were forbidden as unfitting, and we were expected to walk at a sedate pace. It provoked rebellion even from me. And now I was truly suffering.

Nightly, as I knelt by my bed, I said that forgotten prayer for my father. Now it had to be posthumous. 'Please God, bless Papa, who is a hero and deserves all proper heavenly reward.' Secretly, because I didn't think it God's province, I prayed that he would also get an earthly reward in the shape of a medal.

When the telegram and packets duly arrived, I cajoled Aunt Phyllis into letting me see the report of the action in which Papa died. He had been killed on 9 August, after three days of bombardment. In the early hours of the morning his battalion had left their trenches on the edge of the wood and crossed five hundred yards of open space to the heavily mined German trenches ahead, while exposed to fire from German trenches in the wood to their right. They attacked in short bursts and, reaching their objective, faced a tremendous bayonet fight. They won. It was called winning, although in three hours 92 men and 6 officers were killed, and 362 officers and men wounded or missing. Poor Papa. There were many heroes. And not one of them was recommended for even the meanest of awards. I did not require a VC; a DSO would have been quite adequate. But no award— except eventually a measly mention in dispatches—was a bad disappointment. I discovered years later that Papa's commanding officer, who wore a monocle and smoked a cheroot, was crying at the end of the day. But it would have been little consolation for me even then. I put the telegram under my pillow and told William that war was a beastly thing unless one did one's duty. But I could not disguise from myself a feeling that Papa had let me down. Although I tried loyally, I could not convince myself that a man could be a hero without being acclaimed a hero.

We children were not allowed to attend the funeral service, which was conducted with wartime lack of splendour by the Reverend Tiptree. I was left with a sense of absence and restrictions.

Summer was dismal. The only dramatic moment came when Aunt Phyllis, whose energy knew no bounds, ordered all the lawns to be ploughed up and planted with potatoes. The sight of the sacrosanct purity of the lawns reduced to clods of earth wildly excited us children. I quickly submerged any feeling that my father might not have approved. He had loved those lawns. Instead, I joined the other children in a legitimate onslaught on plums and peaches which were at last in season.

Meanwhile Aunt Phyllis, between endeavours at galvanising the local populace into greater war efforts, was trying to solve the question of what to do with me. And the house. Some sort of sharing between the sisters seemed most likely. She was reckoning without my Mama.

The telegram arrived from a remote Irish lighthouse. 'Place booked for Violet on Irish Mail Boat leaving September 13th. Will be met at Dun Laoghaire. Eleanor Hesketh.'

My aunts and uncles, amazed and disbelieving, conferred with the family solicitor, who informed them that my mother had every right to her own daughter. There had not been a divorce. Their brother had never attempted to make them legal guardians. Worse still, from their point of view, he had never altered the will made at the time of his marriage, which left everything—house, grounds, and money—although there was little of this—to his wife.

I was pressing flowers in the schoolroom when a wild figure burst through the door. 'You had a fool for a father and you've got a criminal for a mother! If she wants you, she shall have you. I wash my hands of the whole disgraceful affair!'

Confronted by Aunt Phyllis' purple, furious face and having no idea what she was talking about, I assumed I had done something terrible. A blameless conscience made it easy to be humble. 'I'm sorry, Aunt Phyllis. I didn't mean to.' Then, hearing again the remarks about my parents, I couldn't resist adding, 'But you shouldn't speak ill of the dead.'

Aunt Phyllis, goaded almost beyond rage, was saved from thorough disgrace by the arrival of Nanny and several of the smaller children. Her tone descended several octaves. 'Mrs Fig, you may prepare Miss Violet's clothes. She will be leaving shortly. So will you. So will we all. Tell the other nurses to do the same.' Turning on her heel, she swept out. I finished pressing my pansy into a perfect owl's face and shut my exercise book with a clap. 'I fear Aunt has been overdoing the War Work.'

The mail boat to Ireland, which before the war had left at night, now went by day owing to the danger of German torpedoes. Nanny thought it a better target in daylight and said this was the sort of faulty reasoning that could lose the war. Our date of departure being 13 September only confirmed her worst fears.

At heart she must have known that whatever her loyalty to me, she could never work for Mama and Nettles on a savage island. For one thing, it went against her Christian principles. Besides, a ten-year-old child does not need a nanny. No number of misguided Huns could be the cause of her pale, frightened face. It was a sense of the unknown future.

The whole journey was ecstasy for me: the long train ride, broken by strange shuntings as brave troops of soldiers appeared and reappeared out of the night; the dawn view of the grey waves at Holyhead. I wasn't even nervous at the prospect of seeing my mother again. It was clearly too extraordinary to be seriously considered. I held no grudge against her for abandoning me for so long, nor did I try to imagine why she should suddenly want me back. After all, Father had told me to forgive her. He would have wanted me to go to her. I was still at an age at which children do not expect to understand the behaviour of grown-ups. I was quite prepared to think of my mother as some magical fairy godmother and my departure from a home of ten years as nothing more than a different kind of holiday. I was merely annoyed with Nanny for being such a killjoy when I was having such a wonderful time. 'Do you think she'll meet us herself?' I tugged at Nanny, willing her to react out of her miserable stupor.

'If pigs could fly.'

'Do you think she'll wait on Eureka, then?' I had found out where we were going only on the train journey. Now I pronounced the name of the island where my mother lived with reverence. It seemed to promise the romance and beauty so far lacking in my life.

'Don't cross your bridges . . .'

'Oh, Nanny!'

The crossing, despite our first-class accommodation, was not very satisfactory. Nanny insisted on lying down in her cabin, while I wanted to go on deck. Eventually I became so fidgety that she consented to my going on deck with a nice stewardess on condition I wore two overcoats and wound up my head in a shawl.

'Be careful the sailors don't take you for a Turk or you'll be for it,' joked the stewardess.

All the excitement of the wind and the sea gulls and then, at last, a first sight of land—for a really thrilling moment mistaken for a German torpedo boat. I'm free. I'm independent, I thought. I half-shut my eyes, opened my mouth till it filled with salty air. 'Eureka! I come. Eureka!' I called to the wind, in somewhat self-conscious drama.

Spots of rain fell on Dun Laoghaire quayside. I held Nanny's hand tightly. Amidst the loading and unloading, coils of rope, train tracks, cranes, sailors, soldiers, officials and Irish which the whole non–first-class part of the boat turned out to be, I was glad of the security of the past.

'I'm sure I don't know how they'll find us.' May Fig stood resolutely upright, refusing to leave the shadow of the mail boat before a proper course forward was indicated.

'Oh, they will.' My voice sounded small and unconfident. We were becoming more and more conspicuous as the quay cleared of the other passengers. I wore a dark-blue panama hat, blue linen coat with white collar, black patent shoes and blue stockings. Nanny wore her perennial straight dark coat with the winter rabbit collar exchanged for a band of georgette, and a panama hat dimpled with bumps from the plaits twisted over her head. Our gloved hands gripped each other tightly. We were dressed for a Sunday afternoon in Hyde Park.

'Are you Miss Hesketh?'

A strongly accented voice spoke behind us. We swivelled round, nervously. He was a big dark man with bright blue eyes, wearing a peaked hat and heavy navy-blue sweater on which was written 'SS Eureka.'

'Good afternoon.' Disappointedly, I conceded he was not a German torpedo commander.

'I've got the boat handy.' Ignoring Nanny, he spoke directly to me. 'And the tide'll be turning.'

'More haste—less speed,' murmured Nanny in a flurry. Already she felt in the grip of my mother's impatient, high-handed ways.

'Not for you, Miss, that's certain. The mail boat doesn't take its departure for several hours to come.' The soft Irish tones for a moment disguised the stark message. I understood quicker than Nanny.

'You mean Nanny isn't coming?'

'For a growed girl like yourself?' The man looked at me in a way no servant in England would ever have. But then, he was a captain.

'D'you mean I'm to go all alone?'

'Well, now, I'm hardly a spirit to be discounted myself. Hurry now or the tide'll have turned and we'll have a night ashore.' He signalled to a man to pick up my trunk, took my overnight case in one hand, and started to take my arm in the other. At last Nanny took action. Drawing herself up so that she reached the man's shoulder, she interposed herself with courage and dignity.

'We don't even know your name. You might be an impostor. A spy.'

'Well, now, I don't know what I'd be wanting with you two girls.' The man smiled in an agreeable way. 'Here now. Everyone knows Josiah from *Eureka*.' He turned to the lad who was shouldering the trunk. 'Dan, tell the lady who I am.'

'Sure he's Josiah from *Eureka*,' grinned the boy through gap teeth.

Nanny's pent-up nerves and exhaustion defeated her fighting spirit. My father had asked her to look after me, but he had also spoken of my mother. She had given nearly ten years of her life to me. If there was to be an end of it with no thanks to follow, then she would not stay to lose what remained of her pride. The dark little cabin in the mail boat would still be unoccupied.

'Goodbye, Violet. Be a good girl. Remember Patience and perseverance brought the snail to Jerusalem.' The tears which no one would see rose suddenly, and she hurried away.

The SS *Eureka* was very modern. The drops of rain had passed now, and some autumnal afternoon sunshine made its blue and white paint gleam and its silver railings spark off light.

'The tide seems high enough here,' I said conversationally. It seemed best to win over Josiah before examining the extraordinary implications of Nanny's departure. I knew I should have run after her, given her one last kiss, one last hug. But there was no time. Besides, with the faithlessness of youth I wanted to impress Josiah with my brave independence.

'There's water here, all right. It's at the island we have to worry.' Josiah went off to his steering wheel, leaving me alone in the neat cabin.

So much independence so suddenly was undeniably daunting. I was not tempted to cry 'Eureka' into the wind. I sat numbly beside my small case. Sea and sky battered the boat. I slipped into a restless sleep.

'Five minutes, Miss. The skipper says do you want to see the island?'

Barely awake, I allowed myself to be led on deck. The rushing of waves and wind had stopped now, and we were gliding quietly through the green water towards the sun setting in cloudy streaks of red and purple and grey. At first the island seemed another layer of cloud, in parts golden, in parts dark and mysterious. But as we drew closer, I saw where it began and ended, that the golden was cut corn, the dark copses of trees; and between them smooth dips of green fields. Soon I could even see a turreted castle halfway up what seemed to be a slope, and in front a low white house and several cottages curving down towards the sea and a small crescent harbour. I couldn't decide if the island was big or small. Any usual scale seemed to disappear in the green waves all around and the endless streaky sky. In my dazed state I identified it with the land I'd always imagined lay behind the black mountains of Northumberland.

I saw a vision of beauty floating along the harbour wall. I wouldn't have been surprised if it had floated across the water and landed in the boat beside me. It was dressed for the evening in a long Grecian tunic of rainbow-coloured crêpe belted low with a swag of beading. Dark wavy hair cut short was bound to the head with four or five bands of the same beading, which also trimmed a short cape hanging from the shoulders.

I didn't recognise her, but presumed such a creature could only be my mother. 'Mama,' I tried out under my breath, but it seemed a most inappropriate description. At her side walked a slight brown-haired man. Suddenly breaking free of him, she ran the rest of the way to my boat.

My look of amazement made her laugh with delight. She plucked me off the boat and twirled me about. 'Welcome to Eureka. We're never dull here.' She put her bare arm through my navy linen and drew me swiftly along. 'You remember Nettles, of course.' She pulled at a curl under my hat. 'Now, where did you get that grisly head-gear? I do truly believe the terrible Fig must have chosen it. Here, let us get rid of it once and for all.' She snatched off the hat and with a wide swing flung it into the sea. She paused for a moment and surveyed its bobbing, then cried out in sudden alarm, 'Oh, Lord. I do hope it won't be washed ashore like a dead body.' She raised her voice. 'Josiah, the tide is going out, I trust!'

Nettles held out his hand. 'Good evening, Violet. I'm re-re-relieved you've arrived safely.' The stuttering rs were the first thing that seemed familiar on the island. I smiled. I thought Nettles' brown curls, pale face, and kind brown eyes very sympathetic. My mother was hastening on. 'Darlings! Do come. The baggage can use the donkey cart. I crave to show dear Vi everything!'

We followed a path laid in an intricate pattern of silvery beach pebbles, bounded by pink bricks laid on their edges. On either side thick hedges of wild fuchsia sprayed their dark-pink bells with purple clappers. The path rose upwards in serpentine curves till the wild scabious and grasses of the seashore had given way to the more luxurious greenness above. Then we passed farm gates, arched in great stone slabs and topped by huge mossy balls. It looked far too beautiful for a mere farmyard, but the stooked hay was unmistakable. A little farther on I saw a row of whitewashed cottages, each one carefully thatched and fronted by a small garden, overflowing with marigolds and pansies and garlands of yellow nasturtiums. I had never seen anything like it. I compared the grim granite farm workers' houses in Northumberland, and it seemed this was fairyland.

'It was all designed by a glorious friend of Nettles'. The whole island. Gates, fences, cattle sheds, castle, harbour. He's a genius.'

'Yes,' said Nettles modestly. 'He believes in perfect simplicity. Quite a revolutionary idea, you know.'

'Oh, yes,' I agreed, feeling dull and inadequate.

We passed through a meadow, rich with clover despite the lateness of the year and grazed by a herd of butter-coloured cows. Beyond it, thick grey castellated walls hid all but the topmost turrets of a full-scale castle. A huge iron gate opened onto a perfectly smooth lawn down the middle of which an avenue of interlaced nut trees formed a triumphal arch to a great oak door. As my feet met the soft springy grass, I remembered my own lawn so ruthlessly ploughed at Aunt Phyllis' tyrannical command. How could I ever have enjoyed the sight? Oh, mean-hearted girl! I saw again the stiff back of Nanny, alone in an alien country. As I was alone. Tiredness swept over me, bringing with it a sense of total desolation. Poor Papa. Poor Nanny. Poor me, I thought, and the sobs burst out of me in a very unmagical pedestrian sort of way.

My mother, who still led us like some will o' the wisp, whisked round and came back to me. I collapsed onto the ground, ignoring grass stains—poor Nanny's pet aversion—and proper behaviour alike. 'Oh, oh, oh, I think I shall die too. I'm so dull, and Nanny's gone, and Papa's dead, and Aunt Phyllis ploughed Papa's lawn, and . . . oh, oh, oh.'

Drama was always my mother's strength. Now there was no Nanny to upstage her. 'Darling, darling.' She crouched down so that her robe billowed round us. With spiky ringed fingers she undid my tightly buttoned coat. 'You're all tightly buttoned up, that's the trouble. Look at those great wool stockings. So hot and uncomfortable.'

'I'm dull,' I cried, divining that this was the worst thing in my mother's world. 'I'm dull like my hat. I'm dull like the cousins are dull, like rice pudding is dull, like crossword puzzles are dull . . . dull like poor N—' I stopped; even I couldn't sacrifice Nanny so easily.

'No. No.' My mother held my face, looked at my glistening blue eyes, at my cheeks flushed with passion, at my thick, tumbling hair. 'No. You're not. In fact, darling, now you've shown a touch of spirit, I see you've every chance of becoming a wicked woman.' She looked up at Nettles and laughed teasingly. 'Like me.'

Chapter Two

Hodder & Stoughton's Books.
THE KAISER I KNEW by Arthur N. Davis. Ready Immediately.
AMERICAN DENTIST TO THE KAISER FROM 1904 TO 1918. 10/6 net.
THE WAY ETERNAL by 'Bartimeurs'.
THE NAVY THAT FLOATS, THE NAVY THAT FLIES, AND THE NAVY UNDER THE
SEA. Illustrated. 6/- net.
WINGED WARFARE by Lt-Col W.A. Bishop, V.C., D.S.C., M.C., D.F.C. The
Ace of all Aces.
(Advertisement) *The Times.*   27 September 1918

WINTER FOOD SUPPLY SUFFICIENT, BUT NO SURPLUS
(Headline) *The Times.*   8 September 1919

Harrods
SCHOOL WEAR WEEK.
                    SIX DAYS OF SPECIAL PRICES.
The factor of Quality is surely never more important than in Clothes for
Boys and Girls. Not only does Harrods Quality in school-wear make for ser-
vice which in turn makes for economy, it also encourages the little wearer's
confidence and pride and self-respect. Gym Tunic (J.C. Timmie) in good
quality navy serge 1st size. 19/6.
Knickers. 7/6.
(Advertisement) *The Times.*   8 September 1919

I was collecting gulls' eggs. They lay in messy straw piles on the slanting rocks and tussocks of grass that crowned the cliffs at the back of the island. The birds, angry at such barefaced robbery, circled round screaming with wide-open beaks. If they came too close, I waved a stick or threw clods of grass. Usually I was forbidden this secret part of the island where wild deer darted in nervous groups and the seals popped their heads out from black watery caves. But today Mother was on the mainland. The eggs were to tempt the palates of a party of visitors arriving the following day.

I straightened up and pulled out my dress, which was stuffed into my bloomers. I thought all this fuss rather absurd. But during this long cold winter since the ending of the war, Mother had been dreaming and planning this great victory celebration. Only Nettles had been to London since my arrival.

'Gulls' eggs are not too vulgar, are they, Nettles darling? I remember at London dances it always used to be plovers' eggs.'

'But that's why they're such a delicacy. Plovers' eggs are vulgar.' Nettles was always understanding. As Mother's fixations became odder and more impassioned, he became calmer and more sensible. The only problem from my point of view was that his good sense never actually led him to contradict her.

I looked down at my crumpled dress. From my reading of Angela Brazil, which Nettles brought me regularly from The Times Bookshop, for he was an ally as far as he was able, I was well aware that my mother's insistence on a bright flowered smock topped by a coarse canvas pinafore, both made by Finola, who lived on the hill, was not regulation children's wear. But any complaint met with a lecture on the Principles of Beauty.

I picked up my basket of eggs and started back to the castle. The land sloped up for a while to the topmost point of the island and then down on the way to the sea. Standing on the crest with the spring wind blowing me cool again after all my climbing, I could see over the dark sea to the blue line of the mainland and coming slowly towards me the little dot of the S.S. *Eureka*. I would have to hurry if I was to be down first, eggs delivered, hair properly combed into the natural but untangled curls Eleanor liked. I started to walk down a sheep path as fast as I could without risking breaking the eggs.

It was four years since I'd first stepped onto the island, and I'd never wanted to leave except to go to school. I'd fought that battle early, less than a year after my arrival, when the memory of jolly comradeship with the cousins was still strong. Nettles inspired me when he expressed shock at my lack of education.

'It's hardly surprising I'm a savage', I defended myself, 'when my only education came from a series of silly women. Take the Belgian refugee, for example.' Unfortunately, Mother took the line that if I vulgarised myself by going to school she never wished to see me again—a threat unbelievable in most mothers, but only too likely in mine.

As usual, Nettles found a compromise. Next time he went to London, he returned with a nineteen-year-old pacifist called Augustus Budd. At first Mr Budd's arrival took second place to the news that the previous mailboat had been torpedoed and the stewardess who had kindly led me on deck had gone to a wet grave. 'My darling,' said Mother with a voice of tragedy, 'No one will make me leave this island till the Boche pigs have receded to their sty.'

'None will try, Eleanor dear,' said Nettles reassuringly.

When Augustus came into focus, he turned out to be an exceptionally tall, thin, red-faced, nervous young man, and a great source of embarrassment to his solidly patriotic family because of his antiwar stance. He attended every pacifist march, carrying the most prominent banner, and organised small loud-voiced meetings in village halls round the country. His family felt the police would lock him up soon and if the police didn't, they would. A remote island seemed the best alternative. He was, however, very clever, and had spent a term as a classics scholar at Oxford before throwing it all up for pacifism.

Eleanor, starved of society, even if by her own choice, welcomed him with her best spare room, and an easy acceptance of his creed.

I was less sure. It seemed hard to have a fanatic for my first properly educated teacher. During the three hours we spent each morning in a schoolroom which looked out onto grey battlements and wild blowing sky—the sea view was considered too distracting—I tried my best to point out the error of Augustus' ways. After all, though he appeared insensitive to any personal feelings, pacifism did make my own Papa's death quite without point. I cut out and pinned on the wall the *Times* slogan:

Fight them for your life
Fight them for your good name
Fight as Britain has fought before—for freedom
Fight for humanity.

But Augustus pointed out it was a very old copy of *The Times*, written before anyone really knew what war was about. So then I resorted to simple crude advertisements. 'Your King and Country Need You,' 'Join the Army Today,' and 'What did you do in the great war, Daddy?' I succeeded only in antagonising Mother, who said it spoiled the perfect white of the walls. She became a long-distance member of the Women's International League, and signed, by proxy, petitions and manifestos in support of Lord Lansdowne.

I might have weakened too, for poor Papa's lack of heroism still rankled, and Augustus' knowledge was so impressive in other fields that it seemed likely he was right in this, had I not discovered he had given up pacifist work for the island not because of police threats, but because of parental threats of no more allowance.

'How you dare face us with talk of principles, I don't know.' This ammunition was provided for me by Nettles, who thought one pacifist on the island enough. Augustus, admitting defeat, lectured the farm labourers instead, who were happy to down tools for a while even if it was only to listen to a load of baloney. His nervous, high-pitched English voice was hardly comprehensible to them. Still, they were all fully agreed that they were not going to fight. Certainly not.

Nettles, an American citizen, did try to fight when the Americans joined the war, but his eyes, although he'd never worn glasses, turned out to be slightly squinting and colour-blind, while his stammer on the r inspired little confidence. I was quite upset on his behalf, for they seemed very unmanly reasons to be turned down. Unmanly reasons for my mother's husband. The fact that he wasn't actually my mother's husband I normally ignored, except on the occasions when my mother wished to make a point of her unconventional position. Even then I realised they were an unlikely couple. Nettles was too gentle and unflamboyant to be living in sin in an era when sin with a capital S still existed. Probably my mother had run away with him because he was the only one who would run away with her. I was very fond of Nettles. He was my intermediary with my mother, my bulwark and comforter. Once he confided in me that the war had made him three times richer than he had been before. He was really ashamed of it, I think, but it did not cross his mind he could do anything about it.

My progress down the hillside had slowed. The war had slowed down everything. It had always seemed odd that my mother had given up England for the duration. She, who in Northumberland had been obsessed by her miserable isolation, now chose to spend almost all the time on her own, even further removed from society. Once her brother Eddie arrived, convalescing from a wounded leg. He wore his uniform and several medals with a bravado which did not much appeal to the farm workers and horrified Augustus. But after less than a week he said that he'd rather be in a trench than on an island filled with fools, cowards, and children, and caught the next boat away. Mother smiled after him fondly and called out her love to her parents. This was irony. 'Your grandmother,' she had told me one wet evening, 'won't receive me till I've married Nettles, which is very odd considering a divorced woman can't go into the Royal Enclosure at Ascot or be on the Honours List. She wouldn't be too worried about the Honours List, of course—I mean I'm hardly likely to find myself there—but racing means more to her than any man,'—she paused a moment—'although she's so perverse she might even want me excluded!'

'But Mother . . .' Something about this speech had worried me all along. 'Papa's dead. You're a widow. So it wouldn't be divorce.'

'That wouldn't matter to my mother. It's the principle that counts.'

I now gave up hurrying altogether and sat down on the grass. The boat would soon be entering the harbour. I could already see its scarlet and blue paint and the fluttering figure of my mother standing at the prow. She wouldn't be cross. One of my mother's nicest characteristics was that she was never angry. She never gave in. She was habitually irrational. But she never got angry. I found I loved her quite soon. Not as a child usually loves a mother; the breach in our relationship had been too long for unreasoning worship. She never mentioned my five years without her. Once I plucked up my courage and asked her whether we couldn't pay a visit to Northumberland. I was suffering from homesickness, and I can remember the hot nervous feeling as I waited for her reply.

'Northumberland?' She managed to look quite blank. 'Oh, you mean Tudor's house.'

'But it's yours now. He left it to you.'

'Oh, not really. Nettles arranged for it to be shut up. So dark. Dreary. The sun barely touched it before the mountains covered it up again. That's why I like an island. So much sky, so much sun. Dawn before you've got used to night.'

Love of Northumberland remained a guilty secret. Only Nettles knew it.

One dark winter's evening when the peat fire reminded me of the schoolroom, I wrote to Nanny enclosing a poem. My transition from nursery to drawing room had been so sudden that I sometimes felt a babyish desire for all that security. There was no one on the island whose main aim in life was to look after me. An Irish girl looked after my mother's clothes and mine in her spare time. An Irish housemaid prepared my supper. Lunch I took with my mother. No one told me what to do or what to say. No one said, 'More haste—less speed' or 'Ask no questions and you'll hear no lies.'

I had both written and illustrated my poem, which had a strong flavour of *The Isle of Innisfree*:

I will fly like a bird on the wing
And go to the island where nightingales sing.

I half-expected to see a neat dark figure arrive with the next boat.

Instead I received a letter. The ill-educated writing gave a jolt, but the sentiment was all, apart from her person, I could wish for.

Dear Miss Violet,
I was most happy to receive your work of poetry. Your hand has come on very nicely. And your colouring also. I am sure an island is a very healthy place to be with all that sea air, but I hope you wrap up against the cold winds and your mother keeps well also. I have three children who keep me busy.
Your Old Nanny,
May Fig.

I showed it to Nettles, who laughed so much at the idea of wrapping up against 'your mother' that I managed to control my jealous pangs at the mention of those three children and even smiled. Carefully folding it back in the envelope, I put it away with the telegram announcing my father's death.

And now the war was over. At least I had some sort of education to thank it for. Without Augustus I would not even have known the meaning of the word *eureka*. There had been an anxious moment in 1917 when conscription had been introduced and Augustus' fate—to be a soldier or not to be—hung in the balance. Luckily, it had been a dryish summer on the island, and Augustus, whose long, narrow frame was prone to asthma, caught such a terrible cough from helping shift the hay in the fields—a touch of Tolstoyan imitation which he had never thought would be so useful—that he spent most of his ten minutes before the medical board doubled over in a paroxysm of coughing and choking. This performance so moved the doctors that they even became scared he might be the first wartime recruit to die before their examining eyes.

'Absolutely unfit,' cried one walrus-moustachioed officer. Augustus told the story to amuse Mother, and it soon became a legend to be brought out at any dull teatime. 'Unfit for absoballylutely all.' 'Absoballylutely.' 'At death's door.' 'Hardly ballylutely fit to turn the knob.' 'Absoballylutely.' 'Pluto said absoballylutely no.'

So I had a teacher. My mother had an admirer. By the end of the war, Augustus was desperately in love with my mother. I added to his misery by a thirteen-year-old's teasing. 'Why do you turn purple and stammer whenever Mama appears? It makes you look so very young. But then she is old enough to be your mother.'

'I have decided to return to Academe,' retaliated Augustus, looking as majestic as possible. 'There I will be among serious people.'

'Oxford doesn't need you half as much as we do, darling.' My mother put out a slender arm clad in lamb's wool, sheared and spun and dyed and knitted on the island. 'Oxford's jammed already with the most gigantic brains. Honestly, darling, you'll be the one to make the bathwater overflow.'

Augustus was persuaded to stay the winter. But when the winds had modified to less than Force Nine, and the temperature risen above freezing, he prepared to go again.

'How can you bear to miss the first magnolias?' Mother appealed. It was no good. He had left, looking very uncomfortable in suit, wing collar, and waistcoat, about a month before.

I had watched his departure from the gravel path on the wide walls around the castle grounds. I had walked their circumference till the S.S. *Eureka* was beyond recall. Augustus, for all his gangling passion, whether for pacificism or for my mother, was the nearest I had had to a friend since I'd left England.

Tomorrow, there would be visitors. Perhaps there would even be one for me among them. Nettles usually brought me a present. The last book was a 1917 publication called *The Wonder Book of Children of All Nations*. Despite a large Union Jack on its cover, the preface stated its aim as 'a humble but sincere contribution to the cause of international understanding.' Augustus, who was to leave on the boat's return journey, had snorted derisively and discovered a chapter headed 'The Peoples of Central Europe' which put the interesting thesis that 'all the Central Powers who had caused so much trouble to the other nations of Europe are in different degrees and ways of Mongoloid origin.'

'I leave you in the hands of fools and charlatans!' he had cried. They were his last words to me.

Now I really must hurry. Slipping and sliding, dragging my basket behind me, I took a shortcut into the back end of the castle, over the haha and across the smooth green of the archery lawn.

'The cost of food went up 129 per cent during the war.'

'Oh, Archie! No one wants to know depressing figures like that.' A serious young man's voice was interrupted by a petulant young girl's.

'Sorry, Clematis. It's the Ministry of Information. No outlet now it's been disbanded. Sorry.' He subsided apologetically.

'You shouldn't take any notice of a sister. Her one aim is to shut up Big Brother.' A nasal woman's voice with an American twang came to his defence. 'I'm sure I find it a wizardly riveting bit of info. I shall quote it to all the shopkeepers now, especially Harrods, to keep them up to snuff.'

'But that's the whole point.' Archie couldn't resist dipping in further, but again he was interrupted, this time by a drawling man's voice, very English, very self-assured.

'Bloody hell! He'll be telling us about the League of Nations soon.'

'Oh, but we all jolly well do believe in that, darling Buffy, don't we? I mean it's the Great Hope for the future.' A bright, quick feminine voice.

'Bloody hell, Christobel,' continued Buffy's drawl, 'Isn't it enough to read the *New Statesman* without actually quoting it?'

This bit of dialogue was the most enthralling I could ever remember hearing. I was sitting in the window seat of the drawing room after tea on the day after the guests arrived. I had placed myself behind a long curtain so that I could listen as intently and inconspicuously as possible. Already I could identify the owners of the voices without actually looking at them. All of them were strangers. Uncle Eddie, whom I'd been looking forward to impressing with my increasing brilliance, had left for Canada the moment the war had ended. He had written a letter to his sister full of the 'jolly good show' put up by the Canadian service chaps and how they were leading him to a 'New World.' My mother had given the letter to help line the cook's dog basket and remarked (wrongly, as it turned out) that 'no doubt he would return sooner or later, richer or poorer'. The serious young man was a friend of his called Archie Dare, and the girl who had pulled him up was his sister, Clematis. He was tall and broad and had the sort of fair, short-nosed good looks that one normally associated with sportsmen. Unfortunately, being a tennis and rugger blue does not immunise you against enemy shells. He had been badly wounded early in 1918 and spent most of the past year in the Ministry of Information explaining the peace. Thwarted of his rightful heroism, he had become very serious.

His sister, Clematis, who was a pert blonde version of her brother and whose skirts were already creeping up her silk-clad legs, found him inexplicable. The war was over; there was no need for reminders. Much better to enjoy yourself.

Gay, the American voice, would have echoed this sentiment, though in a more cynical, worldly-wise way. She was recently returned from America, where she had been, till her divorce, Mrs Clarence S. Shipberg, Junior. My mother had known her in the carefree prewar days as the Honorable Gay Heavenly-Smith. The change from a demure debutante in muslin to an American matron with short crimped hair, a cigarette holder, and at least a touch of something artificial on her lips and cheeks had been a shock.

'Oh, dear,' she confided to Nettles, 'Gay does seem rather racy. I do hope the Dares won't be shocked.'

As usual, Nettles was unperturbed. 'Clematis is too silly and Archie too preoccupied. Besides, my dear Eleanor, you are much racier than Mrs Shipberg Junior. Living in sin is, I believe, the moral term.'

'How absurd you are, Nettles. I've never even been divorced!'
Mother gave a triumphant smile.

The obvious star of the guests had been lured by the expedient of
offering him a landing place for his aeroplane. Colonel Buffy
Spooner possessed a drawling complacency which he had collected
after three years of seeing the enemy go up in flames. He had also collected a DSO and VC. His one aim was to fly as many hours of the
twenty-four as possible.

I looked at him, lounging on the sofa, with awe. He had smooth
dark hair parted in the middle, a silk scarf tucked under his determined chin, and rather short legs, which I thought appropriate for a
cockpit. He had arrived several hours after the boat. Thus we had opportunity to gather on the long flat field, grazed smooth as tarmac by
the sheep, and watch his dramatic descent. The farm workers and
their wives and children had also come to watch. When his propellers
stopped whirring, he had waved his cap in acknowledgement of
cheers from the admiring crowd. Then he had jumped out, as agile as
a well-dressed monkey, and posed by a wing of the plane for Gay's
clicking camera. Here at last was my real-life hero.

He had brought with him a very silent friend, also a war survivor—
though in this case, on the ground rather than in the air. His wife had
already arrived by boat. When we were introduced, she looked
amazed at my corn-coloured smock with stockings dyed to match.
'What a charming costume!' she commented with obvious disapproval.

Her hair was coiled stiffly in a Grecian bun at the back of her
square head, and her dark eyes blinked crossly on either side of a long
nose. I supposed it was frustrating to be married to someone as
leaden as Major Roly Royston.

Major Royston had shell shock. My interest in the war had been
resurrected lately owing to Nettles' presents of several boy's adventure books written by a certain Captain Brereton. Though I recognised that Augustus would have condemned the tone as ridiculously
naive and unreal, I couldn't help thrilling to the tales of Frank Riven
in *Under Haig in Flanders—A Story of Vimy, Messines and Ypres*.
There were chapter headings such as 'Foiling the German' or 'Star-
vation or Surrender' and with illustrations titled 'One of them is a
British Officer. Come on! shouted Roger,' or 'They crept along behind the bank, under the lee of which the Tank lay sheltering.'

On the other hand, I hung round the women visitors with a particular kind of fascination. Gay and Clematis could teach me how to
become a woman of the world.

'Ha, Ha! Caught you!' My screening curtain was drawn rudely
aside, and Buffy's oily head was revealed behind. 'Your mama has

deserted us, and Christobel say's there's a whole hour before one can reasonably expect to be offered the smallest cocktail, though Gay says the whole point of inventing cocktails was so that they could be drunk anytime . . .' At this sally there was a shriek of protest from farther in the room, at which Buffy smirked but did not pause. 'Therefore we have voted you our leader to take us for a lovely swim.'

'Somewhere with a nice rocky ledge,' called Gay, 'where I can watch.'

'What a spoilsport! Now, Violet darling. We're all on tenterhooks. Follow my leader.'

'Shouldn't we find towels?' I began doubtfully. It was late, and the sun had already turned a paler yellow.

'Oh, no! Don't let's prepare. That takes away the fun!' Clematis stood in the middle of the room swirling her pleated skirt.

'Come on, then. Through the window. Like naughty children. Not you, darling girl. I'll bet you're never naughty.' Gay, hopping and bobbing, climbed onto the window seat and dropped to the grass below.

I was reminded of Angela Brazil. It was just the sort of escapade Honor Fitzgerald, the wild Irish girl, would get into and earn herself a stern but fair-minded lecture from her magnetic teacher. It surprised me in such sophisticated company. I made a note.

However, it was a beautiful if cool evening, the spring shadows dark across the green lawns, the leaves of the lime avenue almost phosphorescent in their brightness. I decided to take them to Death Cove. Over the fields we cavorted, a cheerful cavalcade, sobered only by Major Roly Royston, whose square face and rigid frame recalled some half-alive Frankenstein monster. Every now and again Christobel tugged at his arm like a puppy pleading for a game, but he fell farther and farther behind.

As we reached the cliff top I picked up my skirts to tuck them into my knickers, but remembered the company just in time.

'Bloody hell!' cried Buffy. 'You'd have to be a bloody sheep to get down there.'

'Oh, no, you wouldn't.' I was making a great effort to overlook his bad language, since Nettles had explained it was the corrupting influence of the war. 'The sheep go hurtling down like skittles; that's why it's called Death Cove.'

'Oh darling,' Christobel trilled with laughter. 'That has put you in your place.'

'Onward,' cried Gay. 'DSOs and officers first, lesser ranks to the rear.'

'Oh, darling,' protested Christobel, for only someone who had just come from America could make such a Bad Taste remark.

Meanwhile I was halfway down, slipping and sliding, catching hold of roots to steady myself and then running a few daring steps. It was a new experience to have someone to impress. The worst that could happen would be a high tide so that there was no pretty beach—or alternatively, a dead sheep, smelling revolting and covered with flies. I was lucky: nothing but beautiful smooth pebbles, blue, pink, mauve, grey, like huge marbles unrolled by the great green breakers.

'It's quite rough,' I shouted upwards.

One by one the party descended.

'Oh, dear. I'm sorry about your trousers!' Buffy had been wearing the whitest of all white ducks, knife-creased back and front with a turnup like a shelf. Now they were brown and green, bagged shapeless, and even torn in one place.

'Hey! You lot! We're sticking here.'

Looking upwards, we saw Roly and Clematis silhouetted on the skyline.

'Don't be such spoilsports!' screamed Christobel.

Far away, Clematis was seen to tap her little diamond-studded wristwatch. Her voice floated down again. 'Cocktail time! Shaky-shaky!' The two figures vanished over the top.

I thought this preoccupation with cocktails very odd, but it was clearly a telling blow to Buffy.

'Bloody hell!' He began to brush down his trousers ineffectively.

With a bump and a bound Gay joined the group. 'Don't worry, mateys. Try a bit of your Prohibition spirit.' From a pouchlike bag slung across her flat bosom, she produced a silver flask whose top unscrewed into a little silver drinking cup. Archie, appearing behind her, expressed amazement and admiration.

'Neat, isn't it? My first present from dear old Clarence Shipberg Junior. Now become a lasting memorial to his'—she paused and trilled her jolly laugh—'abilities.'

I realised then why Mother had been worried, but thought her behaviour not shocking at all but filled with that highly desirable quality of 'brio.' Soon the little cup had passed from mouth to mouth, and even when I apologised for the sun, which had now gone quite off the beach, no one complained.

'We didn't really want to swim anyway,' said Christobel.

'Oh, no.' Gay seemed quite in charge now. 'We must climb that beastly mountain now while the spirit moves us.'

But this proved easier said than done. The main problem was Christobel, who despite her stalwart appearance turned out to be hopelessly unagile, particularly as she was encumbered by her broad ankle-length skirt. The spirit did not move her at all.

'Darling,' cried Gay, who scrambled about quite fearlessly, 'it's a judgment on you for being so unfashionable.'

'It's not my style,' protested Christobel, almost in tears. By this time, halfway up the dark and dusty slope, their tempers were distinctly frayed. Buffy had just trodden in a sheep's dropping, and when I foolishly added one more to my stream of apologies, he turned on me with something very far from a drawl. 'Let's just keep quiet, shall we, and try and solve this one in an adult fashion.'

'Here, I say!' Archie, bringing up the rear, knew bad form when he heard it.

'I'm stuck,' announced Christobel mournfully. 'I'm jolly well stuck.'

'Darlings. Darlings,' called Gay in a soothing voice. 'Surely if Archie pushes and the brave Colonel pulls we can budge the dear girl.'

Now Christobel collapsed entirely. 'I'm stuck. I jolly well am. I'm jolly well not being budged.' She said down firmly and clasped her knees in her hands.

'She jolly well is, you know,' agreed Archie.

Night fell. Quite suddenly it was absolutely dark. Even Gay seemed temporarily nonplussed.

But before despair could settle too heavily, the sound of voices was heard over the horizon.

'Nettles,' I shouted, recognising his soothing tones. But my relief was quelled by the horrid realisation that the whole affair might be justly blamed on me.

I was in disgrace. It was a new experience. Forbidden to leave the castle for three days; forbidden to take lunch or supper with the visitors. 'You have proved yourself a child; therefore you must stay in the nursery.' Mama's voice had been more weary than cross.

I sat with my elbows on the schoolroom table pretending to read *Villette*.

Nettles said to me, 'Your mother likes to make scenes round her; this house, this garden, this island, the people who work here, she painted them all. Still, she needed the visitors, society, beautiful people to complete the picture. So they come. And what happens? You lead them off into an adventure from which they emerge unbeautiful, unheroic, whining, and bleating—totally unworthy to fill their allotted role. In short, you showed them up for what they were.'

'But Gay was wonderful, Nettles. Simply bursting with "brio".'

'That's true. The ex-Mrs Clarence Shipberg, Junior, is the one saving grace. Don't worry too much. Eleanor's already planning a tip-top bathing party among the seals.'

My punishment lasted only as long as my mother's disapproval. I was released onto the Royal Tennis court, specially constructed because Mama thought the original game so much more elegant than the modern version. The men wore whites so brilliant they quite dazzled me as, eager to restore myself to favour, I ball-boyed conscientiously. The ladies, except for my mother, who was playing a passive role in Grecian blue, wore white calf-length skirts over white stockings, tipped by a white 'jumper'—a new invention suggested by the endless socks knitted for the soldiers at the front. Gay, even more fashionable, sported short white ankle socks over sheer stockings so that it looked almost as if she were bare-legged. We all thought it very bold. My mother was suffering the unusual sensation of being under the influence of somebody else. She was toying with the idea of exchanging her classical style for Gay's American modern.

'One must move with the times,' she confided, as I took a rest under her parasol. 'I've been very cut off here, you know.'

'But you chopped off your hair long before anyone else,' I said placatingly.

'In the style of Lesbos, my darling. Not in the forward thrust of woman's new place in society. Do you realise if I'd been in England during last December's elections, I would have been able to vote? That is to have a place in history. I do blame Nettles for not arranging it.'

'But Mother, you don't care about politics. You wouldn't have known who to vote for.'

'The principle, my dear, the principle,' said Mother, not at all crossly. 'The world has moved on since I was shut up first in Northumberland and then on this island. We must learn to catch up.'

I did not argue with her, but secretly thought it was Gay's 'brio' linked to her grasp of New Fashion which was the main attraction. The Irish Question, fully covered by Augustus in the schoolroom, had left her quite unmoved—despite the chief dairyman's having narrowly missed a sniper's bullet on the mainland. I think she lumped it all together with the World War. Politics was the excuse rather than the end. Beauty, chic, style, would remain my mother's yardstick. Nettles' view of her would last. On the other hand, he might not.

'You will come back?' I said to Nettles as I escorted him down to the harbour. I didn't like his stiff white collar and watered hair.

'Don't I always?'

'But this time . . .' I hesitated. He was returning to the real world with Christobel and Clematis and Archie. Archie wore a dashing white-and-charcoal pin-striped suit and cried enthusiastically,

47

'London's threatened with every sort of disruption.' Buffy had already taken Roly off by plane. 'I'm afraid it's only a Virgin,' he'd apologised gruffly to Gay when she'd pinched a last cigarette.

'Gay will keep you company, Vi.'

'Do you think Gay is an altogether good influence on my mother?' Last night Gay had given it as her opinion that 'discipline, school spirit, uniforms, exams, pushes, crushes, hockey, lacrosse are all imperative for the development of a proper twentieth-century cynicism.'

'School?' We had reached the quay, and I looked wonderingly at the boat, the clear green water, and the dark-blue strip of mainland beyond.

'School. That's part of what I shall be doing in London.'

Nettles was away from Eureka for several months. No one except me seemed to miss him. My mother's time was taken up by the Bright Young Things (and not so young, nor so bright if it comes to that) who now filled the island. I watched agape at their antics, which included lassoing the massive stag who patrolled the back of the island with royal dignity. At least, I told myself, it was better than shooting him. Another day the two sexes swapped clothes, causing terrible scandal to the Irish, who without knowing the word *transvestite* muttered belligerently about the Devil and all his works. I was not old enough to know whether they indulged in real orgies. Possibly not. My mother was always more interested in romance than in sex. Gay, of course, was a different matter. Meanwhile, Nettles was striving to settle me in a more conventional mode.

At the beginning of September, when the salty winds were turning cold and the visitors grumbled, 'Bloody hell, Eleanor, peat isn't the same as coal, y' know,' Nettles returned with astonishing information. I was to join my cousins Priscilla, Dot, Daphne, and Hetty at Shoreham Abbey School for Girls. I felt a sudden doubt. Nettles waited for my applause and delight. I tried to remember my female cousins. I had not seen them for nearly five years, had not even corresponded, and could picture them only in clean pinafores doing what their nannies told them. I had had no formal supervision since I'd arrived at the castle.

I had seemed peculiar to them when I lived at Kettleside. What would I seem like now after so long on an island? I had a strong feeling that even my mother's friends were not the cousins' idea of models for proper behaviour.

'Lost your nerve, have you?' Nettles looked at me shrewdly. He was always good at suppressing his disappointment.

'Not exactly. I'm very glad, of course. But I wish I knew about schoolgirl behaviour. Besides, I'll miss Eureka.'

'You'll come back for the holidays.' Nettles sounded unusually firm.

I might have drummed up greater enthusiasm and less honesty if I'd known the trouble he'd taken to get me a ticket back to the world of aunts and respectable schools. My Christian aunts had been most reluctant to accept their vagabond niece (whose acting father was not even married to her mother) as fitting schoolmate for their unsullied daughters. Besides, neither aunt had forgotten or forgiven the matter of the Northumberland inheritance. It rankled particularly that my mother did not even deign to use the house, although, as they both agreed, they would rot before they asked permission to use it themselves. Nettles, showing surprising guile and determination, began by enlisting the sympathy of Shoreham Abbey's headmistress. She was one of those strong-minded ladies who liked to conquer obstacles—especially if they were other strong-minded ladies. Of course, the aunts could not actually stop me coming, but Miss Loxley-Peacock demanded active cooperation. She appealed to them in the ringing contralto which so inspired all us pupils:

'Peace has come to England! At last after four years of struggle, of bloodshed, of sacrifice, Christian Endeavour has conquered the Forces of Evil.' This was borrowed from her address to the assembled school on Victory Day. Loxy-Poxy was never averse to using good words twice. From victorious unity she moved to individual strife. 'The tools of war must be laid down, not only on the battlefield, but in our own drawing rooms.' Finally came a grand appeal to the spirit of Christian Charity. My case was won. I would join Priscilla in Florence Nightingale House. Priscilla would be my protector.

'I'm sure I'll love it, Nettles.'

At last I gave Nettles the reward he deserved. As I hugged him I realised how tall I had grown lately, for his puckish face, smooth and pale from his stay in London, bent easily to mine. As he kissed me, kindly on the cheek like a father, I remembered he was not my father. He was my mother's lover. The ghost of my aunts hovered over me. For the first time I was properly aware of a man's lips on my skin. I pulled away.

'It's wonderfully clever of you to arrange it. Do you think my cousins will be nice? And do you think Mother will be agreeable?' I babbled incoherently.

Mama failed to be agreeable only over the school uniform, which she christened the Abomination of Desolation, soon becoming shortened to the A of D. It consisted of three equally ugly outfits: bulky serge tunic which produced a falsely bulging bosom, teamed with badly cut skirt and black woolly stockings; a hefty coat and skirt which transformed even the narrowest-hipped into a Wife of Bath: and a dreadful silk dress for best with long ruched sleeves and sagging hemline. 'Cheer up, darling,' said Mama with sudden generosity. 'The boater's quite charming.'

'It's not so awfully A of D, is it?' I agreed hopefully.

'Spiffing, jolly spiffing,' volunteered a young male visitor who was very good on the fashionable saxophone.

'Your opinion is better kept for music,' reproved my mother.

'At least we'll all look the same,' I said sensibly.

Priscila met me on the school train. I had been travelling for thirty-six hours and was quite dazed by the noise of the world. Five years of Eureka had receded into a faraway fantasy. The only reality was this bumping and clanking and hissing and shunting. I gave up trying to read or sleep or even eat stale cake. I watched Nettles, who was my escort, reading the financial pages of *The Times* and tried not to think of what awaited me. At last we reached the Shoreham Abbey train at Waterloo. Nettles put me into a carriage and then disappeared hastily from a crowd of schoolgirls attended by maids or mamas. Looking out of the window, I was reminded of my last view of my father, except that this time the roles were reversed. This time I was going to war.

'I believe you must be Violet Hesketh. I'm your cousin Priscilla Overley-Summers. I've been asked to look after you.' The first thing I noticed about my cousin was that she had a different hatband on her boater. Was the plain dark band which Mother had admired incorrect?

'How do you do? I don't expect I should have recognised you.'

'One does change. Luckily, I never forget a face. Welcome to Shoreham. I'm afraid I won't be able to sit with you because you're a New Twit—new girl, you know—and I've got all my friends, but I'll see you're all right the other end. It's only an hour and a half's journey, and we all consider the last half hour quite the most perfect stretch of England.' Ending this speech, she seemed about to leave the compartment, but perhaps taking pity on my forlorn expression, she added more kindly, 'Don't worry, you won't be sent to Coventry in here; it's just that New Twits generally stick together. You know, at the start.'

I didn't know anything, but was relieved when a few more girls aged from about ten to fifteen also wearing dark bands—presumably the New Twits badge of shame—sidled in. I thought that although I hadn't recognised Priscilla's neat pale face, I remembered her manner very well. I had been right to worry whether I might seem unconventional. The whistle blew, and the train began to move. We all sat stiffly, knees together, and wondered if we dared take off our boaters, which banged uncomfortably on the back of the seats. Suddenly a girl burst open the door. Her boater hung from her neck. Behind her she dragged a huge, bulging case.

'Gosh! Let's hope you lot are the New Twits! It's discrimination, that's what it is. This is my fourth school and it's absolutely the worst yet! My guardian says if I don't stick to this one, it'll have to be the last, so there's light ahead. Gosh! Talking of light, do you think I can leave this great white elephant in the corridor?'

The carriage stared tongue-tied at her appeal. She had red hair, bright green eyes, and buxom figure, covered by a suit which looked distinctly unregulation. Our silence didn't seem to worry her.

'It'll have to stay there, that's all, unless one of you's hiding your muscles under a bushel. Girls, I'm Molly Mannering. My real name's Mildred, but I changed that as soon as I could speak. Who are you lot?'

'I'm Violet Hesketh. Call me Vi.'

'Jolly nice to meet you,' cried Molly, taking off her shoes and producing from her pocket a huge bag of pear drops, which she handed round generously. 'Perhaps my fourth and last school won't be so bad after all.'

Shoreham Abbey Select School for Girls stood four miles from the sea in bare cliffside country which was supposed to be very healthy. The sea to which we were taken for a twice-weekly bathe till the end of September lessened my homesickness. From the beginning I was under the dual patronage of Priscilla and Molly. The result, as they pulled in quite different directions, was not altogether comfortable. Priscilla was school monitor, head of the house lacrosse team, deputy head of her house, and well on her way to being head girl. Although much the same age, Molly was responsible for nothing, not even herself; had absolutely no wish to play games; and showed enthusiasm only for learning Shakespeare or Matthew Arnold, which she declaimed nightly for all the dormitory until discovered, forbidden, and punished. Punishment, which was mainly in the form of order marks or missing games, meant nothing to her, so soon she had carved out a rebel's niche for herself outside the system.

I wanted to conform. My years of being on my own had left me with a strong desire to join a herd. Better still, lead the herd. I wanted to swap my navy hatband for a yellow-and-red stripe. I wanted to lead tubes of girls down the highly polished oak floors. I wanted the teachers to admire my intelligence and beauty. I wrote home to Nettles: 'The music teacher, Miss Haverly, who we call Heavenly because she just is, said that I have a natural gift for the piano so you must let me learn. She's got the most beautiful white fingers I've ever seen and she can span an octave and two. Everybody's in love with her!' In fact, most people were in love with the headmistress, Miss Loxley-Peacock, but she was so remotely perfect that one had to have someone a bit closer as second string. Quite a few of the younger girls even admired me, which was most satisfying. My Irish pink cheeks and thick curls were considered unusual and romantic.

All this gave me a strong incentive to succeed. My years of rock scrambling had made me extremely athletic, so that I found games easy and pleasurable. Augustus' three years of tutoring had given me precocious knowledge in some subjects which made up for my total ignorance in others.

'You could do really well,' advised Priscilla over hot buttered toast in her own room, two prefect privileges, 'if you became steadier and stopped seeing that wild Molly Mannering. I wouldn't be surprised if you made the lacrosse team next term, and who knows where that will take you?'

On the other hand, I felt deeply the ugliness and uniformity of our life. I couldn't get used to sharing a room with three other girls. I hated the feeling that they judged me on such silly matters as whether the turnover of my sheet measured an exact foot. I hated lining up to wash my face in cold water. I suffered from whispering and giggling which I always presumed was directed against me. And the actual teaching I found distinctly uninspired, compared with Augustus'. I wrote to Nettles, 'They make us learn by heart as a punishment! Can you imagine "Shall I compare thee to a summer's day" as a punishment? Miss Leatherhome who is HORRIBLE said algebra is more exciting than poetry. Ibsen is absolutely ne parlez pas. Can you imagine!'

'I got three more order marks today,' announced Molly, sucking one of her pear drops in the dormitory, 'and Loxy-Poxy said if I wasn't fatherless and motherless and my guardian ignorant of the ways of girls she would seriously consider'—here she did a very good imitation of the headmistress' measured tones—'sending me away from her select establishment. As it is she will allow me till the end of the term to pull up my socks, roll up my sleeves, button up my collar, etcetera, etcetera.'

'Oh, Molly. You mustn't go!' I needed both my patrons. I swung between them, saved from touching ground where I might have finally decided that my mother was right and school taught a vulgar code of uniformity, where the lowest common denominator became top. Instead, I could never decide for a day at a time whether Miss Loxley-Peacock was the proud acme of womanhood or a pompous old bore, whether the assembled school roaring out the school song, 'Always Duty, Always Virtue,' was the most moving of experiences or the most idiotic, whether the dark-

52

panelled rooms with their occasional flash of stained glass were inspiringly dignified or hideously claustrophobic.

I wrote to Nettles, who'd asked whether I wanted anyone to stay during the holidays: 'Molly Mannering is awfully jolly but I think Mother might think her common—she isn't of course—her guardian's a dental surgeon in Harley Street—but you know what Mother's like. Priscilla is very jolly too, jolly in a different way of course, but there's absolutely no chance of her being allowed to stay with me. And there's no one else. Quite honestly, it'll be spiffing to be on my own.'

Nettles and I corresponded weekly that first term. Mother wrote once: 'Darling, Gay says I'm too shockingly unmaternal. But you can't imagine the business of finding a house in London. Everything's so ugly and dirty. Ugh! But I think I have one now. How are the A of Ds? You must be longing to escape their hairy grip. See you very very soon. Masses of kisses, darling. Your ever loving, Mama.' It arrived special delivery, as we set off to catch the train to London. The school porter ran after me waving it in his hand. He thought it must be a death.

Soon I was emptying out of the train with the other girls at Waterloo station. This time I was part of a mass, lacrosse stick under one arm to be greased regularly in readiness for next term's ambitions, neatly packed overnight bag under the other.

'I wonder if they've sent anyone to meet me,' shouted Molly above the din.

Priscilla tapped my shoulder. 'I think you should meet my mother again. I'm sure she would want it.'

'Introduce her to Nettles,' screamed Molly, who knew Priscilla's attitude to my family history. 'Oh, I say! My guardian's sent the chauffeur. See you next term, morons all! Unless I've been given the cold shoulder. Byee!'

'Well!' said Priscilla.

'I didn't know Harley Street dentists kept chauffeurs,' I said. 'He must be rich. Perhaps that's why Loxy-P—I mean, Miss Loxley-Peacock keeps her on.'

'Really, child.' Priscilla often spoke to me as if she were ten years older instead of barely two. She didn't like it if I reminded her we had romped in the Kettleside rhododendrons together. 'Miss Loxley-Peacock would never be corrupted by mere money.'

'What would she be corrupted by, then?' I dared, for after all we had left school behind. But Priscilla did not answer.

'I can see Mama and Dot and Aunt Letty and Daphne and Hetty.' I followed reluctantly. The other cousins had figured little in life at Shoreham Abbey, since they were in different houses. And I was

53

frightened of meeting the aunts again.

'Good afternoon, Violet. I hear Priscilla has taken you under her wing.'

'Yes, Aunt Phyllis. She has been most kind.'

'We were both delighted to hear you were to get the opportunity to enjoy the company of your peers,' said Aunt Letty.

'Everyone's been very kind,' I repeated. Although perfectly recognisable, they were no longer the huge dark mountains I remembered. Aunt Phyllis, if stouter, was barely taller than Priscilla, and Aunt Letty was quite slight and frail. Molly could have knocked her over like a ninepin.

'Hello, Violet,' said Daphne, who was prettier than ever, and Dot, who was fatter, and little Hetty. .

'Hello.'

It was awkward. The aunts fussed about the children. Their duty was done. They had no intention of meeting my mother, Nettles, or whoever was to meet me, but the station was clearing rapidly and it would be difficult to avoid a confrontation across an empty space. I was uncomfortable too. Aunt Phyllis said, 'It's been very pleasant to see you again, my dear. No doubt we'll meet at the beginning of next term.' She bent and delivered a swift pecking kiss. Aunt Letty followed suit.

'Have a spiffing hols,' said Priscilla as they moved away.

I was left alone. Very soon the platform had cleared completely. Resolutely I called a porter. Before I had decided on my destination, he had wafted me to the station exit. I stood forlornly by my large chest. The last of Shoreham Abbey boaters sped away. Then I saw Aunt Phyllis, Aunt Letty, and their children squashed together in a taxicab. The aunts looked away desperately, but Priscilla's conscience was too energetic. I could see her arguing furiously.

There was very little room for me in the taxicab. The driver grumbled as he laced yet another box to the roof. 'You lot'd be better off with a trolleybus.'

'I'm sure Nettles hasn't forgotten,' I cried out with a gulp in my voice.

'I thought you might be captured by the White Slave Trade and spirited away to a distant land,' sighed Daphne with disappointment.

They all began to gabble excitedly.

'Are my goldfish still alive?' 'Is William home yet?' 'Are we going to have chocolate cake for tea?' 'Has Cook given notice again?' 'Did you get tickets for the Panto?'

I sat quietly. It seemed they traditionally shared the first tea of the holidays at the house of Aunt Letty, whose cook baked a particularly delicious chocolate cake. I decided that whatever happened, I would catch the seven o'clock train that linked with the night ferry. Aunt Letty's house was five storeys high and near to Marble Arch. Inside, it was very dark and heavily furnished. I remembered its waxy smell from previous visits on our way to the seaside.

'Oh, what bliss to be home!' sighed the girls. 'Here, Violet, prop your lacrosse stick there.'

'Nettles wouldn't forget me.'

Nettles would not have. But he was on a boat to America. My mother, Gay, and her friend the impresario Mr Raymond Lark were on their way to meet me. But they had been diverted by lunch at the Savoy. By the time they arrived at Waterloo station, Mr Lark's chauffeur reported not a boater remaining.

The room where the chocolate cake was served overlooked the street.

'Oh look, there's a super smart car stopping outside our house.' Dot pulled aside the net curtains, which were considered necessary despite the room being three floors up. 'Oh, do look at the people inside.' She turned round and lowered her voice. 'Do you think they're *demi-mondaine*?'

'Oh, no!' breathed Daphne.

'Not coming to this house,' said Priscilla the realist.

Daphne and Hetty and Dot crowded round the window. 'The chauffeur's opening the door. He's wearing a beautiful double-breasted pale-blue jacket with a cap with a huge tassel.'

'Can you see them getting out?' Priscilla was too dignified to look for herself but needed information.

'Yes. Yes. Oh, gosh! There's a man first. Very dark, very, very sallow, with black hair too—'

'Do you mean he's from Africa? Oh. Perhaps it's the white slave trade followed—'

'No. Don't be stupid. He's talking English. Quick! Quick! Oh, look! Here come the ladies.'

'Go on. What about them?' Priscilla's curiosity overcame her dignity. She rushed over. Only I remained behind.

'There're two. The first is small with a silver dress on and a short fur cape over it and a skirt miles above her ankles and she's wobbling about all over the place. Do you know, I think she's, she's . . .' Words failed Priscilla. Dot took up the story.

'And the chauffeur's helping her and the man. Do you think he's a gentleman? He's getting the second lady from the car. Oh. Oh. She's so beautiful!'

'Slender and dark,' said Daphne, who still cared very much about appearances. 'Her hair's cut, too, I think. It's a bit difficult to see under her hat. It's sort of flat and black with a rose on the front, and she's wearing the most expensive-looking fur coat. Oh! I would like to look like that!'

'Well, you shouldn't want to,' said Priscilla, resuming her disapproving air as the visitors disappeared under the porch above the door. 'They're going to ring the doorbell. Come on, there's still some cake left.'

'More chock, Vi?'

'No, thank you, Priscilla. I feel a bit sick.' A dreadful thought had struck me. Embarrassment truly made me feel very sick. The two ladies could be no one but Gay and Mother. As the doorbell rang loud and long, I jumped up and rushed to the window. I decided to jump out when the summons came from below.

'It's awfully rich if you're not used to it,' sympathised Dot.

'They're in,' reported Priscilla, who'd taken up a listening post at the door. 'They've gone into the best drawing room. There goes Mama after them. They've shut the door!'

The housemaid came puffing up the stairs. The cousins gaped expectantly. 'Miss Violet,' panted the girl. 'You're wanted downstairs.'

'Goodbye. Goodbye. Thank you. Thank you.' Perhaps if I ran, the truth would never be revealed.

'But who is it, Elsie? Who are they? That man and those ladies?'

'Miss Violet's mother 'as come to collect 'er daughter.' As my cousins fell back aghast, I was already escaping. I flew down the stairs.

'Hello, Mother! Sorry we missed. Shall we go?' I broke into a standing circle, for Aunt Letty had issued no invitation to stay. Mr Lark, famous impresario, was at his most charming to no avail. This flower of the British aristocracy was not to be plucked.

'No, I never attend the theatre,' she was saying when I burst in. 'Never since the flu epidemic of 1918 and seldom before.'

'But the germs are no worse than in church. Not so holy perhaps, but no more dangerous.' At this Aunt Letty turned her back totally, only to be met by the bright face of Gay.

'Honestly, darling, do you really worry about germs? I was in America at the time, but I hear people wore ghastly skin-coloured masks. I'd rather die than wear a skin-coloured mask.'

'Many did,' said Mr Lark, laughing heartily.

Up to my arrival, my mother had been struck dumb by the horror of her sister-in-law's surroundings. My appearance, boater crammed urgently on head, lacrosse stick already gathered from the hall, was the final straw. 'What a wicked, wicked sight!' she cried. 'What have they done to you?'

This was too much for Aunt Letty, now supported by Aunt

Phyllis, whose curiosity, like Priscilla's had overcome her high-principled decision not to meet my mother. 'We picked up your daughter from Waterloo station, where she was quite abandoned, and brought her to the sanctuary of my home.'

'Your home!' Mother's gaze swept round in horror.

'A Christian home,' echoed Aunt Phyllis in a stalwart tones.

'Please, Mother. Oh, please!' I cried. 'Can we go now? Please! We'll miss the train to Ireland. Oh, please!'

Mr Lark appeared to make a decision. Perhaps the dowdy solidness of Aunt Phyllis was too much for even his aristocratic ambitions. 'I shall send you tickets for my latest show,' he announced magnanimously. 'Ladies.' In lordly manner, Mr Lark offered an arm to either lady.

'Darling.' My mother turned to me. 'You not only look perfectly dreadful, but your behaviour leaves much to be desired. Are not children taught gracious behaviour at school?' She smiled at the aunts in gracious farewell and then turned back to me. 'I think you'd better call me Eleanor now that you're so large.'

Mama had given up croquet for archery—or toxophily, as she insisted on properly terming it.

'But darling, you'll develop such a bosom, and you know they're getting smaller and smaller.'

'You mustn't be a slave to fashion, Gay. It's a beautiful sport. Go and keep poor Lark happy. He looks so sad and cold.'

'It is cold. Freezing.'

'Not if you breathe properly.'

Gay disappeared into the castle, her little nose pink and muffled in furry spikes. I was left to admire my mother in peace. It had taken only a few days on Eureka to banish the standards of navy-blue serge and well-greased lacrosse sticks.

'Twang,' went my mother's bow. 'Plonk' went the arrow into the centre of the fat, straw-filled target. Behind it dropped the invisible haha, and behind that, hills sloping cold and green into the sky. The other way lay the castle, above which hung a red ball of sun waiting to drop heatless into the dark winter sea. On either side of the lawn, thick hedges of rich copper beech leaves, which stayed crackling on the branches until the new shoots pushed them off in the spring, shuddered under a chill, salty wind.

'Can I have a go, Eleanor?'

My mother glanced round, surprised apparently to hear her daughter's voice, though I had been collecting arrows slavishly all afternoon.

'But you're such a bundle, darling. Toxophily depends on a fluid line.'

Nettles was not expected back from America this winter. Gay and Raymond Lark were like some double act of his musicals which I couldn't really believe in. I hoped my mother would notice my devotion soon.

'It's my school overcoat. It is A of D, I know. But I haven't anything else. Except summer smocks. And they're too small.'

'Poor ugly duckling. Remind me tomorrow and we'll make up some patterns.'

When she did give me her attention, everything became an adventure. In this spirit she suggested a visit to Finola, who lived on the hill and had a magic touch with a needle.

Unfortunately, Raymond's circulation was not equal to island adventure. I suppose he had expected a smart house party. A freezing climb to visit a dressmaker was hardly the sort of entertainment he appreciated. He had not solved the problem of clothing and wore a well-tailored suit with waistcoat at all times. Lately he had taken to adding his overcoat with astrakhan collar, even inside the house. No one had told him that you couldn't leave an island on demand.

'You're not truly suggesting I mount upwards in the land of ice, in order to see a peasant called Finola.' His black eyes seemed ready to fill with tears.

'Darling, I do think the tides should be made to hurry up,' Gay confided to Eleanor. 'I fear Raymond is turning against us.'

'He's got his moving pictures,' said my mother indifferently. 'Anyway, it isn't the tides. It's the wind.'

'The moving pictures are very exciting of course,' agreed Gay, who had imported the projector herself, 'but he's seen *The Kid* and *Goldrush* six times each and *Riders of the Purple Sage* at least four. In fact, I think he saw it again this morning, so that makes five. And it's hardly a masterpiece.'

'Everyone says Chaplin is.' Eleanor wound a long woollen scarf several times round her throat and over her head, so that it made a stunningly practical turban, and pulled on elbow-length gloves.

'It's not just the repetition. He says the billiard room's below freezing point.'

'Everyone knows islands have temperate climates,' said Eleanor, disappearing into her huge fur coat and then opening the door for the trip to Finola. 'If he moved himself instead of watching moving pictures, he'd soon be warm. Why doesn't he play billiards?'

'Oh, darling. You're so Olympian.' An icy gust of wind blew into the room, making tears start in her eyes. Probably Gay had already made up her mind to leave with Raymond.

'How could they?' I thumped my pillow angrily the night before Christmas. Raymond and Gay had left that morning. I was suffering for my mother. She had even prepared stockings for them. 'Heartless, ungrateful beasts!' Far into the night I poured out the shameful story, scribbling like some lovesick poet.

Over a Christmas breakfast of kedgeree, fresh braised kidneys, and bacon, my mother inspected me with a frown. 'Darling, what have you done to yourself? I hope you're sleeping properly. Sleep is essential for the complexion.'

'The complexion, Eleanor . . .' I faltered, looking in vain for signs of disappointment in her well-rested face.

'Thirty chews, darling, and bear in mind we have a long day ahead.'

My mother was not suffering. The day was to proceed as planned. Mass in the little stone church on the promontory—the priest had come with the boat that took off Raymond and Gay. Eleanor would kneel as she always did once a year and admire the crib made by Finola on the hill and listen to the soothing Latin. Then there would be lunch, no less ceremonial because we sat unaccompanied at either end of the long pine table. In the afternoon we would take a bracing walk below grey skies and swirling sea gulls, followed by a tea party for the farm workers and a buffet supper for the inside staff.

Eleanor would not worry that the same visitors arrived for both. Her plans were made for herself. Her tolerance was selfish. I didn't understand this then. I took her concern that I played my part as maternal solicitude. She cared how I looked; the least I could do was look beautiful.

That evening, I sat at my small dressing table in my red flannel dressing gown. I looked at my face in the mirror. Outside, I could hear the wind in the lime-tree avenue. Underneath it I could sense, without hearing, the noise of the winter sea as it burst on the black rocks. Soon, weather permitting, I would leave Eureka and my mother for the girls of Shoreham Abbey. We would huddle together in our regulation hairy dressing gowns sucking Molly's pear drops. 'Miss Bellchamber's wearing a ring.' 'You don't think. . . ?' 'The ball was going for the net, you know.' 'Oh, we do know.' 'Loxy-Poxy's hair is much redder than yesterday. . . .' 'You can't mean. . . !' Occasionally, under Molly's influence, we became more daring. 'Guess what started with me last vac!' 'You are lucky!' 'Mine started ages ago.' 'You're older.' 'Was it the most fearful shock?' 'Dreadful. I thought I was dying.' 'My mother hasn't told me a thing.' 'My mother pretended to be shocked. She said respectable girls in her day never started before they were fifteen.' 'You are fifteen.' 'Only just.' We talked about menstruation because we could not talk about sex.

We feared menstruation because we guessed it had some link with sex. The blood could have signified the most horrific rape. No one told us to be proud that we were now women. My mother, despite her reputation, talked about beauty. 'Darling, I've told you before about sitting up late. What are you staring into that mirror for? Don't tell me you're taking your face seriously.' She stood behind me looking at her own face behind mine.

'Handsome is as handsome does.' It was Nanny's phrase. Molly liked to lecture any girls who would listen, 'The suffragettes did not fight for a woman's right to curl her hair. We must not let them down. Do you realise during the war a woman worked heavy machinery? Women commanded men. A woman has a stronger body than a man, more determination, more intelligence and sensitivity, without even mentioning the gift of procreation!' We looked shocked. 'Honestly, Molly, don't be so vulgar.'

'Fine feathers make fine birds,' I said out loud.

'Nanny Fig to the life,' said my mother, who was not so silly.

'Do you remember her, then?'

'Of course not. Silly old maid. Dried-up old stick. Women should be like lilies.'

'Neither do they toil nor spin. . . .'

'What else are men for?'

I thought this was the first conversation we'd ever had. 'Mama . . . Eleanor.'

'Yes, darling?'

I wanted to ask about my father. About guilt. But I was too sensitive of her feelings, of my own feelings. I didn't want to know how badly she'd behaved.

My mother sat beside me on the little stool and smoothed back my hair. Embarrassment and pleasure made me wriggle and pull a face.

'Your New Year resolution should be to smile more. It lightens your face remarkably.'

'At school only stupid girls smile.'

'School! When you've finished all that nonsense—'

'It's educating me as a woman to take my place in society.'

'Of course, darling.' My mother smiled soothingly as I broke from her caressing hand. 'That's what I was going to say. When you've finished all that education—we must launch you into society.'

'I'm not sure we mean the same society, Mother—Eleanor.'

'Mothers always mean the same society, dear. The one that will bring happiness to their daughters. The English social scene is geared—'

'I didn't mean social society. I meant . . .' I tried and failed to imagine how Molly would define the society to which we would bring our education. Where would my B minus for algebra fit in, for example?

'You see, darling, look, now. Look how heavy your face is. Smile. Do. After all, it's quite thrilling that we agree on the word you should aim at, even if we may quibble over a definition. My mother and I never agreed on anything. Not even the big things.'

Chapter Three

'Have an angel biscuit.'

'Oh, I mustn't. Isn't this fashion for sashes round the widest point loathsome! Truly, I've got quite a small waist.' Molly sighed dangerously in her skimpy dress, which in the fashion of the early twenties was cut like a petticoat with a plain top and short frilled skirt.

'It's all right for you.' Dot took a cucumber sandwich. 'You're not expected to look slim and pretty! You just have to be clever.'

'I praise the Lord daily for giving me a guardian instead of parents.'

'Tea parties are quite wrong anyway. It's too babyish. You must give delicate lunch parties with a touch of smoked salmon or a cheese mousse.'

I was giving a tea party as practice for being a debutante. Mama's society had prevailed over Molly's. Neither Eureka nor Shoreham Abbey had prepared me for the London season. Eleanor advised: 'Don't worry about the men. Get the girls on your side.' 'I don't know any girls.' 'I understood you went to a girls' school.' 'Don't your friends have daughters?' 'Not likely, darling. And definitely not suitable.'

I had ended up, as usual, with the cousins—plus Molly as moral support. Priscilla and Daphne, who had come out the season before, were supposed to give me advice.

'Oh, dear, my mother was sure it was tea. She won't like me having lunch parties. They'll clash with her own.'

Now that we had a house in London, my mother had become constantly social. Dressed in a flowered silk kimono, she lay toying with a gin fizz in our new oyster-grey drawing room. Luncheon guests ranged from Gay's new husband, Raymond Lark, to Nettles' business friends. Often they did not mix very well, and I would put my head round the corner to see a room divided into two mutually hostile groups. This never worried my mother, but caused Nettles embarrassment if he happened to be there. Nettles was now relegated to the status of visitor to his own house: 'Darling, you've managed perfectly well with a club all these years.' 'You weren't here then.' 'Exactly. We mustn't be selfish. Violet would be blackballed.' 'Not if we married.' '*Pas devant.*' Eleanor looked at me as if marriage were a shocking concept. 'We're too old for romance.'

'You are lucky having such an exciting mother,' enthused Dot.

'The trouble is she married before she really came out. She was presented, of course . . .'

'Of course.'

'. . . and the Queen spoke a special word, but she doesn't know exactly how it's done. It's lucky Priscilla's so absolutely *au fait*.'

'As nothing compared to Daphne,' said Priscilla modestly.

We all but Molly smiled in homage, for beautiful, fashionable Daphne was engaged to the Honorable Rupert Devenish.

'From 1911 to 1915 there were 3,178 divorces. The figures are already double for the last two years,' Molly announced peaceably. 'Young marriages are particularly at risk.'

'Go on, then, Priscilla,' I urged. 'What does one talk about at these delicate lunches?'

'You pretend you talk about men, but you don't really because that's too boring. But you have to pretend so the men get jealous at dances.'

'Marie Stopes has obviated the need for hastily contracted marriage.' Molly tried to catch my eye, but I was cross with her. Any minute she'd shock the cousins into leaving. They were my pass to respectability. In a superficial way, Priscilla fitted the current image of Venus. Two-dimensional dresses suited her cardboard figure, and her smooth pale hair fell easily into a fashionable bob. Molly, on the other hand, still possessed a buxom figure and had not dared let her frizzy golden-red hair out of the earphones coiled tightly on either side of her head. I frowned furiously at her. 'Go on, Priss. Apart from men, what do you talk about?'

'You talk about the dances you're going to, of course. How many to what dinner party. You talk about clothes; who's jollier—Osperat, Septimus, or Lucille—'

'What extraordinary friends!'

'They're dress designers, mutton chop. Not that Mama lets us go to them. Much too expensive. After clothes is finished, you talk about the Summer Exhibition at the Royal Academy. That's an endless subject.'

'But it isn't on yet.'

'I'm just trying to tell you . . .' Priscilla sounded aggrieved.

'That's terrifically useful. Really.' I couldn't resist one despairing look at Molly, who raised her eyes to heaven.

Luckily, a diversion was caused by the arrival of Flo, bearing a fresh pot of tea. Flo, of Harry Lauder fame, had been rediscovered by Nettles on a visit to Northumberland. He had found her living with Kettleside's ex-cook. She had no other home. She had become very thin, almost scraggy, and unlike Molly, she had made a ham-fisted attempt at cutting her hair so it stood up all over her head. Occasionally my mother tortured both of them by making her wear a frilly white cap. 'I'm sure, Ma'am, I look like a turkey cock with a bandage.' Flo had never met my mother or Nettles before he found her. She had never been south of Newcastle. But she had a special kind of rock-bottom confidence which I loved. 'You are posh!' she said when she first saw me. 'Your new dad only got me down here with tales of how you needed me. But you look very well set up without me.'

Nettles had persuaded my mother to accept such an unlikely maid only after he had pointed out how difficult it was since the war to find servants at all. Eleanor became deeply shocked by the situation, and particularly by the advent of the 'Lady Help.' She took to reading out examples from *The Lady* of what she considered the immoral leniency of would-be employers: 'Clergyman's Daughter or ex-VAD, lady by birth, essential for house-parlour work in vicarage. Must be capable, methodical and early riser. Live with family (four). Salary, starting £30 and laundry. Age 24–30 years. No brass or silver.' 'No brass or silver!' she would cry out indignantly. 'And who is supposed to do that, I wonder? The real lady, I expect!'

Flo was certainly no lady, but she soon became my friend again. Molly thought her wonderful and, discovering my mother's obsession, took to buying the *Daily News*, a hardly acceptable paper, and circling snippets about the new enlightened treatment of servants. 'Mistresses often restrict the number of their fires so that their servants may enjoy the full benefit of the coal ration' was one that particularly annoyed my mother when she found it on the hall table.

'There you are, Miss.' Flo plonked down the teapot. 'Enjoy yourselves.'

'Thank you, Flo,' said Daphne in a fair imitation of Aunt Letty.

'Mistresses are much more considerate than they used to be—they or their daughters have washed up in canteens and scrubbed in hospitals during the war,' recited Molly. Flo ducked her head and tried not to smile. She thought Molly a regular caution. Molly had become extraordinarily knowledgeable since she'd won an entrance to St Hilda's College, Oxford. To our immense surprise, she'd become a prize pupil of Shoreham Abbey. Loxy-Poxy, finding material worthy of her own energy, had made her an unlikely pet and soon discovered a large supply of brains remarkably unimpaired. Then it should have been my turn. Instead, after the Christmas holidays, I decided to leave school.

Loxy-Poxy summoned me to her inner sanctum: 'My dear, if you worked you could perfectly well gain a place at university.' The pale aristocratic face on its swanlike neck condescended over the large mahogany desk.

'I know, Ma'am.'

'You know?' An eyebrow arched.

'I mean, thank you. But my mother—that is, I can't shut myself away like a nun.'

Miss Loxley-Peacock, who habitually wore a plain black silk dress with a white collar and a single string of perfectly matched pearls, and knew perfectly well that her younger acolytes called her Eloise, raised her other eyebrow.

'I mean, it suits you. You're naturally beautiful.'

'I'm afraid I fail to see what beauty has to do with continuing your education.'

'I know.' The task of explaining my mother to my headmistress was beyond me. Beyond anyone, I thought. 'I fear my mother—'

'I fear, Miss Hesketh, that you are too impressionable. I should advise you to look for yourself rather than through the eyes of another. But I shall follow your future with interest and expect occasional reports.'

'But why should I ever get invited to any parties, Priscilla?'

A silence fell. Priscilla looked uncomfortable. Finally Dot said in a no-nonsense voice, 'It's a question of social standing, knowing the best hostesses, and of course, letting people know you'll be giving a dance too.'

'You mean it doesn't matter what I'm like at all?'

'It's the mothers who run the show, after all. And they come to all the dances as chaperones.'

'It has to be your own mother?' In vain I tried to imagine Eleanor joining a row of middle-aged ladies gossiping on gilt chairs over bowls of melted mousse.

I was relieved when Priscilla and Daphne and Dot decided to leave. Flo said disapprovingly, 'Didn't stay long, your cousins, did they? After all that preparation I did.' 'No. But they ate a lot.' 'True enough.' Flo popped a last sandwich into her mouth.

I went back to Molly in the drawing room. She was making faces at herself in the mirror above the mantelpiece. 'The whole project is insane, doomed. Against the current of modern Britain. Do you know the unemployment figures for the North-east alone?'

'That's not the point.'

'It soon will be when the workers march on the pleasure domes of the rich. I'm going to spend the summer learning how to manage when the holocaust breaks.'

'You're only doing a domestic science course.'

'Turnip soup and potato fritters. In touch with the heartbeat of the nation.'

'Dover sole and sauce meunière,' I rallied, but sighed all the same. There was no help from Molly.

'Did you have a topping tea party?' Eleanor returned exhilarated from a skirmish with an admirer.

'It has to be a lunch party, and I don't see why anyone should ever invite me anywhere! It's not the girls that matter, after all; it's the mothers!' To my fury, I felt childish tears filling my eyes.

'Oh, Lord.' Eleanor fell back onto a sofa which was spread with a dozen little patterns of silk. They fluttered into the air like butterflies. 'The trials of motherhood. Darling Vi, do you really think you want to come out?'

'No,' I gulped. 'I'm not suited. And it is 1923. We've had a woman MP for five years. Perhaps I should try for Oxford like Molly.'

'The time has come to enlist the help of my family. You're feeling the need for respectable antecedents. What could be better than a belted earl? The prodigal daughter shall return accompanied by offspring. We must go immediately, before Mama comes up from the country.'

I lay on my narrow bed at the top of the house. In a way I did want to be queen of the social scene. Flo came in. Her gaunt mutton-chop limbs bulged through a short black dress and white apron.

'Now, now. What have you got to cry about? A beautiful big girl like you with the whole world at your feet.'

'Do you think it's extraordinary to want to come out, Flo?' I sat up.

'It's the thing for your sort, isn't it? Like the army. It's not a question of wanting.' Flo was never to be a good pupil for Molly's preaching of social unrest. She patted my back with clumsy kindness. 'It's growing pains, that's what it is. I'll give you a verse or two of Harry Lauder.'

'No, thank you, Flo.' A servant's sympathy must be allowed only so far. 'I shall go and cheer myself up with a few Poussins in the Wallace Collection.

Flo was not as impressed as I'd hoped. 'That's right, dear. Be a brave girl. And I'll have Cook make you a nice dish of kidneys for supper.'

I stood on a scrubbed doorstep. My mother gave me an encouraging smile from the taxi. She had decided to send me in to her father alone. Her intentions were good. She was only thinking of my happiness. I raised my white-gloved finger very slowly. But before I could press the bell, the door was opened by a well-manicured maid. Flo could have placed her on the palm of her rough hand.

'Yes, Miss?'

'I am calling to see my grandfather. My name is Violet Hesketh.'

'Step this way, Miss. I'll just hinform His Lordship.'

I was shown into a room clustered thick with furniture, draped with pictures and many layers of curtains. It was very dark and very quiet.

'Good morning, young lady.' I jumped round.

My grandfather was a small, silvery-haired man impersonally dressed in a dark suit and waistcoat.

I gave him the curtsey practised for my presentation at court. 'I am your granddaughter. Lady Eleanor's daughter. We are in London for the season, and I came to introduce myself.'

'What a pity!'

'Oh.'

'What a pity my wife isn't here. She's so much keener on this sort of thing. She doesn't come from the country till April the first.'

'Oh.'

'Not that I've anything against you. Eh. Haven't seen Eleanor for years. Perhaps it's as well my wife isn't here. Lady Hambleside has views. Can I give you a lift anywhere? I'm on my way to the House.'

'Oh.'

'For a spot of luncheon, y'know.'

I wondered if he thought I was a maniac, and we were awaiting the Black Maria. The maid appeared with black homburg, pigskin gloves, cane, and heavy overcoat. I followed him to the door.

'Care for a spot of luncheon, y'know?' said my grandfather.

We sat side by side in the back of a large black car. The smell of polished leather was daunting.

'Eleanor well, I suppose? You're not bringing news of illness or death?' Out of the window I saw my mother jumping up and down beside the taxi. She clapped her hands silently.

'Oh, no. She's in jolly good shape.'

'Always caused trouble. Lady Hambleside was never keen. Most embarrassing—such a charming daughter. Haven't seen Eddie, too, have you? He disappeared to some godforsaken heathen country.'

I realised he had accepted me. 'Are we going for luncheon to any particular house?' I asked charmingly.

'Er. Up.' My grandfather offered his arm up broad, red-carpeted stairs which led after many corridors into a large room with long windows overlooking the river. We were inside the House of Lords. So were many very old men distinguished from my grandfather by bushy white moustaches and an occasional ear trumpet. Our entrance stirred up a series of rumbling 'Herrups.'

'Herrup,' responded Lord Hambleside, making his way to a couple of chairs, adding to those nearest, 'Me granddaughter. In London for the season, y'know.' In reply came more 'Herrups,' plus one 'Fine-looking gel, what?' My grandfather stopped and gave a brief 'herrupping' laugh. 'Only turned up today. Quite a surprise.'

Drinks thus passed till my grandfather rose, muttering, 'A spot of luncheon, what?'

The debating chamber was offered as a postprandial entertainment. 'Care to cast an ear, eh? Guardianship of Infants Bill, I'm told. Not the thing to show us at our best.'

A passing peer overhearing him gave a loud snort. 'Asquith doing his bit for the ladies, what? Herrup!'

The stained glass and heavy panelling reminded me of Loxy-Poxy's study. I wished she could have seen me. I looked down from a gallery onto the somewhat sparse representatives of the British aristocracy. Their lunches hung over them heavily, so that their heads in most cases fell lower than their shoulders and their legs slumped exhaustedly askew. One man stood, legs securely apart, hands behind his back. I tried to concentrate on his words, '. . . effect upon the harmony of thousands of homes where perfect harmony prevails. . . . effect upon the discipline of children who may find a divided authority in the home and may perhaps, as children will, take advantage of it.' Gradually I began to make sense of what was going on. These venerable fellows were trying to decide whether parents should have equal rights over their children. Up till now, fathers had had sole rights. Another peer rose; he spoke magisterially. 'I ask Your Lordships to think what this Bill comes to. A father wishes to send his son to Harrow; the mother thinks Eton best. Or the father says, "All my people have been at Oxford. I should like him to go to Oxford." The mother thinks Cambridge best. You will have them going to the courts . . . to decide to which school or university the boy shall go.' This talk of Eton and Oxford surprised me. Was that really the issue? When I picked up the thread again, another speaker was on his feet, apparently winding up the debate. Although I missed a few words, his message seemed clear and his forthright attitude very different from the previous speaker's. 'The principle of improving the status of women . . . is one which is very important at the present time . . . In nearly every one of the States of the USA this principle of equal guardianship is already law. It is also the law in British Columbia, where I understand it is working extremely well.' Which seemed, to say the least, an anticlimax. But now it was over and I wouldn't know the result. I was only a spectator, excited by a new experience.

'See old Oxford and Asquith taking his fences, eh?'

'Oh, thank you. I was impressed.' The experience was over. My grandfather was tired. He needed a rest in Boodles.

My grandfather looked guilty. I gathered he did not wish to drive me home. He did not wish to accept my existence as a serious proposition. I was to be a mirage that had appeared in his drawing room, provided entertainment for an afternoon. He was terrified of discovering where I and my erring mother lived. He was also terrified of his wife.

'Heavens! I can quite manage. On my own. Please don't bother.'

I walked very fast. I passed out of Parliament Square, down the Mall to Hyde Park Corner. There I saw the cool green expanse of the park and dived into it thankfully. My grandfather, the debate, the unaccustomed wine at lunch, and my ultimate rejection left me dazed, so that ordinary motors and people seemed extraordinary, as if out of a dream. Thankfully, I felt myself enveloped in a completely different world of soft turf, pounding of distant horses, and far away, between the dark-trunked trees, a hint of silvery water.

A man drew near, an Australian soldier left over from the war; he peered at me curiously. A nanny pushing a large blue pram sped past. She was hastening towards the water, gleaming closer and broader through a fringe of trees. The nanny's upright brown back, porkpie hat, and sensible shoes looked as safely institutionalised as the House of Lords itself. Only when pram and nanny were out of sight did I feel some faint recognition. I stopped and then hurried forward. I broke through the trees into the wide parade that bordered the lake.

Again I stopped. For instead of the one nanny I wanted, there were now dozens. Strolling in twos up and down; posed in a central group, prams outward; pushing up a yard, down a yard; sitting in threes on iron benches, prams ranged neatly to the side. Occasionally a nanny broke away to snatch back a toddler too keen on ducks, but mostly the children were confined like dolls to their prams and the nannies, like dark birds, lost in their chatter. Which was my nanny? What I wanted was a brown nanny with a grey pram like that one, not a blue nanny with a blue pram like this one, nor a grey with a brown. Their chatter, the movements of the prams backwards and forwards, the restless groups of pigeons and sparrows, the ducks slipping over the smooth dark waters, the baby's wail quickly hushed or childish voice, all confused me. I decided to sit on a bench for a moment. But as I did so, a new movement started, a procession back from the water which gathered momentum quickly. Two nannies at my left rose simultaneously.

'How time flies.'

'Hardly settled before on our way again.'

'Did you see Nanny Buckmaster . . .'

'Mrs Fig comes from the North.'

So it had been my own dear Nanny hurrying across the park—that determined step, that stiffened back. As I knew it for certain, I saw her again, sitting two benches along, deep in conversation with another nanny although one hand mechanically rocked her pram. Her back was towards me, and I could see under the brim of her hat the little plaited coils of hair that I had once known better than my own head. My heart beat as if I had rediscovered some lost lover.

May Fig and her companion rose to their feet.

'Oh, excuse me . . . I want . . .'

The two prams stopped simultaneously. For one terrible moment I thought I had made a mistake. Had Nanny's eyes really been so small and close together, her mouth so thin, her nose so shapeless, her skin so lifeless? How could I have loved anyone so ordinary?

'Well, I never! Goodness gracious! Gracious me!'

'Nanny! Nanny!' With one part of me I saw how ridiculous it must have seemed—the little plain figure hugging the tall red-suited girl. But from the hug I received all the old nanny messages, the warmth and security wrapped in the same smell of soap and tapioca pudding and the faintest whiff of eau de cologne.

'Well, well, Miss. Taller than Nanny now, Miss Violet. To think I could carry you once!' Out came the reassuring clichés, even if linked to the unaccustomed formality of Miss. We smiled at each other and the ordinariness of her features disappeared. 'Miss Violet Hesketh, my first baby. Nanny Bird.'

'Master Jeremy and baby Charles,' added the other nanny, pointing first to her own pram and then to Fig's. She had a sharp little face below her pudding hat. Not altogether in the first class of nannies, I decided.

'We walk part of the way home together,' explained Nanny.

I walked between the two prams. The sun slanted lower between the trees. 'Do you go far?'

'As far as the crow flies.' I recognised Nanny's way of avoiding questions she didn't want to answer.

'Miles,' said the other nanny sternly. 'It's a wonder she gets here at all. It's not right for a nurse of her quality. Not right at all.'

'But why ever do you come, then?'

Both nannies stopped in their amazement at such stupidity and then decided to overlook it. The other nanny's pointed nose quivered with indignation. 'No references after ten years. How can you expect a proper position . . . It's a wonder she's got where she is. Kilburn to Fulham is a step in the right direction.'

'Chelsea, please.' Nanny was dignified. 'That's enough, Bird. Miss Violet doesn't want to hear your nonsense.'

But it was too late. I had understood. Blushing as scarlet as my suit, I recalled that moment on the Dun Laòghaire quayside when Josiah had turned Nanny away. I had been living bright days on Eureka. Nanny had been fighting for survival. With sudden insight, I saw that tapioca pudding in Kilburn was not at all the same sort of tapioca pudding as in Cadogan Square.

'I'm terribly sorry. If there's anything I can do.' I felt liable to burst into tears at any minute. The events of the day were too much.

'Now, now. Look how you've upset the child. Don't you listen to Bird. She's always one for a bit of drama. I'm in a fine position with a fine healthy baby. Now you'd better run off to your tea. And some day, if you're passing here in the afternoon, we'll have a proper chat.'

'You saw who?'

'Nanny. My Nanny. In the park.'

'Darling. Is that the point?' Eleanor patted a place beside her on her bed, where she was resting. 'Where did my papa take you in that hearse? You've been away for six hours!'

'I'm hungry.' I sat down.

'Didn't you eat?'

'Oh, yes. In the House. Nanny has been badly treated, Mother. By our family. She had no references. She has to walk miles to the Serpentine.'

'In the House. Darling, what fun!'

'But I don't think he wants to know about us really. He said your mother never liked you, and he wouldn't bring me home. That's why I saw Nanny. You never gave her a reference. Because of us she suffered.' My voice rose indignantly.

'A long walk to the park is hardly suffering.' If I'd been less obsessed by Nanny's plight I might have noticed that Eleanor was suffering herself. Total rejection from your family can never be very agreeable. It is not difficult to understand why she went on as she did. 'Besides, angel, how could I give her a reference? I hadn't seen her for six years. And your poor father was hardly in a position to help.' She paused, and then continued in a deceptively mellower tone, 'I did think of having her over to the island once—with you too, I suppose—when poor little Henry was born. But fate intervened.'

'Poor little Henry?'

'Three days in the world. He barely weighed more than a kitten. Such a perfect wasted angel.' It was inconceivable my mother wasn't joking. Yet my mother never joked. My look of horror made her turn her head away almost crossly. 'But darling, you must have seen his grave. On the rise above the castle, looking seawards. It's all written on his gravestone.'

'That grave,' I whispered. 'I thought it was a dog's.' I recalled the little mossy headstone marked by a small grove of nut trees and one wild fuchsia. I had often passed it on my way to Finola's. I had never sensed it was my brother's grave. Half-brother's.

'It's not important,' said Eleanor bracingly. 'It made you the one and only forever. Besides, I never was the maternal type. Motherhood saps the energy. Poor Nettles was cut up, of course. He thought a baby would make me marry him.'

I sat in my bedroom puzzling over the story of Henry. Could my mother really have given birth to a child and even named it, and yet feel so little at its death? If that was so, perhaps she cared as little for her surviving child. Me. My sense of security, which had been undented by six years of mother deprivation, splintered dangerously. The ordinary face of Nanny reappeared again, and with a feeling that it was her sad lot that I mourned, I broke into loud sobs.

'Oh dearie, dearie, weeping again.' Flo's ungainly figure filled the doorway. 'A big girl like you with everything she wants.'

'It was Nanny. I saw Nanny.'

'Nanny? You don't need a nanny at your age.'

'My old Nanny. You know Nanny.'

'Mrs Fig. Well, that's nothing to wet your cheeks about. That's a nice thing.'

'Oh, you wouldn't understand.' I threw myself back on the pillow.

'I daresay I wouldn't. I was earning my living at your age. Takes your mind off your own problems. If it hadn't been for the war I'd never have looked outside.'

'I thought the war was your ruin,' I peered up with a somewhat vindictive look. But Flo smiled reminiscently.

'The road there wasn't half nice.'

I tried not to blush too obviously. 'Did you do your bagpipe imitation and sing Harry Lauder on the factory floor?'

'That was only the beginning. If you'd seen me doing knees up in the Temperance Hall on Beer Street, you'd wonder how I ever came to tie on another pinny.'

'Perhaps because of the ruin part,' I hinted delicately.

'You couldn't say no, could you? It broke my heart to see their brave smiles as they buckled on their Sam Brownes. All the girls felt the same. It wasn't just me. It was different then. Even when I got caught, no one read a sermon at me. I couldn't tell my family, of course. There were people who looked after us. Ladies and all!' Flo sat down on my bed. I moved over tactfully so as not to interrupt her story. A gentle, wistful smile had come over her ugly features. 'It was a lovely time. The baby and me in a little room I shared with two other girls. They even got me a job. In the factory canteen, so I could take the poor mite with me. Everyone made such a fuss over it. The wee creature quite cheered up the place with all the smiling and cooing.'

To my horror, I saw large tears gathering in Flo's eyes. I prepared to flee, but instead she got up herself. 'The end of the war put a stopper on it,' she said sternly. 'Then things were back like they always were. Nasty faces. No work. No work at all for a girl with a baby and no husband. No work. No food. The baby died and I came here.'

'Like my mother's!' The exclamation came out against my will. Flo didn't react.

'Best thing for it.' She seemed suddenly indifferent. She began to bustle clumsily about the room, took out a pair of clean stockings from a drawer. 'You'll be getting me into real trouble soon. Your mother's got visitors. Who's going to let them in if I'm gossiping up here?'

'Mother should get a butler. Besides, it's only Nettles and an American.'

'That's no way to talk. They helped us win the war, didn't they? Now, I came in here to lay out that new dress of yours.'

'Go on, Flo. I'll manage.'

Nettles was not quite the support he used to be. I suppose his fatherly spirit could not altogether survive his banishment from the house my mother and I lived in. That evening he greeted me warmly, but there was no opportunity to discuss the day's events, because he had a stranger with him, a businessman from Boston.

Carter Fitzgerald was correctly dressed in white tie, swallowtail coat, and perfectly creased drainpipe trousers. He had a good figure and a round pale face with prominent dark eyes. His hair was heavily slicked back but, even so, barely avoided breaking into kinks. I saw at once that Nettles did not like him. Nettles had brought business associates to the house before. They must have been quite confused by his relationship with my mother, but they never said anything. My mother was still upstairs.

'Lady Eleanor's real home is on an Irish island. This is only rented for Violet's coming out.' Mr Fitzgerald and I smiled at each other politely. I thought my mother had been looking for a London house long before my season was planned.

The small drawing room was gradually being converted into an extension of Eureka. Simple linen covers had replaced the heavy damasks, and pale clear colours the cluttered darkness of the walls. The warm spring evening came through the uncurtained windows. Mr Fitzgerald looked about as if he felt insecure in the absence of signs of wealth. Flo made a valiant attempt to take his nonexistent coat.

Eleanor arrived. She was dressed in a calf-length white satin dress covered in silver net with a matching train that trailed an inch or two along the floor. She wore long white gloves, a spray of fresh violets at

75

her hip, and three white ostrich feathers bound miraculously to her bobbed head.

Prepared by her title and her island habits for something much more sedate, Mr Fitzgerald was amazed into a literary allusion. 'I guess Prospero must have a hand in your island.'

My comment was less elegant: 'Oh. Oh. How could you be so mean?' The outfit had been created by Septimus for my presentation at court the following week. The headdress was the Prince of Wales feathers compulsory for the occasion. Eleanor could never resist new clothes. She held out a smooth kid-gloved hand to Mr Fitzgerald. 'My gloves too!' I cried.

At that moment the bottle of champagne which Nettles was opening, overagitated by Flo's abrasive handling, exploded into the air.

'Welcome to London,' said Eleanor soothingly as a frothing fountain spurted from Nettles' hands onto Mr Fitzgerald's shirtfront. In such a crisis I had to bury my grievances. A towel was needed, two towels. I ran backwards and forwards. Amazingly, Mr Fitzgerald was unabashed. 'A delightful christening,' he said. Usually this sort of indignity upset Americans most awfully.

When I sat down again, Mr Fitzgerald produced a large, long parcel which he pushed in my direction. 'Mr Nettlefield spoke of you, so I bought this on my way through Paris. All the children had them. But I guess you're not a child. If you're not insulted, I'll give it you all the same.'

I opened the parcel. It was a pogo stick. If not insulted, I was disconcerted.

'On one condition,' continued Mr Fitzgerald blithely: 'you let me have a bounce.' I smiled assent, and Nettles even laughed. Falsely. I could see that this cosy familiarity did not please him. Nor, at first, my mother. Perhaps she was jealous. She rose from the sofa and, plucking the feathers from her head as if she were a peacock making an autumn sacrifice, she flung them into a chair. 'So annoying', she explained, 'for the people behind one at opera.'

'Besides, turbans are chicer,' I said. Tenderly I gathered up the discarded plumes.

Aunt Phyllis and Aunt Letty, Dot and I sat in a row along the leather seat of a large Riley. Large though it was, we were so squashed that we girls were forced forward and up. This meant our three feathers continually brushed against the roof, which was most irritating.

'I know they'll fall off,' wailed Dot, who was red in the face despite a surreptitious undercoat of green powder, which had made Daphne look ethereal if not consumptive.

'Just keep your gloves clean, that's all I ask.' Neither aunt's temper was very good. Aunt Phyllis was making a virtue of her decision to do the right thing by her brother's daughter. My mother, of course, would never be allowed to confront the monarchy with her immorality. In fact, Aunt Phyllis was delighted at the opportunity of this second visit. She had merely allowed herself to be irritated by my mother's attempts to send us off in style. Wearing a strangely embroidered kimono, she had stood on the pavement waving a bottle of pink champagne, followed by Mr Fitzgerald clutching a fistful of glasses. I thought it most unsporting of Aunt Phyllis to drag me into the car and order the chauffeur to drive away as quickly as possible. I fear the sight of another man in my mother's life was too much for her. 'A most inappropriate scene,' she informed Aunt Letty as if we were already in the presence of royalty.

'Sit up straight, girls!' She tapped our hunched shoulders and gave an admonishing twitch to her own three feathers.

The car turned into Pall Mall and immediately joined a long line of similar large cars. We came almost to a standstill. Suddenly a large face appeared at the window. It wore a bowler hat above, whiskers in the middle, and a less than spotless collar below. 'Look, Mum,' it said, 'here's a real carful; the girls aren't half fancy, but give me the mums any day. They're proper smashers!' A huge eye blinked appreciatively.

'Roll up the window, Dot,' said Aunt Letty sharply.

'It is up.' Giggling, I watched as a female face, accompanied by two children, joined the first. This was followed by two smaller versions. They all commented on our appearance, exactly as if we were monkeys in a cage. 'They should do something about it,' hissed Aunt Letty. 'Close off the road.'

Aunt Phyllis nodded in a cold, aristocratic way, as if she were thinking deep thoughts. The whole of the Mall had become a giant sideshow for those Londoners who were never likely to receive the Royal Command. The surprising thing was that there was no mockery in their appreciation. I thought of Flo wistfully fingering my silver train—'It'd make a lovely bridal gown'—and gave the nearest spectator a gracious smile.

Dot's elbow nudged me painfully. 'Isn't that your nanny?'

There stood May Fig. Not prying and peering like the common herd, but on the pavement nevertheless, neat head turned unashamedly to each passing car. It was the first time I'd seen her without a child. It must be past baby Charles' bedtime. 'Nanny Fig!' cried Dot. 'Just look who's in here!'

Nanny turned. Her gaze focussed, and as she took in my silvery gauze, Grecian knot, and long white gloves, she broke into an ecstatic smile. Only I could also see that she muttered, 'Well, well. Fine feathers do make fine birds.' I wanted to say something to her, to bridge the gap between us, but the car put on a sudden spurt and she was left behind.

'If you weren't on the list, Dot, I'd take you straight home. On the doorstep of the Palace. Shouting out to the public street. For any working man to hear,' twitched Aunt Phyllis.

'They should be at work,' agreed Aunt Letty. 'Now the war's over, they think the world's a playground.'

'Still in their uniforms too, some of them. They should know better.'

'Begging for sympathy, that's why they do it.

Almost as soon as I'd recovered from this, we were set down at a porticoed entrance and ushered into a large waiting room, filled with rows of gilt chairs on which were already installed a hundred or more debutantes and escorts. Anxiety, caused mainly by those fatal feathers which were hard enough to control for the majority who still wore long hair, but almost impossible for those bold spirits who wore bobs. Matrons attacked them murderously with huge hair grips. Their victims' agonised faces suggested that death would have been welcome. 'Serve them right,' whispered Aunt Phyllis. 'They don't deserve the honour.'

'She'll be called any minute,' said Aunt Letty, looking to the far end of the room where two Guards officers—chosen presumably for their godlike good looks—called out names of the next to be presented.

I draped my arm more gracefully, poised my head at an appealing angle. At least I was more beautiful than Dot. Dot's favourite reading was *Burke's Peerage*, from which she chose suitably rich and titled young heirs as future husbands. It was considered a perfectly sensible occupation till she fixed her attentions on a particular Scottish baron. Unfortunately, he was not on The List. 'A baron has to be very unsuitable before he's struck off the list,' advised Aunt Letty with an expression of doom.

'I bet that's Scotto,' I whispered, pointing out the elegant guardee.

'Isn't he divine?' languished Dot.

I suddenly thought how Molly would have laughed at the scene. I told myself firmly that she had no sense of British historic tradition.

'Lady Overley-Summers and the Honorable Dorothy Overley-Summers!' Aunt Phyllis rose as imperiously as her nerves would allow her.

'Mrs Arthur Brand-Snetley and Miss Violet Hesketh!' A colonel of the guard turned our names into something resonant and impressive. And there at the far end of a large room, seated nobly on a dais, were Their Royal Majesties.

I felt a dreadful snort of laughter threatening. Beaver! The King wore a beard! I must cry 'Beaver!' The Beaver game knows no exceptions. Molly and I had played it for months. Even Priscilla and Dot had played it. Eventually my mother too. A point a beaver. First to twenty wins. Two points to shout 'Polar beaver'—a white beard; how many, then, to shout 'King Beaver'? Oh, heavens! The snort came out as a little belch; the smile could not be repressed, but might be taken as a nervous ricture.

Flo sighed and sighed as she unhooked my train, then my dress.

'You sound like a bagpipe before the sound comes through.'

'Just think of it. Seeing His Majesty so close. And the Queen. Just think.'

'Close enough to throw a bomb.'

'Don't say such a thing. We had a letter from them once. At the munitions. Thanking the girls for their work. Some thought it stupid. Said they'd hardly turn down the chance to earn so much money. But I thought it lovely of them. To take such a special interest.' Flo's face became rapturous.

'Did you really earn a lot?'

'Not as much as the men, of course. But not far off.' She paused. 'I'd never have come back into service except for the war ending.'

'And your baby.' I felt on the defensive. No one had forced her to our house.

'I was a projectile girl. Earned three pounds four shillings and tuppence, five times as much as they paid before. Mind you, we worked for it, six days seven A.M to eight thirty P.M. and eight to five on Sundays.'

'Three pounds four shillings and tuppence,' I repeated, unsure if that was a daily, weekly, or monthly rate.

'We stuffed ourselves on it. Canteen food wasn't bad—"two Zepps in a cloud" sausages and mash to you for tuppence ha'penny, mince and mash tuppence, beans a penny. It wasn't a bad time. Not a bad time. And always the other girls for a chat.'

I saw she was not going to mention her baby again. 'I heard the war was a dreadful time of privation.' Shoreham Abbey had been full of horror stories. Some of the girls had VAD elder sisters who had seen dreadful things in France or even in London. One girl's sister had lost two stone. Even the aunts described their work for the Red Cross in terms of heroic misery.

'Depends what you start out with,' said Flo casually. 'We weren't wanted after the war. I could see the men's point of view. They'd been fighting in all that mud and blood and all the thanks they got was no job. Of course they blamed us. It's only natural.'

*　　　*　　　*

Molly said my inane way of life was putting a great strain on our friendship. I said living at home with only her dentist guardian as company was making her pompous. 'He's a dental surgeon!' she screamed.

'There you are.' We were sitting in the waiting room to his consulting rooms, whose huge leather armchairs and wide selection of reading matter appealed to us both. We sat there for hours while patients came and went. We gave a very bad impression of the consultant's punctuality. 'I'm only swimming with the stream of my particular class.'

'Only dead fish swim with the stream.'

'You've been reading Confucius again.' Sometimes we couldn't resist showing off to our neighbours, who were far too ill to raise their voices above a whisper.

The day after my first dance, I came to the waiting room to report to Molly. Despite her disapproval, she enjoyed hearing about my adventures.

'It was held in a rented house. In Portman Square.'

'A rented house? After the Palace . . .' A shrivelled lady in furs looked our way with satisfactory astonishment.

'Dot and I are giving our dance there too. It costs two hundred pounds.' Despite my visit to the House of Lords, as expected, leading to no further contact between our household and that of my grandparents, I had already been asked to eighteen dances. Taking the credit, Aunt Phyllis had become benign. 'Now, as long as you don't blot your copybook at your first dance, you'll do very nicely.'

Before the dance, there was the dinner party. I was seated next to my host, Lord Teesdale. His attention was concentrated on the chicken fricassee and the sweetish hock. On my left sat a man whose polite but blank expression was vaguely familiar. He was older than the other escorts, who shared the characteristic of underdeveloped heads and overdeveloped ears. I decided to try one of Priscilla's opening gambits, which ranged from the standard 'I suppose you know everybody here?' to the daring 'Do you like the left or right side of the tennis court?' which apparently resulted in instant intimacy. Just as I made up my mind to try Molly's suggestion, 'Do you think women MPs are a good idea?' he spoke himself.

'Does Eureka thrive?'

It was Roly Royston, the shell-shocked major, who'd been married to that awful Christobel who'd been so keen on the sleek-haired flyer. It might even be possible to talk to him in an ordinary way. Priscilla lived through a whole season without having one ordinary conversation. 'Roly!' I exulted. 'What ever are you doing here?'

Roly was politely unsurprised by my effusiveness. 'They needed an odd man, I suppose. I'm a sort of cousin.'

'I am glad.' I avoided the glance of the competitive pink-cheeked girl on his left. 'I didn't know anyone here before you. Not worth knowing.' This idea seemed to cheer him, and he took several gulps at his wine. 'Is your wife here?'

'She's no longer my wife.' I hid my embarrassment in a large sip of wine, theoretically forsworn in the interest of a sophisticated pallor. 'She wanted a bloody braggart hero back from the bloody trenches. A typical bloody war marriage. Made in bed. Not heaven.'

'My mother and Nettles never married, you know,' I volunteered, to show nothing could shock me.

'Is that so? I didn't know.' My reward was distinct, if not overwhelming, interest. There was a pause. Roly twirled his glass meditatively. 'You're a bastard, then.'

Even for the sake of greater conversational sparkle, I couldn't let that one pass.

'Certainly not. My father was married to my mother. He was killed during the war. At Hooge.' Since I was already scarlet in the face, there seemed no point in avoiding the wine. I drank deeply.

'Hooge. What was he called?'

'Tudor Hesketh.'

'I don't remember him. A lot were killed there. I was only eighteen.'

'I followed the war on all the maps.'

'How extraordinary.' I watched, dismayed, as animation was gradually covered by the original lack of expression. To test him for further use, I said quickly before the curtain came right down, 'You are coming on to the dance?'

'If my hostess insists.'

Despite this disappointing ending, I felt triumphant enough to rush at Dot in the powder room of the Portman Square house. 'How was your dinner?' 'We had a super chocolate mousse.' I adjusted my hair in a negligent manner. 'I sat next to a man I knew.' 'You knew a man!' 'A friend of my mother's actually.' 'Your mother's!' 'He told me all about his failed marriage and sex not being everything.'

Dot's look of horror was the perfect tribute. 'Shh. Honestly. Anyone might overhear. You don't want to get a reputation for being fast. It's bad enough with your mother and everything.'

I smoothed up my long white gloves airily. 'Only dead fish swim with the stream.' We started up the stairs to the dance floor.

'You must point him out to me,' whispered Dot, longing to disapprove in the flesh. 'I suppose he's terrifically good-looking? Of course you mustn't dance with him.'

81

We both looked for a moment at the ungainly group waiting resignedly to do payment for their feeding and watering. 'I bet not one of them's heard of the Black Bottom.'

'You can't do it yourself.'

'At least I've heard of it.'

'I can't see him,' I said anxiously. 'I'll introduce you when I do.'

'Lord, no!' Dot scurried away to the dull safety of her dinner party.

We separated across the dance floor. Lady Teesdale, a formidable woman whose jewels clustered over her bosom like chicken netting over grass, was speaking to her husband: 'It really is too bad of Roly.' 'Sad chap.' 'He has a duty.' 'Yes, dear.' Roly had gone home.

I reported all this to Molly. I dwelt freely on the presence of Roly.

'So what about the actual dance?' The waiting room, which had accepted shell shock with average interest, looked forward to the next instalment.

'There was this fortune-teller called Carmen Rose. She comes from Bermondsey.' 'You can't have danced with her.' 'She goes to all the dances. She said I had an interesting hand with the possibility of many marriages. She keeps a good supply of the *Tatler* for reluctant debutantes.'

'You don't read the *Tatler*.'

'People do strange things under stress.'

I sat next to Molly on a trolleybus. It was very full—mostly with men in short shabby jackets, badly cut trousers, and caps. They were the sort of reason Eleanor forbade me public transport: 'You never know what foul sickness they're carrying.'

Molly took the bus regularly to her cooking classes. It travelled to Holborn via Theobalds Road and the Kingsway embankment. At one point it even dived under the road, which was quite an adventure, since my life was normally circumscribed by Bryanston Square in the north and the edges of Belgravia in the south. West or east, of course, I didn't know at all. 'It's the days that are the problem,' I was explaining earnestly. 'Even if I stay in bed till eleven, which is jolly boring, I've still got till six thirty till I can possibly start dressing for dinner.'

'How Loxy-Poxy would clasp her hands! "Work separates man from beast."'

'It is work. I expect my mother will ask Aunt Phyllis for a progress report at the end of the season. "Interested coronet. Attentive younger son. Beta plus."'

'She's probably trying to give you the respectability she lacks.'

'The only friends I've made are Carmen Rose and Roly, who turns up looking miserable remarkably often. He must have a lot of relations.'

Molly tapped her head.

'I'm trying to decide whether to go slumming!' My voice rose, turning the heads of several passengers.

'Oh, how jolly feeble!' cried Molly.

'Everyone else does it. Once or twice a week. Down in the East End. Helping with orphans and things.'

'Florence Nightingale's interest was drains.'

'I don't want to be Florence Nightingale. I just want to do something.'

'You should be trying for Oxford.'

'How revolting!' Eleanor, in pink satin chemise, stayed poised in shock over a silk stocking she was rolling carefully up her leg. Her pointed red nails splayed away like daggers. 'You can't mean to actually touch slum children. They'll have lice, ringworm, scabies, verrucas . . .'

'Don't be so old-fashioned.'

'Old-fashioned!' Eleanor was stunned. She pulled up her stocking fiercely; a quivering red dagger struck. 'Bloody hell!'

'It's absolutely the thing. Daphne did it twice a week last year.'

'Daphne's engaged.'

'There you are.'

In fact I found the experience of fifty little East End children quite as distasteful as my mother could have wished. Thursdays seemed to come round twice as fast as any other day, be preceded by a particularly long and tedious dance, and last till my legs and back and patience were breaking. Although two of the children did have lice, it was the ugliness and noise that I found most jarring. The dreadful brown-and-yellow rooms where they played; the coarseness of the badly cut, ill-fitting clothes they wore. Their greyish, unhealthy skin; the faint nasty odour that hung around them all, despite the bottles of disinfectant that were daily poured down lavatories, over sinks and floors and even walls.

The superintendent's artistic efforts at decoration—beech leaves stuck into bottling jars—added to the depression. My main duty, to tell uplifting stories from the Bible, proved impossible, since the children knew them much better than I and finished them at a shout long before the allocated fifteen minutes was over.

It was a great relief when August came and my mother announced we would leave for Eureka. Carter Fitzgerald was coming with us. Eleanor said casually, 'Affable enough, like all Americans, but hardly my taste.' Nettles said, in a depressed voice, 'Very energetic, very rich, quite personable, very sociable. No wonder your mother can't get enough of him.' Eleanor regretted, 'Dear Nettles can't get away this summer. He always has worked too hard.'

That summer I was too old for Eureka and not old enough. I mooned about, feeling my problems were central to the world. I spent long hours on the headland watching the sun rising and setting or, more often, the uninspiring grey clouds that covered it. I took long walks on the back of the island, ending up with a huge tea of soda bread and honey in one of the cottages on the hill. I became fat and bored. Meanwhile, my mother strolled with Mr Fitzgerald or played an occasional game of clock golf, which she thought becoming to her maturer years. 'Darling girl. You really should try. It does wonders for the waistline.' I slumped further into my Shetland knit.

Dot wrote that the country house they had taken near Chard, Somerset, was horridly Victorian and her younger brothers and sisters 'a frightful nuisance,' but she'd already got several invitations for the winter season, hunt balls and weekends in Warwickshire, so that really was something to look forward to: 'You remember that pimply Hamish Talbot, well he's staying nearby and honestly he's much better than he seemed in London. He says dancing gives him the bloody jim-jams and his idea of fun is a good bracing walk over nine holes. Golf is the Latest Thing. It comes from America. Hamish promised to teach me but I think I'm too fat as the ball's so awfully small.'

Molly's letters were worse because she was even more enthusiastic. 'I can't tell you how much money I've spent on books. It's quite decided I'm to change to Classics. I've decided to call my first child Ulysses. Dr Marie Stopes, in person, is coming to lecture in Oxford. You jolly well must come down for it. There might even be a riot.'

I wrote back, hiding my misery: 'You won't have a first or last child if you listen to Dr Stopes. We're back in London at the beginning of September. Have you read *The Sheik*?'

Our London drawing room seemed small and stuffy; throughout England there was a sad lack of sky. My mother stood by the mantelpiece with her arm through Mr Fitzgerald's; she had become very respectable lately. Gay made jokes about the change of life.

'Darling. Carter's taking me to America for a visit. So kind of him.'

'Nettles goes all the time.'

'He never invited me.'

'Yes, he did. You said there were only two stretches of water you wanted to cross. From here to Dun Laoghaire and from Dun Laoghaire to Eureka.' 'Was I really so long-winded?' 'Yes.'

'Darling Vi has the most amazing memory,' said my mother abstractedly. I considered it a victory until Carter spoke.

'I'm hoping for the honour to become your mother's husband.'

'Oh, dear,' my mother sighed, and then appealed to me. 'Apparently people get married all the time in America. It's quite a national pastime. If only I could interest Carter in the delights of secret dalliance.'

When they left for America, I felt horribly deserted. I decided to visit Nanny by the Serpentine. We walked up and down beside the greyish water because every time we tried to stop or sit down, her baby thrust up his legs and screamed. 'Poor mite,' said Nanny, with patience verging on stupidity. 'Of course he's got colic with his lungs filled with motor fumes. So your mother's planning to get married again. Very nice. Give you a nice settled home after all these years.'

'They've gone to America.'

'Now, now, Master Peter, there's no good making a face like that.' She joggled the pram about in what I hoped might be hatred, but it was obviously some special nanny magic, for nasty Peter suddenly stopped protesting and shut his eyes.

'Don't you hate my mother?' I burst out.

'That's my little beauty,' cooed Nanny.

'They've left me all alone,' I said in piteous tones.

'Dear, dear!' Nanny clicked her teeth, but the sympathy was mechanical. 'You've got those nice cousins of yours. Oh, you were as pretty as a picture on your way to the Queen.' For a moment she looked at me properly. 'Filled out a bit since then, haven't you?'

'Soda bread's very fattening.'

'You always were a chubby little girl. Your mother would never admit it. "She's just rounded," she used to insist.'

'Nanny, what matters to you most in the world?' I tried one more desperate question, but I knew the answer as I spoke.

'My babies,' she said firmly. And I wasn't her baby any more.

Nettles tried to help. He took me out to lunch at his club, but since I was the wrong sex I barely caught a glimpse of the fine curling staircase or the heavy oil paintings that hung above it. We arose by lift to avoid an area where men traditionally told risqué stories over their cigars. Nettles and I looked at each other sombrely. He had dark circles under his eyes, and his hair had been cut unbecomingly short. He wore one of those black city suits which make depressed businessmen be mistaken for depressed businessmen. I should have recognised that his suffering was greater than mine. He was in the process of losing someone who had acted as his wife for over a decade. He was also in the process of losing a great deal of money. With an unlucky sense of timing, he removed his money from America both for nationalistic reasons and to catch the British postwar boom just too late, when we were already sinking into a decline. I suppose he would have lost it on Wall Street in 1929 anyway, but that was little consolation in 1923.

'I like your new suit,' he said to me.

'It's one of Mother's cast-offs.'

'Your mother's cast-offs are often very nice.' There was a pause while he fingered a bread roll. 'Your hair looks very nice.'

'I think I shall have it cut off.'

'If you ever do decide to try for university, there's a very good tutor I know of in Bournemouth.'

'Bournemouth!'

My main comfort was Flo. She brought me breakfast in bed and suggested ways of passing the day. Without her encouragement I would never have visited Oxford. 'I like to hear that Miss Molly talking. She's not much of a looker, but she brings the blood to your cheeks.'

Molly waited for me in Oxford station. She wore a black gown and a flat black hat. 'You do look extraordinary,' I said jealously.

'It's the law. If I don't wear them, a dreadful thing called a bulldog runs after me and lifts his bowler hat, and then a proctor progs me.'

We walked into Carfax and then down The Broad. I was amazed to see ordinary people in the streets as well as the black bats flying on bicycles or striding the pavements like cold-weather Arabs. We turned into The Turl. 'Heavens!' I cried. 'That looks most awfully like Augustus.'

'Do you know Dr Budd?' Before I could question the awe in Molly's voice, Augustus had recognised me. Pointing a long white finger, he cried in his shrill voice, 'Your King and country need you!'

I shrieked back,

> Fight for your life,
> Fight for your good name
> Fight as Britain has fought before—for freedom
> Fight for humanity.

We shook hands vigorously.

'After I left Eureka,' said Augustus, who always liked a positive subject for conversation, 'I went to see the battlefront. Can you imagine it, there was a thriving business in guided tours. People picnicked in the trenches, laughing and joking, using old ammunition boxes as tables. . . .'

'Good afternoon, Dr Budd,' interrupted Molly aggressively.

'Miss Mannering, isn't it?' Augustus shook her hand.

'Yes, I'm one of your new students.'

'Good.' He turned back to me. 'Doesn't that confirm my worst judgments on human nature?'

'A country that can ban German music, even after the country's been defeated,' agreed Molly.

'How's your mother?' Abruptly Augustus changed the subject.

While I considered how to answer, Molly took my arm. 'We're just going to take tea in my room. Perhaps you'd like to join us. Mr Briggsworthy will be there.'

We strode together towards Beaumont Street. Augustus looked longingly towards the Randolph Hotel.

'He was my tutor before I came to Shoreham,' I whispered to Molly. 'He's considered the most brilliant young don at Oxford,' she whispered back. 'I'm fearfully lucky to get him. He makes a principle of taking one woman.'

Back in Molly's room, Augustus and I chatted about old times while she produced a large bag of doughnuts. Since he was now so important, I didn't think it would upset him very much if I told him my mother was considering remarriage. Any reaction was blurred by a rap at the door. A head popped round the door, 'Miss Mannering?' a deep voice inquired doubtfully. 'Yes, please!' said Molly, bouncing up from her toasting fork.

It would have been hard to find two more dissimilar men than Augustus Budd and Henry Briggsworthy. Although both were tall, Augustus' frame still had a thin and asthmatic bend, while Henry's seemed made of solid oak. Augustus' face was small and pale with close-set yellowish eyes. Henry's fresh-faced complexion, with its good straight features, was topped by yellow hair. I remembered that Molly had said he was a rugger Blue.

'Jolly cosy,' he said, shaking hands all round. 'All we need is a punkah wallah to wield the toasting fork.' Augustus looked at him in bewilderment, or perhaps his mind was on my mother.

'Mr Briggsworthy was brought up in India,' Molly said protectively.

'Only in the hols, you understand.'

'Polo and pig sticking and all that,' said Augustus.

'Sundowners, tiffins, and Burra Khanas notwithstanding,' responded Henry with perfect good humour.

'Have a doughnut.' 'Granville-Barker killed three fairies.' Molly and I spoke together in an urge to combat antagonism. I continued 'It was his production of *A Midsummer's Night Dream*. He painted the fairies gold all over so their skin couldn't breathe, and they died.' It was an item I had read somewhere and suspected was untrue.

'How gruesome.' Henry seemed impressed.

'Did they finish the production?' inquired Augustus. 'One must suffer for Art,' said Molly at the same time. There was a pause.

Augustus stood up. 'What do you think about Oscar Wilde?' He waved his head in snakelike challenge at Mr Briggsworthy. Before we could answer there was a loud crash as his ungainly elbow knocked a pile of books off a shelf. The top one was *Married Love* by Marie Stopes.

'The Gods have answered us,' cried Augustus as Henry, blushing to his neck, bent to pick up the shocking book. 'Do I hear the dull tramp of women's martial feet?'

After this sophistication, the London season, now transferred to wintry weekends in the country, seemed miserably philistine. Hunting had become the passport to success, and since my only recent riding experience was with a fifty-per-cent cart horse on Eureka, I was doomed to failure. Even Roly's gloomy maturity looked better on horseback. I had recently discovered that it was our political leaders who had forced him into the social whirl. After the war, when there was a great deal of unemployment, they had ordained that insurance should be paid to men but not to officers. The assumption that officers came from moneyed backgrounds was flattering but often untrue. The house parties which I so hated were a godsend of good food and clean beds to him. 'As long as I never actually rape anyone and keep my divorce secret, I'll be on The List forever.' He had just come in from hunting, and his cheeks glowed with unaccustomed vigour. One of the problems of being a nonhunting guest was that I suffered terribly from the cold. One morning I discovered that the water in my bedroom in a certain West Country house had frozen overnight.

'You look almost handsome, Roly. You've got a good Wellingtonian nose, solid brown hair, and an upright stance. Perhaps an heiress will fall in love with you.'

'Christobel will crash in her Armstrong-Siddeley.'

'And you'll live happily ever after.'

Marriage was, of course, the theoretical *summa cum laude* for all our social activities. Aunt Phyllis discovered via Dot that I spent most of my time talking to a man already married, and gave me a stern lecture. 'It's not,' she said, 'as if you had all the advantages.'

'What advantages?'

'Don't be clever, my dear; that's not the way to marriage either.'

I'm sure my aunts were not so stupid and repressive as I thought. I had cast them as the Ugly Sisters, with me, of course, as Cinderella and my mother in the unlikely role of Fairy Godmother. They would have called her the Wicked Fairy.

'And when's your mother returning from America, I'd like to know. It's not right leaving a young girl all on her own.'

'I've got Flo. Anyway, Eleanor will probably get married and never come back.'

My worst fears, revealed with nonchalance in order to irritate, eventually were to prove true. Till that time I lived in a curious hiatus of which my only vivid memory is a visit to Northumberland. It seemed my mother had suddenly remembered her inheritance and was toying with the idea of selling it. For some reason Nettles was very upset at the idea. More so than I. My childhood memories had been superseded by Eureka. I was curious, but unemotional.

Nettles, myself, Roly, and Molly set out to visit it. It was an icy January dawn. Roly, unnecessarily loaded with gauntlets and goggles, was to be our driver. We drove because Roly had become suddenly car-mad. He had visited Brooklands Motor Course for a series of thrilling high-speed rides and had suddenly become convinced that there might be a future for him as part of Sir Herbert Austin's racing team. 'You're too old, Roly,' I kept telling him. 'Even if you would look dashing in white overalls and cap.'

'It's practice, Vi. Watch the way I double-de-clutch. Have you ever felt anything so smooth?'

Hence our Buick Six Tourer, which was a popular American car then and lent to Roly by a foolhardy friend. 'Can you imagine, old chap, it cost one thousand, seven hundred and ninety-five dollars.'

Despite Roly's determination to break the 20-mph speed limit on every occasion, it took us till four o'clock the next morning before we reached Northumberland. The discomfort was considerable. We had to carry most of our own petrol with us, since there were few garages in England then, besides equipment for changing tyres—executed by Roly twice with much drama—our luggage, and food and drink.

'The motion of the ship,' Nettles remarked calmly, during a particularly fraught five minutes when it seemed all four wheels were coming off at the same moment, 'precludes carrying the older red wines.' We all, except the wrestling driver, stared. 'From the *Aquitania*'s first-class menu,' he explained. 'The best part of my visits to America are the journeys.'

'Going Cunard is a state of grace,' contributed Molly. 'Such a brilliant slogan.'

'Can't you lot jolly well stop chattering for a moment?' shouted Roly, who was worried for the owner's sake as much as ours.

'You approve of the concept of advertising, I may presume?'

'Of course. I see its danger . . .' Nettles and Molly, oblivious of their cramped quarters, argued happily throughout the journey. It caused me, as I sat map-reading beside Roly, to reconsider my concept of Nettles. For a start, I worked out his age and realised he was only thirty-seven, hardly a fatherly total. Then I saw that his slight figure clad in the fashionable baggy trousers and tight V-necked sweater looked quite as youthful as that of many a dancing partner in Portman Square; while his puckish face, even though the dark curls were still severely cut, was distinctly attractive. Molly certainly thought so. 'How glamorous to have him as a stepfather,' she whispered as we beat each other warm in the midst of windswept moorland this side of Newcastle.

'He's not my stepfather.' I thumped her harder.

'Such a wonderful sense of humour. One can hardly believe he's a businessman.'

'He's losing money at the moment.'

'Ouch! You're murdering me.'

One of the journey's problems was the lack of discreet tree, bush, or large tuft of grass in the windswept moorland the other side of Newcastle. 'I suppose it's all the bumping,' I said to Molly, who had offered to hold up a rug round me.

'You're the reason women will never get taken on a Polar expedition.'

'It's a medical fact that women have better control than men.'

'So why am I freezing my marrow holding up this rug?'

Relations between Molly and me were definitely strained by the small hours when the car finally bumped up the driveway. A moon flitting between streaky clouds revealed an ugly black block standing in the middle of a ploughed field. 'They've never turned it back to lawn!' I cried.

'"They" don't exist,' said Nettles. 'There's only the farm.'

The house smelled as I remembered, only more so, as if the smell had increased in its imprisonment. I could identify wood panelling, damp stone. 'There's no electric light!' Molly, who had been feeling along the walls, let out a shriek of amazement.

'Eleanor always complained about the dark.' Nettles sounded sad.

'She didn't mean the electricity. She meant no sun. Because of the mountains,' I snapped with exhaustion.

We chose white-shrouded furniture in a room I recognised as my father's study and slept till dawn. I thought I might dream of my father. But I didn't. I could barely remember his face.

When I woke, a huge eye-protruding beetle glared at me. I jumped up nervously. 'I shall eat anything that moves.' It was Roly wearing his goggles to induce sleep. 'Let's forage.' We left the other two sleeping and moved through the silent, empty house. Nothing had been altered since I'd left, nearly eight years ago. Tables, chairs, books, ornaments, even clothes waited under the dust sheets. 'I feel as if I've just cut through a rose hedge.'

'There's no Sleeping Beauty.' We were in the bedroom, my mother's room, the room I was born in. A room I hardly knew. I went over to the shutters and pulled them back. A very cold white light came in over the top of the black mountains. It made me realise that the whole house was icy; our breath blew out like steam from a kettle. I began to shiver. Roly, who was standing near, put his arm round me.

I braced myself, knowing he would kiss me. But when it came it was so chaste, lips closed against passion, that I felt gratified instead. 'Now I feel just like the Sleeping Beauty,' I boasted. But I moved backwards.

We went downstairs again, Roly apparently unmoved by my lack of reciprocal passion. We passed the door to my mother's Chinese drawing room.

'That room was always kept locked after my mother left,' I said. 'I expect it still is.'

The heavy door handle turned and the door opened. Nettles came out. He looked very embarrassed when he saw us. I went in past him. The room was dark but, unlike the rest of the house, was not covered by sheeting. The tasselled lanterns swung slightly in a draught from the hall. The yellow parrots gleamed from the walls. I found I didn't want to explore further, so I came out quickly and shut the door.

'I always liked this house,' said Nettles. 'But I never persuaded your mother to come back. I've been up here several times now. It's sad.'

'I'm hungry!' Molly came stamping along the hall. 'Looking at the past always makes me uncomfortable. And when I feel uncomfortable, I get hungry.'

'Of course.' Nettles took her arm. 'We'll go to one of the farm cottages.'

'This was another empire when I was a girl. Far too remote for a visit. Except at Christmas.' We sat in a little kitchen drinking fresh milk and eating homemade bread.

'Her Ladyship was not suited to country life.' The farm worker's wife spoke without malice.

'Oh, but it wasn't that . . .' I started eagerly, about to explain my mother, but realised just in time that it would hardly be appropriate with Nettles actually present.

'I want to know about the secret room,' said Molly, winking at me.

'It's time we went.' I stood up. 'Do we owe you anything for a breakfast worthy of the Ritz?' Our hostess was insulted at the idea, but just before we left took my arm urgently and held me back. 'They say your mother's going to sell. Will my husband keep his place?' I looked at her for the first time. She had a healthy rose complexion, but her hair was going grey and her eyes were anxious. Suddenly I was ashamed of our impulsive romp to the North.

'I don't know,' I said, which was honest but unhelpful. Beyond her the half-cut loaf on the table, the jug of frothy milk no longer looked so positive and cheerful. This was a poor man's cottage. Another Nanny situation confronted me, and this time I was in at the beginning. 'I don't know. My mother's in America.'

'Of course, Miss. I understand.'

This humility made me feel even more guilty. I knew that my power over this woman and her acceptance of my power was wrong. I was an ignorant girl. She was a responsible woman. But I had offered her money and she had turned it down. Turning my back on the situation, I ran after the others, calling like a guilty child, 'I'll race you! I'll race you!'

But when we were within fifty yards of the house, we stopped. A deputation waited for us on the front steps. From a distance they looked like wooden dolls standing in rows, stiff and straight. We clambered across the muddy furrows towards them, and I realised that to judge by its weed-free state the front lawn was still bearing a useful crop. I looked up at the house and saw that someone had been inside and opened the shutters. Just as I had done for the five years after my mother ran away, I found myself looking for the blank windows of her Chinese drawing room. But every window gleamed black and glassy.

'They've opened them.' I turned to the person next to me. A strained face stared at me in the cold wintry morning.

'I should never have come.' Nettles looked ahead at the solemn deputation. Even in my youthful self-centredness I did see he had a point.

'They'll never recognise you.' Molly was in her usual ebullient spirits.

'That's not the point.'

'I know what you mean, old chap.' Roly's voice sounded quite like a real major's. 'Running off with the master's wife and coming back with his daughter. Doesn't look too good, eh?' He gave a strange guffaw.

We all turned to him in astonishment. An important symptom of his shell shock was a terror of any personal remarks, as though people were bearable only if indistinguishable ciphers. Eventually Molly said, 'I don't think that remark was in very good taste, either.' Roly was reduced once more to insensate immobility. 'What I think,' she went on, 'is that Violet, as the representative of the ruling class, should meet the serving class and we should go for a walk.'

'Good idea,' said Nettles, stopping abruptly at the driveway.

My second taste of power, following so quickly after my first, left a much less sour taste in my mouth. Everyone seemed excited by my sudden arrival, so welcoming. Their faces, remembered from airing cupboard or pantry, grinned from ear to ear. They said lovely things like 'What a fine young lady she's grown into' and 'In the height of fashion, I shouldn't wonder.' They gave the impression that they had all found happy employment or happy retirement outside the house, but were ready at a moment's notice to move in with starched aprons, bristling brushes, or gleaming saucepans.

'Flo's quite a London girl now, I expect, poor child.' 'And Nanny Fig in London too. Well, who'd have thought it?' They gathered round cheerfully. No doubt the reality was a very different matter. They must have been desperate for the house to reopen, since there can have been little employment in the area since the war. If I'd been looking for a hint, I would have seen it in the face of one of the old gardeners when I said, 'We simply must put back the lawn.' 'Oh, the state of the gardens, Miss, it do make you weep.' And tears seemed to be forming in his eyes. 'We'll have to do something!' I cried, feeling quite emotional myself, though for all I knew my mother might have sold it that day.

Salvation came. But not from me. Eleanor, in her boredom with all things British and traditional, wrote to Nettles, 'Oh, darling, I hope you're not going to be difficult about Carter. After all, you did introduce us. He's more your friend than mine. It's just chance we're going to get married. But that's not what I'm writing about. It's Kettleside. Such a nuisance. I keep getting letters from agents and solicitors asking me what I plan to do about it. You know I never plan. Could you settle it, my darling? Apparently the roof's falling in, the farm's making no money and no one's shooting on the grouse moors. Well, that doesn't surprise me after that ghastly war and I suppose it'll please you with your views on guns— A brilliant thought has just struck me. Why don't you take over the whole charabanc? I know your finances are bad but I'm sure you could make a living from it. With your business acumen. Take it as fair swaps for Carter.'

Nettles had enough money left to finance a fresh start at Kettleside. Because of his lack of success and Eleanor's departure he was fed up with the City, fed up with London. 'My dear Eleanor,' he wrote back. 'You should treat property with more respect. It cannot be tossed away like a bridal bouquet. The people up there expect a Hesketh. They curtseyed to Vi. I didn't dare face them. And they're right. If you don't want it, then it belongs to Violet.'

Though there was more in this vein, Eleanor merely took the hint that he had visited it as a desire for ownership. 'Who would have thought you were so feudal? Think of the robber barons. Or the King's grant, if you prefer it. Everybody here agrees inheritance is bad for the character.'

About the time Eleanor became Mrs Carter Fitzgerald III, Nettles, for eight thousand pounds, paid into a trust for me, took over Kettleside and within a few weeks had moved permanently North. I never did find out whether he was met by a deputation on the front steps.

In the London winter of 1923, I was fighting a losing battle for happiness as a debutante and fulfilment as a social worker. Only one dirty little boy liked me, and that was because he was so beautiful despite the dirt. 'Miss Hesketh,' the superintendent used to say, 'that boy Goldstein may be a member of the chosen race, but that doesn't mean he can maltreat the little girls.' I put it down to anti-Semitism and found a new grumble for Molly. Just back from her second term at Oxford, she was in no mood to hand out petty sympathy.

'You are idiotic, honestly. Dividing your time between two pointless occupations, hating both and feeling guilty about both. University won't wait forever.'

'How do you know I'm not waiting to get married?'

'Don't be so old-fashioned.'

'All the men are awful. Except Roly, who's awful in another way.' I was suffering at the time from Roly's need to repeat the first Sleeping Beauty Kiss. 'Besides, he's married already.'

'There you are. Loxy-Poxy knows an excellent crammers at Bournemouth. She's certain you'd get into Oxford.'

'The men must be awful in Bournemouth. And Oxford too. Either unmanly like Augustus or an extension of a rugger ball like your friend Henry Briggsworthy.'

'You are obtuse. The men are not the *raison d'être* at Oxford. That's the bliss. It's all *id*. A voyage of self-discovery. I must introduce you to Virginia Woolf.'

'At least she's a woman.'

Chapter Four

'On behalf of the whole of the General Council, and I think in your name, it ought to go out that neither the miners nor ourselves have any quarrel with the people. (Cheers) We are not declaring war on the people, war is being declared on us by the government, pushed on by sordid capitalism.' (Hear, hear) Ernest Bevin speaking in the Memorial Hall to the Trades Union Congress.
The Times.   3 May 1926

BRITISH ALUMINIUM WARE WEEK
DERRY & TOMS
BUY BRITISH GOODS
Today the British Shopping Week begins the great national campaign organised to popularise and increase the demand for British Goods . . .
The Times.   3 May 1926

Charges of spreading false news of police strikes and mutiny of troops, assaults on the police . . . were dealt with at the North London Police Court on Saturday. Ernest Harper, 56, who told a crowd at Highbury Corner that the Welsh Guards had refused to act, was sentenced to six weeks imprisonment with hard labour.
The Times.   10 May 1926

I celebrated passing the entrance exam to read English at Oxford by taking Roly to the British Empire Exhibition at Wembley. I thought it would be a good joke. On the way there Roly told me he had rejoined the army and was leaving shortly for the Sudan. The Empire was not a joke to him.

Between picturing myself a feminine Descartes—an unrealistic image since, despite the excellent crammers in Bournemouth, I had only scraped into St Hilda's—I was playing the part of Sybil Thorndike's Joan of Arc. A Ladies Hairdressing Salon in Bournemouth had clipped my hair 'in the style of a man,' and I was toying with the idea of a stand-up chain-mail collar and silver boots.

Roly had countered my unfeminine need for further education by dragging me from Chaliapin at the Winter Gardens to the seafront, where he delighted the old ladies by bawling,

I love her in the springtime,
I love her in the fall,
But late last night on the back porch
I loved her best of all!

But Shaw's Amazon saint proved too much for him. We had a loud argument in front of a 'Flag Arrangement from Many Nations,' ending with our marching in opposite directions, he in anger, I in mockery.

When we accidentally came once more face to face at the exit, I saw he was part of my misspent past. He bowed stiffly and I said, 'Good luck' with a martial wave.

I was still Saint Joan of W.1 when I arrived at Oxford.

It took a short acquaintance with undergraduate rules and regulations to persuade me manacles were not my line. I complained to Molly. She was not sympathetic. 'Last year we couldn't even go for a punt without heavy chaperoning. You're free. Besides, we're here to work not to play.'

I looked at Molly, at her red hair still plaited around her ears, at her ugly serge skirt and plain blouse, at her sensible shoes and serious expression, and saw this was true. Worse still, I realised that all her friends were girls like herself. I resolved to visit Augustus, whose fight for a new life could be relied upon to stimulate rather than depress.

All Augustus' friends were men. As a don he was in a privileged position and could invite anyone he pleased to his rooms. My first visit was for sherry before lunch on a Sunday. I took a long time over my toilet and ended up in a striped harem suit of my mother's with matching headdress. It had come from Osperat, and every stripe represented at least five pounds. Molly, who dropped in to borrow some cocoa, said I looked like a deck chair. Augustus' rooms were very large and panelled in dark wood. He had half-drawn the curtains, so that the main light came from several black candles burning on tabletops. There was a smell of incense and the soft sound of disconcerting modern music. Four or five other men in the room lounged self-consciously. I was deeply impressed.

'My ex-pupil,' Augustus said in his high-pitched way. 'Her mother saved me from prison during the war.'

I smirked. Several of the men, momentarily forgetting their casual attitudes, jumped politely to their feet. 'No. No.' I waved my hand and sat down quickly in a nearby armchair. There was embarrassment as I sat and they now stood. Nevertheless, I could see that my outfit had struck the right kind of individual note, and after more sherry they resumed the discussion I had interrupted.

'A playwright should never run the risk of being mistaken for a politician.' A doe-eyed youth with a straight dark fringe and a velvet suit spoke.

'Ireland has never been a political matter.' He was contradicted by an exceptionally ugly man with crossed teeth, blubber mouth, and squashed nose. By his thinning hair and confident manner, I decided he must be another don. 'Only politicans think so.'

'The point is, does Synge think he's written a political play?'

'The point is he has written a political play. Whether he thinks so or not interests no one but his mother.'

'The play is all about his mother.'

'Rot. Absolute rot.'

I guessed they were speaking about *The Playboy of the Western World,* which I had recently read. 'The awful thing is,' I blurted out, 'that no modern writers are in the Oxford syllabus. No Synge, Huxley, Lawrence, Shaw, not even Hardy.'

'We all read those anyway.' The ugly man grimaced. 'Ruining our style. The English novel has been decadent since 1871.'

Augustus defended me. 'There's a principle involved. Sometimes you'd think we lived in 1825, not 1925. Violet's quite right.' I felt my face quivering nervously at being the centre of attention. There was a pause, and then the ugly man said, turning his back on me, 'A play that needs police protection is a political play.'

'Synge said it was "an extravaganza made to amuse."'

'He also wrote it was "an event in the history of the Irish stage."'
We were back with *Playboy.* However, I felt my reading credentials had not fallen on stony ground, and next time I proffered a point of view: 'Surely Synge in his introduction makes it clear that it's language he cares about—in reaction against the "joyless and pallid" words of Ibsen.' My voice was steady.

97

Augustus said to me when we were left alone in a room smelling of smoke, sherry, and guttering candles, 'We're not used to women, you know. Leonard, that's the ugly one, always gets aggressive when he's nervous. It's because his father worked for the post office and his mother took in washing. There's quite a few of those here now. But he's the cleverest. He's been in Oxford for seven years now. Every time we think of turning him out he wins another essay prize.'

'Do you mean he's still a student?'

'Oh, yes. On an eternal scholarship. I suppose the evening was too boring.'

'You know perfectly well your friends are the most interesting in Oxford.'

'Oh, are they?' He paused. 'That's a dashing outfit you're wearing. Reminds me of your mother.'

It took me the whole of my first term to realise that Augustus was trying to protect me against the disappointing discovery that his friends were more or less homosexual. He assumed that being my mother's daughter, I looked on all men with romantic interest. In fact, very few of the group remained homosexual for the rest of their lives. The majority were attracted by the company and way of life more than the sex. It was a turning against the Henry Briggsworthys even more than a turning against women. In later life only two out of a changing group of about twenty didn't marry at least once. At the end of my second year, I myself received no fewer than six proposals. It was their last term, so that they felt a sudden desire to conform with the rest of the world.

Augustus' rooms became the centre of my world, which caused several lectures from Molly in my first year. 'If you must frequent a man's college,' she said, 'you should favour Magdalen, which is the shortest walk over the bridge and besides, has the most lovely garden.'

I made Augustus laugh at this. But Leonard threw back his head. 'Let us not be arrogant. Let us be content to emulate the uncensorius sun that rises over Wadham and sets over Worcester.' I must have looked unacceptably impressed, for Augustus quickly added, 'In the words of Raymond Asquith.'

It was their playing with words which most attracted me. And oddly enough for someone so outspoken herself, what most repelled Molly. I took her for lunch one day and it was not a success. She wore her ugliest ruched skirt and most ferocious expression. Everybody behaved very badly; Leonard said over and over again in a refined voice,

*　　　*　　　*

98

There once was a Fellow of Merton
Who went down the street with no shirt on
He would titivate shyly
His membrum virile
For the people to animadvert on.

And when she eventually took some notice, he apologised in a loud drawl, 'So sorry, absolutely got it on my brain. Not the right place for sex. Too, too annoying.' In fact, I was more shocked than Molly.

'They think they're so witty and daring,' she said to me as we left, 'but actually they're like children.'

I couldn't explain that they had put on a special show for her benefit. 'I'd still rather have children than pompous old cats.'

'At least we're serious. Your men friends only know how to play.'

But where else could we play if not at Oxford? We never took ourselves half as seriously as people have since. The President of the Union expected recognition. The rest of us expected a breathing space before becoming irretrievably adult. Youth was not given power at that time.

Molly was already adult. 'I do like being introduced as Miss Mannering and introducing Henry as Mr Briggsworthy.'

'Like putting up one's hair.'

'I know you think I should cut it off . . .'

'Just look at the difference it made to me!' I wetted my hair nightly, and pushed in heavy grips, so that in the morning fashionable waves broke across my forehead.

'You wait. I'll have my First and you'll have—'

'Memories. Memories of love . . .'

Molly drove me to a frivolity which was something of a pose. For although I certainly didn't work as many hours as she did, I spent four or five mornings a week in the Bodleian trying to make sense of Anglo-Saxon. I went at a time when I assumed members of the Augustus set were recovering in bed from the previous night's excesses, though now I think it quite likely they too were working in unobtrusive privacy.

I could never have fallen in love under their cynical gaze. He was called Gordon Cheviot-Blythe, and he was nearer a Henry Briggsworthy than an Augustus, being over six feet tall, blond, broad, and very masculine. He was trying to understand Fowler's *Modern English Usage*. We stared at each other across a table. Since we had not been introduced, it was naturally impossible to speak. Most of the girls at Oxford were in love with him, and a high proportion of the men. He had the looks of a Greek god, he was a rowing Blue, he was unattached and supposedly not without brains. 'Not the sort of brain you admire, Vi, but quite adequate for the rest of us,' a girl called Edith Spinks said spitefully. She did not shake my conviction that Gordon and I were made for each other.

One Saturday morning I was having coffee with ugly Leonard and another friend in the Cadena Café. They were indulging in a touch of 'pleb baiting' over their breakfast. This was a sport aimed not at the townspeople but at an unfortunate member of the university. The game was to make up a verse about him (women were too uninteresting to stimulate even ridicule) and recite it loudly enough for the subject to hear. If he recognised himself and turned round, a point was scored; if he remained unaware, a penalty point was incurred; if he turned round and then left the café out of rage or embarrassment, two points were scored; and if he had enough gall to approach with objections, then two penalties were incurred, for he had clearly been wrongly identified as a 'pleb'.

That morning both William and Leonard were obsessed by a large man, only half visible behind other breakfasters, but that half clearly garlanded by a luxuriant red beard. It was a noteworthy sight, since beards were almost totally out of fashion.

'Perhaps it's the King!' I cried.

'Wrong colour,' said William, who was working hard on his limerick.

'In disguise.'

'He's wearing a commoner's gown.'

Eventually the verse was finished. It was on the lines of Aldous Huxley's quatrain:

Of decorous behaviour,
He was a true believer.
He'd imitate our Saviour
And cultivate a beaver.

Leonard recited this several times, gradually getting louder until almost everyone in the room had turned round except the man with the beard. By this time we were both egging him on between hysterical giggles. Suddenly the bearded gentleman scraped back his chair and strode towards us. As he strode, I did have a faint sense of recognition, but lost it under the full impact of the great red growth.

'Sirs,'—he stood before us, stroking the hair with a magisterial manner—'I gather you admire this beard. Seeing as you look a rather hairless group, allow me to present you!' And with that he swept off the beard and flung it on our table. While Leonard and his friend goggled at the awful thing, I looked at the unadorned face. It was Gordon Cheviot-Blythe.

It was an amazingly uncharacteristic performance. Normally he was a gentle, unassuming young man. He had worn the beard for a bet. Gentle, unassuming young men, once acting out of character, tend to go further than the other sort.

'Wait, do wait!' I chased him out into the High. I could not let him identify me solely with his tormentors. 'I'm Violet Hesketh. I am sorry. You were magnificent.'

Gradually he returned to his normal self. 'Gordon Cheviot-Blythe. I'm worried about the beard. I borrowed it from OUDS.'

'I'll take it back for you.'

So we made our own introductions after all. Leonard and the others were furious at my defection. 'With his beard he had a certain Tolstoyan mania; without it he looks like a bandleader.' But nothing could stop First Love.

Second Kiss, I remember, took place in the Moorish Tea Rooms. This was a perfectly respectable place in the Banbury Road, which had become The Place for Romance because the lighting was low and it was designed with several alcoves where courting couples could feel alone. Not very alone, as waitresses passed backwards and forwards with cups of tea and cream scones, but between sentries, there was just time for a fairly chaste kiss.

'Oh, Gordon, do you love me?'

'You know I do. I'm absolutely bats about you!'

Stars whirled, bells rang, this was altogether better than Roly's sentimental attempt. Throughout the first two terms of my second year we held hands and kissed in suitably secluded, but not dangerously isolated, places. These were mainly outdoors, such as a punt on the River Cherwell, or up the tower at Horton-cum-Studely, or near the Trout Restaurant at Iffley. Never, never in his rooms. There was no question of his asking me to go to bed. Bed would have killed Romance. We disapproved of The Somerville Fast Set, who wore picture hats and long skirts and admired Augustus John. Even my Augustus was much keener on the purity of early Florentine paintings and frescoes, which were not yet in vogue. On the other hand, Augustus was always ready to spot the Bandleader's vulgar confidence, and when I dared admit to shock at some of the passages in *Women in Love,* he denounced me as bourgeoise and worse still, 'unpresentable.' I suppose he sensed the limits of my physical relationship with Gordon. D. H. Lawrence believed that happiness for women lay in yielding submissively to the dark sexual urge of strong-loined men. An absolute lack of passion was definitely unfashionable. Later I discovered there was a lot of ribaldry about the Bandleader's baton, which they were nice enough to curb in front of love's acolyte.

By the end of my second year, even I was becoming bored with Romance. Despite Gordon's spectacular rowing successes, I could not disguise from myself that the prospect of a series of Commem dances in his sole and very jealous company lowered my spirits.

'Oh, Violet, Violet,' he sighed. 'I don't believe you love me any more. Surely we should be engaged.'

'Not now, Gordon. Can't you see I'm enjoying these strawberries? Why don't you take a walk or something? It's a lovely night.'

Actually it was raining. But he went out anyway and sat sulking on a large roller abandoned on New College's lawns. Seizing my opportunity, I filled in every remaining dance on my card. Molly and Edith Spinks, who led all the other girls who were in love with Gordon, thought I was behaving very badly. 'Really, Vi, can't you be serious about anything?' Dot, who had come from London for the dance, was so moved by his noble brow that she quoted Coward's lines,

> The way that he uses
> Ingénues is
> Really a sight to see;
> He binds them across his saddle tight,
> Regardless of all their shrieks of fright
> And carries them upside down all night,
> He never did that to me.

My cousin Dot had become irritatingly sophisticated. After three years of being 'out' in London, she had got unnaturally thin, wore silver tube dresses, and smoked all the time. Even the most unlikely candidates became Bright Young Things at that time. She put her changed image down to perseverance and eventual success at golf.

'He never did that to me either,' I said dourly, referring to the song. I couldn't describe how boring Gordon was over long periods, so I didn't try. In fact we made up our differences that particular evening, and the final climax was more or less engineered by Augustus and Leonard.

Gordon and I were walking back from dinner at the Mitre—by this time, chaperoning rules had relaxed. It was a hot night, and we'd spent most of the time arguing about being engaged. It ended up with my shouting, 'What's the point of being at Oxford if you're engaged?' To which he replied, as usual, 'Clearly you don't love me!' To which I said nothing. In this uneasy silence, broken only by the usual Oxford bells ringing somewhere or other, we walked down the Broad.

Just as we reached Queen's College, whose doors open directly onto the pavement, there was a tremendous noise of shouting and singing. Half a dozen figures hurtled out onto the pavement, amongst whom I recognised my friends. They blocked our way, lurching and staggering in such a parody of drunkenness that it would have seemed funny had Gordon not been so cross. I remember

102

that they had been attending a so-called meeting of one of their drinking clubs, dedicated to the advancement of German white wine.

'They've been at the Hockey Club,' I explained to Gordon.

'What?' He loked amazed, and his lack of quick understanding infuriated me.

'Augustus!' I announced our presence with a loud hail. 'Make way for a lady.'

'Vi!' bawled Leonard, who always looked drunker than anybody else. 'It's beautiful Violetta and the Bandleader!'

At that the whole disreputable gang started shouting and swearing how they must save me from a fate worse than a fate worse than death. As Gordon stood stiffly, they danced around pretending to be musical instruments and imploring him to conduct them.

'Get it up then, Gordy! Don't waggle it around. Give us the beat.'

'Take us to the high notes . . .'

'Float away on the wings of song.'

'One two three four. One two three four.'

They launched into imaginative renderings of 'When Day is Done' and 'Bye Bye Blackbird,' neither of which I would have thought they'd even heard of, and were just starting an imitation of Dame Clara Butt singing 'Land of Hope and Glory' when I could contain myself no longer and burst into hysterical laughter. This was the last straw for Gordon, who totally lost his temper and began to hit out wildly.

'Save me, save me from the Mad Bandleader,' cried William, dropping to his knees. But Leonard put up his fists in a pugnacious manner and went for Gordon.

'Oh, just look at Leonard!' screamed Augustus in his high-pitched voice. 'It's Jack Dempsey taking on Carpentier.'

In a moment there was a wild mêlée in which it was not clear who was fighting whom, except that Gordon in his lovelorn state was not giving as good an account of himself as he should have been. This became clearer still when a nonbellicose club member, circling outside shouted, 'Proctor!' Drunk or not, they heard this cry and left with surprising speed. I stood by the wall too dazed to run. There at my feet lay Gordon. At first I thought him dismembered, but then I saw it was something infinitely worse. It was the first and last time I was to see him without trousers. Even at that moment I saw the classic perfection of his straight white legs. At the same time, I realised First Love was gone forever.

I did manage to drag out the end for another dramatic morning. In fact, all I did was ride fast down the Banbury Road on a cycle heading towards the Whitham Woods. But a note I left in my room, 'Hate Oxford, gone West, don't follow,' gave Edith Spinks her chance. She rushed to Gordon with the news that I was threatening suicide. Molly then went to Augustus, who, suffering from a dreadful hangover, was in no mood to take a proper perspective. 'You realise you've ruined Vi's life with your riotous behaviour.'

Meanwhile, I had become hot and tired of bicycling and stopped on a grassy verge for a rest. Here I was joined by a young man I vaguely knew as a friend of Gordon's. We lay in the sun chewing grass stalks and talking of Wordsworth's misapprehensions of the universe.

Suddenly an extraordinary procession advanced along the road. The leaders had flashed past us before we took much notice. 'Was that Gordon?' said his friend desultorily. It was only when I recognised Augustus on the back of a motorbike driven by Leonard that I realised they were hunting for me. By that time Gordon had gone a long way past us, overtaking with his rowing Blue's muscles even the previous leaders. We stood up among the grass tops and poppy heads and waved. Gradually the riders returned. All was explained, all forgiven, and we repaired to a nearby inn for some much-needed refreshment. When we realised that Gordon was still bicycling fast into the distance (was he at last planning to bind me 'across his saddle fast'?), it was generally agreed it would be more tactful not to recall him. Only I noticed with guilty relief Edith Spinks slipping away to her bicycle. First Love was now truly over.

So was the first flush of my university career. The third and last year loomed ahead with a distinctly bleaker attitude. Many of Augustus' protégés had entered the cruel world, and although Augustus remained, he was hard at work on a book. Molly had gone to teach the most amazing variety of subjects at the new Reading University. 'How could you, Molly? They don't even have an entrance examination.' 'Don't be snobbish, Vi. An enormous proportion of them become teachers, which I consider the Highest Calling and is certainly a lot more useful than most Oxford undergraduates.'

'I thought all your friends here were becoming teachers,' I said sulkily. The dreadful need to 'do something with my life' was being borne in, and I didn't much like the possibilities.

'The traditional women's professions, I know. Teaching and nursing. It is depressing.' Molly was always willing to discuss A Woman's Role. 'The pay's bad too. But at least since the Burnham Scale a teacher knows what she's likely to get. It can't suddenly dip with unemployment. Graduate men teachers start at £240, graduate women at £225, although it's more different by the time you get to Heads, £606 versus £486. The most shocking fact is that nursing is so badly run, when it's one of the few professions run by women.'

'Yes,' I agreed in an unshocked voice. I found it difficult enough to identify my cause with Molly's friends at St Hilda's, let alone the potential teachers at Reading. Like almost all men and most women, I did my best to laugh off the whole question of women's equality. I remember the fun I had over Molly's proud announcement in her first letter that there was a women's rowing team. 'Can you imagine,' I giggled to Augustus, 'girls in singlets and shorts, shouting, "One two, one two?" It's too silly.'

'You seem silly enough to imagine it for me,' replied Augustus, holding his pen in a menacing way. He was quite right. In the first weeks of my last year, sadly short of distractions myself, I tried desperately to distract others. I was so dissatisfied with my lot that I even regretted refusing the last-minute marriage proposals of Augustus' friends. I wrote to one of the most pressing, but an extremely cool, if witty, letter from Cholmondeley Boys' Preparatory School soon cured me of that fantasy.

I went to London in search of light relief, but found only Raymond Lark and Gay, who were anything but the latter, having just lost several thousand pounds in a musical about Santa Claus and an iceberg. 'We shouldn't have opened in August,' wailed Raymond. 'Managements are so stupid,' I agreed sympathetically. 'He is the management,' explained Gay briskly. Against my better judgment I allowed them to return with me to Oxford, which they insisted would act as a tonic. It probably did for them. They installed themselves in the Randolph and gave huge lunch and dinner parties for anyone in a gown. They embarrassed me so much that I refused to introduce them to any more of my friends. Upon which they took to loitering in Christ Church's Peck Quad, where they had established that there existed the highest ratio of peers to plebs. When they finally left, having captured a postgraduate student to create a musical out of *Beowulf,* we were barely on speaking terms.

Meanwhile, I kept up fairly regular working habits, but might have been driven to something more properly ambitious had not Leonard the ugly, the drunken, come to my rescue. Prize essays having at long last let him down, he quite suddenly abandoned his men friends and took up with a member of the Somerville Fast Set. He moved out to live with her in a stone cottage near Burford. The girl's name was Araminta. She had large, vacant blue eyes and curly black hair and came from a reputably rich Mancunian family. She had already been at art school in London, and no one could understand how she'd ever got into Oxford. She didn't stay long, being sacked for climbing into college every night for a week and breaking every other rule possible. 'Climbing in every night deserves a medal, not a rebuke,' she was supposed to have commented, though I never heard her say anything as sharp all the time I knew her. She wore the biggest hats and the longest skirts, and if Augustus John had ever met her, he would have gone mad with desire. As it was, all the men who were interested in that sort of thing fell in love with her.

She managed to convince her parents, who had never ventured beyond Stratford, that she was still at college, so that her allowance could be used to buy the cottage, support herself and Leonard, who was now writing a novel, and entertain. Many women were jealous of her beauty, but I liked her from the beginning. She was so gentle and generous.

The cottage was not big enough for more than one or two to stay, but it had a huge, sloping lawn on which she gave all-day parties, warmed by huge bonfires if the weather was cold. In the winter she wore flannel petticoats under her long skirts and exchanged her floppy straw hat for a strange fur toque. But she never ran races as we did or burned her mouth on scalding mugs of soup.

I had just swallowed a burning gulp of pea soup at one of these winter festivities when she introduced Howard to me. 'We lay together among the poppies.' I swallowed my soup with difficulty and acknowledged the truth. It was Gordon's friend. Araminta's eyes became as focussed as they ever did, her eyebrows arched, and her mouth pursed. She loved introducing people.

'I suppose you wouldn't like to finish my soup,' I said to Howard, and I remembered with nostalgia, although it was barely six months ago, our last meeting, when I had been the centre of so much attention.

'You look thinner,' Howard said to me.

'It's worry.'

'Over Finals?'

'No. Over what to do afterwards.'

'You're reputed to have a rich mother.'

'She's married an American. Anyway, that's a terrible thing to say.'

'You're beautiful.'

No one had ever said it to me directly like that. Looking into my eyes. The nearest who had come to it was Flo last vacation, when I'd put on a new dress and paraded it for her. But she had said, 'You're beautiful, Miss.' Howard's compliment was not hampered by the wrong class or the wrong sex. His 'You're beautiful' gave me my first purely sexual thrill, and I immediately fell in love for The Second Time.

'What ever's the matter, Vi?' Leonard's face swam before my exalted gaze.

'I've just met an old friend.'

106

'The Risen Christ? Hello, Howard.' Leonard's personality had become even more abrasive since the start of his new life. I put it down to the strains of marriage. For it was generally understood that after a few months of living together, Leonard and Araminta had got married—although no one knew quite where or when.

'It's a magnificent bonfire,' said Howard, as Leonard continued to glower beside us. I sometimes thought he increased his bad temper because it suited his ugliness, but when I suggested it, he replied, frowning horribly, 'Gargoyles smile.'

'The bonfire's all right.' One of Leonard's poses was that the guests were entirely for Araminta's benefit and if he had his way he would be working all day. He therefore made a parade of doing the jobs as if he were a servant. It also was likely that the father's money left a gap in their household management. 'It's well fuelled.'

'Magnificent,' repeated Howard.

'Oh, no!' I exclaimed, consciously ruining Leonard's next line. 'Don't tell me.'

'Twenty-five pages. Twenty thousand words.' One of Leonard's 'I am a genius' performances was to throw his latest output into the fire. Occasionally he did it in public, although I had never been near enough to see if there was actually ink on the pages.

'Such a pity.' Araminto circled round us. '*These Barren Leaves* made him realise Intellectual Sexuality is passé.'

'Huxley's a charlatan,' growled Leonard, moving away to stoke up his novel.

'It's probably jealousy,' I said to Howard.

'Do you always impute the lowest motives?' Howard had a habit of directness. It made him seem more perceptive and intelligent than he was. He was not very tall, but well-proportioned, with regular features and brownish colouring. He always reminded me of someone, and a decade later I realised it was Nettles. He was not an obtrusive sort of man, and but for the circumstances of our first meeting among the poppies and his way of making personal remarks with wide-open eyes, I would never have noticed him.

That winter we met frequently at Araminta's, and it was on a rug in a barn she had brought into use as snow covered the lawn that I had my first initiation into sex. We were both helped and hindered by the amount of mulled wine inside us. Without it, I would never have let sex happen; with it we were both too muzzy and sleepy to try for much more than a token deflowering. Nevertheless, I felt passionately romantic about the whole event. Howard thought me beautiful. Howard loved me. I was really in love with his love for me. The massive stone barn with a load of mouldering hay in the back was very much the background for a Thomas Hardy heroine.

107

My staggering nausea when we woke up in the freezing dark at about seven o'clock, and I realised I should be eating supper in Hall, though doubtless due to excess of alcohol, gave me a sensation of passing through new frontiers. It seemed ages since I had disapproved of the Somerville Fast Set. Now I could hold my own with Araminta and talk about D. H. Lawrence without a sense of make-believe. That was the plus side. On the other hand, I could only just hide from myself that I didn't want to repeat the experience.

'It's always difficult first time,' Howard had whispered into the darkness. At present I felt content to rest on my laurels.

'It's so difficult for us to be alone' was a line I used freely over the next few months. Luckily, it really was difficult, though I had to use all my ingenuity to prove that it was impossible for me to join a skiing party over Christmas. Work became a major excuse and eventually even a reality. 'Darling, you're so beautiful, so hardworking, and I love you.' Howard's attentions certainly won me my degree.

While we, the young brains of Britain, worked out our sex lives, our country was on the verge of crisis. I suppose some of the more political undergraduates knew there was a General Strike on the way, but the first I heard of it was when Howard burst into the Cadena Café shouting, 'We must go to London immediately!' Thinking this a new plan for elopement, I began to mumble, in my usual way, about 'fifty-five minutes of Milton and sixty-five minutes of Marvell.' 'This is history!' he interrupted me with unusual gusto. 'We must be in the capital. We must give the nation a helping hand!'

It was the beginning of May. The next day I had letters from Molly and Dot. Molly exulted that at last old Baldwin would have to take out his pipe and face a few realities. Dot announced plans to succour strike-breaking lorry drivers by a vast canteen service set up in Hyde Park and serviced by such glamorous waitresses as herself. 'Darling, you must come. It'll be the best fun ever. Do let me put your name down! There'll be shifts. And if you don't come in now, you might find yourself stuck with some dreary lot of pre-debs or the awful young marrieds who talk about their beastly little children all the time.'

Howard was even more enthusiastic. He could have been the original for the 'Plus Four Boys.' The moment the strike was announced, he rushed up to London and signed on as a bus driver. Chalked on one side of his bus was 'Flappers Only' and on the other 'Ladies Only (White Cargo).' Quite probably he used the whole episode as an attempt to prove his manliness.

When I asked Augustus if he planned any participation, he waved his hand dismissively. 'If the Great Unwashed want time off for a bath, then who am I to pull out their plug?' Araminta, on the other hand, with the kind of peaceful optimism that made her the perfect companion to some and infuriating to others, decided to throw a Strike Party, remarking that 'I hear the miners are playing games with the policemen, so it can't be all that serious.' She then proceeded to send a card headed 'Strike Party' to the Official Oxford City Trade Union Committee. I can't think what the workers can have thought of this invitation 'to drink a glass of wine on the lawn and admire my new Henryi Lilies.' But in the end a representative did arrive. He was a shy first-year undergraduate who was helping the Oxford Strike Committee help the City Trade Union Committee, but since he could neither drive nor organise, and certainly not address public meetings, he had, up till Araminta's party, found no outlet for his idealism. The invitation must have been a great relief to him. Unfortunately, he became so drunk under the pressure of being the workers' representative at such a fashionable gathering that he passed out under the Henryis. He had never mentioned politics. Araminta woke him sweetly saying, 'I always find the scent rather overpowering myself.' At which he sprang to his feet and ran off.

Nevertheless, his presence did make me think a little more deeply, and I decided to visit London. I went straight to Hyde Park. It was a strange sight; lorries stretched all the way from Marble Arch. Quite a lot of tired-looking men in dirty macs lounged about, and I hoped they might be desperate revolutionaries, till I caught sight of several Old School ties. Inside the tent there was a pleasant air of activity with distinctly more waitresses than those to be waited upon. Judging by the waitresses' water waves and slinky hips, I guessed I had lighted on Dot's 'smart unmarrieds' shift.

'Oh, yes. The Honourable, isn't she?' 'That's right.' 'She's washing up. With the Colonel and the Chink.' My guide pointed with a long cigarette holder.

'Give us another cuppa, dearie,' begged a man gloomily playing Patience. 'He's not even a Special Constable, I'm afraid,' the girl mouthed before gliding away to do his bidding.

In the back of the tent, Dot flung down her drying-up cloth in a gesture of welcome and relief. 'How blissy! I thought you might not come. We're frightfully unbusy. Colonel, darling, you won't mind if I take a moment off.' Her distinguished fellow washer-up, sporting a spotless uniform ajangle with medals, nodded his white head in agreement or resignation. 'You are a sweetie!' Dot took my arm and dragged me back to the tables. 'We all do a turn at washing up. Even the draggiest men-about-town. Most frightfully democratic. The Colonel's a dab hand at "The Red Flag."' She stopped and looked round at the dark murky space. 'You should see us when we're full. Hello, Mr Smith.' She waved at an ancient man reading a battered copy of *The Bystander*. 'I never thought serving bacon and eggs could be so jolly!'

After sampling a cup of tea I left Dot, despite her assurances that a huge contingent of Police Specials was expected at five. 'Darling, they're fearfully elegant. The horseback sort wear topees, and carry the most divine truncheons!' I went to Selfridges, where I was to meet Howard. A large crowd stood round a ticker-tape machine, their mumbled expressions of confidence in Baldwin occasionally interrupted by a man with a loud-hailer who shouted incomprehensible news items. I was staring vacantly at passing buses, wondering that the level of humour ran no higher than signs reading, 'This Bus Goes Anywhere You Like' or 'No Fares and Kind Treatment' or 'Joy Rides to the West End,' when I felt a heavy hand on my shoulder. I turned round hoping, I think, for revolutionary attack, and there stood Roly. In full uniform. Before I could do more than gulp, Howard pushed passed him and gave me an enthusiastic kiss.

'Darling! The bus is waiting at the stop. See you at your house in an hour.'

'Who's the bus driver?' Roly asked as if we'd seen each other a day ago instead of over three years.

'Howard Shakespeare. I thought you were in the Sudan.'

'North West Frontier. Back last week.'

'In time for the revolution.'

'I'll tell you what. I'm on my way to the docks.' Roly was bigger and older than I remembered. He was also very sunburnt, which gave him an alien look. Nevertheless, his unquestioning acceptance of my presence there, and his heavy stillness, were unchanged. He had some army business at the docks which took us past the police at the barrier. Groups of striking workers nearby muttered as we passed and one even spat, but Roly, presumably used to much worse on the North West Frontier, took no notice. Inside, the deserted silence was broken only by the tramp of a Guards officer patrolling. We walked along slowly. In this quiet centre of the whirlwind, I looked at Roly and found that the years had made communication with him even harder. At what point did Oxford and the North West Frontier meet? It was a relief when I heard a faint sound. 'What's that?'

'What?'

'Music.' We followed the gentle strains, which gradually turned into 'Dear Little Buttercup.'

'It's a long time since I've heard Gilbert and Sullivan,' said Roly. He sounded sad. I wished I could find something to say. We entered a huge dark warehouse and there discovered the Guards band playing a selection to no one but the rats. The conductor's baton waved magisterially, the trumpets gleamed, the men's cheeks blew in

110

and out.

'Everyone's doing their bit,' said Roly after a while. He looked up at me, so I smiled a meaningless confident smile.

'Do you remember how we used to sing songs on the promenade at Bournemouth?' He didn't answer.

We made our way back to the barrier, where if possible an even stranger sight met our eyes. Down the road towards the barrier straggled a band of several hundred young men in the last stages of intoxication. Above them hung a pall of smoke from their cigarettes; bottles and cans of beer fell from their hands as they attempted a martial swing. Their staggering progress, three steps forward, two steps back, and their sudden convulsive clutchings at one another's shoulders, even the occasional collapse into the gutter, made them resemble some heroically wounded contingent. But their healthy, if glazed, red faces and their smart tweed jackets and Oxford bags proclaimed them the flower of young manhood. Their leader, a genuine old soldier in full uniform who was striding along as if commanding the smartest regiment in England, reached a Guards officer at the barrier. The old soldier gave an impeccable salute.

'Varsity Squad. Reporting for escort duty. I think you'll find them a fine bunch of lads, sir.'

My attention from whatever the Guards officer found to reply was diverted by my suddenly noticing that the largest and drunkest of all the 'lads' was Molly's friend Henry Briggsworthy. 'Henry!' I exclaimed.

Roly looked understandably horrified. 'You don't know any of them!'

I began to see one or two more faces I knew. 'They're Oxford undergraduates,' I said. Meanwhile, Henry had weaved his way towards us and was now pressing his face against the wire that separated us.

'Kept inside for days,' he blabbered. 'Lord Howard de Walden's house in Belgrave Square. Only just been let out. The Varsity Squad, y' know.'

'But Henry, you're all drunk.'

'Are we? Are we really?' He looked round in a surprised, blinking way. 'Yes, I daresay we are. Nothing else to do for days. Except drink. Kept us locked up for days. Only just let out.' He waved his hand, which brought a bottle of whisky into his view. 'Care for a drink? No? I think I will. Very smart address, of course. Belgrave Square. But they shouldn't have kept us in so long. Not good for discipline, eh?'

'No,' said Roly dryly.

'Ah.' Henry saw Roly's uniform with fresh energy. Hampered by the bottle, he began the road to a salute. Perhaps luckily, he was interrupted by the Old Soldier's giving up the battle to convince the officer that he was leading a prime working force and issuing a loud command.

'Squad a-ttention. Backwards march!' At which his surprised but willing cohort, doing their very best to obey this order, collapsed more or less wholesale into the road. Roly and I picked our way around the chaos.

'Poor Henry,' I said. 'He will be ashamed in the morning. Would you like to come home for a drink?'

'He won't remember in the morning,' said Roly. 'Those chaps never do. I'd love a drink.'

Howard was sitting in the front hall while Flo, with a very ferocious expression on her face, stood over him. 'Thank the Lord you're home, Miss. This gentleman'—she cast a disbelieving glance—'says he's a friend from University, but I took the liberty to keep him from the drawing room. It's a lawless time when they have tanks out from the barracks.'

'Do I look like a miner?' Howard rolled his eyes. I think he was quite flattered at the idea.

'It's a lawless time,' repeated Flo stubbornly. 'All on my own in this big empty house.' Avoiding her reproachful look, I pushed Roly forward. 'You remember Major Royston, don't you?'

'Nice to see you safely back, Sir.' Skirting Howard warily, Flo took a key from her apron pocket and unlocked the drawing room. 'You'll be wanting cocktails, I expect, Miss.'

'Gosh, what a terrific idea!' Howard flung off his mac, and I looked to see if he really was wearing plus fours. The funny thing was that at the time I wasn't at all put off by his boyish enthusiasm. I was merely jealous that he was doing his bit. Nevertheless, I couldn't resist immediately telling him the story of the Varsity Squad. 'Bounders!' he cried. 'Scoundrels! They're the sort who're giving this country to the Bolsheviks.'

As I began to laugh at his ferocious expression, he became crosser. 'I can tell you it's no joke driving a bus round all day.'

'Busmen have to.'

'That's not the point. As a matter of fact, I'm thinking of trying for a train. Trouble is they're not too keen on us civvies. Some silly ass tore up half the line between here and Henley. Probably another of that Varsity Squad.'

While Howard and I chattered on about the strike, Roly withdrew deeper into his silence, and an expression of distaste settled over his face. I was on the point of deciding not to suffer on his behalf anymore—after all, who was he to come in like a thundercloud?—when he stood up suddenly and said, 'You know, I married again out there, Violet.'

I stared at him. 'I didn't know.' I could not think of an appropriate comment.

'It must have been frightfully hot out there.' Howard looked sympathetic.

'Dreadful,' agreed Roly. 'Not fit for a cat, let alone a man . . . let alone a woman.'

'Who did you marry?' I said, trying to match their conversational tone.

'No one you'd know.' Roly looked harassed again. 'I'm going back after my leave.'

'Constant heat gets you down.'

'I don't see what heat's got to do with getting married.'

'Don't you?' Roly stood up, quite clearly feeling he had done all the explaining possible.

'But Roly, I've only just found you!' I cried out at last. But it was too late. The expression on his face was as rigid as in the early days of his shell shock. I saw he was going to leave. I wanted to sing to him, 'But late last night on our back porch, I loved her best of all!'

I went with him to the door. I kissed him on the cheek and said, 'I'm glad you're happy.'

'I didn't want to write to you.' He gripped my arm so that it hurt. Here was the confidence. 'I knew you'd understand if I told you. A man needs a wife.' But I didn't understand. I didn't understand the feeling of mystery he had created, the references to heat, nor the look of shame that had accompanied his pronouncement of the word 'wife.'

Howard and I looked at each other when he was gone. Howard said challengingly, 'You know, they call us the Bentley Boys.'

I retaliated, though my heart wasn't in it. Even then I sensed I would not see Roly again. 'They say that the coal miners' leader— A. J. Cook, isn't it?—when he was negotiating with Baldwin took out his dentures and gave them a good clean.'

'Revolting!' said Howard, complacently.

'Molly says strikebreaking is cutting the throats of the poor.'

'The Soviets. They aren't the real poor. Anyway, the BBC is the real strike breaker. We'd be lost without that.'

'You sound like that idiot at the *Mail* who started the whole thing. He gets £34,000 a year. What does he know about the real poor?'

'What do you know about the real poor?'

'What do you?'

This produced silence while we both racked our brains for poor of our acquaintance. Flo seemed a possible candidate, but her clear identification with the privileged against the strikers made me hesitate. Besides, the worst hardship she was suffering at the moment was loneliness during my absence at Oxford. She had become pathetically clean and spruce-looking lately. Howard, whose family came from Sherborne, a smallish town in North Dorset, may have had a few candidates from the land, but if so he did not consider them poor enough to convince me. The truth was neither of us knew any poor at all, real or otherwise.

'It'll all be over soon,' I said.

'Yes.' Howard stood up gloomily. I felt sorry at having deflated his excitement. It was Roly's fault. If I felt angry with him, it might kill the sadness.

'We could go down to Fleet Street?'

'You need a pass. Or rather, you have to be a member of a union. Printers and Papermakers.'

A very heavy silence fell. Our agreement that the strike would end soon made us suddenly face the horror of Schools and the Great Unknown that yawned afterwards. Howard shouldn't have felt the blankness I did, since as the son of a firm of solicitors, he had his career mapped out for him. Yet I saw my feelings reflected in his face.

'Oh, Vi.'

What would we do without Oxford? Without the Cadena Café? Without the narrow streets and noble buildings? The colleges which looked after you like a mother? Why had I ever laughed at the rule at Lady Margaret Hall which forbade female students to go on a bicycle ride with a male unless chaperoned by two others of the same sex? How could I ride my bicycle here—in London? How, without Araminta and her parties, would I ever meet anyone, except Dot and the cousins, again? How could I live in this house haunted by the absence of my mother? How would I ever get a degree? And if I did get one, what would I do with it? Why wasn't I like Molly, who had principles? What would Loxy-Poxy think of me? How could Augustus admire me anymore? How could anyone admire me any more? Even Roly had left me. Why should anyone love. . . .

'Oh, Vi!' Howard knelt on one knee in front of me. In his urgency he had knocked over my 'sidecar', which made a dark lozenge on my mother's pearl-grey carpet. 'Oh, Violet, will you marry me?' Would the carpet disappear under its vile potency? I wondered. Howard gazed with his most wide-open sincerity. 'I love you, I love you, I love you.'

Chapter Five

If in the light of the Christmas festival we consider our national life, we become aware of signs that we are beginning more readily to recognise its true ideals . . . that the country and the Empire can achieve their true development and discharge their proper influence in the world only as they are controlled by higher considerations than those of money or power.
(Leader column) *The Times*.　　24 December 1927

THEATRES

LONDON PAVILION.
The Greatest Stage and Screen Spectacle, 'Uncle Tom's Cabin' with enormous Negro Plantation Stage Show.
SPECIAL PRICED Matinées for Christmas Shoppers.
The Times.　　23 December 1927

Sir, It is to be hoped that the Commission of Bishops which has been appointed to inquire into the question of divorce will do nothing in a hurry . . . People are already growing more and more disgusted with the prevailing loose views concerning marriage, and there is bound to be a reaction before very long. Furthermore evil always destroys itself in the end. I submit that the present moment, when things are on the downward trend, is not the time to legislate . . .
(Letter to the Editor) *The Times*.　　8 June 1931

Howard's father sat in his garden wearing a panama hat and a white linen jacket. He looked as solidly English as the Dorset stone house behind him. He looked as if he always looked like that before lunch on a fine summer Saturday. Howard said that when he wasn't at the office he was at home, and when he wasn't with his partner or a client he was with his wife. He was a ritualistic man. Howard was his only child.

'Good morning, Sir. This is Violet Hesketh.'

I had no experience of ordinary middle-class country life. I saw that Howard, compared with his father, was a wild tear-away. The fifteen-inch Oxford Bag which was more or less *de rigueur* for young men of my acquaintance was a shocking gesture of defiance. An engagement to an unknown bride must have been a bombshell. Yet such was Howard Shakespeare Senior's contentment that he rose from his comfortable wicker chair with a warm smile.

'My wife hoped you'd arrive in time for lunch. We always have boiled ham on Saturdays.'

'I love boiled ham.' The air smelled of honeysuckle, lemon verbena, and boiled ham. Bees buzzed in the sun. It had been overcast when we left London.

'I hear you're one of this new race of women who take degrees. My wife is most impressed. She always wanted to be a doctor, you know.'

'I'm so sorry.' Howard nudged me, and I saw this was a family joke.

'I've lived in Sherborne since I was a girl,' stated Mrs Shakespeare, as if that put everything right. No one here would ask me what I was planning to do with my life.

Molly had been most irritating about Howard. We had driven specially to Reading to tell her the news. Our car, The Bed Pan, as the Austin Seven was commonly known, broke down twice. Instead of greeting us with a nice restoring cocktail, she had produced a bottle of Bovril, quoting with a bright smile, 'Don't get tired, drink Bovril.' At our bitter looks she explained she was now really a vegetarian, but had made a special exception for us. When Howard went to the lavatory she gave me a lecture about 'the duties of a woman with a degree.'

'But I don't even know I've got a degree.'

'Don't be obtuse, Vi. Women have fought to be in your position. Would you like to see a photograph of forced feeding?'

'It would just remind me I'm hungry.'

She was a little more appreciative when Howard described at length his ambition to be the best country solicitor ever. Although even then she felt compelled to make various boring remarks such as 'The first woman was called to the Bar in 1919.'

'She never used to be so priggish,' I said to Howard on our return drive.

'She seemed very sensible,' Howard pooped his horn at a old man standing like a sheep in the middle of the road. 'Just too fat.' The old man moved very slowly away and as we passed shook a gnarled fist at us. 'Extraordinary,' said Howard hiding his embarrassment, 'how people resist progress.'

'She's stuffed full of vitamins and women's rights.' I had never thought of Molly as sensible. 'She told me there's as much goodness in a handful of nuts as a great lump of steak.'

'My mother would be interested.' Mr Shakespeare's main relaxation in life came from estimating the working order of his own and others' gastric juices. Owing to the thinness of a partition wall, I later overheard his views only too often. He was a bit of a bully with his wife:

'No movement. No movement at all. I must have slumped tonight. Edie, did you notice if I slumped?' 'No, Howard.' 'No, you didn't notice? Or no, I didn't slump?' 'I don't think you slumped.' 'I must have slumped. There's no other way to explain it. I've asked you to tell me if I slumped.' 'Perhaps it was the cheese.' 'It could be the cheese. But then, I allowed for the cheese. I had a second helping of spinach expressly to counteract the cheese. Perhaps it was two eggs at lunch. . . .' And so on and on. With poor Mrs Shakespeare sounding more and more exhausted.

The particular obsession also explained Mr Shakespeare's regular habits, his four-times-daily walk and his habit of making announcements about the food. Perhaps he thought we all needed time to make allowances to suit our digestive juices. Howard would never laugh at his father. Or even discuss him.

I should have been more sensible when at our first meeting he offered us a part of his house, 'I know it won't seem a big house compared to what you're used to, but there is a very nice spare bedroom and Howard's old nursery as your own place to sit. My wife would be so pleased.'

Mrs Shakespeare should have been pretty; she had soft hair, a rosy complexion, and bright blue eyes; but constant preoccupation with her husband's digestion had left her with a nervous, hunted look. She never sat still for more than a minute and often trailed off her sentences halfway through with an appealing look of apology. I used to finish them for her, until Howard accused me of mockery. Which was not true at all, as I felt a great deal of sympathy with her. By this time Howard had started doing the four-times-daily walk with his father.

'We'd love to stay here.' Howard's voice was firm, and I smiled

117

brightly. We'd already discussed the idea on the way down. I liked the look of the house. It seemed to me a charming doll's house, with the great advantage of someone else to do the work. I overlooked the yellowing wallpaper, the antimacassars and hunting prints, for the pretty garden, the golden stone, and the warm welcome.

'We plan to get married as soon as possible,' said Howard in that same firm manner.

'I suppose it's difficult for Miss Hesketh's mother to arrange a sailing,' said Mrs Shakespeare.

'Please call me Violet.' It seemed best not to try to explain my mother.

All my friends tried to stop me marrying Howard. Augustus explained it as marrying on the rebound from a poor second-class degree. He was still too much wrapped up in his book for ordinary human contact, but advised, 'If you must marry a dullard, marry a rich one.' And he offered to find me one of his stupid students from Christ Church. Leonard said, 'You're a fool, Vi. Howard has already reached the zenith of his life.' 'Araminta should never have introduced us, then,' I said defensively. Neither of them gave me the one reason I might have listened to.

Flo never got over her unlikely conviction that Howard was a revolutionary. He naturally spent a lot of his time in the London house—though delicacy forbade his actually spending the night. 'We are engaged, darling. Let us not cause speculation.' 'There's only Flo to speculate.' One evening I heard her voice coming from the kitchen.

'What I can't approve is his not being a gentleman. Up in Northumberland he wouldn't have been offered more than a glass of sherry before lunch.'

'Flo! How dare you!' Her loyalty to me and mine to her had stretched too far. I burst into the room. 'Oh.' Opposite her sat a middle-aged man in his shirt sleeves; In front of him sat a half-drunk cup of tea; behind him hung a white butcher's overall. I had obviously interrupted a much-repeated scene. At my shrieks, he jumped to his feet in miserable guilt. I glared at them both.

'Oh, Miss Violet. This is Mr Lyons, our butcher. It's a long ride up the hill, so he was just refreshing himself with a cup of—'

'What right have you to discuss my private life with a stranger? A butcher!'

Flo's face went as red as her hair. 'Cecil isn't a stranger, Miss. Cecil's my fiancé!' At which she burst into tears and fled from the room. Cecil and I were left to stare at each other with equal embarrassment

*　　　*　　　*

Molly even let me down when I brought her a problem I considered just up her street. 'You know when you had that Marie Stopes craze . . .?' It had struck me that the last thing I wanted from union with Howard was hordes of little children. My ravishingly beautiful cousin Daphne, who had now been married four years, had four children. I could see no reason for it other than to please the heart of their grandmother—Aunt Letty drooled over them disgustingly. At last, I thought, here is my chance to show Molly a bit of real feminist spirit.

'That was an awful long time ago,' Molly looked flustered.

'I expect things have moved on wonderfully. I'm idiotically old-fashioned.'

Molly looked even more flustered, 'I was in the middle of preparing a paper on the use of the British Broadcasting Corporation in schools. It could open out a whole new teaching era.'

'One simply can't leave it all the man any more.'

'Of course, Havelock Ellis makes some very interesting points in *The Psychology of Sex*.'

'It's not the theory I want.'

'Dr Stopes did have a clinic in Holloway.'

'I don't have to go to prison first, do I?'

We were interrupted by the door's opening noisily and a head's peering round at us. 'Awfully sorry! Jolly busy, are you? Call back in a tick.'

I stared rudely. Molly had always been surrounded by a hearty gang of women. But none before had actually dressed like a man, looked like a man. I looked with horror at the short bushy hair and gross chest flattened under a stiff shirt. No wonder Molly was so little interested in my marital problems. Molly stared at me defiantly. I stood up. 'See you at the wedding,' I said, and to show I understood the situation, 'Please bring your friend.'

I was married at St Mary's, Wyndham Place, on October 5 at 12 noon. Flo and Cecil were married at St Mary's, Wyndham Place, on October 5 at 4pm. It was a happy thought that caused some confusion. My mother misread the telegram I sent her, and arrived just in time to see Flo making her entry up the stone steps. St Mary's is a pretty, round church with pillars, built by Sir Robert Smirke in a lighter mood than when he created the British Museum. My mother was so pleased at having come to the right place that it took her a long time to realise that she was not attending her daughter's wedding. I saw her point, for most of my guests had, either as a gesture of politeness or out of drunken frivolity, returned for Flo's ceremony. 'My darling child,' my mother kept saying, 'why on earth did you choose brown for a wedding dress? An unflattering colour at the best of times and really not symbolic of purity.'

'This is my going-away dress, Mother. I have tried to explain that I'm already married.' 'You don't appear to have a husband.' 'Howard, slide along the pew. Show yourself to my mother.' All this took place in whispers that echoed round the church. When Eleanor finally understood, she gave a loud congratulatory kiss and cried, 'Never mind, my darling. I absolutely promise to be there next time.'

My reception had taken place in the same rented house in Portman Square that Dot and I had shared for our coming-out dance. It was an appropriately unlucky omen. The aunts had thought it lent respectability to my choice of church. They admired Howard; 'Such a steady, reliable sort of young man. After all, it's not as if Violet needs to marry for money.'

This was an aspect of things that I wished to clear up with my mother. For although the house in London, with all running expenses and Flo and now Cecil thrown in, was paid, otherwise I was given a not very large allowance with no indication of what might follow. Eleanor was still only in her forties and looked remarkably spry in a gold lamé dress trimmed with fur and topped by a gold cap sewn with seed pearls. The skirts were well above her knees, exposing legs clad in shining silk. She kissed everybody she met.

At the reception, I had approached Nettles on the subject. His answer was muffled by a barrage of sneezes. 'I have a recurring damp patch in my bedroom.'

'I heard the farm was making a fortune.'

'Tiles and drains fly off the house as fast as I stick them on. Do you believe in poltergeists?'

'More likely the aunts' baleful influence. Have you reseeded the lawn?'

'My first action. But I still get the odd potato out of it. Tenacious things, potatoes.'

I had not seen Nettles for several years and liked his more weather-beaten appearance. The red nose and watery eyes were a pity, of course, but he seemed to have become more substantial. I even liked his old-fashioned suit and shabby patent shoes, clearly not renewed since his removal from London and my mother. The truth was, and I had no intention of holding it against him, that he had bought my inheritance for a pittance. After all, he was the wrong person to ask about my prospects. 'It was very nice of you to make the journey.'

'Your fiancé seems very . . .' he paused, and we both looked at Howard, who was talking to his father. The resemblance in their twin tailcoats was striking. Nettles did not finish his sentence.

'We met at Oxford.'

'I guessed that.' Nettles blew his nose, and I felt a sudden urge to confide a little. He was the nearest I knew to a father.

'I suppose everyone has misgivings on their wedding day.'

'Your mother had them before we reached the stage. I presume she isn't that raven-haired creature dressed as a peacock?'

'That's Araminta.'

'Of course.'

'Araminta introduced me to Howard.'

'She reminded me of Eleanor in our early days on Eureka. I hope you don't mind me mentioning these things.'

'I'm quite grown up now.' But I did think it tactless of him to live in his past with my mother when we were celebrating the start of my future. 'I'll introduce you to Araminta.'

'You were asking about money. Most of your mother's inheritance went into Eureka. I expect you thought it was mine.' He began to sneeze again so violently that I had to take several paces back.

'We're spending our honeymoon on Eureka,' I shouted, but I don't think he heard above the noise. Strangely enough, when I reminded him of that cold years later on another wedding day, he completely denied it. He'd never had a cold in his life, he insisted.

My wedding guests were a remarkable sight on our return journey from St Mary's. Molly and her friend strode beside Araminta's peacock tail. Leonard nudged me, 'Don't they know it's dress suits for a wedding?' The aunts walked on either side of Augustus, who, with a new potbelly above his long thin legs, looked like some prehistoric bird. First Aunt Phyllis and then Aunt Letty rocked away with enjoyable shock as he told one risqué joke after another. Behind them came Nanny Fig escorted by Nettles. I was glad of having tracked down Nanny. I knew that if no one else remembered this day, she would; she would be thinking what every bride wants to hear; 'How beautiful Miss Violet looked! How radiant! How happy! How distinguished the groom!' As usual, she seemed smaller and thinner than I remembered, but her eyes gleamed with all the old vitality. She was my link with the past.

Howard's relations moved *en bloc* like a soldier's square set against the enemy. Edie Shakespeare had been kept busy at the reception giving reports on the jellied ham and stuffed quail, and she looked distinctly green. Howard Senior, on the other hand, having decided champagne was an emetic, was thoroughly enjoying his one and only visit to London.

My mother, however, was very cross at having missed the reception. 'But sweetheart, I must meet all these wonderful friends of yours. I've travelled the Atlantic.' She appealed to my nearest neighbour, who was still Leonard.

'Yet still as sparkling as a diamond.' He bowed gallantly.

'If only I was young enough to be a flapper.'

'Ride in a sidecar instead of drink one,' said Leonard. My mother tipped back her head to laugh. She was very thin now. Her head looked as it it were held on by strings, like a puppet's.

'Besides, I haven't had a drink all day.'

This seemed unlikely to be true. However, it reminded her that the huge chauffeur-driven Rolls that waited for her outside the church contained not only my wedding present—a Tiffany lamp, which collapsed into a thousand fragments when we attempted to lift it from its box ('Such a rough crossing' sighed my mother. 'It's a wonder I survived')—but also three magnums of champagne. 'What bliss it was to be in Fortnums again. I called in there to stock up for the house on my way here.' Since Fortnum and Mason could by no stretch of the imagination be considered on the way to St Mary's it began to seem as if her late arrival had not been entirely due to misapprehension.

I decided to overlook it. 'Let's go to the house, then. Those who wish to continue celebrating.' It was only Howard and I who had to go to catch the train and night ferry to Ireland. The others were too concerned with enjoying themselves to give us much of a send-off. My last view was of the convergence of my mother and Nettles. It seemed inconceivable that they had lived together for all those years. She kissed him. Her lips moved. I would have liked to have known what she was saying. Would they talk about me?

'Well, darling, we've done it.' Howard beamed with pride. I beamed back. The train ride, followed by a berth for two in the boat, was as romantic as I'd planned. It was helped by my enormous nostalgia for those childhood crossings. Nothing seemed changed except me. I looked at the shining platinum band on my finger and removed a silver horsehoe from our pillow. 'I suppose the attendants know our guilty secret.'

'Unless they put silver horseshoes on everyone's pillow,' said Howard a little snappishly. I'm afraid he was feeling the strain of things to come. In fact, all things considered, it went reasonably well. At least his performance didn't make a mockery of my new crêpe de chine nightdress. Enjoyment is based on expectation. I went to sleep feeling pleased with myself, caressed, loved.

Our good humour with each other lasted till we reached Eureka. No one can imagine how quickly paradise can degenerate, how quickly an uninhabited castle becomes uninhabitable—particularly on an Irish island in October. The farm was all right. It worked, in a lazy enough manner, as it always had. The cows were milked twice a day, a sheep was killed on Mondays, the eggs were collected from the chickens—if not every day. Cheese hung draining in the dairy; a great pile of potatoes filled one whole shed. But Josiah and his sparkling boat existed no longer. The gardeners had gone back to the mainland, leaving one man to scythe the grass when he could find a whetstone. The castle was dank, unattended; only the faithful Finola came down from the hill to open a few windows. Round the shores of the island the sea gulls swooped lower and fiercer as if waiting their chance to regain their empire. All this could have been wonderfully romantic had it been high summer instead of low autumn. I tried to convince myself and Howard it still could be.

'Oh, look! Have you ever seen such vast blackberries? So late in the year, too!'

'Is that another greenhouse under them?'

'That's where Mother kept her archery equipment. It was so wonderful. The bright target set up on the smooth green lawn. Drinks in the house. The sunset catching the top of the tower. People laughing, shouting. Once when I was still a child I led a whole group of them down a sheer cliff. I was the Pied Piper, but luckily we returned.'

I suppose I was irritating with my mostly falsified memories. They pointed up the difference between what had been and what was now. Despite my descriptions, Howard had not appreciated how isolated we would be. He looked at the rough grass, spiky with dark nettles, and then at the thick grey clouds above us. 'I'd better get that fire going.'

Owing to lack of servants, Howard appointed himself chief fire maker. It was inconceivable anything could be so difficult or take so long. When he wasn't doing it, he talked about new methods. Until my honeymoon I had loved the smell of peat fires.

I wandered about muffled like a Sherpa in my smart new sweater. I climbed to the back of the island and searched vainly for the seals. Once I thought I saw a deer, but it turned out to be a large and probably dangerous wild dog. Howard and I began to see less and less of each other. Like prisoners forced to spend their sentence in the same cell, we eked out our relationship. I walked. He bent over his fire. Great waves of smoke rose up from either side of his head. 'Are you sure you won't end up like a smoked trout?' I had come in for lunch: potatoes and mutton cooked by Finola. This diet, supplemented by eggs, cheese, soda bread, and quantities of milk, was already altering my figure. One terrible morning, I had wondered if the fate worse than death might have happened; but Howard, despite my earlier fears, was assiduous with his precautions. Our sex life, like our days, had fallen into an unavowed but well-ordered routine. Every other day, under the great heavy blankets and puffy eiderdown, we solemnly copulated. If we fell asleep before performing on the proper evening, we made up for it the following morning. This was a little irritating, as it took us a day or two to get back into evening order, but we managed it. Occasionally I wondered if I were missing some of the glories of love, but it seemed too worrying a possibility to explore.

We were to stay a month. After nearly a fortnight, Howard said to me over toasted soda bread for breakfast—it had been one of our mornings for love, so we were feeling warm towards each other—'Why don't we pay a visit to Ireland proper? We don't have to stay here all the time.'

I was irrationally astonished at the idea. 'We never used to go to the mainland.'

'That doesn't mean *we* don't have to.' I tried to remember why we hadn't gone to the mainland. Was it because we had liked it so much on Eureka? Had Howard and I so little in common that we could manage only a fortnight on our own?

'The boat only goes once a week.'

'It goes tomorrow.'

'It doesn't come back for a week.'

'That's all right.'

'I'm not coming.'

'That's a pity.'

At least Howard caused our first separation.

The first time I went to stay in London without Howard, Mrs Shakespeare was very much upset. 'I've done my Christmas shopping in Sherborne for twenty-five years.'

'Vi knows London better,' Howard exercised tact. We were having a warm drink and digestive biscuit before retiring to our respective bedrooms.

'There's not much to know in Sherborne.'

'Quite.'

'I haven't spent a night away from your father in twenty-five years.' The thought of eight thousand one hundred and seventy-five nights in Mr Shakespeare's bed was appalling. I decided to stay away a week instead of four days. I remembered one of Araminta's comments: 'If you marry security you mustn't expect romance.'

'When I was married my friends congratulated me on marrying a man with a desk job. Some of them who married soldiers or sailors hardly saw them year in, year out.' Although Edie was a thoroughly unselfish person, she could not imagine any other situation but her own. The possibility of freedom would have made her own lot unendurable.

'Anyway, I'll be back for Christmas.'

Howard was as cheerful about my departure as I had been about

124

his from Eureka. Our sex ratio had now fallen to once every three days and sometimes only twice a week. I liked the twice-a-week routine better, as it allowed for a little more variation. One night I had caught myself thinking with relief that I had at least two sex-free nights ahead. This was disconcerting and not appropriate for the picture of young married bliss I was painting for the world's benefit. So I decided to visit London. My mother, who would have been my best excuse, had suddenly decided to return to America.

She phoned me on the Shakespeares' new telephone, which had been installed to celebrate our arrival. 'Darling, Carter's going into politics. You know what that means. He'll need a woman to keep him on the strait-and-narrow. Everyone's in New York at the moment. If I was younger I would become a film star.'

I recognised that this last idea was prompted by her jealousy of Lady Diana Cooper, whose *Virgin Mary* was hitting stage and screen. It was insensitive of Eleanor to leave London just as I planned my arrival. I had thought we might get to know each other. I had thought we might amuse ourselves with visits to *No, No, Nanette* and *Lady Be Good*. Fred Astaire seemed about as far away as I could get from Howard.

When I suggested this, she said, 'Carter's sister Grace wears silk pyjamas all day and sings 'Dance, dance little lady' over breakfast to keep her face supple. I do think you should try a vitaminised face pack, darling. I'll send you one from America. It's a great relief to know your future is assured.'

In the end, I went to see Tallulah Bankhead play in *The Green Hat* with Molly and her Friend. I liked the play but thought the famous forehead too cathedral-like to be beautiful or even charming. Molly and her Friend were in ecstasies. I read out a newspaper article: 'Tallulah B. gets more female fan mail than any male rival.' This silenced Molly, but Friend said huffily, 'I don't know what you're trying to prove.' We were standing, at this point, outside the theatre, and a cold wind was not improving our tempers. I did not plan to invite them to my house.

'Heavens,' said Molly, who was staring at the road, perhaps hoping for some *deus ex machina*. 'What a huge car!'

She had struck lucky. Leaning out of a window, like portraits bursting from their frames, were Gay and Raymond Lark. Although I had not seen them since the unfortunate Oxford visit, I didn't hesitate. 'Gay! Gay! It's Violet.' The car, which had been touring slowly by, came to an immediate half and the two figures bounded out.

'Hop in, all of you! We were on our way for a spot of supper at the Ritz.'

It always amazes me what those in search of company will accept.

'What a coincidence you should pass,' I said. Getting into their car, I was reminded of my trips with them as a schoolgirl.

'Not at all,' Gay's little cat face turned to rest on the top of the seat; heavy makeup knocked twenty years off her age. 'We tour all the theatres every night. Raymond likes to see what everyone's up to.'

Raymond showed no embarrassment at this shameful admission. 'You didn't happen to see my *Stocking Tops*? Not many did. It's Cochran. There's not room for C. B. Cochran and Raymond Lark.'

'Practice makes perfect,' Gay gave us all an encouraging smile. We were arriving at the Ritz, and as we entered the revolving doors she manoeuvred it so that she and I went round an extra turn and were spun out again onto the street. 'Keep off the subject of Cochran,' she hissed. 'Raymond thinks all his problems are due to him.'

'But he seemed quite resigned about *Stocking Tops*.'

'Cochran does have flops too. He brought *Chauve-Souris* all the way from Paris and what business did that do?'

'I've no idea!'

'Look at his *Cowboy Rodeo*. Where was that when the Society for the Prevention of Cruelty to Animals had finished with it?'

I found myself pushed back through the revolving door. Gay tripped after the others. She tossed a cheering thought over her shoulder: 'I heard that you were getting married.'

'I am married.'

'You are married!' I was spared immediate explanation by our arrival in the dining room.

'My usual table, waiter!' Raymond was proclaiming with a flourish. 'There's not many men who could take on four women.'

'Three,' whispered Gay. Raymond never believed in taking too much notice of other people's appearance. He thought it a sign of weakness, a weak feminine trait. Miscasting was always one of his problems. His later big successes came from the simple expediency of hiring a casting lady.

'Vi's got married, darling.'

'That's wonderful. Waiter! A bottle of champagne! So where's the lucky man?'

'He's in Dorset.' I did not particularly want to explain Howard to this gathering. 'I've come up to do some Christmas shopping.'

'Who do you buy presents for?' asked Molly, as if seriously concerned.

'Her husband will expect something,' said Raymond heartily. 'Gay bought me tickets for a Cochran show last year.'

Gay gave me a meaningful look.

'Violet's husband, Howard, is a solicitor,' said Molly. 'So is his father. Vi lives with her parents-in-law.'

'Country solicitors are the backbone of England,' said her Friend, scornfully.

'There was a country solicitor in one of Raymond's plays,' Gay began doubtfully. 'I'm afraid he wouldn't have made a single vertebra. But then, the play didn't last long either!'

'What I'd like to start next,' said Raymond, forking over his smoked salmon so that the whole plateful was reduced to one little omelette, 'is dramatise an Edgar Wallace.' He popped the salmon into his mouth.

'Surely CBC's started already.'

The evening was not, to say the least, awash with merry laughter. Nevertheless, a week or two back at The Laurels made me think of such cosmopolitan entertainment with intense longing.

There's no doubt it's very hard to marry out of your circle—particularly when you've chosen the man because you thought he was right in the middle of the circle. I had met Howard at Araminta's party. Everybody I thought interesting at Oxford was there. He knew them all. He appeared to be accepted by them all. Unfortunately, when he became a solicitor in Sherborne, he was nobody's friend.

On one of my many visits to London during that winter of 1926 for 'shopping', 'checking the house,' 'attending the first night of my friend Mr Lark's new production,' Leonard took me out to lunch. Araminta was in the North trying to wheedle some more money out of her parents. She had just found she was pregnant and was worried about the expenses involved. She had decided she was having twins.

Leonard came to London almost as often as I did. He said undergraduates were beginning to bore him, particularly as it seemed as if Augustus had put him up for some sort of lectureship. On the other hand, the silence of a dead countryside stultified any real possibility of creative work. He might have to wait till the spring. This naturalist line of argument annoyed Araminta considerably. She pointed out the crocuses, snowdrops, Christmas roses, holly berries and added that since she had conceived in December, no one could call it an uncreative time of year. She may have gone North in a huff.

Rejecting our country homes (though mine, encircled within the other stone houses of Sherborne, seemed almost suburban), we met for a metropolitan lunch. Flo and Cecil, happily married in a huge house hardly ever occupied, had spent days preparing a special banquet. Flo had turned into a respectable cook/housekeeper as soon as she married Cecil. Harry Lauder and 'The Bluebells of Scotland' disappeared. Even her hair lay noticeably flatter. I wondered if this meant she was not happy. After all, Cecil was at least fifteen years older, nearly bald, authoritarian, and even, I suspected, quite lazy. All he ever did, as far as I could see, was carve the joint, carry the heaviest scuttles, and bring up the wine from the cellars. At best, I thought, it must be a marriage of convenience. With my present interest in the subject. I couldn't resist putting it to Flo.

She looked at me with total incomprehension. 'But Miss Violet, Cecil's a wonderful husband! I'm the luckiest woman going.'

'Well, of course, I see that,' I said hastily.

'If he says he'll be back in half an hour, he's back in half an hour; if he says he'll bolt up the door at ten, he'll bolt up the door at ten; if he promises to help me down the stairs with the shopping, then he'll be near the back door when I call; if he had a drink in the evening it'll be no more than a pint, or two at the most. Now how many men can you say that about? With the temptations he has all around him. All those bottles lying down where Mr Nettlefield put them.' I agreed that Cecil's temptations were almost unendurable, but Flo now was determined to finish the catalogue of his virtues. 'And how many men could you trust with money as I can him? He looks after your mother's money and your house as if it was his own.'

'Yes. Yes, Flo. I never doubted it for a minute.'

Yet I still felt she hadn't told me whether she loved him. It took me several months of seeing just how happy she was before I understood that she had told me after all. It was just that love to her was a very different thing from love as I saw it, as I wanted it. The virtues in Cecil that made him her love object were almost the same ones in Howard that increased my lack of love daily.

Over my lunch with Leonard I brought up this question of love among the working classes. He gave me a spiteful look. 'On the basis of Oscar Wilde's dictum: "If the lower orders don't set us a good example, what on earth is the use of them," your servants seem to be behaving with impeccable good sense.'

Having dismissed long ago as unimportant the information that Leonard's father was a postman and his mother took in washing, I continued blithely, 'It's not as if Flo hasn't ever felt passion; she had this wildly romantic affair with a soldier during the war. She even had a child. So how can she now settle for second best, such a dull second best? She actually pretends it's exactly what she wants. You'd think love depended on good behaviour!'

'If you're going to talk rot, pass me some more wine.'

'The truth is, Leonard,' I said in the end, when I saw that no fascinating generalities would arouse his interest, 'I'm fed up with Howard.'

'I didn't think you'd found a sudden kinship with us men with feet of clay.'

128

'He's driving me insane.'

'How passionate.'

'That's just what it's not.'

'I told you not to marry him.'

'But you never gave any reason. If you'd given me a good reason I'd have listened.'

'The reason was not very suitable for nice young ladies.' He was joking, but I was very serious.

'Do you mean there was a special reason?'

'Not really.'

'Look, I'm an old married woman. You can tell me now.'

'As a matter of fact, I assumed you knew. Everyone else did. It was Araminta who said you wouldn't. Which makes it sound much more important than it is. After all, Howard's not the only one. Look at me, shortly to be father—of two.'

I think Leonard, despite Araminta's warnings, still didn't believe he was making a revelation. Or if he did, he assumed I would not mind much. After all, we had first met with Augustus and his friends who were without exception homosexual. He told me about his affair with Howard as if it were a bit of a joke—perhaps it was to him.

'I always thought Howard an unconvincing aesthete. He folds up his clothes too neatly.'

'You mean you and Howard went to bed together?'

'That kind of buggering around.'

'That's why he was a friend of yours?'

'Has he other charms?'

Suddenly it all became clear to me. I had been deceived by appearances. Howard had been coloured by the glow of Araminta's parties. But he had only been there at all because of a short-lived affair with Leonard.

'Don't look so desperate, Vi. A girl like you needs a lot of security. That's what Araminta said.'

'So you were all talking about us. Laughing. At the wedding.'

'Oh, no. Howard's very nice-looking. I never thought he was too convinced about the charms of his own sex.'

'Bloody hell. Bloody hell, Leonard. He doesn't like sex with women either!'

The truth, which I'd been hiding from myself for some time, burst out.

'Oh,' said Leonard, looking serious for the first time. He poured me some wine. 'What are your views on divorce?'

Unsatisfactory sex might not have mattered if life at The Laurels had not been so boring. For days at a time I would pretend to be Edie; go shopping in the morning, visiting in the afternoon, sit quietly sewing

129

in the evening while Howard *père* and *fils* discussed their week's cases. Such was my good behaviour that Edie asked me if I was 'off colour' and Howard offered to find if there was a horse for me to ride. Sometime I would even convince myself there was something dignified about Edie's acceptance of this simple way of life. Then it would all seem pointless: a world designed by man for man's comfort, sweetened over by lack of real hard work—although in some ways this was the worst trial. In one of my black moods I wrote to Molly, 'It's all negative, with expectations of nothing but death.' Molly wrote back an oddly critical letter saying that most women in my position had children and it was typical of me that I had to be different. This made me crosser. 'It's certainly no thanks to you I'm not rearing third-generation dreadful Howard Shakespeares. I suppose with your friends you don't have to bother. You should be the last person to lecture me on the duties of motherhood. At least Howard's got a penis!'

A few days later I walked with Howard to his office. He was surprised and pleased. When we reached the door I took his arm. He pulled back slightly.

'I'm going to London.'

'Again?'

'For a month.'

'I love you, Vi.'

'You try. Leonard stays in the house when he's in London.' I looked him in the eye. He looked away. 'You'll be late,' I said with hypocritical sympathy. I had given him his chance. 'A break might save our marriage. I'll come back.'

My friendship with Leonard grew incidentally. First, he was 'that ugly friend of Augustus', then he was, surprisingly, 'Araminta's lover/husband, and she gives such extraordinary parties'; next he turned out to be, even more surprisingly, my husband's ex-lover; and finally his occupancy of my house whenever he was in London made him during 1927 the man I saw most often.

Araminta was not well during her pregnancy. She spent most of the nine months in bed. Being ignorant, by choice, about anything to do with babies, I showed more sympathy than I felt when she returned from the North. She lay, palely beautiful, on a nest of embroidered shawls in their cottage outside Oxford. When Leonard was away, a woman came in from the village. Admirers still visited her from the university, but a lot of the time she was desperately bored and lonely. I half-assumed it was a new act put on to make the parties she still gave more romantic. She did look lovely, on a silken dais, her usual flowing costume gracefully accommodating her swelling lump so that she seemed particularly Madonna-like. Most of the men that day I visited her were desperately in love with Araminta, wishing only to kiss her hair, and never guessing she had spent the last months wishing she were dead. 'You're so tranquil,' they would say. I said it myself. We gazed into her round blue eyes as if they were crystal balls. 'So calm. So serene. How do you manage it when everyone else is so fidgety and the world is such a mess?'

It never crossed my mind to disapprove of Leonard's London visits. Nor to feel guilt when he introduced me to Noël Coward's *Dance Little Lady*—'Strange how potent cheap music is',—and *Twentieth Century Blues*, rather than sit at his wife's bedside. I don't think I was ever as self-centred again as during that period of my life. Gay Lark said to me wonderingly one evening, 'You were such a serious little girl, so intense. I'd never have guessed . . .'

'Guessed what, Mrs Lark? That I'd sing too?'

A feeling that Howard was waiting to catch me if I flagged gave me a wild urge to play. Howard never had the wit to say, 'Certain women should be struck regularly, like gongs.' After all, this was the Roaring Twenties and I was still only twenty-two. Not that I was anywhere near the centre of the roar. I hedged my bets and disguised my uncertainties by flitting from one world to another. I could never be discovered because I was never fully committed. Leonard introduced me to a raffish world of writers and artists. Dot brought me back to the debutante world, four years on—the faces were as boring, but the behaviour more racy.

From Dot, I rebounded back to Oxford and Augustus who, now that his masterpiece, unread by any of us yet, was safely in proofs, found time to collect round him another groups of talkative intelligentsia. When their brand of humour, however brilliant, began to seem effete and unkind ('I'm more dined against than dining'), I would do a last turn, and land up, pale and exhausted, in Mrs Shakespeare's drawing room. Poor Edie was endlessly patient, discreetly curious. Perhaps I was leading her Secret Life. Howard explained my absence by a nearly fictitious story that I was being a journalist. It was true that I had become a very occasional stringer for the gossip column of a large-circulation daily newspaper. My best story, which brought me near fame in certain circles, was about my cousin Daphne's husband's younger brother, the Honourable Julian Titchfield, who got a First at Oxford. "*An Honourable and a First*" read my caption. "First time the Peerage comes Number One. The Daily—offers a badge printed Forward with the People for anyone who can find an earlier example."

Poor Mrs Shakespeare's hope that I would have a baby and settle down didn't have a chance. We did have happy moments, sitting in her garden on an early-summer evening with the lemon verbena and the catmint by the kitchen door, and the lavender bordering the path and the bright pansies blinking under the old-fashioned roses. Like most Englishwomen, Edie showed creative talents in her garden which were never apparent anywhere else.

But I never let those movements last for long. 'Sherborne must have the highest birthrate in the British Isles,' I would say, as Edie stared lovingly at her marigolds. The gold turned to brass. Anyone who could say nasty calculating word like *birthrate* was clearly not in the mood to produce a pink bouncing babe.

'Children are a blessing,' she would say helplessly.

'That's what you've been told. What blessing is Howard, cluttering up your house, and me causing you endless worries?'

'You know we love having you both here.'

'Perhaps you do. But that's because you've been told you're lucky. What you'd really like to be doing is quietly getting on with your gardening and reading Ethel M Dell when your Howard's safely at work.'

'I'm not that old or silly,' she would say weakly.'

At which point my Howard would lean out of the window of his nursery, where he was working, and shout, 'Stop bullying Mother. Isn't it time for supper?'

And I would rise ungraciously and see if the maid wanted help with laying the table. I didn't mean to bully Edie; I meant to educate her. But any real education would have had to start with a denunciation of Howard Senior's treatment of her.

'If my parents irritate you so much, why don't we move out? I could just about manage a house of our own now.' I did my best to see Howard as little as possible. Our sexual confrontations had receded to a very occasional skirmish, usually ending with Howard saying in a huff, 'Well, if that's how you feel, I won't bother.' As if it were my lack of enthusiasm . . . Well, I suppose, by then, it was.

'I like this house,' I said. I saw that his offer was a trap to catch me for longer periods. 'I like its stone portico and its arched eyelids. I like the view of the Wingfield Digby hills from our bedroom window. I like the sound of the train, passing the Old Castle. I like Sherborne. The Abbey is magnificent, the bandstand in the public gardens amusing, and Blue Vinney from Moulde and Edwardes perfection.' Howard's father never touched it. 'I even admire the white-haired battle-axes who still wear cotton stockings and corsets, though I do find their stiff-collared, stiff-necked husbands a bit much to take. I like Sherborne School, the pompous youths in the pompous courtyard. And I definitely like your mother. I love the way she treats flowers as if they were children and talks about children as if they were flowers.'

'Then why do you bully her?' Howard obstinately rejected my rhetoric.

'Because I can't stand her acceptance of your father's superiority. He's like something out of the nineteenth century.'

'Because you have a guilty conscience.'

'You're pretty nineteenth-century yourself.' It was some time since Howard and I had had enough contact to even argue.

'My father has a weak digestion. He needs special attention.'

"Ever heard of the Anderson technique? If it was his digestion he could cure it easily enough. It's his mind.'

'People have foibles as they get older.' This was a concession. I looked up surprised, but he moved so that I couldn't see his face. 'I'm coming up to London with you next week. I deserve a holiday. It's been a year.'

His circumspection was irritating. If he thought coming with me to London would save our marriage, then why had he waited a year? 'You become more like a country solicitor every day.'

'I shall enjoy coming to London.'

'Are you sure you can afford it?' He had continually refused to use any of my income.

'Staying in your house, if I may.'

'With Leonard?' I said maliciously.

'If necessary.' He lifted his head and stared at me. I was impressed. 'We could catch the nine forty on Monday. I've written off for tickets to *The Garden of Eden*.'

'It's a funny time to go to London,' I said in a mellower tone. I decided not to tell him I'd already seen *The Garden of Eden* twice. It starred Robert Maudesley with a silver beard and black eyebrows and Tallulah Bankhead with her skirts at least six inches above her knees. 'Most people leave London for the country in August.'

'I don't move in those circles.'

I decided to reward his honesty. 'Leonard isn't there either. Araminta's having her baby anytime now. He's required at the bedside.' Howard looked genuinely pleased. 'Tell your mother I'm the friend of a putative mother of twins. She might forgive me.'

'My mother loves you.' This was quite a day for home truths. Perhaps Howard in London, away from the constant example of his father, would be a different person.

'Flo won't be very nice to you.'

'I don't need Flo to be nice to me.' He turned to me with his old clear gaze.

If Howard wasn't a totally different person in London, he was certainly easier. Household expenses were on me, which meant he couldn't object to all the nice luxuries I enjoyed. He even paid a recal-

133

citrant Flo a graceful compliment on her new recipe, brought from America by my mother, of absinthe ice cream. He didn't know London very well, so I took him to all the places I had visited as a teenager, which meant a heavy diet of museums—the Natural History Museum with its dinosaurs; the Science Museum, still a new idea; the Victoria and Albert, which was always my favourite. *Pace* Raymond Lark, we even went to see C. B. Cochran's Young Ladies in Noel Coward's *This Year of Grace*. 'But they're quite curvy,' Howard said in a pleased voice. 'I thought fashions were all tubular like a cigarette.' 'It's Clara Bow,' I said, 'and those Hollywood vamps. Thank God, I'll be able to eat bread again.' 'You always look right,' said Howard gallantly.

We slept in my mother's room in the big silk-draped bed; and whether it was these sumptuous surroundings, escape from his parents, or the champagne, we managed a night or two of respectable ardour.

On our third night we tried conversation instead of sex. We were both tired and rather drunk after a party to celebrate Baby Overley-Summers' engagement to a peer. Now Aunt Phyllis had equalled Aunt Letty's success with Daphne.

'I never could decide why you married me,' mumbled Howard.

'Because you called me beautiful. No one called me that,' I mumbled back.

'But they must have. That chap, that rowing Blue . . .'

'Your friend. He kissed me in the Moorish Tea Rooms. But he didn't tell me I was beautiful like you did. As if it was a statement of fact. He said it like a compliment. I fell in love with you because of the way you said You're beautiful. I married you because I was frightened of leaving Oxford.'

'I still think you're beautiful.'

'Do you? It's different now. I know you too well. I know your past and future, the way you knot your shoelaces and brush your teeth. You can't be an oracle. It shouldn't be a statement of fact anymore. You should know me well enough to pay me a compliment. I've no idea what to do with my life.'

'I don't understand.'

'I'm asleep. I'm talking nonsense.' My eyes were closed. 'I don't want children.' I was nearly asleep. So was Howard.

'There's a girl secretary in the office. She thinks I'm wonderful. A god. She worships me. She's got very fair hair and very fair skin, and whenever I talk to her she blushes.'

'That's very nice.' Did he really think he could make me jealous. 'Why don't you tell her she's beautiful?'

'Because I'm your husband. And I love you.'

The day before we were to return to Sherborne was particularly bright and sunny despite its being 1 September. The whole summer had been hot, encouraging a revolutionary fashion for sunbathing. I was unreasonably proud of my own delicate golden colour. I put on my slippery Celanese underwear with a definite feeling of God's in his Heaven and all's right with the world.

'Let's take a boat down the Thames. Flo can pack us a picnic.'

Howard seemed pleased by the idea. I wore a dress that had thirty-two round buttons down the back and he did up every one without a murmur. How many husbands could you say that of? I tried on a pink cloche hat with a rosette above my left eye, but discarded it in favour of the wind in my hair. What was left of it. My hair had reached its very shortest shingle. I put on red lipstick, a different colour for top and bottom lip, a touch of mascara—and splashed on the Ardena Skin Tonic which my mother had left behind. She had told Flo with great pride it cost her two dollars fifty, although the ingredients were worth only three cents. It was typical of her to forget it. Or perhaps it was the vitamin face mask she'd promised me.

'You look . . .' Howard began, and then paused. I laughed at his puzzled expression. I knew he wanted to tell me I looked beautiful.

The boat left from a pier beside the Albert Bridge. It was still early in the morning, and our fellow passengers were almost entirely women with children. The smaller ones wore straw boaters and sailor suits. I looked at Howard to see if he showed any dangerous symptoms of paternal desire. He appeared more irritated by their noise.

'We'll sit right at the back,' I said. 'Children always go to the front.'

They were idyllic, our last moments of harmony. A throwback to my own childhood trips in the SS *Eureka*. Howard didn't speak, and if I shut my eyes I could imagine that soon the long low shape of the island would appear behind its cloudy streamers of red and grey and bluish-purple. I had banished our honeymoon from my mind, so I could imagine the smooth castle lawns as they'd always been, the soft plunk of tennis balls, of croquet balls, of the arrows into straw— games were so much more leisurely then, I thought to myself, particularly for women. Now when I went to house parties, I was expected to take off my stockings and run around quite as fast as the men . . . Unwillingly, I found myself returning to the present. The breeze was softer and warmer than any Irish wind. Yet on a July day there was nowhere gentler than the cove right at the back of the island where I had lain watching my seals shaking their sleek heads, or the spot just behind the harbour where I could see the *Eureka* crossing from the mainland.

This time my romantic memories were gradually interrupted by the noise of music which rose above the excited cries of the children.

'What a disgusting spectacle,' said Howard. I opened my eyes and saw that he was looking along the side of the boat. My view was obstructed by the saloon, but I gathered that the noise, which seemed to include singing voices as well as music, was coming from an approaching boat.

'Not very harmonious.'

'Drunk.'

'At this time of the day?'

'They look as if they've been up all night.'

His voice was so disapproving that my curiosity was aroused. I stood up and peered round the side of the boat. It certainly was a remarkable sight. Despite the sun, the boat was wreathed with garlands of different-coloured light bulbs. On the deck a solitary man played an exhausted mixture of 'Dixieland Blues' and 'Tea for Two' on the piano. Around him stumbled a few figures, imagining that their one step forward, one step back was the best Black Bottom ever. Around them sprawled a further group of semiconscious creatures. They were singing. On the whole the men looked slightly better than the women, since a dress suit retains a certain amount of dignity at all times, while silver lamé with hip swathings torn and diamanté shoulder strap sprinkled on the floor looks quite awful.

'No coats, no ties,' said Howard.

'Look at that one with her bandeau over her nose.'

'Disgusting,' repeated Howard. I was quite prepared to agree with him. It gave me a pleasant sense of superiority to feel my cleanly clothed limbs. But I couldn't help looking to see if there was anyone there I knew. It must have been a very good party.

'No wonder we get strikes,' said Howard, eyes glued. 'It almost makes one sympathise with the working classes.'

This was going a bit too far. I was just about to say that we didn't have Prohibition here, and I bet a miner put back a pint or two, and why didn't he try reading *Sons and Lovers*, when a huge voice yelled, 'Vi! Vi!'

The boat was alongside us now, so there was no mistaking the pale ugly face of Leonard. 'What are you doing?' I called idiotically.

'I was looking for you. I've been looking for you everywhere!' He waved a half-empty bottle above his head. All the children, who had naturally rushed to the side of our boat where the fun was going on, turned their round faces towards me.

'Violet, go inside,' ordered Howard, as the mamas and nannies tried to drag their charges away from such an unedifying spectacle.

'Violetta! Darling Vi! It's so wonderful. Such wonderful news! I wanted you to be the first to know!'

'He's making a fool of you,' hissed Howard.

'You're not my nanny,' I shook off his hand crossly. The awful

136

truth was that the sight of Leonard had brought me alive again. The self-centred pleasure of clean Celanese and skin tonic, the dreams of a childish past all disappeared into the real, living excitement that Leonard created. Meanwhile his boat had almost passed ours. Desperately he ran to the stern.

'Vi! Vi! Wait for me. Tell them to stop.'

'I can't,' I began to laugh. The confrontation of neatly dressed children and upper-class drunks was too funny. 'Come to the house for lunch!'

Too late. Leonard had jumped, bottle and all, into the water, dirty and dark and turbulent. He disappeared. Oh, God. It crossed my mind that here was Howard's moment. If he'd jumped in too, and executed a brave recovery, he would have seemed marvellous, heroic. Too late for that now. Leonard's head bobbed up, and an efficiently calm sailor from our boat, whose engines had now stopped, held out a boathook. Leonard, his ugly face with its low brown, squashed nose, and small eyes looking positively ghoulish as water streamed from him, was hauled over the back. A ragged cheer rose from the other boat, which was answered by a shrill squeaking and clapping of hands from the children.

Ignoring Howard, I made my way towards him. The pool of water spread over the varnished floorboards. 'I can't swim.' Leonard said with a surprised expression.

'I'm not surprised with all that in you,' said the sailor in a jocular tone.

Leonard felt in his jacket pocket and brought out a sodden pound note. 'Saved my life.'

'Much appreciated, Sir.' The sailor disappeared and soon the engines started again.

'What ever was it you have to tell me so urgently?'

Leonard looked solemnly at his feet. His big toe stuck out of a waterlogged sock. 'Lost a shoe. Can't remember.'

'You must remember. It's probably cost me my marriage.'

'Ah, Howard. Dear Howard. Told him folding clothes takes the life out of them.'

'What did you want to tell me?' I squeezed his soaking shoulder. 'You do look awful.'

'Reminded me.' A smile split his face. 'Araminta had twins. Twin girls. Today. No, yesterday. Came to tell you. Looked awful, all three of them. Wanted you to know first.'

'Seems someone else got in first.' I pointed to the receding fairy lights. Leonard staggered to his feet.

'September the First Club. Special all-night do, to see autumn come in. Seemed appropriate at the time. Fatherhood, autumn of the years!'

'Leonard was celebrating fatherhood,' I explained to Howard, who'd appeared magisterially at my side. 'Araminta's had twin girls.'

'They're called Clancy and Nancy,' nodded Leonard. Either for support or out of comradeship, he put out a wet hand to grasp Howard's shoulder. Howard jumped back like a kangaroo. 'Honestly, Howard, you nearly sent me back overboard.'

'Either you come with me now, or it's all over. Over! I've had enough! Enough!' His eyes were fixed on me with a mad stare.

'Honestly, Howard. We're on a boat.'

'It's over! All over!'

Leonard slumped against me on a public pavement. 'Doesn't look worth saving, Miss,' said one witty passerby.

'I can't just leave him, Howard.'

'Why not?'

'You were his lover, not me!'

Howard stared at me with ashy hatred. We came back to the house in separate taxis, and it took him a very short time to pack his case. In silence. When he had gone I sat in the drawing room, whose simplicity and pallor now seemed dreary rather than fashionable, and felt sorry for myself.

'How do you like me?' I turned to Leonard's simpering voice. He was posed, hands behind head, dressed in my mother's silk kimono. He had brushed his wet hair back from his face. I had left him unconscious on the bed.

'Frightful.' I began to laugh hysterically. Then cry.

'Oh, Christ!' Leonard sat down with his legs apart. He was no longer drunk. 'Araminta was crying at the beauty of birth; what are you crying about? I rely on you to keep your emotions under control.'

'You should put your knees together in a skirt,' I sobbed.

'I bet Howard would.'

'It's not funny. He's my husband. I love him!'

Leonard looked sympathetic. 'Oh, dear. That does make it more complicated. Are you quite sure? I mean I know he loved you . . .'

'It's even worse if I didn't love him.'

'You women are so devious. Araminta only loves me because I pay her no attention.'

'I am pleased about the babies.' My tears were less choking.

'Perhaps you could be their nurse. We'll need help.'

'I don't like children. Especially babies.'

Leonard looked surprised. 'I thought all women did. An inborn urge. Of course, I don't.' He was clearly relieved I had stopped crying. 'You don't expect Araminta will want me to kiss them, do you? Frankly, I adore them in principle but the practice would be a bit much.'

'I think I might like other people's.'

'They say it's very nice to be a grandmother.'

A pause fell in which I felt relaxed enough not to begin to cry again. After a bit I said, 'Well, now I've got through one marriage at the age of twenty-three, I can begin a life of decadence.'

'Try me,' said Leonard fairly seriously. It was a valiant offer considering what a dreadful hangover he must be suffering.

'No,' I said, I like to think with good motives. How would Araminta ever forgive me? 'I've got a much better idea.'

Leonard followed me up to the bedroom. I picked up my mother's bottles off the dressing table and began to throw them about. The Ardena Skin Tonic went first. As it smashed against the chest of drawers a refreshing odour arose. 'Two dollars fifty,' drawled Leonard, to whom Flo told everything.

'Three cents,' I replied, letting fly a jar of cold cream, an ivory hairbrush, and the chair cushion.

'Try the bathroom,' advised Leonard after I had turned over the chair, stripped the bed, and scattered around all the contents of the wardrobe. 'Things are harder in the bathroom. More satisfactory as missiles.'

He was right. Bars of soap, toothbrushes, toothpaste, mugs, bath essence went flying through the air. They crashed with excellent sound effects, and some left gorgeous explosion marks on the shiny surfaces. 'I suppose it would be more fun to throw them at him,' I panted.

'Or at her,' suggested Leonard understandingly.

'It's the action that counts. Not the target! Mother or husband. What's the difference?' I aimed a jar of bath salts at the ceiling. The crystals descended on my head like coloured hail.

'None of us use enough physical energy,' said Leonard. 'We would all feel much better if we did. Look how tremendous Araminta felt after childbirth.'

'I think that's the grand climax.' I brushed the pink and blue and yellow crystals from my hair.

'Like confetti.'

'No one threw confetti when Howard and I got married.'

'You looked too cross.'

'You were all enjoying yourselves too much.' I thought of my wedding. I had met the vicar only once and could not remember a word of his address. I had said 'I do' without giving a thought to 'till death us do part.'

'My impression is you were enjoying yourself too.'

'I was too young.'

I sat down on the side of the bath and looked at the confusion I had created with pleasure.

'Now I suppose I'll have to clear it up.'

'Honestly, Vi,' Leonard looked shocked.

'I can't leave it for poor Flo, can I?'

'She's a woman of the world.'

'Cecil wouldn't like it.'

'Nonsense. I bet she throws Bovril at Cecil most breakfasts.'

'Oh, Leonard. It's all such a waste.'

'It was a wonderful show.'

'I meant my marriage.'

'I know.' Leonard scooped up a few bath crystals and flung them in the air.

I went to recuperate at Leonard and Araminta's cottage. Ignorance made it possible to overcome my prejudice against babies. Cries and gurgles alike were equally meaningless and uninteresting. It must have been pretty galling for Araminta, since Leonard took much the same attitude, but she bore it well, spending most of her time in bed with a twin sleeping on either side of her. There was a slow, gentle girl from the village who fed them, changed them, and bathed them, but she was so frightened of Leonard that we hardly ever saw her. They were exceptionally good babies. Sometimes she sat in her pillows with one at either breast. This was a remarkable enough sight to make even Leonard and me take notice. Our faces were an even mixture of admiration and repugnance.

'Do you think you'll ever tell them apart?' I said.

'Clancy's greedier,' said Araminta, and I saw repugnance exchanged for curiosity in Leonard's face.

Loenard became preoccupied with Araminta's lactation. This was not difficult, since two babies meant an almost constant milk round, so that Araminta's breasts seemed always damp from a feed just given or a feed in prospect. 'Nature's not as efficient as a tap,' said Leonard speculatively. It interested him in a way the babies didn't. He continually questioned her about the feeling it gave her and whether she thought it was a different sensation a cow felt on her daily milking. He had been reading a lot of D. H. Lawrence lately, since his own novel was not going well, and he had proved to his own satisfaction that Lawrence's whole approach to life was due to mamillary deprivation.

'Then his mother's got a lot to answer for,' I said.

'Just listen to this,' Leonard read out a passage excitedly: '"The queer cowy mystery of her is her changeless cowy desirableness."'

We all agreed heartily, and in response to Clancy's squirms, Araminta shifted her to the fuller right breast. Our latest discovery was that her right breast produced more milk than her left.

'The extraordinary thing,' he repeated several evenings running after plentiful *vino barriero*, 'is that he hasn't allowed Frieda milk in those huge bosoms.'

'There's time yet.'

'He never will. Doesn't dare. It would simply be too much. If he fell in love with a dirty old Mexican cow, what would he have felt for the human species?'

'Perhaps he doesn't want a baby?' suggested Araminta.

'Perhaps he can't,' Leonard shifted his tack.

The next day he made a huge bonfire and burned all his novel because it was too like Lawrence, and if you liked that sort of thing, Lawrence did it better.

'How can I work, Araminta, with a cow in my house? Milk, milk, night and day that's all we think about, talk about. I see it everywhere, smell it everywhere.' His enchantment with lactation ended abruptly.

'I shall start a new comic novel,' he announced. 'Lawrence has no sense of humour, though some people get a lot of laughs out of him. My book will be a satire on London Society loosely based on *Gulliver's Travels*.'

'You'll never be a good writer till you admit what you are,' said Araminta. 'You can't waste your whole life.' She looked at me, and although she smiled, I felt suddenly uneasy. It was clearly time I left. Since I did not want to reveal too much of myself to Araminta and I didn't want to blame her for my marriage, I went up to my little room and cried for twenty minutes. Then I packed my case.

141

Chapter Six

WOMEN'S FREEDOM LEAGUE—24TH ANNUAL CONFERENCE
The conference passed a resolution strongly repudiating the suggestion that the unemployment problem could be solved by the removal of any women from industry. . . .
A message was sent from the conference to the Prime Minister reminding him that the next honours list would be a suitable occasion for the realisation of his hope to create the first woman peer.
The Times. 20 April 1931

THE DEAN OF ST PAUL'S ON DIVORCE
He declared that he was not prepared to be so dogmatic as to say that Christ would not have sanctioned release from marriage in very hard cases. It was conceivable that He who said that the sabbath was made for man, not man for the sabbath, might have said, had He been confronted with a hard case, 'Marriage was made for man, not man for marriage.'
The Times. 7 June 1931

PARIS FASHION-SECRETS AT OLYMPIA
THE EMPIRE BRIDAL PAGEANT SETS FEMININE HEARTS AFLUTTER!
The Times. 20 April 1931

Guilt was not very fashionable in the twenties and thirties. Perhaps we were still rebelling against the Victorian variety. We called that hypocrisy. A year after my separation from Howard, Molly and I buried our differences. Molly was always the most serious influence in my life. Her 'Friend' had disappeared several months earlier for 'a more adult' life in Paris. Molly merely commented that she had been 'in danger of becoming doctrinaire.'

I smiled, remembering how doctrinaire Molly herself had always been. But this was a new glowing creature, the dark ugly dresses exchanged for skirts covered in bright whorls and dashes. Around her neck hung a string of turquoise beads which matched her shining eyes, and her hair was coiled into a rich red-gold sausage, so that against all the fashion trends she looked nearly beautiful. Molly was in love.

The man she loved was George Briggsworthy, cousin to Henry, last seen breaking the dock strike. 'Even at Oxford I knew that Henry had some deeper meaning in my life. But I never guessed it would be George.'

George Briggsworthy was big and handsome in an English Squire sort of way. His face was saved from fatuousness by a strange beaky nose and wide forehead from which he watered back his yellow hair. He would sit listening to Molly propounding some new theory with an air of stupefied bliss. 'She's so original,' he would say to me. 'So brilliant, so sympathetic, so unlike a woman.' They were a very unlikely couple.

They had met because George had decided that after three years of trying to run his farm, he needed some theoretical training. He had inherited the five-hundred-acre farm in 1922 when he was in his earlier twenties. He was now in his last year at Reading, after which he would return properly equipped to grow barley for the rest of his life.

By rights of True Love, Molly should have gone with him. Unfortunately, in 1922 George had not only inherited five hundred acres, but also married a wife to go with them. He had been an introverted young man with no particular aims and suddenly he had become the master of a very good livelihood, for it was a beautiful, prosperous farm, with a stunning Georgian house and about half of a village. A wife had seemed a good idea. His mother had sent him off to a few dances, and a few months later he was at the altar.

This cadet branch of the Briggsworthys were Catholics; had always been Catholics. Divorce was out of the question. 'But surely, Molly,' I asked, 'George doesn't believe all that mumbo jumbo? It's all right for his mother, nice and consoling for a widow. But he's got his life in front of him.'

'You always did like to blame others. When George married that silly child he wasn't very Catholic. Just like any other unthinking upper-class product of a Jesuit school. But when the shallow little bitch ran off, he turned to religion. There's a very pretty chapel attached to his house, and he used to go there and sit for hours in the semidarkness.'

'He should have taken to drink.'

'It would have been easier'—Molly's patience was almost unbearable—'but not like him. He may not be very academic, but he thinks. I know some brilliantly clever people who never think—about the things that matter. George thinks with his heart.'

'What does he love with?' I was embarrassed by her emotion.

'George can't abandon all his beliefs and principles just because he falls in love. He believes marriage is a sacrament.'

'Do you mean he would take his wife back? If she popped home sometime?'

Molly turned away from my horrified expression. 'We did hope for an annulment at one point. But it seems impossible.' Realising Molly was on the verge of tears, I went over and put my arm round her shoulder. 'Oh Vi! I'm so happy.' Tears threatened to overwhelm her. 'I love him and he loves me. It's a miracle. Why should one be so greedy and want even more? Think of the martyrs. They never had half as much earthly happiness. The Blessed Margaret Clitherow, my namesake, was gay as a cricket while her body was squashed flat under a door loaded with eight hundred weights. Please don't tell George I've been crying, will you? It's so much worse for him. So much worse for a man, whatever modern psychiatrists say.'

'Do you mean, you don't even—'

'Oh, we do. We have. But of course, it's wrong. George suffers terribly. Terrible, terrible guilt. It makes him haggard and miserable. Not immediately. He's happy immediately. But a few hours later. I've looked up things, I've told him about French Catholics and Italian Catholics, but it doesn't help. God stayed with him when he was in trouble; now he must stay with God. Oh! Even the Blessed Margaret had a husband and children before she was martyred.'

I often accompanied Molly for a weekend at the Briggsworthys. Despite the charged emotional atmosphere, I felt refreshed by the orderliness of the house and surrounding countryside. A circular lawn swooped up into a wide vista of golden corn alternating with green fields filled with fat cows. The farm buildings were half-hidden in a dip; only their red tiles gleamed picturesquely in the dusk. In another dip sprang a luxurious growth of burly trees, some, like the roofs of the cattle sheds, already turning a brilliant red. Rabbits ran in the woods, pigeons flew in the sky, chickens cackled in the farmyard. The only disconcerting, because un-English, sight was the triangular

145

chapel attached to the end of the house.

George and Molly spent a lot of time holding hands. I suppose the Catholic Church didn't consider it carnal contact. Beggars can't be choosers. Mrs Briggsworthy was an important feature of evenings at Didcot. She was a fat but anxious lady with grey hair, a dark dress, a spectacular string of pearls, and another pointed nose.

'Violet dear, would you mind looking at the clock on the mantelpiece?' 'So sorry. Am I blocking your view?' 'You do have a watch on your wrist, Mother.' 'Sometimes it runs fast.' 'So does mine.' Molly alternated smiles with frowns.

'Dear Father is never late.' Mrs Briggsworthy seemed always to be awaiting some priest or other. 'It doesn't matter, Mother.' George looked more harassed than unhappy on these occasions. He had his inner strength. Molly needed me.

'I had hoped for a quick visit to the chapel before we dined.'

I conceded to Molly that if George's mother hadn't put her son off religion, nothing would. When Mrs Briggsworthy's priest finally arrived, she would fuss over him ridiculously and be deeply upset by what she considered his early departure. After her disconsolate retirement to bed, George began the great wrestle with his conscience. Being conscientious and in love, Molly wrestled alongside him, but she couldn't help offering him the apple too, in a dimpled knee or the flash of a suspender. Skirts were on the side of the Devil in 1928. While George wrestled, his looks getting blacker and bleaker every minute, I—invited, as I soon realised, to be the referee between the two—chatted merrily and drank crème de menthe. Occasionally this wearing mighty battle would be exchanged for a long period of defeat or victory, which produced in either case that look of health and happiness which I had first seen in Molly.

'It's so ghastly. For both of you.' When George had stamped off to his room, Molly and I would sit up till two or three talking. Sometimes she would say jolly things like, 'It must be awfully boring to be married,' which would give me endless opportunities to describe just how boring it was. We even managed a few good laughs over Mrs Briggsworthy's quest for the Priest of her dreams, although that fun was liable to be cut off by a remark like, 'You shouldn't joke about priests. They're God's representatives on earth.'

'They're men too.'

'Human.'

'Men. Honestly, Molly. Please don't go mad too.'

'I'm not. I've found one way to stop this dreadful fight that's tearing our love apart.'

'Annulment?' I spoke hopefully, knowing her face looked too resigned for that. 'Renunciation?'

She sat up fiercely. 'Never.'

'Murder?'

'I can't think why your jokes cheer me up. I've decided to become a Catholic myself.'

I sat back astonished. 'But that doesn't solve anything at all. In fact, it'll be worse than ever. Instead of one load of guilt there'll be two.'

'Don't you see, we'll be on the same side then, fighting the same fight. The worst thing is this feeling of being torn apart by a force that should be good. I've started my instruction now. There's a priest in Reading who puts a great emphasis on Love. Don't smile, Vi. I can't tell you how much happier I've been since I started.'

I did laugh, though never maliciously and not really truthfully. For I was pretty unhappy myself and looking for some answer. The Catholic Church was having a revival, almost a vogue. People much cleverer than I and with more sane reasons than Molly were being converted. Perhaps it could help.

'All it gives you is guilt,' I would grumble to George.

'It's not a question of what you can get out of it,' he would answer pateintly. 'You must learn to give first.'

One day I had driven with George and Molly to Reading from the farm. I had an hour to wait before the train to London. 'You can sit in on my instruction if you like,' Molly suggested casually. It was November, about four o'clock on a dark, cold Monday, with promise of rain or even snow. I was wearing a light silk dress under a fur coat, because I was going direct to a party. The party was to celebrate publication day of Augustus' book. I was looking forward to seeing some of the Augustus Oxford crowd. The publishers, who were new and fashionable, would certainly invite as many of London's literary lions as they could. Part of the reason I accepted the invitation to meet Father Wilson was that I thought my other preoccupations would preserve me from becoming overimpressed.

'Is it very cold in here? I'm afraid this fire is hopeless. Would you like a nice cup of tea? Don't take off your coat.' I was surprised to find a man of the soul so concerned about the needs of the body. By the time he had finished stoking the fire, finding tea, drawing curtains, fussing about a slight cold Molly had started, and advising her to encourage George's new interest in tall trees, it was time for me to leave. I felt a mixture of disappointment and relief. Relief because Father Wilson had not turned his priestly eyes on me and said, 'And what do you believe in, Mrs Shakespeare? It is *Mrs* Shakespeare, isn't it?' And disappointment because, so I told myself, there seemed nothing there to solve Molly's problems. Only ordinary cheerfulness. When I asked Molly whether that particular session had been useful, she said, 'Oh, yes! We talked about transubstantiation, which is my absolute bugbear.'

The publication party was held in the upper rooms of a literary association. From the street, I could hear the noise and see black silhouettes in the long lighted windows. They moved about jerkily like marionettes, mechanical arms lifting their champagne glasses up and down, heads nodding, hands shooting out to acknowledge an introduction. It was easy to pick out Augustus. He was much the tallest and stooped about like an agitated crane. The rest seemed curiously alike, the men in cut-out evening dress, the women in draped sacks.

The first person I recognised, as I topped the wide curving staircase, was Nettles. I couldn't think why he was there, till I remembered it was he who had employed Augustus as my tutor on Eureka. He looked distinctly more prosperous than he had at my wedding. His hair was shorter and somehow seemed thicker, his face was ruddier, and a thickening round his waistline gave him more substance—which, oddly, made him look younger.

'Vi! I'm sorry about your marriage,' he said immediately, as if he wanted it out of the way.

'I'm not.' I made a face and handed him my coat. 'It was a mistake from the start.'

'Well, then, I'm glad it's over.' We went into the large room together. 'I hoped you'd be here.' He looked at my face and then a long string of ivory beads I was wearing, 'I like your necklace.'

'They were given me by an admirer.' I drank a sip of champagne and looked at the other guests.

'It's very clever of Augustus. The publishers must think a lot of the book to give a big celebration like this.'

'That's what they hope we'll think.'

'I don't know many people here. I came to see you.'

'I'm very well. Living in Eleanor's house still. You could always come there.'

'I leave Kettleside so seldom. I love it up there. You could come to stay.'

'No, I don't think so. But thank you for the offer.' For ten or fifteen years after I grew up, I was incapable of holding a proper conversation with Nettles. Maybe I was waiting till I could forget his relationship with my mother and see him for himself. Certainly I had not come to Augustus' publication party to talk to him. He tried again.

'I had an inquiry about you.'

'Who ever from?'

'Nurse Fig. She was very upset about your separation. I expect she was looking forward to little Violets.'

'Nanny!' For a moment he did break through my preoccupation with the party. 'Is she well?'

'Oh, very.'

But then I began to feel trapped. What did Nettles want from me? I moved away uncomfortably. We had not been intimate for years. This was not the moment. 'Oh! Sorry Nettles. There's someone I must talk to.'

Leonard was leaning against a wall, looking satanic and drunk. He was probably suffering because it wasn't his publication party. He began the moment he saw me. 'Augustus is ghastly. Don't talk to him. Particularly not about his book. The effort at humility nearly kills him.'

'Augustus is naturally humble.'

'Then he's a master of double bluff.'

'Is Araminta here?'

'Do you mean you've managed to avoid seeing her? As a matter of fact, I was going to ask if we could spend the night at your house. All of us.' He pointed to a corner. There sat Araminta, looking more serenely beautiful than ever, with a twin on either knee. They were identical, with their mother's round blue eyes and high foreheads and their father's scowling, quizzical expression.

'You seem to have done it. Araminta's beauty and your brains.'

'They sit looking at each other for hours on end. They probably think they're looking at themselves.'

'Very bad for the character. Of course you can stay.'

'No friendship can survive patronage.' Leonard was looking gloomily over my shoulder. 'Augustus got me that lectureship.'

'How goes it?'

'Perfect. Top-hole. Tailor-made. I have rooms too, so I can escape the imbecility of a family.'

'Is that why I've hardly seen you in London?'

'Yes.' Since Leonard was now obsessed by the view over my shoulder, I turned round. I only just avoided catching Nettles' eye. He was still standing alone. Augustus' pouting head was visible above a crowd of people who all seemed to want to shake his hand.

'I bet his asthma's better,' I said, remembering his old red-faced narrow bending.

'Vi!' Augustus saw me and came over immediately. 'They say the better the champagne, the worse the book—draw your own conclusions. I'm just so relieved to have got rid of it. Like childbirth, I'm sure. Araminta and I have been having the most revealing conversations. She's one up on me. Though by the time I'd finished, I'd really done two books. Have you seen it yet? Oh, well. I'll make sure you have a signed copy. I may never write another. I'm glad you got rid of that dreary Shakespeare. Positively makes one believe in the Francis Bacon theory. Do come and meet Henry Nettlefield; he's shy but terribly worthwhile when you get him going. Oh, God. He's almost your father. The champagne *must* be good. Come and meet the publisher and see what presales figures you can wheedle out of him. Do you think twelve and six the most horrifying price?'

The publisher was quite young and said he had high hopes of Augustus' book because the academic market was expanding so fast. I thought it a limiting approach. 'Won't you try it on the general public?'

'If it gets good reviews.'

'That's why you have this party?'

'We want people to know about us. I suppose you don't know any unattached writers?'

I wondered how drunk Leonard was. 'Leonard Trigear is writing a novel. He's very brilliant.'

While the publisher set off after Leonard with exemplary zeal, I approached Araminta. 'You look like the Madonna with Attendant Cherubs.'

She smiled delightedly, and for a moment the need for sympathy battled with the desire to present an unflawed picture. She must have decided she had enough unallayed admirers, for the smile wilted. 'They like an audience. At home they're more like devils. Clancy, that's the fatter one, grabs everything from Nancy, Nancy retaliates by pinching or biting her, and then they both start screaming.'

'What you need is a May Fig.' I said it idly, but immediately saw that it was true. 'You met her at my wedding. The nanny with a heart of gold. Nettles knows where to contact her. You remember Nettles . . . .' I failed to find a proper description and pointed instead to where he now stood talking to Augustus.

Araminta turned round, but continued to look gloomy. 'We haven't got a green baize door. She'd hate it.' She sighed wistfully. 'I want to paint again. What bliss to be free. We couldn't afford her anyway.'

'Don't worry about money. I owe her a huge debt. Couldn't you clear out those trunk rooms at the back?'

'They're so small. There's the barn, of course. But it's freezing in winter.'

'If we said it was temporary, I'm sure she'd overlook the lack of square yards.' I hurried over talk of the barn, ill-omened scene of my first union with Howard. 'Then she'd get so attached to Clancy and Nancy that she wouldn't want to leave.' I became aware of four huge blue eyes staring at me. I bent over to talk to them. 'You'd love

150

Nanny Fig. She'd make you eat semolina and wash your hands.' In unison two fat little fists shot out and, before I could move away, grabbed hold of my ivory beads, which were swinging in front of their faces. The string broke and the heavy beads dropped like bullets to the wooden floor.

'You see what I mean,' said Araminta, without attempting to move.

Around us people began to drop on their hands and knees. It was a very long necklace with a lot of beads, and they had rolled far and wide over the shiny floor. Soon most of Augustus' guests were crawling about the floor. It might have been some lewd party game. I thought how funny we must look from the street, like pigs hunting for truffles. Going after a smallish bead hiding in between two floorboards, I nearly crawled between Nettles' legs and, avoiding them, came head to head with the publisher.

'So they're your beads,' he said, noting the broken string in my hand.

'I'm most terribly sorry,' I replied, admiring the thickness of his black hair.

'Don't be sorry, please.' He sat back on his heels grinning maniacally. 'It's the most brilliant ruse. No one will ever forget this party now.'

I retrieved the bead and sat up too. 'You're pleased?'

'Over the moon. Up to now it was a quite boring run-of-the-mill affair. Roger Fry stayed for an hour, Lytton Strachey flew in and out, and Osbert Sitwell cancelled at the last moment. Just look at it now. Look how much better-tempered people are. Look how much more friendly they have become.'

I looked. I hadn't met any of the famous. 'I see what you mean. You'd think it was a family party.' Giggling, shoving, and bumping had taken over from a thorough search. Even quite old men were snuffling through chair legs, if not ladies' legs.

'With the British you just have to find something to break the ice.' I took my eyes from a dowager crouched like a great toad under the drinks table to look at him again. 'Yes,' he admitted. 'I'm Polish. I made Moore out of Mrozek. Now I must go and see there's enough champagne. Thirsty work, crawling.' He rose up and disappeared out of my view. I continued crawling until I recognised some vertical legs. I straightened up too.

'Might have guessed you wouldn't be helping.'

'Silly buggers,' Leonard swayed slightly. 'Half of them will never get up again. Did you send that publisher to me? Silly bugger!'

'Yes.'

'Augustus is a patronising bugger.'

'It wasn't Augustus.'

'I said I might consider The Moore Press for my novel. But only if he promises not to put a picture on the cover. Terrible new fad for pictures on books. I'm a writer, not a painter. What do I want with a bloody picture on the cover? Misleading the public, that's what it is. You look very pretty this evening. I suppose the twins broke your beads. Did you a favour, of course. Know the chap who gave them to you. A second-rater. Second-rate taste. Second-rate string. Typical. Can't think why you reject a first-rate chap like me.'

'How is the novel?' I knew his inevitable reaction.

'Christ, Vi, you know better than that. Think I need a drink. Care for a drink? Just the moment while the other silly buggers are at ground level. There'll be a stampede when they stagger up.'

I let him go. Ever since the episode of the September the First Club, he had propositioned me with a greater or lesser degree of urgency—usually when drunk. I treated it as a meaningless habit, but it still embarrassed me, particularly when Araminta was so near at hand. I was afraid that one day when she wasn't at hand and I was drinking too, it would happen by mistake.

'Why so pale and wan, fond lover?' Leonard had done a brief circle before the drinks table. 'Forgot to tell you. Araminta's pregnant again. Probably bloody triplets this time. Triumphantly miserable. She says it's another bloody girl. Can girls be a support in your old age? Only good for darning socks and producing grandchildren. What I need is a wage earner. Take her to Marie Stopes sometime, will you?'

'Honestly, Leonard. You're perfectly capable of doing something about that yourself.'

'Oh, no! I'm not getting trapped into a conversation about that. Christ, there'll be nothing left of a man if women have their way. Anyway, it's not nice to talk about that sort of thing at parties.' He bent suddenly closer. 'Do you know Araminta's the most beautiful woman in this room? Silly bitch.'

He reeled back to the drinks again and I resolved to get in touch with May Fig. I looked about for Nettles. But now I wanted him, he'd gone. I walked to the door, but there was no sign of him. As I returned, a stream of people rose from the floor to press beads into my hands. Mr Moore, ex-Mrozek, had been right. Their mood was very different from before; the formality of a London soirée was gone; ties and hair askew, eyes glittering, voices high. I caught the excitement too. At that moment I saw the admirer who had given me the beads entering the room. He came straight to me.

'I'm late. Had to stay for a division.' He was a young Conservative MP. 'Looks like a good party. Where's your author friend? Want to stay a bit longer or go straight to supper?'

This Member of Parliament, Jack Logan, was my first experience of the openly ambitious male. The friends I had made at Oxford despised vulgar ambition however much they secretly wanted success. Jack was interested in power, prestige, and money—not necessarily in that order. His family had been small tailors for generations, but his father now employed thirty men and owned three shops. Jack was a complicated man. One of his complications was to present himself as a straightforward fellow. He was genuinely shocked that I was already separated from my husband at such a young age, and yet could not understand why I hadn't slept with him yet.

The truth was that although I was flattered by his attentions, I didn't trust him. I didn't think he was capable of real love. I was bored, lonely, and self-centred when I first met Jack. He was ambitious, lonely, and self-centred. I took him over and introduced him to Moore and Augustus. He explained the reason for his late arrival and lack of evening dress, but did not ask the name of Augustus' book. He was one of those people who saw a situation only in terms of themselves. But no one took offence. Mr Moore wondered if he was thinking of writing a book. He told him the name of Augustus' book.

'Good. I'll see if we can get it for the Commons Library. Must take Vi away now.'

When we got out into the street, I realised I had drunk a lot of champagne. The cold air felt wonderful. I put my hands into the pockets of my fur coat and jangled the piles of loose white beads. When we sat face to face in the restaurant, I would test if Jack noticed their absence. I always wore them with the same red silk dress printed with little Chinamen.

I waited till he had ordered and we had got our wine. 'Do you notice anything odd about me?' He never noticed precise appearances. Once when I'd wrapped my wet hair in a bath towel, he'd admired my new hat. Suddenly I decided to make it important. If he noticed that the beads he'd given me with many protestations of affection no longer hung in their usual place, then I would go to bed with him.

'Jack,' I said, 'do you see anything different about me tonight?' I sat back and stared at him. I kept my fingers from touching my naked neck. He didn't appear to be attending. He was tasting the wine, unfolding his napkin. Eventually he gave me a glance.

'Where are my beads?'

Of course, if I hadn't had so much champagne, I'd have realised he could hardly have failed to hear them jangling in my pockets all the way down the street to Soho. But at the time it seemed fate.

On the other hand, it was typical of Jack that he should win me by a trick. Not exactly a lie, but not a straight contest either. He was a politician through and through.

We made love in my mother's bed, since his bachelor flat was spartan; he spent his money publicly, on clothes, in restaurants, on taxis. I could feel his ambitious energy driving him at me, and it was a relief after Howard's lack of conviction. Everything wouldn't stop if I stopped. I could relax and enjoy myself. It wasn't much more than that. Afterwards, as we lay side by side in the dark, I found myself thinking about Molly and George. I wondered how they could let their whole lives be dominated by a relatively short, relatively unimportant act. Then I remembered Father Wilson's cheerfulness. He presumably never made love at all.

'Do you do this often?' There was not much humour in our relationship or Jack would have laughed at me.

'I think you're a terrific girl.'

'I think the same about you.' I wished for that moment that I could love Jack. Perhaps I could if I tried really hard.

Our cordiality was oddly formal. Jack tried to become more intimate. 'You don't hate me?'

'Definitely not.'

'We've made a beginning.'

We were both beginning to falter. Just before I fell asleep, I wondered if I should do something about Flo's finding us there together. I forgot that Leonard and his family were supposed to be staying.

One of the most useful corollaries to Jack's ambition was his efficiency. When I woke up the morning after Augustus' party he had already left, leaving no trace of his presence save a nice flattering note written on House of Commons notepaper, offering me lunch that day. Since it was still earlyish, I didn't bother to dress but went down in search of Flo and breakfast.

In the dining room I found breakfast and Leonard.

'Good morning, my dear. At least not so good. It's wet and cold with a vile east wind. You don't happen to possess a spare mackintosh, I suppose? Interesting party last night. I've been giving consideration to your friend Moore. There's something to be said for the right sort of newish, smallish publisher.'

I saw that he was in that very talkative mood which takes people when they have awakened early; found, surprisingly, that their head aches less than suspected; been out for the papers; finished breakfast; found nothing particular to do; and still had no one who would listen to them talk.

'Where's Araminta and the twins?'

'I was drunk. They preferred a lift with Augustus to the cottage. I

passed out in your guest room very early. Hence my good spirits!'
Was he making a special point that he had not heard my own dual
arrival? He considered Jack an illiterate bore.
'Pass the coffee, Leonard.'
'I happen to know a bit about The Hogarth Press. In six months
Orlando's sold eight thousand one hundred and four copies. Extraordinary for a clever book like that. Coming from publishers who
more or less print it themselves. They say the parcels Virginia Woolf
ties up are so knotty that only someone as neurotic as she can untie
them.'
'That's not very funny.' The coffee was restoring me to life.
'Anyway, she's been writing for years. I bet the early ones hardly sold
a copy.'
'She made thirty-eight pounds per annum in her first six years of
writing. And that includes American sales. But then *Mrs Dalloway*
did better, and *To the Lighthouse* sold nearly four thousand copies
last year. My point is that if The Hogarth Press can do so well without even trying, then surely Mr Moore, with a bit more business in-
itiative, could do really well.'
'Isn't it a question of the authors?'
'If I'm to be a writer I've got to earn money by it. Araminta's a cor-
nucopia. She won't stop at three children. The Woolfs have Freud.'
'Please.'
'What?'
'Freud. My mother has found a Freud substitute. I don't want to
think about her.'
'Certainly not.'
'Too late.'

My mother wrote, when I told her about my separation:

. . . dear Dr Blumberg—such a sympathetic Freudian, without
him I'd never survive at all. Carter's in politics now. He should
never have married me. I should never marry at all. What he needs
is an Eleanor Roosevelt to attend Democratic Luncheons, endure
the Women's City Club, write the odd line for "The Consumer's
League" etc etc. What a bore that woman is, dowdy, ugly, dedicated and doing everything for a husband who treats her abomin-
ably. What hope is there for a frivolous woman like me with the
soul of the 1890s? If I talk about Chanel's new grège-brown jersey
suit, they look at me as if I'm mad. She's put the women's cause
back a millennium. Blumberg says we should divorce, so I expect
we will—if Carter convinces himself he's near enough to the
bottom of the political ladder for it not to harm his reputation. I'm

155

compiling a list of suitable second wives. So far I've got Frances Perkins, Chairman of the Industrial Commission, Nell Schwartz, Bureau of Women in Industry and Molly Dewson, who has a reforming finger in every pie. If I have to listen to another speech from the Woman's Committee for pre-Convention activities, or eat another slice of blueberry pie with heavy cream, I shall scream. Blumberg says I may have a love-hate relationship with blueberry pie, but he tends to the romantic. Only a European like Blumberg can understand what centuries of civilization were needed to create the leisured classes.

Foolishly, I responded:

Darling Eleanor, I can't tell you how leisured I am myself. Now that we're both short on husbands, why don't I come and keep you company? We could be extravagant in New York, stay at the Ritz and shop at Bloomingdale's and Saks Fifth Avenue. I'm a quarter of a century old and I've never left the British Isles.

I shouldn't have tried. The answer came back immediately, as if fearful I might set off at once.

Darling child, what an adorable idea. But you know, no one goes to New York in the summer and quite frankly, I prefer Bergdorfs. I would ask you here, the swimming pool's divine, but couldn't put you to so much trouble. Blumberg, who has absolutely changed my life, says we shouldn't meet for a while as he's at a particularly delicate moment of analysis. Such a pity darling, as I'm absolutely longing to do a Lindbergh. Did you know flying's one of the basic sexual symbols? I do really think you should try and find yourself an analyst. Blumberg says Eureka (incidentally, that's outside the British Isles) was my attempt to re-create the Garden of Paradise, in other words a step backwards into the pure unspotted world of childhood. Carter and I will be divorced as soon as Blumberg says we can meet without wrenching my psyche. Don't you think you should get divorced too? I always did think your brown wedding dress a bad omen. Who is Cecil? Not an amour, I hope. Such a dreadfully common name. Don't expect me to write again for a while, my darling, Blumberg says I must cut away from the past. He also suggests that I stop your allowance. Too much of an umbilical cord. Of course you can keep the house. All love, my darling child.'

A postscript scrawled on the envelope added that thanks to

Blumberg she now loved Blueberry pie though not as much as cranberry sauce, and that she had learned to play bridge.

On this note, contact between us was broken for another five years. Unless I count a newspaper clipping she sent me, commenting on the marriage in Saratoga Springs, N.Y., between Moses A. Blumberg and Lady Eleanor Hesketh Fitzgerald.

Lady Blumberg is a daughter of a very ancient and aristocratic family. Dr Blumberg, who does not become Lord Blumberg in consequence of his wife's title, tells me he does not plan to discontinue his work as a Freudian analyst. The couple are planning to build a residence 'somewhere along the Hudson,' so Dr Blumberg can commute to his newly acquired offices in New York. We wish them all good luck. Lady Blumberg was previously married to Lord Hesketh, a Scottish Knight, and Carter Fitzgerald, the popular Democratic Governor.

The immediate result of her Freudian-inspired cutting of the umbilical was that I had a largish house and no income, to support either myself or it. I looked at Leonard embarking on his second breakfast and decided there was no point in asking his advice.

'The problem with politics,' said Jack, when I asked his advice, 'is that one must act with perfect probity. At the very least, be seen to act with perfect probity. Therefore, since I cannot move in with you and pay you my pittance of rent, I suggest you divide the house into three flats and find others. The alternative would be to marry me.'

I thought this very charming of him. His offers to marry me had never been very convincing and might have died away altogether in the face of my lessened prosperity. The suggestion of flats was such a good one that I decided not to tease. 'I am married, and you need a house in Birmingham to woo your constituents, not in W.1. Augustus definitely should have a London *pied-à-terre*, and there must be many others. You are clever, Jack. I should think you'll end up a Minister, at least.'

'All politicians think they'll end up Prime Minister.' said Jack seriously. 'If a politician denies it he's either a liar or a fool.'

'You don't seem like other Conservative politicians I meet.'

'The separation of parties is largely artificial. Look at us now. Conservative out, Labour in. Two hundred and sixty-one against two hundred and eighty-nine. The Liberals have more power with their fifty-nine.'

'You're just cross because you're further from Prime Minister. Wrong ladder in operation.'

'I agree with a lot the Labour Party do. And they do with us. Take voting for women workers above the age of twenty-one. What party do you think brought that in?'

'Don't know.'

'Power. Class. Money. That's the real difference.'

At last I was in tune with world affairs. Everyone was about to be a great deal poorer. That autumn Wall Street crashed. Money became the okay subject in the smartest drawing rooms. Augustus took the top floor of the house. Owing to the success of his book he was richer than before. When I showed him the small sloping rooms, handed him a front-door key, and explained he had use of the drawing room, he became sentimental. 'Do you remember how I loved your mother?'

'You were thinner. Your nerve ends were closer to the surface.'

'And Pacifism. What happened to my pacifism?'

'The war ended.'

The change in Augustus' appearance was remarkable. From being an exceptionally thin youth, he was making a rapid transition into an exceptionally stout man. At this interim stage the new flesh was still carried by his great height, so that he looked imposing rather than stout. 'I'm not sure this bedroom fits you.'

He patted his stomach contentedly. 'All my life I've hated being shrimpy. At least Oxford's given me something.' He sat down on the bed, which creaked ominously. 'I never meet interesting women anymore. I gave up my female students. Their essays were such a portentous length.'

'No women at the Hockey Club?'

He brightened up, 'Last week the Hockey gave a fancy-dress party. Leonard, dressed as a priest, recited the best part of *Ariadne in Naxos* backwards.'

'What were you dressed as?'

'The costumery wasn't explicit. I had a white wig and two beauty patches.'

'I suppose you don't know if Leonard is living with Araminta?'

'On occasions. Come to think of it, Leonard said he had borrowed his priestly mannerisms from a friend of yours. I didn't know you mixed with the clergy.'

Father Wilson had become my friend. About the same time as Jack became my lover. Everyone teased me about him, and even Molly thought it odd I saw so much of him without showing any desire to become a Catholic. 'If he doesn't worry, I don't see why you should,' I used to tell her firmly. 'But are you sure you aren't wasting his time?' 'Surely I can have a friend who's a priest?' 'But that's just where you've got it wrong. Father Wilson must always be a

158

priest first.'

As well as being a parish priest, Father Wilson had various duties concerned with the Catholic hierarchy. He came up to London most weeks either for a meeting at the Palace of Westminster or to sit in on some committee. His geniality was the other side of a determined, worldly mind. At first I was often surprised at the extent of his contacts, until eventually I grasped that he was a much more powerful figure than he ever showed.

Then I was surprised, like Molly, that he had spent so much time on me. He would appear usually at tea-time, his brown robe twisted and sometimes spotted with dirt, his sandals scruffy rather than saintly. His face beamed at me. The large undistinguished features were coated in a darkish red colour as if once he had been a drinking man, just as his girdle encircled the solid stomach of someone fond of his food. Yet when I knew him and he was already in his early forties, I never saw him drink more than a couple of glasses of sherry or eat more than a hasty bite or two.

'Any sign of Friar Tuck?' Dot would say before kicking off her shoes and unrolling her stockings, and I didn't try to explain the disguise. After a few visits we had discovered Flo was named after Flora Macdonald and had been brought up a Catholic. Soon she was paying a regular Sunday visit to church, led off on the arm of Cecil, who took her as far as the porch but never ventured in himself. 'He's a fine man,' Flo would say. 'He has no need of the Church, and so I tell the good Father.' She made Father Wilson her best pink cakes, and when she had a miscarriage of a longed-for baby (she never again became pregnant), he knew before I did.

Once, almost in passing, I discovered he had known my father; he had met him during the war. But I don't think that was the reason for his interest. Half an hour spent in my company fortnightly, though it figured large in my empty life, was one of a succession of contacts in his heavily filled days. Yet I never felt on an assembly line of processed souls. When I told him about Howard, I felt it was the first intimate story of a failed marriage he had ever heard. 'You set yourself a much harder task', he responded simply, 'by marrying so young.'

Marriage was on my mind again—not that it was ever far from a woman of the twenties and thirties—because my cousins Dot and Priscilla had taken my second-floor set of rooms. Dot had a job as fashion adviser to the same paper which intermittently employed me. For the first time she felt the pleasures of earning an independent living. With typical irony, her old admirer Hamish chose this moment to make a determined effort to win her as his wife.

Dot and I remained good friends despite our basic incompatibility, which seemed almost insignificant when Priscilla was around. Priscilla had been working away as a civil servant 'in Tax, my dears' ever since she didn't marry after her third season. She was fast becoming the sort of state employee who was then considered the unselfish backbone of Britain.

Dot had become even more excessively fashionable since her job. In 1930, when we were entering a time of terrifying economic depression, she would wear to work 'Vionnet's silk-crêpe afternoon dress, black-and-grège print, crossed and knotted at the waist' or "Schiaparelli's black-and-white diagonal tweed, white shantung shirt buttoned onto the skirt." 'But darling,' she would say, 'I get them half-price. It would be criminal not to wear them'. Over breakfast, which we quite often shared, since she seldom left the house before eleven, she would quote reprovingly, 'All smart hair is longer, but long hair is not smart.'

'Jack wouldn't notice the difference,' I defended my still very short locks.

'Remember the beads,' crowed Dot, to whom I had told that story. Under Dot's influence (and cut prices) I became very smart for a short while. Jack said he was embarrassed to take me to the House of Commons. How could he possibly make a serious speech about unemployment when I came in looking a million dollars?

'A million dollars ain't worth nothing these days.'

'Ha!' Jack was very gloomy and troubled. I suppose most politicians were in the months before the National Government. It was causing a strain on our relationship, which was still a fair-weather business. I gathered enough to realise that his allegiance to the Conservative Party was fighting a new battle with his allegiance to his working background. He saw relations, and even his own father's business, backed against the wall, and he couldn't help feeling their best help would come from a properly organised Labour Party. Instead, of course, the very opposite happened. On 23 August 1931 a National Government, which included Conservative, Liberal, and Labour members, was formed under the leadership of Ramsay MacDonald. The National Government candidates, including himself, were returned with 497 seats, and what remained of the Labour Party could put in only 46 members.

It was a very odd time to resign from the Conservative Party and throw in one's lot with an apparently decaying Labour Party. But that's what Jack did. It was the first time he acted out of principle, and it turned out to be the most brilliant move of his career. Just before he took the decision, I went with him in the winter of 1931 to the House of Commons. Before listening to the debate, we had tea.

'The English are a funny race.' Jack looked gloomily round at the chomping faces. 'The evening after the election, the King went to see *Cavalcade*.'

'Even a King can enjoy Coward.'

'Not when the country's in a state of ruin. Quite properly, he was met with a jingo demonstration.'

'You can't have changed enough to be glad about disorder.'

'It's more complicated than that. Have you heard about Tom Mosley's New Party?'

'You're not going to join him now?'

'Don't be childish. Shall we go and jeer at the noble Lords first?'

'Don't be childish.' I remembered that long-ago visit when I had been escorted by my grandfather. 'The past doesn't interest me.'

The Commons debate had already started when Jack and I separated, he for the benches, I for the gallery. 'It's what remains of the Labour Party trying to annul the new Unemployment Insurance Regulations,' he explained. 'What ever does that mean?' 'It means someone's sticking up for the working classes.' He gave me a bitter look and walked away.

The first obvious thing I noticed was the lack of Hon. Members on the Government side. From the Labour benches, men rose to paint a picture of penury and humiliation, as British workers went before Public Assistance Boards to have their resources scrutinised. Everything was taken into account: the pension already paid to disabled ex-servicemen, the house bought after years of saving by some thrifty mine worker, the £80 invested by a woman which would have to support her—while the woman who blew a £250 inheritance on a trip to Canada would get unemployment payment.

As the evening went on, I became more and more infected by the rhetoric of the left. The most fiery speech came from Mr Aneurin Bevan. An Honorable Member, who was also a Noble Lord and who laughed when Bevan suggested that the sort of means-test operating 'will undermine the foundations of home life in this country, as nothing else could do,' was given a short lecture on his own experience of unemployment in 1923, ending with the words 'I do not want to threaten the Noble Lord, but had he been nearer to me at that time, I should have wiped the grin off his face. We know that the Noble Lord has no need to pass a means test. He and his family have thriven upon the proceeds of banditry for centuries.'

After the furious objections to his ungentlemanly attack had died down, he continued, 'It is not possible for us at this moment to influence the course of legislation, because we are not able to send influential deputations to the Prime Minister. It is not possible for us to bring subterranean pressure to bear upon him. It is not possible for us even to inflict upon the Government any fear of a defeat in the Division Lobbies. All we desire to do is to warn them that if they persist in the course which they have adopted, if they continue to inflict injury upon the poorest members of the community, then not even their swollen and monstrous majority will protect them from the Nemesis to come.'

I felt like cheering. At the same time I had a distinct sense that Mr Bevan and his friends were beating their heads against a brick wall. And that they knew it.

'How about something to eat?' I jumped as Jack tapped me on the shoulder.

When we got onto the stairs I burst out, 'But why were there so few of the Government to listen to all that misery?' As I spoke, I noticed quite a stream of Members, smiling and joking, with butts of cigars and red faces, advancing towards the chamber. Jack looked at them too.

'A dinner was being given for Beaverbrook. They'd rather attend that. Now they'll come in and vote against the annulment.'

I stared. 'It's worse than the Lords.'

'It's democracy.'

We stood in the great marble hall, looking very cross and out of place among all the jovial Honorable Members. I noticed that none nodded to Jack.

'Let's go somewhere else,' he said abruptly. 'I'm sick of this place.'

'I'm not surprised.'

Yet the odd thing, the shameful thing, was that as soon as we got out into the cold of Parliament Square, the drama of the working man's plight seemed to lose its grip on me. By the time we reached a restaurant, I didn't even want to talk about it. My passionate involvement with the debate was a tribute to the playwright; my total identification with the causes of the left was due to the greater persuasiveness of the actors.

'Oh, Vi.' Jack put his head in his hand. 'What am I to do?'

'Have a drink.'

'You saw it too. Even with no political interest, you understood it. They make you shudder, don't they? Shudder!'

I looked down at the menu. I was embarrassed by the spectacle of emotion in a man whom I had relied upon for strength. I was not willing to enter his struggles. I didn't love him. 'I was just an audience,' I said, firmly squashing Judas-like sensations. 'I don't understand the ins and outs.'

'The ins and outs?' Jack looked amazed. 'You understood perfectly well the main point that the very poor are to be squeezed dry to keep the middle classes going.'

'Surely if you believe in the capitalist system—'

'If you believe in the capitalist system!' Jack mimicked me. 'You heard the descriptions of what it's like to stand in line for money to buy food for your family and be treated as if you were a beggar. And I must go back and vote against them!' He put his head in his hands.

'Obviously the system isn't perfect.'

'It's archaic. Insulting! Earlier this afternoon the Prime Minister deigned to put in appearance. And guess what held our attention?'

I looked pleadingly at the menu as Jack's anger mounted. 'Can't we eat?'

'We were wondering why the Victoria and Albert Museum was now closing at six o'clock on Thursday and Saturday instead of at nine o'clock. And the answer we got, from no less a person than the Parliamentary Secretary to the Board of Education, Herswald Ramsbotham, was that the Museum had stayed open till ten o'clock and "the evening openings had been discontinued in the interests of national economy." This sort of thing is taken seriously while starving men are humiliated—'

'Museums are serious,' I interrupted mildly, hoping, I suppose, to divert him. Indeed I did direct his wrath from the House of Commons to myself.

'Even if you're not interested in politics, you should be able to see the difference between pretty pictures and food for the starving.'

I began to get angry. 'Food for the mind, food for the body. It's easy to see which you're interested in.'

'Yes, I am. More interested in dead workmen than living culture snobs!' He banged his palm on the table so that everything on it clattered and jumped. By this time I was happy for the battle to be joined as loudly and publicly as possible.

'So that's what you think I am,' I shouted. 'A culture snob. Well, let me tell you what I think of your bullying, uncivilised—'

'Go on, say it, working class!' Jack screamed back. It was a classic quarrel, absurd because we each supplied ammunition for the other. Jack's 'culture snob' referred in a general sense to those who visited museums, while I had not planned an attack on his working-class origins, which anyway were more exactly lower-middle-class. Nevertheless, we may have understood each other's subconscious, for neither of us bothered to deny the accusations. The odd thing is that our differences had not caused us to quarrel before. We had always been remarkably good-tempered with each other—lack of passion, I suppose. The passion was supplied by the House of Commons Unemployment Insurance Debate. Ironically enough for someone as unconcerned as I was then with public events, my private life was twice affected in a major way by a political situation. I married Howard because of the General Strike; I finished with Jack because of Unemployment.

Our fight in that unfortunate restaurant lost nothing from lack of practice. 'And while we're on the subject of the mind versus the body—'

'We're not on the subject; we are trying to conduct a logical—'

'You pretend to be interested in the body, but it's all in your mind—'

'If I stripped naked now and posed on the table, I'd interest you no more than a fly. There's a time for that sort of thing, isn't there—'

'Your naked body is about as relevant to this discussion as a fly—'

'Discussion?'

'Women are so self-centred!' he yelled. 'They never think of anything else but how they feel, how they look, how other people think they feel, how other people think they look. Why can't they ever look out into the world like men do?'

'Women are how men want them. Obedient-wife material, good-mother material. We might as well be sensitive about ourselves, since no one else is—no man, anyway. Be a good wife. Be a good mother. Ugh!'

'You don't want that. And you don't want anything else either. Women are stupid!'

'Women are what men make them. Of course we'd all be Prime Minister if we had the chance. Look at my education. What chance did I ever have? No one would have given a boy an education like that.'

'Your moronic idiotic mother would have given Ramsay MacDonald an education like that.'

'That's the fault of her lack of education.'

'How much education do you think Ramsay MacDonald had? He didn't need education.'

'I thought you despised Ramsay MacDonald.'

'Ramsay MacDonald has nothing to do with it.'

'I'm not the one who introduced the subject of Ramsay MacDonald.'

'You know I hate Ramsay MacDonald. Here's a typical example of woman's inability to function except on a personal level.'

'Ramsay MacDonald is not my personal level, even if he's yours. I don't sink so far.'

'If you mention Ramsay MacDonald once more, I shall never see you again!'

'Who shall I mention instead then? Your friend Herswald Ramsbotham? As a matter of fact, I'm not sure Herswald Ramsbotham isn't an anagram for Ramsay MacDonald!'

This provoked Jack into the final crescendo. He leaped to his feet and screamed, 'That's it! Ramsay MacDonald! You said it! It's all over!'

'Herswald Ramsbotham! Herswald Ramsbotham! Herswald Ramsbotham! Don't you see? It never began.'

I returned to my house to find Dot and Hamish finishing off a bottle of champagne. 'A last fling.' Dot pulled a face. 'The wedding is set for March. St Margaret's, Westminster. All the trimmings. You can be chief bridesmaid.'

'Matron,' I said dourly. 'Married women have to be matrons.'

'How interesting.' Hamish stared at me.

'Not very.'

'I meant,' said Hamish, still curiously, 'that I didn't know you were married. It must have been very sudden.'

It was then that I decided to get divorced. It was not, as Dot always thought, because the happy example of her shining bridal eyes and confetti inspired me for a second attempt, but because I realised the whole Howard affair had never existed. I could never have killed a marriage. But nothing had ever been there to kill. I visited a solicitor called Mr Ladysmith.

'Do you mean your husband has never, er, taken another woman to bed since you left—er, he left you?'

'I don't know for a fact, but I think it fairly likely.'

Mr Ladysmith was young, with huge black eyebrows and hair which, despite heavy watering, popped up suddenly in little turrets over his head. His mind was like that too. He tried to keep it calm and controlled as befitted something as boring as a divorce case, but it kept leaping in excitement as if he were investigating the most dreadful murder.

'Not a fact. But you think it likely. I see. I see. A problem confronts us. Yes. Yes.' A new tuft of hair shot up centre right, so that he was encircled by turrets like a king in a game of chess.

At that time, before the Matrimonial Causes Act of 1937, which allowed three new causes for divorce—wilful desertion, cruelty, and insanity—there was only one way to dissolve a marriage: adultery. The problem, of course, was that *I* had committed adultery and that Howard hadn't. Yet despite my lack of charitable feelings towards Jack, I could hardly let him take the blame for the breakdown of our marriage when it was over long before I met him.

'Talk to your husband,' advised Mr Ladysmith.

'He doesn't want a divorce.'

'Make him feel manly.'

It became clear that much the easiest solution would be for Howard to agree to be found *in flagrante delicto*.

165

With Mr Ladysmith's advice in mind, I took the train down to Sherborne. My morale, already low, was made worse by the selection of magazines I had bought to cheer myself in Waterloo Station. It was no surprise to find the new sixpenny magazines, *My Home*, *Wife and Home*, *Woman*, advocating a life of shopping, cooking, knitting, and bringing up the children; but it was a bit much when the shilling glossies, *Homes and Gardens* and *Ideal Home*, rammed in the same message. It seemed to me that it was only a few weeks ago that women were the bright hopes of the future; that satisfaction could be found, and even should be found, outside a husband's enduring love and a quiverful of babies. Even Father Wilson had not been so dogmatic when I'd told him my plans. 'I'll pray for you,' he'd said, and added that he was also praying for Molly because she was suffering particularly at present. 'Perhaps you should see her?' I hadn't. My own problems seemed enough. I threw the unwelcome propaganda down with disgust and tried to go to sleep in the corner of the carriage.

Howard and I met in his offices. My first reaction was surprise at how good-looking he was. I had quite forgotten his large eyes, his regular features and excellent figure. I was digesting this when a very pretty fair-haired secretary came in with a file. Before she left, she cast him such a look of adoration that I was reminded of almost our last agreeable conversation before we broke up. The golden girl in his office who thought him a god. Her vivid blush as she saw me looking convinced me. This was either the same worshipper or an indistinguishable successor.

The knowledge gave me hope. Perhaps Howard had fallen after all. Perhaps a little urging from me would tip the balance even if he hadn't. Perhaps he'd read the propaganda too and was just longing to be the master of a nice domesticated slave. 'What a very pretty girl, Howard.' To say that I had estimated wrongly would be an understatement. My tentative inquiry was met with cold astonishment and disgust. Fury was reserved for Miss Chaffey's defence. She was, apparently, pure as the driven snow, virtuous as a nun, delicate as a lily, etc, etc. It seemed I had put my cause back some way. We parted enraged with each other.

Nevertheless, the presence of Miss Chaffey, handled in the right way, did eventually provide an answer to the problem. Even if Howard didn't have her or want her in any intimate sense, he certainly did not want to appear in front of her as a pathetic cuckold. Where I failed, Mrs Shakespeare succeeded. 'He does want to appear manly, Vi dear. You can't take everything from him. Just tell your chap to make the appropriate arrangements, and you can start looking for a new man right away.'

'For God's sake, Edie. I've just got rid of a husband and a lover.'
'Well, then, you'd better find something sensible to do with your life.' It was the first time she had ever reproved me.

Chapter Seven

HOLIDAYS FOR WORKING WOMEN

Sir—May we again appeal at this holiday season to the generosity of your readers, who have in the past enabled us to provide seaside holidays for some of the poor working women of London . . .

Some will tell you they did have a holiday once, but so long ago that they have forgotten when. 'Of course I knew there were such things as 'olidays,' said one woman when describing her utter bewilderment at being offered the chance of one, 'but I never dreamt I should ever 'ave one myself.'

£2 will pay for a fortnight's holiday at the seaside for one woman, and an additional 10s. will enable her to take her baby with her.

(Letter to the Editor) *The Times.*   5 July 1935

DIARY OF THE SEASON 1935

A record of the chief Social events arranged to take place during May, June, July, August and September. Neatly bound; convenient in size ($4\frac{1}{2}$ × $3\frac{1}{4}$) and interleaved with blank pages for personal notes. Price sixpence.

(Advertisement) *The Times.*   5 July 1935

CHRISTIANITY TODAY

Sir—It seems to me that there will be no general return to religious observances till our clergy, and those who teach our young, press home the fact, simply, constantly, and forcibly that the Church is a living society with a divinely given authority and a supernatural mission full of glory & romance.

I am, Sir, your most obedient servant,

W. Ashley-Brown, Chaplain (on leave),

Indian Ecclesiastical Estab., Archdeacon of Bombay,

Seameadows Cottage, Eccles, Norfolk.

(Letter to the Editor) *The Times.*   5 July 1935

Immediately after my divorce, I felt a great surge of joy and energy. I played my first game of golf with Dot and Hamish—cosily installed in a horrid little house in Hertfordshire—and amazed them by my prowess. I realised that most of my problems had been caused, or at least aggravated, by a lingering guilty attachment to my marriage. I went round quoting Vera Brittain and Virginia Woolf on the role of women.

Nettles arrived on my doorstep one Sunday in September. It was dusk, and I had been practising calisthenics in the drawing room. I opened the front door. He carried a Gladstone bag in one hand and a neatly rolled umbrella in the other. I stood there, panting, in my tights.

'The harvest was good,' he said as if already in the middle of a conversation. 'All in and stored away. The cows have calved, the men are well, the house is rainproof, and the sheep can look after themselves.'

If a fifty-year-old man can look like a lately descended Mary Poppins, he did. I began to pant and laugh at th same time. His humble look of happiness became uncertain.

'Are you entertaining?'

'In my tights?'

'These days . . . .'

'These days, we're into swagger coats and English spun-silk "washing frocks" in fashionable stripes.' As he looked amazed, I pulled him in and explained. 'I used to rent rooms to my cousin who was a fashion writer. Now I only have the civil servant cousin. And the don above. Augustus, that is. You can borrow his rooms, I'm sure. That is, if you've come to stay. He never comes. He thinks he comes, but in fact he's tied to Oxford's apron strings.'

Nettles' appearance had enormously cheered me. I gabbled gaily as he followed me into the drawing room. Nettles looked round curiously at the room. The needle of the gramophone was knocking regularly against the card in the middle of the record. It was a noise I often ignored for minutes at a time, but now it sounded sharply insistent. When Flo came in and switched on the lights, I saw the room in a series of odd shapes and angles, as if I had never seen them before. I watched her pleasure at seeing Nettles. Her broad, ugly face, which I had known for so many years, seemed to form itself into new lines of sensitivity. When she called in Cecil, I noticed the way he stood solidly beside her as if he were there to support her happiness or sorrow. For the first time I saw that they loved each other.

All this happened because Nettles had appeared at my door, and I was ready to meet him.

'Tomorrow,' I told him, 'we're going to stay with Molly and her illicit love object near Didcot. Mrs Briggsworthy is opening a fête at

Little Bidding. You don't mind going to the country again, I hope?'
My concern was real. What if he vanished into the air as suddenly as
he'd appeared?

'I'm totally in your hands.' With a gesture that seemed to me symbolic, he took off a pair of dark-rimmed spectacles he was wearing
and put them in his pocket.

We sat down opposite each other in the pearl-grey drawing
room which my mother had created on the way to escaping
him, and I didn't think of that at all. Nettles, now in middle age,
living a healthy but monastic life at Kettleside, had never looked
better. His russet tweed suiting with its soft flannel shirt and shiny
brogues may not have been very fashionable, but it suited admirably
his curly hair, thinner but only slightly grey, and his coppery-
coloured face. He looked like a nice healthy farmer, which was, I suppose, what he had turned himself into.

George, with his guilt and nervous beaky nose, was also a farmer.
'George Briggsworthy has a few hundred acres. I gather it's like
inquiring about a man's bank balance to ask exactly how many.'

'Your mother has asked me to keep an eye on the farm at Eureka.'

'Has she?' I said, suddenly cool. 'You won't, of course.'

'Probably not,' he conceded. 'I don't really have the time. I might
go once. Out of curiosity.'

'It's most depressing. I spent my honeymoon there.'

That made him notice me. 'Perhaps it was not the fault of the
island, but of the man.' He smiled shyly, and I immediately felt all
would be well after all.

'I'm divorced now.'

The next morning we took a train from Waterloo. I tried to forget
it was the same line that went to Sherborne. Molly joined us at Reading. She dragged me out into the corridor. Her face was flushed. 'I
had a letter from George this morning. We haven't met for a month.
He'll be there at the station. Do you think these bright stripes appropriate? He thinks I'm a stunner in anything. It's Reading's best.
Sometimes I wish I was richer. Do you know my guardian's ill? I keep
having this unworthy thought he'll leave me something. When you reach
my age it's such a fag having to think about money. Of course, you don't.'

'I do since Blumberg. Don't be so hysterical.'

She plunged on regardless. Her eyes stared wildly out at the flashing countryside. 'I even find myself missing the comforts of George's
home as well as him. It's so easy to be corrupted. I can't tell you how I
hate my three little rooms—do you remember how exciting they
seemed in Oxford? Now I long for a home and a maid and even a
cook. Sometimes I look at that oafish white loaf and think if I have to
cut another slice . . .'

'Whole-meal bread's much better for you.'

'I live on red wine. My students think it's medicine. They think cider's daring. They seem so young now. Have you ever thought of having children yourself, Vi?'

I turned to Nettles, sitting quietly in the compartment, and raised my eyes to heaven. He smiled encouragingly and called out to Molly, 'Didcot next, if I remember a right.' I made a mental note to ask him when he had stopped stuttering on the letter *r*.

George did not meet us at the station. Mrs Briggsworthy had fallen down the stairs, and he had driven her to hospital.

'Oh, God,' Molly prayed as she dipped her finger in the holy-water stoup outside George's front door, 'make her stay in hospital for rest and observation.'

In such an emotional atmosphere, how could my love fail to increase and multiply? Mrs Briggsworthy did not return with George from the hospital. Molly and George disappeared. When they reappeared for lunch, his face beamed like a schoolboy's, hers showed signs of prolonged tears. In between swooning glances and roast beef, they discussed with words of gravest worry in voices of greatest happiness who should now open the fête. 'They count on my mother. They won't know what to do without her.'

'She makes such a topping speech.'

'The same one.'

'They like it better every year.

'You'll have to get up and say what happened. Unfortunately, my mother fell downstairs.'

'They'll love that.' George gave up his unconvincing lines of worry and began to giggle. His pointed nose wiggled at the end. 'Have you noticed how the very young and the very old adore disaster? They're all old ladies at the fête.'

With this jolly conviction, George cranked his car and we all piled in. 'I always liked your friend,' Nettles said. We sat together in the back while the lovers tried to hold hands across the gears. 'Do you remember when we drove up to Kettleside?'

'I was the young lady of the manor and you ran away.'

'I haven't got enough servants to fill even one row of the front steps now.'

'No pulling of forelocks? No curtseys?'

'It always embarrassed me. How could I have family retainers when there was no family left? If you come up you'll have to use a disguise, though you've changed so much none would recognise you. Mrs Shakespeare.'

'Don't call me that. When did you stop stuttering on the letter *r*?'

'When your mother left me.'

Fêtes always produce intimacy. People have to react originally to an original situation. Nettles found himself buying lavender bags, embroidered table runners, and a bag of tomatoes grown through seaweed. He guessed the weight of a homemade chocolate cake. Eventually he even judged the baby competition. In reacting to the babies freshly, he did the same to me. He turned out to be an inspired baby judge. Mothers glowed under his attentions. 'How can I possibly say one is more beautiful than another? They're all perfect.'

'Thank you so much,' I said, after a red-cheeked curly-haired creature had been declared winner.

'I've always loved babies. The great sadness of my life is that I have no children. That was one of the main reasons I wanted to marry your mother.' He smiled. 'However, since she neither wanted more children nor to be married to me, it was a fruitless desire. Now I produce calves and corn.'

I took heart from the information that he had wanted to marry Eleanor not out of love for her, but out of love for children. 'You should have married my friend Araminta.'

I was not willing to remember Henry's headstone on the hill. Quite soon after my mother told me it was her dead baby's burial place, I had reverted to my original belief that it was a dog's grave. Childhood memories are odd. I'll never know whether she made up the story. I never asked Nettles.

'Let me buy you a cup of tea,' said Nettles. We sat side by side on a low stone wall that bounded one side of the small paddock where the fête was being held. The village hall sheltered our backs from a coolish wind, and the mellow September sun shone upon our faces. The villagers chinked heavy china cups around us, and a woman wearing a hat of Edwardian dimensions handed round rock cakes at a penny the pair. I was glad Nettles sat beside me, rather than Howard, who would have been too much part of the scene, or Jack, who would have made me feel guilty about the starving mass of unemployed.

'My friend Araminta is a tremendous baby factory. Unfortunately, her husband's taken against the assembly line. She's that very beautiful girl you saw at my wedding.' I did not say that he had mistaken her for my mother.

'Your friends are very obsessive.'

'I've never thought so.'

'Look at Molly. She hasn't left George's side all afternoon. And that MP friend of yours.'

'What?' Why should Nettles know about Jack? He might know about his public life, because his speeches were often reported, but why should he know about our friendship? 'Obsessively caring. For one political party or the other. I suppose you're a very eligible bachelor in Northumberland?'

Nettles laughed. 'Miss Tiptree still thinks so. Everyone else has given me up. Too old.'

'You don't look old.'

'I'm too comfortable to be young. I've become self-satisfied from making the farm run properly. It was in a terrible state. No money put into new machinery, far too many men employed, old buildings, bad balance between dairy crop and sheep. Now it's all set to go. Another ten or fifteen years and it'll be a first-rate farm.'

'Such a long time. An age,' I sighed. Because I had done nothing with the first three decades of my life, I clung to the possibility of instant change.

'I distrust overnight success. I made money overnight during the war. I lost it, too—all except what I spent on the farm.'

'People don't talk about money much.'

'People don't talk about the fundamentals.'

'They don't dare.'

'You had an odd childhood.' Nettles got up off the wall, took our two cups back to a trestle table, and then returned to me. 'I blame myself.'

I thought of my childhood from when Eleanor had left me at Kettleside. I thought of the years spent entirely on Eureka and the years spent partly there and partly at Shoreham Abbey. I thought of that twilight time in London before I decided to go to Oxford. 'When I was a girl you were about the only person who was any use to me. Only you and Augustus ever talked to me sensibly. You didn't kill my father.'

'It's no excuse, of course, but your mother's a very dominating woman.'

'I'd guess Blumberg can cope.' I stood up restlessly. 'Why do we always end up talking about Eleanor? Neither of us have seen her for years. She's got no interest in us; why should we be interested in her?'

Nettles looked surprised. 'She's what we've got in common.'

I began to walk quickly towards a coconut shy. 'No, she's not. She's the past. We've got plenty of other things in common.'

Nettles took my arm and forced me to stop and face him. 'Of course we have,' he said gently. 'We've got . . .' We looked at each other, and although in our closeness I saw the crisscross lines of fifty years and the slightly greying stubble on his chin, I also saw an expression in his eyes which made me realise he finally saw beyond the fifteen-year-old daughter of his mistress. I didn't want him to smile, and he didn't. Instead, a look of nervous doubt suddenly masked his features. 'I'll try and win you a coconut.'

174

'I'd like that.' The nervousness made me even more certain about what I'd seen.

That evening began demurely. We all rested and bathed. A feeling that we had done our duty by Little Bidding gave us a childlike virtuous glow. George, who had clearly decided to lose the nighttime battle with his conscience, carved up a haunch of his own sheep. After dinner and a great deal of red wine, we decided we must play a game.

'Don't be so middle-class!' exclaimed Molly to try her power.

'Have you never heard of Musical Chairs at Cliveden? Lady Astor always gets the last chair.'

'Your cousin Henry Briggsworthy plays games all the time,' Molly said lovingly.

'No one except the unemployed aristocracy have the energy left for games.'

'Or Prime Ministers,' said Nettles mildly. 'I play chess with the vicar. He's hardly upper-class, though I believe he went to Charterhouse.'

'We'll play Charades!' cried Molly, flinging her arms around so that we all jumped. 'George and I will go out first.'

'They are an enthusiastic couple,' said Nettles when we were left alone.

'They're making up for lost time. Do you take religious scruples very seriously?'

'I go to church. You must remember the church at Kettleside. Quite feudal. There's still a pew which says Hesketh.'

'They have a chapel here. Tomorrow morning George will persuade us to go to Mass. A priest comes over each week and joins us for kidneys and bacon afterwards. I enjoy it, though it must be embarrassing for George.'

'Embarrassing?'

'If he doesn't go to communion, one knows he slept with Molly the night before.'

'There are other sins. Perhaps he had a midnight feast.'

'Perhaps. Do you think they'll ever come back?'

'I don't mind.'

'Nor do I.' We sat in silence on either side of the fire. Between us a low table was piled with various books and magazines. Nettles picked up a volume and took out his horn-rimmed glasses. I looked at this sign of advancing age and found it didn't put me off at all. On the contrary. I remembered how his squint and colour-blindness had stopped him fighting in 1916. He flicked through the pages of the book. 'Strange to find Arden's poems in a gentleman farmer's drawing room.

Beethameer, Beethameer, bully of Britain,
With your face as fat as a farmer's bum;
Though you pose in private as a playful kitten
Though the public you poison are pretty well dumb,
They shall turn on their betrayer when the time is come.
The cousins you cheated shall recover their nerve
And give you the thrashing you richly deserve.

'I don't think Arden's as politically committed as everyone else seems to be. It's just that politics are fashionable. It's probably Molly's book.'

'Does she really want to marry him?'

'They're coming back. Intelligent, independent women always fall for the most unlikely men. Aren't you lonely in Kettleside?'

'Occasionally.'

George was wearing a skimpy piece of tiger skin which revealed too much of his very white skin. Molly looked more attractive in a selection of capes and gowns circa 1870.

'It must be the "I Want to Sin" girl,' suggested Nettles.

Would you like to sin
With Elinor Glyn
On a tiger skin?
Or would you prefer
To err
With her
On some other fur?

'Wrong. He doesn't wear the tiger. They lie on it.'

'Tarzan. He's Tarzan Lord whatever-he-was!'

'Woola, woola, woola, woola!' George beat his chest obligingly.

Molly grabbed his bare arms emphatically. 'He is not Tarzan.' They looked lovingly into each other's eyes.

Charades usually follow the same pattern of idiocy. After we had successfully guessed George and Molly's eve-oh-lute-shun, Nettles and I went from the room. For a moment I was cast back to the time at Kettleside when I was a child and Mama and Nettles had giggled outside the door. Had I crept out from bed one evening, hung over the stairs watching them, shivering with cold and terror of Nanny Fig's detection? Resolutely I shook off Eleanor's ghost.

'Let's be something shocking!' Nettles was ready to oblige. 'Confessional.'

I played Father Wilson talking about the all-healing power of love to Nettles' lesbian Mary Magdalene. Fatuous though it was, we did manage to shock George, who suddenly rose like a ruffled eagle and left the room. 'It's just nerves,' cried Molly, racing after him. 'You understand, Vi.'

'Well, that's that, I suppose.' I unwound the silk patterned shawl masquerading as a chasuble.

'It wasn't very tasteful,' said Nettles. 'I'm sorry.'

'So am I.' We looked at each other and began to laugh.

Becoming ever more absurd, we swooped about the room to George's out-of-date dance records. We played 'When Day Is Done' by Ambrose and his orchestra over and over again, as loud as George's antediluvian gramophone would allow, taking turns to wind it up until our arms were as weak as our legs.

Eventually we collapsed onto the Daghestan hearthrug. I don't know who touched the other first, but I remember the feel of Nettles' hand on my shoulder and his leg under my hand. From that first touch it was inevitable we made love. The sense of coming home was intense. Yet each kiss, each touch, seemed perfect in itself, so that I had a feeling of slow motion. We lay mouth to mouth for what seemed like hours. When we changed position, it was like finding another way to complete the same puzzle. Our bodies were warm, close to the fire yet never burning. When we undressed, our clothes slid off obediently. He touched me gently; he held me firmly, protectively. I felt weak, strong, grateful.

I dressed for Mass on a dull, cheerless morning with a feeling of foreboding. I imagined four guilty persons sitting in a grim line, carefully avoiding the eyes of their last night's partners. I tried to soften the blow, to smile at the image, but the face staring at me in my dressing-table mirror looked far too terrified. Instead, I wrapped my head in a scarf and went downstairs. I was late. No one was waiting for me. Was this a bad omen or were they kindly leaving me to extra sleep? I ran along the stone-floored corridor which ended with the door to the chapel. It creaked horribly when I opened it. The priest had his back to me, but the others turned. I saw only Nettles. To my astonishment and confusion, he smiled at me. A smile anywhere would have been wonderful; a smile in church was breathtaking. No one smiled in church in 1933. Nettles, that most conventional of all men, smiled broadly. I rushed forward. Stumbling apologetically but determinedly over George and Molly's legs, I knelt beside him. His hand found mine and pressed it warmly. It was all going to be all right.

It was not, unsurprisingly, as easy as that, though that particular morning was merry. Whatever the state of our souls, we ate breakfast with ravenous appetite. The priest, unusually, was Father Wilson, and I remember thinking like a naughty child that he wouldn't be so

177

friendly if he'd known how we'd spent the previous evening.

After seeing him off, we took an immensely long walk round the fields. The weather had not lifted and we were surrounded by a dripping mist, so that even the trees turning now from green to bronze were shaded with grey. The trees were the point of the walk. George was fast becoming a world expert on trees. That morning he was interested in girth. Producing a tape measure from his pocket, he conducted us on a tour of the Hertfordshire giants. Absurdly, we talked of nothing but trees. 'Hold that end, Molly, my dear. No, no. Don't walk round after me.' 'I am sorry, George—I'm in a dream today.'

'So am I, so am I,' I could have echoed. Nettles, dressed in astonishingly ancient plus fours and a green weatherproof cape, had declared his love for me. He was in shock, I suppose, half horror-struck at the implications, for he was a man who liked to carry things through. Why, for example, had he hung on to Eleanor so grimly when it had been obvious for years their time together was up? Peculiarly, he had a strong belief in marriage, an urge to be faithful. His parents, who had both died during his teens, had been idyllically happy together. Love to him meant marriage. He walked by my side under those great spreading trees.

'Surely, George, this one must be something special?'

'Surprising, perhaps, in southern England, but hardly special.'

And Nettles' mind was on marriage. I wanted only to touch him, to be near to him. The walk lasted a very long time. I remember it through a veil of silvery mist like a dream, as if we were all much younger, in some teen-age *Grand Meaulnes*. We were giggly in a hung-over sort of way, unwilling to return to the sobering reality of Sunday lunch and the week ahead. George kept looking at his watch even as he led us farther from the house.

'This is a horse chestnut.'

'A horse chestnut,' repeated Molly, as if he'd said something quite extraordinary.

'I would have thought it was a Spanish chestnut,' remarked Nettles. I smiled at him as if he'd made a brilliant point. Neither George nor Molly noticed our ecstatic state; it was too parallel with their own.

At the end of the day, when dusk was thickening the mist and we were packing in preparation for catching our train back to London, I drew Molly into my bedroom. She immediately assumed I wanted to hear the latest state of play in her love affair. 'How can I ever make the final break when it feels so wonderfully right when we're together? I feel good, not bad. I feel morally good. The guilt only comes later . . . when . . .'

'Molly—'

'Maybe women are more pragmatic than men. Maybe I should change jobs. . . '

'Molly, I'm in love with Nettles. He loves me too.'

To do her justice, once she heard my news her attention was overwhelming. 'But darling, he's almost your father!' I was to hear that line too often to make it anything but painful—even in retrospect. 'I know he's fearfully attractive. I thought that years ago, when we went North together with that poor pale-faced major.'

'I was a child then.'

'Exactly my point. And he was your father.'

'Not exactly.'

'Not exactly but very nearly. Please don't follow my example and get in a muddle.'

'He isn't married. My mother would never marry him.'

'Oh, God. Back out before it's too late.'

'It is too late.'

Again, once I had convinced Molly of this, she was ready to make the next step. I had never brought my problems to her before.

'The trouble with you,' she said in a resigned voice, 'is that you don't take enough interest in world events.'

'I can't see what that has to do with falling in love.'

'Nettles is an escape. He'll take you to Northumberland and you'll both pretend it's 1903 instead of 1933. I've started teaching politics. England's in even more of a mess than I am.'

'I'd hardly see George as a man of the age. Measuring chestnuts on five hundred acres near Didcot doesn't say 1933 any more than raising grouse in Northumberland.'

'George should have been a priest. He's totally apolitical.'

'You have to admit I tried. Look at Jack. A Member of Parliament. Our relationship collapsed over Ramsay MacDonald. I bet you've never discussed Unemployment Insurance with George.'

Molly sighed. 'I've explained to him that it's immoral to be apolitical at time like this. Do you know Spender's poem, 'Oh Young Men'?

> Oh young men, oh comrades
> It is too late now to stay in those houses
> Your fathers built where they built you to build to breed
> Money on money . . .

'I wish I cared about something outside myself.'

'It's my search for an identity. Did you know I'm illegitimate?'

'What?' My voice of amazement and, I suspect, horror, made Molly laugh.

179

'It's a strange thing about school friends. One doesn't have much interest in the past at fifteen, and by the time you're old enough to know better, the present takes up all the time. I'm illegitimate. I was brought up by my mother till I was six, when she died. I never knew my father. My guardian was a friend of my mother's. Poor chap, he was such a bachelor. Can you imagine what it must have been like to be landed with an ebullient six-year-old?'

'You did seem different from the other girls at Shoreham Abbey.'

'Loxy-Poxy knew. It appealed to her sense of the dramatic. "The rate of illegitimate to legitimate mortality in the first week of life increased from 170 per cent in 1907 to 201 per cent in 1916! You're lucky to have survived, my dear." I didn't feel lucky to have survived.'

'Do you now?'

'Mostly.' Molly tried to look brisk and uncaring, but I was aware of her sadness. I rushed into speech.

'It's extraordinary that neither of us show any interest in producing babies ourselves.'

'You need more basic security. Though I wouldn't dream of bringing a child into the world, as it is now. It's not all sour grapes.'

'All principles are based on personal experience. Personal experience comes first. I shall marry Nettles!' I must have looked absurdly triumphant, for Molly overcame her sadness and said that I was the sort of silly remnant of the upper classes who made it impossible for England to face its problems and move into a new gear.

'I'll never understand why you became involved with George.'

Again Molly sank back. 'Probably to do with my need for security.'

'The only thing secure about George is his farm. He's a bundle of neurotic anxieties.'

'I like his profile.'

'You've never cared about appearances.'

'He loves me.' It was Molly's turn to look triumphant.

'Other men must have loved you.'

'Not really. There was Ivy.'

'Your Friend?' Molly had never talked to me about her lesbian friendship. I had assumed she was ashamed of it.

'I've always liked women. I get on with them better than men. They're generally more interesting people. If it wasn't for sex, I don't think I'd ever want a man. It was sex that was wrong between Ivy and me. I often regret we're no longer friends.'

'But you love George.'

'Love. Love. It must be possible to live without it. Why does one fall in love? You tell me. You've just done it!'

Many people did try to explain to me why I fell in love with Nettles. No one knowing my history or Nettles' could possibly credit the simple truth that I fell in love with him. The psychiatrists employed by my mother on Dr Blumberg's recommendation all—quite naturally when you think who was paying them—explained my 'infatuation' in terms of Eleanor. 'Maternal jealousy—or rather, jealousy of the mother—is one of the potent forces of this generation.' Nettles and I were the only people who knew that the peculiar thing was not that he fell in love with me, but that he had previously been in love with my mother.

'I had my incarnations muddled,' Nettles said as we sat in the house which he had tried to enter as her husband. 'I loved the little bit of you in her. Now I've got all of you.'

Above us we could hear Augustus' weight creaking the floor-boards in his slant-roofed sitting room. My exhilaration was undimmed by the horror in my friends' faces as I told them the great news. It had been Augustus' turn that afternoon.

'Do you think Augustus is pacing the floor in misery? He's making a dreadful noise.'

'You could have prepared him more.'

'He's a Philosophy don. It should be just up his street.'

'Are you sure, Violet, you're not playing a game? Sometimes I think I'll wake up one morning and you'll have vanished.'

'Like Eleanor, you mean?'

'We weren't going to talk about her.'

'Everyone else does.' I felt a sudden cold bitterness dispelling the happy clouds of love. 'Augustus more or less assumed I was only doing it to spite my mother. Which is patently idiotic, since she never wanted to marry you and has been married twice since to other men.'

'I don't want you to alienate your friends,' said Nettles in a worried tone of voice.

'Don't be ridiculous, darling.' I gave him a hug. 'You go back to Northumberland before the cows get brucellosis and I'll tidy things down here and join you. My mother and pacifism are the only two causes Augustus ever espoused, the only things he's ever truly loved, and now at the same time his attitudes to both are getting a thorough shake-up.'

'I don't see what pacifism—'

'The "They Must Not Fight" mentality that's hit the country. If the *Sunday Express* got the message, then where is poor Augustus?'

'He could line up with Molly's friends. The poets. The intellectuals.'

'But their hearts are in Moscow. One can hardly see Augustus fitting into a Communist state. Besides, he thinks them poseurs.'

'Auden, Day Lewis, Spender, poseurs?'

'Poetic animals posing as political animals!' Augustus had descended. His large frame shook with indignation. He approached us waving a copy of Claud Cockburn's *The Week*. 'It makes nonsense of British law. They say anything without regard to truth or honesty.'

'You sound so old, Augustus.' I could never get used to his new form. The amount of tweed needed to clothe him in an appropriate three-piece suit—waistcoats were essential then to hide the vulgarity of braces—would have done for a normal father plus a couple of sons. What I couldn't decide was whether his nervous, hypersensitive personality had merely been disguised by the padding or had disappeared further underground.

'I'm not older. In spirit I'm years younger than these chaps. The cynicism of this chap Cockburn. It's journalism that's killing the goodness in Britain. If you can call this scandal-mongering journalism. Been in America too long, these chaps. Given him a hankering for a communism that doesn't exist out of fairy tales. Reds—blundering, murderous reds. I'd as soon have Gandhi tell us what to do as this chap.'

'Gandhi?'

'Mohandas Karamchand Gandhi. Mahatma Gandhi. The little man in his khaddar.'

'Poor Aunt Phyllis nearly died at the idea of good King George shaking the hand of a man in a loincloth with well-worn bony knees and bare toes. We had to wear long white dresses and three feathers.'

'He nearly died too. With the cold.'

Nettles looked on. I had promised him to stay in London for at least six months before joining him, so I was intent on proving that none of my relationships meant a thing. No one except he knew my true worth. With him, I would become a real woman, a woman of principle.

When Augustus had taken himself to his club, looking for a bit of action, I decided the moment had come to break the good news to Flo and Cecil. Flo had always taken Nettles' side against my mother, and since she had married an older man, she was predisposed, I thought, in our favour.

I was wrong. My announcement, 'Dear Flo, isn't it wonderful, Mr Nettlefield and I are to be married!' was met with a look of horror. When she had left the room still without any rational response, Cecil stayed to explain. His embarrassment was even greater than Nettles'. His circumlocutions were so labyrinthine that only heightened sensitivity made understanding possible.

'I'm hardly likely to marry my stepfather, am I?' I cried indignantly.

Cecil's unhappiness increased.'Of course not, Miss. I should guess it's against the law, for one thing . . . '

'The law has nothing to do with us! Mr Nettlefield has a right to get married, just as much as you!'

For a moment there was a distinct possibility that my aggression would turn to tears. Nettles squeezed my arm. Cecil backed towards the door with almost as much horror as Flo had shown earlier.

Nettles and I sat on the sofa. His brave stand gave way to gloom. 'It's madness. What possible right have I to marry you?'

'You're not exerting rights when you marry someone. You're showing love.'

Nettles continued staring at the carpet. Mechanically I noticed the stain made on the day I became engaged to Howard.

'What would your poor father say? Poor Tudor. First I take his wife, then his daughter. What is it about your family? I can live perfectly well without women, you know. I have for years.'

'I need you. Don't you see? Probably I want you more than you want me.'

'With your mother, I had the excuse of youth. Now I'm old.'

'Don't be so maudlin. Selfish. Self-pitying.' My anger reappeared. Perhaps that was Nettles' aim.

'No one can understand what we're up to. It seems ludicrous, obscene, incestuous.'

'We're not marrying for other people. No one ever understands other people's marriages. Anyway, it's too late to worry about the incestuous bit. That side's already done. We're onto more serious things now.'

I was interrupted by a birdlike tap on the door. Cecil entered with a tray. He handed us a drink. We produced tentative smiles. 'Flo is planning a caramel custard with fresh cream for dinner. She hopes you're not going out.' Our smiles became more certain. Flo's caramel custard was a sign of approval we badly needed.

The following morning we received my mother's reaction:

The Present is made up of the Past. I am your Past. You must create your own Future. A mother should sink like the Moon as the new Day of maturity dawns. Your ever-loving Eleanor.
P.S. Dr P.R. Goldman is one of Emmanuel's ex-patients.

'She sounds like Carmen Rose, the fortune-teller at my deb dances.' I attempted a jolly satirical laugh. 'Does she really think I'll go to a psychiatrist recommended by her third husband, whose attitude to me was clear from the moment he persuaded her to cut my allowance?'

'Would you go to a psychiatrist of my choice?'

I'd bitten off a decisive lump of toast and marmalade before that one sank in. I had trouble in swallowing it. 'At least she's paying. I'd rather spend your money on a villa in Tangier.'

Jokes and diversions failed equally. I ended going to not one psychiatrist, but two. This gave people like my aunts the excuse for thinking I had gone mad. 'My dear niece, Violet. Such a tragedy. But then, with a mother like that . . . We always treated her like a daughter, but now I hate to imagine . . .' I enjoyed imagining Aunt Phyllis bustling with energetic irritation and Aunt Letty more controlled and correct, but at heart just as annoyed. I didn't credit them with a sense of moral outrage which I'm sure they truly felt. Oddly enough, they, like Nettles, mentioned my dead father, as if it were on his behalf that they felt the greatest shock.

My only real worry was that Nettles would finally lose his nerve.

'I refuse to come between you and all your friends and relations.'

'I've been praying for someone to come between me and the aunts for years!'

We were walking in Hyde Park. It was a grey day, with flat clouds moving above the trees. They reminded me of a procession of coffins. I stood watching them reflected in the waters of the Serpentine. Nettles, at my side, stirred restlessly. He clapped his hands together. It was a cold as well as a grey day.

'Your aunts have been kind to you. You mustn't be cruel. Why can't you love?'

'I love you.'

'Sometimes I think you use me. Your love for me should teach you to love others.'

'You sound like Father Wilson.'

'Who's Father Wilson?'

'You know who Father Wilson is.' I walked quickly away along beside the trickling waves. Stepping closer, I allowed the soles of my feet to tread down the fringe.

'You'll get wet!' Nettles called after me.

'I want to get wet. I can quite understand King Canute. He was a very irritable man. I thought at least you would understand.' Now I stamped in the thin shivers of water, so that little sugary whorls swished up on either side of my shoes. They were shoes I was fond of, with a bar across the front secured by a row of three pearl buttons, so it was a satisfactory action of masochism. 'If you loved me you would understand. Molly would understand.'

Nettles seemed relieved instead of annoyed by the greater understanding of Molly. 'She's so fond of you.' He came close to me and put an arm round my numbed shoulders. He pinched them warmly.

'I barely know you as an adult.'

I put my arm through Nettles' and led him to a bench. 'I do love people. I love Nanny. It was here, sitting on this bench, that I saw Nanny again.'

Nettles looked uncomfortable. 'I've done so much harm. Poor Nanny.'

'It was Eleanor, not you. You tried to help her. Besides, she's very happy now. Araminta's children think she's a god. When you go back to Kettleside, I shall enlist Araminta's sympathy. Leonard's so seldom there now that she needs a companion.'

Nettles touched my hair at the back of my head. 'What will you do all day long with me?'

'Have babies.' The firmness with which I announced this was misleading. I said it to convince Nettles of my solid intentions and because it seemed the natural corollary to marriage. Unfortunately, it threw Nettles into even greater anxiety. He put his head into his hands. His words were muffled: 'Do you think our past will be put right in their future?'

'Father Wilson places the emphasis on love. He instructed Molly when she joined the Church.'

'I didn't know Molly was a Catholic.'

'She wants to share George's load of guilt.'

'Don't talk to me about guilt.' Nettles did not at that moment give the impression of a man lucky in love. His bowed head with the hair just thinning on top, his narrow hands clasped tensely on his knees, his voice soft and gloomy painted a picture of a man condemned. I even felt a twinge of guilt as I remembered how he'd arrived on my doorstep strong and confident only a few weeks earlier.

Father Wilson was waiting for us in my drawing room. He often turned up in this way when I'd been talking about him. I could see he had come after several meetings hoping for a quiet cup of tea. It didn't seem the moment to burden him with my intentions. Despite his obvious tiredness, I couldn't help noticing that he was quite definitely in a younger age group than Nettles. This comparison disconcerted me, for it was the first time I had seen Father Wilson, despite all his generous humanity, as a man as much as a priest. It gave me a sense of bravado as I made the introductions.

'Father Wilson—Henry Nettlefield.'

'We met over breakfast at George Briggsworthy's' said Nettles, holding out his scone.

'I'd forgotten.' I thought of that day and turned away, embarrassed.

'Have a scone,' said Father Wilson, hitching up his robe and offering the plateful that Flo had already provided.

'I don't mind if I do.'

'I remembered all about you,' continued Father Wilson amicably, but with a deliberation that made me gulp nervously. Perhaps now would come the soul-searching question, the moral condmnation which I had always awaited. He might look like a youngish man in a food-strewn robe with a cord that was unravelling by the minute, but he spoke with the voice of God.

'Flo's been talking to you,' I said as nonchalantly as possible.

'You've been talking to me. You told me about your mother, about Eureka, about school. Naturally I got to know Mr Nettlefield. I didn't realise who he was at George's. I hope you enjoyed your walk through Hyde Park. I used to walk there just after the war when it was filled with Australian and American soldiers. Do you come down to London often?'

It was clear that I was not going to say, 'Nettles and I are engaged.' Instead we began an agreeable conversation about the changing face of London. 'It's the cars that have made the most difference. The noise and stink.'

'The tramcars are abominable.'

'No worse than a horse-drawn carriage over cobbles. And smellier than a cowshed.'

'My cowsheds aren't smelly.'

We moved on to the farming community. 'The only reason that we haven't given up growing wheat altogether, with Australian and Canadian so much cheaper, is that the British variety makes such good biscuits.'

'Biscuits. How absurd.'

'Arable farming's disappearing—unless you count sugar beet, which the government subsidises, or peas, which fit well into the new passion for canned food.'

'Not long ago I was taken to see the pea shellers in Covent Garden. Have you ever seen that exploitation of your sex, Violet?' Father Wilson leaned forward suddenly and adddressed me with such intensity that I reacted almost as if it was the feared question.

'No. Surely it's done mechanically.'

'Grandmothers, most of them, sit on wooden planks, or upturned baskets on the ground, splitting open pea pods with rheumaticky old fingers. Their shoulders, covered in old black overcoats, permanently hunched; their withered faces frowning under round black hats. They get paid tuppence per quart of shelled peas.'

'That's terrible,' I said honestly, for it did seem terrible, but I could no more relate their condition to my own than I could have a sparrow's.

'Of course women do the dirty work. My sugar beet is hoed by

186

women. While they accept low wages, they'll always do the dirty work.'

I looked at Nettles with a faint stirring that this was a more personal issue. 'You pay old women to crawl along on their hands and knees. All day.'

Nettles shrugged. 'They're not all old. I can't change the system single-handed. Anyway, they're lucky to work. Unemployment never falls much below three million these days, and it's particularly bad in my area.'

'Even on the land?'

'Cattle, sheep, grouse. They don't need much attention.'

'The truth is that Britain's prosperity is not based on agriculture at all. We're a highly industrialised nation. It's pure sentimentality that attaches so much importance to the land.'

'I like sentimental people.' My habit at this time of giving every general statement a personal meaning must have limited my conversational value. Both men stopped and looked at me politely.

'Well,' said Father Wilson, hitching up his robe again, 'I must be going.' Perhaps some religious instinct prompted him to leave before an unacceptable situation was placed before him. Instead, I received a warm smile of approbation—lead, kindly light . . . 'Ah, my dear Violet, when you decide what to do with your life, you'll beat us all at the game.'

And then he was ushered out by a fluttering Flo. His departure left Nettles in the agitated state of foreboding which I was becoming used to whenever he met a new friend or relation. 'He's right, of course. You've got so much in you to give. How can I tie your youth and beauty to an old has-been like myself?'

'I don't think Father Wilson places a high value on youth and beauty.'

'Even priests do that.'

'You're just thinking of the embarrassment of an announcement in *The Times*,' I said in more bracing tones. 'An announcement in *The Times* isn't obligatory, you know.'

'Nor is marriage,' replied Nettles in an even gloomier tone of voice. 'But people generally do it.'

Between my bouts of psychoanalysis, which were amazingly unproductive, since I knew just enough about myself to put up a steel curtain, I visited Araminta and her babies. My new ambition of marriage and children made her relevant again. I found that the babies were babies no longer. Nanny had lined them up in the doorway to greet my arrival. All three were dressed in identical blue Viyella dresses, thick with white-and-pink smocking; white cardigans and socks; and

187

black patent shoes. The identical twins, Clancy and Nancy, with rippling pale-brown hair and Araminta's huge blue eyes, stood on either side of an identical smaller version. I shut my car door and bent to get my case from the boot. When I turned round, someone had shaken the kaleidoscope. Araminta had appeared from the house dressed in one of her timeless flowing robes. Clancy and Nancy, who must have been about seven years old, ran towards me screaming with all their lungpower. Behind them came the youngest, dragging at Araminta's dress and also screaming. Nanny, arms folded, had not moved. I noticed to my surprise that she did not seem disapproving and even smiled slightly.

'You're my godmother, aren't you?' Clancy arrived first.

'You haven't given her a present for years,' said Nancy, arriving second. With the two identical faces peering up at me, I realised that apart from the wide beautiful eyes there was a lot of Leonard in their determined faces, although the short nose and rubbery mouth seemed charming on them. At least, it would have been with less vengeful expressions.

'I haven't been to see you for years.'

'That's no excuse. Augustus Budd gave me his collected works last year and I was only six.'

'Clancy! Nancy!' Araminta arrived, expostulating mildly above the undiminished shrieks of her youngest.

'What's she called?' I patted the child in an attempt at soothing sympathy, noting as I did so that the children's welcome had banished any possibility of a civilised reunion between adults.

'Henrietta. Don't you remember? She's suffering from earache and jealousy.'

'It has turned cold.' I looked round at the garden. It was just before lunch, but the frost had barely melted off the grass. 'Is it really years since I've been here?'

'Must be. Three or four. Since Leonard caused your marrage with Howard to break up.'

'He didn't really.'

'Didn't he?' She stood vaguely, watching the children as they began to trace green patterns on the lawn. I noticed she was shivering. Her timeless robe looked more fitted for summer than for Christmas. It was typical of her to ignore physical realities; I found it both irritating and restful. 'Nanny's been looking forward to giving you a big hug for days.'

Nanny's hug was a success, as she immediately found plenty of room for disapproval. 'Terrible thin you've become, Miss Violet. Not enough good country air and good country food. Soon fatten her up, won't we, Ma'am?'

'I think Vi looks ravishing. So fashionable.' Araminta led me to a huge log fire, and I wondered whether her compliment was ironic. I had not realised what a barrier to the finer feelings children create. When Nanny was in charge, the girls looked and behaved like something out of the *Tatler*. The moment Araminta appeared from the barn where she spent most of the day painting tiny precise oil paintings of moles and squirrels and other furry things, total confusion took over. She would blink disingenuously at their antics and then approach calmly, smiling as if the plaits of one were not being wrenched off by the other—'Did you have a lovely day, darling?'—adding, however ungracious the reply, 'Oh, good, darling. And now shall we do something lovely?'

I remembered how the same thing had happened at her parties. While she wafted round, Madonna-like, we shouted and harangued. At first I couldn't think how either adult stood the din. Then I noticed that they did indeed 'do something lovely' with Araminta. One day she had them all gathering fallen leaves and sticking them into patterns; the next they had a feather hunt, or they made pink fudge, or sewed a purse decorated with beads. Although some of the objects were messy and in the cold light of the following day seemed nothing but the scraps they were made of, at the time they glowed under Araminta's enthusiasm.

'I love making things,' she told me. 'It stops me having babies.'

'I wouldn't have thought there was much chance of that at the moment.'

Leonard was not in residence. From the aspect of Araminta's bedroom, which was all aflutter with feminine draperies and garments, I guessed he had not been for some time. I was sleeping in his dressing room, where I had discovered a mound of letters, stuffed unopened behind the bed. I wanted to talk to Araminta, but I was not yet sure if we could be friends. I began to see that the years since our last proper talk had changed her more than me. Her vagueness covered an implacability that made me feel she had made various decisions about life while I still kept my options open.

'I haven't seen Leonard for years and years. How is he?'

'I thought he passed through London quite often.'

'If he does, he doesn't see me. Our relationship foundered over my Honourable Member.'

Araminta sighed, and paid her husband the compliment of putting down a piece of tapestry from which I had assumed her inseparable. 'He's selling whisky. In Poland. The last letter I had was from the Polonia Hotel in Warsaw. The whisky he sells comes from a town near where I was born. Very special.'

189

'Leonard's selling drink?' I could think of no appropriate comment.

'Didn't you know?' Araminta sounded surprised. 'At least it's a job.'

'Isn't it dangerous? One hears such awful stories about Eastern Europe.'

'Leonard doesn't tell me. He hardly talks to me. Even when he does come back.'

Araminta took up her tapestry again but this time stabbed at it crossly. 'We had a row over *Lady Chatterley's Lover*. I removed the book when Nanny arrived, and one way or another it got burned. He screamed the house down. He'd promised it to some student. I said it was pointless drivel for those who'd got no balls. He said he daren't have balls if every demonstration produced another baby and did I think pregnancy attractive. It was very childish and ended up with him telling me about his latest love. It was probably all an excuse because he'd got fed up with lecturing. He abandoned it in the middle of term. I expect you found all those letters from Augustus. He thinks Leonard's wasting his life. Leonard gives me no forwarding address, so I shove them under the bed.'

'But he writes to you?'

'Postcards. Letters twice a year. He even encloses money. Usually foreign. My bank at Oxford view me with deepest suspicion.'

'It all looks so nice here. The furnishing. The childrens' clothes, the food.' I floundered. Araminta's face wore a bitter ironic look which I had never seen before.

'The so-called furnishing is an illusion.' She swept her hand round the room, 'My pictures, a broken sofa covered in a worn-out coat, bedcovers and straw pretending to be carpets, two garden chairs with cushions made by Nanny; their dresses are also made by Nanny and smocked by me. Nanny is seldom paid except when my father sends a present; he thinks a husband should look after his wife, so he doesn't send more than a present. Their school is virtually free—surely you noticed their Oxfordshire accent? And the food . . . Do you usually get served bread and soup for supper?'

'It was delicious,' I said weakly.

'Once when Leonard was drunk, he said he's employed by the secret service.'

I laughed. 'But his novel never materialised.'

'He got as far as proofs with Augustus' publisher, Moore or whatever he's called, but the flames proved irresistible even then.'

'Mrozek.' I remembered our conversation over the beads broken by the twins.

'There're several letters from him upstairs too. I opened a few once when I had nothing better to do and he still seems convinced Leonard's a genius. Personally I think I'm nearer one.'

I laughed again. There was an awkward pause. Araminta had not been joking. It crossed my mind for the first time that no one spends long hours in a draughty barn who does not take her talent seriously.

'I wish you'd give me a guided tour of the—of your studio someday.'

Araminta became relatively serene. 'Augustus gets me commissions once in a while. It pays a few bills.'

So there was money involved. Araminta the vague, the beautiful, the abandoned, could take on the world. 'You are clever,' I said jealously.

'Don't worry. My patrons despise my paintings. They hang them in the spare bedroom or the lavatory. Everyone's afraid of seeming sentimental!'

I was attempting to lead into a revelation of my own affairs of the heart, but Araminta was too deeply involved in her train of thought.

'I can't understand why Leonard and I ever married. He says my little animals made him puke.'

'He thought you were the silent, undemanding, beautiful—'

Araminta interrupted me impatiently. 'Oh, Vi. Surely you've got over the idea that beauty is of any importance at all? He killed a little hamster I was keeping as a model. Of course, he was drunk.'

There was a pause. Araminta picked up her tapestry, Nanny went out to fetch cocoa and biscuits, and I looked into the fire. I wondered at what point I had stopped taking pleasure in my friends. I thought of my new love for Nettles and took heart. After a while, I began aggressively. 'I suppose you and Leonard will get a divorce, then?'

'Oh, no!' Araminta's amazement was profound. She covered it with her vague look. 'We couldn't do that.'

'I thought that. Until I did it.'

'But your case was quite different. For one thing you had no children, and for another it never was a marriage at all. You each married pictures of the other in social surroundings. You didn't know the first thing about the real person underneath.'

'No,' I said sulkily, for it was impossible to deny the truth. I should never have begun this conversation without telling her first about Nettles. She should know I was vulnerable too.

'Leonard knew more about Howard than you did.'

'That's true, anyway!'

'Oh, that. That shouldn't have been important.'

'It was the last straw.'

'If you and Howard had talked before you married, you'd have known about his little fling and then you either would or wouldn't

191

have married on that basis. My marriage and yours are quite different. Leonard and I respect each other. We adore each other. One day we'll come together again.' She looked up and without changing her tone said, 'Ah, there's Nanny with the cocoa. Drink and be merry, for tomorrow ye die!'

I saw that Araminta would be the most discouraging of everyone if I told her about my engagement to Nettles. She was the married one, the mother. I was classified as not the marrying sort.

'Shh, dear.' Nanny plonked down the steaming tray. 'We had a robin in the kitchen this morning, and as if that isn't enough you start talking about death.'

'Don't be such a peasant.' Araminta managed Nanny in the most surprising way. I would never have had the courage to mock her nannyisms and yet she seemed to thrive on it. Now she trotted away cheerfully.

'Doesn't Nanny rebel against being scullery maid?'

Araminta looked worried only for a moment. 'But it's not a question of status here. She's one of the family. She just feels terribly needed.'

'You sound like my analyst.'

But even that clue didn't nudge Araminta into prying. She thought I was strong and independent.

On Christmas morning, Araminta re-created the past with a party on the frosted tufts of her lawn. It was bitterly cold despite a bright sun and a vast quantity of mulled wine. Augustus was a prominent guest. I found myself envying his girth and thinking that age takes the romance from unnecessary discomforts. The food was smoking on the bonfire; the children were dressed in double-knit wool from head to toe; the guests, young and old, had come expecting something wonderful. Araminta wore a djellaba made of heavy tasselled velvet which had covered her bed till the day before. I was fashionably dressed in my sleek astrakhan-trimmed coat, with matching hat pulled sideways to reveal a ripple of expensive perm. It made me neither warm nor happier. The skin on my face stretched cold and tight like that of a plucked chicken. I felt unsociably disinclined to make conversation with the village vicar or the teacher of the primary school, or the young lord of the manor who looked ridiculously astonished at events, or the two or three dons and students Augustus had invited out from Oxford, or Araminta's farming admirer from down the hill. I was missing Nettles. I still had not told Araminta about him. I would have liked to talk to someone I knew, like Augustus, but he was far too busy anticipating Araminta's needs to attend to me. In the end I divided my time between little Clancy and the mulled wine.

192

Over the past week I had come to appreciate the clarities of a seven-year-old's mind. 'Why are you talking to me instead of the grown-ups?'

'Because I like you.'

'You don't like children.'

'I don't think of you as a child anymore.'

'I'm your godchild.'

'That's a spiritual relationship.'

'Are you planning to be a mother yourself? Women usually do.'

'Nanny used to tell me that too, when I was your age.'

'Nanny loves babies. She wishes Henrietta was still a baby.'

'There'll never be enough babies in the world to satisfy Nanny.'

'I think it's very sad Nanny can't have babies of her own.'

I stopped and looked at her. Neither I nor my cousins would ever have considered a nanny's feelings in that way.

'Will you have babies?'

'You have to marry first.'

'Daddy usually comes back for Christmas. So you are planning to get married?'

'In the spring. I'll be a farmer's wife.' I put down my empty glass and beat my ice-cold hands together. 'Do you think we could sneak inside for a moment or two? Just to warm up.'

'Oh, no,' said Clancy censoriously. 'Mama wouldn't hear of it.'

'That was my plan.'

'If you're going to be a farmer's wife you should get used to the cold. My mother has a friend who's a farmer—you can see him over there.' She stared at me consideringly. 'You look wrong for a farmer's wife.'

Clancy was the first person, apart from Nettles, to question my role as a farmer's wife. 'Are you really only seven?'

'Everyone asks me that. It's being the elder twin. I'm very ambitious.'

'Ambitious?'

'Oh, yes.' Clancy sighed, her thoughts elsewhere. 'If only I was a boy.'

We both looked up, attracted by an unusual sound. We were just in time to see Araminta throw a full plate of turkey over her gentleman farmer. The cream sauce lingered in glistening drops on his tweed. His face above his inappropriately white collar looked ready to dissolve into tears. I remembered that the turkey was a Christmas present off his own farm. Was this relevant? While I stared, the scene frozen for a second, Clancy cried, 'It's Daddy!'

Her shrill scream set us in motion again. Araminta began to apologise profusely. Apparently the turkey had been not thrown with intent, but dropped in surprise. The farmer stopped looking as if he wanted to cry, and showed instead childish frustration. Leonard, laughing like a hyena, with his three daughters hanging on to his coat, strode into the centre of the grassy circle. I expected him to crack a whip and watch us perform.

Then I noticed, several steps behind him, a slight dark girl muffled in a heavy overcoat several sizes too big for her. Her large dark eyes fixed worriedly on Leonard's back as if she suspected he might disappear into the ground. Leonard appeared to have forgotten her. He patted his daughters' smooth fair heads in a surprisingly fatherly way and then greeted Araminta, who was still placating the farmer with a dirtyish dishcloth.

'Happy Christmas!' called Leonard. 'I'm parched.' He took out a whisky bottle. 'Add a bit extra to that cup of yours, my love.'

Araminta looked at him over the farmer's shoulder, the dishrag trailed over his face. I saw at once that she would always wait for Leonard. Yet her cool was queenly; no one would have guessed she hadn't seen him for nearly a year. 'And your guest too. Perhaps she's hungry and thirsty.'

'Oh, her. She's called Katynka.' Flinging off his daughters, Leonard went and fetched the girl. 'Araminta, my wife—Katynka.' He spoke very slowly and carefully. 'Katynka came with me from Poland.'

'She can go back there.' The audience, for we felt united as observers, gasped as Araminta, who never raised her voice above a gentle trill, screamed violently. Leonard, I must say, gaped less than the rest of us. The poor girl shrank so far inside her coat that she was barely visible.

'Now, now.' Leonard addressed Araminta, but took the girl's arm. 'We'll go into the house till you feel more hospitable. I don't think Katynka can stand much of this English heartiness.' Preceded by a running band of children, they disappeared quickly into the house.

Almost immediately Araminta returned to her usual tranquillity. She pressed little presents into the hands of departing guests— knitted animals for the children, homemade silver bells for the ladies, and crocheted mufflers for the men. She beckoned me over and whispered, 'Isn't it typical of Leonard to come marching in like that expecting a hero's welcome? And with his tart, too!'

'Do you think . . .?' I began, for the girl had looked far too young and frightened to be anything as energetic as a tart. But Araminta had moved on. The real ferocity of her first reaction was forgotten; now she was the calm but ill-used wife. I looked around. The guests would soon be gone. The grass under my feet had begun to crisp as if the frost that had lifted for the morning were beginning to descend again.

A huge fire roared up the chimney of the little sitting room. Leonard bent nearby throwing on more and more crinkled pieces of apple tree. His ugly face, lit by the flames, looked as demonlike as ever . He had grown much thinner since I had last seen him and wore a strange mauve suit apparently made of felt. As I watched, one of the logs cracked like a pistol shot and several embers flew out onto the rug.

'You'll burn the house down!' I cried.

'I thought it was you out there.' Leonard stamped on the embers imperturbably. 'We can't have Katynka dying of cold now she's escaped the Fuehrer's clutches.' The girl was crouched in the corner staring at the fire. Clancy, Nancy, and Henrietta sat close by, staring at her. 'Is my lady wife singing a pretty tune?'

'Honestly, Leonard . . .'

'So she is?'

'I wouldn't say that. Her description of your companion, who . . .doesn't speak English I presume?'

'No.'

'. . . was hardly flattering. But she does seem resigned.'

'Good. I suppose she thinks she's my lover. I plucked her out of a ghetto in Warsaw. Quite a feat, though I don't expect you to appreciate it. Dare we bring in some of those mince pies?'

'What about the turkey given by Araminta's admirer?'

'The thing about Araminta is she knows how to look after herself.'

'Do you really represent a whisky manufacturer?'

He glanced at me casually. 'Yes.'

Araminta arrived bearing a tray of tempting remainders. She went straight to the huddled figure in the corner. 'My poor child.' She unbuttoned the huge coat and took a hand in each of hers. 'I suppose Leonard hasn't given you anything to eat for hours, nor any sleep either, by the look of it. Start with a cup of nice steaming soup.'

I looked at Leonard, who shrugged. 'She doesn't understand a word of English,' he said to Araminta.

'You don't understand a thing about young girls,' she replied in a governessy manner. Again I caught Leonard's eye. This time he winked complacently and leaned forward to take a handful of mince pies.

A man's presence in the house altered the tenor of my visit. Araminta made better food, with a higher meat content; I dressed more carefully and tried harder with my conversation; the girls showed off by drawing and painting continual offerings for their father (who usually scrumpled them up or trod on them); and Nanny put on her silver-winking buckle belt and most correct manner. The girl slept downstairs and soon became Araminta's assistant. She cleaned the copper pots with great vigour. Her doglike devotion to Leonard spread to Araminta.

Although it was perfectly clear that Leonard had returned only for a rest cure, he and Araminta were like young lovers. She floated around with a constant half-smile; he touched her whenever they were close. I attacked her about it one afternoon when we were trying to hack off frozen sprouts from their horrid stalks. The odd-job man grew them but would not pick them. 'How can you let him use you like this?' I blew crossly on my cold and sore fingers.

'For a shilling an hour, how can I complain?'

'I don't mean the gardener.'

'Oh, Leonard. It's wonderful what he's been doing. He doesn't tell me much, of course—it's all very secret. But he's helping Jews escape the dreadful Nazis.'

'But you were furious when he appeared.'

'I was probably showing off. Look how clever he was bringing that poor little Katynka. Just what I needed around the house. You know, both her parents and her older brother and sister had vanished by the time Leonard got her. Such a lucky escape!'

My inability to tell her about Nettles made me cross with them both. I can only presume I was better company than I thought. Clancy and I spent hours playing complicated games. She was the only one who cared enough to find out about Nettles.

On the Sunday before I left, Augustus was invited to tea. The three of us went for a walk while Araminta baked scones. Augustus and Leonard immediately began to discuss the situation in Europe. We balanced along the sides of fields ploughed into hard brown ridges and through copses of black leafless trees. It was the first serious conversation I'd heard about war. Nettles and I were too concerned about ourselves to talk about anything else. The picture painted of a Europe threatened by the twin monsters of Mussolini and, worse still, Hitler became darker as the sky above us turned to night. The men walked very fast, shoulder to shoulder. I began to blunder about, cold cheeks whipped by barren twigs and my legs by sharp brambles. Neither man seemed to notice. Excited by Leonard's horrible predictions, they strode on ahead, only stopping to wait automatically when I fell a long way behind and then continuing again before I had properly caught up. I picked up disjointed comments: 'Even two years ago at an antiwar congress in Amsterdam ...' and 'My worst fear was to be beaten to death accidentally by Storm Troopers ...' and 'Any fool in New York or Berlin or Vienna knows more than a professor in London.' Once I shouted into the darkness, 'Why don't you talk to me?' But my words did not reach them. I thought that if even the prospect of war turned men into such insensitive brutes, what would the actuality bring? Yet nothing could be worse than this struggling to grasp a new horror while my body was tortured by a cruel winter countryside.

One secret part of me upbraided myself for having become such a mindless bore that I could not enter a serious conversation, but another longed for the undemanding middle age of Nettles. He had known one war and survived it. I would go to him in Northumberland, raise babies, and forget all about Europe's troubles. 'Please, please,' I cried, 'let's go home!'

I felt sad and cheated. I should have been glowing with love.

'I'm going to marry Nettles!' I announced when we got back to the cottage.

'Oh, yes,' said Araminta, looking surprised at my vehemence. 'Augustus told us. I wondered when you'd bring it up.'

Chapter Eight

In everybody's memory but mine, 20 January 1936 was the day King George V died. For me it was the day my first child was born. While the nation listened to Stuart Hibbert, the BBC's chief announcer, repeating every hour, 'The King's life is drawing peacefully to a close,' I was heaving and gasping on my bed at Kettleside. Even Nettles admitted he became mesmerised by the ticking clock which took over the air-waves when Hibbert left off. I was quite amazed by the amount of pain a woman was expected to bear.

Araminta and Nanny had specially come up for the event. 'One can hardly expect your mother to do the honours,' Araminta had written, 'under the circumstances. I was cut out of your wedding, but I certainly don't intend to miss its happy results.' She failed to mention that she also was pregnant. Nettles, who drove her, Nanny, the three children, and Katynka from Newcastle station, also failed to mention it. He may not have noticed. I saw it the moment she took off her cloak.

'But Araminta, why didn't you say? You're enormous! It must be due any minute!'

'Heavens, no!' She smoothed at her tummy as if to decrease the swelling, although I recognised on her face that irrepressible smile of satisfaction. 'It's your baby that counts. After all, this is just number four.'

'I don't see what difference that makes.'

'I couldn't be more than six months, could I?'

'Yes!'

'I always get big. Bigger each time. Don't let's talk about me. You look wonderful!' She bent forward to straighten my pillows. I was to be the centre of attention and centre of attention I was till King George decided to die.

Poor Nanny didn't know whether to be sad that her King was passing on or happy that a new baby was on the way. According to Nettles, whose role in my life she had accepted with reserved dignity as if nothing could shock her any more, she kept recalling the happier days of the King's Silver Jubilee. 'Barely eight months ago there was dancing in the streets, trees were planted, that lovely new train which goes over two hundred miles an hour was called Silver Jubilee, and so was that dear little monkey born in the London Zoo . . .'

'Perhaps I should call the baby Rex as a consolation,' I suggested in the early stages of contractions before pain had defeated my sense of humour. Despite the pain, childbirth was the first experience that didn't disappoint me. Araminta darted in and out the room with an expression of ecstasy. 'Isn't it wonderful! You're getting on so fast!'

'So fast?' I croaked.

'So well, anyway,' she conceded. She thrust at me a little present made by Clancy. 'They say the longer the birth, the better the baby.'

It became a countdown as to whether I would produce or the King pass away first. The King just made it by a couple of minutes. At four minutes before midnight, my firstborn's first experience of the world was drops of warm water as the midwife's tears dropped on her naked tummy.

Nettles was allowed into the room. He took my hand, and his felt weaker than mine.

'It's a girl,' he said.

'What shall we call her?' I whispered.

'Oh, Violet!' he replied. I nodded, pleased and touched. A few days later, recalling the conversation, I realised that he had not heard my faintly whispered question, and was merely exclaiming to me in wonderment. But by then it was too late. The baby had become little Violet.

Little Violet weighed a whacking nine pounds, for no one had suggested a small baby might make my job easier. On the other hand, after the birth, there was no suggestion that I could stir from my bed for at least ten days. Nanny, with strange cooings and chuckles and an apron like cardboard, which looked horribly uncomfortable for a tiny soft-skinned creature, removed her from me between the four-hourly feeding times.

Despite Araminta's example all those years ago in Oxford of natural intimacy with the twins, it did not strike me that separation from my baby might be the cause of the terrible depression I began to suffer. But Nettles, when he was allowed to visit me, called it post-birth blues, and Araminta, who should have understood, said how lucky I was to have Nanny and what a treat it was to watch her at bathtimes. I was not allowed to attend bathtimes. I had just decided to rebel and was shakily searching for clothes when Katynka, face as ashen as the day she arrived, burst in, closely pursued by the three little girls. I leaned on my bedpost. 'What ever is it?'

'Araminta's baby. It arrived!' Luckily her tenses were not reliable, but by the time I ran tottering to Araminta's room, where she had collapsed after an energetic session of scone-making, it was clearly within a few minutes of arrival.

It being the 1930s, my first reaction was of horror that the girls had seen so much of the indelicacies of childbirth; my second, relief that Nettles was out of the house; and only my third a panicky wish that I had been in a position to learn more from my own birth. 'I can see it!' I remember exclaiming to Araminta, who was being terrifyingly brave. 'It's got dark hair.'

'Then it must be a boy,' she puffed back.

'Just hold on. Hold on,' called Nanny, who was desperately

collecting bowls and water and scissors. Her face was nearly as red as Araminta's.

'I can't. I can't another moment,' whispered Araminta. My surprise and amazement as a perfect little boy slid out was such that I gaped and grinned like an idiot. Far from being ugly, as I'd been told new babies were, he was perfect, a nice pink, and as Nanny picked him up and snipped the cord, he gave a healthy cry. Since I was clearly no use for anything, Nanny placed him on Araminta's stomach. He lay there quite contented, his little fingers curling in and out, and even made as if to put his thumb in his mouth. It was the first time I had seen a naked baby. While what worried me most about my own baby, bundled as she was in shawls and nappies, was her extreme fragility, what immediately appealed to me about Leo was his strength. He looked ready to crawl up to Araminta's breasts.

So Araminta and I found ourselves in possession of more or less twin babies, and it became clear that even Nanny could not segregate three small children and two babies from their mothers. Suddenly I had my baby to bathe and walk in the grounds. At Nettles' suggestion, I assured Araminta, who seemed remarkably well but stuck by her six-month story, that there was no question of her moving south for several months. This delighted her, and she immediately enrolled Clancy, Nancy, and Henrietta in the village school, causing amazement among the local community, who still believed that Kettleside children were unique in some undefined way. I was glad to be able to help Araminta.

I summoned Flo and Cecil from London, where they had been keeping my paying guests happy. They were so full of the King's funeral that it took some time to turn their minds to the births. But soon they had settled in. Flo took over the cooking duties from Nettles' Northumberland lady, who returned to cleaning, and I had suddenly set the scene for a multifamily establishment.

It was a woman's world. In the thirties, a woman with babies and young children entered a world where a man was not expected to follow. I had realised I was pregnant almost as soon as we had arrived at Kettleside. This fact had overshadowed our marriage from the beginning. The house, not shrouded in white as I had last seen it, but painted a colour I christened 'bachelor banana,' was interesting for the future, not for the past. I quickly painted my dingy old nursery in brilliant primary colours and whitewashed my mother's Chinese drawing room. 'It's the lightest room in the house,' I explained energetically. 'Perfect for a children's playroom.' Already I was preparing to put my relationship with Nettles second to our children. He did not discourage me, relieved, perhaps, that the pressure was off. 'Burgeoning,' he would say, 'burgeoning,' patting my stomach with his eyes looking out of the window. I never minded his anxieties as long as I could feel his love.

Our evenings had been quiet. As darkness drove him in from the fields or moors, we would turn on our huge radio set—the main component of Nettles' bachelor establishment—and listen to the BBC's six-o'clock news. Nineteen thirty-five was not a jolly year, despite the end of the Depression being given the Jubilee seal of approval.

In March, Germany repudiated the military provisions of the Treaty of Versailles. In June, when I was two months pregnant, Baldwin, whom I'd disliked ever since the General Strike, became Prime Minister of the National Government. In September, when I was five months pregnant, the Nuremberg Laws outlawed Jews in Germany. In October, Mussolini invaded Abyssinia. And in December, when I was as fat as a whale, there was the nasty affair of the Hoare–Laval Pact. Almost worse than all these fairly remote disasters was the Home Office's action of instituting Air Raid Precautions. War came nearer.

It was a good moment to take cover in my reproductive organs. I remember my amazement, as I sat knitting baby clothes by the radio, to hear that a woman had actually intervened in a Foreign Affairs debate to demand adequate armaments. 'What,' she asked, 'would the feelings of the women be if this country were invaded from the air, if we had aeroplanes of a foreign nation overhead and our aeroplanes going up to fight not merely against fearful odds, but against hopeless odds?'

Nettles did not share my amazement. 'They're not women, they're Honorable Members.'

'I wonder what Jack thinks of them,' I said in a voice of nostalgia, for all that London life seemed disproportionately long ago. I could even mention Jack without upsetting either of us. 'I suppose Nancy Astor was there even then.'

'Mavis Tate's my favourite.' Nettles lit his pipe in what I tried not to see as a Baldwin gesture. 'She's a pilot herself and always pressing for night training.'

I sighed and looked down at my knitting. 'Bootees are all a matter of casting on and casting off.'

Nettles patted my tummy and smiled. 'Burgeoning, burgeoning. Shall I fetch you a glass of milk?'

Milk, once the two babies appeared, became the unlikely theme for the years leading up to the war. Araminta and I produced it; Nettles produced it at one remove—his cows were his main delight; and babies and children consumed one or the other product. I remember saying to Araminta, when she and I were feeding little

203

Violet and Leo in side-by-side armchairs, 'Won't Leonard be appalled at all this domesticity?' She tugged away Leo's head from her breast. 'What makes you think Leonard will come here?'

Our first visitor from the world outside came in August when Molly arrived. She was expected; her companion, a dark-haired beauty who looked twenty but turned out to be twelve, was not. 'I found her,' said Molly, 'in your house. Someone had dumped her there. Possibly her father.'

I stared, speechless. My bemusement, common to feeding mothers, reached new heights. It was the hottest day of the summer, and we were sitting on the lower lawn, which had once been Eleanor's rose garden. In my childhood it had seemed a daringly remote part of the garden, almost too far for Nanny to catch me. Now she sat a little apart on a bench rocking a vast pram which housed a baby at either end. The twins were giving English-grammar lessons to Katynka, and Henrietta was playing in a sandpit I'd just installed—uncovering in the process several interesting roots of hybrid tea roses, one of which proved itself on the bare soles of many children to be the vigorous and thorny *Frau Karl Druschki*, much beloved of my mother. Molly, dressed in a linen suit with vaguely military overtones, and her companion, who wore black stockings as I had as a child, did not fit in with the general holiday atmosphere. 'What do you mean, my house?'

'You still own the London house, don't you? Augustus certainly thinks so.'

'Oh, that house.'

'Christ!' Molly looked round. 'It's a bloody children's playground.' Seeing my bewilderment, Molly began to be irritable. 'Surely Roly told you, didn't he? It's his daughter and your house. Both your houses. I'm merely the carrier pigeon. If you hadn't told me to pick up your fur coat, I'd never have been involved at all.'

This sort of semi-explanatory argy-bargy might have continued longer if the girl had not announced solemnly, 'My name is Isabella Royston.' She stopped and gulped, for now she was faced by a solemn audience of ten, as the children, sensing drama, lined up with Katynka on one side and Nanny with her round-eyed charges on the other. 'My father is Major Roland Royston.'

'His friends call him Roly.' Molly nudged me meaningfully.

'I haven't seen your father for ten years. Is he well?'

'My mother died. But he is as well as can be expected. He brought me to England and then returned to Egypt. He said you would look after me.' The precise, almost exaggeratedly precise, accents of a twenty-year-old threatened to dissolve into the blubbering of a twelve-year-old.

'Isn't that dreadful?' Molly nudged me again. 'About her mother, I mean.'

Slowly I rose to the occasion. I tried to remember entertaining old ladies on the seafront all those years ago in Bournemouth, and our trip to Kettleside in the borrowed Buick Six Tourer culminating in The Kiss. 'Come into the house,' I said, taking her arm. At that moment I understood with sudden intuition the look of shame with which Roly had announced his marriage just before our final parting. His daughter's skin was golden; beside the other pink-cheeked children, she looked almost brown. Except for her blue eyes, one would have thought her Indian or Egyptian. Poor, correct Major Roly Royston. He had found a girl to keep him company on the North West Frontier. Probably she was the reason he never returned to England. And now I had inherited the result. Isabella. Beautiful Isabella. I kissed her affectionately. Her unblinking blue eyes were disconcerting at such close quarters.

'Lord, what a monstrous Regiment of Women!' cried Molly, as we all trooped across the lawn. She paused and then added in her most provocative tones, 'Which certainly makes a change from my next destination!' It was difficult to focus on Molly's excitement. The world outside existed only through the BBC's sound waves.

By dinner time, Molly's inner tension had become so great that it had to burst out, whatever the circumstances. Dressed in an orange silk dress, she looked like some heaving premonition of a parachute. 'You must have heard of the War!' she burst out. 'You're not that cut off!'

'Of course we have,' I replied confidently, though actually unsure to which war she referred.

'I've broken with George because of Spain. I've broken with the Church. It's a time when no gesture is theatrical. There is only one more logical step I can take. Why shouldn't I, if I believe, as I do believe, that this is a war fought between Good and Evil, Right versus Wrong? If Wrong wins now, it will be the end of Europe. Here we have indisputably a military dictator trying to crush out of existence a democratically elected government. If our country is so weak that they bow at the sight of force, then we must show ourselves strong. If the Catholic Church enters politics, supports with all its might the side of Evil, then we must stand up against it. Politics is not a word here; it is the soul, the voice of conscience. No one who is able-bodied can withstand the call!'

Molly's passion impressed us all. She seemed to be talking about something quite different from the BBC's Spanish Civil War. There, Franco was a Spaniard trying to unify his country—a very faraway country. In Molly's waving hands and shining face one saw a Holy War in which we all could be counted. With guilty relief I thought of little Violet and how a feeding mother would hardly be much use on a battlefield.

'Have you discussed it with Father Wilson?' I said weakly.

'Did you discuss it with Father Wilson when you decided to marry Nettles?' replied Molly sharply. That was a punch below the belt. I could see that Molly was applying a wartime code of behaviour. I glanced at Nettles nervously. He did not look put out. 'You don't even see Father Wilson any more. Who are you to bring up Father Wilson?'

'But do you think you can actually do any good? I don't doubt your sentiments—'

'I can drive an ambulance. Peter and Paul weren't the most obvious candidates for church leaders, were they, but that didn't stop them answering Jesus' call.'

'I don't think you should use so many Christian analogies under the circumstances. Anyway, you can't drive.'

'Under the circumstances anyone can drive.'

My scepticism, greater, I think, than either Nettles' or Araminta's, was based on a feeling that Molly didn't really mean it. Such an old friend couldn't be about to do something so dramatic. One only *heard* about people who did that sort of thing. But Molly was perfectly serious. The formalities for joining the International Brigade were minimal. Even though in theory Britain led twenty-seven other governments in a policy of non-intervention, it was quite easy to dodge the authorities. All you had to do was present yourself at a Communist Party recruiting office and you could be on your way to battle in a matter of hours. One of Molly's left-wing friends at Reading was already on his way.

'The fighting force will be mostly unemployed miners,' she cried, 'but some of us must go too, so that we can make the brave anti-fascists understand that not all of Britain is as lily-livered as our government!'

'Oh, dear,' Araminta sighed heavily, and propped her head on her hands. 'Are you sure it's as simple as that? In my experience nothing is ever quite so obviously right. It seems an awful pity to give up your faith and your lover. Couldn't that be rather a wrong thing to do? For your soul, I mean?' Only Araminta's gentle, swaying voice could have made this point in a way that conciliated Molly more than it angered her.

'One must make sacrifices,' she said. 'Besides, I'm tired of talking.'

After that dinner, we didn't talk about it much more. Molly put herself on a training course, borrowing a bicycle for long sessions over the moorland lanes. She refused all healthy protein, saying she must get used to a life of bread and pasta. It was an odd contrast in feminine occupations to see Molly doing knee bends in the old nursery while Nanny, sitting quietly in a corner, resolutely completed her Jubilee sampler. It has hung in my bedroom ever since, a decorative piece incorporating pictures of guns, palaces and yachts,

> Prince of sportsmen, brilliant shot,
> But happiest aboard his yacht.

I remained in my maternal cocoon, waved Molly goodbye with more smiles than tears, and found, against all maternity folklore, that I was, while still feeding Violet, once more pregnant. Though in principle pleased, I was aggrieved to be sick and fat again quite so soon, and felt sorry for little Violet, whose solitary splendour would be so short-lived.

Consequently, when Nanny was found sobbing over royalty for the second time in one year, my sympathy was based on a selfish panic that if Nanny collapsed, the whole domestic edifice would go with her. Katynka, who came to fetch me, failed to understand the significance of a King's passing—particularly as another who looked much the same was there to replace him. Now, if we were becoming a republic, that might be something to cry about . . .

'Mrs Simpson's won,' I announced to Araminta, who arrived looking more exhausted than usual, since the school holidays had just begun.

'Or lost.'

'This is no time for irony.'

'Oh, dear, oh, dear. Perhaps we should have prepared Nanny.'

'Isabel's just as bad, says it means the end of the Empire.'

'It's Nanny that matters. Just before Christmas, too. I was hoping to have her full attention while I weaned Leo.'

'She's weeping into Good King George's Jubilee march-past.'

'Weaning is more good job than weeping,' suggested Katynka, whose Polish pessimism made her creative at difficult moments.

Weaning was our present preoccupation. Just as at the beginning of the year our conversation had revolved round how to increase the milk flow, now we talked of binding our bosoms, cold compresses, a pill someone had heard of. We took ourselves very seriously.

Araminta was still called several times night and day. 'It's your cows—their milk's too stimulating, Nettles,' she would say, in her agonised rush from the room, breaking the unwritten law that a man was not involved in such things. Sometimes I contemplated my nipples floating on the surface of the bath and thought that the whole world had reduced itself to these two brown teats.

Weaning was my excuse for being so unkind to poor George when he arrived in search of Molly. I kept thinking, as I watched his shoulders shuddering, what bliss it would be to stay buttoned into a dress all day. As he explained with tears in his eyes that Molly was the only thing that made his life bearable, I sneaked a look at my watch and deliberated whether I should try to skip the ten o'clock feed.

'Molly calls the war Totalitarianism versus Democracy, or Force versus Liberty, or Barbarism versus Culture, but I call it Catholicism versus Atheism.' He looked at me hopefully as if I might find some solution.

'I suppose it is Fascism versus Communism,' I said, showing more interest now that I had definitely decided to discard the ten o'clock feed. I noticed how his blond English ordinariness had become dominated by his odd beaky nose, so that his looks no longer belied his nature. 'Have you got much thinner?'

'That's not the point. Molly pretended to me that she'd got a journalist's credentials. But that's impossible. She'll go to the front line and get killed. Then I'll have her death on my conscience as well as everything else. I sent her there, you know. I expect she wants to get killed!'

'You are conceited.'

'What?'

'I said you're conceited. Do you think the whole International Brigade consists of people escaping unhappy love affairs?'

'They're mostly unemployed mine workers. And you can't put Molly in that category!'

'Others go too, you know. There's even talk of Attlee. Do you think he's suffering from lovesickness?'

'He's a man like anyone else.'

I saw that he was buried under a huge cloud of self-pity and self-importance. At least my lack of sympathy made me hardhearted enough to give them a few sharp jabs. By the time I'd painted a spirited portrait of Molly's intellectual worth before she'd met him, her political affiliations, work in the General Strike, etc, he was certainly more subdued. However, before I could take my opportunity to move from the particular to the general—'Why do men assume women incapable of acting out of principle?'—there was a knock at the door.

Nanny, with that special nanny's look of dire foreboding, summoned me. Little Violet was not as keen to discard the ten o'clock feed as I. 'Poor mite. She'll cry away all the fat on her.'

'Sorry, George. Babies take precedence.'

'I long for a baby.'

'I'll be back in a moment.' I hurried after Nanny. But I was immediately enveloped in the warmth of Violet's round cheeks, her spiky dark hair, her grasping hands, so I didn't return that evening.

George took consolation in long solitary walks on the moors. When he returned with flaming cold cheeks and filthy boots, he followed me round talking about things he usually kept locked away, about his possessive mother and his competitive boarding school and what it was like to inherit a farm. He probably realised I was too busy to pay much attention. Still, it did filter through my motherly fog that Molly was not as important in his scheme of things as he thought she was. Or as she thought she was. If Molly had not fallen in love with him, they wouldn't even have been friends.

After George had left and I had finally established my two feeds a day, there was a short period when I had time to notice Nettles. I couldn't help seeing that he looked older and not very happy. Worrying dreadfully as I did over every one of Violet's hiccoughs and now the imagined problems of my new pregnancy, I found it took a great effort to uncover new areas for sympathy.

'But I'm the luckiest chap alive!' Nettles, lying at my side one early morning—at night I fell to sleep so quickly there was no chance of conversation—seemed touched and surprised. 'I've everything. A beautiful wife and child with another on the way. Enough money, four hundred acres . . .'

'Why do you look so—worried then?'

'Doesn't everyone these days?'

'I hadn't noticed.' There was a pause while I beat my brain into action. 'Do you mean the war?'

'Which war? I've lived through one war.'

'But you're not political. What do the Spaniards mean to you?'

Nettles got out of bed and put on his Noël Coward dressing gown that had been my wedding-anniversary present to him. 'I went to a meeting in Newcastle the other day. In Newcastle.' He emphasised the word in a surprised tone, and it was true that in those days one hardly associated the tough industrial town with an international conscience.

'They're not supporting the Republicans?'

'Spain is only a trial battleground for something much worse.'

Although this point of view became perfectly clear to everyone later on, there was still a strong English tendency to an ostrich-like burying of the head. Neville Chamberlain was no accident. His views were shared by a large portion of the British public.

Despite Nettles, I might have continued feeling the same way myself, if Leonard had not come North with sabre flashing. He arrived the day after his son's first birthday. His timing put Araminta into one of her rare furies.

'If you had to remember you were a father, couldn't you go the whole hog and discover your only son's date of birth? Or at least make it less obvious you didn't know!' The reunion took place at breakfast time, and Araminta, still dressed in a Japanese robe, with the girls ranged behind her and a squalling baby under either arm, was an impressive sight. I watched from the stairs. I thought Leonard, who always looked bonier and uglier than I remembered, must fall in reverence before her rippling dark hair, flashing blue eyes, and matriarchal bosoms.

He did no such thing. Instead, a look of incredulity mixed with disgust gradually gave way to a smile—at best ironic, at worst plain nasty. 'I didn't know you had twins,' he said.

'It's not! It's Vi's!' screamed Araminta, splendid matriarchy losing control as she thrust little Violet's bawling red face towards Leonard. He took a step backwards. 'Virgin birth,' he said, which I presumed was a reference to my refusal of his advances.

'And she's having another!' screamed Araminta. 'You leave me alone to fend for myself as if I was a cow or a sheep for nearly two years, and then you suddenly walk in and start throwing around insults. What have you ever done? Persuade your precious downtrodden Poles or whatever they are to drink as much as you do! At least we're making something. A happy, secure home . . .'

At this point I noticed Katynka's sallow face of more than usual misery. It must have been very difficult for her to see her saviour welcomed back to such an ignoble squabble. The twins, on the other hand, were definitely enjoying themselves, and I could see them estimating their chances of missing a good portion of school. As Araminta continued to paint a picture of our contented family life, I found myself curiously reluctant to announce my presence. My large, complacent stomach seemed to underline all she was saying only too effectively, and I didn't want to be on the receiving end of Leonard's satirical gifts. I lingered further behind the door.

At first he seemed incapable of reacting. As if his breath had been taken away. Then he looked round at all the gathered children. 'Yes,' he hissed dangerously, 'I see what you're saying. But you should try and see what I'm saying too.'

'How can I? Whisky salesman! Drunk!' Araminta's clear intention of letting off a bit more steam was interrupted as Nanny arrived to take the two babies upstairs for a bath.

'Good morning, Mr Trigear.' Her precise politeness and neat uniformed figure made a ludicrous contrast to the disorder of the scene.

Leonard sat down on a chair. I assumed he had given up the battle until he began to speak.

'Coming here's like coming to Never-Never Land. Do you know Germany introduced conscription last year?' He looked up at Araminta, who stared at him defiantly. 'No. Or even if you do know, it means about as much as that Butlin holiday camp opening at Skegness. There're two wars on already, three monsters ready to carve up Europe, and you carry on about a baby's birthday as if it was all you think of.'

'It is all I think of. If you were in my place I defy you to think of anything else. We listen to the BBC news.'

'We listen to the BBC news,' Leonard mimicked her. 'That makes you feel better. In common with most of your compatriots. Until conscription comes here, no one will blink an eyelash. Let Mussolini grab Abyssinia, let Hitler squash the Rhineland! What does it matter to us? It's all happening a long way away. If France is happy to sit behind its Maginot Line, why should we worry when we've got a whole sea between us? Typical! That's what you are! Typical!' He jumped off his chair and glared at poor Araminta as if she represented the mass of complacent island dwellers. 'Selfish! Stupid! Narrow-minded!' He shouted and, swivelling about, marched in German goose step towards the door. This was too much I burst into the room.

'But what are we supposed to do? Throw the children out of the window and sharpen our knives?'

'You've made your bed, not me.' Leonard gave a Heil Hitler salute, but didn't look round. The children, perversely treating him as a Pied Piper, parted for him and then closed in ranks behind. We could hear them following him to the front steps and then hesitating there, as he continued his retreat down the drive.

Araminta and I were left to stare at each other. 'He's gone,' she said. And as I wondered who would cry first, I found tears dripping down my face.

'It's just because I'm pregnant,' I sobbed. 'You should be crying, not me. Who does he think he is? The Prime Minister?'

'Oh well,' said Araminta, putting out a consoling arm. 'We may be selfish, stupid, and narrow-minded, but at least we're not selfish, spiteful, and mean-minded.'

We both began to giggle weakly. It did not strike either of us that he could not have gone for good, since the incredibly expensive taxi that had brought him from Newcastle had already left and he was hardly likely to walk the forty-odd miles.

In fact, he met Nettles along the way and spent an energetic morning reviewing the crop-rotation system and the new mechanical milking machinery just installed. He reappeared at lunchtime in excellent humour, kissed Araminta warmly, played with Leo, and produced strange dirndl-skirted dolls for the girls. 'What a wonderful husband you have,' he said to me with a smile. 'And a nice little place to live in, too.'

Araminta seemed happy to accept this transformation. But I was angry. However, apart from reinstigating the argument, if it could be called that, there was little I could do. I also remembered that Araminta and Leonard tended to an explosive reunion. Probably it cleared the air of resentments collected during their separation.

Leonard had visited Spain. None of us thought to ask why. He had seen Molly. It was typical of Leonard to hold back this information for a whole day.

'Was she fighting? Was she fighting, Leonard?'

'She was trying to save the world.' He sipped at his balloon of brandy with infuriating calm. 'No, actually she was cooking beans. They'd dug a hole in the ground and filled it with coals so the smoke wouldn't be seen—'

'Do you mean she was near the front? She *was* fighting?'

'She was cooking. Part of a group. Near the Ebro. They were planning to blow up a railway line the other side of the river. Perhaps even hold the area a bit before another Republican column arrived from the south. She was part of it, all right, even if she wasn't planning to kill anyone directly. I admired her. She gave me this letter.' He pulled out a folded piece of paper from his jacket and handed it over. There seemed no reaction great enough for the news that my old friend Molly, whom I'd mocked in this house only a few months ago, was actually taking part in a real war. My naive excitement might have appeared ridiculous to Leonard, but he was generous. He left me to read it in peace.

'Comrade Vi, darling Vi, everything has become narrowed to this patch of countryside. I know it better than anywhere in England. There's a farmhouse that I've looked at so much that I think it might disappear. We may have to attack it. I spend most of my time cooking and washing which is strange. But I'm better at sleeping on the ground than anyone. We still talk here. Not politics like in Reading. We talk about food and bed bugs. Tell George that I'm much better here than I was before. I'm in the Aragon but I mustn't write more. The aeroplanes are the most frightening things. But I shall certainly return when I'm no longer helpful. Reassure George I will do nothing silly. I don't want to kill anyone. My love to you all. Molly. Arriving in Barcelona was the most astonishing experience. Funny. I find you the nearest I have to a family.'

Nettles said as we lay in bed that night, 'What do you feel when your friends become involved in world events and you stay at home?'

'I can hardly be jealous.'

'I just wondered.'

I lay on my back so that my tummy made a nice pillow in front of me. 'I've other responsibilities. Apart from my own babies, there's Katynka and Isabel. And Araminta's brood too, in a way.'

Nettles turned towards me and held me in his arms. It was comforting. His love had seemed so much when I had nothing and I would not now let it be too little.

'I'm glad you're not upset.'

'Good night, darling. I hope Molly is safe.'

I worried about Molly. My present absorption in birth had given me a respect for the gift of life. Besides, George had been anything but reassured by my news about Molly. When I tried to cheer him up, he gave as explanation his mother's collapse with bronchitis. 'Surely that's good news.'

'You're so hard, Vi. I don't believe you care a jot whether Molly lives or dies.'

'Don't be puerile.'

'Father Wilson was asking after you.'

'I invited him to stay.'

'How could he? How could you?'

'He didn't accept. Don't be so pompous, George.'

Our exchange ended without reconciliation. So when a telephone call came from him early one April morning in 1937, guilt added to my natural fear as I assumed that something dreadful had happened to Molly.

I stood in our hallway—the area of the house considered uncomfortable and public enough to be a suitable place for the telephone—dressed in one of Araminta's robes and felt my knees begin to tremble. The line was bad, but I couldn't mistake the words.

'She's died. She absolutely died. Just like that. No one expected it. She was perfectly well the day before and now suddenly she's dead. It's the most extraordinary thing. I can't react. I can't believe it. Although there's absolutely no doubt. She's dead.'

The ice-cold draughts helped to turn my skin to goose pimples, and a sudden flurry of action from the baby made me feel so sick and faint that I had to sit down at once. 'Wait a minute,' I said into the mouthpiece.

I lowered myself gingerly onto the cold stone floor, and as I did so it struck me that there had been something strange about George's voice as he told me the dreadful news. Was I imagining it or had there been, mixed with the surprise, a tone of elation? Surely even the worst

213

line couldn't turn despair into its reverse. Hardly daring to hope, I picked up the receiver. 'George?'

'Yes.'

'Has your mother died?'

'Has my mother died? Of course my mother hasn't died. What ever makes you think—'

'George?'

'Yes.'

'Who has died?'

'My wife.' And on he went again about the absolute overwhelming surprise of it and how she'd been at a party the night before with her latest man and everyone had said how well she looked. 'She did drink a bit too much, of course, and take the odd sleeping pill.' She had simply died in her sleep. Drink and drugs. An accident. No fuss. Looking her best. On top of form. Surely the way she would have wanted to go.

I was too preoccupied with trying to resurrect Molly after those dreadful seconds of death to react at all to the real news. Eventually George noticed my silence. 'Vi?'

'Yes.'

'Are you still there?'

'Yes.'

'You see, I had to tell you because Molly isn't here.'

'I thought Molly had died.'

Now it was George's turn to be silenced. Even so, it wasn't long before he was pointing out what the girl's death meant. By this time I had recovered enough to be shocked that a good Catholic should shrug off death so easily.

'But that's half the point of being Catholic,' cried George. 'It takes the sting out of death. We can rejoice that she's gone to a better world.'

'You wouldn't rejoice if it was Molly.' At which point the line went dead.

'What was all that?' said Araminta, finding me on the floor.

It struck me that my odd physical condition was not entirely due to shock. I looked at Araminta with that special mixture of excitement and apprehension. Before I even spoke she had reached for the phone.

'It's going to come quickly, isn't it?' I put my hand to my back half-smiling as a sudden pain caught me.

'Yes. As a matter of fact, very quickly.'

'Oh, Lord.' Araminta began to bang on the phone. 'The phone's dead. What ever did George do? Why are men such fools?'

'Nanny'll have a fit if she has to deliver another baby without a doctor.' I began to laugh helplessly and felt myself enter that private world of producing babies in which all outside problems seem infinitely remote.

A large, healthy son, named Tudor after my father, took over my life. Once again I entered the tunnel of night feeds, tentative walks blinking against the sun, and strange daytime dreams. No man can ever fully understand the trancelike condition of young mothers. The exhaustion, the total emotional commitment, the sudden passions of fury and ecstasy. Communism, pacifism, or fascism, the obsessive triplets of that era, were mere words compared with the experience of motherhood.

I made one visit to London that year of 1937. It was late September. A warm, sad time, with the harvests just completed and the leaves already turning. Nettles couldn't leave the farm, but Flo had accompanied me to baby-sit Tudor, whom I was still feeding.

Molly and George were getting married. I had not seen Molly since her return from Spain. She had not been well enough to come North. 'So humiliating,' she had written to me. 'Anywhere but the International Brigade they could have put me on a charge for it. Don't tell too many people.' She had trodden in a pan of boiling fat. The burn had been serious, particularly with the primitive medical services available at the front. The barber-turned-doctor had tried to cure her by regular purgatives and the advice to take as much exercise as possible. Luckily, she had ignored him, but by the time she got herself removed to a reasonable hospital in Barcelona it was doubtful whether they'd even save her leg.

'I thought I was going to die,' she wrote, 'which is of course what I thought I wanted when I went out there. But when it came to it, I found I had absolutely no intention of giving up. I don't know what it was. Partly an instinctive urge to live, partly a feeling that if I was going to die, I didn't want my last experiences of the world to be so miserable and so alien, and partly that I had seen men and women in far worse positions than myself who absolutely knew that life was the most precious gift of all. If they clung on to life and even to beliefs about what sort of life there should be, then why should I be so frivolous as to let it slip. I was one of the lucky ones. I had a home to go to. I had someone who loved me. I had a country I believed in. I was the luckiest person in the whole of Barcelona. I determined to live—and live with my body whole. I told the doctor not to cut off my leg and I bribed the nurses for extra rations of bread. The next day someone brought me George's letter about his wife's death.

'Oh, Vi, I haven't helped Spain—who can help Spain?—but Spain

215

has helped me. The sadness, the dreadful torturing lack of hope, the hatred, the lack of food, the lack of milk. What would you do if your baby wanted milk and your breasts went dry because you were exhausted and starving and you couldn't buy any milk anywhere, whatever you offered? I saw mothers and babies in that state. I think if I ever do try and help anyone again, I shall bring food not guns. How could we all be so greedy?'

Molly had gone to Spain for political motives and come away convinced that the only proper motives were humanitarian. I did not let her appeal strike me too hard. She was ill, emotional, she had undergone a terrible experience. She would feel differently when she had been in England a few months—when she was married. I never doubted that she would marry George, although at first she would give him no answer.

'Give her time, George,' I would advise as he wrote in despair. 'She may say it doesn't seem very important, but a few months in England will change her mind.' It had taken only the summer. She had been recuperating in George's house.

We arrived at my London house, which I hadn't seen since my own marriage, at about six in the evening. Perfectly timed, I thought, for Tudor's feed.

'Oh, heavens,' I said to Flo. 'What ever is Augustus doing?'

Augustus, now the most elegantly clad mountain one might behold, was standing on the pavement surrounded by his pictures, books, several umbrellas, a suit on a press, and a tall pile of soft homburgs. When he saw us—or, as I soon realised, not us but our taxi—he began to wave one of the umbrellas frantically. We had barely stopped before his head was poking in at the driver and urgently directing him to Euston station.

'Augustus!' I shouted, trying to bundle out Flo, who was getting tied up amongst our packages. 'It's us. It's me. It's Vi! What ever are you doing?'

At last I had his attention. 'Vi! Thank God. You can take over. I can't bear it another moment. Do tell that creature to lower his voice.'

'You can't tell babies things like that.' No scene at that time was unaccompanied by the yells of a baby.

'How very uncivilised.' For a moment a surprised contemplation of Tudor dimmed the urgency of escape. We stood together on the pavement.

'Let's go in,' I said, 'and you can tell me the matter,' which proved a mistake, for he immediately resumed his hysteria and began piling his things into the taxi, which, since our things were not yet unloaded, caused instant chaos. 'If you won't go in, tell me what's wrong here.'

'I can't go in.' Augustus dropped his voice to a whisper. 'She's in there waiting for me. I only managed to escape because she's taking a bath. She can't follow me out with no clothes on. At least, I hope she can't.' He looked up at the windows with apprehension.

'Not Priscilla!' I said. 'Not Cousin Priscilla fallen in love at last?'

'Oh, no. Nothing as simple as that. In order to escape her constant demands I've been to see Charles Laughton in *The Private Lives of Henry the Eighth* twice a day for three days.'

'Why don't you go to something else?'

'It's a wonderful film.'

'That's all right, then.'

'You don't understand. She's obsessed by this Peace Pledge Union thing. She wants me to accompany her to all the meetings. She says she's not used to being without a man. And she knows how deeply I feel about it, since, after all, I converted her all those years ago in Eureka. If I hear the name Canon 'Dick' Shephard, I shall cut my throat—or hers! Which, incidentally, is as scrawny as a second season's woodcock.'

Only my mother could have reduced a distinguished scholar, famous throughout Oxford for his wit and sangfroid, to this quivering heap.

'Why ever didn't you tell me?'

'It's ghastly! She thinks I'm still in love with her. Well, you know what I feel about women.'

'Why didn't you tell me?'

'You seem so—busy these days. Besides, she wants it to be a surprise. She's terrifyingly demanding. Thank God you're here. I can go with a clear conscience.'

As we talked, the driver had piled his baggage into the taxi, and before I could say more, Augustus too was inside and on his way.

'What about Molly's wedding?' I shouted.

He stuck his head out of the window, 'Tell her I've gone to Spain!' His manic laugh floated behind him. I turned to Flo, the curious spectator of all this, and was reassured by her enthusiastic, 'Well, I never.' I reflected that it was just as well that it was her rather than Nanny I had brought with me. Nanny's views on my mother were not touched by charity.

One of the nice things about the maternal tunnel is that it provides good cover for difficult situations That is why, of course, some women never come out of it. By the time my mother rose from the bath, I was installed on the drawing-room sofa with Tudor latched on my breast. Surprise was on my side. I felt I deserved it, since my

217

mother had never acknowledged either of her grandchildren's births, nor, indeed, my marriage to Nettles. I don't think I had ever expected her to enter my life again.

'She's coming!' Flo darted in excitedly and then fled down to the kitchen. I sat regally, hoping Tudor wouldn't choose this moment to burp or choke or otherwise reduce my tranquil beauty to a distasteful nursery scene. I needn't have bothered. My mother, like all really self-centred people, never noticed other people's efforts to present themselves in a certain light. She hesitated at the door, recognised it was her daughter, and flew towards me.

'Vi! Darling! And a baby!' She hesitated again, giving me time to readjust my first impression that she had come straight from the bath, head wrapped in bath towel, body wrapped in bathrobe, and realise she was in fashionable turban and coat. Never slow to sense a sartorial judgement, my mother stopped her advance to pose. She gave her turban a little push. 'Nice, isn't it? Talbot's violet-and-green grosgrain turban with matching scarf. Not very new, of course, but Blumberg wouldn't let me wear it. He liked me dressed in black. His Jewish mother complex. Such a relief to be rid of him. Not that I have anything against Jews; in fact, I'm just off to heckle one of those vile Fascist meetings, which is another reason why I can't be in black. Wouldn't want to give the wrong impression!'

Any misgivings over my own superficiality were easily dispelled by association with my mother. I saw at once that unless I actually mentioned Nettles, or produced him at my side, she would never introduce the subject. My fears that association with an analyst might have altered this were clearly unfounded. Fourteen years and two marriages in America seemed to have worsened her dress sense, given her an unconvincing American accent, but left her as much like a child as ever. 'Do sit down,' I said. 'Tudor won't be long.'

'Tudor?' questioned Eleanor, coming closer to peer at the baby. 'Hardly a tactful choice of name. I hope you're not becoming obsessed with the past. I've had enough of that with Blumberg.' At close quarters I saw one reason why Augustus was unwilling to escort her to the meetings. Makeup, laid on as if by a colour-blind Sioux, decorated her face from forehead to chin.

'What have you done to your face?'

Sitting down beside me, she directed a wistful smile over my shoulder. 'It's my disguise. I'm so glad you like it.'

'What do you mean, disguise?'

'From Blumberg, dear child. I ran away from him. Horrible man. He's put the private detectives on me. They'll never expect a fifty-three-year-old to look like this.'

I began to suspect that my mother had moved over the border

218

from merely being difficult to actual insanity.

'In case anyone asks you, I'm calling myself Pansy Childe-Harold.'

Walking through London with my remarkable mother was one of the experiences I would least like to repeat. Suited figures materialised from doorways with the regular swing of weathermen, while ladies of the night hissed most unwelcoming suggestions. I began to think the Peace Pledge Meeting was total fantasy and Eleanor was either playing out some sexual game or else torturing me for marrying Nettles. Then, somewhere far too deep in Soho, we arrived at a small hall adjoining a church. 'Here we are!' My mother produced a compact and directed a few extra puffs of powder at her face. 'Any for you?'

'No, thank you.'

'Hitler patronises the natural look. All those Nordic cows. It's my only point of sympathy with that poor deluded Mitford girl. They say that at a Party rally in 1934, a German Party rally, the dreadful man in charge of foreign press relations wiped off her makeup, with his own handkerchief. How can an English girl allow herself to be so humiliated? A peer's daughter, too.'

Inside the gloomy greenish hall was gathered a small group of men and women—not including the famous Canon. They welcomed my mother eagerly and pressed towards her the collection box, which she filled with an uncounted packet of dollars. They were discussing their decision to join a meeting to be addressed by Mosley in the East End—not, I was glad to hear, that night, but later in the week. Eleanor bravoed enthusiastically as it was announced that one hundred and thirty thousand people had renounced war through their organization and discussed ways of avoiding ARP exercises. I tried to keep her quiet in a corner while a visiting member described what it had been like to take part in the International Peace Conference at Brussels the previous year. Since I was there, I might as well listen. The meeting broke up with exhortations to us all to patronise the Union's bookshop at Ludgate Hill and to buy and sell the journal *Peace News*.

It was a jolly, unradical meeting—not the thing to appeal to Eleanor on a regular basis without the lure of confrontation with the Fascists. My own uneasy stirrings of a social conscience were soon overwhelmed by the realisation that Tudor's ten o'clock feed was already overdue.

'But darling! Twice in one evening?' Luckily, my mother had offered supper to a hungry-looking man, so I was able to escape alone.

By midnight that evening I was, despite my strange surroundings in Augustus' pictureless rooms, very sound asleep. I was awakened by a tremendous crash at the window. There in the street, murkily lit by a gas lamp, stood the hungry-looking young man, arm upraised to hurl another missile.

'You'll wake the baby,' I shouted crossly.

'It's your mother,' he mouthed, pointing to a heap on the pavement. Before I could react, Flo appeared from the basement, and the two of them dragged Eleanor inside.

The drawing-room light revealed her garish makeup, now augmented by blood. 'Oh, God.' I sat down on the sofa, noticing also how horribly pale and ill the boy looked. I hoped he'd had his supper before whatever had happened, happened. I saw I would have to take my mother more seriously. 'She's not dead.'

'Oh, no.' The boy sat down too, and I thought how inappropriate his worker's revolutionary gear of cloth cap and boots looked in the muted *eau-de-Nil* of a bourgeois drawing room. 'She would go to this meeting. It had nearly finished as we stood outside. I tried to stop her saying anything.'

'What sort of things?'

'Feeble things, really. 'Fascism means War.' That sort of thing. Of course they wouldn't stand for it.'

'No.'

'They came out in a rush and more or less trampled her underfoot. The police couldn't have done a thing. Even if they'd tried, which they didn't. She was very lucky not to be more hurt.'

I looked doubtfully at the splayed limbs and macabre ruins of a face. Flo appeared with cotton wool and water. 'Shouldn't you have taken her to hospital?'

'Oh no,' said the boy firmly, but with a shifty look. 'I ought to go.'

Flo finished wiping off her face and looked up. 'I'm afraid, Miss, Her Ladyship's been overdoing liquid stimulation.' Her expression of disapproval changed to sly pleasure. 'You could light a tray of Christmas puddings with her breath!'

Eleanor had become an alcoholic. She had always been a thin well-preserved woman, but now the thinness of her arms and legs was made to seem malformed, attached to a thickening waistline and puffy face. Even at my most optimistic I couldn't see her looking after herself, and how could I possibly offer her a home in the house she had abandoned, now owned by the lover she had abandoned?

My few days in London were filled with the sort of gloom that, although in my case personal, fitted in only too well with the atmosphere in London. It was, in fact, a consolation to find myself for once in step with everybody around me.

220

Only Tudor's sweet face and happy waving arms reminded me that a day's train journey would take me back to the world of Kettleside, which in retrospect seemed utterly idyllic. I began to understand, if not agree with, Leonard's fierce reaction to arriving there.

We left for Molly's wedding with no answer to the problem. Like a child, my mother was completely careless of the future. Her only fear was that Blumberg would discover her. 'But he's your husband, Eleanor.'

'Not after the things he's done.'

'The things,' naturally, turned out to be stopping her drinking, and my sympathy for Dr Blumberg rose higher, but not high enough to stop me writing a pleading letter. I had few hopes of it. Surely he could have stopped her flight to England if he'd wanted.

'Now,' I said, straightening up my mother in the train seat and adjusting her ubiquitous toque as if she were a doll. 'We will enjoy ourselves at Molly's wedding. But not too much!'

'Yes, darling,' said Eleanor meekly.

Molly and George were being married by Father Wilson in the small chapel adjoining George's house. We did not see them before. I was so concerned to keep Tudor and my mother quiet that without Flo's horrified hiss, I might not have turned my head to see her come up the aisle.

'That's never my Miss Molly!'

Instead of an exuberant redhead with large bosom, larger hips, and a fresh pinkish skin which made her look in her twenties rather than her thirties, Molly was now a small and thin person, with hair cropped unfashionably short round a pale face and above hunched shoulders. She walked quickly up the aisle as if trying to diminish her limp, although that served only to emphasise it. She looked totally different from the Molly who was my friend. I told myself she had always been short, that her cream suit, double-breasted with wide lapels, showed her usual endearing lack of clothes sense. As the service started, I remembered with nostalgia the girl who had bounced into the Shoreham Abbey train, cheeks bulging with pear drops. I remembered our conversations in the dentist's waiting room, her determination that I should go to Oxford, her first flush of love for George, her exuberant exercises in the nursery at Kettleside before she left for Spain.

Now Father Wilson was overseeing George's clumsy attempts to put the ring on her finger. Despite her shrunken state, it looked too small for her, and as he pushed it, I saw her wince.

Father Wilson bent to help, and the ring slid on easily. I looked at Father Wilson in his robes of priesthood, the representative of Jesus Christ on earth, 'joining together' George and Molly 'that no man might put assunder,' and I felt embarrassed about my own marriage. I imagined he regretted the time he had spent with such an unregenerate sinner. I had not invited him to my wedding. I had invited him to stay at Kettleside, but only in the knowledge that he would not come. And he had not. I looked round at the congregation, but apart from Mrs Briggsworthy, I didn't recognise anyone except one large man whose dull good looks seemed vaguely familiar. Suddenly just as Father Wilson was launching into a sermon about the different kinds of love, he leaped to his feet, pushed past two old ladies sitting by him, and staggered hastily out of the church. The stagger reminded me that he was George's cousin Henry Briggsworthy, last seen leading the University Squad's retreat from the docks during the General Strike. Clearly it had become a habit.

My spirits rose. At least my mother would not be the only eccentric. Living in the company of children, the most conventional of human beings, I had forgotten how full the world was of weird behaviour. At the same time, I caught a word or two of the sermon—'acceptance of another's failings demands almost as much love as acceptance of your own'—and remembered that Father Wilson would never take the rigid disciplinarian attitude I was fearing. If he disapproved of my marriage, he would not disapprove of me. Hate the sin and love the sinner. I smiled, and Tudor in good-natured imitation gave me a huge smile back. I took him from Flo and hugged him. There must be some good in producing such a saintly bundle.

The service was over. Molly came down the aisle, and her happiness recaptured the spirit of her childhood. I looked over my baby's downy skull and knew her after all. 'I think she looks wonderful,' I said to Eleanor. 'It suits her to be skinny.'

But Flo, noticing her limp for the first time, looked ready to burst into tears. 'Such a lovely young lady she was! All wasted away to nothing. She looks twice the age she did only last summer.'

'Don't say that, Flo. It's her wedding. Don't say unhappy things.'

'You always were a harbinger of doom, Flo,' said my mother with satisfaction. 'I'm reassured marriage hasn't changed you.'

'I'll thank you, M'lady, to remember I'm not employed by you anymore.'

'I still own the house, I do believe,' replied my mother sharply.

'But not that in Northumberland anymore, and that's my proper place of work. We are only here visiting, and if Your Ladyship don't like . . .'

Why Flo had to choose a small echoing church to show so much unwonted spirit, I couldn't think. Clearly the last few days of hiding bottles from my mother, putting her to bed, and generally putting up with her whims had taken its toll. I waited till we were outside the church, and then thrust Tudor at the still arguing Flo and sent her ahead to find somewhere to change him. I took my mother firmly by the arm and led her for a couple of turns round the rose garden. What she needed, I thought, was a touch of air to cool her down.

Unfortunately, when we stepped through the thick box hedge, which I remembered turned that part of the garden into an appropriately secret room, we found it already occupied. Worse still, it was George's mother. Worse still, she was crying, and worse still, she had seen us. There was no going back. 'Ah, Mrs Briggsworthy! What a surprise! Shouldn't you be receiving the guests?'

'They can't make me if I don't want to' came the sobbed reply. A pallid stream ran down her Pancake makeup. 'Let her parents stand there.'

'But she hasn't got any parents.'

'Exactly!' Her voice rose to a shriek. 'I wish I was dead!' The sobs increased. This was not promising. I looked at my mother, who was watching the scene with undisguised pleasure. It struck me that although one was so large and flaccid and the other all sinew and bone, they were both about the same age. Even, perhaps, from the same sort of background.

Adjusting her toque to a rakish angle and swinging her narrow hips, my mother approached daintily along the stone path. 'Dear lady.' She reached the bench where Mrs Briggsworthy slumped. 'How we young widows are made to suffer!'

Mrs Briggsworthy looked up. A ray of hope lightened her wet jowls. 'You too?'

'Nineteen fifteen,' said my mother, sitting down beside her. 'No one can understand what we suffer. My daughter here understands nothing.'

Mrs Briggsworthy looked up at me and scowled with honest dislike.

'Totally self-centred,' continued my mother. 'No understanding of anything but material—'

'No feeling for the spiritual.' Mrs Briggsworthy brushed away the last tear. 'George is just the same. I've given up my whole life to him, and what does he do but marry a succession of unsuitable hussies? At least, the first has the good taste to take her chance with God, but now there's this Molly, a cripple no less, back from fighting for the Republicans. For the Republicans! Against everything my son believes in . . . She's taken arms against the church, against the Pope . . .'

'Yes, yes,' said my mother soothingly. But Mrs Briggsworthy had hardly started. As I backed away, I heard her begin again

223

enthusiastically, 'Of course, now she pretends to regret it, otherwise the good priest would never have married her, but how can . . . ?' I left them and ran up towards the house.

The queue of guests, if there had ever been one, had dispersed, and I looked among the crowd for Molly. As at every wedding, the guests seemed not to know each other or the bride and groom. I heard one guest say, 'She had polio as a baby . . .' and another 'Both his first two wives killed themselves . . .'

I found Molly sitting on a gilt chair, an expression of oblivious bliss on her face. George hovered above.

'Oh, Vi,' she murmured as I appeared. 'Wasn't it silly to think I didn't want to marry?'

'You've earned the right.'

'Oh, yes.' She caught my hand. 'Father Wilson's searching the house for you.'

'She's in pain,' George whispered in my ear. 'All the time.'

'Oh don't, darling.' Molly patted my hand as if it were a puppy. I realised that her face was not only blissful but saintly. 'Where is that gorgeous baby I saw in church?'

'Flo's changing him. He's called Tudor.'

'After your father. How lovely!'

'I didn't know you remembered.' I was touched.

'You never knew how he died, what he suffered, did you? Not really. You told me once that he disappeared in a wall of flame. But war isn't like that.' I watched for a change of expression as we entered this dangerous area, but Molly only sighed and, dropping my hand, took up George's instead.

'We're all so lucky. Georgie, darling, do get me another glass of champagne. Vi doesn't seem to have one at all!' Then she turned back to me. 'I haven't forgotten,' she said. 'I still believe what I wrote to you from Spain. But today I'm getting married.'

Although I hadn't been criticizing her even in my thoughts, I was embarrassed that she felt a defence necessary, but she wouldn't listen to my expostulations. 'I'll tell you my great plans another day,' she said. 'Now do get me that beautiful baby and do find Father Wilson.'

I found the two together. They were gurgling at each other in a clear expression of mutual admiration. I was reminded that neither of my children had been baptised.

'Well, my girl, what have you been up to?' Tudor grabbed my finger and rammed it into his mouth. 'And I hear this is the second shining new soul.' He turned his attention from the baby. 'I've missed our chats and'—he gave Flo's arm a squeeze—'those cups of tea.'

'So have I. There's so much to do in Northumberland, so many

children, I hardly have time to talk at all.'
'You should try and get a little peace to yourself. Even if it's only ten minutes.'
'I never know how you manage to do so much.'
'If I can do anything for you?'
But I couldn't ask him about baptism. I wasn't a Catholic, and even if I had been, the children would presumably have been illegitimate and hardly eligible for the grace of a spotless soul. Instead, we talked about Molly and George, and what a good person she was and how her experiences in Spain had made her better than ever. And he asked me if I had read anything of Simone Weil, who coincidentally had also hurt her leg in a pan of fat. So we got onto the war, and I asked his opinion about the Peace Pledge Union and described my visit to one of its meetings. I realised that he might be able to help me.
'My mother's in the London house at the moment. Her marriage has collapsed. And so has she, in a way.'
'Physically or mentally?'
'Both.' I was reminded with a sense of guilty alarm that she and Mrs Briggsworthy had not reappeared from the garden. 'Perhaps I could introduce you?'
A shrill stream of giggles rose above the box hedge surrounding the rose garden. 'She was crying when I left. That is, Mrs Briggsworthy was.'
'Some improvement, then.'
Only the most charitable could have thought so. They were still sitting side by side on the bench, but at their feet in a line stood three empty bottles of champagne while a fourth, still apparently full, was upraised in my mother's hand. 'Have some more, darling, do.'
'Oh, I shouldn't.' Giggle. 'But I do feel so much better. What a dear boy Henry is. Now. Just the teeniest, weeniest little drop . . .'
'Bottoms up!' cried Eleanor filling her own glass.
'I'm so glad you ran away from that dreadful Homburg . . .'
'Blumberg!' shrieked Eleanor merrily.
'Humbug. Oh, I don't know what I'd have done without you!'
My own instinct to turn and run was hindered by Father Wilson's priestly presence and the colour of Mrs Briggsworthy's face, which burned a fierce puce under her fashionable cartwheel hat. Even allowing for the mauvish dusk, it did not look healthy. Besides, we were already spotted.
'Oh, look,' trilled Mrs Briggsworthy. 'Here's that terrible girl again, and guess what? She's brought a man!'
'My daughter.'
'Not your daughter!' The red face split into peals of disbelieving laughter. 'You couldn't have anyone so disagreeable as a daughter.'

'And that's not a man, that's a priest!'

'My mother always had good eyesight,' I apologised to Father Wilson as we advanced.

'What interests me is the line about poor Henry,' said Father Wilson. 'You saw his premature exit from the chapel. Like many obsessionally conventional men, he has a very wild side.'

'You mean he drinks?'

'That too.'

'Good evening, Father. May we offer you a glass of bubbly?' My mother had a maddening ability to appear suddenly gracefully sober until the total collapse.

'Aren't you feeling the cold out here?' Father Wilson was gentle.

'Oh, Father. It's you.' Mrs Briggsworthy had no deeper shade to blush, but she sat up straighter and put her knees together like a little girl. One of her shoes knocked over a bottle of champagne, which broke noisily on the paving stones. I bent to pick up the pieces at the same time as my mother. Our foreheads banged painfully. She was anaesthetised by champagne. I was not. What sympathy I had for two silly old ladies began to disappear.

'It was dear Henry,' Mrs Briggsworthy rattled on above my head. Her attempt to control her voice sent it up and down in a scatter of squeaks and rumbles. 'So polite and generous. Enough to turn one against one's own son. I haven't seen him since he was in short trousers. Of course, he's changed quite a bit . . .'

I became aware that my mother was goggling at something behind my back.

'Where is he now?' asked Father Wilson.

'Back in short trousers,' said Eleanor with the smile of a successful hostess. 'What an exciting party this is. I'm so glad I was invited.'

'Cock-a-doodle-doo!' There stood Henry, stripped to his underpants.

Mrs Briggsworthy gave a shriek of delight. 'That's him! Just how I remember him. Such lovely strong legs he always had. Even as a boy.'

Our presence seemed to be encouraging events rather than subduing them, for suddenly Henry gave a wild yell—something like 'Sundowners, Tiffins, and Burra Khanas! Polo and Pigsticking and Pickling Poisonous old ladies!'—and, tearing off his underpants, ran through the rose garden into the wide open spaces beyond. The sight had a devastating effect on Mrs Briggsworthy. In a moment she appeared totally sober, sober but shaken, like a woman in shock. 'Oh, dear, oh, dear,' she kept saying, 'and such a nice young man. So generous with his bubbly.'

Seizing our opportunity, we led the two ladies firmly towards the house. 'Ah,' said Father Wilson as if with sudden inspiration, 'a lovely evening for a swim.'

Mrs Briggsworthy looked at him with gratitude. 'Did you hear that, Eleanor, my dear? The silly boy was going for a swim.'

'Bit chilly, darling, don't you think?' said my mother uncompromisingly, but she put her arm through Mrs Briggsworthy's.

'It never does any harm to make a friend—particularly at their time of life,' said Father Wilson, taking my arm.

'Even my mother?'

'She needs a companion and Mrs Briggsworthy needs an occupation. They're perfectly suited.'

He was quite right. Mrs Briggsworthy did not take to drink, but she did take to my mother. At first they divided their time between London and Didcot, joining ranks at the bedside of 'poor dear Henry'—'such a handsome boy, too, and such a nasty hospital.' But within a year, my mother had the brilliant idea of moving to Eureka. 'It always was my only true love,' she enthused. 'Besides, Blumberg will never find me there.'

'That terrible man would set bloodhounds after her if it would help.' Mrs Briggsworthy's eyes were saucers. 'How happy I shall be to end my days in a truly Catholic country!'

I had long ago lost confidence in Blumberg's bloodhounds and agreed fervently, though hardly daring to hope the rigours of Eureka would suit their pampered psyches.

I had underestimated their eccentricity and toughness. They found a castle to live in—even if, as in *The Sleeping Beauty*, the briars were growing over the battlements. They found an odd selection of slaves whose Irish brand of eccentricity and good nature suited them perfectly. However, Nettles' reaction when he heard the news may have been the most accurate. 'Ah,' he said, with an unusually cynical expression, 'she spent one happy war there and now she's planning on another.'

War sat on the horizon like a horrible turkey, its gizzard already gobble-gobbling our precious future. Araminta moaned about the house. 'How can I possibly paint little furry things when people are advised to murder their beloved pets in case of war?'

'But Mummy, they give a lift to the National Spirit,' said Clancy with her usual bracing practicality.

'I only sold three last year.'

'You give too much time to Leo. When I'm grown up I shan't waste my time having children.'

We were all sensitive on the subject. Molly was proselytising her conviction that it was a sin to bring new lives into a world on the edge of total holocaust.

'But she's a Catholic,' I said to George, who was naturally distraught. While Molly organised meetings, he was paying one of his soul-baring visits to the North.

'You've heard of the safe period, haven't you? The Church allows that.'

'That's all right, then. Everyone knows it isn't safe at all.'

'It is for us.' His flat tones brooked no denial.

'Oh, dear,' commented Araminta later, 'it probably means she's infertile. From what you told me of her physical change, it's quite likely.'

'In that case she's sensible to make a cause out of it.'

'Yes.'

'Poor George.'

'Some men like difficult women.'

'Yes.'

There was silence as we both considered what amenable wives we were. 'Oh, God!' I burst out. 'If I don't have something else to think about but children soon, I'll go stark, staring mad!'

As the turkey's gobbles grew louder, my dissatisfaction with my passive role in life, which had been solaced by the role of feeding mother, suddenly resurrected itself. I felt the whole country was doing something of national importance, except me.

'You're a farmer's wife,' said Nettles, alarmed by my vehemence. We trod the lawn which had only recently recovered from an earlier war. I kicked at the grass crossly.

'Do you know that they estimate sixty thousand dead in the first sixty days of war?' I left Nettles struggling not to take my remarks personally, and ran across to where little Violet, Leo and Tudor wiggled about in the sandpit. By the time Nettles caught up with me my good humour was restored. 'I can't help loving them,' I said. 'They're so tough and jolly. Even when they cry, they don't seem unhappy.'

Nettles put his arm round my shoulder. But he was too sensible to disregard my display of dissatisfaction. 'I know it sounds corny and unfashionable, but why don't you join the WVS?'

'A-B-C-D!' shouted Violet, who, with all the older girls to fuss over her, was endearingly precocious. 'E-F-G-H—!'

'The WVS?' I said. I began to laugh. 'The spirits of Aunt Phyllis and Aunt Letty must haunt this lawn. Do you think they'll want me?'

'Of course.' Nettles smiled too. 'You've got a titled mother.'

'Not a very respectable titled mother.'

'You're a respectable married woman with two children. What you need, Vi, is less self-consciousness and more self-respect.'

'All that from the Women's Voluntary Services?'

Chapter Nine

The King has sent four binoculars towards the collection which the Ministry of Supply is making for the Army. The Prime Minister could not attend the Lord Mayor's luncheon yesterday owing to an attack of gout.
The Times.   10 November 1939

WARNING TO WOMEN WHO MAKE UP
NON-WATERPROOF EYEBLACK
The attention of women is drawn to the fact that the temperature conditions obtained inside the facepiece of the mask cause the eye-black to run, leading to smarting of the eyes, profuse tears, and spasms of the eyelids. This produces an urgent desire to remove the mask, with dangerous results if gas is present. (Issued by Ministry of Home Security)
The Times.   10 November 1939

WORLD EVENTS IN ALLIES FAVOUR—FRIENDLESS NAZIS
As they look out tonight from their blatant, clattering, panoplied Nazi Germany, they cannot find one single friendly eye in the whole circumference of the globe Not one! Russia returns them a flinty glare; Italy averts her gaze; Japan is puzzled and thinks herself betrayed. Turkey and the whole of Islam have ranged themselves instinctively but decisively on the side of progress. The great English-speaking Republic across the Atlantic makes no secret of its sympathies . . .
(Extract from a speech by Winston Churchill)
The Times.   13 November 1939

IF YOU ARE THINKING OF MAKING A WILL PLEASE REMEMBER ST DUNSTAN'S.
(Advertisement) *The Times.*   23 November 1939

'But you can't want to huddle with those fussy women day in, day out?' Araminta received the news of my enrolment in the WVS with disdainful disbelief.

'You would love them. They never stop creating. Vests out of socks, socks out of vests, blankets out of socks and vests. Sometimes I think the same wool goes round and round, endlessly unpicked and knitted up again, without anyone actually wearing anything.'

'Then how can you—'

'I admire them. They care.'

'You've got your children, your husband. You care for them.'

'Nanny does.'

'At least you could do something that won't bore you stupid.'

'I think you've forgotten there's a war on.'

I was an odd choice for a WVS centre organiser. I had never interested myself in local affairs, and there must have been intense gossip about my background and marriage and my strange household. Probably they were desperate. There was an idea around that you had to have the right accent to head any organisation. It may have been based on the sound economic principle that we were the only people likely to do it for nothing. Most suitable candidates had already been snapped up by the Red Cross or the Women's Institute. We were a new venture. I liked that.

Our first problem was the Phoney War. If we'd known what we were suffering at the time, it would have been easier. The war had been so long coming that everybody had plenty of time to work out idiotic prognostications. Churchill's cheerful prophecy that three million Londoners would flee from the blitzed capital into the Home Counties was typical. The thousands of cardboard coffins specially ordered for the holocaust, the eight thousand tubercular patients sent home from the sanatoria to make room for the bombed, the radio transmitters dismantled, television taken off the air, cinemas and theatres closed, and of course the evacuation of children, mothers and babies were all based on the assumption that normal life would end abruptly at the outbreak of war.

'It is evil things that we shall be fighting against, brute force, bad faith, injustice, oppression, and persecution,' announced Mr Chamberlain at 11.15 on that first Sunday morning, and most people got their first and last thrill of fear for a year as a siren screamed warningly. It was actually caused by a single French aeroplane arriving off schedule, but it didn't stop people jumping out of their baths, dashing out of church, and thrusting their children into dustbins.

My anxiety came from an excess of property. It was all very well driving into Newcastle and organising salvage collections, clothes and toys for the evacuated poor, or whist drives for the Spitfire fund, but I had an uncomfortable feeling that my main asset to the nation was a large half-occupied house in the country.

The papers at that time were full of advertisements for individuals or organisations looking for a 'funk hole.' Not that they called it that; they were merely removing themselves from the centre of action in order not to 'embarrass the government with their useless presence.' I decided to close up the London house until it might serve a role in the war effort, and offer the unused part of Kettleside as a funk hole. 'Large empty wing of Northumberland family home wishes to serve its country. Safe area. Business groups, charitable foundations, artists, mothers, children, babies, foreign evacuees all considered. Rental dependent on applicant.'

The advertisement reflected the varied interests of my household. Araminta, the eternal Earth Mother, now stout though still beautiful, wanted only babies—if possible without their mothers. Araminta's attitude towards the war was basically one of relief. It meant that at last Leonard's absence was fully justified. Now she need no longer worry that she was a deserted wife (or even worry that she didn't worry she was a deserted wife), because almost every woman was or soon would be in the same position. Now she could undisguisedly revel in her queenship over women and children.

The twins, Clancy and Nancy, just entering their teens, were still identical in appearance, their thick chestnut hair cut short with a bushy fringe above their round blue eyes and pointed faces. But their expressions were habitually so different that it was easy enough to tell them apart. Nancy had inherited Araminta's misty gentleness, which in her case seemed to conceal nothing but goodwill. She was used by the others like an underhousemaid. Clancy, on the other hand, frowned and pursed her small mouth just as Leonard did, and was always aggressively involved in some project which stopped her being of any help. We all longed for her to grow up, live her own life, and stop pestering us.

Katynka, now nineteen, but still indisputably Polish in a way that belied her years in England, wanted only European refugees. I tried to explain that although we British welcomed them here with all sympathy, we had to recognise the danger of infiltration by spying Germans. Even her own position became a little precarious at the height of the 'put them in internment camps' fashion. Eventually, and to our surprise, Leonard succeeded in getting her a British passport.

The sixteen-year-old Isabel, my shell-shocked Major Roly Royston's daughter, was also in an ambiguous position, for though we knew her mother to be dead, her father had not made contact since her arrival four years ago. Isabel, being a romantic child rather young for her age, invented sagas of his heroism in some little-known

231

army not unlike a Saharan version of Robin Hood and his Merry Men. Her hero worship reminded me of my own belief in my father during the First World War and convinced me that Roly was already dead—without honours. On the other hand, her desire for Kettleside to become a recuperation centre for wounded officers may have been a simple girlish need for masculine company and admiration. She was very striking, and in a strange way her dull, blocklike character (which made me wonder if we had done Roly a favour by assuming shell shock to be the cause of his problems) added to the effect. The blue eyes in her dark golden skin were more compelling than ever. Even Leonard quailed before their gaze, and little Violet used to push at her eyeballs and say 'Eyes, eyes!' in a wondering voice.

The smaller children naturally had no opinions on added occupants, except as far as Nanny had managed to indoctrinate them. Nanny had no doubt at all that it was a terrible idea to invite strangers into our home. Although she never seemed to change physically, her manner had become gradually more gruff, which we knew covered a heart of gold and assumed covered a basic contentment. Like all good nannies, May Fig was unbelievably conservative. Her loyalty was reserved for her 'family,' and the world outside could be consigned to outer darkness for all she cared. Her similarity in this respect to Araminta was the basis for their excellent relationship. By 1940, Nanny felt she had already accepted far too many changes. She looked on my advertisement as an incredible act of folly. She commented darkly and quietly—so as not to embarrass Nettles, whom she now worshipped—'It's Lady Eleanor speaking through. Always restless. Never content with what she'd got.'

Nettles did not express a definite opinion on my plans. I think he spent the years of our marriage in a constant state of surprise. He had gone up to farm the land at Kettleside after my mother's departure for America with a feeling of retirement. He had expected to live quietly with reasonable satisfaction for the rest of his days. He had not expected to fall in love. He had not expected to get married. He had not expected to have children. He had certainly never pictured himself surrounded by such a circus of women and children. He simply accepted what was offered without question. Of course he loved me, and I never doubted it. Yet he had obeyed my mother's summons. And he didn't love her.

I assumed that his surprise at what my love had brought him was flattering. I presumed that he enjoyed the teeming world that had sprung up round him, supported by his generosity. I presumed that it gave him a feeling of power and strength. Yet he took very little part in communal activities, in the picnics we conducted up to the moors or the games of cards in the room that had been my father's study. He pleaded farm business, field inspection, or accounts. He went to chat with Miss Tiptree, my old friend and governess who now looked after the village school.

When I announced my intention of filling Kettleside's every nook and cranny as my war effort, he merely said, 'I leave that side of things to you, my dear.'

Apart from Nanny, the most vociferous protests came from Flo and Cecil. Cecil, a good East End Londoner himself, was enraged at the idea of 'vagabond Cockneys slashing the furnishings and pocketing the silver.' Araminta's vague thoughts on the perfection of small human beings and my even vaguer ideas on the Right of every man, woman, and child to freedom from danger were met with a barrage of practicalities.

''Ygiene, ma'am. Basic 'ygiene,' said Cecil, raising his eyes to heaven. 'A butcher learns the unpleasant side of life.'

'What he means, Miss Violet,' interposed Flo, 'is bed-wetting, lice, filth, and shocking table manners.'

'And where would they get fish and chips from 'ere?' added Cecil, as if that settled it all.

None of this had any effect on Araminta. 'Just imagine their excitement on seeing where an egg comes from!'

'They won't know what an egg is,' said Cecil.

'They'll pop it in shell and all,' said Flo.

'All they want is fish and chips,' repeated Cecil with even more dire foreboding.

'We don't know who will answer our advertisement,' I replied briskly.

There were only two replies. One from Molly to ask whether this was my way of avoiding any real contact with the war. The other from a London publishing company that wanted to move presses, books, and editors into safer and, one got the distinct feeling, more congenial surroundings.

The letter was odd. 'The Literary aspirations must never be confused with social, yet the writer is a recorder of society and the publisher his amanuensis. I have always, Mrs Nettlefield, felt an affinity for the moors since I chose it as my name.' I recognised Mrozek, the erstwhile Pole and Leonard's would-be publisher.

I told Araminta, who groaned and said that the task of stuffing his unopened letters under the bed in their Oxfordshire cottage at a time when she was particularly miserable had put her right off him and on no account was I to let him cross the threshold.

It was towards the end of 1939. The weather was very cold. We were suffering from the boredom of the phoney war. There was rationing and likely to be more. There was the blackout—luckily not a big problem for us, since Kettleside was well provided with shutters, but a disaster for Miss Tiptree, who had the responsibility for the Vicarage's huge casement windows; the schoolhouse's, which were pointed in ecclesiastical imitation; and those of the church itself. She confided in me that the temptation to follow the example of the cottagers and leave uncovered the windows that backed onto the street, thus evading the eye of the local policemen, was sometimes intense. Katynka often went down to give her a hand. They were striving to cover the Vicarage's most recalcitrant window, at the top of the staircase, with a piece of black paper on a wooden frame when the doorbell rang. The doorbell had not rung for at least forty years. Miss Tiptree dropped the frame, and Mrozek, or Moore, entered the door to a volley of Polish imprecations.

By the time Katynka had escorted him to me, she was determined we should become the wartime headquarters for The Moore Press. At this time Felix Moore could have turned any woman's head, let alone a young isolated girl's with wild dreams of her fatherland. He was in his early forties, the exaggerated thrust of black hair and pallid skin that I remembered from Augustus' publishing party now toned down into a sleeker, more fashionable, yet conversely more foreign version. When most of us were resigned to a drabness in clothes that matched the drabness of our outlook, he was almost exaggeratedly well dressed in a dark coat trimmed with fur, a high-brimmed homburg, soft, thick gloves, and narrow, highly polished shoes. But more than his appearance, his manner had that particularly attractive combination of interest, intimacy, and danger. I had just come from the children's tea and felt nonplussed. I did know immediately, however, that I would not allow him to take over Kettleside. For I was quite certain he would do nothing less than take it over. He could hardly be expected to fit in with our child-oriented community.

'This is Felix Moore. You know him! Isn't it an astonishment? He's been telling me an amusing tale of the twins' breaking your necklace.'

Moore bowed and kissed my hand. 'You brought Jack Logan. I've seen quite a bit of him lately. You know he's been made a junior Minister, no doubt.'

I felt myself blushing—something I had not done for years. I did not know Jack had been made a minister, and I could not reconcile the memory of how that particular evening had ended with my present homely image. Felix Moore had a gift for sensing this sort of split in a woman and enjoying the feeling of power it gave him. I heard myself inviting him to stay the night. It would be easier to refuse him over dinner. Despite myself, I was excited by the prospect of company, and when Nettles came into our bedroom he found me

dragging out a forgotten dress of red silk patterned with Chinamen.
Nettles smiled good-humouredly. 'All this in honour of Miss
Winifred Beauchamp.'

I had forgotten that a visiting Regional Organiser of the WVS was
coming that night. A colleague of Aunt Phyllis. My relations with
Aunt Phyllis had improved considerably since she had decided I was
mad and deserved pity (after my marriage to Nettles), and that I was
repentant (after I joined the WVS).

'I'm not dressing up for Aunt Phyllis' friend,' I said. 'A publisher I
once met called Felix Moore has arrived in answer to my advertisement.'

'I read the letter. I even remember his party. You don't want him.'

'He's here. Katynka found him wandering in the village and
brought him up. Miss Tiptree can talk to Miss Beauchamp.'

When Nettles left I turned back to the mirror, but Miss Winifred
Beauchamp weighed on me. Now there was no chance of an evening
of light relief. The air would be heavy with the voice of Duty. I
enjoyed my work in the WVS. I enjoyed driving into Newcastle with
a carload of petrol-conscious women who also needed transport; I
enjoyed the drumming-up of support in the villages, addressing little
groups of women over cups of tea and fish-paste sandwiches; I
enjoyed getting going our mobile canteens in the Newcastle station
and our own plans for future evacuation. Nevertheless, I wished that
Aunt Phyllis had chosen to send her *alter ego* another night. I put
away my silk dress and found the skirt and black sweater I usually
wore in the evenings. I was now ready to be stern with Mrozek.

I was stopped outside the drawing room by a breathless Katynka.
'You can't wear that.' She eyed my outfit with her usual un-English
directness. 'We're dressed all up. Felix has a green velvet coat with
buttons of pearl he brought from Poland, and Miss Beauchamp is the
Lady Winifred, called as Winnie, and she's young and dazzling
English with strings of pearls and a man called Poops. When Araminta asked did he like Spam and chips, he said the Strand Palace
called it "Ballotine de jambon valentinoise" and it was all the rage.'

'Do you mean Araminta isn't cross about Mr Moore?'

Katynka stiffened. 'Why should she be?' She paused and then
brought out one of the less obvious reasons why Araminta should be
softened by Mr Moore. 'He's brought an astonishing book by Mr
Harold Nicolson called *Why Britain Is At War*. I go tell Flo to lay
two more places.'

Everything that Katynka had reported was absolutely true.
Winnie was the foreigner's conception of the English rose, with
smooth blonde hair, a perfectly complexioned oval face, and long,
long legs. She was also nice and sensible, and talked about Aunt

235

Phyllis as 'that good old stick.' They had met in the Red Cross, from which she'd been seconded to enliven the WVS. 'Gosh, I was miffed. Being sent off to all the fuddy-duddies. I didn't know there'd be people like you involved.' Her confidences over dinner won me round. On her other side sat Poops, whom I can remember only as the first in a series of nice young men who were besotted by Winnie and were treated as younger brothers. We talked, of course, about the war. Mrozek saw it only in terms of books. 'My orders have never been so high. If I can get the paper, I'll have people reading who've never even opened the Bible.'

'They waste most of it dropping those idiotic pamphlets all over Europe.' said Nettles.

'Keep them in lavatory paper for the rest of the war,' said Poops.

'It'll be troops soon,' shouted Katynka bellicosely.

'What you don't understand, darling,' I said, 'is this is a World War. You can't just have one jolly great battle and finish it all. We've got to prepare ourselves for years. Mr Moore's books are important for the morale of the country.'

Katynka glared, as Mrozek, who sat on my other side, glistened at me. 'Have you ever thought of writing a book yourself?'

'About "padding splints for the First Aid Post, knitting squares for blankets, and making pyjamas for the local infirmary"?' mocked Katynka. She was quoting from the WVS bulletins which I used to bring home to read. We were never destined to get on well.

Araminta sat next to Poops, who reminded her of her undergraduate adorers. 'I paint,' I heard her say to him. 'I would like to be an accredited war artist.' I wondered how her precise little animals would fit in with records of 'Constructing an Anderson Shelter' or 'Salvage mounts up in Bermondsey.' At various times I had felt jealous of Araminta, but now I felt only sorry for her. I was glad to see her flushed and happy. After all, it was an evening of light relief.

After dinner Mrozek took off his jacket, revealing a disconcerting width of shoulders for his slight figure, and said, 'So! Where is the billiard table?' When we looked surprised, he threw up his hands. 'But every English house has a billiard table.'

So did Kettleside. But having so few men in residence and so many women, usually pregnant, and children, we had forgotten all about it.

'The room's not blacked out!' cried Miss Tiptree obsessively. Luckily, there were shutters, and soon Poops and Nettles were in their shirt sleeves too, and we were having a game of 'roll the red' which is nothing to do with billiards, very bad for the baize, but gloriously exhilarating.

After a while I found myself collapsed, exhausted, next to Mrozek

236

on a bench below one of the many supercilious stuffed fish that hung round the walls. Mrozek offered me a sip of his brandy. I saw that the moment had come to deny him Kettleside. He might even now be assessing this room for his printing press. 'I should tell you—'

'Don't.'

'What?'

'There's no need.'

'You don't know what I was going to say.'

'Yes, I do. The truth is, it wouldn't do.'

'Oh.'

'I don't want to come here. You may breathe a sigh of relief.'

In fact I felt suddenly nonplussed and strangely offended. 'If it's not an embarrassing reason, why don't you want to come?'

'Too cold.'

'What?'

'Freezing in here.' He blew out, and I had to admit that a puff of white appeared on the air. 'The presses would freeze up. My workers would leave.'

'I must be used to it.'

'Probably.' He looked stern, as if I had failed him. I was too fuddled and tired to react sensibly. He assumed my silence was disappointment, for he suddenly took my hand and smiled winningly. 'I'm here on false pretences. I've already decided on a lovely house near Reading. I knew who you were. I was coming into the area and I was curious to see a woman who threw up a future prime minister to bury herself in the country.'

'You mean Jack. He's just a dim memory.'

'Why are you blushing, then?'

'We were never very close.'

'He doesn't think so. He sent his love.'

'I don't believe you.'

'Ha ha. No. He didn't send you his love, but he does remember you.'

'Is he married?'

'Why do women always want to know if men are married? No, he isn't married.'

'You wouldn't ask that if you were married.'

'I am married.'

'Oh, really. That's too bad.' I was thinking of Katynka. A married man shouldn't flirt with nineteen-year-old girls.

'I haven't seen my wife for nearly twenty years. I left her when I left Poland.' He laughed, and feeling I already knew too much of his personal life, I jumped up. At the same time, Katynka pulled Mrozek's arm, exhorting him in Polish to play up and play the game.

The noise level rose higher. Poops, who had one of those public-school photographic memories, began a competition for the best advertisements of the war.

'Your Courage, your Cheerfulness, your Resolution will bring us Victory!'

'Take care of your gas mask and your gas mask will take care of you!'

'Out of Battledress into Moss Bros.'

'Patriotic down to the Pantees! These slick little pantees, beautifully embroidered with the "Washing on the Siegfried Line" and the slogan "England Expects . . ." might come in the category of "improperganda," but as a gift for any lingerie drawer they're certain of a rapturous welcome!'

We all became more and more hysterical, and none of us noticed Nanny's stiff figure standing in the doorway. She must have waited her moment, for her words fell into a lull: 'I'll have you know there's a war on!'

This was awful, for they were the very words to send us into paroxysms of laughter. Even Nettles, even I, who knew how it would hurt my beloved Fig, could not control ourselves. Through my tears of laughter, I saw her draw her flannel dressing gown closer and fold her arms. Perhaps, I managed to hope, she would merely dismiss us as naughty children. As she turned her back, the pigtail no longer so thick as it used to be but still as long, caused me particular distress. But still I could not call out to her.

The minute she had gone I became suddenly, icily sober. 'Oh, dear,' I said to Araminta. 'Couldn't you go to her either?' She gave me one of her vacant, meaningless smiles that still had the power to infuriate.

'I couldn't be bothered,' she said. 'I just couldn't be bothered.'

I knew what she meant. It had been our evening off.

Leaving the men and Winnie planning to set up a game of bridge, we started up the dark, cold corridors. The uncarpeted back stairs led directly from the billiard room to the nursery wing. Our noise must have awakened one of the children. I tried to remember whether I had ever been awakened as a child by the click of billiard balls or male voices made loud by too much brandy. I didn't think that was my father's style, though vague memories of my Uncle Eddie made it seem possible. In those early days, one of the voices would have been Nettles'. Avoiding this line of thought, I turned to Nanny again and thought that in those days she would never have dared stand like an avenging conscience.

'Let's hope she's found a child to comfort her,' said Araminta.

'It's freezing here.' I was remembering how Nanny had warmed

238

the nursery that first Christmas when my cousins arrived. My guilt grew stronger, but I said, 'Mr Moore says it's too cold for his presses. He won't come.'

'Good. I'll never forgive him for encouraging Leonard. Aren't there any light switches along here?'

'My father wasn't very keen on electricity. The windows here aren't blacked out, anyway. Feel your way along the bannisters.' I felt the house around me a cold, dark womb. It frightened me, as if I might become submerged again in the loneliness of childhood. I felt again my anxiety when my mother had disappeared, which then I had hardly dared admit. I felt opened to my father's misery at being deserted, and my own childish grief at his death grew into an adult emotion. I felt the tears filling my eyes, and although I tried to tell myself it was tiredness and too much to drink, I knew it was true sadness. 'Poor, poor Nanny,' I said to Araminta in a choking voice. But now we had come through a door into the lighted nursery corridor and I could not let the ghosts overwhelm me.

'I can hear her,' said Araminta. She was crooning to little Tudor some unrecognisable dirge, a composite of nursery rhymes and Nanny's sayings. 'She's all right,' whispered Araminta, in a bitter tight voice. 'She only wants babies. We should cry for ourselves.''

'I was.'

'I always used to think you so unfeeling. I used to make excuses for you because of your extraordinary mother, and your dead father. But now I'm beginning to think Nettles is thawing you.'

'I was always frightened.'

'If Nettles does thaw you, I expect you'll leave him. You're like Leonard in that way. You don't really care about people. At least, you do. But they don't hold your attention unless they're serving you in some way.'

'Don't say that, Araminta.' We walked quietly to the children's room and watched through the open door as Nanny walked slowly up and down, Tudor cuddled round her neck. He was quite big now, and his legs clasped round Nanny's waist and his arm round her neck. I noted that I felt absolutely no jealous desire to have him cuddling me. 'I love Nettles,' I whispered. 'I love little Violet and Tudor. I love Nanny. People are all I've got. Don't say they don't matter to me.'

'If you don't want me to.'

Nanny turned and saw us. Her face was calm and untroubled. She mouthed at us, 'Wet his bed. I've changed the sheets.' We mouthed back, 'Sorry, Nanny.' And she nodded her head in acceptance and whispered, 'Good night!'

'I knew it wasn't the war,' said Araminta.

239

The next morning I took Mrozek for a walk round the gardens. It had snowed heavily in the night, and the rhododendron leaves were weighted to the ground. The skies were still thick, as if more snow were to come. 'Do you think you'll get out?' I said.

'I've got plenty of petrol. All you have to do is pay six and six instead of one and six for pool petrol and Hey, presto! your tank is full.'

'I meant the weather.'

'Alternatively, you can strain out the red dye from commercial petrol. I know you meant the weather. I was just teasing you into awareness before I made my symbolic utterance.' He stopped and, bending down, cleared the snow from a Christmas rose that was almost buried. 'You ask whether I shall get out and the answer is that those who wish to get out will always find a way.'

His Polish accent and intonation was more pronounced than last night. It stopped him seeming absurd. I remembered what was happening in his country at that moment. 'You'll have to explain your symbolism more clearly,' I said. 'We live a very unliterary life up here.'

'You know what I mean.'

'Is it about the war?'

'Not directly. Though the war could be the means.'

I sighed. 'My mother was always obsessed with escape.'

'I've never had the honour of meeting your mother.'

'She escaped all over the place. And she's ended up on one of the smallest islands in the world.'

'Every man is an island.' Mrozek gave his Polish bow. 'But I shall look forward to seeing you again in London.'

'When this war is over?'

'If not before.'

'Why do you say that?' He didn't answer, and we turned and started back to the house. The clouds had broken slightly, and I could see that Mrozek wanted to set off. 'Give my farewells and felicitations to your inestimable husband,' he said. 'You are lucky to have a happy marriage.'

'Yes.' Annoyed by his patronising tone and aware of the contradiction from his previous remarks, I turned to the car. There in the front seat, waiting patiently, sat Katynka. 'But you can't!' I cried out automatically. And although I was addressing Mrozek, Katynka answered. 'Araminta knows. She's going to tell Leonard. I'm not going forever.'

'I need a new assistant,' said Mrozek smoothly. I saw it was pointless to argue and none of my business, but couldn't resist crying, 'I

240

shouldn't be surprised if you end up as enemy aliens!'

'Oho!' said Mrozek, clearly enjoying himself as he got into the car. As he drove slowly through the snow, his face appeared from the window. It wore a gleeful smile. 'See how easy it is to escape?'

'What was all that about?' said Araminta, coming up with a contingent of children.

'Apparently you know. Katynka's gone. She's under-age. You could have stopped her. You know that dreadful Mr Moore's married. He'll just seduce her and leave her.'

'You are angry. I didn't think you particularly liked Katynka. I can't tell a girl of nineteen who's not even my own daughter how to run her life. She's Leonard's responsibility, and he would tell her to go.'

'How can you be so passive?' I cried out angrily. I turned away and, gathering a large snowball, threw it straight at Araminta's face. We were both astonished. The snow covered Araminta's hair and neck. She brushed it away and looked at me in disbelief. The children round her shrieked with joy.

'Look what Mummy's done to Minta!' 'You are bad! Bad Mummy!' 'Mummy's a snowman!'

I was terribly apologetic. 'How could I? Oh, Araminta!' My anger had gone. Even her own lack of righteous anger did not annoy me. My absurd, uncharacteristic action had put me in an excellent humour. I brushed Araminta down, played with the children a little, and then went in to get ready for my journey into Newcastle. I was going to write up the Monthly Narrative report and looked forward to detailing every item we had collected and supplied:

To the Forces	
Scarves	527
Helmets	310
Body Belts	76
Socks (pairs)	340
Cuffs (pairs)	134
Steering Gloves (pairs)	369
Mittens (pairs)	188
Sea Boot Stockings	5
Bed Socks (pairs)	21
Gloves (pairs)	18
Pullovers	6
Long Stockings (pairs)	2
Full sized blankets	32

After this I would write:

I think you will agree that this is a very creditable figure for a centre of our size. We are in very close touch with the Missions to Seamen and garments are sent there for seamen who are brought into the port from ships which have been victims of warfare.

A few weeks later we received an official letter from the Civil Service commandeering the whole of Kettleside as a rest home for recuperating naval officers. Nettles acted swiftly. Three days later, all but the best spare bedrooms were filled with half a dozen land girls. A very efficient letter then went to the Civil Service explaining the situation and offering the remaining rooms to needy officers. Araminta and I couldn't help wondering whether Nettles had planned this all along, as indeed he had a perfect right to since his own young farm workers were continually joining up despite their special status. The girls, who came in a random selection from Newcastle's poorer areas, were big and quiet and very hungry. The biggest and hungriest eventually turned out to be pregnant, which at least satisfied Araminta's requirements. Flo, despite the struggle over food, really enjoyed commanding a regiment. She lectured them about her own role in the First World War and, when Mary's pregnancy was discovered, became, to those who didn't know her own history, inexplicably protective. It was Mary who was responsible for peeling the potatoes and cleaning the leeks for pease pudding, which I hope never to see out of a nursery-rhyme book again.

About this time, Leonard paid an extremely short visit. He called pease pudding 'piss pudding.' He stayed just long enough to make Araminta pregnant again. I hardly saw him, for I was becoming more and more involved with my WVS work, often staying a night or two in Newcastle. I was planning the 1940 Evacuation Scheme, which after the problems of 1939 was a much more sensibly organised affair, with an emphasis on communal feeding, proper medical supervision, and supplies of extra clothing. The other day I came across a letter from a headmaster thanking the WVS for clothing we had sent for evacuated children. 'They are so happy,' he wrote, 'except when the mothers come.'

Then Lady Reading came to Newcastle. She stood on the station platform, a stalwart figure in her bottle-green uniform and maroon badge, and said to me, 'We could do with your sort in London. Winnie thinks so. We're expecting things to hot up now.' The now, I presume, referred to Dunkirk. It was May 1940 and at last, nine months after war had been declared, the waiting seemed to be ending.

Lady Reading had come up to open our second canteen in the

station. She had already inspected a guard of honour with representatives of the Navy, Army, WRNS, and WAAF. 'Come to the Cookhouse Door' had been sounded by a bugler of the Royal Artillery, and a WVS pennant had been broken by a Petty Officer RN as Lady Reading unlocked the door of the canteen.

This kind of arrangement, which before the war would have seemed absurd, now seemed full of significance, and when Lady Reading spoke to me my mind was so full of bugles and bakers that I stared quite stupidly. Eventually I said, coming to the point more sharply than I meant, 'But I'm married. I've got two young children.'

'Ah,' said Lady Reading. 'Winnie didn't give that impression at all.' She began to turn away, for she was the sort of woman who didn't believe in wasting her time. I felt as if a spotlight had swept across me for a moment. I wanted the moment to continue.

'It's not quite like that,' I cried out. 'I might be able to come. I'd like to come.'

Nettles and I shared the large bed that my mother had shared with Tudor, my father. Too much of my marriages, both my marriages, had been spent in my mother's beds. At least she had not slept with Nettles in this bed. The bedroom, which had a wide alcove incorporating three long windows through which the chilly sun streaked on hopeful mornings, was always very cold. Even in summer. By contrast the bed, which was huge and soft and lumpy, seemed very warm.

Nettles was a nice person to sleep with. His feet were always warm, and his hands, and all the parts of my anatomy which tended to heat up only for short periods after heavy exercise. He was also good at lying awake, and talking over whatever was on our minds. In this way we kept in touch with each other even if we had been mostly apart during the day or even for several days.

We were on good terms physically in other ways too. It was always easy making love with Nettles, so that it happened without any particular signals and ended with us happier together and closer. The only problem from my point of view was my fear of having more children. Yet I did nothing about it beyond watching the time of the month. It seemed a long time since I had insisted on Howard's precautions. Now the idea of birth control seemed almost immoral.

The night of my meeting with Lady Reading, I lay in bed with Nettles and wondered how I could possibly have thought I wanted to go to London. I murmured to Nettles, 'Winnie Beauchamp suggested me to Lady Reading for a London job. Isn't that extraordinary?'

'She must have thought you'd be a help.'

'I've got a husband. I've got children. I told that to Lady Reading.' Nettles put his arms round me and held me closer. 'I know.' We were silent for a moment. Then he said, 'Perhaps Winnie thought you were getting bored with making shrouds and Treasure Bags.'

I couldn't help giggling. 'My main task is to persuade mothers not to use their Baby Protective Helmets as general holdall. We found one containing bus tickets, cooked meat partly eaten, a pair of lace curtains, postcards, a drinking glass, and a complete civilian respirator.' We were both sleepily silent again. Then I said, 'The funny thing is, if I had to deal with any of this sort of problem at home I'd be bored silly.'

'But you don't actually deal with it.'

'Not literally. I see it gets done.'

'Efficiently.'

'Yes. I suppose so. Yes. Very efficiently. I like organising people.'

'That's why they want you in London. The war in England is all about efficiently organising people.'

'But anyone can do that. If they're lazy enough. All my life I've been too lazy or spoiled to do anything else.'

'You manage to be popular as well as getting things done.'

'You have to develop charm to disguise laziness.'

'That's why they want you.'

Again we were silent. We might even have fallen asleep for a moment. Then I suddenly said in a self-pitying tone, 'You sound as if you're encouraging me to go. You don't want me to go, do you?'

'No.' Nettles grunted and still held me close. I tried to push him off a little.

'What do you mean? You can't just say "no" like that.'

'I mean that after thirty-five years you've found something you're good at and that gives you satisfaction, and now that you've been offered an opportunity to extend your experience, I'm not going to be the one to forbid you.' He had finally allowed himself to be pushed away, so that his voice was no longer muffled in my hair but spoke out clearly into the dark.

'But Nettles, darling,' I cried, grasping his shoulder, 'I can't leave you. I can't leave the children. What would I do without you to chat to? Without the children waking me up with a kiss in the morning?' I appealed to him piteously: 'I don't want to leave you. I don't want to go to London. I was miserable in London. You made me happy!'

'Don't go, then.'

I was miserable before I met you. I would be miserable without you.'

'They're not the same thing.'

244

'I love you, Nettles!'

'I love you, darling.' We rolled together, and I kissed him eagerly as if it were the last opportunity.

The tears swilled out of my eyes and ran down my face. I really and truly felt desperate with misery. At the same time, I did not try to stop them or hide them. If I had been feeling misery without hope, I would not have dared show my grief.

I was standing on Newcastle station waiting for the train to take me down to London. Like everything in wartime it was late, giving me extra time to see what I was leaving behind. Despite the evening hour, everyone had come to see me off: the children, Nanny, Araminta, Nettles—even Flo and Cecil.

I've never been very good at seeing people whom I most love when they are close, and now a space had appeared between us. I was leaving; they were staying. Even physically they were already moving from me, so every few minutes I would find myself isolated while they talked to each other about things that no longer concerned me.

'Oh, Nettles!' I cried through my tears, 'If only the war hadn't started and the WVS didn't exist and we hadn't decided to open a second blasted canteen. Surely one is enough. Look at it, over there. There's positively no trade!' This made us both laugh, though rather hysterically, and we turned together to look at the children.

'They don't care,' I said, becoming mournful again. 'They won't even remember me in a couple of months.'

'Little Violet will.' Violet was five now. I watched her as a stranger. She stood close by Nanny, who carried Tudor. Her hand was tucked securely, bossily, into Leo's hand. They both had dark hair; elongated eyes that varied from green to grey to hazel; stubby, rather prominent noses; and plump rosy cheeks. They were dressed alike in cream flannel coats with a double row of pearl buttons and Peter Pan collars, inherited from the twins. I think they thought they were twins too and when I was gone no doubt Violet would completely adopt Araminta as her mother.

The thought made the tears roll afresh, and Nettles said, 'Why don't you go and talk to one of your WVS girls over there? She might take your mind off it.'

'It's so difficult to make your own road,' I said, hardly knowing what I was saying. 'And Violet's too fat. Look how her feet pop over her button shoes.'

'Well, why don't you talk to Nanny about a diet?' suggested Nettles, which showed that he was upset, because if there was one thing calculated to put Nanny and me at loggerheads, it was the subject of diets. Besides, the idea that she would listen to any advice at my point of departure was clearly absurd. She had accepted the plan only when she had been convinced that I must be looked on as a soldier going to the front.

'I hope no one sees me looking like this,' I said, rubbing my face.

'They'll probably think you're seeing me off to the front,' said Nettles, echoing my thoughts.

'In civvies?'

'I could be a war reporter risking my life for *The Times*. That would explain my age, too.'

'Oh, Nettles.'

'Everything will be fine, darling.'

I began to feel better. It was now almost dark. The dark made the station seem dramatic rather than depressing. Flo and Cecil brought cups of tea from the Reading canteen, and Nettles produced a flask of whisky, which he poured liberally into the mugs.

'The train will have to come sometime,' pointed out Isabel.

Araminta, who'd been wandering about with the twins and Henrietta, reappeared. She accepted a cup of heavily laced tea and said with a misty smile, 'I've just realised that your mother left you at exactly the same age as you're leaving little Violet.' She drank thirstily from her cup.

I began to laugh hysterically.

Nettles said, 'Oh, really, Araminta,' and Nanny, coming up eagerly for a nice cup of tea, pursed her mouth disapprovingly. 'I'm glad you've found something to laugh about. I was thinking of the night that you and I, Miss Violet, stood on this very platform and watched your poor dear father, Major Hesketh, go to his end.'

I stopped laughing. Araminta said, 'I'm sorry, Nettles' in a not very convincing undertone, and the train, with no more warning than a sudden shriek from Tudor, came rushing into the station.

There was nothing else to do but say goodbye. This I did hastily and unsatisfactorily, failing to take a proper last look at the children or concentrate as Nettles and I kissed. Even when I was on the train, I was so intent on getting my cases and myself into a corridor which was already packed full that I pulled down a window only in time to see my family already disappearing away down the platform. It seemed this train should not have stopped at Newcastle at all. The few minutes that had given me time to jump on had been to relieve an engine driver who had fallen sick. Somewhere at the back of my mind, even after I had made all the arrangements to go to London, I had reserved the right to change my mind at the last minute. But now the last minute had gone, and Araminta's words would stand as an epitaph.

The long journey South lasted till dawn. Our train seemed

all but expendable and was relegated to a dead-end siding every time a VIP train thundered up behind us. It gave me plenty of time to consider the justice of Araminta's view. By the time I found myself six inches between a line of sleeping WAAF, my tears had gone. But I could not sleep.

Certainly Araminta had every right to make a judgement. In effect I had left her the responsibility of my children and, indeed, my husband. When I had told her my plans, her face had shown a curious mixture of shocked disapproval; pleasure at, as she saw it, my failing; and a certain quickly dismissed jealousy. Since then she had shown only the disapproval, but the fact that she had never tried to dissuade me made me sense still the pleasure that the prospect of total responsibility gave her.

'You never find time to paint now,' I tested her once as she picked spring cabbage from the garden.

'I don't mind.'

'You used to mind very much. Is it the war?'

'Don't be silly. It's Clancy. She's much better than I ever was. There's no point in me doing it.'

'What do you mean? Do you mean you get the same satisfaction from Clancy's drawings as from your own? You can't mean that!' I was astonished.

'More. Because she's better.'

'But surely that just makes you envious?'

Now she was astonished. 'Of course not. That's the whole point of children. To carry on from where you left off. And be better. If possible.' With heavy, decisive gestures she gathered up the huge pile of green leaves into her apron and carried them towards the kitchen door. Just before she was out of earshot she turned suddenly and called out, 'Self-sacrifice, Vi—or in other words, motherhood!'

I was pleased to have made her rise and shouted back quickly, 'You sound just like Nanny!'

This was almost too near the truth. I had Araminta living in Kettleside because I needed her nannylike qualities. She knew this, and although in one way she felt rightly insulted, in another it stopped her from the feeling she was living on charity. She paid her way with Earth Mother warmth.

Although I cared very much about my children, they always seemed quite separate from me—almost remote. I could never understand why little Violet should feel particularly attached to me. I always assumed she would love whoever was nicest to her, and I only very seldom felt jealous pangs. Tudor was still a baby, more Nanny's than mine. I didn't feel guilt over leaving them. They would be well loved and protected, and it was not as if I would be gone forever or even for long.

I put my head against the back of my seat, and as the night cold pressed through the windows I became glad of the huddled figures on either side. It was only when a grey dawn showed our slow arrival into a cheerless London that I thought of what separation from Nettles really meant. The officers had begun to talk softly to each other, which made me feel particularly alone. Then one of them, a reddish-faced girl who had irritated me in the night by snoring contentedly, produced two thermos flasks of tea, which she offered round.

'We're going on leave,' she said to me. She indicated my WVS uniform. 'I suppose you're going on duty.'

In a moment I felt myself part of a great team of women doing their part to win the war. It was nice of the WAAF to make me feel this, for the Forces, particularly in the early part of the war, felt a natural snobbery towards the voluntary organisations. Besides, I was at least ten years older than the oldest of them, and might have seemed stand-offish with my fashionable hair and expensive luggage—bought for my first honeymoon.

As it was, we all tipped out merrily into Euston station. One of the girls read out, laughing, a huge poster stuck up on the wall opposite: 'Is Your Journey Really Necessary?'

Chapter Ten

Buckingham Palace has been hit by a delayed action bomb of heavy calibre which damaged the royal suites and destroyed the Princesses' swimming pool.
The Times.   12 September 1940

CHURCHILL'S WORDS OF CHEER: 'LET GOD DEFEND THE RIGHT'
These cruel wanton, indiscriminate bombings of London are, of course, a part of Hitler's invasion plan. He hopes, by killing large numbers of civilians, and women and children, that he will terrorise and con the people of this mighty Imperial city . . . Little does he know the spirit of the British nation, or the tough fibre of the Londoners whose forebears played a leading part in the establishment of Parliamentary Institutions, and who have been bred to value freedom far above their lives.
The Times.   12 September 1940

COSIES FOR NIGHT-CAPS
Sir, Now that we are apparently to have a return of the four-poster in the shape of a substantial table placed over our beds, may I suggest that the ancient accompanying night-cap should reappear in the form of a large, well-stuffed tea cosy? It is obvious that some special protection for the heads of sub-table sleepers is urgently needed, for we have been told that a gentleman who had slept under his dining table was so overjoyed on waking to find himself unbombed, that he sprang up and knocked his head with such violence against the table that he was insensible for hours.
Your obedient servant, J. Menburn Levien.
The Athenaeum, Pall Mall, SW1.
(Letter to the Editor) *The Times.*   15 October 1940

Darling, darling, darling,

I am here, in the house. I've blacked out one floor which is all I'll use. I shan't bother to connect the telephone—not yet at least. It's strange and eerie but I'm not worried. Just now an ARP warden called. He knew this house was empty so was surprised by the drawn curtains. He was nice and friendly—rather like an older Cecil. I made him a cup of tea and he said he or his mate comes round every evening at about this time so I could always call if I was worried about anything. The war has made people much more approachable. (Wardens get paid £2.10 per week, incidentally.) I went to the WVS Headquarters at Tothill Street, which will be a tricky journey when trouble comes. I'll probably get myself a little car. Trouble—the Blitzkrieg, I mean (I've started to use the warden's euphemisms!) is expected fairly soon—probably before the end of the summer. Everybody thinks me very brave (or mad) to be coming into London just when most people are trying to get out. I smile proudly and hope inwardly that I will be some use. For the next few weeks I'm 'learning the ropes,' going to the various departments and meeting the people there and seeing what they do. I start tomorrow at the clothing depot, at 88 Eaton Square. Then the Polish Refugees Committee for warm clothing, run by Nina, Countess Granville at 33 Belgrave Square. Today I was only called upon to decide what to do with a large quantity of sultanas and cream cheese sent for evacuated children from the Victoria Ladies Golf Union in Australia!!

Eventually I'm to be a Metropolitan Regional Organiser. Tomorrow I'm going to a showing of a film made with the cooperation of the WVS called 'Britannia is a Woman'. I saw Winnie Beauchamp who I'm sure will be a terrific friend.

I can't tell you how extraordinary London is—particularly, of course, at night when the blackout comes down. There suddenly seems more sky even than in Northumberland. The warden told me the moon is full tonight, so in a moment I'm going to go upstairs to Augustus' flat and look out across the city. Good night, my darling. I miss you, miss you. All love, V.

I did miss Nettles that first night. My pleasure in human contact with the warden (who later drove me mad with lip-smacking delight in stories of carnage) proves that. Yet almost immediately after, the change in the London around me made the change in my own personal life seem almost insignificant. Almost everybody I met was separated from her husband or lover or mother or whomever she cared most about. One evening when I arrived home exhausted after a day spent driving my new Austin 8 round London arranging for church halls to be available as receiving centres in case of 'trouble',

Molly was waiting on my doorstep.

'I heard you were doing something useful at last,' she said, noting my uniform and exhaustion with satisfaction. It was a typical Molly greeting after two years in which we had only corresponded.

'Sometimes I wonder. Come in. I'm in the process of turning most of the house into a clothing depot, so you'll find it a bit of a shambles!'

We sat in the kitchen and I made toast while Molly uncorked a bottle of wine I'd discovered in the cellar when scouting its possibilities as a bomb shelter.

'I see you have butter,' said Molly.

'Flo sends it down. I can't stop her.'

'She'll get you into trouble.'

'I keep telling her that. But she's so pigheaded. She'll be delighted I met you. She's always thought you perfect.'

'That's because I treated her as a human being.'

'How's your farm life?'

'The dairy's gone. It's entirely cereals now. More labour-intensive.'

'I didn't mean that. I meant how is George? How are you and George? He doesn't come up for a progress report any more.'

Molly put down her toast reflectively. She had never regained her buxom, bouncing figure since her Spanish experiences, and her character seemed to reflect the loss. Although she was as spirited as ever, she did not shout or physically dominate any more. Her face was quite pale and pinched, and her hair looked less red.

'It's strange,' she said, 'how marriage used to obsess us all. Even at Oxford. The absolutely brightest girls were dead set on making a good marriage. I was just the same, whatever I may have said. The moment I fell in love, even though it was with a man clearly quite unsuitable and anyway already married, I simply had to get him in my clutches. Or get me into his. Looking back, it seems to be quite extraordinary.'

'You were in love.'

'Madly. Passionately. I know. But why did I want to marry him?'

'He was Catholic. He wouldn't have it any other way.'

'That's not entirely true. I was a much stronger character than him. I still am. I could perfectly well have fixed it. But what did I do? I became a Catholic. And why did I do it? Because I wanted to be married.'

'Does that follow?'

'Not entirely. Of course, one of the best things that came out of all that was my conversion to Catholicism. I'm working for a Catholic organisation run by Father Wilson now, you know. But that still

251

doesn't explain why I married George after I came back from Spain.'

'You loved him.'

'No. I didn't. Not any more. Not like before, anyway.'

'Perhaps you were just tired.'

'I thought I owed it to him. The truth is, I'm not the sort to be married. I'm too keen on leading my own life. Not that George and I are on bad terms. Quite the contrary. We're very good friends. Not particularly close friends, but good friends. We're very pleased when we run into each other. Sometimes I wish I could become a nun!'

'Oh, Molly!' She had spoken so seriously that I had to believe her, and I couldn't help remembering ironically when she had cried out the same thing at the height of her passion for George. 'I'm sorry,' I said in the end, rather lamely.

'Oh, don't be sorry,' she replied quickly, taking a drink of wine. 'It's what's called Growing Up, I believe, and Facing Realities. I suppose you're the same, anyway. You and Nettles, I mean. Now that you're living down here on your own.'

'Of course we're not!' My annoyance at her assumption that we were in the same, as I saw it, failed boat was so immediate and obvious that it embarrassed us both.

'Oh, dear,' said Molly. 'Now it's my turn to be sorry.'

'No,' I said stiffly, but determined to explain further, for I could see my anger had only made her more convinced that she was right. 'I love Nettles more than ever. And he loves me.' I paused.

'Well, that is nice,' said Molly.

'There is a war on, you know.'

Molly decided to try a different angle. 'I saw Leonard the other day. He doesn't spend much time with his wife.'

'That's not Araminta's choice.' I tried to get the crossness out of my voice. 'Though I don't think she minds.'

'He said he was going to drop in on you soon. You used to be very good friends, didn't you? Everybody thought you were having an affair. Were you?'

'No.' Since my marriage to Nettles I had seen Leonard only on his brief visits to Kettleside, Araminta, and his children. He had irritated me by his disturbing casual presence, coming from a world I didn't want to know about and he didn't talk about. On his last visit he had left Araminta pregnant. 'What's he doing in London?'

Molly shook her head. 'He never tells one things like that. Except, of course, to say he's selling this particularly good brand of whisky. I presume it's something secret. A lot of men have got very boring lately because they're doing something secret. However, it would be wrong to assume all boring men are doing something secret.'

'They may be just boring.' We smiled at each other. 'Leonard was never that,' I found myself saying. The prospect of a visit from Leonard now that I was on my own in London, away from Kettleside, seemed a positive bonus. I felt as if there were two Leonards, one who upset the happy household in the North and another who was my 'good friend,' as Molly put it, in the South. 'I suppose Leonard used to be the nearest thing I had to a friend who was a man. It was he who prompted me to escape from Howard.'

'What about Augustus? I thought he was your real old friend.'   .

'He didn't approve of my marriage to Nettles.'

'Who did?'

'Molly!'

She laughed at my expression. 'You are funny. I know you're a model of respectability now—apart from abandoning your husband, that is—but that's no reason to disown the past. Come on, now, be bold. Now is the time to get it straight. What made you marry your mother's lover?'

I was just opening my mouth to scream at her cynicism when an air-raid siren wailed longer and louder than I could. By early August, 1940, I was used to the sound of the siren, but it still had the power to interrupt any train of thought. I was immediately thrown back into the war. Our conversation seemed part of a prewar self-indulgent obsession with personal trivia. Now we were made of sterner stuff. I crammed my WVS hat back on my head, and Molly, picking up her bag, started briskly for the door.

'Don't you take cover?' I said.

'I've got to get back to Dagenham. This is still the rehearsal. We'll know when the real thing's starting.'

'It's real enough over Kent and Sussex. My cousin Dot hardly dares play a round of golf. And that means it's serious.' We were walking, as we spoke, down towards the front door. 'Do you know there's a special rule for a ball displaced by enemy action?'

'Don't you want to know what I'm doing in Dagenham?'

'I'm sorry. The siren makes me gabble nonsense, I'm afraid. I presumed it was something to do with Father Wilson's job.'

'It is. You must visit me there, darling.' She set off down the street. Feeling brave, for although the siren had stopped at last there was no sign of the All Clear, I stood and watched her go. After she had turned the corner I heard a number of planes some distance to the east, but no roll of bombs followed. Soon the All Clear sounded, and I went up to make a cup of tea.

August was for me the most frightening month of the war. We knew by now what bombs could do. Three hundred civilians had been killed in one of the few daylight raids at the beginning of July on Wick and in Hull. We could see the German planes practising the night run across Bristol, up the Welsh border into Merseyside. We knew that the blackout had no effect on the gleaming waters of the Thames, which would lead them to London as if it were a sitting duck—or 'a fat cow', as Churchill called it. The sirens seemed to be going day and night. I was extremely busy and soon learnt to follow a quick dive for the shelter by life as usual. One evening in late August I heard the Philharmonic Orchestra at Central Hall. Winnie at my side, whispered, 'Whenever I listen to music I begin to cry.' Which indeed she did, with huge, silent tears. I noted for future reference how thin a veneer was her jolly capable manner.

I broke down only once myself. It was my own fault. I invited myself to spend a night with my cousin Dot and her family. I pretended it was for a rest from London. In fact I was drawn by the Battle of Britain, in full cry above their heads. I felt like the schoolchildren who, evacuated from Southampton to Dorset, felt happy only when the battle moved to rage round them—We're 'in things' now, they told their headmaster. I wanted to be 'in things' too, or I would feel my present way of living was not justified.

When I arrived at Dot's, I was affected by something quite different. Dot's three little boys were mirroring the fight above their heads with a complicated game of Spitfires and Messerschmitts on their garden lawn. 'We shall fight in the air!' screamed the middle boy. 'This is A Last Appeal to Reason!' screamed the elder.

'That's a reference to Hitler's Reichstag speech. The boys are horribly clued up about the war,' said Dot proudly.

'They'll soon forget it,' I said, watching the smallest boy spreading his arms like wings and exploding into loud engine noises. He was exactly Tudor's age. Dot had put up two deck chairs for us on the terrace, and as the real planes disappeared into sudden silence and a blue sky, we found ourselves faced with either her children or each other's company. I stared at the little boy.

Dot said, 'I would never have recognised you.'

'It's the uniform.'

'No, it's not. It's age.'

'You've got fat again.' I reflected that although Dot was my favourite of the cousins, none of them brought the best out in me. She sighed, but I sensed complacency.

'It's the children. And no time for golf. I can't think how I ever managed to be that tubular slim flapper.'

'One does revert to type.'

'You haven't. But then I wouldn't really know what your type was.'

She heaved herself up. 'I'd better make us some tea.' Her stoutness was accentuated by a garishly scarlet and blue dress with large square

254

buttons over a pocket on each bosom. Her dark hair was rolled up right round her head like a continuous sausage, with a high wave in the front.

Seeing where I was looking, she patted her head, 'It's the Victory Roll.'

As she went inside, I turned to watch the children again. When she came back I was sitting with tears pouring down my cheeks.

'It's all Aunt Phyllis' fault that I came to London,' I sobbed. 'If she hadn't sent Winnie to Kettleside, Winnie wouldn't have recommended me to Lady Reading and Lady Reading wouldn't have issued a command.'

'Aunt Phyllis always was a meddler,' said Dot distractedly. She put down the tea tray and began to shout threats at the older boys, who had begun a fierce quarrel.

'It's your youngest one,' I hiccoughed. 'He reminds me of Tudor.'

'What a funny name.'

'I haven't seen him or spoken to him for over two months.'

'The telephone's in the hallway.'

The thought of telephoning Kettleside had never entered my head—partly, I suppose, because I still had no phone in the house. I got through immediately, which in wartime was a surprise. A squeaky voice answered the phone. It was little Violet.

'Violet, darling, this is Mummy.'

She said, 'What?' several times loudly, then, suddenly screaming out 'Mummy!' dropped the receiver. I could hear her cries of 'Mummy! Mummy! It's Mummy!' receding into the distance.

When I got back to London I wrote to Nettles.

Darling, darling, darling,
    I spent a night with Cousin Dot and her three boys, which made me unbearably homesick for family life. I telephoned, but Violet said hello and ran away. Now I'm back in London it's not so bad. I'm mainly concerned with seeing the shelters are reasonably hygienic at the moment. Some people live there, which makes it hard.
    In the East End, under the Stepney Arches I found one gigantic shelter, the Tilbury Shelter, where people were sleeping on cases of margarine. That put it under the jurisdiction of the Ministry of Food, and in the end I had to get Lord Woolton down himself before I could get it removed. Quite a lesson in the problems of bureaucracy! I must say he was very nice. Incidentally, did you know that till Dunkirk and the Germans were almost visible to our Ministers, women's unemployment had actually gone up instead of down? It was just the same in the First World War apparently.

No one wanted women's services till it was almost too late and then they can't do without them. Have you lost any land girls to Ernest Bevin yet? They call him Mr Pankhurst here! I hope the harvest is going well and your harem is proving helpful as well as hungry. Now that Flo's stopped sending butter I live off WVS soup and buns. I enclose a new recipe for Araminta mainly consisting of 40 pounds of potatoes and served with a jam sauce. Very good for those eating for two. It's called Fadge. You'll hate it!

All, all, all my love, darling, and big XXXXs to the children and Araminta and Nanny and Flo and Cecil and everybody. The big battle should be on any day now, but don't worry, I'll be sensible!

Love, love, love, V.

Saturday, September 7, was a gloriously fine day, and after a working lunch I decided to walk through Hyde Park, now zigzagged with trenches, and across Kensington Gardens into Queensgate. I might scrounge tea from Winnie, who had a flat there. The bombers came, 357 of them, at five o'clock. Of course the sirens had already gone, and I was safely in a rather empty public shelter. It was the first and only big daylight raid of the war, which made it memorable. However, during the actual hour I sat there between a silent soldier and an ancient noisy man, my main sensation was guilt, for here I was, in my WVS uniform but without my gas mask. What a shocking example! I emerged worried lest it should be gas, not bombs, that had fallen.

I was quite unprepared to see smoke and flames rising from shattered buildings not more than a few streets away. The bombers had dropped their main load on the East End, destroying much of Woolwich Arsenal, the Docks, Millwall, Limehouse, Rotherhithe, Tower Bridge, and West Ham Power Station. But then, for no apparent reason, a solitary plane had crossed the City and Westminster and bombed a crescent in Kensington.

'Cor, blimey!' said the ancient man.

'You get on home,' I said, hoping to sound efficient. 'I may be needed.'

By the time I arrived at the crescent, a fire engine and an ambulance were already at work. There was also, in these early days of the war, quite a large group of people watching. Among them, I recognised Leonard. I hesitated for a moment before I approached him. He looked so much absorbed in the scene, his dark, thin face with its rubber lips was frighteningly still. I knew the look from his daughters when they were planning some particular evil.

'Hello, Leonard.'

He turned his head without moving his body. 'Oh, hello.' He turned back again. I was surprised by quite so little interest till I realised he hadn't recognised me in my uniform. 'It's Vi.'

He swivelled round now and looked at me properly. 'So it is. You do look hideous. Why ever couldn't you join something with a decent uniform like the Wrens?'

'Digby Morton designed it.' I stared stupidly at some flames which were suddenly sprouting from a ruined window.

'There you are.' He looked down at my feet. 'I suppose I should be glad you're not wearing ankle socks.'

'Quite a blaze, isn't it?' I tried to match his bantering tone. A wall crashed down from somewhere, throwing up a fog of dust.

'I just came out from one of those buildings. I won't tell you which because it was secret. Though I don't think it matters much any more.'

'Do you mean you know some people in there?' I remembered the expression on his face.

'I did. There's not much we can do now.'

'What about the homeless—' I began doubtfully.

'The place is swarming with do-gooders.' He took my arm and started marching me away. 'Come on. I need a drink. As a matter of fact, if it will salve your conscience I suppose I qualify as homeless now.' He nodded back towards the rubble.

'You were living there too?'

'I'd gone out to buy a bottle of whisky.' Smiling oddly, he led me away.

By this time it was getting on for seven o'clock and I felt unlike wandering about London looking for a drink. It would be dark soon.

'Why don't you come to my house?' I suggested. 'It's not what it used to be,' I added as we started walking northwards. 'Your old bedroom now holds two hundred and fifty pairs of men's pyjamas allocated for Gibraltarian refugees, three hundred night-dresses for child evacuees, and one hundred items assorted under-clothing.'

'All designed by Digby Morton.'

'I did suggest a WVS label. But my girls are too busy stitching wings into airmen's uniforms to have time to sew them in.'

'Your girls,' mocked Leonard.

We walked silently, and as we left that preview of nightmare farther behind, I found I needed to take his arm and cling to him.

'You always made fun of me,' I said.

'You like it,' he said, moving apart as I tried to find my key for the front door. 'I mock everyone, even myself.'

'Even Araminta.'

257

'Even Araminta.'

I thought as we went up the stairs—feeling our way in the gloom, since the blackout was not yet up—that if I was to be serious about this meeting with Leonard, I should continue the discussion of Araminta, mention her new baby, raise the question of Katynka and Mrozek. But I felt curiously reluctant to talk about any of his responsibilities. I knew it would break this strange interlude of intimacy between us, and I didn't want to. I knew he wouldn't if I didn't.

We sat either side of my kitchen table. I had opened another of my cellar's bottles of wine. Leonard, presumably, was thinking of his colleagues who had not got out of that Kensington crescent, but I felt myself floating in a sort of vacuum, almost mindless. Yet in a curious way very happy. I soon learned that this is a common effect after an escape from a raid, although often the happiness is hysterically energetic rather than calm. I saw Leonard there opposite me, but it was several minutes before I became properly aware that a part of my mood was composed of growing physical desire. I had often been attracted by Leonard at odd moments in the past before I had met Nettles. But I had never felt anything like this intense need before. His periodic overtures had become almost a joke between us.

Now as I sat within a foot of his face, which from the first I had labelled ugly and unattractive, I found I couldn't even trust myself to speak. Nor could I look at him, for what if by any dreadful chance he was feeling the same thing? If he wasn't he might not notice the state I was in, but if he was he certainly would.

I stared down at my wineglass and told myself it was a purely circumstantial feeling, due to my first real air raid, and my separation from Nettles. I willed myself to overcome such weakness so that I could get up without falling over and go out of the room. Once I was out of his presence I was sure it would pass in a moment. He'd said I looked a fright, I told myself; he couldn't be feeling the same. Testing myself, I began to slowly raise my head.

As I did so, the second siren of the day began to scream. The surprise made me raise my eyes unprepared to Leonard's, and in that second I saw he was feeling exactly the same.

'Violet,' he said simply. And coming round to me, pressed me close.

'It's nothing,' I said, pretending I hadn't understood. 'The siren always frightens me . . . With Molly the other day . . .' I remembered what Molly and I had been talking about and tried to pull away. Leonard held on to me. He kissed me. Now there was absolutely no doubt what both of us wanted.

I was terrified. I was quite clear about who I loved and it certainly wasn't Leonard. I didn't want to hurt Nettles. I didn't want to hurt

258

him with Leonard, who I didn't care about. If only I could get out of his presence, it would all be forgotten.

'Where do you shelter?' Leonard held me still. 'In the cellar?'

'Yes. Please, Leonard. Please not. Please just go.'

He looked at me surprised. 'I can't go. There's a raid on. It's serious now. They mean business. We'd better get downstairs.' He began to push me out of the room, never letting me out of his grip, so that my will was weakened by his touch.

'Go to someone else's cellar,' I pleaded. 'Go next door. They've got a huge cellar.'

He laughed. And stopping at the top of the stairs, gave me another kiss. In one hand he held the bottle of wine. I could feel it pressing into my back. I would run ahead of him into the cellar. Perhaps that would break the spell. He followed me closely. The mattress lay ready prepared on the floor.

I saw that my only hope was to talk about Nettles and Araminta and Katynka. If I'd done that at the beginning this would never have happened. It was all my own fault.

'Don't flutter about so,' said Leonard, setting down the wine. 'I'm not going to rape you.'

'You don't understand.'

'I'm Leonard. We've known each other almost since we were children. Over sixteen years, anyway. Come and sit down. Talk to me.'

I knew if I went close to him it would be worse, but I couldn't shout across the cellar about Nettles and Araminta and Katynka. So I went into his arms, and he kissed me again and put his hands on my breasts. And then said, in a rational schoolmasterly voice, 'Speak, then. Explain to me. Am I affronting you?'

'No,' I whispered, wanting his hands to stay on my breasts. 'But I love Nettles. Nettles means everything to me. Before I had Nettles I was nothing. I love him. I love him.'

'Of course you do. I love Araminta too. But this is different. Isn't it?'

'But I don't want it,' I cried out. 'I don't want to hurt Nettles. Nor myself.'

'He won't know.'

'I don't want to deceive him. I love him.' I began to cry.

'Oh, dear,' said Leonard taking his hands away from me, which made me cry even more.

'Hold me just for a moment,' I cried. 'Then we'll separate and pretend it's never happened.' Leonard put his arms round me, and this time, since we were going to part, I kissed him. We were too old to stop then. I thought fleetingly, longingly of that big warm bed in

259

Northumberland, and then we were both undressed and it was too late.

Two hundred and fifty bombers came to London between 8:10 and 4:30 AM, when the All Clear sounded. Three mainline stations were put out of action. 430 killed and 1,600 severely injured.

I told myself the next morning, as many a faithless wife has done before and since, that the war was responsible. That now I knew what could happen, I would see it didn't happen again. I more or less said this to Leonard over a five o'clock breakfast.

'Heavens, Vi,' he said. 'For a nearly middle-aged woman, you're amazingly idealistic. Do you want me to say everything? You don't love me. I don't love you. I probably don't love anyone—except possibly Araminta because she's so crazy and female. But I like you tremendously. More than ever now. Not less, as your romantic novelists might assure you. And you, for some reason, find me interesting. You always have found me interesting, but now that you're more sexually aware you find me attractive too. Does that make it clear enough? We're friends. Don't worry. I promise not to make love to you ever again, unless you absolutely plead to me or we get caught in another air raid. Okay?'

'I'm sorry.' I looked down at my coffee.

'And please don't be sorry. I enjoyed myself and I got the feeling you did too.'

'Yes.'

'Then button up your uniform and go and see what the filthy Boches have done now. Your girls will be waiting for you.'

I smiled wanly. We went out into the city just as it began to lighten for another beautiful early-autumn day. But this time there was a red glow in the east even before the sun topped the horizon.

'I wonder what's gone,' I said. As I stood on the pavement with that view in front of me and some knowledge of what I must do in the day, the night's adventures really did not seem too important. Except that I was tired. And even that tiredness vanished as the curious after-raid exhilaration took me over. 'I'll give you a lift to the tube. I must get to Tothill Street. I've got to see the canteens are properly placed and the reception centres working smoothly.'

'So that's what you do, is it?' We drove towards the red sky, through the tunnel of a still dark Oxford Street.

'You'll get a tube here,' I stopped the car. Leonard got out. He smiled at me through the window.

'Someone told me WVS stood for Wives, Virgins, Spinsters. I'd better tell him he's wrong.'

I smiled back. 'We're considering a slogan: "The women who never say no".'

Later that day I was helping sift through the rubble of a street in the East End when I found a little child's pink handbag. Before I had decided what to do with it, a black huddled figure, more like an animal than a woman, snatched it from my hands and, clasping it to her, ran off down the street. I hurried after her through bricks and glass, avoiding a flaring gas pipe here, and hanging wall there, but she had gone.

I tried to forget everything in some good hard sweeping. A broom would have made an appropriate emblem for the WVS. I was considered impatient and rather high-handed. But my impatience got things done. When a recalcitrant vicar refused to open his church hall, I was called in. When a young member became hysterical at the sight of blood, I was called in to slap her face. One afternoon I was called in to quell a near-riot among some refugees quartered in Earls Court: they had suddenly noticed the whole roof was made of glass.

There was no time to think about personal problems. No place for selfish guilt. My worst experience was in Lewisham. There had been a bomb on a school there. So many were killed that the mortuary couldn't put them together quickly enough for the parents to identify them. They were waiting outside, usually the mother with a friend or her own mother. Our people, the WVS, were taking them into the mortuary when it was their turn. I went in twice. After that I couldn't go in again. I found a table and made arrangements. It taught me a lesson about the value of oversensibility. There was one fat old lady, who had joined the WVS because nobody else would have her, who went into the mortuary seventeen times. And each time she was giving love and support. I couldn't do that. I told myself it was because I had young children myself.

That evening, oddly enough, a letter came from my Violet. It arrived via a postman of about sixteen with a wan, lifeless face. He rang the bell and when I took the letter said, in a Cockney voice, 'This makes a change.'

'What?' I said absentmindedly. At which point he fainted. I dragged him inside and washed his face. When he came to, he said immediately, 'That's the first letter I've delivered in weeks.'

'From my daughter.' I had opened the envelope and seen the childish capitals. 'Been off sick?'

'No such luck. I couldn't find no letter boxes to put the letters in. Nor no people, neither. Shoreditch. Whole streets flattened. My own Auntie Evie's house went first, and my mum and dad's lost its roof. You can't be a postman if there's no place to put the post, can you?'

'So they've brought you up West?'

'That's right.'

'Where do you sleep?'

261

'Dickins and Jones's basement, if I'm on the early shift. That fills up quick. Or the tube sometimes; if my mate's kept me a place. The shelters last. Can't think a bit of brick thrown up in a few minutes would keep out Jerry.'

People kept working because they needed the pay. My postman dropped in quite often afterwards, drinking tea and even spending a few nights in my basement.

Little Violet's careful note, in which I recognised Nanny's prompting, 'We all hope you are doing your duty without losing too much sleep,' seemed infinitely remote. It would have been different if they had been in any danger. Invasion was the only scare. Nettles wrote that he had been trying to teach first Cecil and then Araminta how to remove the distributor head, leads, and carburettor from the car according to the Ministry of Transport's order 'Immobilisation of Vehicles in the Event of Invasion,' but had decided it would be easier to blow up the car.

I usually arrived home before six, when the siren went, made tea, and then descended to the basement till six in the morning, when I heard the All Clear. Quite often there would be a lull in the attack round about nine, and I would go upstairs again for a wash. I would see from my window other people who surfaced, taking their dogs for a quick walk round the block, and I would note where the worst blazes were this time. Where my work would take me in the morning. I very seldom went out at night. My moment always came at dawn or before as autumn drew in. One morning, after a night of tremendous noise so that I could actually feel the walls of the house shaking as if there were an earthquake, I emerged knowing that those headed by Nettles, who said that I was mad to sleep on my own, were absolutely right.

As I came upstairs, I found that glass and dust covered every surface. The dust got into my mouth, making me cough. I went down to the front door to find it blown in and Winnie just arrived on the doorstep.

'You've been lucky!'

'Depends how you look at it.'

On one side of my house there was a huge hole, into which most of the street seemed to be falling. On the other side, the roofless walls of another house stood gaping open. 'What rotten taste in wallpaper,' I said, trying to keep my voice from shaking. 'And just look at that bath. It can't have been cleaned for weeks.'

'There was nobody living in those houses,' said Winnie meaningfully. 'What we need is a cup of tea.' She took my arm.

'The gas will be cut,' I said. But by some freak it wasn't, and although the water pipes were, I always kept my kettle full. We swept off the dusty, glass-covered table and sat across it in the position of all my wartime conversations. I noted how Winnie's creamy beauty seemed quite unaffected by living conditions. 'How do you keep your hair so shiny? Oh, God!' I leaped to my feet. Even Winnie looked worried. I raced downstairs. 'My car! Did you see what happened to my car?' Even with the constant detours for bombed roads, I could get around twice as quickly as on the totally unreliable public transport.

Winnie found me standing on the pavement gaping with amazement. 'Look! My little car stood on the very edge of the crater, its windows shattered, its boot and all its doors blown open by the blast, but otherwise quite untouched.

'I told you you were lucky,' Winnie smiled at my face. 'Brush off the glass and I expect you can get in and drive it away.' Which is exactly what I did. When I came back, having been halted pretty quickly by a fire engine trying to stop a fire spreading to a church—the church I was first married in, as a matter of fact—Winnie was busy shaking off the uniforms.

'I don't mind the dust,' she complained, 'but I can't kill our members with fragments of glass.'

'I'm staying,' I said. 'Lightning never strikes twice.'

'Tell that down at Limehouse.'

I indicated the stacked piles of clothes. 'I can't leave this lot, anyway. What if there was a fire?'

'They'd burn.'

'We'd get out our stirrup pumps . . .'

We laughed at each other and got down to work.

So Winnie stayed with me, and when I was homesick I talked about Nettles and the children.

Although the loss of life was less than half that expected, 5,730 killed in September, the damage to property was much greater. This meant a tremendous need for organisation of living quarters. Our enemies, in order of importance, were sleeplessness, hunger, and finally shrapnel and blast. Bombs hardly figured. If you caught a bomb, you didn't know it.

Blast was something none of us had been prepared for. I found it a fascinating but not frightening phenomenon. Even when one of our workers was blasted almost from her husband's arms as they stood at the doorway of their house, I felt no creeping ghost of the future. Perhaps it was the image of my little car, doors and boot open but engine ready to spark into life, that deceived me.

I was most frightened of the full moon on a cloudless night. I had to stop myself staring heavenwards every few minutes. The worst raid before the pressure moved to the North was on the full moon of

15 October. Four hundred planes crossed and recrossed, leaving a nightmare of destruction.

The next morning Leonard came into the WVS headquarters. I introduced him to my harassed colleagues and was surprised to find I felt no embarrassment. He was an old friend who'd come to see me. He wanted to know if I had any message for Nettles or the children. He was on his way North and would drop in on Kettleside to see Araminta, who was now six months pregnant.

'She's not very well,' he said.

'I'm sorry,' I said. 'I can't think. Sit down a moment. I'll get some tea.' I half-wondered whether I felt any of that dangerous attraction, but was too busy to concentrate. I scribbled a note for Nettles, a line for Araminta and Nanny and Flo, and a funny picture of me for the children. 'And will you say that Winnie Beauchamp's probably being posted North? So she might come looking for a bed.'

'They'll ask whether you're coming home for Christmas.'

'How extraordinary.' I looked at Leonard sharply. 'How extraordinary for you to think a thing like that.'

He shrugged. 'I'm getting old.'

'It depends on our Hunnish friends,' I said. 'I suppose they can't go on for ever. Say I'll try.'

We kissed, and I did feel a jump in my body as if it recognised the past. But again I was too preoccupied to consider it further. 'Tell them I love them all.'

Leonard saluted. 'To the Women who never say No. Well, hardly ever.'

I smiled. 'We never did adopt that slogan.'

'I thought you might not. Goodbye, darling. Keep Smiling Through—or to bowdlerise the words of our great leader, "I can see the spirit of an unquenchable woman".' Leonard went to the door, and to the amazement and delight of the office, he began to sing raucously:

> There'll always be an England
> And England shall be free
> If England means as much to you
> As England means to me.

I didn't go up to Kettleside at Christmas. I intended to. I had collected a crate of presents—mostly consisting of clothes pinched from the WVS dump and toys pinched from the American offerings. Some had little labels saying 'to increase the feeling of a personal link between the children of the two great Democracies.' But too many other workers had decided to spend Christmas at home.

I spent Christmas Eve decorating an evacuation centre in Bermondsey with very old tinsel lent by a theatrical costumier, and Christmas Day at another centre eating plum pudding made with flour, water, powdered egg, about two sultanas, the same amount of nuts, crushed biscuits, a great many threepenny bits, and a huge amount of vegetable dye, which had turned it a purplish colour. We doused it with brandy to make it palatable, and the dye oozed out in sinister rivulets.

I didn't get away for New Year either. On 29 December the fire-bombs burned up much of the centre of London. Eight Wren churches went in one night. It was one of the few times that I came out to help support the Services before dawn and the All Clear. The smoke and flames rolled up so high that it seemed impossible anything could survive. I was making cups of tea in our mobile canteen parked in a square in the City and found tears blurring my vision. At first I honestly thought it was the acrid smell of burning all around, but gradually I realised that that would not explain my feeling of misery. In a pause between wet tea leaves which seemed to be coated somewhere up to my elbow, and steaming water which mixed phantasmagorically with the smoke around me, I suddenly understood that I was crying for London. It was the night that the survival of St Paul's, rising out of the smoke like a giant unifying umbrella, became a symbol of triumph over the Blitz.

So I did not go to Kettleside for New Year. I consoled myself with the knowledge that Winnie was there. Dazzling, efficient Winnie would take my place.

Eventually, at the beginning of January, I emptied my office— which meant kicking out four workers who had urgent queries for me—and by some miracle managed to get a line through to the North. Araminta answered. 'It's Vi. How are you?'

'How are you? What a surprise! We've still got plum pudding made out of—'

'No, don't tell me.'

'And presents from the children made out of—'

'I know. I'm sorry.'

'Quite. There's a war on. We know. Little Violet cried for ages.'

'Don't be so horrible, Araminta.'

There was a pause. 'I expect I'm rather emotional.'

'It's an emotional time.'

'I didn't mean that. I meant me in particular.' She paused again.

'The baby. You can't have had the baby yet!'

'Not exactly.' Her voice stopped being cold and became rich and proud. I realised she had had the baby.

'Boy or girl?'

'Both.'

'What?'

'Twins. I had another set of twins.' She began to laugh—I must say, rather weakly. 'I've been longing to tell you. I absolutely couldn't wait to hear your mixture of horror and healousy. Twins, Vi. Quite individual, with fluffy hair like birds' feathers and delicious fat little tummies. Oh, I do love babies!'

'When were they born?'

'19 December. What a miracle it all is! Even Leonard's pleased. You know he came up for Christmas? Well, when they started coming and we realised they were twins, I had to go into Newcastle Hospital, so Leonard drove me and then he actually watched them being born.'

'Leonard!'

'The hospital had just filled up with a contingent of sailors with oil in their lungs, so there wasn't anyone to operate the gas and air. His family's absolutely riddled with twins, you know. The midwife said with a history like his, it's amazing I've had two single babies. Did you know he was a twin but his opposite number died?'

'No.'

'He's not the man to have an affair with,' said Araminta, echoing my own thoughts disconcertingly. 'No,' she went on, in such a firm manner that for a moment I even wondered if Leonard could have told her about us. It was not impossible. Although I would be humiliated, they were quite likely to use it as another brick in the strange surface of their marriage.

'Can I speak to Nettles?' I said quickly, which, to my surprise, produced a silence not unlike those earlier in our conversation. 'Isn't he in?'

'I expect so. I expect Winnie will know where he is.'

'I'm so glad Winnie's staying. She's such a wonderful person. She must cheer up Nettles. Give her my love, won't you?'

'If I were you, I'd give her something quite different.'

'What ever do you mean?'

'Nettles has fallen for your wonderful friend,' said Araminta coolly. 'It's perfectly natural with you away all this time. She was here over all the holidays and all the weekends before that. She's back again now for another weekend.'

I did not believe Araminta, but even the thought of Nettles' loving someone else gave me a terrifying feeling as if I'd just fallen off the top of a cliff. 'You're emotional,' I said, using my Regional Organiser tone of voice. 'You've just had a baby. Two babies. Why do you suggest things like that, Araminta? It's not right of you.'

'At mealtimes she can't take her eyes off him.'

'I can quite see she might get stuck on him. After all, she's young and there're not many men around. But don't go inferring from that that Nettles'—I began to feel angry—'cares about her.'

'After supper they sit close together on the same sofa. They play games.'

'You have to sit close together if you're playing games! You shouldn't say things like this on the telephone.'

'You don't give me much chance in person.'

'You could have told Leonard. He would have told me.'

'Leonard?' Her emphasis was so filled with possible layers of meaning that I did not pursue that one. But she laughed and said, 'Leonard might easily encourage it. He believes in everyone's freedom to do what they think best. Providing it doesn't hurt someone else.'

'But it does hurt someone else. Me. I love Nettles.'

'Perhaps Nettles is giving you a warning.'

I became suddenly very angry. 'Shut up, Araminta! Your silly suppositions! I don't believe a word you've said. Get back to your babies and your bosoms! I've got a job too. Tell Nettles I'll ring him this afternoon at four.' I slammed down the receiver.

'Oh!' exclaimed one of my WVS girls, popping in the moment she heard the telephone ting. 'You are a lucky one having such a long call without being cut off.'

'I'm not so sure,' I muttered. I grabbed a pile of files from her and threw them one after the other to the floor. 'Fuck!' I screamed. 'Fuck it all!'

My curses, which were heard all over Tothill Street, turned out to be unexpectedly productive. I was immediately ordered to take three weeks' leave and, whatever I did get, right out of London. 'You mustn't be ashamed,' I was told. 'Anyone with your record should expect a crack-up.'

'But I've not cracked up,' I shouted. 'It was nothing to do with the war, with my work. It was something quite separate.'

'Yes, dear,' one of the older organisers soothed me. 'I'm afraid we've abused your public-spirited unselfishness and now you're paying the price. A short break will make all the difference.'

Like the soldier who proves he is too mad for army service by protesting his absolute joy at the prospect, my insistence on working only made them more determined I should go.

It felt odd to be sitting at my kitchen table in the daytime. It wasn't daylight, because to save time I had my blackouts permanently closed. The obvious course of action was to go to Kettleside. I wanted to see the children now that I took time to think about it. I wanted very much to see the children. But that was selfish. Of course they wanted to see me, and Violet cried when I didn't come, but the truth was that they would be very much upset by a short visit. My work with the evacuation of small children had taught me that. I remembered the postscript from the Sussex headmaster coping with East End children: 'They are very happy and settled except when their parents visit them.' I should not go to my children until I intended to stay with them for more than a week or two.

I had to see Nettles. Quite apart from Araminta's despicable insinuations—I needed him near me. There was my night with Leonard to be erased.

The siren went, and as I collected my things together to go down to the basement I realised how much I had missed him, his support and kindness. Perhaps I was heading for a crack-up. On the other hand, I didn't want to meet him at Kettleside. The air would be poisoned by Araminta's accusations. If Winnie was there, my good friend Winnie who'd spent many a night in my basement listening to me talk about Nettles, I couldn't help looking on her with suspicion. I had only known her for a year, after all, since Aunt Phyllis had sent her up to Kettleside. Perhaps she was not as nice and straightforward as she seemed. Araminta would be proud and complacent with her babies; I knew the feeling from my own experience. She would assume I had come to answer her summons. She would nudge me and look for occasions for a further heart-to-heart. I couldn't bear that. My love for Nettles was far too precious to be made public. Worse than that, Leonard might still be there. One could never make any sense out of his time off. If he wasn't there now, he might suddenly appear. Even if he hadn't told Araminta about our night, she would certainly have told him about Winnie.

As I reached my front door and turned to go down to the basement stairs, I decided quite definitely that my reunion with Nettles would not take place at Kettleside. The question was, Where? At which point there was such a thundering on the door that I dropped the biscuits and the WVS bulletin I was carrying, and only just managed to retrieve the wireless. For a second, I even madly thought the bombs had caught me; then, just as madly, I thought with a wild thrill that it was Nettles.

The door opened and revealed a huge, portly man with pallid, anxious face. He took off his steep homburg and revealed a nearly balding head. 'Oh, Lord. Why is everyone else so calm? Why did I ever come? Why did no one tell me that London was a heap of rubble? What man does to man! At least you're here. May I come in? Will the house stand?'

It was Augustus, clearly regretting his departure from Oxford. I pictured nostalgically the gardens, the meadows, the river.

'Come in. Don't worry. The siren always goes ages before the planes come over.'

'I'm not worried. I'm terrified.' He looked at the filthy stairs. 'And to think I lived here once!' He peered into the drawing room piled high with bundles of bedding. 'Protected against the blast, I see. Good. Good.'

'Oh, Augustus,' I took him down the dark stairs. 'That's WVS bedding.'

'Huh.' He just stopped himself tripping. 'I heard you were encouraging the war.'

We reached the basement. 'You can't still be pacifist. Even you must see that Hitler has to be beaten.'

'What about the Russians? That's what I say.' He settled his huge bulk comfortably onto the mattress.

'Not communism,' I protested. 'Not this evening. I just haven't the strength to argue.'

'War's no excuse for laziness,' He raised himself onto his elbow. 'What we need is alcohol. When did you say the planes come?'

'Laziness!' I thought of the last few months.

'Intellectual stagnation. An invitation for any charlatan who calls himself a politician to take over.'

'But Augustus, what are you talking about? This is war. We don't need politicians—'

'What we need is alcohol.'

'We need a war leader like Churchill. We can't afford to think of anything else. We can't afford to think at all. We've just got to fight.'

'Bunkum! Do you think politicians stop being politicians just because there's a war on?'

'Yes.'

'My God. You've been sorting jam too long.'

'I don't sort jam.'

'What do you think your friend Jack, now Minister, is up to? Knitting shrouds?'

'You don't knit shrouds.' Feeling nonplussed by this mention of Jack, I offered to go up and get some wine. When I came back, he looked up from the WVS bulletin.

'Don't sneer,' I said quickly. 'It's very important work. We've a million members now.'

'I wasn't going to.' His aggressive mood seemed to have passed, perhaps now that he felt physically safe. 'I'm impressed. Women have a remarkable power for doing things. Men talk about them.'

'It's because you're looked after by women when you grow up.'

'And by men when you're grown up. The college servants won't let me lift a finger.'

'Perhaps the college servants would make good WVS members.'

'No. More army. They're obsessed by rank. Not like you lot.'

'Natural communists. If women ruled the world, you'd really have cause for worry.'

But Augustus didn't take me up. 'They say Hitler's got a plan to knock out the intellectual manpower of England. I wonder if it's true. And if it is true, I wonder whether I'm on the list. And if it is and I am, I wonder if that makes me feel better.'

'Listen. They might be coming to get you now.' The sound of planes came rumbling closer, followed by the staccato rap of our ack-ack guns—which always made me feel better, though they did little good—and finally the dull thunder of falling bombs. 'They're quite far away,' I said. 'Sounds west. Might be after the factory belt.'

'Good,' said Augustus, who seemed to have quite lost his former fear. He sounded almost absentminded. He always lost touch with his surroundings when his mind was occupied.

'Mind over matter,' I murmured, and yet as I looked at his huge body, a monument to his delight in good food and drink, it was not a totally appropriate comment.

Augustus, carrying on his train of thought, continued, 'It's lonely in Oxford. It's lonely in College. It's lonely being a pacifist.'

'Join the Home Guard, then.'

He smiled and patted my knee. 'It's nice talking to you, Vi. I expect that's why I came to London, though I thought it was to make arrangements for my elegant country mansion. Or else to satisfy my curiosity.' He seemed about to go off again into his problems, but then decided against it. I expect he found it difficult to talk about himself—even while sheltering from bombs, which tended to make most people exceptionally candid. Instead he gave me a congratulatory look which reminded me suddenly of the days when he taught me Latin on Eureka, and said loudly, 'I'm glad to see you've split up with Eleanor's lover.'

'Augustus!' I jumped to my feet. My face must have looked as furious as I felt. He put up his hands beseechingly.

'*Pace! Pace!* Don't send me out to my death. Rather stab me here.'

'It's not funny.' I was not having my rightful anger ridiculed. 'We've been married over five years. We've two children, and I'll not have you making cynical bachelor remarks!'

'And what do you mean by that?' But seeing my fury, he gave in. 'I'm sorry, I really did think you'd parted. Someone told me so. Or that's what I thought they said.'

'We haven't. I was just planning a reunion in some country idyll. Perhaps you can help us. What's all this about a country residence?' I said this not very seriously, but mainly to turn the questions onto Augustus. To my surprise, he looked worried, but burst out unhesitatingly:

'Of course you must borrow it. It's a small manor house in a village five miles from Oxford. The most terrible folly, of course. It's been rejected for war use by the Civil Service, the army, and the Canadians. But I couldn't let the poor dear go to rack and ruin. It cost next to nothing.'

'So you'll live in it?'

'Even the army rejected its sanitation as beyond repair. The word "killer" was used in the report, I believe.'

'The army have the most frightfully high standards. The batmen set the tone.'

'The Canadian army suggested blowing it up. That's when I stepped in.' He looked humble and apologetic. 'I'm so humiliatingly reliant on those college servants, I'm afraid. But if you and'—he paused and took a deep breath—'your husband could find some use for it, you're indeed more than welcome.'

'A manor house in the Oxfordshire countryside would seem like heaven compared with this,' I said.

Augustus heaved himself upright. 'Does your cave run to a lavatory? I fear this wine is more of an irritant than a stimulant. Oh, how the flesh does take over as youth recedes!'

'It should be better than the WVS "Honeymoon Houses",' I said gaily to Nettles over the telephone. We agreed to meet in Oxfordshire.

While I was waiting, I went to visit Molly in Dagenham.

'I'm supposed to be on holiday,' I explained pathetically. 'I've cracked up.'

'What?' Molly didn't even bother with such obvious nonsense. 'Do you think you could lend a hand in the schools? They were closed down after evacuation and a lot of the children disappeared and now, of course, the children are all back again. It's a terrible muddle. There're so many, you see, because this is a modern estate specially built for families. And now the Irish are pouring in to work the factories, the whole thing has become even more congested. That's where I come in, of course.'

'There're no basements,' I said, interrupting her with a sudden nervous realisation. 'For sheltering?'

She looked surprised. 'We've got proper shelters under the tennis courts, but no one ever goes into them. We don't get much bombing here. We get the sirens, all right. Every evening as the planes go over to London. Sometimes I stand at my bedroom window and watch London burning.'

She told me then how she too had watched St Paul's rising above

271

the smoke. To her it had seemed an image of Christianity triumphing. We talked continually during my visit, and I realised that Christianity—or rather, Catholicism—had now become the only thing in Molly's life. She no longer cared about her husband or herself or her friends—except as Jesus bade her. She was totally without worldly ambition too—except for the spread of her church. She had, in effect, dedicated her life to God. She could have been a nun after all.

This did not mean she had become a boring or uninvigorating companion. On the contrary, she had all the energy and enthusiasm of people who know what they want out of life—or rather, what they want to give it. She was an appreciative listener for my blitz stories, and even let me talk about Nettles once I had made it clear how seriously I took our marriage.

'After all,' she said, 'your marriage to Howard was such a ridiculous thing. You could probably even have had it annulled.' It was so long since I'd considered my first marriage that I was nonplussed by this remark. However, seeing it made Nettles more acceptable to her, I quickly agreed. 'I was a child,' I said. 'I married for all the wrong reasons. Or for no reasons at all.'

Our conversations usually took place in a community centre. One evening Father Wilson came over to me, smiling and warm as ever. 'I heard you were here. I'm giving a talk about "Loving your Neighbour in Wartime." I can't tell you what a terrible time some of these POWs are having. I hope you'll listen.'

I assured him I was looking forward to it, and as he went up to the stage I thought that, as ever, he'd made me feel that he understood me completely and that if I gave myself to his cause all would be well. That was what Molly had done. When I was unhappy I had felt threatened by his interest. Now I could face him more boldly, for my work had given me confidence. For some people salvation has to come from inside themselves. Molly would have disagreed.

When Father Wilson had finished speaking, he came over to me again. 'Do you think I went too far?'

'You have to hate in order to fight, don't you?'

'These people aren't fighting. They're working.' He indicated the groups of people round the room. 'They're working for the money. They're mostly Irish anyway. Italy is Catholic.' He stopped and smiled at me. 'I'd better not start again. I last saw you at Molly's wedding. I hear you've been busy since.'

Before we could go further, Molly interrupted with an anxious, excited face. 'You've done it this time, Father. Half the men have left already. You simply mustn't order them to imagine Jesus Christ as a German.'

Father Wilson turned to me. 'Molly is a remarkable woman, but occasionally worries overmuch about numbers. One soul rescued is worth a lifetime's work.' He turned back to Molly. 'Violet and I were just recalling your wedding day.'

'Not my marriage,' protested Molly. 'Not now. I've got the tea to serve, for one thing.'

I couldn't help feeling that Father Wilson was much sterner with those inside the fold than those outside. However, when we reached the urn, instead of saying more to Molly he began to question me about my mother. Was she still living with George's mother on Eureka? Did she still drink as much? And how was her health? I answered him yes, she was still on the island; apparently she drank just as much, but without doing any damage to her health. The two old ladies were quite content, except when they enlivened the monotony of life by a fierce quarrel and refused to speak to each other for a few days. I was surprised at his interest.

I suppose he noticed it, for putting down his teacup, he addressed Molly and me in reproving tones. 'I don't know how you girls come to the idea that you can discard people. Especially your mother, and your husband.'

'My mother discarded me,' I said, thinking that after all he must consider me at least halfway in the fold.

'My husband is going mad,' Molly let off a huge burst of steam from the urn.

'Mad?' I'd always thought George was one of those people who could go mad, given the right circumstances.

'It's his cousin. You remember Henry Briggsworthy? He's moved in with George. Or rather, they've moved out together into a couple of rooms just the other side of the chapel. The Canadian army has moved in.'

'That's enough to drive anyone mad.'

'Mad and drunk. You remember him at Oxford?'

'I remember him at your wedding. He ran naked through the rose garden.'

'George needed a companion when you left.' Father Wilson held out his cup for more tea.

'Don't tell me you believe charity begins in the home, because I just won't believe you.' Molly slopped milk into his saucer and said, 'Sorry,' unconvincingly.

'But I do.' Father Wilson took out a folded piece of a Catholic newspaper and put it into the saucer so that it soaked up the drips. He took a sip and then said to me gently, 'I hope dear Flo is well, and your husband and family?'

'Yes,' I replied, turning away.

When I got back to the rooms I shared with Molly, there was a letter from Nettles waiting for me.

Darling V,
   Can you believe the bad luck? I'm in bed with some sort of silly tummy problem which makes me feel quite wretched and quite incapable of movement. Of course it will be better in a week, but then our week will have gone. Can we arrange it for later? Or perhaps you'll decide to come up here after all? There's no need to on my behalf. Winnie is being an excellent nurse, but I can't help hoping to see you. Why my beastly body lets me down just now I can't imagine. I was so looking forward to seeing you. Perhaps it's old age! Ring me when you can, my darling, darling, adorable Violet. Love and hugs, Nettles.

I was just lying back for a tearful consideration of all the most gloomy inferences from this letter when the telephone call box in the hall rang. Crossly, because I expected no call and I didn't want my misery disturbed, I went downstairs.

It was Winnie calling from Kettleside. Only Winnie could have tracked me down. Her voice with its cheerful good nature soothed me despite everything. 'I've just got Nettles' letter,' I said.

'He was worried he'd made it sound too worrying. He asked me to ring. He doesn't want you to come up. The weather's dreadful. Freezing and wet. He's determined to come for a recuperation to Augustus' mansion, but he wants to leave it till April.'

'April!' I was horrified.

'When the weather's nicer.' Winnie had begun to shout, but even so her voice was fading into a rattle like ack-ack fire.

'I must come up!' I screamed. Her protests were unintelligible.

I had already packed my bags when Molly returned. She read the letter. I told her about Winnie's call.

'Poor Nettles. It doesn't sound to me at all as if this Winnie's trying to nab him.'

'You don't think so?'

'She'd never have rung you. Go back to the war till April. It's only for a couple of months. You were keen enough to leave him for it.'

I felt differently about my work in 1941. The drama and initial excitement, even the fear had left me. Now I had a more sensible idea of what people meant when they talked about duty. Even on the terrible night of 19 March when 751 civilians were killed and 1,170 injured, I found myself keeping slightly apart from the tragedy of it all. To the outsider I may have seemed more involved because my lack of fear made me unwilling to spend any more hours sheltering in some dank

274

basement. Now I worked through sirens—in company with many others who after five months of continuous bombs were feeling much the same as I was.

But my reaction was also personal. Although I had accepted Nettles' plan, I felt a constant ill-defined worry which I knew could not be settled till we met in April. At the same time I was beginning to be frustrated by the limitations of an organisation reliant on part-time women.

There were moments of pride. We were proud when the Queen came to our clothing depot in Eaton Square. We were proud when we raked in the last £500 needed to make up the money for our third Hurricane. We were proud and amused when our fame reached India and His Highness the Nawab Ruler of Bahamalpur presented us with a mobile canteen. I had my last moment of private satisfaction when a taxi driver I instructed to take me to Tothill Street—my car, surviving blast, had finally succumbed to shrapnel—refused to accept any payment. 'You ladies in green,' he said, 'I don't know what London would do without you. Last night, my wife and kids were bombed out. One of your lot took them over. Found them beds, food, even washed their clothes. And you know what struck my wife most, shocked as she was—there were real fresh flowers on the table. Imagine that! In a war. In March. Fresh flowers!'

April came at last. Nettles had written of a heavy snowfall in March, so I was terrified it would make the journey impossible. But April produced enough sun, and after dealing with last-minute requests for 120 white gloves for traffic control and an unlimited supply of cotton reels needed for use 'in the construction of Army telephonic communications,' I set off for Oxfordshire. I had a distinct suspicion that the WVS was not using my capabilities to the full. It was difficult to avoid the realisation that however hard I worked, I was basically making up for deficiencies farther up the line, in the Council, the Forces, or the politicians. I needed to be farther up the line.

I had arranged a lift to Oxford with some evacuated children. They had the gaunt greyness of blitzed London. One of them cried for the whole journey. We'd all just been immunised against diphtheria and typhoid. I hoped I didn't look as bad as they did.

Chapter Eleven

Hope! Faith! Confidence! in Times of Stress. 'Aspro' calms and comforts.
(Advertisement) *The Times.* 9 May 1941

PARLIAMENT: WVS AND POLITICS

Sir H. Williams (Croydon S.N.) asked the Home Secretary whether members of the Womens Voluntary Service were free to express their political opinions and to engage in political activities when off duty. . . . Mr Morrison said that . . . members of the service had, so far as he was aware, the same freedom of speech and action in regard to political matters as other members of the community.
The Times. 9 May 1941

WOMEN OF THE EMPIRE

Sir, It is time the Government of our country took the women-power of the Empire into account. British women are in the front line and have proved not only their courage but their ability to rise to any and every emergency. When will the Government give the lead to authorities throughout the country and appoint women as well as men to creative posts?
Yours etc., Evelyn Emmet
Amberley Castle, Amberley, Sussex.
(Letter to the Editor) *The Times.* 14 May 1941

Dowager Lady Sysonby wishes to LET her charming Regency House, 7 miles from Bath; bus route, 4 sitting, 10 bedrooms, 4 bath, electric light and heating; large, well-stocked garden; garage for 2 cars and chauffeur's rooms; three maids left; linen and plate. 23 gns. per week inclusive.
(Personal column) *The Times.* 6 June 1941

I was dropped at the driveway of Babstock Manor in the late afternoon. It had rained. The sky was still streaky, the air fresh and damp, but some yellow sun was beginning to pierce the clouds. The driveway was overgrown with dark rhododendrons budding with mauve-and-pink flowers. Occasionally a tall yew tree crested the flat shiny leaves, as if once there had been a more formal design. The surface of the road was a bright orange, pitted with soggy holes. I noticed with foreboding that my impractical high-heeled shoes, on which I had used most of my coupons, had exchanged their smart shine for a sandy dankness. I remembered, for the first time since he'd made them, Augustus' remarks about the house's sanitation and feared that our reunion would fester in an odour of decay.

The driveway turned sharply, and I found myself faced by a vast spreading carpet of golden daffodils. Their brightness made it seem as if the sun had come out fully. I was so dazzled that it took me a moment to see the small stone manor house behind and, sitting on a low wall in front, Nettles.

He jumped up the moment he saw me, and I barely had time to notice he was thinner—but then, we were all thinner in 1941—before we were together.

Neither of us spoke, but as we stood there in each other's arms, I was aware not only of his closeness but also of the daffodils at our feet and the house behind us, even the sun, and I felt that all would be well.

'I've lit a fire,' he said as we walked arm in arm to the house, 'in what I take to be the drawing room and in our bedroom.'

'Oh dear,' I laughed rather hysterically, 'is it as bad as that?'

'The sanitation is remarkable,' said Nettles. 'Remarkably extensive. The Canadian army put in five bathrooms and seven lavatories before they decided the house was hopeless.'

'They must have used up all the rooms.' I began to laugh again. I felt so wonderfully joyous. 'You are well, aren't you Nettles? I was so anxious.'

He didn't answer me immediately but pushed me forward into the house. 'Of course I am. Right turn to the fire.'

'Look,' I said as we entered a low, long room with mullioned windows in which a large fire blazed, 'the sun's brighter than the flames. Isn't that wonderful?'

'You see'—Nettles pulled me down beside him on a sofa so that we sat pinpointed between fire and sunlight—'I was putting off my visit for the spring.'

'That's what Molly said.' I kissed him. Refusing to recognise that he had grown older in less than a year, that his eyes had a sadness I didn't remember. I decided not to ask him about his illness, about

Winnie. Not for a while, anyway. And I think he made the same sort of decision, for we both drew back for a moment. Then I said, 'We'll be happy together. Two weeks of utterly selfish happiness.'

And he said, 'I want to hold you forever. I want you lying beside me. I want you to be mine again.'

'We'll go upstairs and stay there for a week.'

As we went up the wide, shallow stairs, which were uncarpeted and surprisingly polished, I thought that already my night with Leonard was erased. Even five minutes with Nettles made me realise how different our affection was. 'I love you,' I whispered in his ear.

'I'll tell you what I think of you later,' he said.

'A bathroom for every day of the week!' I cried out because I felt too happy and we were faced at the top of the stairs with a row of new shiny doors.

'And a rest day on Sundays.' Nettles led me through a wide doorway.

We slept together after making love. It was dark when we awoke. I lay for a long while trying to believe in our happiness. I went over our meeting again and again. I could not believe I had really seen that row of newly painted doors outside the bedroom. Eventually I got up, careful to avoid waking Nettles, and crept onto the landing.

'It is ridiculous, isn't it?' He came and found me sitting on the floor smiling idiotically. He crouched down beside me. His arm rested along my shoulder. 'I love you too,' he said.

'I'll get us some supper,' I said. 'If there's any food.'

'There's everything.' We started down the stairs together. 'Except a telephone.'

The weather became ridiculously hot for April. Nettles worked in the garden, clearing great stretches of tangled vegetable garden as a thank-you for Augustus. We talked about Kettleside, the farm and the children. How we wanted them to grow up and how lucky little Violet was to have Nanny for her physical needs and Miss Tiptree for her mental needs. I pointed out that I'd had them too, but Nettles answered that I hadn't had the advantage of a mother and father. This made me very happy for various reasons, but firstly because it implied that he did not feel I had deserted them or him. And if he didn't feel deserted, then how could he have taken up with Winnie? I even dared tentatively to mention her name. He was cutting through a great bramble at the time, but he did not suddenly slice his hand or prick his finger or show any other signs of emotion. Once again I decided to leave the subject alone. He spoke affectionately of Araminta and the new twins. He said Leonard had been much more amenable to the sight of his offspring than usual, actually holding them on one occasion—and since I didn't trip over my hoe at the mention of his name, I suppose that should have worried me. But it didn't. He told me, which I hadn't known before, that they had two recuperating airmen in the house. The beautiful golden-skinned blue-eyed Isabel Royston had been delegated to attending their welfare, with the result that she was besotted by each in turn. One was handsome and one was amusing. The handsome one had lost an eye, the amusing one a leg. At the moment she favoured the legless, amusing one, but we both decided the black patch would win in the end.

We slept and ate whatever strange food the village shop happened to have in that week, and except for the number of planes which passed high in the golden air, we managed to forget almost entirely about the war. We had agreed not to bring a wireless. If a German had appeared in our lane and in lieu of hidden signposts asked the way to Oxford, we'd have assumed without question that we were now an occupied country.

But we were as optimistic about the war as about everything else. The idea that the blitz continued in London and that I would soon return to it seemed absolutely unbelievable. I said to Nettles, 'This is the happiest time of my life. It's much better than our honeymoon. I suppose that's wrong when so many are suffering and dying.'

'No,' he said simply. 'I don't think so. I'm glad.' I turned to him and noticed again that sadness I'd seen when we first met.

'You're tired.' He'd been working all afternoon, and he held a glass of water in his hand. 'Gardening's supposed to be for pleasure.'

'It is.' He smiled.

The next morning Augustus arrived on a bicycle. He was scarlet in the face, perspiring heavily, and more or less crash-landed in the driveway. Trying hard not to laugh, I dragged him inside the house.

'I've come to apologise,' he spluttered.

'Oh, dear. It must be something dreadful to get you on a bicycle. Have you sold the house over our heads?' That was the only possibility I could take at all seriously.

'It's that uncouth Polish import of Leonard's. No wonder the Germans smashed them up. She stopped me working for a whole morning.'

'Katynka?'

'Silly name.'

'Silly girl.'

'She came to me after Leonard about some hysterical story. Some man. Her father. One or the other, I don't know. I don't know where Leonard is. Who does know where Leonard is? But she went on and on, and in the course of it all I found she'd wheedled out of me where you were. So now she's on her way here. Hotfoot, since I've got her bike. She hasn't arrived yet, by any chance?'

'Not unless she's hiding.'

'She wouldn't do that. More's the pity. That's his name, incidentally. Moore. You don't happen to have a bottle of wine open, I suppose?'

'I'll call Nettles in and we'll have lunch. We love your house, Augustus. Don't worry about Katynka; I can cope with her.'

Despite Augustus' terror of Katynka's appearing, we had a wonderfully enjoyable lunch. When Nettles appeared, Augustus cried out as if rehearsed for the event, 'You have my only house and my only woman friend, so you'd better have my friendship too!' They shook hands with absurd enthusiasm. The food was particularly revolting, some kind of tinned cockles or mussels in tomato sauce, but we drank so much wine that when I produced my masterpiece, a whole genuine onion, Augustus recited over and over again the cook's ode so that in the end we all knew it and shouted in unison:

O pungent root, so lately dear to me,
Though bulbous, aromatic rarity . . .
Today thou art a treasure vainly sought . . .

Since Augustus was clearly incapable of ever mounting a bicycle, we proceeded drunkenly to the village, where by some miracle a delivery van was returning to Oxford. We heaved him in, waving cheerfully even as he thrust a clenched fist through the window and shouted, 'Give that to the Poles! Who needs a guilty conscience? Not me!'

In fact, I felt perfectly able to cope with any histrionics from Katynka. I was certainly not going to allow her to spoil my idyll with Nettles. I had always felt her place in my household was stretching our generosity to the limit. Our only connection was through Araminta, and although she had always worked to help, I had never actually liked her. She was so foreign, sinuous, and outspoken. She was an un-English dun colour—all over: hair, skin, and eyes—and when she got excited threw her body around. The more I thought about her on that warm drunken afternooon, the more prepared I was permanently to sever our connection. Let her rely on Mrozek, since she had chosen him!

Nettles had gone into the garden and I was making a pot of tea when there were passionate pantings at the window.

'Oh, you are there!' She was through the door in a moment and, before I could take up appropriate repelling action, had cast herself onto the floor at my feet. 'Only you can save me!'

'Honestly, Katynka . . .'

'I adore him! I love him! He is everything to me! The world! I am not living before he comes! I am now the living dead!'

'Felix Moore is . . .' I tried again.

'My father!' she shrieked. 'My father I love! I love my father!'

I subsided into a chair. 'So you should,' I said under my breath. But it was no good. Irony could not cope with real despair. I put another cup of tea on the tray. 'Get up, Katynka, do. The floor's awash with earwigs.'

The story was that Mrozek had not, as he had told me, married on arrival in England; that he was already married, with a daughter in Poland. Leonard had discovered for him that the mother had died and offered to bring out the daughter. But when he arrived with Katynka, Mrozek had persuaded him not to reveal his identity, since he was in no position to look after her, but to hand her over to Araminta. Now that Katynka was grown up, he had decided to unmask himself. He had decided a sudden revelation would be too upsetting, which was why he had captured Katynka from Kettleside to work at The Moore Press.

As Katynka talked, protesting at intervals her undying love for her father, I began to feel that my first reaction had after all been the right one. 'You should love your father,' I said firmly.

'Not like this.' Katynka clutched her stomach and bent double. 'This is a love with my body.'

'All girls feel that about their father,' I continued briskly. 'Usually when they are too young to realise it. Because you have only just met your father, you are naturally older. That makes your feelings more intense, perhaps more physical. But there's nothing wrong in it. When you fall in love with a man who is not your father, you'll find it quite different.'

'But I fell in love with him when he was not my father.'

'He always was.' I spoke even more severely. 'Your body knew.'

'Do you think so?' Katynka stopped writhing about and actually sat down on a chair.

'Of course I do. The relationship with a father is just as exciting as with a lover. More so in many cases because it lasts longer. You should be celebrating that you have found a father who you— admire, not tangling yourself in emotional self-indulgent knots.'

'Could I have a cup of tea now?'

'Certainly. And some food. And then I want you to go back to your father and start again.'

I was determined not to allow Katynka to tell her story to Nettles. Despite my firmness with her, I felt greatly upset. It had brought back all the emotions of my falling in love with Nettles. In an odd way her experience had been the exact reverse of my own. I had fallen in love with a man whom I had thought of as my father, and therefore unavailable, but who in fact was not. She loved a man whom she took to be available as a lover, but who in fact was her father. It was an aspect of our marriage that had always concerned me and always would, and the last thing I wanted was to relive it during this brief interlude of happiness.

Luckily, the reverse of Katynka's sudden passions was sudden calms. Within a few moments she had entered a dreamy state of self-absorption. After several silent cups of tea and slices of bread, she informed me that she wanted to see her father again to judge whether what I said I was right. I gave her money, more food, a sweater and, taking the bicycle from under a hedge, pointed her in the direction of the station.

'Incidentally,' I said, as she loaded up. 'You upset Professor Budd most dreadfully.'

'He is too fat,' she answered decisively. 'Besides, he stole my bicycle. He should pull himself together or he will begin to rot.'

This showed me more clearly than anything else that she was herself again and perfectly capable of rising above Hitler's Poland, British Rail in wartime, and incestuous love for a father. I waved her off with tremendous relief and a feeling that my head was about to drop off.

'Why did we drink so much at lunch?' I groaned to Nettles. We stood holding cups of tea by some old raspberry canes.

'Because we were happy.'

'It's strange,' I said. 'Our happiness was built on us being alone together, away from children, away from Kettleside, but now I feel restless again.'

'You said you wanted to visit Molly's husband at Didcot.'

'We'd have to borrow bicycles.'

We set off early, determined to cover the twenty-five miles by lunchtime. The sunny weather had changed to a light drizzle, and Nettles had the strained, thin look again, which I was still determined to attribute to overwork in the garden. We rode side by side, pedalling slowly. Nettles held a large map on his handlebars, since the signposts had mostly been removed, and if we did see one standing, we assumed it was spun in the wrong direction to foil the Huns.

After about fifteen miles, we stopped and I unpacked a thermos flask and a packet of sandwiches. The rain had ceased and we sat on Nettles' coat. The grass was already long around us, and a weeping willow, growing out of sight of stream or habitation, spread its delicate fingers above us. I thought this could be the happiest moment of my life—selfishly happy. I said so to Nettles, who looked pleased, but when I asked whether it was for him too, he said yes, but he missed the children.

'Little Violet,' he said, 'is both grown up for her age and very

283

childish. She has learned from the older children to carry on an adult conversation or train of thought; she reads books far too old for most six-year-olds; but she is also very dependent on people. She won't do what she's told, and she cries if anyone is cross with her.'
'I'm surprised at Nanny,' I said defensively.
'Nanny is very busy. Violet must learn to fit in.'
'How strange. I so longed to fit in. And there was no one ever to fit in with—until I met you.'
'Tudor's quite different. He reminds me of your Uncle Eddie, Eleanor's brother.'
'I don't remember him.'
'They look the same. Dark curly hair and blue eyes.'
'I thought Tudor's eyes were green and his looks came from you.'
'Eddie went off to Canada after the First World War. I've never seen him since. He was my friend and why I met Eleanor.'
'I don't want to talk about her.'
'I would like to know what happened to Eddie.'
'I want to bicycle again.' The whispering willow fingers had lost their charm.
'I don't think you have to worry about Tudor.'
'I wasn't.'
We bicycled on. Thin clouds collected high above us and stretched like a muslin cloth over the sun. We lost our way several times, once finding ourselves unpleasantly close to a military enclosure with barbed-wire rolls and notices painted with skulls perched among the spikes. Even more unpleasantly, we skirted an air base, so that for about twenty minutes we were surrounded by threatening noise. Eventually we passed into peaceful country again and,-with inspired map reading, managed to avoid any signs of human habitation for about an hour. By this time it was after one, and I suddenly had my doubts about the expedition. Would George be able to produce lunch for unexpected guests? Would he want unexpected guests? Would mad and drunk Cousin Henry be unacceptably mad and drunk?
'Shall we go and find a nice pub for lunch?'
'Certainly not. I'm looking forward to returning to the place where we fell in love.'
All was restored. We rode through the white-painted gates, now noticeably more rusty than in the past, at half-past one. We were immediately saluted by two officers in unfamiliar uniforms strolling towards us. The front driveway was filled with cars and jeeps.
'I can't think why they saluted us,' I said, feeling very hot, tired, and dirty.
'Perhaps it was ironic.'

'I'm sure Canadians don't have that sort of sense of humour.' I was struck by a wild suspicion. I wheeled round on my bicycle. The officers were now marching briskly towards the gates. 'It's George,' I cried. 'Don't you recognise him? And Henry. George! Henry!' I called, and began to bicycle as fast as I could after them. 'George! Henry! George! It's me! I've come to see you.'

Nettles got off his bike and stood watching me. It must have been a weird sight, for the two soldiers reacted to my cries by breaking into a jog which soon turned into a fast run. The more I shouted the faster they ran. Despite my exhaustion, I put on a spurt and overtook them just before the gates. I quickly jumped off my bike and, swinging it like a barrier across their path, took up an aggressive attitude.

'It's me,' I said again, my panting making me crosser. 'What ever are you doing? Do you think I'm a German or something? Though if that's the case it doesn't say much for the army!'

They both stopped, though I noticed that George kept a firm hold on Henry's arm. I must say his face was filled with pleasure and relief when he recognised me. Henry, on the other hand, looked fixedly ahead with a furious unheeding scowl.

'Vi!' George took off his cap. His blond hair was cut very short and stood up like ruffled feathers in the wind. That, with his beaklike nose, made him look more birdlike than ever. 'We thought you were something important to do with the Canadian army. At least, Henry did. He thought you might reprove us for our unmilitary bearing.'

'Is that likely?' I said, with scorn.

'Henry doesn't need things to be likely. Quite the reverse.' George was humble, and I had the strong impression he wanted me to stay and was afraid I might flee.

'And what about your uniforms?' I said mellowing. 'They're a little unusual, aren't they?' As I looked closer, I saw that they were totally unbelievable.

'Bits and pieces from the acting chest,' said George apologetically. 'My father's coat, my uncle's medals—you know the sort of thing.' He darted a quick look at Henry, who stood statue-still, apparently unhearing and unseeing. 'Keeps him happy. Inferiority complex with so many soldiers around. Medically unfit.'

'I should think so,' I said. 'If you're not going anywhere special, perhaps you can reverse march and allow us to visit you.'

'I'd love that.' George was so pathetically grateful at my restored humour that I even began to feel guilty. The situation did not seem to be of his making. I indicated Nettles leaning on his bicycle.

'That's my husband. I expect you remember him. We've come from near Oxford. I want to tell you about Molly and all sorts of things.'

285

'I'll give Henry the order. With any luck, I'll get him strolling off duty rather than marching. Officers of Company B, about turn and reverse march to quarters! At ease! Off duty! Stroll!'

As George bellowed these odd orders, which nevertheless did turn Henry to face the house, I had a distinct feeling of déjà vu. Only as we reached Nettles did I recognise it as being a remembrance of that occasion during the General Strike sixteen years ago, when Henry had arrived at the docks with the drunken Varsity Squad.

George was living in the stables, at praying distance from the chapel. On our arrival he dismissed Henry to his room, advising him his buttons needed a good polish and his webbing a good whiting. He offered us lunch. A slightly helpless tone in his voice made me look at Nettles, who was sitting, exhausted, in a chair, and offer to get it myself.

'If you really think . . . The trouble is . . .' We went together to the kitchen. Even my WVS training had not prepared me for quite such a scene of squalor. Saucepans, plates, ashtrays, glasses, cups, frying pans, all filthy, were piled in the sink and on every other available surface, including the stove, and inside an open fridge.

'I'm afraid the woman who does for us hasn't been in lately. She's in mourning. Her son was killed a month or two ago. She did say she'd send her daughter, but the Canadians put her off. I'm out on the farm a lot, and Henry's not capable . . . Of course, you can't expect everything to be the same in wartime.'

'But how do you eat?'

'Out of tins now. From the Canadians. We've discovered tinned food is just as nice cold as hot. It's all precooked, you know. Occasionally they invite me in for a hot supper. I've got a ham hidden away somewhere, and I know there's some bread. It's just a question of finding a plate and a knife.'

'Don't worry, George. I'll cope. You go and talk to Nettles.' As he retreated thankfully, I wondered how the English upper classes had survived for so long; and then, recalling that he had offered us ham, an unheard-of luxury, and that he had just found himself a free charlady, I decided it was not so odd after all.

Over bread and ham and George's protestations of undying gratitude for my help, I attempted to introduce the subject of Molly. Gradually his unwillingness to talk, where always before their problems had been our main topic, made me realise that the situation had changed.

He had possessed Molly, if only for a few years, and it had not been the answer to life. Although he did not blame her, he was disillusioned and once again had fixed on the Catholic Church as the only possible saviour. I thought it odd that both Molly and he had come to this conclusion, and yet instead of bringing them together it had driven them farther apart. I half-suggested this and he immediately understood, saying, 'But Molly's an active Christian, a soldier of Christ, and I'm a contemplative. I believe in the power of prayer primarily.'

'But what about Henry?' I asked. 'Looking after him's active Christianity, isn't it?'

'I'm fond of Henry. He's part of my family.'

He wouldn't answer any more, turning away from me, and it was only later, when he began to ask about our children, that I realised the real problem between Molly and George was still their inability to produce children.

Henry was very like a six-year-old boy. When he felt secure, he lost the stony silence and became playful and excited. He was not violent, George explained, but very sensitive and easily hurt. This was why George couldn't put him in a mental hospital, for without a constant sense of his affection he would commit suicide. George had found someone who needed his love.

After lunch he looked at his watch and, since it was now four o'clock, suggested diffidently that we join him for tea at the house. He had been invited to meet someone, he said, but he couldn't remember who it was. It would come back to him. We declined on grounds of the long ride home and had actually mounted our bicycles when he came running after us. 'It's your uncle, Vi!' he shouted. 'Or rather, his son! In the Canadian army. You must stay!'

It was most peculiar to be sitting in George's drawing room with half a dozen Canadian officers, one of whom was my first cousin. I felt spectacularly scruffy and tired beside their gleaming youth. It was a relief, at least, that George had exchanged his uniform for tweeds and firmly locked Henry into the stables.

Eddie Pemberton, as he was called like his father, did not resemble Tudor in any way. Instead of being thin and dark, he was tall and fair and very Canadian. We were all excited by the coincidence of our arrival, and by the way Eddie looked at Nettles, I felt sure he knew the family history.

'My father died,' he said, 'five years ago, when I was fifteen, but I've always wanted to get to England. I guess I was the only person glad to see war declared.'

It struck me that his ideas of England must be pretty odd if they were based on tales of my family, and George and Henry's establishment. 'You know my mother lives with George's mother on her island?' I said.

'Eureka.' His glance went to Nettles again.

'Two batty old ladies,' I said firmly. 'One crazed with drink and

287

one crazed with religion.'

'That's a bit strong Vi,' protested George, but I changed the subject to my uncle. He had been run over by a train at a railway crossing while supervising the arrival of a consignment of grain. Eddie Junior described him as the owner of a large mill, though I had the feeling that a second meeting might produce a slightly different description. At the moment, I had a strong urge to go home. Eddie arranged for a soldier to drive us, bicycles and all. He apologised profusely for not being able to take us himself, and his warmth was so endearing that I told him about my work at the WVS and invited him, when he came to London, to look me up in Tothill Street.

As we left, I confessed to Nettles that he had made me feel old and tired. 'He's so fresh-faced and confident.'

'He's nineteen. He wants to conquer the world.'

'Uncle Eddie ended under a train.'

'I can't find my past, my Eddie in this Eddie.'

'You were getting your generations confused.'

Nettles took my hand.

After our visit to George, I had a sudden panicky feeling that our honeymoon holiday time was running out. I lost all desire to see anyone from outside, and we reverted to our country routine. The only communication came from a postcard from Katynka, saying with strange formality, 'Thank you for your help. My father and I have moved to an arrangement. Yours, Catherine Moore.'

Then, the day before we were to leave, two letters arrived. One came from a WVS colleague expecting my return, and asking if I'd heard of the terrible bombing from 16 April to 19 April. On the first night alone, over a thousand had been killed and eighteen hospitals damaged. The other was from wartime Civil Service department pointing out that my unoccupied house was a fire risk and what did I plan to do with it?

Suddenly the interlude was over and the war was all around us again. I showed the second letter to Nettles, asking his advice, and he said that it all depended on the state of the house. Seeing a way to put off our separation, I suggested immediately, 'Why don't you come and see?'

If he had demurred at all, I'm sure I would have realised that it was a silly reason to drag a man into the blitz, but he, perhaps feeling the same as I, instantly agreed. I had got out of the habit of considering London a dangerous city. It was where I worked, and I wanted to talk about my work.

First of all, we would celebrate. I planned, with the excitement of the reprieved prisoner, the night we should share in London. 'We'll go to the Café de Londres,' I crowed. 'I shall get my hair permed and

288

you'll wear a suit. Did you pack a suit?'

My childish elation at the prospect of a meal cooked by someone else in surroundings where one was expected to relax and enjoy without guilt persisted through the sadness of closing up Babstock, and the hour's train journey that took five. It was only when we took a tube from Paddington, and found many of the stations already filling with mothers and children preparing for the night ahead, that I looked at Nettles' tired wondering face and began to have doubts.

He saw me looking and said, 'Let's have our celebration tonight and look at the house before I go tomorrow morning.' I agreed, realising he couldn't face a gloomy look at bomb damage without a good night's sleep. The walk from the tube to my flat was bad enough. It was late afternoon, the sky already growing dark, helped by a thickening bank of clouds. To an old hand in the blitz that was a happy sight, but to a newcomer like Nettles it merely added to the desolation of the scene.

'This part of London is relatively unscathed,' I protested, as his eyes turned from craters in the ground to gardens ravaged and without their iron railings, to houses sliced in half like cheese, or churches burned into prehistoric skeletons. 'Well, at least that won't happen much more.' I pointed to the blackened ribs. 'Not now we've got the fire-watching properly organised. Since January the men have been conscripted to guard every untenanted building. I'm pressing for women to do their rota too. Even now many wives who have minimal family responsibilities get off without doing any war work at all. It's all the men's fault, of course; they like to think of England's women keeping the home fires burning. Service wives are an absolute scandal. They get exempt from absolutely everything in some idiotic sentimental theory that our fighting men's morale is of number one importance. There's a war at home too, you know!'

I stopped, because we had reached my flat, and turned to Nettles. His face wore a slightly surprised, slightly amused look. I laughed. 'I suppose I'm back on the job.'

'I'm glad to see you in operation firsthand.'

'I want to talk to you about that.' I took him a block farther along to where a little shop had been damaged.

He read the govenment notice pinned to the boarding round it: 'WARNING! LOOTING. Looting from premises which have been damaged by or vacated by reason of war operations is punishable by death or penal servitude for life. Is there much looting?'

'More than anyone admits. That's awful, of course, but even worse is the government belief that they can bully people into behaving properly. What you've got to do is train them.'

'In a war?'

'After the war.' I began to speak eagerly, trying clumsily to find words for something I had never articulated before. 'I want to get involved in making people think what it means to be part of society. Particularly women whose scope up till now has been limited to the kitchen, or if you're better off, the drawing room. I want to make them realise that they've got as many responsibilities to society in general as the men, and more reason to care, as it's their babies who go out into it. I want little Violet to grow up realising that she can do anything she wants in the world, just like a man. That she has an actual duty to use her talents. That marriage is only part of life, not an end in itself. I don't want my daughter to waste thirty-five years of her life like I did.'

Again I stopped, as we had returned to the flat, and again looked at Nettles. Although he looked interested rather than reproachful, I corrected my last sentence: 'Thirty years of my life. If I hadn't met you, I would never have escaped from myself. Oh, darling Nettles, don't look sad.' I leaned forward to kiss him.

'I don't feel sad,' he said. 'I feel pleased. And proud.'

I laughed, feeling pleased and proud myself. 'There's a better notice down the road. Outside a bombed but still operating barber's shop. "We've had a close shave. Come and get one yourself."'

Cheered with each other and the times, we went upstairs and prepared for the evening. No siren had yet gone. At about seven-thirty, as we stood on the corner of the street and a real-life taxi like Cinderella's coach appeared to take us to dinner, Nettles said, 'Everything seems right tonight. I'll soon begin to believe the destruction is all cardboard. A stage set.'

'Before the lights go up.'

We got into the taxi and I told him where to go.

'It isn't even raining.'

'Only that lovely big mattress of clouds above us.'

The taxi driver, who was talkative and knowledgeable, took us down streets with a minimum of the usual irritating diversions. 'Always well to be early at the Café de Londres,' he advised. 'It's a popular spot—a lucky spot, if you know what I mean. No one expects anything to happen there. Although the tables in the middle get taken first, if you know what I mean. Given the choice, the customers prefer to avoid the window tables if you know what I mean.'

He had made very clear what he meant, but Nettles and I in our euphoria thought him a ghoulish old goon, and joked as we went into the restaurant about the pleasure people took in fearing the worst. I told him about my ARP warden whom I imagined languishing miserably without a receptive audience for his horror stories, and Nettles told me about one of the land girls who insisted upon wearing

290

a helmet because she had heard that German pilots took a particular delight in machine-gunning women field workers.

We were placed neither in the centre of the room nor by a window, but by an Emergency Exit, which we both agreed should satisfy our driver. Most tables were already filled, almost entirely by men and women in service uniforms. The black and white of the waiters, the khaki and dark blues of the customers seemed inappropriate to the crimson walls and the gaudy little red lamps on each table. It was so long since I had eaten out without wearing my own dark WVS uniform that I wondered for a moment whether this would spoil our evening.

'Don't you wish you were escorted by a dashing young officer with a couple of stripes on his arm and a baton under the table?'

'I saw one like that,' I said. 'He was my first cousin.'

'And he made you feel old and tired.'

'Quite.' I laughed. Looking around again, I had a strong sense of the transitoriness of the scene. I imagined that the clothes people wore, the uniforms and tailcoats, were made of paper, hung round their shoulders by little clips, ready to be lifted off for another scene. And that scene, I thought, consciously working on the image now, would be the end of the war. Then these unreal figures disguised in paper uniformity would become clothes in their true colours and reveal themselves to be like us, real people.

'We're the only real people here,' I said. 'The others are playing Charades.'

'The war seems to me like that, often. Because I'm outside it, I suppose. But I'm surprised you feel that.'

'It's the strength of your personality.' I watched Nettles smile. 'I feel as if a puff of smoke could blow away all these important military men with their moustaches and serious self-satisfaction.'

'Do you mean you think the war's near ending?'

'I don't know. I don't think so. It's not as simple as that. Just a feeling that the stage might fill with smoke like when the genie comes, and when it clears, there'll be another set of characters.'

The glowing redness of the room, the swathed and tasselled curtains did give the restaurant a fairly obvious resemblance to a theatre. Our waiter brought us wine and bread. As we ordered, he lectured us enthusiastically about Lord Woolton and his Ministry of Food. When Nettles told him he was a farmer, he became very excited and kept repeating, 'We're both fighting on The Kitchen Front, then! Both members of the great Kitchen Front army!' He shook Nettles' hand several times and advised us that a rare consignment of liver had just arrived.

The liver, deliciously crisp and delicate-looking, with even a blob of something resembling butter on the top, had just arrived when the siren went. Nettles looked at me for guidance. Not being a Londoner, he didn't know what action to take. I looked round. No one appeared to be moving. Our Kitchen Front waiter appeared at Nettles' side.

'If you wish, sir, we have a basement shelter.'

Nettles nodded at the other diners. 'What about them? Will they go?'

'A few might. But mostly they won't want to interrupt their dinner. A nice evening out and a proper meal is really quite an event for them.'

'So it is for us,' I said.

'Begging your pardon, Ma'am, but they may be more used to the air raids than you or your husband, seeing as you come from the country. That's why I presumed to advise you of the existence of our cellar.'

'Thank you'—Nettles smiled at me—'but it is a celebration for us, and I think we'll stay with the others.' He took my hand across the table. 'My wife is an old hand at this sort of thing.'

So we began our liver, which was as delicious as it looked. In the next few minutes several tables became empty, but not enough to alter the atmosphere. Only the number of waiters seemed considerably lessened.

We didn't particularly listen for planes or falling bombs as we ate our food. No one else seemed to either. When there was a crumping noise and a very faint juddering under our feet, a few people looked up, but the whole reason for coming to the Café de Londres was to forget the war. No one wanted to think what could be happening outside.

Nettles and I had finished our main course and were talking in a desultory manner about Violet and at what age she could start at Loxy-Poxy's boarding school when there was an almighty loud noise; the building shook, went dark; glass clattered down like hundreds of falling chandeliers; and a large object flew past me and landed on the floor.

Then there was silence. The suddenness of the noise, its abrupt end, left me momentarily dazed. I knew I was unhurt; I knew that a large bomb had fallen very near at hand, but not actually on the building, but I was incapable of taking any action. Others round me must have felt the same, for it was a full two or three seconds before people began to move and talk. There was no panic, no screaming; it appeared no one was hurt. Candles were found and lit; tables that had overturned, righted.

I said to Nettles, with that shaky excitement of escape, 'That was a close one.'

The moment that he made no reply, I knew he was dead. In a way it was extraordinary that I knew, because all round me the sounds of relief mounted. In my own private silence and darkness, for there were no candles yet near, I felt down at the object that had flown past me. My hands felt the cloth of his suit and his face. I put my fingers inside his jacket and under his shirt. There was no heartbeat. I felt his wrist. There was no pulse.

Methodically, as I had been trained, I knelt across him and tried to breathe life into his mouth, but there was no reaction. I crouched near him while around me the confusion and excitement grew. I knew I would be found soon or that I must call somebody soon, but I wanted to be alone with him as long as possible. I knew only too well the routine for a wartime death. I didn't want him carried from me.

I sat quietly, not crying, sheltered by our table. Gradually, as I sat, I became aware of a cold wind behind me. I looked around and saw a hole where the emergency door had been. Through it I could see encapsulated the terrifying scene that follows after a big bomb has fallen. The towers of jagged masonry, the flames beginning to spurt like gypsy fires, the black lumps of survivors, the various services beginning to arrive and rush to work. As if you could do anything to help when tragedy struck.

I leaned my head on Nettles' breast and began to weep. They came soon with candles, although I was already lit by the blaze across the road. I sat up and let them lift him up.

'It was the blast,' I said dully. 'It stopped his heart.'

'The emergency power's gone,' someone shouted.

'Blast's an extraordinary thing.' A woman in WRNS uniform was beside me, holding my hand. 'It just picks people out like God. He wouldn't have known a thing.'

'I knew someone who was standing with his wife at their front door and the blast picked one out and left the other quite unharmed,' a voice said before being told to keep quiet.

Someone else said almost in tears, and I think it was our waiter, 'But no one else was even scratched—not even scratched.'

'It doesn't matter how it happened,' I said, gripping hard to my Wren's hand; in an odd flashback, I pictured her as the officer who had shared the train compartment on my journey down to London. 'He's just gone. That's all. I'm sorry, but I think I'm going to be sick.'

Everyone was very, very kind, and I needed desperately to hang on to someone living. After I'd been sick they brought me brandy, which gave me strength to look at Nettles again. I know that soon my numbness, which clutched at their presence, would have to dissolve. I said, 'Please don't have him put in the same ambulance as those

hurt in the bomb across the road. He's not bloody like they will be.'
Luckily, my Wren understood this and found an empty ambulance. There was not a big raid that night, so it was not too difficult.

Then I told her I was a member of the WVS and could she get hold of someone from Tothill Street to help me? She said yes, and of course it was Winnie who was in the office and came down to the hospital. As we sat in some dreadful grey corridor waiting for the formalities to be completed, I found myself glad that she loved him, if she loved him, and even able to accept that he might have loved her a little too. It made her more able to share my mourning.

'I don't know why I brought him to London. There was no need for him to come to London. I could perfectly well have arranged about the house myself.'

'Don't upset yourself.'

'But don't you see? It was my fault that he died. I asked him to come to London.'

'He wouldn't have come if he hadn't wanted to.'

'I don't know. Nettles is . . . was so passive. He always did what people expected. I wanted him to come to London, so he came. He didn't want to come to London himself.'

'He wanted to come because you wanted to come. That's a good enough reason.'

'What I'm saying is, my selfishness killed him. If I hadn't . . .' As my excitement and self-accusation grew, Winnie became quieter and more controlled. We were interrupted by the doctor, who said something that if I'd been less wild might have struck me as odd. 'When a man's time is up, there are worse ways of going.'

'I shall take him back to Kettleside,' I said to Winnie later in the night, as we sat up in her flat drinking endless cups of tea, 'and have him buried in peace and dignity.'

The train ride to Northumberland was without doubt the worst twelve hours of my life. I can never forget it. I can never enter a train without thinking of it. Winnie came with me.

We started out in an air raid, which meant absolute darkness and a pace not much faster than a crawl. In earlier days a proportion of the passengers might have left for shelters, but by now there were so few trains and so little room that the possibility of bombs seemed much less terrible than the certainty of another long wait. We had been pushed on by a group of servicemen, standing behind us in the station. They were going on leave and carried kit bags with sharp corners. Although by chance we were facing a door, the rush of men shoved us right through the compartment and into a corridor on the other side. By the time we struggled round, the men had filled every space in the compartment, including a recumbent body on each luggage rack and one underneath each seat. We were obviously doomed to the corridor. Even the lavatory was filled with servicemen.

'I'm sorry,' said Winnie, who had given herself the role of protector.

'It makes no difference,' I said.

On one side of me a vicar, identifiable in the dark by his white collar, said, 'The war does not encourage chivalry.'

'You would have thought, when every minute might be their last . . .' began Winnie, and then stopped.

'They probably see themselves as heroes,' said the vicar.

'They can't see anything,' I said, 'in this dark.' A small blue light was switched on.

'Missed us this time,' said the vicar, who looked hardly out of his teens. He settled down with satisfaction on his case.

'I'm glad I brought some food.' Winnie sat down on one of our cases and I joined her.

'I suppose we're lucky to be sitting.'

'Train's not full yet.' The vicar seemed determined to join our conversation. 'It's got at least two more stops before we head north.'

'I think I'll try and doze,' I said to Winnie.

Physical discomfort, misery, and exhaustion battled for an escape. In the end I nodded into a black reflection of the train's stumbling progress. I felt as certain that the journey would never end as that my thoughts would never break out of the lines in which they had become fixed ever since Nettles' death. My selfishness had killed him. My determination to have things the way I wanted them had brought him to his death. My head seemed to burst with this everrecurring conviction. The revolving of the train's wheels echoed it and reinforced it.

We stopped at the first of the vicar's stations, and as he had said, more people squeezed in, thrusting us closer together in a dreadful stuffy, though cold, intimacy. We started off again, and like the train my thoughts gave a jerk and shifted into a slightly different gear. If it hadn't been for my suspicions about Winnie, I thought, I would have gone up to Kettleside and Nettles would have been nowhere near London. I began to turn the blame from myself to Winnie. I could feel her sitting beside me protectively, occasionally answering the talkative vicar but always ready to help me. Who was she, a stranger, to come and interfere in my life? The train stopped for a second time. It was still, apart from clankings and groanings and hissings and bangings, for nearly an hour. My thoughts spun faster. When at last the train started again, this time going at quite a respectable and therefore noisy speed, I shouted at Winnie, 'You and I killed him!'

'What?'

I couldn't repeat it. Winnie had heard the last part of the sentence, not the first. She shouted back, 'You mustn't go on thinking like that. I was afraid you were still thinking that. Think how happy you were together.'

'I can't,' I screamed back, for now the noise was immense. It sounded as if we were going through an eternal tunnel. Besides, I liked having to shout. It relieved the pressure in my head a little. 'I can't! It's all spoiled!'

Winne didn't reply for a moment; then she came closer. I could feel her fair silky hair next to mine. 'I'm going to tell you something,' she shouted.

'No.' I was suddenly terrified she would explain to me about herself and Nettles. Perhaps she thought it would lessen the burden of my guilt.

'No!' I cried. 'I don't want to know! Don't tell me!'

But Winnie was a methodical sort of person; she made decisions only after weighing all the pros and cons, and then she stuck to them. She grasped my shoulder. 'Nettles was going to die soon anyway. He had cancer. The doctor gave him less than six months to live.'

I took in what she said at once, and recognised that all the signs had been there for me to see. Winnie was offering me comfort, but although I knew that would come, now I cried back angrily, 'Why didn't he tell me? Why do you know? I'm his wife!'

Winnie didn't try to lie. 'I was there,' she said. 'He didn't want to upset you unnecessarily. He was going to tell you when he came down. But I suppose he hadn't yet—'

'We were so happy,' I said, and although I spoke quietly Winnie heard, for she answered.

'I expect that's why he didn't tell you. He always wanted you to be happy. He felt guilty about marrying you, I think. He never quite believed you weren't the child he knew first.'

'That's not true!' I said. 'We were husband and wife.' I suddenly understood clearly what the relationship had been between Winnie and Nettles. At least from her point of view. She was the loving companion who understood where the difficult wife did not bother to, who listened and sympathised, and knew things that the husband never told the difficult wife.

'Don't be ridiculous, Winnie,' I said sharply. 'You're younger than me. You're less than half Nettles' age. If anyone's a child to him, you are. You were.' I stopped. The fact of Nettles' death struck me again, and with it the realisation of how inappropriate this squabble over his memory. Let Winnie feel she had a special place in his life. She was right. I hadn't been there to help him when he'd learned he must die. I had, however, been with him at his death.

'I'm sorry, Winnie.' I took her hand. 'I didn't mean any of that. I don't know what I'd do without you. I expect Nettles felt the same.'

'Oh, Violet.' Winnie squeezed my hand, and by her connection to her body I felt rather than saw that she was beginning to cry for the first time.

I held her still, but could think of nothing to say in consolation. I was glad when we were interrupted by a small child being handed over our heads towards the lavatory. It was a boy about three years old, very sleepy and already damp.

As Winnie and I settled back onto our suitcases, I began to think of how I would tell the children about their father's death, and to wonder whether they were old enough to take it in. This made me remember my own reaction to my father's death. I supposed it was not particularly unusual for a woman of my age to lose a father in the First World War and a husband in the Second. Yet in my case it was unexpected, because Nettles was too old to fight. And now I discovered he would have died anyway. Certainly I would not tell this to little Violet now. Perhaps later. You can't mourn for two deaths. Nettles had been killed by bomb blast, not by cancer. I was not even sure that 'he would have died anyway' was much of a comfort at all. If I were a little six-year-old girl whose memory hardly stretched beyond war time, I would rather my father died a victim of the London Blitz to take his place with the lists of innocents that shrivelled away of some slow disease.

The train had been going fast now for quite two hours, and I began to feel that we might, after all, arrive. Winnie opened her picnic bag, and I found I was even hungry. The vicar, who looked so longingly that we had to offer him a sandwich, began to seem less irritating. We were in the country. It was dark, it was cold. But I felt the freshness of the air and a lessening of my guilty despair.

This feeling lasted till we slowed down again and drew into York. An air raid was in progress. We could hear it quite close. Our little blue lights went out, and a nervous female voice nearby asked whether we shouldn't lie down on the floor as regulations required. This produced some hollow laughter, since there wasn't a square inch free on the floor. A loud male voice suggested to cynical snorts that she nip off to the station canteen for a nice, bracing cup of tea. Our vicar said, 'If Hitler stopped tea now, he really would be winning the war.'

We were halted outside York for nearly four hours, occasionally being moved from one line to another, which only raised our hopes fruitlessly. The darkness never broke, although the noise of the raid passed quite soon. The others in the carriage were surprisingly quiet. Perhaps they were all as sunk in gloom as I was. A new sense of self-reproach had come to torture me. Why had I not spent the last months of Nettles' life with him in Kettleside? Surely some wifely instinct should have told me that they were all-important. Instead, I had made them all-important to me alone. After our previous conversation, I couldn't talk to Winnie about this, so the terrible rotation of guilt began again. After several hours sitting in this deadly black vacuum with the noises in my head louder than any other sound, I found myself thinking that only Nettles could straighten me out. He had encouraged me to go. He had not wished me to return.

Now he lay in the guard's van, wound in cloth and nailed into a box of wood. This was an image I'd managed to avoid all the journey, but now it came so strongly that I could not get rid of it. Tears began to stream down my face. I was glad no one could see me.

'I want to see if Nettles is all right,' I whispered to Winnie.

'What?' Her voice of amazement told me what I knew. The corridors were wedged with people and cases. Only a child could be lifted hand over hand. 'Don't cry.' Winnie came closer to me.

'I can't stop. It's the thought of him all alone. I can't bear it. I want to be with him.'

'You said you didn't want to.'

'I want Nettles near me.'

The vicar, who was listening, spoke into the dark. 'You might be able to walk along the platform. If we ever get onto a platform. I know what it is about pets. It's their helplessness. A dog, is it?'

Winnie tried to stop him tactfully, but with a feeling that I wanted him to take a little share in Christian suffering, I said defiantly, 'No. Nettles isn't a dog, since you wonder. Nettles is the name of my husband, who was killed by a bomb yesterday. We're taking his body to our home to be buried.'

My plan misfired, for although the vicar was confused and upset, I was far worse. The statement of facts seemed so cold and impersonal. What difference did his death make to anyone except me? He might just as well have been a dog. I began to sob uncontrollably.

I suppose my hysterical statement had been heard fairly widely in that quiet darkness for soon after this two soldiers appeared out of the compartment and gave Winnie and me their seats. I slept then. We both slept till a bright May dawn woke us up only a short distance from Newcastle.

Looking at Winnie's pale, strained face and her lank, flattened hair, I remembered how I had thought her unchangeably armoured when she had come to me that morning after my house had been bombed.

Now I saw why she always cried at concerts. She looked at me wanly, and I managed something near a smile. 'We'll do all right,' I said. 'We're strong.' I said it to console her. But after I'd said it, I realised, extraordinarily, that it was true. At least about me.

I never after that moment lost my belief in my basic ability to survive, despite the agony of the next few months and the unalterable sadness it left behind. I had grown strong during my separation from Nettles. I had paid for it, with sad irony, by using up the last year I could have been with him. Without that time of independence, I could never have borne his death.

Araminta could not understand my attitude. She tried to make my grief ferment into self-hatred. She even told me how Nettles had suffered when he had been ill and I was in London. We sat on a rug one warm afternoon. It was the first day of June, nearly three weeks since Nettles' death, and I had just found myself able to read again. I had brought out a newspaper, hoping to see what had happened to the war since I had left it for my own battlefield. A few yards away, her new twins slept in either end of the large pram. Araminta looked up from a frock she was smocking for little Violet in obvious reproach. 'Of course, you will stay here now.'

I saw that I was not going to be allowed to read. Araminta thought me recovered enough for a full frontal attack. She disapproved of newspapers anyway. She even tried to divert us around the time of the BBC news. I folded up the paper and sat on it.

'We shall all have to clarify our positions,' I said.

'It's your house now. You're head of the house.'

'Oh, Araminta!' Her head was bent over the smocking, and despite my appeal she refused to look up. 'That's true, of course, in one way. But you've been running the house ever since you came here.'

'What about the farm?'

'We'll get a manager.'

'In war time?'

'We're part of The Great Kitchen Front,' I said facetiously, and then, remembering where I'd last heard the phrase, began to feel very unfacetious indeed. I looked at Araminta, at her solidity, her confidence, at her pale moon face with the dark hair pulled back into a piece of ribbon. Despite her fatness, she seemed younger than ever. Innocent. I remembered that it was her story of Winnie that had stopped me coming back to Nettles and felt a sudden hatred for her. I leaned forward and said viciously, 'You killed Nettles just as much as I did. If you hadn't made up those lies about Winnie and him, I would have come up here and he would never have been near a bomb!'

Araminta looked at me, dropped her sewing, put her head into her hands, and burst into tears. I did nothing. I watched her. We sat like that for several seconds. Then one of the twins woke up and began to cry. I said, 'A baby's crying.'

Araminta sobbed out from behind her hands, 'You don't know the strain I have to carry. You don't know what it's like having all these children . . .'

'You like babies.'

'And women and stupid land girls and no men. At least there was Nettles, and now there's no Nettles. You'll go. Of course you'll go. Why should you stay? I know I'm lucky to have such a wonderful home; I am grateful really. If only Leonard came more often . . .'

The other twin woke up and began to cry. Araminta continued to sob. I was reminded of my baby period. I put a hand out to Araminta's heaving shoulders. 'We used to be friends,' I said. 'Do you remember when we used to talk of nothing but milk?' Her sobs began to diminish, although the twins' wails increased.

'The trouble is I'm still like that and you're not.' She got up slowly. 'I'd better pick up one of these. They're probably hungry.'

'I'll hold one while you feed one.'

'Oh, thank you, Vi. I'm sorry.' She looked at me with wet-eyed gratitude.

'I'm sorry too.'

We sat on the rug. Araminta had one baby at the breast while I rocked the other. He was hungry and thrust his mouth hopefully towards me. I felt no pang that there was nothing there for him. I watched Araminta be soothed by the other baby's sucking. 'I'm sorry I made it an accusation before,' I said. 'But did Nettles love Winnie?'

Araminta stared peacefully over the top of the baby's downy head. 'Not as much as she did him. They probably made love because they liked each other and were lonely. Loneliness makes people take second best. You were his first love.' Seeing my face, she stopped. 'You did want to know, didn't you?'

'No. I don't know. . . . I don't want to think Winnie slept with him.'

Araminta sighed. 'I suppose you wouldn't. I've got used to that sort of thing. It doesn't seem very important to me anymore. As long as Leonard doesn't tell me.'

Almost glad to be diverted into feelings of guilt from misery and hatred, I said, 'But I always assumed Leonard told you everything.'

'Only when we have a row.' I wondered whether I should mention my night with him to this calmly philosophical creature. It would be nice to have it off my conscience. But some instinct held me back. 'What I would hate', Araminta went on, 'would be to know for certain that he had slept with, for instance, you. I would hate that.'

There was a pause. I stroked my twin's head uneasily. 'What about me and Winnie, then?'

'Before, I was warning you. I have only told you now because Nettles is dead.' She took the baby from her breast. He was half-asleep, and his head lolled forward as she sat him up to pat his back. She put him back in the pram and took the other twin from me. I lay back on the rug and looked at the sharp blue sky above me. Far away I could hear noises of the bigger children playing at a swing we had fixed to a large tree. I pictured the scene: Violet with her thick plaits flying up as high as she was allowed; Tudor trying jealously to escape from Nanny's grasp.

When I'd told Violet about Nettles' death, she had reacted not with the painful bravura I remembered from my own father's death, but with a quiet self-possession. 'Is he in Heaven yet?' she'd asked, and when I said, 'Probably on the way,' she wanted to know whether I meant Purgatory. I was surprised she knew about Purgatory, and reflected that there was a lot I didn't know about my daughter. After she had settled the whereabouts of his spirit, she became very much interested in all the details of the burial service.

It was tempting to think I had a place here to fill. I stood up. 'I'm going to see the children.'

'Tell Nanny,' Araminta said, 'I've fed the twins and I'll be along to help with tea in a moment.'

I wandered up towards the swing, which was on a grassy mound just behind the house. Already the shadow from the mountains was falling across it. For a moment it seemed changed into a guillotine, with the silhouettes of Nanny turned into executioner and the moving figures of the children into spectators.

I thought how my mother had left this black shadow for light and independence, yet had ended up on an island, in lunatic, meaningless isolation. I wasn't like her. I didn't want to escape the world. I wanted to become its servant. Yet how can we ever tell how far we are programmed by our mothers? Perhaps I was deluding myself with ideas of selfless duty. Perhaps I was another failed mother, failed wife.

I neared the mound, and Nanny became navy blue and three-dimensional again. She saw me and said, 'So there you are, Miss Violet,' which was the same greeting she'd used ever since I was a child. I recognised the comfortable mixture of pleasure and reproach.

The children saw me, and Tudor ran down the hill with his arms uplifted, wanting to be twirled about. 'It's my turn next, Mummy,' shouted little Violet, who was waiting impatiently while one of

Araminta's brood swooped backwards and forwards. 'Wait and see how high I go! I can catch a leaf from the tree! Well, nearly.'

I swung Tudor and, carrying him, went up to join Nanny. I gave her Araminta's message, and we stood together watching the children. 'I can't help thinking about poor Mr Nettlefield not being here to see them anymore.'

'Don't, Nanny. You'll make me cry.'

'That's only natural. There's no mourning without tears.'

I thought of the funeral service, when all the women, including Flo, Nanny, and the land girls, had wept copiously. 'He had quite a send-off,' I said.

'And I wouldn't be surprised if we're seeing you off again soon.'

I turned to Nanny, surprised myself at the calm matter-of-factness with which she assumed my departure. She was staring at little Violet, watching her vain efforts to catch a leaf. I suddenly wanted her to decide what I should do. Apart from my mother, of all the people in the world, she had known me longest. 'Don't you disapprove of me going away?'

'You can't make the moon square.'

'But do you think I should stay?'

'It's not what I want . . .'

'But I'm asking your advice, Nanny. Do you think I should stay here and help look after all this—the children, the house, the farm? Or do you think I should go back to my job in London? If I go back to that job, there'll be another afterwards. And then another. I'm asking you, Nanny, to advise me.' As my voice rose in urgency, I must have squeezed Tudor, whom I still carried, because he suddenly dropped out of my arms and raced towards the swing. 'Take your eye off him for a moment . . .' muttered Nanny as she set off at a fast pace after him. But she was too late. Already Tudor was within inches of Violet's swinging feet, and in a moment the tip of her red leather shoe had caught him in the middle and sent him tumbling down into the grass.

Nanny reached him at once, picked him up, bawling and cross. 'That's what comes of staying out too long,' she said. 'Now, now. You're not hurt. Stop crying, and we'll go in for tea.'

I hadn't moved as this little scene unfolded, for I had a strong sense of *déjà vu* from my own childhood. Then, as Violet was parted reluctantly from the swing and they began to move towards the house, I realised my mind was made up.

I would go to London. I would move away from the WVS. I would not be a slave to the war any longer; I had given it enough. I would try to enter politics. I was a strong woman. I could get things done.

Nanny had led the children away by now, the sounds of Tudor's crying ceasing abruptly as they entered the house. I sat on the swing and looked up to the red glow that the sun had left behind when it dropped behind the mountains. My mother and I were similar in one way. Neither she nor I could be satisfied with the role of mother and wife. She had ended with nothing.

I had found an alternative. Perhaps one day it wouldn't be the alternative. Perhaps a woman would be able to do both.

I pushed the swing gently backwards and forwards, watching the sky turn from red to purple. Araminta appeared, hurrying up the path pushing the pram in front of her.

'The answer lies with our children,' I called out cheerfully.

She didn't stop, but shouted back, 'But that's what I'm always telling you. I suppose that means you're going to stay.'

'Not at all. It doesn't affect me. It's just nice for them.'

She wouldn't answer anymore, and after she also had disappeared into the house, I sat a long time on the swing, thinking with peaceful hope about the future.

Part Two

Chapter Twelve

HANCOCK—News received DICK. Hospital ship destination Australia. Molly returning England in Empress of Australia.

ROBERTSON, Major D.B.C. 2/2 Goorkhas, POW Changi, arrived safely Dehra with battalion: 'All in good heart; health pretty good.'

TOWNSEND GREEN, Sub-Lieutenant Kenneth Aubrey (Squeak) RN. Late HMS Exeter. Cable received from Calcutta 'Good health; Home by Christmas.' 'Jads', Wadhurst, Sussex.

(Personal column) *The Times.*   1 October 1945

EVENING DRESS
Sir, It would be interesting to know whether maîtres d'hôtel are acting legally in refusing to admit clients not wearing evening dress. To many of us their action seems a gross impertinence. Yours Faithfully, D. Thompson. Overseas Club.

(Letter to the Editor) *The Times.*   29 September 1945

WOMEN'S DUTY IN PUBLIC LIFE
As women were going to the polls for the first time in France yesterday, the Pope in an address specially directed to women and broadcast by Vatican Radio said 'Courage, young Catholic women . . . Carry on your work without allowing difficulties to disturb, humiliate or discourage you; be the defenders of the home, the family, and society.'

The Times.   22 October 1945

VICTORY brings nearer the day when I'll return, meanwhile use my STORK COOKERY SERVICE.

HOT CAKES for COLD DAYS, ROLLS, BUNS, GIRDLE CAKES AND SCONES . . . All approved by the Ministry of Food.

This is the third week of ration period No. 4.

(Advertisement) *The Times.*   31 October 1945

My mother told me he had been killed by a bomb.

If it hadn't been for the coffin, brought with horrid ceremony to our peaceful little church, I would have pictured my father living elsewhere happily ever after. I wasn't allowed to the funeral, but I stood in the rain soon after and looked at the raw grave. The yellow wreaths were monstrous. Even more monstrous was the idea that my loving father was lying under them. I tried to pretend it was all a trick. Like magic. He had gone wherever my mother went when she wasn't with us. Once she telephoned me, but I was so excited I ran away and when I came back she was gone.

I knew if my father had been alive he would have been at my side. I didn't appreciate the idea of a lofty perch in Heaven from which, according to Nanny, he looked down to see if I was being a 'good girl.'

I decided to show him how much I needed him here below. I was so angry that if for any reason I was awakened out of sleep, I would scream and kick out. I made a fuss about eating, so that I got unchildishly thin. My clothes irritated me, and I pulled at puffy sleeves and tore off bunchy socks. I scowled, pulling my brows down low and pouting my lips with what must have been comic effect. No one laughed. Nanny said, 'Violet is being unnecessarily trying.' I was never called Vi like my mother. 'She must learn to consider others.' Araminta, who, owing to overweight and overwork, was being trying herself, sighed deeply. 'Can you wonder, poor child? So skinny, too. We must see she gets enough love.' Nanny decided that I was old enough to leave the nursery and become a little girl. This new freedom allowed me to do things on my own, so that if I became unreasonably cross there was only myself to be cross with.

My first free act was to fall in love with Isabel Royston. I thought of her when I ate my food, when I made houses for my dolls in the shrubbery or ran down the driveway to school. Isabel made up for the lack of my mother, although no one could have been less like her. Because of her odd background, she had escaped any real education, and was obsessed by two things: her appearance and her soldier. Her soldier, Captain Hubert Creswell, with a black patch over one eye, had lain in a bedroom along a side corridor for nearly six months. His companion, who had only one leg, had left recently.

The idea of this manly island in a sea of women filled me with wonder and curiosity. I often watched Isabel gliding away in the captain's direction. She usually carried a bowl of soup or soft milky pudding to soothe some romantic internal injury.

His room was out of bounds to the little children. I set off in the gap after school and before tea. It was late autumn, a windy afternoon; the leaves had rustled above my head and tumbled along beside my running feet. Inside the house, wartime saving forbade lights till the sky had dimmed to total blackness. Feeling my way up the back stairs, I began to tremble with nervous excitement. My mother called the mountains God's blackout. I almost wished I'd brought along Henrietta, Araminta's third child. But then she would have made me her servant. She was so bossy. Boys, like Leo and my brother, Tudor, would not see the point. Anyway, I wanted to share a private adventure with Isabel.

Isabel was about seventeen. She looked older. She was very beautiful. She had long dark-golden limbs, large breasts, straight black hair, and brilliant turquoise-blue eyes. I suppose she had a nose and mouth too, but no one noticed it after seeing those eyes. She very seldom spoke, but when she did she had a precise un-English accent left over from her youth around the Empire, which gave her most ordinary remarks—she never said anything that wasn't ordinary—an extraordinary impact.

I crept along the corridor listening for the sound of male tones. I reached the bedroom door without hearing them. It was not closed properly, so I pushed it open and stepped quietly inside. I looked towards the bed and in the dim light saw dark hair haloed on the white pillow. Captain Creswell's hair was pale brown. I came closer and recognised Isabel, blue eyes staring at the ceiling, face more beautiful than ever. Beside her, I now saw the one-eyed Captain. He was not wearing his black eye patch or I'd have noticed him earlier. My little girl's mind spun with rational explanations. The obvious one seemed the most likely.

'Were you feeling tired, Isabel?' Captain Creswell sat up so suddenly that I saw him wince with the pain. He grabbed his patch from his bedside table.

I came to Isabel's side of the bed and said, 'Or maybe you were cold?' Isabel, who hadn't moved before, now turned her head toward me.

'Hello, Violet. What are you doing here?' Her voice was pleasant and calm as if she'd met a friend out shopping.

'Sometimes dark makes me feel cold. And it's very dark in here. You don't look tired.' I was determined to have my explanation.

'I'm getting out now,' said Isabel. And as she lifted the bedclothes and slid out her legs, I was relieved to notice that she was fully dressed. For some reason, perhaps because Captain Creswell's pyjama jacket had been unbuttoned until he had noticed and quickly buttoned it up, I'd thought she might be undressed. I had never seen a grown-up woman undressed.

Nevertheless, I said severely, 'You shouldn't get into bed with your clothes on.'

'I took my shoes off,' she pointed out nicely. She was being very

309

nice altogether, bending over me now and smoothing my hair from my face.

Captain Creswell regained his composure. He was nice to me too. He accepted my offer to put on the bedside light, and Isabel drew the thick blackout curtains. He said, 'This is cosy, isn't it?'

And when I suggested it would be even nicer if we had something to eat, he produced a toffee. A toffee at that point in the war was quite a rarity. 'You can sit on the end of my bed if you like,' he said.

I giggled. 'But not get in it.' He smiled, not altogether successfully, and quite soon Isabel said it was my teatime.

She took my hand and led me along the dark corridor. When we reached the top of the stairs, beyond which we could see the lights of the kitchen, she crouched down and whispered, 'This will be our secret, Violet.'

'Oh, yes!' I breathed excitedly. There was a little pause. I held my breath as she kissed my cheek.

'About the bed.'

'Oh. Yes!' There was another pause. 'Isabel?'

'Yes, darling.'

'I can visit you again, can't I?'

'Well . . .'

'I do really want to.' I could feel her considering. 'You don't want people to know you're cold and tired, do you? Araminta's got so many worries already.'

Isabel made up her mind, gave me another kiss, but this time rather less loving and more businesslike. 'Of course you can come. But I'll bring you along myself. There, now, off you go!'

And off I went. More in love than ever—a prospect of endless intimacy with Isabel ahead, for I did not consider a bedridden, one-eyed man much of a rival.

Unfortunately, our illicit threesome had a built-in obsolescence. Captain Creswell—or Hubert, as I was taught to call him over games of Ludo and Snakes and Ladders—could not remain in forever. His eye was healed, if non-existent; his stomach complaint might be never totally well but could not keep him in bed for much longer.

He began to pace his room in his crimson dressing gown. Then one sunny afternoon in early November, he came down the slippery backstairs and entered the Chinese drawing room. My mother had painted it white and called it the playroom, but we knew it had been my grandmother's favourite room and she had called it the Chinese drawing room. Against its white walls Captain Creswell looked thinner and paler than seemed possible. He wore a tweed jacket with leather patches at the elbows and began to smoke a pipe. Isabel combed the tobacco for him and pressed it tenderly into the bowl of his pipe. She wore a blue knife-pleated skirt and white ankle socks. When she bent over, the pleats bunched together over her golden calves. Hubert and I stared admiringly.

Araminta, who was having trouble with the land girls, chanced upon this scene when she came to snatch a quick cup of tea. The love affair which had blossomed in an upper room could not be trimmed to drawing-room conventions.

'Isabel! Have you been curling your hair?'

'What?' Isabel looked round, surprised. Araminta had chosen an odd method of reproof. Isabel's hair was noticeably without curl. Araminta became more irritated. She hated being brought out of her natural calm. She felt ugly, ridiculous, old. It was particularly annoying that Isabel, who meant nothing to her and remained as impassive as she liked to be, should be the cause of it.

'I shall tell Mrs Nettlefield it's time you pulled your weight round here.'

'I'm afraid it's my fault, Mrs Trigear.' Hubert approached with humble politeness. Unfortunately, he forgot to put down his pipe, and as he waved his hand apologetically, clouds of smoke blew across Araminta's face.

She retreated, grimacing. 'Would you mind not smoking in here, Captain Creswell?'

'I'm sorry. I—'

'I'm pleased to see your health so much improved. No doubt you will be rejoining your regiment soon?'

'I'm afraid my eye—'

'But leaving us?'

'Hubert hasn't even been outside yet!' I cried out. I had gradually sensed that my happiness was bound to his presence.

'Violet! What ever are you doing hanging round the grown-ups?' Araminta's anger turned on me. My father had been dead for some months now. Now even the little children were against her.

'Isabel isn't a grown-up.' My defiance was the last straw. Araminta collapsed in an armchair and burst into tears. Her long hair, which was knotted back, came loose and straggled down her back. Her voluminous skirt, muddy at the hem where she had been picking greens, trailed on the bright-blue flowered carpet. Tears spouted down her face. The sight of such demoralisation in the one upon whom we all depended was terrifying. I began to cry even louder than her. Captain Creswell, with the look of a man who, bravely surviving near-death, had at last found true terror, concentrated on trying, unsuccessfully, to put out his pipe.

Isabel was apparently unmoved by the scene, turning one white ankle sock this way and that meditatively. Finally, she approached us—not, as I thought, to comfort, but in order to make her voice heard.

'I've decided I want to go on the stage.'

As Araminta stopped crying in amazement, I stopped also.

'Captain Creswell knows one or two people in ENSA. It's all very respectable. One of them is an old friend of Mrs Nettlefield's. He's called Raymond Lark.'

'Raymond Lark was never respectable.'

'He is now. Hubert says he wears a uniform and spins a coloured globe to decide where to send his artistes. Hubert is hoping to work for him. Hubert was at RADA before he joined the army.'

'Ah, Hubert.' Araminta stood up suddenly and looked as if she might walk away without further comment. I knew her in this mood. If pressed for anything, she would say 'I'm a painter. Go away.' Usually she relented. I saw Captain Creswell was unnerved. He began to protest.

'Of course, I want to marry Isabel.'

Araminta looked at Isabel. Isabel looked away. Araminta started to walk towards the door. Hubert and I followed anxiously. Hubert said, 'I've prospects and a little money. My father owns a cinema. More than one, actually. That's why I know Raymond Lark. There's going to be quite a boom in film-making after the war. The American influence, you know.' As Araminta had reached the door, he grabbed her arm, but her expression of frozen hostility made him remove it hastily. He cried out, 'I love her!'

I said, trying to help, 'He does, he does! They lie together in bed. They go to sleep together when Isabel's tired. It's just like a Mummy and Daddy!' At which point I burst into tears again. I didn't have a Daddy. And a Mummy only on occasions. Captain Creswell retreated back across the room, though this time he had more than mere tears to run from, and Isabel said calmly, 'So now you know. Hubert and I are lovers.'

'They are. They are,' I sobbed. 'And I are too!'

'She's so beautiful,' mumbled Hubert. Araminta opened the door. It looked as if she would go out without reacting at all. Then she changed her mind, came back, and looking now as calm as Isabel, sat down on the chair. While we all waited nervously, she stared out at the mountains blurring into the darkening sky. Then she said, 'I don't know why you think I should care. Do what you like. People seem to think I'm a well of compassion. I'm not.' There was a pause. No one spoke. The room had become quite dark, and my eyes fixed on the yellow fringes to the Chinese lamps. We had brought them back quite recently. I thought vaguely that grown-ups did not seem as happy as one would expect considering they could do anything they wanted, and wished someone would switch on the lamps.

Araminta began to speak again, and although I did not really understand, I heard how vindictive her tone had become. 'I just hope you're taking precautions, because if you think I'll look after some illegitimate half-Egyptian brat you're absolutely wrong. Do what you like, but don't rely on me to pick up the pieces!'

We were all silent again. Isabel standing, Araminta sitting, stared out of the window. Hubert began to play with his pipe, batting it against the palm of each hand. Then down the hallway I heard brisk footsteps advancing. I would recognise them anywhere. It was Nanny come to see where I'd got to. She would be cross because the others had already started tea and I had caused her an unnecessary journey. She would thrust my hands under the icy tap and rub green soap over them till they stung. I could almost hear her tut-tutting as she came. I looked round the room. Araminta was cross too, and Isabel was going to run away with Hubert. I sidled across to Hubert and looked longingly up at him. 'Take me too, please?'

'What?' He moved away and stood beside Isabel.

Nanny's steps came closer. There was a knock at the door. I cast a desperate look at Isabel. For some reason no doubt unconnected with me, she smiled. In that instant before the door opened, I decided to leave Kettleside when she did. Ah! I would run away!

'Come in,' said Araminta.

'So there you are, Miss No-Sense-of-Time.'

'Better late than never!' I shouted, and evading her pinching fingers dashed out from the dark hallway and towards the comforting lights and smells of the kitchen. Even as I ran I made a mental note of the need to secure a torch and plenty of food.

I had collected two pieces of toast discarded by Tudor, two imperfect pears, and one temptingly rosy apple, when any plans were disrupted by the arrival of my mother.

'Ah, Violet. I'm glad to see you taking up music.' She had caught me at the piano, in which I was hiding my runaway rations. I hoped she couldn't smell the toast. I put down the top hurriedly. 'Playing the piano is a great solace. Unfortunately, I never learned. My mother tried to teach me, but she was a bad teacher and I was a bad pupil. It always ended in tears.'

I looked beyond where she stood in her neat black suit (she never wore a colour again after my father's death), for I realised she would not talk like this for my benefit alone. Not even after several months' absence. I saw a dark male figure. 'Who's that?'

'Who's that? Who's that?' She whisked round with a briskness of the world outside Kettleside and took the man's arm. 'Little Violet's manners are not usually so lacking. This is Jack Logan, an old friend of mine. A very important man. A Minister in the government. Shake hands nicely.'

The man came forward and bent down. I liked grown-ups who came down to my level, so I looked on him more kindly. He did not start as a tall man; he had thick grey hair, a largish nose, and bright brown eyes. He said, 'When your mother and I first met I wasn't at all important.'

'We had absolutely nothing in common.' They laughed to each other.

'Do you now?' I asked.

He gave me a serious look. 'I hope so. Your mother and I have both changed a good deal.'

'So have I. Araminta says I'll outgrow my strength if I'm not careful.'

He patted my head sympathetically and then stood up and looked at my mother. 'Your mother's a remarkable woman. If only she'd get her allegiances straight.'

'*You* may want me, but will anyone else?'

'After the war finishes . . .'

They forgot about me and talking hard, began to walk away. I took my rosy apple from the piano's entrails and followed them disconsolately. I saw that my plan for running away was the sort of babyish fantasy that Tudor babbled out in his dreams.

'Come on, you pale little shrimp.' My mother held out a hand behind her back. 'Come and introduce Jack to Tudor and all the others.'

I ran after her and caught the thin fingers tight. When they didn't curl round mine, I pushed them round with my other hand. I must make her take me away. I liked being thin when she called me 'shrimp'.

My mother had come for Christmas and to resolve the question of what to do with Isabel. Captain Creswell had already button-holed Raymond Lark. He came up to spend a night with us at Kettleside. Both in uniform, she in the WVS overcoat, he in ENSA khaki, they took a stroll round the garden. I tagged along behind them.

'How is Gay?' asked my mother.

'Spirit unchanged; wonderful girl. How is Eleanor?'

'On Eureka.'

'Your mother was always original.' He shivered and his

314

fat fingers fought the stubborn top button of his coat into the hole.

'I'm so glad you're doing so well.'

'What?' He looked cross. 'I was before this blasted war. Can't think why I ever agreed to this ENSA business.'

'Serving your country . . .?'

'Hmmm.' They had come to the edge of the park, and before them stretched rough grass and crackling brown bracken. I hoped they would go on, but Mr Lark turned back firmly.

'I gather from Hubert, a dear boy, that you look on his beloved as your daughter.'

'My own daughter is not quite six.' My mother moved away irritably. 'Violet. Please don't walk in front of me. . . . What?'

Raymond Lark, who'd been expressing sympathy over Nettles' death, realised she hadn't been listening and snapped, 'Do you want me to help about this girl Isabel or not?'

My mother was immediately apologetic. 'What exactly could she do? She's never performed in her life. Except in private. Araminta said she had no idea what was going on.'

'Hubert's father owns a string of cinemas.'

'So I understand.'

'After the war I'm hoping to work with him.'

'So what can Isabel do?'

'I need an assistant.'

'I can't have her living with me in London. My flat's too small. She'd drive me mad.'

'Hubert is living with us at the moment.'

'Marry Captain Creswell, live with you . . .' My mother looked at her watch.

Raymond sighed. 'Women are so much more efficient than men. Gay will be delighted to have Isabel. It will remind her of happier times. She has arthritis in her hands and finds it difficult to cut bread. A pair of willing hands will be most welcome.

My mother smiled sympathetically. It was difficult to imagine Isabel being a help around the house.

When my mother told Nanny about Isabel's imminent departure and marriage to Hubert, she pursed her lips.

'I always did say she didn't get that dark skin from any Englishman. Married! At her age!'

'I've told you before, Nanny. Her father, Major Roly Royston, was a very good friend of mine.'

Nanny ignored this. 'Still, I can't say it won't be a relief to have her off my hands. At least that Katynka was a help. All that Isabel does is unsettle the children. Look at your little Violet, now, following her round like a shadow.' She stopped abruptly.

Invisible behind a chair while others were being discussed, I couldn't help reacting to my own name. My mother turned. 'Ah, there you are.'

'I'm always where you are,' I said, firmly defying Nanny. 'I want to be with you all the time. I do not want Isabel. I want to stay with you.'

'Well, you can't!' my mother snapped suddenly.

'Well, well,' said Nanny, meaning the opposite. There was a pause while we estimated each other's strength of will. Then my mother walked over to a mirror and pressed a wave of hair over her forehead. Looking at her face, she said in a sad voice, 'I'll be staying over Christmas.'

I pressed home my advantage. 'And the Minister. Will he stay?'

'No.' My mother began to pace round the furniture of the room as if she were marking out a route. 'He's busy.'

'Busy. Busy. Busy,' intoned Nanny, disguising her relief that my mother was staying and the Minister, a sort of man she didn't understand, was going.

'Busy, busy, busy!' cried my mother, and sat down in a chair with her legs stuck out straight in front of her. I immediately sat down on her lap. She tried to push me off, but I was too strong.

'This won't get the baby fed.'

'Oh, Nanny do stay. I want someone to talk to.'

'I'm here,' I insisted, bouncing a little, which was difficult because her legs were so hard and taut. 'Talk to me.' So she did, and because she really needed to unburden herself, she explained about meeting Jack again and being introduced to the Labour Movement and how it seemed to link with her new feelings for social service. She told me about the Beveridge Report and the better world that would come so that people like Flo and Cecil and even Nanny would always be looked after. I had been sucking my fingers until this point, luxuriating in the unaccustomed closeness of my mother's body, but now I began to take a little notice. 'But you look after Flo and Cecil and Nanny,' I objected.

'That's true. But it should be their right. Not my favour. It should come from the State, not from individual good humour. People don't like presents.'

'I do. Actually, I was going to tell you what I wanted for Christmas.'

My childish confidence did not appeal to my mother. Already her interests were turning to the general good at the expense of the particular. 'All over the world little children will be doing without presents this year,' she said seriously.

316

Mother's stay lasted for over a month, which was a record length of time. She was often sad, remembering, as she told me later, that if she'd come back the previous Christmas, my father would have been there. She would have left earlier, except that she was booked to speak at a large meeting of the Women for Peace Movement in Newcastle.

On Boxing Day, Leonard arrived at the house in an ambulance.

Araminta, already on the point of a nervous collapse, had to be put to bed before he was. His dark face, which frightened all us children, was made even more satanic by a swathing of white bandages. He had a small silver flask which he put to the hole between the bandages when the ambulance men carried him into the house. I imagined it filled with blood.

The only one of us not frightened of him was the eldest twin, Clancy, who followed him up the stairs asking questions. She was about fifteen and spent the whole time wishing the war would end and she could start becoming a famous painter. By the time Leonard was laid in the bed beside Araminta's, she had established that he was suffering from head injuries which needed rest but were not as bad as they looked, and that he had lost the little finger of his right hand.

'I am glad you're not brain-damaged,' enthused Clancy. 'I wouldn't have found it at all useful in a father. Now, I think to lose a finger positively distinguished. When can we see the stump?'

Leonard never told anyone the details of his accident. Just as he never told anyone that the injuries continued to give him headaches for the rest of his life. He had not seen my mother since Nettles' death, and they both felt it ironic that he should be the one to survive. I saw my mother now in a new role. She carried trays up and down the stairs, she chased the land girls out of their rooms, she wore slacks and tied her head in a scarf. She never sat down except to plan meals, occasionally eat them, and oversee the older girls' homework.

Araminta grew noticeably weaker at the sight of her efficiency. The whole household quailed.

'It's all or nothing,' she said, rubbing her hands together. 'If I'm doing a job, I like doing it well. Let's get these Christmas decorations down. They're only gathering dust.'

Nanny watched with awe for a day or two, and then she picked a quarrel. For a week they did not speak. Nanny said Araminta's twin babies should be put out into the garden every afternoon; my mother said it was inhuman in the snow and besides, the pram wheels made the hall floor filthy.

We children retreated out of the battlefield into Araminta's room. Leonard and Araminta seemed to be getting on very well. She made a patchwork quilt or darned socks while he listened to the wireless or played chess. They didn't talk often, for conversation was considered bad for Leonard's head and communication was never Araminta's strong suit even before her breakdown. She also cried several times a day, which no longer amazed me as it had the first time, and we became accustomed to mopping her up with one of Leonard's handkerchiefs.

We reached New Year with this unusual arrangement. Then one morning my mother, having scourged Flo over the amount of fat wasted in the pans and Cecil over the needless use of electricity, came marching up to Araminta and Leonard's bedroom. She flung open the door and stood there in her black trousers and jacket like a military inspector. We all felt guilty.

I slipped down from Leonard's bed, where Leo and I were learning to play chess, and hid under it. Araminta, who was having a smallish cry, watched over sympathetically by Tudor, who was stroking her cheek and saying 'Poor Minta,' stuffed her handkerchief under her pillow. Henrietta and Nancy, who were playing Snakes and Ladders, dropped the dice. Only Leonard, whose bandages made his face expressionless, and Clancy, who was sketching, remained impervious.

My mother's eyes flashed scornfully. 'There is a war on!'

Leonard began to laugh, which came out of his hole in ironic bubbles. My mother looked at him incredulously and then stamped her foot. This made Tudor laugh. He was a jolly little boy, fat and pink, with a very loud voice if thwarted. Now he caught Mother's legs and shouted, 'Got you! Got you! Got you!' Her look of incredulity deepened. I was afraid she might turn on Tudor, whom I considered it my duty to protect. I crawled half out from under the bed. This was a mistake.

'A zoo! That's what this is!' She came over, with Tudor still struggling to hold her legs, and gripped my shoulder. 'Why can't you sit on a chair like normal little girls?' I stared up at her stupidly.

'There aren't any chairs up here,' said Leonard mildly.

My mother dropped me, broke loose from Tudor, and strode to the door. 'Spoiled! You're all spoiled! I'm going . . . I'm going . . . I'm going to Newcastle!'

We all knew she wanted to go to London.

Leonard began to laugh again, and my mother slammed the door behind her. Tudor began to cry. I crawled back under the bed and lay there with my heart beating loudly. I realised that there was no hope of my mother taking me away. Besides, I didn't want to go to Newcastle; I wanted to go to London. I saw no reason ever to come out from under the bed. There was a creaking noise above my head as Leonard leaned over and put on the wireless. A man's voice said, 'Here is the News, and this is Bruce Belfrage reading it.'

318

There was a further creaking, and two feet in hand-knitted purple socks descended to my eye level. The hem of Araminta's flowing nightdress was shaken down to cover them as she said, 'That's that. I suppose it's time I got better.'

The voice on the wireless said, '. . . pigs at Windsor Castle who live entirely on kitchen waste were visited this afternoon by Her Royal—' interrupted by Leonard, who, patting Araminta's hand consolingly, said, 'Holidays have to end sometime. Besides, I won't be here much longer.'

'. . . near the oil wells of Persia and Iraq,' said the voice.

'Tidy up the room, now, girls, and I'll take you soon to get the milk from the farm.' Araminta drew back the curtains fully, although no more light reached me under the bed. 'Now, now, Violet dear.' Her large pale face with gentle blue eyes came down to my level. 'You mustn't be upset by your mother. She's very tired and worried about all the work she should be doing for people outside this house.'

I was excited by this adult explanation of an adult's behaviour. There was even an implication that she was in the wrong. I shouted, 'I hate her! I hate her! She doesn't love me! She's horrible! I'm going to run away. I'm going to take Tudor and run away!'

I had overplayed my hand. The face was withdrawn abruptly, and I found myself propelled from the room in a very ungentle manner. As the door closed behind me, the voice, which had been struggling on during this commotion, remarked, 'The News is followed by The Brains Trust, in which Julian Huxley, C.E.M. Joad, Commander Campbell, with guest Anna Neagle and Question Master Donald McCullough—'

Stamping my way down the stairs, I decided it was extremely unbrainy to be a child in wartime.

The only thing I had to look forward to was my birthday on 20 January. Even in wartime I could count on some sort of celebration. One afternoon my mother picked me up early from Miss Tiptree's school. She came briskly into the classroom where I sat with fifteen other children and said, 'You do look a fright.'

I ignored this, not being at an age to care about beauty. 'You never collect me. Is it something important?'

'A birthday treat,' said my mother in preoccupied tones. 'Why is your nose so red? And your tummy. You shouldn't have a tummy like that at your age.'

'It's the cold,' said Miss Tiptree. 'And the bad food.'

'It's not my birthday for six days,' I said anxiously. Was it good news or bad news? Certainly it was odd to see my mother in her smart black suit standing up by Miss Tiptree in her old woollen cardigan.

'You may have noticed it's snowing,' continued Miss Tiptree, trying for irony. But she had been bossed about by my mother since they were twenty and five respectively, so it came out merely as a defensive croak.

'Appearances aren't important,' said my mother, who obviously thought they were. She flicked her gloves against her palms. 'Come on, Violet. I'm taking you to hear me address a meeting of the Women for Peace Movement in Newcastle. Most educational.'

Her car, a small grey Vauxhall with a red stripe along the side, was parked outside the school. It was still running, puffing out white exhaust into the leaden air.

'This is cosy.' My mother jumped into the driving seat and smiled at me like someone who had decided to overlook trivialities such as unattractive colouring and fat stomachs.

'I would have put on my party dress if I'd known,' I said ingratiatingly.

'You don't have a party dress. Do you?'

'No.'

We drove through the black-and-white countryside at a speed which convinced me that a Women for Peace meeting was more exciting than it sounded. My mother had put on a grey lumpy coat which I knew was made of squirrels. Above it her face was set and pale, as it always was now unless she brushed it with rouge. I willed her to smile, and after a bit she did. 'I hope you've got cat's eyes, darling. We won't make Newcastle before it's dark.' The black and white began to merge into a formless grey. At the side of the road, great mounds of snow banked towards the trees. We passed through a village, and I was enough a child of the war not to find its unglimmering dark strange. My mother began to look depressed. The car slid slightly across the road.

'It's beginning to freeze. Oh, dear. I hope enough people turn out.'

We reached the outskirts of Newcastle and saw the huge bridge ahead. I pressed my nose against the cold windowpane and peered out for the black waters of the Tyne. Instead, I saw vast ships slotted in the estuary like sausages in a can. 'Look, Mummy! Look! I've never seen so many ships.'

'There is a war on.' My mother sounded harassed. During those five years I heard that sentence said by many different people, but always in the same harassed and uncertain tones. As if they were waiting to be told that it was all in their imagination—There is no war.

'I know, Mummy,' I said. 'Can we buy my birthday present?'

'Oh, really!'

'Can we?'

'No.'

We entered the town and a whole new depth of blackness. There was little traffic, but whenever a car passed, or a tram, I started and strained to see it pass along the road behind us. I thought it a miracle we hit nothing.

'That's the station.' My mother's voice sounded bright suddenly, as if she were giving me a guided tour of the city. We were nearing City Hall.

'I don't like the station,' I said, its pillars and porticos reminding me of waving my mother goodbye and of my father giving me a consoling hug.

'Nor do I,' agreed my mother; 'stations are gloomy places.' But her voice still sounded gay. We parked the car and walked quickly through streets marked by unmelted lumps of snow standing like white policemen at junctions of the road. There were few people about, and when soft white flakes began to float down from the black sky, I felt as if we were in the Ice Queen's country. I thought of poor Hans and the splinter in his eye.

'Here we are!' My mother glowed. We were inside a hall. Her face was pink without rouge, and melting silver stars were caught in her hair and squirrel coat. The lights were so bright that I couldn't see properly. A man's voice said, 'Hello, Violet. I'm glad to see you've kept your mother company. I was worried about her on the drive.'

It was Jack Logan. The Minister. Around him were grouped several women in heavy coats, and beyond them stretched an endless row of empty chairs.

'Let's have something to eat before they start arriving,' said my mother, smiling.

'Hilary's got the sandwiches,' said someone. 'And I've got the tea.'

'Did you have the most frightful journey?' said my mother to the Minister. 'Little Violet and I were just remarking on the gloom of railway stations.'

'I came from Manchester. Inspecting factories. All I ever do is inspect factories.'

'People work so hard,' sighed my mother. I took another fish-paste sandwich and tried to decide if the strangeness of the occasion made it a birthday treat.

'What am I going to say?' asked Jack.

'No Churchillian phrases.'

'The Mayor's wife's arriving,' called someone.

'Next time we'll have the Mayor.'

My mother gulped her tea. 'I did want another sandwich.'

I sat in the front row of City Hall with a kindly old lady wearing a towering purple hat. She kept feeding me sandwiches, which I was too shy to refuse, although I was beginning to feel sick. Despite my lack of contact with my mother, I identified with her glory on the stage surrounded by ministers and mayors' wives. I was terrified she might do something silly.

In fact she was confident, strong-voiced, even strident.

I put my hands to my face and felt it burning. The hall was hot now and half-filled with people who clapped enthusiastically. My old lady nudged me and whispered 'Now, dear, listen hard.' But I couldn't. I looked at the people sitting on either side of her on the platform. I looked at Jack.

I had found Jack and my mother in bed together when he visited Kettleside. When they saw me they had shown no embarrassment, like Captain Creswell and Isabel, so I had gone away again without being too upset.

I was concerned about only one thing. 'Mama, are you going to marry Mr Logan.'

'No, darling. Mr Logan's not the marrying sort. He's too old.'

'But what about you?' I didn't like to mention my father's name.

'Your father was the only man I wanted as a husband. Now he's dead, I shall never marry again.'

'Good.'

'Mr Logan is a great friend and a great help with my work. Do you understand?'

'Yes, Mama. Thank you.' Sometimes my mother's directness could be comforting.

Hot clapping surrounded me. My mother had finished her speech. But there were many more speeches before we were released into the cold night. Mr Logan was coming to stay at Kettleside again. He patted my hand. 'You must be very proud of your mother.'

'Why?' I asked, not hostile but invigorated by escape from City Hall. I thought my mother was right: he was old; but I liked him all the same.

'Because few women have her gifts.' My mother laughed, but the ironic trill did not disguise her satisfaction.

The following day my mother disappeared from my life for a long period. I was not particularly surprised or upset. I was becoming a precise, bossy little girl, with a strong urge for order. I drew little patterns on pieces of paper, which I coloured neatly, and had a special place for each of my toys. I was obedient when it suited me and disobedient when it suited me. Nevertheless, I wanted praise. Leo and Tudor were rowdy little boys, tough and good-natured. I found their noise irritating.

Then Miss Tiptree taught me about books. From seven onwards I lived two lives. Books and the ordinary world. I far preferred books. I began to eat again, and one day Araminta pinched my cheek and said, 'You're not so unlike your mother after all, darker and paler, without her lovely curls, but your eyes are a really lovely green.' I glowed and felt even more convinced I was Mary Lennox in *The Secret Garden*.

Nanny found my self-containment unnatural and insulting. 'Come and join the other children,' she would insist.

'In a minute.'

'Mind your eyes don't fall out.'

Araminta, after her short-lived capitulation to my mother's efficiency, took up the reins of government again, and it was only several months after Leonard's departure that Clancy, remarking on her increasing stoutness, made us all realise she was pregnant yet again. 'Not another beastly baby,' I said.

The final three years of the war made no impact on me. My mother's life, her visit to America as an adviser on the Plans for Aid to Europe, and her sadness mixed with relief when a V-2 finally caught the house in London, reducing it to a pile of rubble, were only reported incidents. *The Secret Garden* and *Red Shoes* were reality. Then Isabel sent us a postcard: we must see her starring in a film called *War Blues*. We all became very excited and drove in to Newcastle. Isabel acted the deeply patriotic wife of a pilot who eventually was killed. She rolled her huge eyes in dreadful sorrow, and was made up and dressed in such a way that she looked thirty-nine instead of nineteen. I hardly recognised her, but thought her incredibly beautiful. Despite the projector's breaking down at the most tragic moment, I cried and fell in love with her again for several weeks. The land girls who had all come too, some with their boyfriends, sighed with admiration and said it was 'a scream' to think they had slept under the same roof as a real film star.

Leo and Tudor who, never reading books, were unaware of the division between fact and fiction, could not believe our hardheartedness in recovering so quickly from the death of Isabel's pilot husband. They had become plane-spotting mad, and when the war began to drag to its slow conclusion they were filled with impatience. 'It'll be so boring when the war's over! What will we do?'

My mother's grey Vauxhall came fast up the driveway. Leonard's head stuck out of one window. They had just driven up from London. They stopped with a flourish outside the house, and my mother stuck her head out of the other window. 'The war's over! The war's over!' she shouted.

I noticed that Leonard's crinkly black hair was now entirely grey and that my mother's forehead was hung about with silver strands. They both had the same look of exhaustion and excitement, and seemed baffled by the Kettleside atmosphere of disaffection. My mother, bustling about, managed to discover a Union Jack, which she chivvied us into draping over the front gate.

'The war's over!' she cried again, hugging my stiff body.

Leonard poured himself a large drink and sat in what had been my father's study. 'That's my father's study.' I hung about him, unsuccessfully trying to summon up indignation. My father had died four years ago when I was almost a baby. The emotion wouldn't come.

Leonard and my mother had met the night before. They told us they had celebrated together. I noticed that they kept touching each other and that Araminta was in a very bad mood. My mother took no notice. She was filled with exhilaration and impatience at the coming elections. She said to Leonard, 'If people don't want change now, then they're not worth helping.'

First she had to put her family affairs in order.

'Violet and Tudor,' she said with a firmness we had grown to expect of her. 'I'm taking you to Eureka to meet your grandmother. She's sent me a telegram. She is not well; in fact, she may be dying. It'll be a long, uncomfortable journey, so bring plenty of books and sweaters.'

'What about Leo?' objected Tudor.

'He's going to London with his father and his elder brothers and sisters. Leonard wants them to see the bomb craters, and Araminta needs a rest.'

'I want to see the bomb craters!' shrieked Tudor, grabbing our mother's arm. 'I don't care about stupid islands with stupid old ladies!'

In the end, the pilgrims to Eureka consisted of my mother, me, Molly, George and Henry Briggsworthy, and suddenly, at the last minute, Jack Logan, who had to pay an official visit to Ireland and thought he could get a bit of relaxation on the way.

He was under a sad misapprehension. The journey itself, even without the eccentricities of the pilgrims, was bad enough with all the soldiers of the world on the move. The Minister could get us no preferential treatment.

Henry Briggsworthy, whose insistence on wearing his bizarre army uniform embarrassed me deeply, was more successful. His majestically mad bearing and his rows of medals became suddenly convincing in the confusion of the times. Whole carriages emptied at his arrival.

He was very mad. He couldn't sit still for more than a few seconds and marched up and down the corridors. He called my mother 'Queen Mab.' George said if he had left him behind, he would have killed himself. We were all reasonably nice to him except Jack, whom I overheard saying to my mother, as they stood in the corridor of the train watching black smoke belch past their faces, 'What he needs is a good thump round the ears. Pampered aristocracy! He should take a look at parts of Liverpool or the East End or even Didcot . . .'

'He's not unhappy, he's mad,' said my mother, smiling, although I knew she was getting fed up with the 'Queen Mab' thing. Henry had begun bowing whenever she appeared.

'Huh!'

'I do believe George only brought him along to protect himself from Molly.'

'Molly! Why would he want to protect himself from Molly? She's the best thing around here.'

With this I totally agreed. Molly seemed to be a very special sort of old woman with her bush of fading red hair, her limp, and her bent, almost hunchbacked shoulders. Her specialness came from the vitality of her bright blue eyes, her unselfishness when it came to food or comfort, and her willingness to talk to me or play cards for as long as I wished. She was the first adult who had treated me as an adult. I was enslaved.

'Molly has turned into a saint,' my mother sighed to Jack. 'She always had principles, but her impatience stopped her becoming too good.' She moved her head back as a black tongue of smoke licked at the window. 'On the other hand, she's not particularly nice to George, and he is her husband.'

'Under the circumstances she's remarkably nice. I wouldn't be surprised if George went the same way as his cousin.'

'The Briggsworthy mad streak . . .' My mother sighed more feelingly than before. 'Don't come to the island. I'm beginning to be terrified of the raddled ghosts we'll find there.'

We arrived on the quayside at Dun Laoghaire in an extremely inhospitable dawn. It was raining, windy, and very cold. This was particularly unfortunate because Henry had spent the whole night parading across the deck, obeying unseen commands to wheel round, halt, present unseen arms, and the rest of it. George had tried to restrain him for a while but had then given up, retiring below to be very seasick. The Minister, who had a berth, said, 'With any luck, he'll throw himself over the side!'

My mother, refusing the Minister's not over-enthusiastic offer of his berth—'No dear; you're working tomorrow'—settled down with Molly over a beer-swilled table. I was wrapped in a rug near them.

All round us soldiers and sailors played cards, drank, slept, snored, and occasionally were sick. On the whole I thought Henry, marching in the pure cold air above, was more sensible than any of us.

But dawn and *terra firma*, which we found invigorating, caused him to collapse in sudden total exhaustion. He lay along a bench on the quayside facing the ship and fell into a semiconscious sleep. He was immovable. George, his kindly yellowish face and pointed nose twitching with anxiety, tried to lift him without success.

An official car arrived for Jack. The sight of its black sleekness and an efficient-looking driver surprised us all.

'Perhaps,' said my mother, recovering her poise with a pull or two at her neat black suit, 'you could drop us off at the harbour first. The little harbour where the boat goes to Eureka. We'll come back for George and Henry.'

The rain had stopped when we stepped out of the car into the deserted village street. A faint yellow suggested where the sun would be if it came out. This cheered us. 'I'll try and come later.' Jack drove off in the car. Its bonnet gleamed with droplets of rain.

'Now,' said my mother, energetically dispelling our sense of abandonment, 'to find Josiah. You two can stroll down to the boat.'

We found the boat easily enough. It was a heavy, potbellied creature smelling of grease and tar. But Josiah proved unobtainable. He had joined the Royal Navy two years ago and had not been seen since. I could see that this particularly depressed my mother. She had been relying on Josiah from some childhood habit. But at length Pat—a poor substitute, with few teeth and fewer brains—and a boy of about my age, shoeless and coatless, were stirred from their beds. They went over to the island about twice a week, they said, with provisions or a priest. Molly nodded sympathetically. But it was difficult, we must understand, with a war on.

'It's not on,' my mother objected, to which Pat agreed, but with a reserved air, as if we did not fully appreciate to which war he was referring.

'Oh dear.' Molly and my mother sat together just outside the boat's small cabin. 'How I longed to come to this island when we were children. Every holiday I prayed you would invite me.'

'I thought my mother would disapprove of your less than aristocratic origins,' said my mother with her worried look.

'So that was it.' Molly caught a wiry coil of hair that had sprung loose in the wind. 'I never thought you were a snob.'

'I wasn't. She was. Everybody was from her background.' There was a pause. 'I'm beginning to think she's not dying at all. Probably sensed I was making something of my life. The telegram was gibberish. She never even wrote to me after Nettles' death. Perhaps she didn't even get my letter.'

'I suppose it doesn't matter to her who's dead or alive. I dread seeing my mother-in-law.'

'I'm not surprised.'

'Perhaps they're both dead.'

'No such luck.'

I was surprised by this conversation. Surprised and shocked. Surely Pat would have informed them of a death. I pressed forward to see if they were joking, and my mother caught sight of me.

'Look, Violet!' she cried suddenly. 'Look at Eureka. See how it merges with the clouds and that streaky slither of sun. Don't you think it magic? Don't you?'

'Is that a castle?' I peered forward obediently, trying to separate the building from the trees.

'Go on! Go to the front! Stand up there! Let the wind blow through your hair!' I stared at my mother's excited face.

'Poor child, she's tired,' said Molly.

'I can't,' I said. 'Henry's there, and George. There's no room.'

'It doesn't matter.' My mother relapsed out of her fierce enthusiasm. 'I was such an idiotically romantic little girl. We'll be there in a moment.'

The sea was very high when we arrived at the harbour, so that it was easy to jump from the side of the boat onto the quay. I did so with the boy and, since there was no one to meet us, helped him coil the heavy ropes around the bollards. Henry, head high but knees low, strolled past me. 'Thank God, he's off duty,' said George. I laughed.

The island had suddenly revealed itself to me as a miracle. It was nowhere. It was as far away from the nursery of Kettleside as anywhere or nowhere in the world. Above us I could see sloping fields in which sheep and cows, goats, and even a pig all seemed to be grazing together.

'There's libertarian farming for you.' George saw where I was looking. We started upwards. Henry, even though off duty, had already disappeared round a corner. Behind us I could hear my mother talking excitedly to Molly. Pat and the boy were unloading the boat. They thumped provisions and our cases onto the quayside.

George walked so fast that I had to run. He began to talk to me about trees. 'You'd have thought lime trees would want limey soil, but actually they like lime-free.'

'I wish Jack hadn't gone,' I said. 'Now we're not as many men as women.' George stopped and looked at me with amazement.

'What an extraordinary thing to say.'

'It just struck me.'

He started walking again, but stopped talking about trees. He was probably still thinking about them though, because he always had a passion for trees. We had entered a sort of wooded grove, beyond which we could see the soft grey of the castle walls. Everything was overgrown. Our path was sometimes completely barred by brambles brought low with the weight of blackberries. George crushed them under his shoe, and my mother and Molly, hardly noticing, talking hard, stepped neatly over them. There was a gate through the walls, but there were so many spars missing that it was hardly worth opening.

'Just what I feared,' announced my mother loudly, abruptly turning her attention from Molly to all of us. 'Gone to rack and ruin. Worse than when I was here with horrible Howard. And it was bad then. Unless it was him.'

'Where's Henry?' said Molly, looking at my mother disapprovingly.

George pointed above our heads. 'He's all right.' Henry was standing to attention on the top of the wall, his left hand in a rigid salute.

'I suppose that means the ship's going,' said my mother.

'He doesn't know his left hand from his right,' apologised George, still watching Henry.

'I think your mother may be coming towards us,' said Molly quietly. We all turned our eyes swiftly to the castle. Under a wild avenue of lime trees which sprinkled the air with crisp golden leaves stepped a tiny prancing figure.

'Lazarus!' exclaimed my mother. 'Thank God Jack didn't come.'

'She does look in good physical shape,' admitted Molly, for the figure tripped towards us like a lighthearted child.

'Jack didn't say he wouldn't come at all,' I contributed.

'Henry's in good physical shape,' said my mother gloomily. 'Perhaps they can gambol about together.'

'Vi!' cried Molly and George in the same reproving tones. And they exchanged their first sympathetic look of the journey. Sometimes my mother was too coldhearted.

My grandmother started to talk excitedly from several yards distant. She had quite forgotten we were coming, despite her own dramatic summons and the telegram announcing our arrival. She had just happened to look out of her tower window and there were dear Pat and his boat speeding along the crests of the waves. She had jumped out of bed and come rushing out immediately. You never knew what that dreadful Pat might bring. Once he had brought an inspector from the Irish Tax Department. He hadn't stayed long. . . .

I inspected my grandmother. She was not as small as she'd looked from a distance, but very thin. She was wearing an all-in-one knitted garment rather like Churchill's famous siren suit except that it had a hood. The hood flapped closely round her cheeks, but still didn't disguise the wrinkled hollows under her eyes and her chin. Bristly white curls, almost alarmingly alive on one who seemed otherwise so old, bounced across her forehead.

'So you're my granddaughter!' She pointed her finger suddenly at me, and I noticed that her eyes were young too, a brighter and younger blue than my mother's.

'Yes.'

'Don't forget to call me Eleanor.'

'No.'

'We've had no breakfast,' said my mother. 'We're cold and tired and hungry. Can't we at least go inside?'

'I was going to collect some gulls' eggs,' said my grandmother reproachfully, but she spun round to face the castle. 'If you're so impatient, we'll make do with bread. Stale soda bread to sharpen your molars. Finola won't be down for an hour or so.'

She darted ahead, and we followed more slowly. Even Henry was lured down from the battlements by the idea of food. At the great wooden doors Eleanor, as I obediently tried to think of her, spun back to us. 'Don't you want to know where your dear mother is?' This time her finger was directed at George. It struck me, now that I had got over her odd appearance, that her voice was even odder. It was a mixture of Edwardian aristocratic and Jewish-American, plus her own habit of never quite completing any words. They hung without consonants as if they disappointed her and she could not be bothered to spend any more time on them. Or perhaps over the years on Eureka with Mrs Briggsworthy as her main audience, she had lost interest in communication.

'No,' said George in answer to her question about his mother. And then he amended it: 'Yes, I mean. Where is she?'

'Guess.'

'Please, Eleanor.'

'In church.' Eleanor waved her arm. Her gestures, unlike her words, were complete and commanding. 'On the hill. Praying. It's a saint's day—I forget which.'

'Every day's a saint's day.' Molly exchanged another of those sympathetic looks with George.

'How interesting.' My grandmother blinked white eyelashes at George coquettishly.

'I'm not walking over there without breakfast,' said my mother. Her voice was military.

'Nor me,' said Henry. We all looked at him, for he never spoke. Gallantly, he bowed us through the castle door.

'Well, well,' said Molly, taking George's arm. They hurried through thistles and brambles towards the church on the hill.

My mother wanted to leave Eureka the moment she saw that Eleanor was not dying. Eureka meant her childhood when my father was living with her mother. It meant her unhappy honeymoon. Now her mind was on politics. She had actually been accepted as a candidate; she should be canvassing. I understood none of this and was amazed when she told me she was trying to arrange for us to meet Jack in Dublin.

'But I love it here,' I protested. 'We've only just arrived.'

'I've got a lot to do.' My mother walked on the seashore while I, shoes and socks in my hands, jumped the frilling waves. 'You've met your grandmother.'

'And Mrs Briggsworthy.' I watched a wave splash up to my knee and catch the edge of my skirt.

'That's not the point.'

'She's so fat that when she kneels down she can hardly get up again.'

'She's probably hoping to die on her knees.'

'You shouldn't say things like that.'

'Don't be such a prig. Don't let Molly and George teach you to be a prig.'

'I like them!' Another splash ran up my thigh. What would Nanny say?

'That's not the point either. Anyway, I'm trying to get out. You can stay if you like. There's no food, the beds are damp, and the milk is crammed with brucellosis.'

'What's that?'

'Hallucinations.' She walked a little way up the beach, and when she turned back the sight of me splashing and jumping at a distance must have softened her, for she called, 'I'm glad you're having a nice time, darling. I used to love it at your age.'

The next day, at about the time when Eleanor started to drink—she did it quite openly, fetching herself a glass and a new bottle of Irish whisky—I noticed a boat starting from the mainland. I was by myself, sitting on top of the round hill behind the castle. George and Molly, with their newfound understanding, had gone to search for deer on the back of the island. Mrs Briggsworthy was praying. My mother was writing a speech. I wondered if she knew about the boat. But I was too lazy to tell her. It was a wonderfully bright autumn afternoon, with those specially Irish black clouds passing over so fast that they had no time to drop any rain. I decided to follow George and Molly, in the secret hope that the boat would have come and gone by the time I returned. I stood up from among the tall grasses and found myself face to face—well, face to chest—with Henry. He was standing with his peculiar stillness staring out to sea. I couldn't think how he'd crept up on me so suddenly.

'I hate this bloody island,' he muttered. I realised, with a nervous thrill, that he had taken off his fancy-dress uniform and was wearing an ordinary sweater and trousers. His mania, which I'd always treated as a kind of playacting, almost a joke, now seemed serious, even threatening.

'I was just off to find George—Molly,' I said moving away from him.

'You won't find them.' He talked fiercely, but his eyes were still fixed on the sea.

'I might.'

'You won't. They don't want to be found. Don't you see? They've gone off to be alone together. They've gone off to kiss and cuddle.' He turned round suddenly and grabbed my shoulders. 'That's what men and women do when they're in love—didn't you know? Didn't you know?'

I was very frightened now. His brown eyes were wide and staring, his face red, his mouth twisting and muttering. His fingers hurt my shoulders.

'They are married,' I stammered.

'Huh! Huh!' he shouted in my face. 'And who's been living with George all these years? Me! Me! Not that bitch. And now she jumps into his bed as if it was her right. She doesn't care if he lives or dies. I care!'

'George cares about you very much,' I said. 'He told me so.' I heard my own high-pitched, wheedling tone with surprise. It worked. Henry dropped his hands and turned back to the sea.

'I like the sea,' he said moodily but quietly. 'It doesn't change. You can trust the sea not to change.'

'But it does,' I said, my need for truth overcoming my good sense. 'It's rough or calm, and it goes in or out.'

'It doesn't change,' said Henry, ignoring me. 'There it is, day in, day out.' He started to walk away, stumbling a little as if in a trance. 'Day in, day out,' he repeated. 'Day in, day out, always there.'

I was tremendously relieved to see he had forgotten about me. The boat was closer now, but this did not seem to interest him. He was walking away from the harbour towards the caves and beaches on our left. I decided to make a more urgent search for George and Molly; Henry might do something odd.

Ever since my father's death I had known that even adults were vulnerable.

When Henry and I parted, he lurched across the fields with his eyes

331

fixed on the sea. Meeting no one, he climbed three stiles, two gates, pushed through a copse, and finally reached an uninterrupted view of the sea. He was at the top of a cove, about sixty feet above a shingly beach. He started down a narrow sheep path, but after a few feet the path crumbled away into nothing. In the old days a farm lad would have noticed this and put it right before a sheep hurtled off the edge. By the time of our visit there was no one to care.

Henry stood at the point where the path disappeared for some time. A trampled sprig of sea wort showed where he waited. Then, presumably with his eyes still fixed on the bright green water, he took a dive off the edge.

At about six o'clock the boat docked and Jack got off. He looked at the flushed sky, for the high-flying clouds had vanished, leaving a perfect, clear evening. He looked at the luxuriance of the trees and shrubs, at the pleasantly grazing animals, at the perfect formality of the stone castle. He wandered up the hill, sniffing the unpolluted air and wondering if he should throw up his career and become a farmer. He even considered my mother in the role of farmer's wife.

Within half an hour, he had been introduced to a pulpy corpse, a drunken hag, a religious maniac, and a hysterical child. My mother, cold as ice, was down at the farm making arrangements over the wireless. George had collapsed in guilt, while Molly had joined her mother-in-law in the chapel.

The chapel was a converted stone barn on a spar of the island. It was almost windowless, very black inside with a small red light burning. In the end all of us, except Eleanor, gathered there. It was too dark to take the body off the island before the morning. George said prayers. They were in Latin, and his voice went up and down, up and down, echoing against the stone walls. I sobbed, persistently, annoying my mother.

When we came out into the tranquil night, she put me on one side of Jack and took the other herself. The Briggsworthys were still praying in the church. We walked across the empty field.

'Now you see my problem.'

'What?' Jack sounded surprised. I tried to stifle my sobs in order to listen better.

'Muddles and drama!' Her voice was savage. 'How can I do anything surrounded by muddles and drama? How can I hope to become a Member of Parliament?'

'How can you think of that now?'

'I must. You don't understand. Men can't understand. You're made differently. Muddles and drama don't get into your bones. They lie outside. You enter them for a while and then you pass through the other side, unchanged. Women can't do that. Women

332

get dragged under. I am *not* going to be dragged under. I have a feeling about this election. I know no one thinks we'll win, but I think we will. I think people are fed up with the way England's run. They're fed up with the blackout, the blackout imposed by the ruling classes. They're even fed up with our victorious leaders. It's the press who think Churchill's a superman, not the people. They've had enough of rhetoric. They want changes; they want people who care. I care. I want to be part of the changes. I want to bring light. And look at me! In the middle of nowhere, surrounded by hysterical old women and children, mourning the loss of a silly fool crazed with self-pity who jumped off the edge of a cliff. It's not fair! It's not fair! I can't think why I ever came here. At least, I can think—so that I would never have to come again. And look at what it's led to! It's impossible! How can I ever be a sane, responsible person when I'm surrounded by lunacy? Oh Jack, take me away. Please take me away!' She burst into tears.

Not understanding most of what she said, I understood that I was part of what she wanted to leave, so my cries started afresh. Together we reached a crescendo of tears. Poor Jack! Never had his ability for feeling superficially been more useful. Nor, it must be admitted, my grandmother's supply of alcohol. We stumbled back to the house and I toasted the end of my childhood in Irish whisky.

My mother had now been nursing a Birmingham constituency for the Labour Party for a couple of years. Her enthusiasm had been so great that at one point she was even debarred because she'd been disseminating party political propaganda, which was forbidden during the war. But now she was poised for electioneering and the election. Her confidence in victory, which was shared by almost no one throughout the country on either side, was, I suppose, simply the intensity of her need. Yet she had worked for years with a cross section of women, seeing them in their homes, addressing them at meetings, organising them into working parties, so maybe she did know more than most.

After the horrible fiasco of our visit to Eureka, we all, except my mother, arrived in London numbed and without energy. She had absolutely refused to bring Henry's body back on the train despite George's pleas, so he was left to the chapel on the hill and Mrs Briggsworthy's prayers. As soon as we reached Victoria station, my mother started to give instructions. 'See you at the Lyons on Piccadilly one o'clock,' she said, and then disappeared.

Molly and George were not speaking to each other at all and little to anyone else. He left us for Waterloo station and Didcot almost at once. Molly took me to Madame Tussaud's. The celebration bunting with which poor pitted London was still decorated was at odds with our mood of mourning. I wondered if we might begin to smile a little. I said tentatively, 'It's nice Henry's buried facing the sea.'

Molly turned to me, surprised. 'Are you thinking of him still?'

'Well . . . yes. I thought . . .'

'That's why I'm so gloomy? Not at all, darling. I'm a Catholic. Catholics believe in life after death, a better life after death. Particularly for someone like poor Henry. Oh, yes. This world is only preparation for the next. Lucky Henry! We should be celebrating.'

'Should we?' I dared a franker gaze at the flags. 'They are lovely, aren't they?'

'I'm gloomy because I made the mistake of looking for happiness in this world. George and I were getting on well together. After years of being apart. And now it's all wrecked. It's my own fault; I should never have been so naive. Now George really hates me. He blames me for poor Henry's death.'

I saw that after all it would not be tactful to smile at the flags. I tried to look sympathetic. I said, 'But you're married.'

Molly laughed. She paused and then laughed again. 'You're quite right. Ah, well, I expect Father Wilson will keep me busy. Let's go and see how war has affected the Chamber of Horrors.'

When we arrived at the Lyons in Piccadilly, there was a note from my mother saying she had had to rush up to her constituency and would Molly and I look after her guests. 'Miss Loxley-Peacock seems to be offering a solution to the problem of Violet's future.'

Not having known I constituted a problem, I was somewhat piqued by this, though not as much as her male guest was by my mother's non-arrival. He was Eddie Pemberton, a Canadian, my cousin. She had rung him only a couple of hours ago and invited him to lunch. How could she have gone away?

On the other hand, Miss Loxley-Peacock was simply delighted to see Molly again. Her pale, regular features reminded me of my mother's, although her smooth dark-red hair and deep, level voice were far too calm. Molly was delighted to see her too. She cried, 'Oh, dear old Loxy-Poxy!' I gathered that she was a headmistress and that Molly had been her star-pupil. Since they were removed into another world of excited memories, there was nothing left for Cousin Eddie but to face me.

'I hear you've come from a most unpleasant experience.'

'I'm not thinking about that anymore.'

'You're not.' He looked nonplussed. He was not used to precise English accents combined with my little-girl conviction.

'No. He's gone to a better world. I'm thinking about my future.'

'Oh. And what's that?'

'It's linked to her.' I indicated Miss Loxley-Peacock, who was listening to Molly and eating the thinly sliced white bread and margarine which was all we'd been given so far. 'I think she's a teacher.'

'I never had much schooling. Although I have a literary ambition.'

'What's that?'

'I mean to write a book.'

'My mother has political ambitions.'

'My book will be about the Old and New Worlds. My father's experiences in Canada.'

Although it didn't sound a very interesting subject, I responded politely, because I could see it was something he cared about. 'Perhaps I'll read it when I'm older. My father was killed, you know. Four years ago.'

'Then we have something in common. Mine's dead too. He was run over by a train.'

I looked at the round reddish face, the short, clean fair hair, and the friendly expression and decided I liked my cousin. 'I may write a book too. Will you visit London on occasions?'

'I'm going to live here.'

'You two seem to be getting on very well.' Molly's gloom at the second collapse of her marriage had receded under her old headmistress' attention. She looked quite young. Her blue eyes flashed, her hands chopped the air. 'Miss Loxley-Peacock has a proposition for you, Violet.'

'Your future,' said Eddie, winking at me.

My future was a place at Shoreham Abbey. The school had been removed from the South Coast for the war and was returning there—rather late, owing to slight bomb damage—for the new school year. Miss Loxley-Peacock would escort me in person the very next day.

'But I have no clothes,' I cried, thinking that after so much tragedy and confusion on Eureka I couldn't possibly set out on my future without first touching base again.

'We'll buy some this afternoon.' Molly sounded jealous. 'You're so lucky to start Shoreham at a decent age. What bliss! Eight years of Shoreham Abbey ahead.'

'You didn't think so at the time.' Miss Loxley-Peacock smiled archly.

'I'll have to go home first,' I wailed. 'Nanny will wonder. So will Leo and Tudor and Henrietta and Flo and everybody. The twins like me to give them their bottle.'

'I don't think they're listening,' said Eddie. 'Your mother must be quite a fixer.'

'She's going to be a Member of Parliament,' I said, resigning from the task of deflecting my frog march to Shoreham Abbey. Besides, a heavily lipsticked waitress had brought our food, and the mashed

335

potato looked good enough to eat.

> Those who have the will to win
> Cook potatoes in their skin
> Knowing that the sight of peelings
> Deeply hurts Lord Woolton's feelings

recited my cousin, trying to cheer me up.

I thought nostalgically of the limited horizons of the war. Already it seemed a long while ago. 'She's a Labour candidate,' I said.

'How extraordinary!' Eddie indeed looked quite amazed. 'From her background? You can be certain, then, she won't get in. No one's even heard of the Labour Party.'

'I hadn't heard of Shoreham half an hour ago, and yet now it's my future for the next eight years. So why shouldn't it be just the same for the Labour Party?'

Molly lifted her cup of tea in a salute. 'If my mind had been half as clear at your age, what wouldn't I have done?'

'Not got married, for a start,' I replied, made bold by the success of my last remark.

'There is a certain truth in the proposition that men don't last'— Miss Loxley-Peacock gave her tinned peas a look of dissatisfaction—'but it mustn't be taken to extremes.'

'Find me a woman who can do without a man!' Eddie seemed disconcerted by the serious tone of the conversation. 'I intend to marry and I expect no trouble in finding a bride.'

'Women have the vote too,' said Molly. 'And women know what's needed in this country.'

'In that case,' I shouted triumphantly 'I bet you anything Mummy wins!'

Chapter Thirteen

PROTEST AGAINST FILM

Dr. Edith Summerskill, in her presidential address to the annual meeting of the Association for Married Women, advised members to protest against the showing of the film 'No Orchids for Miss Blandish'. In her opinion the film . . . would pervert the minds of the British people. She deplored, too, the fact that this film had been produced by a British firm merely for commercial profit.

The Times.   19 April 1948

TIME FOR DECISION

The Government have to make up their mind about the Russian pressure on Berlin, about the dockers' threat to wreck exports and cut off food supplies, and about the obligations which the Americans have attached to Marshall help . . .

The Times.   28 June 1948

SLOGANS ON COLLEGE WALLS

At the five women's colleges of Oxford University yesterday, every available member of the staff was engaged in removing slogans which had been painted in letters 2 foot high on the walls during the night. One slogan was in Latin.

The Times.   14 June 1955

I liked Miss Loxley-Peacock. She made Shoreham Abbey a pleasurable experience—at least until the days of William Sidebotham.

On that first train journey we sat opposite each other—a terrified nine-year-old girl in a prewar uniform made for a twelve-year-old, and a conservatively dressed woman with heavy white powder and hair too red for someone on the road to retirement. Suddenly she leaned forward as if struck by an important thought. She tapped my knees, which even under the heavy serge were blue and shaking with the cold of the unheated carriage. 'Aha!' she cried. 'It's a wonder your mother didn't send you to one of her great government schools!' Although I didn't understand the reference, I saw the victor's smile and returned it heartily. A bond was formed: I was a hostage snatched from the indiscriminate jaws of socialism.

Miss Loxley-Peacock said, 'My girls have personality!' And it was true in a way, except that we all wanted our 'personality' to be hers. One girl even dyed her hair red. Her punishment was to wear a paper bag night and day. At night it crackled whenever she turned, keeping the whole dormitory awake. Loxy-Poxy still believed in discipline. So did I.

When I went back to Kettleside I infuriated Araminta with my attempts to rationalise her romantic disorder. 'Why do we all eat breakfast at different times?'

'Because we all want it at different times.' Araminta couldn't move away because I was holding up a skein of wool while she wound it into a ball.

'It's quite easy. All you do is bang a gong at the agreed time and then clear away in half an hour.'

'We'd never agree.' She flicked the tail of wool off my hands.

'And the other thing is, about the Sweet Ration . . .'

Araminta tossed the tightly bound ball of purple wool in the air, and I saw her eyes follow its progress admiringly. However harassed, she never lost her pleasure in textures and colour; it was all of the painter she had allowed to remain in herself. Now it gave her the spirit to cut off any remarks, 'Ask the Minister!' she cried.

The Minister to whom she referred was no longer Jack Logan, although he still was a Minister—indeed, now in the Cabinet as Minister of Employment—but my mother. My mother's rise through the ranks of the Labour Party was meteoric. No more so, perhaps, than that of Harold Wilson, who was made a Junior Minister as soon as he was elected to Parliament and President of the Board of Trade within a few years; nor that of Patrick Gordon-Walker, who, becoming an MP in a bye-election after the war, was in the Cabinet by 1950. But it seemed more dramatic in a woman. Particularly one like my mother, still very good-looking and with an

338

unusual background for a Labour politician. She came in with the tide of victory she'd forecast in 1945. Into the Lords' Chamber, since the Commons had been bombed out of existence. By 1947 she was already a Parliamentary Under-Secretary, exerting influence even in the Cabinet, since her chief sat in the Lords. Once when I asked her about her success she reported a conversation she had had with the Prime Minister at about this time. As a woman, she was seated next to him at a lunch held in the House of Commons. He was talking nostalgically of Haileybury and 'Univ', his school and college.

'Your father still alive?' he said to my mother.

'Died in 1915.'

'1915?' The Prime Minister's face cleared with enthusiasm. 'Killed, was he? In the war?'

'Yes.'

'At Gallipoli, perhaps?'

'No, Hooge.' Sensing a slight disappointment, my mother added quickly, 'Leading his men over the top.'

'Ah, yes. Leading his men. Great thing to have a father like that. Heroic.' The Prime Minister beamed with admiration and, according to my mother, brought up the memory of her father whenever she was being difficult or he had any doubts about her capabilities or beliefs. Vague echoes of her childish disappointment over the manner of his death washed up to her. It had taken over thirty years and a Prime Minister to reinstate her father as the hero in her life.

The goodwill of the Prime Minister was obviously useful, but even more so was the direct patronage of a Cabinet Minister. Her affair with Jack Logan had become occasional; he preferred younger, more passionate women. But their friendship had grown even stronger. They were now colleagues. My mother's grasp of politics and manipulation of people impressed Jack—although also occasionally annoying him.

'It's your feudal blood,' he would say, half-jokingly. 'Centuries of organising the peasants.'

'What nonsense, Jack! Most of the Ministers went to public school; you're the exception.'

'What about the people? The way you manage your party workers. It's disgraceful. They'd kiss the hem of your black skirt if you let them. It's not socialism.'

'It's charm,' said my mother, smiling, who would never have admitted such a thing a year or two ago. 'And past association with Flo.'

The major problem my mother had faced was how to get on with the rank and file of the Labour Party. The worst struggle—ironically enough, since it was the occupation which had given her the spur to succeed in politics—was to overcome the right-wing image that her years of work with the WVS had given her. It did not matter particularly to the Members of Parliament. But she had to get to the House of Commons first. And it mattered very much to the ordinary party workers, who even in the middle of war time could see that the WVS was run by women of the 'wrong class' and the 'wrong views.' Luckily, in 1942 my mother had become very interested in the Women for Peace Movement, which was distinctly left-wing. As she began to work actively for this and the Labour Party, she had naturally found it impossible to work for the WVS. Those who thought about this change of direction put it down to the tragic circumstances in which she had lost her husband. Women, unlike men, are expected to act not out of principle but out of personal motives. It was considered natural she should suffer a revulsion against the war and even understandable that she should be more interested in creating a new society after the war than in continuing to serve under its yoke.

Some of this, no doubt, was true. On the other hand, my mother had learned through her work with the WVS that she wanted to serve in public life, and when, with my Father's death, she realised that this was to be a lifetime's ambition, she had looked round to see where she could do most good. The practicalities of the WVS were no longer enough for her. She wanted to affect the structure of society. She had opted for the Labour Party.

Even the Labour Party couldn't turn down such an eager and determined convert. But it was her first speech from the floor at Conference which made sure she would be an MP. The press put her on the front pages. Suddenly her appearance and manner, which had seemed a disadvantage, became an asset. She was known. She spoke fiercely, sincerely for the principles of socialism. She was a star. Not for long, but for long enough to get her elected. Even the most dour-faced constituency party worker likes to feel that he has hooked a Member of Parliament who is famous throughout the country.

Once my mother had her own life spinning onwards—no one was surprised when the 1950 election found her actually inside the Cabinet as Minister of Health and Housing—she occasionally found time to worry about me. I was not what she'd expected in a daughter. Instead of being plump, rosy-cheeked, curly-haired, shining-eyed with inexhaustible energy, I was dark, thin, and quiet. I knew she found me watchful and sly. I didn't really feel myself to be like that. But I could see I gave that impression when she joined us in the holidays at Kettleside or came to visit me at Shoreham Abbey—incidentally (or not incidentally) delivering a lecture about socialism and nationalisation which horrified the parents only slightly less than it did Loxy-Poxy.

That particular visit was shortly before the advent of Mr Sidebotham. I have sometimes attributed his presence to that speech. Miss Loxley-Peacock felt the ground shiver under her feet and looked for support. She hit on William Sidebotham. I could not understand how she could consider marrying such a pale, bald man. The absurdity of Sidebotham seemed inexcusable. Bad taste. Bad taste was something one would have thought as far removed from Loxy-Poxy as a man. Yet the two came in together, and other things too.

She moved out of the school proper and into a gardener's cottage in the grounds. In the good old days she arrived at morning assembly with a look of total dedication, as if she had just risen from direct communication with God over the fate of her girls that day. We listened, hardly breathing, watching that pale powdered face and immaculate red halo as if she were indeed a goddess.

Now she arrived in a hurry as if she'd come from jobs quite unrelated to the school. Her hair was slightly fluffy, as if, sacrilegious thought, it had lain on a pillow. Much worse, as the days went on a grey line began to show, gradually spreading backwards to the crown of her head. That in itself would have been enough to finish her in the eyes of teenage girls to whom appearance was vitally important. But then she began to make references in her addresses to men.

The idea that men should figure in an address from the Shoreham Abbey stage would have been laughable, if it hadn't been so serious, a few months ago. The unspoken belief was that men, with the unavoidable exceptions of Fathers and Brothers, did not exist. Gardeners and plumbers, being workers, were not, of course, what we meant by men. Men in literature were acceptable, but there was a strong feeling that, for example, the male characters of Shakespeare were much improved by being played by women. Miss Loxley-Peacock had a special manner with Fathers and Brothers at Open Days, a sort of charming patronage, which we all tried desperately to imitate—usually with hilarious results.

'Is there something wrong with your eyes, Sis?' Tudor asked me sympathetically, on receiving the look. I used to pay Tudor the compliment of believing he created his lack of originality as an antidote to my mother.

And now in front of the whole school, this terrible, untidy, half-dyed Mrs Sidebotham was excusing her lateness on grounds of fixing a collar stud into her husband's shirt. A thrill ran through the school. We crept to our classrooms in shocked silence. She had made herself ridiculous. The spirit of Shoreham Abbey had departed. That evening I wrote a letter to my mother demanding to be removed at the end of term. Several other girls did too, although since we wrote

341

in shameful secret—the horror was too great to share—I didn't know at the time.

It was the summer term of 1951 and I was sixteen. I had just taken my School Certificate exam. I felt sure I would pass. The grounds of Shoreham Abbey had never looked more beautiful. The lawns, which spread over four or five acres, were a perfect brilliant green; the large trees, planted a hundred years ago when the house had been a gentleman's residence, cast grand Victorian shadows. There were a cedar, its great trunk dividing into sinewy limbs, a Wellingtonia, with its soft orange skin pitted by picking children's fingers, a vast oak spreading shade over half an acre, and two tall monkey puzzles, already becoming unfashionable but too strong and perfect to cut down. I loved the monkey puzzles. But that day, with the problems of Miss Loxley-Peacock's faithlessness and my future to consider, I preferred the tranquillity of the oak. I sat on the grass. This was strictly forbidden. For once I didn't care. The other girls had gone down to the sea for a swim. It had been hot and dry for several days, so the ground was hard. I laid open my copy of *Richard III*. We were performing it as the end-of-term play. I was playing the title role. Clearly Miss Loxley-Peacock did not believe in typecasting, since I was exceptionally tall and straight-limbed. 'Now is the winter of our discontent . . .' I mouthed half-heartedly. Molly Briggsworthy would have made an excellent Richard III, I thought.

When we made our trip to Eureka, she had been bent, lame, and greying. An especially nice old lady. Six months later she had come to visit me at Shoreham Abbey.

She stood in the hall waiting for me. She was very very pregnant, a jutting ledge of flesh, which in the fashion of the times was accentuated rather than disguised by a short boxy jacket. 'Dear Violet! I've been meaning to come down for so long . . .' She rocked towards me like some upside-down toy clown, apparently quite unaware of the feelings she might produce. I backed hastily, terrified 'that' might touch me. I was torn between wanting to get out of Shoreham Abbey, so that no one would see my shame, and not wanting to go anywhere public, like a restaurant or a park, where other people would see. How could they not stare? I thought, staring myself. How could Molly do it to herself?

'How could it happen to me?' was Molly's own often reiterated complaint. Everyone knew she was barren. That was mostly why her marriage had broken up. How could one act of love produce a child when years of intimacy had failed? The doctor said it was a common medical example of the late fertility cycle. Father Wilson said it was the Will of God to teach her humility and love. My mother said it was George's superpotency after years of celibacy. Eleanor said it was the

342

Irish air. George, after a prayer of thanksgiving in the family chapel, said it was the spirit of Henry being given new life in Molly's body. It showed God had forgiven them for causing Henry's death, and it made him very happy. This attitude made Molly so angry that any possibility of a further reconciliation between the new parents became impossible.

'I won't go near him!' she screamed. 'It's bad enough giving me a baby at my age. But when he starts this ridiculous reincarnation claptrap . . . Even if his chosen one wasn't a lunatic, it would be insupportable.'

'A baby should have two parents,' suggested Father Wilson.

'One at a time,' snapped Molly.

'Give it to Araminta,' suggested my mother, who was much the most sympathetic of Molly's friends. Funnily enough her suggestion had the immediate effect of making Molly do a complete *volte-face* and decide she wanted the baby after all. 'Her enthusiasm won't survive nappies,' said Araminta.

But at the time Molly came to visit me, she was proud of her condition, sharing my point of view only in a determination to believe it a virgin birth. Down with men!

As I thought of Molly that sunny evening under the oak tree, I was struck by the thought that although she had made herself absurd, the cause of it, the baby, had been quite lovely. Everyone had admired my photograph of the tiny boy with his white skin, blue eyes, and mass of reddish-gold hair. He wore a long white embroidered robe, for he was being christened by Father Wilson and I was godmother.

'I baptise you Benjamin Disraeli Benedict Thomas St John Briggsworthy,' Father Wilson had intoned, dousing his narrow head with water. A little later he had suffered another sluicing when George, who had refused to come to the ceremony, baptised him personally in the chapel at Didcot: 'I baptise you Henry George St John Briggsworthy.' For some reason his parents both agreed on St John, which is why, I suppose, when he was old enough to care he abandoned both Henry and Benjamin and called himself St John.

At the age of sixty-five, Loxy-Poxy could hardly hope to produce a St John. It did not strike me she might be looking for personal happiness. Happiness had not yet displaced duty as a worthy ambition. I would send another even more insistent letter to my mother.

I embarked on 'Now is the winter of our discontent . . .' with such passion that the rooks rose off the pines at the end of the garden. 'I that am curtail'd of this fair proportion, cheated of feature by dissembling nature, Deform'd, unfinished . . .'

Unfortunately, the summer of 1951 was hardly the time to concern my mother with my problems. The Labour Party majority had become so small as to be hardly workable. They were tired, ready to win again or give up the struggle. All the talk was about when they should hold an election. My mother favoured hanging on, but she was in the minority. Jack looked at her and said, 'Women have such tenacity.' To which she replied honestly, 'I've only been in the Cabinet for a year. There's so much I want to do.' In the Cabinet the Prime Minister said, 'If we're out, we'll be out for years.'

At least, I consoled myself, she would come down to see me act the hunchbacked king. A glance at the wreck of Loxy-Poxy, a glance at the humble Sidebotham, and she would whisk me away. My brilliant interpretation of poor Richard's tortured nature would convince her I was no longer a child. Luckily, mirrors were banned from Shoreham Abbey, so I could not see my own absurdity as five foot and eight healthy inches bent unwillingly under a plaster-of-Paris hump and a black crêpe-paper cloak. My main worry, apart from remembering the words, was that my paper breeches would split. Loxy-Poxy believed as little in spending money on costumes as she did in typecasting. 'I want no soft bedding for my girls!' she would say, banging her hand on the table, and we all imagined her and Mr Sidebotham on a hard mattress.

One of the rules of the Shoreham Abbey Open Day was that it should not be open. No child was allowed to make contact with her parents till after the major event of the day, which was held at 2:30 PM. This gave a frantic air to the show as performers and audience sighted each other in the oak-beamed assembly hall. I passed Lady Anne's speech 'Foul Devil, for God's sake hence, and trouble us not' searching across the row of faces for my mother. She wasn't there. However, near the back of the hall sat Araminta, arm in arm with a young man who looked about the same age as her eldest twins. My disappointment and curiosity made me return to her during anyone else's long speeches. So as Buckingham began, 'My Lord, this argues conscience in your Grace,' I was looking in the right direction when the door at the back clanked loudly and my mother, dressed in a shiny scarlet mackintosh, made a dramatic entrance.

'Alas, why should you heap . . .' hissed the prompter. Reluctantly I returned to Baynard Castle and thus missed the moment when Araminta, catching sight of the scarlet mac, rose majestically to her feet and, pushing herself and the young man past many knees, disappeared out of the room.

Such a late, noisy arrival by any other mother than mine would have caused ostracism among the teachers and deep shame to the child. But my mother was a Cabinet Minister. The red mackintosh was a defiant gesture. Even towards the end of Labour's golden years, the symbolism of Red, The Red Flag, had still the power to move.

We stood together with cups of tea and buns in the dining room. I was still wearing my costume, inflamed with what I confidently assumed to be my success. 'Why were you late? Why aren't you wearing a hat? Where has Araminta gone to?'

'Your enunciation was very clear, darling. I could hear every word,' said my mother. But I saw that she was directing politicians' smiles over my shoulder at parents and teachers. 'Clear enunciation' was as bad as the prize for 'Good Attendance' traditionally won by the stupidest girl in the school.

'It's no good smiling here. They're all rabid Conservatives. They only admire your power, not your views.'

'I'm sorry, darling.' She switched her full attention to me and even managed to look slightly guilty. 'It's your big day.'

'It's probably just a habit,' I said kindly, which, to do her justice, made her smile. 'Where has Araminta gone to?' I repeated.

'I'm afraid she's avoiding me. She didn't think I was coming. You're quite grown up now; you might as well appreciate these things. She's angry with something I did. Years ago now. But she's only just found out for certain.' She paused, and although I looked inquiringly, she obviously decided I was not quite old enough to hear everything, for she said, 'Anyway, she's having the change of life. You know about that, don't you? It makes you irritable.'

'Talking about change . . .' I was reminded of my problems.

'Oh, yes. Poor darling Loxy-Poxy. It is so extraordinary that even the most intelligent women still fundamentally believe that the answer to life is a man. Any man. Still, you mustn't begrudge her her happiness. I've arranged for you to go to a crammer's in London. I'll go and have a word with her now. And then I must be off. I've got a car waiting. You'll come back in the train, won't you? Or perhaps Araminta will reappear?'

Araminta did reappear the moment my mother, after warm, if brief, greetings to Loxy-Poxy, was safely in her official car. Araminta still held her young man tightly by the arm. Besides noting that the eye patch seemed vaguely familiar, I was too excited by the thought of leaving Shoreham Abbey for good that very afternoon to think of anything else. 'I'm going,' I cried out. 'I'm leaving school! Mummy's arranged it all. Isn't she wonderful?'

Araminta's lack of response made me take more notice of her. It struck me that she had never visited Shoreham Abbey before and that she had left Northumberland only three or four times in all my life.

'Get yourself some tea, Hubert,' she commanded her companion. 'Come and sit down with me, Violet. I want to talk to you.' I noted

345

that her face was pinker than usual, her hair was elegantly styled in a modern chignon, and she was wearing a smart silk dress of a very different style from her usual flowing robes. It made her look unexpectedly small and slim. Nevertheless, despite these signs of outward organisation, she emanated none of the calm which, apart from her occasional periods of breakdown, usually came from behind the straggling hair and sloppy dress. Now she seemed nervous, hyperanimated; her blue eyes flicked around as she pulled me down beside her on a hard school bench.

'Who's Hubert?' I said before she could speak.

'Oh, he doesn't matter.' She looked cross. 'You know him, anyway. Isabel's husband. Ex-husband. You remember him, surely? You were quite besotted, the three of you . . .' Her voice trailed away into thoughts.

'In the war!' Vague memories stirred.

'Of course, of course. I told you. He's not important. I just happened to bump into him in London a few days ago. He drove me down. He has a car. Isabel got married again today. I think he's well rid of her. But he was lonely.' Her blue eyes directed across the room to where Hubert was queuing for tea with a speculative expression, but then returned suddenly to mine. She sat close to me and pressed my hand. 'I don't want to talk about him. I want to talk about your mother.'

'Oh dear,' I said, remembering now my mother's explanation. 'I like your dress.'

'That's part of it. I bought it at Harrods. It's a model, the most expensive dress in the department. I would have bought it whatever it looked like.' She stroked the silk covering her knee.

'It looks very smart.'

'I had my hair done too. And a manicure. I bought four pairs of shoes and cashed a very large cheque. That's where I met Hubert. In the Harrods bank.'

'What a coincidence!'

'Things like that happen in London all the time.' This was said with such meaningful bitterness that I foolishly asked, 'Like what?'

'Like your mother having a dirty affair with Leonard!' To my horror, I saw the possibility of tears in her quivering face. The need to stop this seemed far more important than the significance of her words. It also gave me a sudden total recall of the Hubert episode, for he, of course, had coincided with Araminta's great crying period.

'We all love you!' I cried wildly. 'I don't know what we'd do without you.'

'Oh, darling, darling! How can anyone so understanding have a mother like yours? You looked so fine up there on the stage. I was so sorry to leave. All my own children think I'm too silly for words, particularly now I've found Hubert. Why shouldn't I have a boyfriend? Everyone else does. I'm not that old; he's not that young. Clancy was quite sympathetic till I brought Hubert back. You would think I was cradle-snatching. Anyway, he's not important, but if I want him I'll have him. He thinks I'm beautiful. And now I can't have any more babies, there's no reason why I shouldn't if I want to. Is there? I can have lovers as well as anyone else. Clancy says my metabolism has become unbalanced by too many babies and that I'm suffering from withdrawal symptoms now that I'm past the age of having more. She says it's ridiculous to worry about what your husband did years and years ago. But your mother was my best friend, Violet. Still is my best friend. I knew they were attracted to each other, but I never thought they would actually sleep together. But they did in London. More than once. When I was far away in Northumberland, bringing her son and daughter up as if they were my own children. I've paid her back a hundred times for giving me a home. Oh, Violet, your mother is a hardhearted, scheming woman! Be warned. I've come to warn you, and I have!'

We must have looked a very odd couple: the miserably embarrassed schoolgirl with hump sliding off one shoulder, and the hysterical forty-six-year-old woman. Hubert—or Captain Creswell, as I now remembered him—joining us with his good eye fixed gloomily on the slopping cups of tea, fitted in very well. 'It's cold,' he said.

Araminta's outburst seemed to have calmed her, for she went pale again and drank the cup of cold tea silently.

Hubert said, 'I never thought Isabel would marry again. I could understand her wanting to be free to concentrate on her work. It wasn't much of a marriage anyway, once she started living in Hollywood. But I didn't expect her to marry again. Now they've got my son. He's only a baby.'

'She's so famous,' I said helplessly. I saw there was no point in expecting any reference to my performance.

Captain Creswell looked at me for the first time. 'Exactly.' His voice sounded remotely more cheerful at my understanding. Araminta put down her teacup and nodded agreement. 'Like the Minister.' I felt I had passed some test. I took off my hat and shook out my hair.

Araminta stood up. 'We're going to Venice. We're going as lovers to the most romantic city in the world. It might teach your mother a lesson.'

In the course of an hour or so, Shoreham Abbey had changed from occupying the central place in my life to becoming a mere backcloth. Even my friends, most of whom would be staying on till they were eighteen, seemed uninterestingly callow. I was the confidante of a distraught woman and the ex-husband of a film star. It seemed likely they were living in sin. However, it was probably better for my peace of mind not to examine that aspect of the matter too closely. Definitely not mention it to any of the girls at Shoreham Abbey. As I saw Loxy-Poxy approaching us, I inquired hastily, 'Aren't tickets to Venice awfully expensive?'

'That's why I drew all that money out of the Harrods bank,' said Araminta with a return to her old placidity. 'I've made a beautiful hat, all covered with cabbage roses.'

'Ah, Mrs Trigear.' Loxy-Poxy arrived graciously, hand outstretched. 'After so much correspondence, we meet at last. And you have brought . . . your son, is it?'

Poor old thing, I thought, looking without emotion at Loxy-Poxy's greying hair and shiny face. It's terrible when a woman lets herself go. Then something in her expression reminded me of all the times she had helped and inspired me, so that with a sudden generosity I added to myself, I'm glad she has a husband to look after her.

My confident adolescent heart swelled to encompass all the lonely women who had no Mr Sidebotham, no Captain Creswell. I did not think of my mother.

Araminta and Hubert dropped me off at my mother's flat. She was sobbing again, with defiance and too many gins in a pub we'd stopped at on the way up. The flat was empty. I went to sleep on the very comfortable sofa. A couple of hours later I was awakened out of an exciting Freudian dream about snakes and bulls by a small boy shouting repeatedly, 'Toast, toast, toast! With cheese! With cheese!'

This was a typical pattern for future association with my mother. All arrangements were planned with generosity and carried out with precision; cars were available; tickets bought; a warm flat waiting; drinks and glasses laid out; a place for me at the crammer's (or at university, or a job) lined up; money ready in an envelope, even very often accompanied by a note (not always handwritten but always personally signed)—but only very, very seldom, my mother herself. Instead there would be someone else, someone very appropriate whom I wanted to see, but who was nevertheless not my mother.

On this occasion it was Molly. She was fretted by motherhood, but still glad to see me. 'Hear you've been placating the lovebirds. You do look well. Quite buxom. You used to be such a weedy thing. Is that all you, or are you wearing one of those new foam brassière things?'

348

'Of course not,' I said with a mixture of indignation and embarrassment. I was very proud and self-conscious of my quite considerable breasts. They were bigger than my mother's already.

'Sorry. No offence meant. You look marvellous, anyway. Such a trim waist, too. I suppose there's no hope of seeing your important mother? How could you know? I've just been giving this little monster an outing.' She indicated St John, who was tucking into his cheese on toast. 'He lives with his father mostly. I never was one of nature's mothers. I'm much happier looking after the deadbeats Father Wilson's found for me down in the East End.' She gave another ferocious look at her son, who had cheese up to his eyes. 'Other people say he's sweet, but I find him terribly irritating. Luckily, George has found a saintly ex-nun to look after him. Do you think he's sweet?'

I looked doubtfully. 'The cheese doesn't help. But his curls are nice. Isn't it very late for him to be still up?'

Molly sighed. 'Strange to think neither Vi nor I can put up with our children. We were taught to assume motherhood would be the absolute *raison d'être*. At least, I think we were. Although, come to think of it, her mother certainly didn't believe that, and I never had a mother . . .' As she trailed off into a thoughtful silence, I felt very sorry for myself. It was all very well feeling your mother didn't care, but not so good to be told it as a matter of fact. Molly looked up. 'Oh, dear, what is the matter?'

'My mother is very good to me,' I said in a stifled voice. 'And to Tudor too. She's just very busy.'

'Oh God. I *am* sorry; I quite forgot. You're so unlike her . . . I was talking about myself. Really, I was making up stories. Please don't take it personally.'

'I don't—but you shouldn't say that about my mother.'

'Oh, darling.' But I would not let Molly's hugs warm me.

'But my mother especially wanted to see me here, at the flat.'

'Of course she did! Come on, St John, we've got to take you back to Our Father nearly in heaven and ex-Sister Bernadette.'

I retired to the small spare bedroom, thinking my mother would have to woo me when she returned. This she did easily, appearing at midnight with a cup of hot chocolate. The adrenalin pumping through her veins after what had obviously been a fiery meeting with a colleague filled the little room like electricity. I woke up shaking.

'Here,' she said, thrusting the steaming mug at me so that, feeling obliged to take an immediate gulp, I burned my mouth. 'Isn't it exciting? You'll be starting at the crammer's just when the election's on. I'm sure it'll be October or November now. Of course, I'll be away in

Birmingham quite a bit, but you won't mind. At the weekends you can deliver pamphlets and wear a huge red rosette. You'd like that, wouldn't you?'

'Araminta's going to Venice,' I mumbled dazedly, trying to enter the spirit of the thing. 'She's made a hat with roses all over it.'

'She won't hate me after that. Good. A hat? Conservative ladies wear hats. Oh, dear!' She sighed suddenly, and some of the adrenalin evaporated. 'I fear it may be no good being optimistic this time.'

As usual, she was right. On both counts. Araminta's animosity towards my mother was cancelled out by gondolas under the Rialto. The Labour Party was thrown out at the elections.

I'm ashamed to say that, despite wearing a gigantic red rosette for the duration of the six-week election campaign, I was delighted. I thought, quite wrongly, that if she was out of office, she would have more time for me. The truth was that she had got into the habit of being busy. She could not help herself. The knowledge that she was being busy about things that were no longer of great importance to the country merely made her irritable. Besides, the supports of ministerial office—the chauffeur, the civil servants—were no longer available. Therefore, since she insisted on being as busy as before, she had less spare time rather than more.

We met most often at the excellent parties she gave. Sometimes she looked at me with surprise. She couldn't get used to the idea she had a nearly grown-up daughter. One evening I brought an admirer. He was called Paul and was teaching Latin at the crammer's before going to Oxford. When my mother met him she said, 'Ah, another Augustus!' which I thought an odd comment. Augustus Budd was also at the party and he was tall and gross and voluble, while Paul, although tall, was exceedingly thin and far too shy to be voluble. I liked him because he took me to the theatre and the cinema, because he said I would have no trouble passing 'A' levels or getting into university, and because he said I was beautiful.

In fact, my rather large breasts on my otherwise slim figure suited the fashions of the time for huge, bunchy skirts clasped into a wide belt below a tight sweater. My body looked much older than seventeen, although my small, neat face disconcerted me with its look of innocence. Even scarlet lipstick made no difference. But then, I was innocent. Paul never tried to kiss me.

Strangely enough, Paul's shyness left him when he was faced by my mother's important friends. He told the Shadow Minister for War, who happened to be Jack Logan, that he thought National Service should be abolished for men with an IQ over 100 and two years' study of Latin and Greek substituted.

Jack said, 'Then you'd have half the miners in the classroom.'

I said, 'But that's what you're doing, Paul.' And Paul said, grinning, 'Unlike politicians, I only argue from personal experience.'

'I suppose you failed your medical?' Jack was spending a flattering amount of time on an individual.

'No good for the mines, if that's what you were thinking.'

My mother held her parties in our little flat. She invited about a hundred people, fifty more than could reasonably fit. The heat and noise were terrific. My mother went round in a long black sheath saying happily, 'I never thought I had so many friends.' Inevitably, a large proportion were political associates, but there were also her old friends: Augustus, celebrating his fifty-sixth birthday and sixth book; Molly, who'd forgotten to take off her hat but was enjoying herself very much; Leonard, just back from South America; Winnie Beauchamp, whose rise in the Civil Service had paralleled my mother's in the Labour Party; and Felix Moore, whom she persisted in calling Mrozek.

She reintroduced me to him: 'You remember my daughter, Violet? In Kettleside. The new generation.'

'Then a babe in arms.' Mrozek, as I also called him, was still a very striking man. According to my mother, his foreignness, his accent and formal manner had become more pronounced over the years. 'In America they're beginning to discover the power of the person who is neither child nor adult. They call it a teenager.'

Paul and I looked surprised and not very pleased. Paul already thought he was an adult, and I felt myself one that evening. I was not keen on the idea of a purgatory on the way to heaven. I did not recognise the possibility of a teen-age heaven.

'Never mind.' Mrozek patted my hand. 'One day you will work for me. All the beautiful young girls do.' He looked at my bosom with undisguised admiration.

I blushed, embarrassed. A girl on his left smiled at me. 'Don't worry. He's a sheep in wolf's clothing.'

Mrozek turned away.

With surprise I recognised the girl as Clancy, Araminta's eldest daughter. It had been years since she'd visited Kettleside.

'Yes, it's me. I'm doing some illustrating for him. You remember Katynka, his daughter? She tamed him. They live together—between her marriages. She's over there; look. She's thinking of marrying that chap she's with. He's Russian—very White, though. He writes books about ballet for The Moore Press.'

'I suppose publishing is purely a matter of public relations,' said Paul jealously. He put his arm through mine. He would never have dared in private.

'It wasn't, till Felix came on the scene.' Clancy looked round the room. 'You've got to have people before authors.'

'At parties.'

'Everyone likes parties.' Clancy looked round again, but this time with a dissatisfied air. I noticed that she was attractive despite ugly bunched clothes, inappropriate for the evening; a ragged haircut; and no makeup. I licked my own lipstick approvingly. Pale, naked lips in 1952 were as shocking as lipstick in 1902.

'You don't?'

She shrugged. 'I'm going through an artist-in-the-garret stage at the moment. But when I'm at one of your mother's parties I want to be top of the pile. That's what parties are for. To sort out success and failure.'

'Everyone's a success here.'

'The trouble with me is I've been Felix's lover for too long.' She glanced at my face. 'Oh, sorry. Are you too young for that sort of thing? Neither of us is married. It's quite all right. Felix never will be married while his dear daughter's around. Do you hate anybody?'

'No.' I dismissed the thought that I sometimes hated my mother.

'While I'm drawing my little animals I dream of shooting Katynka. Although she's so slimy a bullet might slide in and out without her noticing. I'm sorry; I'm drunk. When I'm not drunk, will you come and see my paintings? My garret's in Cromwell Road. Most unbohemian. My father says it's absurd to waste your time on a man more than twice your age. Incidentally, I hear you saw my mother during her little fling with young Hubert.'

I blushed. 'I would love to see your paintings.'

'Anytime, anytime.' Clancy waved her hand generously, and, before I could turn away, crumpled unconscious at my feet.

People did not always pass out at my mother's parties, but it did happen often enough not to be particularly remarkable. It must have been due to the heat or the crush, for the drink never flowed very freely. Paul and I eyed Clancy lying on my bed, very white and thin under her ugly clothes. I exclaimed with partly alchoholic passion that I had had enough of my mother and her parties. I wanted to go to Kettleside, read Donne, and walk in the pure cold air.

Paul was most sympathetic. He said my mother meant well, but that her friends were far too sophisticated for a girl of my age. 'What you need is a good dose of contemporaries.'

'You make it sound like Eno's. I had contemporaries at school. They bored me.'

'Ah.' Paul put his arm round me, but since we were in private, apart from the unconscious Clancy, it had a tentative feel. 'The right sort of contemporaries. At Oxford there's nothing but the right sort of contemporary.'

I arrived at university just when it seemed possible that the war could be pushed into the background and a new, forward-looking society created. It was still very tentative. Mrozek's American recognition of youth as a state in itself rather than an uncomfortable hybrid between childhood and adulthood had not come in time to give us confidence. We still assumed we were lesser versions of our parents, and most parents still lived in the shadow of the war.

But my mother's independent attitude to her children, and her social mobility—for between her background and her politics, she straddled the upper and lower-middle classes—gave me an unusual freedom. Without really trying, I found myself part of a small group of undergraduates who were determined to think for themselves. I had found the right sort of contemporaries, but they were not the sort Paul had in mind. He began to look on me with suspicion. He feared I might turn out to be 'ambitious'— a very dirty word in the early fifties.

Needless to say, my new contemporaries' first conclusion concerned sex. The older generation's attitude to sex was absurdly hypocritical. We would be more honest. Without our talking about it explicitly, it was understood that we should all sleep with whom we wanted without shame or guilt. This was fine as a general principle, but left out the two things which concerned the women just as much if not more than the sexual act: love and pregnancy. I spent much of my first year making excuses for not making love, while trying to give the impression to those not directly involved that I was. This was made easier by my lack of deep feeling for any of my admirers. I hid from myself that I had merely exchanged one sort of hypocrisy for another.

I found our second principle much more straightforward. This was a reaction against the usual view that working was caddish and must be done in the greatest secrecy and never, if possible, be referred to. We enjoyed our work, talked about it, and even, great leap of the imagination, planned how we would put it to good use in the great world outside. Paul was right to be suspicious. He complained, 'I don't know how you can muck in with that lot. They're so brash.'

'They're real.'.

'Oh, honestly!' We remained friends, but found it less exasperating to meet in London during the vacations.

Then in the winter of 1954, I fell in love. He was called Mike Oakley, and was one of the wave of grammar-school boys to hit Oxbridge. Not that you would have guessed it. It was not fashionable then to betray humble origins, and his rendering of 'Friends, Romans, countrymen' on the Playhouse stage, which was where I

353

first saw him, was as patrician as that of any Mark Antony of the time, and a great deal more so than in the later theatre.

He also performed in the Union, where he had just become Treasurer. He was an extrovert undergraduate. He was also very good-looking, which mattered to me then. He was five years older than I, because he was in his last year and had done two years' National Service before he came up, and he had already passed into the Civil Service. Everyone looked at him and said, 'Why not the Foreign Office?' But he remained adamant. 'Oxford's a playground. When I go into the real world I want a real job.'

I knew I was in love with him. Why else was I hanging over the public gallery in the Union week after week? Why else did I alternately ignore his presence in a room and confront him with some absurd argument?

He hardly knew of my existence till the night my mother came to the Union to oppose the motion that 'Chastity is an outmoded form of behaviour.'

I was invited to the dinner beforehand. My mother and I were placed on either side of Mike. Like all the officers of the Union, he wore evening dress. His strong reddish face with its high forehead, straight nose, and rounded chin looked like a Roman medallion above the severe black and white. On his right, my mother's neat, lively face also rested on a nest of black and white. She was happy at being the centre of attention again, in a place which matched the House of Commons for jolly formality. There is none such good company as the out-of-office Minister. I think she was glad also to have me near her, indisputably a grown woman, a responsibility no longer. She glanced at me often and smiled as if she were an ordinary, proud mother. I was wearing a cherry-red silk dress with a tight waist, three-quarter-length sleeves, and calf-length skirt. I had pinned back my carefully waved hair so that my greenish eyes gave my otherwise ordinary features a special glow. I felt that I looked like a princess—or even a queen. Only a few months ago we had sighed over the coronation of Queen Elizabeth. As we gazed hour after hour at the television we told each other we were watching a great advance in the technological age. What we were really seeing was a dream princess being turned into a dream queen, just as the rest of the country did.

So I sat in the Union's dining room, happy in the knowledge that I looked like a princess and everyone thought so, even my mother. This dream was encouraged by our removal to the Union's debating hall. I sat in the dark gallery like a lady of old, while the men (and my mother) jousted in the glare of the open lists below. Wrapped in this slightly wine-tinged fantasy, I did not listen to my knight's fighting words. I had almost forgotten the evening's motion. I was brought back to reality by a heavy nudge in the ribs from my neighbour and the realisation that faces from all over the hall were turned towards me. My mother was speaking, which was another reason I had not been listening.

'. . . about some fictional notion of purity out of *Parsifal* or *Sir Gawain and the Green Knight*. This motion is not a literary conceit; it is about flesh-and-blood women and even men. You laugh. But look again on my daughter's face. Is Chastity the pale, cold, repressed creature that has been painted for us tonight? Or is it the glowing face of life and beauty? Look for yourself!'

My mother's strident professional politician's voice rang through the hall with hideous clarity. Look they did.

'What we are talking about is something more important than a mere sexual act . . .' Some of the faces returned to my mother, for in the fifties one did not expect to hear such language. I wondered if I could slip away.

'What we are talking about is innocence. Innocence and goodness.'

I feared any movement would only draw more attention to myself. I stared down at my mother. Again I stopped listening. Her words were no longer directed at me. I suspected that I had missed her most embarrassing remarks. Worse than embarrassing. I tried to analyse my misery, but succeeded only in analysing my mother's behaviour. That was simple. Over dinner, she had registered the princesslike quality I had been enjoying myself. Later, it had come to seem a useful debating point. She was not to blame. I was punished for an inflated ego.

I did slip away. I couldn't bear to look down on the gilded knights who had seen my shame. I sat in the marble gloom of the ladies' lavatory. I looked with loathing at my jutting bosom, my cherry-red lips. If only she had been wrong! If only I hadn't been a virgin! Unbearable word . . . Then I could have giggled with my lover. Now I was branded in front of the whole university. Virgin! In front of Mike. Mike, whom I'd taken such trouble to impress with my modern freethinking attitudes.

As I sat there, miserably licking my wounded pride, the one possibility that never crossed my mind was that my mother could be right. That I did have the beauty of innocence. That my reluctance to sleep with any of my admirers added up to an unadmitted and admirable wish to wait for someone I could really love. That Mike, like most men of that time, would be more attracted to me rather than less. I was humiliated. That was all that mattered to me.

My mother was triumphant. They were drinking coffee in the

Randolph Hotel after the debate. Knowing my absence would be noticed, I hovered, self-effacing, on the edge of the group. Whether or not because of my 'virginal beauty,' the motion that 'Chastity is an outmoded code of behaviour' had been, against all the odds, resoundingly defeated. They were now discussing the reasons women were still not admitted to the Union.

'We did have a debate on it a few years ago,' Dr Summerskill's son insisted. 'The pro-women lobby were hooted out of the hall.'

'They've had us there in the House of Commons for over thirty years.'

'Women MPs are a special breed.'

'Am I? Am I?'

At length my mother gave up the struggle and went up the ornate stairs to bed. First she kissed me. 'Darling, you looked so beautiful.' I saw her affection with surprise.

Mike approached me. He pulled at his bow tie. 'I'll get rid of this gear and then take you back to St Hilda's.'

'I have a bike.'

My barely audible mumble did not put him off. 'So have I.' He was cheerful and firm.

Oxford was very dark and empty at night. We rode along side by side with our front lights weaving yellow patterns on the road. I hated the silly balloons of red silk skirt on either side of my bike. As we passed Christ Church Mike said, 'Have you ever made love in a churchyard?'

I assumed I had misheard him. 'What?'

'There's a wonderful tombstone in there with a nice grassy square in front of it. The dear departed was called Theophilus Clifford. I've always wanted to make love with Theophilus Clifford as a bedhead.'

'Oh.' Was he serious? Had he not heard my mother? Was he being kind? He couldn't have disbelieved her. Surely everything had showed in my face?

He crossed the road to the church and leaned his bike against it. 'I'll show you it, anyway. The other part's optional extra.' He leaned my bike against his, switched off both their lights, and took my hand. It was pitch black behind the church. Only the tombstones showed a shadowy grey. Mike led me forward unhesitatingly. When we reached the tombstone, he put my finger into the engraving and made me trace out the name of Theophilus Clifford. Then he sat down. I sat down beside him. I stopped thinking what it all meant.

'I love names,' he said. 'It's strange you're called by the same name as your mother. Or don't you think so?'

'I'm used to it. Sometimes it's confusing. It'll be easier when I marry.'

'Oh, you plan to marry, do you? I thought you were part of that *avant-garde* lot.'

'We don't disbelieve in marriage.'

There was a pause. Mike took up my hand again. 'Well, how about it?'

My heart began to pound very hard, and despite the cold air and the cold stone, I felt boiling hot. I wanted to say, 'I love you, Mike. Please let's make love.' But the evening had produced too many barriers. I needed to know more about his attitude. I put my fingers back into the TH of Theophilus and said in a low voice, 'Didn't you hear what my mother said?'

He sounded surprised. 'Quite fun, wasn't it? She's a good speaker. But I'm not very interested in your mother at the moment.'

'I mean about me.'

'About you? Oh, that stuff about innocence and beauty? You did look beautiful. That's when I decided you were worthy of Theo.'

I decided to brave all. 'About chastity. Virginity. I am a virgin, you see.'

I distinctly heard Mike gulp. He dropped my hand and sat upright, then took my hand again. 'I never thought.'

'You mean you didn't believe her?' I was now desperate to get exactly what he did think cleared up once and for all.

'I just assumed . . . With your friends . . . After all, she was only making a debating point.'

'It was the truth.'

Poor Mike. He tried to laugh, though it came out as another gulp. 'Well, that's very nice. Good for you.' There was another pause. 'Then I expect you won't want to use Mr Clifford's amenities.'

'Yes.' A car passed beyond the church, and a short wave of light passed over Mike's face. 'No. I do want to. I want to very much.'

'You do?' I could sense he was playing for time. The situation was not quite as he'd imagined. 'Why?'

Should I answer honestly? A declaration of love from a girl he hardly knew might be the final straw. 'Because I'm bored with being a virgin.'

'Oh.' I felt his interest slacken and die.

'You don't want to now, do you?'

'It all seems—cold-blooded.'

'Yes.'

He was still holding my hand, and before it was too late I put our joined hands to my face. The contact was so wonderful that I decided not to worry whether we did make love or not. This was enough. We sat still for a second or two, and then Mike leaned forward and kissed me. It was very gentle and not in the least cold-blooded. I felt quite

357

certain that without knowing it he loved me too. Slowly we began to undress each other until in the dark and damp and absolutely freezing cold of a January night we were completely naked. It must have been love.

We were so happy together on that grassy bed below the stone slab. Afterwards we both lay quietly together for a few minutes until we simultaneously began to shake with cold.

'We'll have to go,' said Mike, 'or we'll end up closer to Mr Clifford than we bargained for.'

'We couldn't be closer,' I said, meaning to each other. He understood and kissed me again. We dressed quickly, but not quickly enough to stop our treacherous shaking limbs. 'I'm warm inside,' I protested.

'Come on. Run! Jump!' Holding hands, we jumped from grave to grave. My feet woke up and tingled every time they met hard stone. 'Now I'll take you back.'

We bicycled away from the church, and looking back, I knew I would never bicycle past it again without remembering. Unless it all turned into an unfulfilled dream in the morning. But I didn't expect that. Theophilus Clifford wouldn't allow it.

'Too late for a respectable entrance,' said Mike as we reached St Hilda's. 'Over the wall with you before we're spotted by a jealous female don with a machine gun.' Mike wouldn't allow it either.

'I usually take off my dress first.'

'Usually? I don't like the sound of that!'

We kissed, and he flew me to the top of the wall. 'I'm so happy,' I called as I scrambled down the other side. My dress floated like a huge scarlet parachute.

'Goodnight, darling Violet.'

'Shhhh!'

Chapter Fourteen

For women undergraduates (and the Torture of the Cage is too gentle for those who call them undergraduettes) the Trinity Term at Oxford is a sort of beautiful agony.
The Times.   30 April 1956

The conference was treated to a display of spirited Welsh oratory from Mrs Mary Clement, of Swansea. Housewives wanted something more than the spiritual reward of being told they were the backbone of the country. They did not want supercharged sports cars and platinum mink, but they did want cheaper household goods that would make their lot an easier one. . . . Mrs N. F. Hinks, of Birmingham, was not too bothered about cheaper household appliances. 'They are very overrated, and when the old man fiddles with them they never go again,' she declared to a roar of approval.
The Times.   12 April 1956

Royal Court Theatre, 'Look Back in Anger' by John Osborne. This first play has passages of good violent writing, but its total gesture is altogether inadequate.
The Times.   9 May 1956

My mother wore black to my wedding. I thought she might have made an exception on that day. I assumed that it reflected her earlier opposition. 'You're too young.'

'I'm twenty.'

'Much too young. Even I didn't throw up my Oxford degree for my marriage.'

This looked as if it might be our first serious conversation. We were having lunch in the House of Commons. Every few minutes someone waved at my mother or my mother waved at someone. Perhaps this was keeping her on her toes. 'Who was he?'

'It doesn't matter. It wasn't a real marriage. I just wanted to continue Oxford. As you do. It isn't possible.' A wave.

'I don't want to continue Oxford. I want to leave it. Mike was my Oxford.' This was true. In the year since Theophilus Clifford brought us together, we had never been parted for more than a day except in the vacations, when Mike went home to his parents in Birmingham. He worked there, he told me, and I would be a distraction.

My mother also worked in Birmingham. 'I'm not ambitious like you.'

'Of course you are. You're much more sensible. Here am I struggling to get women a better deal.' An acknowledgement. 'I'm a member of the Royal Commission on Marriage and Divorce, you know. And here *you* are throwing yourself away for the sake of . . . what?'

'Love.'

'What?' My mother looked so surprised that I nearly laughed. She gave a distracted wave.

I took pity. 'Actually, there is another reason.'

'My mother, if you can call her that—she never let me; at least, Eleanor's no hypocrite—was in America when I decided to make my first idiotic marriage. If only she'd advised me as I'm advising you.'

'I'm going to have a baby.' Seeing her expression, I added quickly so that there should be no doubt, 'I want the baby; I want to be married to Mike. We love each other.'

My mother was defeated; the combination of love and a baby, two aspects of the woman's role she had taught herself to pay attention to only on paper, put an insurmountable barrier between us. She saw I was a lost woman. In the fifties young girls from good backgrounds did not have abortions. She looked round the emptying dining room. 'Thirty per cent of teenage brides are expectant mothers.'

'I'm twenty.'

'Mike is a charming and intelligent young man.' My mother never found it difficult to accept change. She took my hand across the table. 'We will make it a wonderful wedding. Here in the Commons.

Your brother can be best man. You won't mind if I ask some representatives from my constituency?'

'Not at all. They might encourage Mike's relations.'

'Ah yes. He comes from Brum.' My mother was vague. She had found the easiest way to assimilate her late call to socialism was to pretend there were no class distinctions. This worked well generally. It worked well with Mike, but irritated me.

He wouldn't even talk about his parents.

'Why don't you ever talk about your parents? I'm interested in your parents.'

'They're boring.' Mike loved me, but he didn't feel the need to explain himself to me.

'How do I know that?'

'You'll see them at the wedding.'

'That's not the point. I want to feel part of the family.'

'Wait till you see them.' Although he had predicted it, I was still surprised. Because I loved him, I saw it as a sign of strength.

'I never do see them.'

'At the wedding?'

'Ah, the wedding. Sometimes I think it's my mother's wedding, not mine at all!' Mike laughed. He thought my mother wonderful.

The first guest to arrive in London—a full fortnight before the ceremony—was Eleanor. She had not left Eureka, apart from an occasional day visit to the Irish mainland, for nearly twenty years. She was a Rip Van Winkle in London. There was even some facial resemblance, since a few threads of silver hair hung from her chin. More remarkable than any natural sign of old age was the artifice she used to disguise it. The morning after her arrival was spent dyeing her hair a pale mauve. She then powdered her face the colour her hair had been, put mauve shadow right round her eyes, and topped them by thin black crescent eyebrows.

She dressed in a variety of once elegant clothes *circa* 1930. Her story that she had discovered them packed and unworn in a trunk the day before leaving Eureka was borne out by the odour of mothballs and the creases of years. However she seemed so pleased with her appearance that none of us had the heart to dissuade her. Besides, she had a sharp tongue and at the slightest hint pointed out how clumsy our fifties bunches and folds were compared with her own sophisticated tailoring. She was also stern with the changing landscape—she exclaimed with equal horror at the bomb craters, which we no longer noticed, and the buildings with which some had been filled, which we thought bold and utilitarian, if not exactly beautiful.

'They look cheap and insecure,' she protested, dancing in front of one block of flats. After an alcoholic lunch, she was in aggressive mood.

I was forced to notice that the concrete was already dripping with dark rain stains and the steel window frames did look very insecure indeed. 'We can't all live in castles.'

'I'm sure those red and blue blocks looked very pretty on paper.'

'Utilitarian. Cheap. We're trying to rebuild a country, you know.'

'Give me the Peabody buildings!'

'The state *is* Mr Peabody now. It's a much healthier situation.'

'Thank God I'm rich, anyway.' The younger generation seemed far too serious to my grandmother.

We were on our way to Harrods to buy me a wedding present. Eleanor had visited her solicitors two days after her arrival and discovered that a minor forgotten asset had become over two neglected decades a major asset. She was rich. Her reaction was total childish exuberance. She immediately moved out of Raymond Lark's luxurious Kensington House where she had installed herself after one look at my mother's flat—'I suppose that's a utilitarian chair?' Raymond Lark had been an equal disappointment. 'I thought he might have changed with all these letters after his name. I'm sure he worked hard enough in the war for them—so brave, all of you here in the hurly-burly.'

'I was still in Northumberland.'

'But he's still a boy! So vulgar. Talks of nothing but success and money—not that I have anything against money.'

'He's the most successful film producer in England.'

'He hates films. He once sailed away from Eureka on Christmas Eve in a Force Nine gale to avoid watching any more films.'

'I expect he'll be knighted.'

'Of course, they were silent films. And poor Gay. Hardly alive. Arthritis—twisted as a corkscrew.'

'It's nice he's stayed with her.'

'Nice he's stayed with her!' She looked at me with amazement. 'Gay Heavenly-Smith is worth twenty times Mr Raymond Lark.'

'She's been crippled for years.'

Eleanor stopped in the street and looked at me severely. 'You must take into account the past. Without Gay's support Raymond would still be a barrow boy.'

'Yes, Eleanor.'

I gave up arguing about the place of the past. When Eleanor left the Larks' she moved into the Hyde Park Hotel, saying the deb dances every evening reminded her of her halcyon youth. Besides, it was equidistant between Fortnum and Mason and Harrods.

'Shopping in civilised surroundings is the last prerogative of the old.' She smiled graciously at the Harrods doorman.

'You're not old.'

'Aha! Tell that to Ivy Briggsworthy. I've spent too much time in the company of another old lady to ignore the reality. Thank God I quarrelled with her or she would be here now. She would not approve of my present.' The sly look that accompanied this information made me uneasy, particularly when Mike, whom I had not expected to see, suddenly appeared from behind a castle of canned partridge soup.

'Your grandmother invited me.'

'Forward to the sports department!'

Eleanor had decided to buy us each a longbow and a set of feathered arrows. Perhaps I should have guessed from her outfit, which consisted of a green tweed suit with matching trilby pulled to a rakish angle accented by a tuft of orange tail feathers. These brushed across her powdery cheek, becoming white-tipped and leaving behind a brownish patch of bare skin. Mike and I watched as she insisted on the senior black-coated assistant's producing more and more bows. Old no longer, sinews hard as a goat's, she bent every one, even insisting, to our terror, on fitting the arrow into the notch.

'I wanted to persuade her to buy us a bed,' I whispered to Mike.

'What a magnificent display!' he replied out loud. I saw he had given up taking my family seriously. Eleanor shimmied under his admiration and said that she hoped we didn't want steel bows because even if they were more accurate, they had none of the beauty of wood. 'You should have seen me when I first ran away with my lover to Eureka. How graceful! Your mother, poor girl, never had the line. Toxophily is all a matter of line, you see. The sport of Gods! The sport of Youth.' She suddenly became old again and handed over the chosen bows to the baffled assistant. 'Send them to my hotel. I shall shoot the sluttish chambermaid with them.'

'What is your hotel, Madam?' asked the assistant humbly.

I had a strong feeling that this wedding celebration was going to unearth more skeletons from the cupboard than I would find comfortable. Although Eleanor had refrained from actually giving her lover's name (not, I'm sure, from any desire to spare my feelings), I knew perfectly well it was my father. I had had the whole story from Flo years ago. With Eleanor such a remote figure it had not upset me particularly, seeming more like a Hans Andersen fairy story than reality. Now, with my mind set on marriage and my body set on motherhood, I was struck by the disturbing thought that Eleanor could easily have been my own mother, as well as my mother's mother. I realised I had never told Mike the extraordinary circumstances of my birth.

We dropped Eleanor at her hotel and, resisting her request for drinking companions, returned to my mother's flat. We made love in

363

her double bed, which was more comfortable than my single. Her work obsession was sometimes useful. The room, though small, had lots of windows, and we hadn't drawn the curtains. As we lay there, half asleep, bathed in the cold grey light of a London winter afternoon, the sun suddenly came out, painting the bed and the whole space around us a brilliant gold. Bathed in this radiance, I told Mike the story of my father's two loves. He kissed me and patted my naked stomach.

'You're sensitive because of this. You'd like the world to be perfectly regulated for your baby. Our baby. I've always heard motherhood turned women into emotional jellies.'

'I don't like a secret past. A dark past.'

'It's better than a dark present. Or even a dark future. What do you know about my past? I might be the illegitimate child of a gypsy girl and her dwarf father!'

'Don't tease.' Instinctively, I put my hand to my stomach. It met Mike's hand. He laughed.

'You would have been delighted by the idea of circus in-laws before you started the baby. Don't worry, darling. My parentage won't harm the baby or us any more than yours will.'

He spoke with a solid kind of conviction that warmed me and made me feel slightly foolish. The yellow light flickered and went out. My mother would be back soon. I opened my eyes and rolled over to hug Mike. 'I do want you, darling.'

'I love you. At least we're well set up with Cupid's bows.'

I sighed, but this time without fear. 'You wait till you meet the rest of my mother's friends and relations.'

I had not yet realised that one of Mike's basic characteristics was a deep lack of interest in people—that is, people in general. He loved me faithfully and deeply. He was preparing to love our child. He would love anyone I ordered him to, and he liked most of the people he admired. He liked my mother for her guts. But he felt no social duty at all. People in society might as well have been animals in a zoo. If they wished to communicate, that was fine by him. If not, that was equally fine. It was why he was so successful at Oxford, and why he attracted me. Even when he was being most energetic and apparently ambitious, I sensed underneath a rocklike indifference to all but his own standards. It made other undergraduates seem childish.

I began to understand this on our wedding day. By the great day itself, I could see it only in terms of the guest list, which like some horrible monster seemed to grow in every direction. My head spun with names, divided roughly under Family, Political, and Friends, but cross-referenced in a most taxing manner. When Mike looked at me with loving eyes, I said, 'Do you think it matters you've got almost no one your side of the church, darling?' or 'If Jack Logan insists on making a speech, can we limit it to five minutes?' Mike never answered, but looked at me with patient indulgence.

Nevertheless, I thought I was enjoying it all till the moment I stepped into the shiny limousine heading for the House of Commons. We had progressed barely more than a few streets when there was the most sinister rippling feeling followed by a cold draught down my back. My wedding dress had burst open like a ripe plum.

Tudor, who seemed to me very young for nineteen—or perhaps it was just that he was doing his National Service and unused to female company—burst into loud guffaws.

My mother cried out with the look of despair she now reserved for unyielding inanimate objects, 'It's the zip! There's nothing you can do about a zip!'

Dress falling round my shoulders, tears falling down my cheeks, I wailed, 'I've been checking it every day. But the last few days everything became so frantic. How could it have grown so big in a few days?'

'It?' enquired Tudor, no longer laughing.

'My baby, you silly fool! You don't think I'm marrying for love, do you?' My mother leaned back in the seat and put her hands over her eyes. 'Well, I am!—but I'm also pregnant! And don't look at me with those round eyes. It's 1956, and you should know the facts of life by now!'

My mother removed her hands from her eyes and seemed to groan. 'Oh, God,' said Tudor, and I saw they were referring to the driver. It was my mother's ex-ministerial chauffeur. The back of his neck had gone bright pink.

I began to laugh as well as cry. 'We can't sit here all day. I'm not going to get thinner, the dress is not going to stretch, and the zip can't be mended.' My laughter began to get out of control. 'It stretches from my neck nearly to my knees. The dressmaker said it would act as a corset!' I bent double with laughter, and the top half of my dress fell into my lap. Surreptitiously the chauffeur, who was really a friend, swung his mirror sideways so that I was no longer visible.

'Shall I slap her face?' said Tudor hopefully.

'There'll be hordes of photographers at the House of Commons,' said my mother. The idea encouraged her to collect her thoughts. 'This dress is useless. Are you set on being married in white, Violet?'

'Yes.' I tried to stifle my giggles. A sudden image of Mike and me marrying in some unknown, unattended church flashed before me.

'Back to the flat,' commanded my mother. 'I was quite fat when I first married.'

So it was that Mike found himself greeted at the altar in the crypt of the House of Commons by a bride dressed in the height of fashion 1927. 'It'll please Eleanor,' I mouthed, having gone through so many moods by now that I was ready to answer his surprised smile by a brave front. 'I love you,' he mouthed back, and he told me later that his expression was nothing to do with the dress, which he hadn't noticed, but a reaction to the sudden realisation that he would be my husband in a few minutes.

'Are there ghosts here?' my page boy asked my bridesmaid, as we came out into the vaulted stone corridor under the debating chamber.

'Oh, yes,' she lisped, 'the ghosts are everywhere.'

'Everywhere?' the little boy repeated nervously.

'There's one. Look now!' Eleanor, powdered and robed, whisked past pointing fingers.

I smiled, and nudged Mike. 'I'm surprised she didn't point out me.'

My mother's wedding dress was very beautiful. It fell from diamond clasps at my shoulders in silky tiers. It reminded me only slightly of a ruched curtain. Flo was the first to comment on its origins. Mike and I stood at the doorway of a heavily flocked public room receiving a queue of guests. Flo said, eyeing Mike, whom she instantly recognised as failing the Eton/Christ Church test, 'I only hope it's not a bad omen, seeing as your mother hardly made a success of her first nuptials.'

'How ever can you remember that day all those years ago?'

'I'm hardly likely to forget my own wedding day, am I?'

An embarrassed Cecil hurried her on.

'It is our wedding, isn't it?' I whispered to Mike.

'It's certainly mine. Here come my parents.'

It was when I met Mike's parents that I began to appreciate how extraordinary was my mother's success in the Labour Party. As I looked at her greeting Mike's parents like a hummingbird in front of two moorhens, I remembered how she had described the scene as she faced the selection committee.

It took place in a cheerless set of rooms in the middle of Birmingham. At first she had hesitated outside with a feeling that this was the Communist Party headquarters, for half a dusty window was pasted with red flags. However, she was seen and quickly drawn inside— mostly by women's hands, for she was on the short list at their insistence. She had pulled herself together, looked them in the eye, and cried out, 'I want you to forget that I'm a woman! I want you to forget I'm a war widow! I want you to remember only that I am a Socialist!' The walls of Jericho fell before her call. 'A politician must be half actress,' she told me.

'I'm so very glad to meet you,' she was saying now to Mike's parents. Although she was not a tall woman, she seemed to bend from an elegant height. 'Of course, I know your part of the world well. I spend more time in the Brum Station Hotel than I do my own home.'

'Hotels won't do you any good.' Mike's mother looked concerned. She had a nice, deeply wrinkled face with Mike's blue eyes turned a palish grey. She put her worn hand on my mother's black silk sleeve. 'There'll always be a bed for you in our house.'

'A bed, a cup of tea, and a good beef sandwich,' Mike's father nodded.

'Come on, Mum, Dad!' Mike chivvied them good-humouredly. 'You're holding up the procession.'

'Oh no,' I protested, embarrassed, for his parents' expression had changed from warmth and happiness to awkward self-awareness. But my mother took Mrs Oakley by the shoulder and kissed her on both cheeks. Before Mr Oakley could hide she'd done the same to him, so that they spun past us towards the drinks in a confused haze of pleasure.

I looked at Mike. He was staring at my mother with what I took to be admiration. 'Don't forget who *her* mother is,' I whispered. 'At least, your parents won't disgrace you. I can't believe you're such a terrible snob.'

'Of course I'm not. I've told you before, they just don't interest me. We've nothing in common. I know they are my parents, but I don't feel as if they are.'

'Would you rather have Eleanor?'

'Can't you understand? Your parents, my parents, your mother's parents are of no particular interest to me—as parents. If they're interesting people, they interest me. You're obsessional.'

'You're unnatural.'

It was an awkward moment to argue about the child/parent relationship. Guests, known and mostly unknown, shook our hands, kissed my face, and exclaimed over my startling choice of wedding gown.

'It's my mother's,' I said over and over again, and saw their faces soften appreciatively.

'It's my mother's,' I said to Leonard Trigear, who had arrived late without a tailcoat.

He gave a huge guffaw. 'You're obviously not superstitious!' He put his hand to his head. 'I'm sorry; I've got a rotten headache.'

'It's my mother's,' I said again to a woman in red tulle and under my breath to Mike, 'Family first, wife next, child next . . . Why ever are you marrying me?'

367

'Because I love you.' One of Mike's most heartening abilities was his frequent statements of love. I, who could say it so seldom however deeply I felt it, was invariably knocked into grateful silence. But I had little time to enjoy its healing properties, for a shriek accompanied by a bump heralded the second dramatic event of the afternoon.

Eleanor, so drunk that she could hardly stand, was having a fight with Ivy Briggsworthy. Ivy Briggsworthy, fourteen-stone tower of prayer and soda bread, had arrived from Eureka two days before in order to look after her dear friend. It seemed her dear friend was not keen on her attentions.

'I have never,' said the Shadow Foreign Minister, who had just shaken my hand, 'seen two old ladies fighting before.'

'And what's the difference from two old men?' challenged my mother, looking him in the eye. But her boldness could not disguise the awful sight.

By the time Mike and I arrived, Leonard, Araminta, Clancy, George Briggsworthy, Molly, and two ushers had failed to pull them apart.

'They're crazy,' panted Molly, who, judging by her pink face and unravelling hair, was the most enthusiastic referee.

'They're enjoying the attention,' said Leonard, retiring with a terrible frown which at the time did not seem particularly significant.

'But they'll kill each other!' I said.

'No such luck.' Leonard put a hand on either side of his head and shook it. None of us had time to notice.

Eleanor, all ajangle with a turquoise beaded number, was making staggering tilts at Ivy, who stood like a mechanical beast, lifting her hands up into the air and then, as Eleanor retreated, down again. When Eleanor came too close or hurt her too much, she kicked out with stout black button shoes. It was Eleanor's shriek as the pointed toe met her calf that had first attracted our attention.

'What's that aged crone holding in her hands?' asked Mike.

'Champagne,' I said.

'Who cares if Eleanor drinks herself to death?'

'That aged crone, it appears.'

Beyond the inner circle of the involved stood an outer circle of spectators, who clearly felt no responsibility to interfere. Among them I noticed Augustus' tall bulk and next to him, my old friend Paul. For the first time I saw why my mother had picked them out as similar types, for they both wore exactly the same excited yet remote expression of ringside spectators at a good boxing match.

'Look at those two!' I cried to Mike angrily. 'Unconcerned. Quite unconcerned.'

368

Meantime my mother had appeared with Jack Logan at her side. 'You take Eleanor, Jack, and Mike will take poor Ivy.' Her calmness and command made it clear they would not fail. 'Bring them to the Lady Members' Room. I'll go ahead and make sure you're allowed in.' I watched as the two idiotic and bedraggled women were frog-marched out.

'Poor Violet.' I felt a hot hand squeezing mine.

'I expect she enjoys it.' I looked towards where my mother had left the room.

'I didn't mean her.' Araminta's voice was surprised. 'I meant you.' She looked round. 'Actually, I think it's been a terrific success—in terms of entertainment. A little exhausting, though.' She pushed in-effectually at her hair. 'Leonard says I've made a spectacle of myself, but I was only trying to help. He's so bitter. He's not very well, either. He's never been very well since that head injury. But he'd never let me help him. I suppose you wouldn't like to sit down for a moment?'

We sat down side by side on gilt chairs. I said, feeling amidst all the turmoil there was one thing I could hold on to and that it might also divert Araminta from gloomy thoughts of Leonard, 'I'm pregnant'.

'Oh, darling. Why ever didn't you tell me before? How wonderful! I'm sure it'll be a girl. Is that why you're wearing that funny dress? Not that you don't look beautiful. I've always said you had lovely eyes. You would like a girl, wouldn't you?'

'I don't know.' Her response was almost too enthusiastic. 'I haven't thought.'

'No. Of course not. Well. To think of it: Vi a grandmother.' I looked up at the excited faces of my wedding guests. Molly was talk-ing to a priest whom I recognised as a friend of my mother's. He looked tired, particularly beside Molly's gesticulating volubility. I remembered that he was called Father Wilson and that he had cancer.

Araminta saw where I was looking. 'Inexplicable, the lengths people go to make life bearable. At least, Molly is successful, I sup-pose.' She sighed deeply. 'People are inexplicable.'

At the far side of the room I saw Mike return and search for me. I remembered with a hot feeling of pleasure the matter-of-fact way he had been able to say, 'I love you.' I turned back to Araminta. 'I think it's your generation who are inexplicable. All I want is to get married and have a baby and do some work, and Mike's just the same.'

'Just like me.' Araminta patted my knee, but her remote look had descended, as if despite her agreement my straightforward ambitions sounded as inexplicable to her as anything else.

'I'm going to cut the cake.'

Before I reached the red-coated majordomo, viciously armed with knife in one hand and hammer in the other, I was waylaid by Clancy. She took my arm and said, peering anxiously over my shoulder, 'Have you seen my father?' Because her face was usually pale and strained, I didn't take too much notice.

'I spent the last ten minutes trying to stop your mother from thinking about him.'

'You won't have seen him, then?'

'Not since the fight.'

I started towards the cake again, but Clancy clung to me still. 'What's the matter?'

'He's ill.'

'I don't know your father.'

'No one does. He's been complaining of headaches for weeks. Terrible headaches. You know he's got this girlfriend?'

'No.'

'She came and told me about the headaches. Now Augustus says he was being sick in the Gents. He couldn't speak; he couldn't even turn the taps off.'

'Didn't Augustus do anything?'

'No.'

'Typical.'

'That's not the point. Apparently he staggered out and now he's vanished.'

'Perhaps he's gone to his girlfriend.'

'She's away this week. Actually, she's a friend of mine.'

'I'm very sorry, Clancy. But it is my wedding.' For a moment I thought she was going to burst into one of her rare but terrifying rages. Instead she let go of my arm and even attempted a commonplace smile.

'I'm sorry. It's not fair to worry you. I expect your mother will help.'

The speeches began. Jack Logan talked about democracy and the inevitability of Labour's return to power. His audience became restive. They wanted some jokes about marital bliss. Mike whispered, 'Your mother's the only one to stop him. Where ever is she?'

'Leonard's ill. She's looking for him.'

Jack said, 'Some of you may have heard of the Suez Canal . . .'

Mike wrote on a piece of paper, 'Don't forget to thank the bridesmaid and page.' The majordomo passed the note to Jack, who was saying, 'If Imperialism has been discredited then . . .' He stopped in mid-sentence.

'Are you sure Tudor isn't supposed to thank the bridesmaids?' I whispered to Mike.

'He can propose the toast.'

I'm still glad, not guilty, that I forced the third drama to be played at least temporarily off my stage. Mike and I had that moment to remember when the glasses were raised to our health and I cut the cake and he kissed me. Even though my dress was not my own, Eleanor and Ivy were locked in the Lady Members' Room, and Clancy and my mother were tracking down the House of Commons green carpets for a fallen Leonard, I had my shining moment. 'I love you, Mike.' That was when he kissed me. 'I don't care about anyone else.'

'That's very sensible.' He smiled at me, disbelieving but happy.

An usher led me along the wooden-panelled corridors. We were trying to find an alternative changing room to the overflowing Lady Members' Room. 'I'm afraid it's only a cubbyhole,' said the usher.

'It doesn't matter,' I replied gaily.

But it did. For Leonard lay snoring in his own vomit on the floor. 'Oh my God. Oh my God.'

Leonard, private and mysterious Leonard, had a very public send-off. An ambulance wailing up to the House of Commons draws crowds. My black limousine with white streamers moved aside; my bright crowd of well-wishers was swamped by a mass of excited doom-gloaters. Mike and I had to leave. We were catching a train to Venice. Mike was on one side of me, Mrozek, for some reason, on the other, and Molly bringing up the rear.

Leonard was carried out on a stretcher. Around him were my mother, Araminta, Clancy and several more of their children, and Augustus. All except Augustus were crying.

I realised I was too. 'Leonard said I'm not superstitious,' I sobbed. 'I hope he's right. What a marriage day!'

'He hasn't died yet.' Mike's voice was comfortingly unchanged.

'Better if he does.' Mrozek's head followed the stretcher as it reared upwards into the ambulance. 'I never did get him to write that book.'

'What did he do?' Mike took my arm.

'My mother wore black!'

'Poor Leonard.' Molly was dry-eyed and stern. 'He so wanted to be a great novelist, yet he never even finished one book.' She paused as the doors were slammed on the ambulance. 'Except in the very early years, and then he burned them. It seemed quite a witty thing to do at the time.' She turned round as George approached with their son. 'Didn't it, George?'

'I didn't know him then.'

'Oh. Now I come to think about it, neither did I really. Vi must have told me. I often thought Vi and Leonard so well matched.

371

Such a pity Araminta got there first.'

'Vi would never have been content with any man,' Mrozek looked towards my mother's black figure.

'It doesn't matter now,' said George, and I noticed his face wore the same stern expression that Molly's had before she started thinking of the past. 'I don't think he's been a bad man. Just unhappy. St John and I shall go to Westminster Cathedral to say a prayer. Will you join us, Molly?'

'What a good idea.' Husband and wife exchanged an identical calm, sad look. They were well matched only in tragedy.

The chauffeur opened the door for Mike and me and we got in. As the car started to move after the ambulance, my mother came running towards us. Her black chiffon dress swirled round her ankles. 'Goodbye, darling,' she called. 'Goodbye—don't think about poor Leonard. He wouldn't want mourning.'

'But Mother, is he dead?'

'In spirit, darling, in spirit.' Her face was pale and tear-stained.

'Don't stop,' I said to the chauffeur, who was slowing down. I looked through the rear window at the figures grouped behind me in the roadway. My mother's waving black figure was out in front, followed by Mrozek, bulky and concerned, and behind him Lawrence, Molly, and St John in a row. Behind them I could see Mike's parents, waving with an attitude of horror-struck embarrassment.

The rest of the guests, unsure whether to smile or mourn, whether to cheer us away or disappear tactfully themselves, stood bunched together in the doorway.

'I hardly knew Leonard,' I said, wiping my eyes. 'Even though his wife was virtually my mother. Once he came to Kettleside all wrapped round with bandages, and I thought he was Satan.'

With such a beginning, it was difficult not to be introspective on our honeymoon. Besides, Venice turned out not to be the ideal location, for I was suffering from a late bout of morning sickness, except that it struck at any time of the day, and I could hardly bear to travel by boat. A gondola was particular torture.

Mike's professed contentment mirrored, I think, his low expectations of a honeymoon. He never believed in holidays. Or, in fact, any line of action that he considered an escape from reality. That was for lesser, weaker men.

I thought mostly about my baby. I knew Araminta was right and that it would be a girl. I had already planned to call it Ethne. At the same time, I carried with me the image of my mother as I had last seen her, alone in front of that little horror-struck group, wearing black, face disfigured with tears. I began to think about her life and see how much she had suffered. I tried to talk about it to Mike, but he couldn't understand. He assumed it was part of my family obsession. We were eating grilled fish against a background of crystalline rain. Already I was fairly certain that the mere sight of the glistening eye and quivering gills was enough for my uneasy stomach.

'Your mother's a strong woman.' Mike crunched bones with his white teeth.

'Out of desperation. Don't you see? Women aren't meant to be strong. God made them to relax and have babies. And love. And look after their family.'

'I never knew you were a reactionary.'

'Of course, women should work too. But they can only do good work if they're already proper women, not some sort of ball-less man.'

Mike wasn't convinced. He looked at me indulgently. 'I hear the baby talking.'

'I'm sorry for her.'

'I've no objections, darling. Don't look at me like that. Everyone deserves pity. Even your magnificent mother.'

'I feel sick.' I pushed away my plate defeatedly.

'That makes a change,' said Mike without rancour.

We returned to our bright new flat and almost immediately the shiny black telephone rang. 'That's probably someone to do with my work,' said Mike eagerly. I picked the phone up. The pips went, followed by the heavy clonk of pennies dropping into a phone box. It was Molly.

'I didn't want to spoil your honeymoon, and anyway, she's much better now. It was worry over Leonard. He should have died immediately.'

'Are you talking about my mother?'

'Of course.' She sounded surprised.

'What's wrong with her?'

'Shingles. Though there's more to that than meets the eye ... there's something basically wrong with her, I'd say. Though she won't.' The pips went.

Molly was just round the corner. She had been trying out a church in Kensington. She was with us in five minutes.

'Is it Sunday?'

'Ah. There you have the other half of the story.' She became silent for a while, moving round our solid Albert Hall Mansions flat with a look of amazement. I followed her proudly, noting as she did the simple good taste of our black-framed chairs and low tables. The curtains were printed with a vaguely cubist pattern in red, blue, and

373

orange. We had not been afraid of plastic or laminated steel or any of the other postwar materials. I waited for praise.

'It doesn't look very comfortable,' she said, sitting down in a hammock-shaped chair threaded with strips of black plastic.

'If you want chintz,' I said sulkily.

'Oh, I don't want anything.' Molly smiled. 'It's a great deal more comfortable than my stuffy little room. Anyway, I expect it's modern.'

'There's nothing wrong in being modern.'

Mike said, 'Would you ladies object if I did some work?'

'He's so polite,' sighed Molly as he left the room. 'Although I would have liked him to hear the news.' I thought I noticed a gleam of exhilaration showing through her usual charitable briskness.

'What news?'

'Your mother is under instruction.' Now the gleam widened to a blaze.

I hesitated. 'Do you mean under instruction for the Catholic Church.'

'What else?'

'She might have been learning to drive.'

'This is not a matter for joking.'

'Not to you.'

'What is the matter, Violet darling?'

'Nothing.' I relented slightly. 'I do sometimes resent my mother always being the centre of attention.'

'Daughters feel that about their mothers. Your mother felt it about her mother.'

'About Eleanor?'

'Don't sound so surprised. Eleanor was quite a girl. Still is, in her own way. Look at how she tried to wreck all your mother's nice wedding arrangements.'

'*My* wedding.'

'Quite, darling.'

There was a pause, in which I noticed that my behaviour had dimmed Molly's exhilaration. I had not thought she could be affected by anyone's attitude. 'Would you like a cup of tea?'

'No, thank you, darling. I've gone off stimulants again.'

There was another silence, which I finally broke. 'Why ever should my mother suddenly want to become a Catholic? She's been through her conversion to socialism years ago.'

Molly leaned forward eagerly. 'That's what Father Wilson and I have to discover.' She pulled anxiously at a piece of crisp grey hair which now showed only the faintest shadow of marmalade. I saw she was not as confident about the conversion as she had first seemed.

'I'm not against her becoming a Catholic,' I said encouragingly.

'Father Wilson thinks it may be her reaction to being out of office,' Molly cried out in a burst.

'Oh, really. Isn't that a bit hard on her? Besides, she is Shadow Minister of Housing. That's not exactly a sinecure. Particularly now, when more houses are being built than babies born!'

Molly shook her head. 'Father Wilson isn't usually a cynic. And of course he recognises it was all set off by the horror of poor Leonard's death. He lived on for a week, you know. Your mother spent more time in the hospital than Araminta. Araminta couldn't bear it. She kept talking about a head injury he once had, years ago. It was almost as if she wished he had died then. He should have submitted to her love more often. Poor Araminta. He couldn't speak at all. Personally, I think he had already gone to God—or at least started on the road to God. I fear it may be a longish journey for Leonard.'

'How dreadful. I didn't know.'

'He hadn't started the journey on earth, you see. At best, that seems a practical error. Still, your mother said that she had never seen him so peaceful, even when he was twitching and writhing. He was never very attached to the world.'

'How terrible.' I put my hand on my baby's tummy.

'But it wouldn't be if it brought your mother to the Church, gave her some peace, would it?' The glow was there again. 'Father Wilson's dying too, you know. Of course, we all are from the moment of birth.'

I kept my hand on my stomach for safety. 'Strangely enough, I was thinking how unhappy Mother seemed when we were in Venice. I suppose I was removed enough to be objective.'

'No one can be happy in this world.'

'I am!'

Molly leaned forward and patted my knee. 'Yes, darling. With your polite, loving husband and nice flat and baby coming. But no one can be truly happy until—'

'But you can't just dismiss all the things that matter to me! You haven't got them; Mother hasn't got them. That's why you're unhappy. That's why they don't seem important to you.' I felt suddenly near tears.

Molly looked distressed. She stood up and put her arm round me. 'I'm sorry. I *am* sorry. I didn't mean to upset you. I suppose I hadn't taken into consideration your position. You're right, I don't often think about husbands and babies now. What I wanted was to ask your advice about Vi. Whether you thought she might be serious about joining the Church. I thought you would be the one to know best. I suppose what you've said is true. You've the possibility of worldly happiness now. It's probably quite a responsibility, too. Your mother and I never managed it. Why should you be upset? It was bad enough your beautiful wedding being filled with tragedy.'

'Oh, Molly.' Now, to her horror, I did burst into tears, sobbing so hard for all the problems of the world that she immediately rushed out to find Mike. I could hear them talking above my sobs. Molly was guiltily apologetic. 'I didn't realise. I suppose I could have talked to Tudor. I mean he's nice, but . . . Oh, dear, I am sorry . . . Shall I make some tea?'

By the time this arrived—Molly had to extract our new tea set from a packing case—I felt recovered enough to joke about that well-known stimulant, wood chippings.

Mike, on the other hand, now wanted to talk about 'the place of religion in our scientific era.' I left them to it and, going into the little room designated as nursery, stood dreamily planning the position of the cot and the colour of the walls. Remembering the distance between the nursery and my mother's room at Kettleside, even if she had been there and not working in London, I was glad to think my daughter would have only a thin wall between us. When she was very small I would bring her into my bedroom.

After an hour or so, Mike reappeared. He had the energetic, smug look of someone who's had a good argument. By now I was lying on my bed. He came and sat beside me.

'She's gone. Interesting woman. Did you know she got her limp from the Spanish Civil War?'

'How ever did you get onto that?'

'We talked about all sorts of things. Another extraordinary thing. One of your mother's oldest friends will be my boss at the Civil Service. Winnie Beauchamp. There's a name from the past.'

'I like her.' I tried to show appropriate interest. 'How did you get onto her?'

'Religion. Molly was saying that some women—men too, of course—have an inborn sense of Christianity which gives them a code of behaviour without having to try too hard for it. Often they may not even go to church or follow any formal relgion. She gave Winnie as an example.'

'I would have thought she went to church every Sunday.'

'There you are. That's exactly the point. She behaves as if she does. The other kind of woman is your mother, who is desperately in need of something to make sense of her life. She tried socialism.'

'She still is a Socialist.'

'Of course. I'm sure she'll never change. But it hasn't worked for her personally. She's not happy.'

'I told you that in Venice.'

Mike smiled. 'Of course you did. But you didn't have a theory to back it up.'

'So now you think she needs to become a Catholic.'

Mike got up and walked across the room. He picked up my brush and ran it across the top of his thick hair. 'It sounds as if Molly's brainwashed me, doesn't it? I don't think anyone needs to become a Catholic. I was just talking theoretically.'

'Oh.' There was a pause while I thought that for some reason—perhaps because I was a woman, and a pregnant woman—I couldn't understand the point of talking about people in theory. I laid my head back on the pillow, closed my eyes, and let my thoughts drift. I felt Mike come and lie beside me on the bed. I put my hand out to him. 'Would you mind if Ethne slept beside our bed?'

I remember Ethne's birth for so many things, mostly contradictory. The warmth and security of my bedroom; the feeling I had of standing on the edge of a bottomless pit whenever I considered Ethne's fragility; Mike's unbelievable excitement and support; his total lack of interest in anything physical to do with birth, baby, or me. My mother's parallel inadequacy, even disapproval, when faced with a nappy or a nipple; the sudden and extraordinary revelation (or perhaps even birth) of her loving interest in me.

It began with my determination not to remove to Kettleside. 'There's Araminta and Flo and Nanny and cots and night-lights and babies—a whole nursery world just waiting to be used,' persuaded my mother inaccurately, but with conviction. Araminta had not had a baby for at least ten years.

'I want my own baby to be born in my own home.'

'But it's so small here.' My mother looked despairingly at the bright square room. 'You'll hear every cry.'

'I want to hear every cry.'

'Poor Araminta.'

'I'm sorry for Araminta, but I'm not having my baby to cheer her up.'

'Nanny will be in despair!'

'I'm not having the baby for Nanny either.'

'What's the point of keeping Kettleside going if no one uses it?'

This appeared to be a *cri de coeur*, but I was adamant.

'I'm not having a baby to make sense of Kettleside. Anyway, the farm makes the money to keep it going. And it's Araminta's home, not ours.'

My mother looked up surprised. 'Yes, I suppose that's true—hers by right of occupancy. She's lived there now for twenty years. She used to think Leonard would come and take her away one day, but he never did. And then there were all those children.'

'So Kettleside is her home.'

'Yes. Although it will eventually go to Tudor. If he wants it.' My mother sighed. 'You must do what you want,' she said.

I thought that this was the very first occasion on which my will had been stronger than hers. 'But I'd love Nanny to come down here for the first few weeks.'

'Oh, darling!' cried my mother, kissing me on the cheek. 'I'm sure you won't regret it.'

Nanny's sayings reminded Mike so painfully of his mother that he hardly came near the baby for a week. Nanny was old now. I worried at first when I saw how her cup shook on the saucer. My mother, who'd collected her from the station, stood over her protectively. I thought we might be looking after her instead of she after the baby.

But the moment Ethne was born, a strange transformation took place. Her eyes glowed, and her famous silver buckle appeared winking at her waist. Her little room became a baby's sanctuary. She smelled of talcum powder and soap flakes. Her only concession to the passing years was a pair of blue fluffy slippers which my mother had given her for Christmas.

I couldn't have done without her, for it was a difficult birth, which left me quite incapable of doing more than hold Ethne to my breast at four-hourly intervals.

'You're a perfect example of why women have to be more resilient than men.' My mother sat on the edge of my bed. She had come straight from her constituency and looked tired and pale. I noticed, for my mind was on such things with the deflation of my own stomach, that she had become thin lately. She had never been fat, but now she was positively boney. I might have said something, but she was so keen on making her point that I didn't get a chance. 'You were so eager to do everything yourself,' said my mother. 'So keen to be strong and in control. And what happens? Your body lets you down.'

I shifted slightly in my bed to get more comfortable and considered. Before Ethne's birth I would have assumed my mother's remarks were meant to express my failure, her victory. But since Ethne's birth her attitude seemed to have altered. She admired me.

'Ethne's very well, anyway.'

'I'm going to go and see her now.' My mother stood up and with her usual military gesture pulled down her black skirt and twitched her hand backwards to inspect the straightness of her seams. She saw me watching her and smiled. 'You don't know what it is being in a man's world all the time. Like being on the stage. One mistake and they'll say, "Ah, just like a woman!" It's a strain. Sometimes I'm so tired.'

I had never heard my mother admit to weakness before. I wondered again if she was ill. But a question unasked once never gets a second chance. She was thinking of something else. 'When I come here,' she said, 'and see you, so happy with your lovely baby and your clever husband, then I feel better. I always said you were strong-minded. Your father thought you would need a lot of attention. We were talking about you when he was killed. But it seems to me you've managed very well without it.' She smiled again and slipped out quickly from the room.

I felt tears starting in my eyes, and although this was a daily post-natal event, this time they were accompanied by a heaving chestful of emotion. When Mike returned, I flung myself into his arms. 'My poor mother! She's got nobody. Nobody! She's so alone!'

'Let's see. Who were you crying over last night?' Mike sounded quite a lot less sympathetic than usual. I took it to be an attack on my mother.

'Just because she's successful and—'

'You know I admire your mother.' He got up and went to the door. 'Anything to eat? I'm starving.' Over his shoulder, 'I saw *Look Back in Anger* tonight. You and your mother may be part of the past.' He beat his chest suddenly, grinning. 'Jimmy and me! We're the new men.'

'At least, I'm married to you,' I answered, not really understanding but oddly glad after all that he wasn't going to listen to my moans about my mother. She wasn't ill. After all, Eleanor was thin as a rake and she looked set to live to a hundred. I lay back in my pillows and fell into a sleep that might have lasted for hours if Ethne had 't interrupted it with her usual hungry yells.

'Ah,' I said sleepily as Nanny bore her in with that doting nanny's hunch. 'The Future arrives. No coldness, inattention, separation, rules, or regulation.'

'I don't know about that.' Nanny found a free hand to help me undo my nightdress at the shoulder. 'It may do when you're grown up, but what children need, babies no exception, is a good dose of nursery training. Running wild never helped any child. Nor mother, if it comes to that.'

'Your whole life's been about that, hasn't it Nanny? About order. You were lucky having your kingdom at Kettleside.'

'I don't know about that.' Very gently she handed Ethne down towards me. 'I was away from Kettleside twenty-five years. I only came with Mrs Trigear when you were born.'

'Oh,' I said, not interested enough to pursue the question.

379

I looked down at Ethne's head and felt the painful pleasure as her mouth pulled at my nipple. 'Love,' I said decisively, so decisively that she stopped sucking for a second or two. 'Love,' I repeated as she continued again. 'That's the first necessity. That's what we all need. That's why my mother will join the Catholic Church. That's why Mike married me. That's why Araminta gave up painting, for babies. That's even why you, Nanny darling, look after babies. That's why Ethne's the luckiest baby in the world. Because I'm going to absolutely swamp her with love!'

Chapter Fifteen

TV snacks and cocktail canapés are delicious with Burgess Anchovy paste on buttered toast.
(Personal column) *The Times.*   13 May 1957

NIGHT RIOTING AT HASTINGS—POLICE SENT BY AIR
About 70 police reserves were flown here this evening after clashes during the day between Mods and Rockers. Screaming mobs of hooligans broke loose along the seafront . . . Screeching girls scratched and tore at the police as they made their arrests, and at one point four policemen were on the ground being punched by a howling mob.
The Times.   3 August 1964

MORE U.S. ADVISERS TO GO TO S. VIETNAM
(Headline) *The Times.*   28 July 1964

My mother was right. Women can't control their lives. I couldn't make myself into the perfectly loving mother I yearned to become. After Nanny left, I struggled on for a year ironing nappies with a bright smile, even ironing the nappies' labels—infallible sign of mother madness. I raced to Ethne's every cry nightly, careful not to disturb Mike—for he went to work, and besides, I was not of the generation that expected a man's help. Quite the contrary, it would have been an admission of defeat. Instead, I smiled outwardly till it grew hard and inside began to hate equally Mike, who was impervious to my aims and my suffering, both of which he considered unnecessary and exaggerated, and poor little Ethne, who under such a wealth of motherly attention wailed or chuckled or spat just like any other baby.

I remember the afternoon I snapped. It was just after Ethne's first birthday. Clancy, who was her godmother, appeared to give her a birthday present. She had a large portfolio under her arm. She wore a smart beret jammed over her shaggy fringe and round blue eyes I thought how young and energetic she looked. Although I had weaned Ethne months ago, I still felt as if I smelled of milk. The whole flat smelled of milk. 'I'm sorry I didn't make the birthday party. The Moore Press suddenly decided they needed six illustrations in a week's time.'

'My mother enjoyed it,' I said dully.

'So did mine. That's what it's for, isn't it?'

'I thought I was doing it for my own enjoyment. Fulfilment. And Ethne's, of course.'

'Oh.' Clancy looked surprised. 'Anyway, I've brought a collection of my best drawings and I thought I'd like you to choose one for her present. Then I'll get it framed.'

'She's asleep,' I said, still cast in my lethargy.

'You were expecting her to choose, were you?' Clancy threw open the portfolio. 'Really it's a present for you.'

I took this in. I had become so obsessed by Ethne that it was quite strange to consider doing something on my own behalf. 'I suppose her artistic sense isn't fully developed.' I smiled. For the first time in months it was directed at myself.

'She's only a baby.' Clancy opened the portfolio and drew out a first picture. 'I'll make a cup of tea while you're looking.'

I suppose I was eager for distraction, but Clancy's mysterious undergrowth world, filled with little animals which were not quite mice or moles or squirrels, with their anxious beady eyes and their eager questing snouts, immediately appealed to me. The nearest similarity I could find for them was in Arthur Rackham's world among the tangled roots of great trees. I wanted to invent stories for them.

I said so to Clancy. She stretched out her legs, which were clad in strange corduroy breeches, and frowned. 'If only you would. I can't tell you how annoying it is. Here I am pouring my soul out into my drawing—even if they are only little creatures. And there's Felix—or Mrozek, as you and your mother call him—picking up any pretty girl who takes his fancy and asking her to "write a few words to go with clever Clancy's picture." It's such an insult.'

'Why don't you write the stories yourself?'

Clancy got up and marched up and down aggressively. 'Never ever have a love affair with your employer.' She turned back to me. 'Because he doesn't take me seriously enough. He thinks any young fool can write like a genius. Except me, I'm all artist, no writer.'

'Go to another publisher.'

Clancy collapsed again. She lifted the lid of the teapot. 'Oh, God! I've forgotten to put any tea in. I should, of course.' There was a pause. 'But I love Felix. Ridiculous. He's old, unfaithful, insulting, lying . . . I love him. I suppose the truth is that in the last analysis I'm not really ambitious. After all, I do my pictures. I have that satisfaction. What does it matter if no one sees them? Or if, when they do, they're side by side with the most dreadful drivel? When you think of it, women have generally done things without reward. Look at my mother.'

'Yes, but she had babies instead. She chose to give up painting.' I found to my surprise that Clancy's attitude was making me very angry. It was a long time since I had cared about anything but my baby. 'You owe it to your talent to see your pictures are shown off properly.'

'What I need is someone to write some good stories. Someone who will work with me. I meant it when I asked you to help, Violet.'

I subsided. 'But—'

'I know you've got a baby. And a husband.'

'Yes. . .' I was struck by the realisation that I had been listening to Ethne crying in her bedroom for several minutes. Normally I was in there at the first snort. 'Ethne's crying.'

'Yes,' said Clancy, unconcerned. 'Babies do, don't they? Mother's always did, anyway. So will you seriously consider becoming an author? Of a sort, anyway?'

'But will Mrozek take me seriously?' To my amazement, I realised Ethne had actually stopped crying. Indeed, I could hear the bubbling noises that were her attempt at singing.

'Oh, yes.' Clancy returned to her bitter tone. She stood up. 'You'll qualify as a pretty young thing. He has a theory he altered your mother's life by persuading her to take on the world, so you can tell him he's got to do the same for you.'

'That sounds as if I should hate him.'

'He exaggerates. I'm sure she would have gone into politics anyway. They never had an affair, if that's what you're thinking. Quite odd, actually, that they didn't. I'm sure they were attracted.'

'Do you think a lot about Mrozek's affairs?' I asked curiously.

'You are innocent. Anyone does who isn't sure of their man.' She became brisk again. 'I'll tell you all about what it's like to have an unhappy love affair sometime. But now I'll give Ethne a kiss and be on my way. Please, darling Violet, help me with my books!'

When Mike caught me with my brand-new exercise book and self-conscious face of concentration, he said, 'What a relief! Does this mean I'll get a woman again instead of the First True Mother?'

Not exactly. My principles of free expression for Ethne remained the same. She was still supremely important, but now I was able to use what I noticed about her in my books. I based my stories on her constant desire to creep under chairs, beds, tables, into cupboards, cases, laundry baskets, all in an apparently deep need to hide. I thought about this, noticed it was true of other children as well as Ethne, and decided it was the small person's defensive action when faced by a large and inexplicable adult world. They wanted their own small, secret places almost like animals. Here was my link with Clancy's world, with her cosy nest among the tangled undergrowth, with her little burrows deep in mossy banks. Her drawings were more complex than Little Grey Rabbit, more fantastic than Beatrix Potter. Her animals were not real animals; they had the look of children hiding in their mother's wardrobe. With this in mind, I began to write.

When I told Mike what I was doing he said, 'I thought you were going to finish your degree.' He smiled, as if it weren't very important. 'At least, children's books will please my mother.'

'I may please other people too,' I said defiantly. By this time I'd finished several stories. 'There's been a very good reader response at The Moore Press.'

'Original and captivating,' said Mike, still smiing.

'That sort of thing. You must get over the idea that you're the only person doing any serious work.'

Mike shared my mother's ability to change. Perhaps the security of the work structure he'd chosen gave him the confidence. Once he saw that I had embarked on a career that was serious to me, even if he could not take it quite seriously, he gave me every support and encouragement. When the odious Mrozek sent Katynka round one afternoon to persuade me to alter a sad ending, he primed me with such a lecture about the artist's integrity that Katynka went away without concessions. When Clancy and I, driven to fury by Mrozek's haphazard production of our books, decided we must publish them ourselves, Mike offered all our savings to finance us. It turned out to be an excellent business investment. But that wasn't obvious at the time.

We would never have stayed so long at The Moore Press if we had not been entangled in a web of personal attachments. When I told my mother about my first book, she said, 'Oh, darling. How kind of Mrozek! But I do hope this doesn't mean poor Clancy's still running after him.'

'She is not running after him.'

It was a Saturday. A sunny July afternoon, and I had persuaded my mother to a walk in Hyde Park. Every now and again I was struck by the unhealthy life she led and tried to do something about it. Father Wilson had died recently, and she was expecting Molly to call in later for a cup of tea. They were discussing the possibility of creating a travel award for priests in his memory.

I persuaded her to leave a note for Molly. 'Molly needs fresh air too,' I said. 'You've probably both forgotten how children force one into relaxing walks.'

'Thank God,' said my mother, but she smiled all the same.

I pushed the pushchair while Ethne tottered ahead of us. We found a bench facing the oily waters of the Serpentine.

'Won't Ethne fall in?' said my mother, in the tradition of grandmothers, more anxious than I.

'She's frightened of the ducks. She won't go too near.'

'I remember when these benches were reserved for the nannies. No mother would have dared approach. Certainly not sit down.'

'Did Nanny come here? Our darling Nanny?'

'During her time away from us. Her bad time. I found her here once. When I was quite young. The English class structure used to be reflected rigidly in the nannies' hierarchy. Nannies who worked for families of the wrong class or wrong income bracket might just as well have carried a bell and shouted "Leper!" At the time, I was horrified and ashamed that my mother should have caused her suffering. But later I began to hate the whole system.'

'Nanny would be horrified herself if she knew she had converted you to socialism.'

My mother laughed. But I could see she wanted to sit quietly on a bench and think of the past. This nostalgia was a new, upsetting trait in her character. A mental sign of growing old. With it came a tendency to accept old-fashioned received opinions. It was only a tendency, but I saw it as a sign of weakness. Why, for example, did she talk about Clancy's running after Mrozek? It did not reflect her true feelings about a woman's relationship with a man. It was a throwback to her past. Strangely enough, although I always found her strength difficult to cope with, I found this tiny weakness unbearable. I would worry her about some innocuous statement until, for the sake of peace, she would admit she had not been concentrating.

'Women are not invariably "running after men",' I said, 'if they're not married. They may choose not to be married.'

My mother looked up, surprised at my aggresiveness. 'Don't tell me Clancy doesn't want to marry Mrozek?'

'She doesn't. Not when she's being sensible. But that's not the point. It's your assumption that in any love affair it's the woman who's suffering. It's such a humiliating attitude.'

'I don't know. In my young days, girls weren't expected to suffer love deeply because they were too pure and virginal. At least, I've given them feelings. Like a man.'

'But you still assume they're at a disadvantage.'

'Do I?' My mother was not very interested. She was off duty, and these matters did not concern her personally. Although she was still only in her fifties, I doubt if she'd had a love affair for several years. She wanted to think about Nanny all that time ago. However, she sat up and made an effort. 'I may get it all wrong, darling, but apart from Dr Summerskill, no one's done more than me to fight for women's rights.'

This was true. She had argued endless bills on divorce, birth control, property rights, family allowances, either in the House of Commons or on platforms round the country. It was unfair to attack her because she couldn't feel it.

'The thing I've cared about most,' she said, turning to look meditatively over the back of the bench, 'is the right of women to work.' I saw her eyes sweep across the pattern of widely spaced trees. 'I'm glad you're working, darling. And getting properly paid for it.'

'But you don't take my work seriously, and I'm not—' I began inevitably, but was interrupted by my mother's jumping suddenly to her feet. For a second I assumed Ethne had fallen into the water, and then I saw coming towards us, between the trees, Molly. Her limp oddly accentuated by the distance, she looked more gnomelike than ever. Her grey hair had grown rather long and stood up round her face in a frizzy halo. At her side, looking like the realisation of an Aubrey Beardsley cartoon, rolled Augustus Budd.

My mother went to meet them. I picked up Ethne and followed. We stood among the trees. Ethne clasped my neck and stared at Augustus and Molly in terror.

'Augustus gave me lunch. A very good lunch, too. Wasn't it

strange, we were dining alone in the same restaurant? Afterwards, we found your note. Guess what? Mrs Briggsworthy's died.'

'Oh, no.'

'Don't panic. George has decided to sell Didcot and live on Eureka.'

'I've told her it'll be the last she'll see of him.' Augustus kissed my mother on the cheek. Ethne let out a yell as he approached me.

'Take no notice of the professor. He's just been told to take off six stone or we'll see no more of him.'

'Oh, poor darling!'

'Your friend exaggerates. I had the teeniest of warning twinges and I made the mistake of seeing a specialist. That's why I'm in London. You look well. Hardworking as ever? We were confounded to discover you were enjoying the sun.'

'It's Ethne,' I said proudly. 'She's the lure.'

'They both are,' said my mother, looking at us affectionately. 'You wait, Molly. You'll miss St John if George takes him to Eureka.'

'He won't. Anyway, I can take him out from his boarding school here if I do. My plan for my old age is to grow more and more eccentric in the cause of the Lord.'

'Holier,' suggested my mother, smiling. She took Augustus' arm. 'Molly's been impossibly holy ever since she started her home for ex-prisoners and prisoner's wives.'

'It certainly doesn't seem to have curbed her earthly appetites,' Augustus beamed. I thought his face was an unfortunate red with the remaining wisps of his colourless hair.

I let down Ethne onto the grass, and as she staggered off we all began to follow a strange cavalcade among the trunks and shadows. I lost interest in their talk and watched Ethne picking a piece of grass, testing it on her tongue, flicking it across her palm, dropping it, running, circling round and round with her hands in the air till she was giddy. 'Mama! Mama!' she cried delightedly as she wheeled crazily and finally toppled onto the grass. I picked her up and flung her, scared and laughing, into the air.

'The odd thing is you didn't become a Socialist during the Spanish Civil War. When everyone else did.'

'I was having babies,' said my mother, and they all turned to look at me. 'But not so much fun,' she added. We smiled at each other.

'The Spanish Civil War turned me into a Catholic,' said Molly with an odd little skip. 'Why did you become a Catholic, Vi?'

My mother didn't answer. She seemed to be thinking of something else. Her head was tipped slightly backwards and her eyes stared up at the undersides of the leaves.

'It's so hot,' she sighed.

'Not under the trees,' I objected. But Molly took her up.

'So it is!' she cried. 'Far too hot. Come on, Professor. Take my arm. We'll join the ducks in the cooling waters of the Serpentine.'

'It's not allowed!'

My mother and I returned to our bench while Molly and Augustus paddled like children in the shallow pond.

'Oooh. It's cold!' screamed Molly. Augustus held her arm gallantly. She began to kick up her legs.

'Oh, dear. Shouldn't we stop them? Like trippers on a beach. Surely they hardly know each other.'

'They had a good lunch,' said my mother, not unkindly. 'Plenty to drink. They're forgetting themselves. It does everyone good to have a spree.'

A spree it might have remained if Ethne had not seen a duck-free path to the water and taken a sudden dive to Molly's sparkling fountains.

'The baby!' Augustus let go of Molly's arm and bent to rescue Ethne. Molly overbalanced. The bottom of the pond was greasy with greenish slime. She lunged at Augustus. Augustus pushed Ethne towards me and then lost his balance.

He fell like a huge statue, throwing up spray and tidal waves which sent faraway ducks quacking even farther away. I watched with horror as he didn't rise. The water lapped over his elegant suit.

Ethne shrieked in my arms. Molly and my mother tried to lift Augustus' face out of the water. He was so heavy they couldn't roll him over or pull him out of the water. Some passer-by came to help. One went to find a keeper. Ethne continued to scream.

Augustus had looked so happy prancing in the water with Molly.

Molly kept shaking her head. 'We talked of nothing serious,' she said. 'Just ridiculous gossip. If only I'd known. We should have had a serious conversation. Of course, I didn't really know him. If only we'd talked seriously. So ridiculous . . .' I found her reflective tones oddly upsetting. How could she put him in the past so quickly?

'He was trying to help Ethne,' I said, hugging her wet warm body.

Augustus lay now on the grass, his eyes closed, his huge frame calm. There seemed no point in giving him the kiss of life. Molly was right. He had gone.

'I suppose he found if difficult to be really close to anyone,' she said, taking my mother's hand. A large crowd began to gather. They chattered and pointed.

'Yes,' said my mother as calmly. 'He tried when he was younger. But he was too intellectual. He couldn't bring his brain and his body together.'

'Such a big body. He would never have lost six stone.' They both looked at Augustus, whose wispy hair was already beginning to dry in the hot sun.

'We can't just leave him there!' I cried.

My mother patted my hand consolingly. 'He was very thin when I first knew him. He couldn't fight in the First World War because of his asthma.'

I saw that neither my mother nor Molly saw death as heightened drama.

'Perhaps he still had asthma,' continued Molly gently.

'He didn't think he was important enough to talk about.'

At last an ambulance came. I ran over to it. The stretcher-bearers tried to carry Augustus to the road, but after a few paces they set him down again. One set off to drive the ambulance across the grass.

The other smiled at us apologetically. 'The water doesn't help.'

The ambulance bumped towards us. Ethne shrieked now with delight. The crowd was enormous. In order to escape it, we all got into the ambulance. I hugged Ethne, who at that moment seemed frail protection against the future.

'It's all death,' said my mother at Augustus' funeral. 'It used to come unfairly. But now I'm old and I must expect it.'

'You're not sixty yet.' My mother turned at my miserable voice. She looked surprised. 'Don't worry, darling. I won't collapse or anything. In one way it's a relief. I'm like everybody else. Work. I still have my work.'

But I saw that she took little pleasure in it any more, and I wondered whether, when and if the Labour Party did eventually get in, she would have the energy to fight for her place in the Cabinet. She had already been ten years out of office. It was a long time.

I began to look at my own life. I was a success. My writing had made me confident. I made decisions. I decided I didn't want another child. Ethne had been too much of an emotional experience to repeat. Mike didn't mind either way. I decided Mike was the love of my life, whom I hoped to keep always at my side, but that it was just possible I might need some other man to give me the things he could not. We were so different. He was solidly ambitious, interested in his job, in politics, in discussions about subjects that he considered important. This did not include people. He did not want to talk about friends—not that we had many—about us, or even, very much, about Ethne. He left that sort of emotional frill to me.

Strangely enough, this characteristic which had so attracted me when we first me—it had made him seem strong and mature compared with other young men—now thoroughly annoyed me. I understood the origins of the attitude very well. It was a reflection of his father's attitude to his mother's gossipy chat about the neighbours. That was woman's talk. Much as I appreciated my mother-in-law's many excellent qualities, it was hard to be cast in her role.

I said to Mike, 'Why don't you ever talk about my work?'

'I do.'

'Only the business side.'

'What else is there to talk about?'

'The people involved. My relationship with Clancy. Hers with Mrozek. Why he behaves perfectly one minute and like a perfect louse the next.'

'But that's not important.'

'But it is!' I cried. 'If we could understand that, we could understand why he's such a good publisher in some ways and such a rotten one in others!'

'He's a good publicist,' said Mike impassively. 'I don't need a breakdown on his love life to know that.'

'You're like a—a rock!' I cried in frustration.

'And what's wrong with that?'

Usually, nothing. But sometimes, after I'd been with Clancy, drinking wine over some new idea or at one of Mrozek's famous publicity parties, I felt the need of someone who would not always appeal to my better nature. Someone who would allow me, even drag me, down a few rungs. Even before I met Eddie in February, 1961, I was looking for a lover. Once I met him, an affair was inevitable. I wanted a lover. On the other hand, I didn't want to lose my perfect husband. My loved husband. I used to wake at night sweating with the fear that Mike had found out. I knew without any doubt that if Mike ever found out he would, quite simply, leave me. There was no prevarication or compromise in his nature. He would see it in straightforward terms. I loved someone else; therefore our love was over. Marriage over. Goodbye. Even now I remember the terror I felt if he even looked at me oddly. In fact, I can now remember it more clearly than the love I felt for Eddie.

Eddie and I met at one of Mrozek's fashionable publishing parties. He was broad and tanned and fair, with the sort of athletic good looks that made me unsurprised that he had just come over from California. Mrozek said, 'Violet writes stories about the most delightful creatures. You ought to get Disney interested. Eddie's in films.' I scowled furiously at his retreating back.

Eddie said, 'Haven't we met before?'

'I suppose you say that to everyone.'

'If they're pretty enough.'

People had similar silly conversations all the time at Mrozek's parties, but as it turned out Eddie was quite right. He was Eddie Pemberton, my cousin.

'We had lunch just after the war. Your mother didn't turn up.'

'I was a schoolgirl. You were going to be a writer.'

'Was. As Mr Moore puts it, I'm "in films".'

'Do you know Isabel Royston?'

'Isa? *The* Isa! No one knows her. Not even her lovers. I know her son, though—poor little blighter.'

'He must be grown up by now.'

'He was grown up at six. In one way. Hollywood does that.'

'His father once consoled himself with the mother of the girl who does the illustrations for my 'delightful little animals.' Actually, they are neurotic incarnations of my daughter's . . .' I stopped abruptly. I realised I did not want him to know about my marriage and my daughter.

'Your daughter? You have a husband too, presumably?'

'Oh, yes.'

'Not divorced?'

'Oh no. He just doesn't come to publishing parties. He says it's my working life. But actually, it's because he doesn't like people.'

'Do all the English say "actually" as often as you do?'

'I don't know.' My voice was depressed. Now he would see me only as a wife. In a minute he would ask what Mike did. There was a pause. Despairingly, I decided to re-introduce him to my mother. They could talk about old times.

'Would your husband let you have dinner with your cousin who doesn't know anyone in London?'

I had the curious sensation that my body was turning into a mass of feathers and might blow away. I found that I was gripping his arm.

'Are you sick?'

Sick with love. I smiled weakly. When I fell in love with Mike I had not known about physical love. As I held Eddie's arm, I knew we would become lovers. I made one attempt at staving off the inevitable. 'You can come home for supper. Mike won't mind.'

'I thought he didn't like people. I want to take you out on our own. What's the best restaurant in town?'

I recovered myself and smiled into his eyes. 'I expect I was sick with hunger.'

'I've had enough of this party!'

Then I knew he was feeling the same as I. He had only just arrived. He had met nobody. We passed Clancy as we reached the door.

I called, 'I'm off!'

Clancy stopped and turned round. She looked at Eddie; she

391

looked at me. She knew me very well. She said, 'Oh, Violet,' in a voice that warned me of danger and sympathised with my happiness.

'See you tomorrow!' As if tomorrow existed. Arm in arm, we stepped out into my fantasy of love.

It wasn't only fantasy. Although I knew even when most besotted that I could not exist without Mike and our home, and that I had existed and could, even would, exist without Eddie, it wasn't only fantasy because Eddie was a very practical person. It was he who pointed out that there were several markets other than publishing for Clancy's and my creations. He had that refreshing American belief that anything is possible. All it takes is ambition, hard work, a touch of luck, and a speck of talent.

He had come to London hoping to set up a film. He had adapted an Evelyn Waugh novel. He said that Hollywood was just beginning to realise the enormous talent that lay waiting to be financed in England. 'It's fashion,' he said—quite correctly as it turned out. 'The sixties are for England. The secret is to be in the right place at the right time. Better still, be ahead of the game. I'm just ahead of the game now. You wait and see.' Strangely enough, despite the accuracy of his predictions he seemed able to do everything but set up his own film. Our relationship, therefore, covered a frantic, rather unhappy period in his working life, although such were his golden charm and confident manner that I hardly realised it at the time.

On the other hand, whatever he tried to do for other people turned immediately to gold. He told Clancy and me that first we should get into the expanding children's television market, and that second we should look into the spin-off market for our sort of product, such as buttons, T-shirts, posters, or even toys and puppets. This sort of thing was almost unheard of in England in the early sixties. We found it difficult to understand that Clancy's weird drawings and my odd stories constituted 'a product,' like bicycles or Brillo pads. At heart, despite our frustration with Mrozek's unreliability, we still considered ourselves lucky to be doing what we enjoyed and being published. 'After all, one of his biographies won the James Tait Black Prize only last week.' We knew there were our contemporaries —much cleverer, many of them, with degrees and qualifications —who did absolutely nothing except look after their husbands or children or at best served humbly in some assisting capacity. We should not complain. People in serious jobs like my husband, Mike, slogging away in the Civil Service, or my mother, in the Labour Party, had the rights. We had the fun.

This attitude infuriated Eddie. 'Of course what they're doing is worthwhile. But no more so than what you do. And as it happens, what you do has a much bigger business potential. Do you think a businessman doesn't take himself seriously? What you can be is original creators and businesswomen!'

Clancy and I looked at each other and giggled weakly. We often reacted to Eddie's confidence this way. Clancy said, 'Do you want to be a businesswoman, Violet?' Our discussions usually took place in her 'artist's garret' in the Cromwell Road.

'I don't know. Do you?'

'Oh, shit!' Eddie rolled off Clancy's divan, where he had been stretched out, and stood up. 'Everybody wants money!'

Eventually, shamefacedly and humbly, we went along to the BBC.

Within a year we had our own daily five-minute spot. Our book sales increased by a thousand per cent, and a year later we had finally made the break and set up our own business. We called it 'Secrets', which was the name of our television programme.

It was 'Secrets' that enabled me to keep my relationship with Eddie secret from Mike. That and the fact that he was my cousin. My exhilaration and inaccessibility could be put down to the excitement and success of a new venture. Mike knew that I saw Eddie often, but he also knew that he was advising us on the film side. If my mother had guessed, I don't think I could have gone on. I would have felt too ashamed. But my mother saw me as the mother of her darling Ethne. She was not interested in peoples' sex lives. Not even her daughter's. In many ways she was my best cover of all, for she often invited us over to the flat together or for lunch at the House of Commons. Sometimes when we had come straight from two hours together in Eddie's bed I used to think our glowing bodies must give us away. But she never guessed. It was hard enough for her to get used to the idea that I was being a success.

To do her justice, once she had grasped the idea, she was very pleased for me. Even more so for Clancy. Or rather for Araminta. 'How wonderful,' she said, 'that Araminta's talent should at last get its reward.'

I said nothing, although I found her attitude absurd. Araminta, poor old thing, now left almost alone with Nanny and the younger children in Northumberland since Flo and Cecil's retirement, had nothing whatsoever to do with Clancy's success. I was not in the mood to give credit to upbringing or genes.

'When will there be an election?' I asked, knowing that on this subject at least she was still sound.

'Another year or so, I suppose.' She sighed. 'It's such a struggle.'

'You're not thinking of giving up?'

'After waiting so long? Certainly not!' she answered staunchly, but I recognised the defensive note, showing the vigour rose out of duty rather than inclination. But before I could press her further, she began to press me about Ethne's education.

We tended to argue about Ethne's education to avoid arguing about her religious education. At least, that was how I put it to myself. I always assumed since my mother's conversion that she was longing to get some holy water over her beloved granddaughter's curls. But now I'm not sure I was right. For she seemed to believe in a very different sort of Catholicism from Molly's proselytising faith. She never brought up the subject herself, although perfectly ready to discuss anything that arose out of a general conversation or answer any questions I chose to ask her.

I asked her once why she never brought up the subject of religion as Molly did, and she answered that for her it was a very personal affair. She didn't know yet that it was the answer for everybody or, if it was, that she was capable of putting it as it should be. The priest, she said, who had influenced her to become a Catholic had hardly ever spoken of the matter directly. Not until he sensed she already believed.

'Ah, the famous Father Wilson,' I said a little mockingly.

'Famous Father Wilson indeed,' said my mother smiling. 'He'd turn in his grave at the idea.'

When Ethne was seven, we were arguing about private schools versus state education. In principle, we were agreed. In this democratic age we did not want to put Ethne into a selected circle of children who would consider themselves an elite, but in fact would have no way of coping with the big world outside. Comprehensive schools, the new Holy Grail of the Labour Party, beckoned on the horizon. One was opening shortly very near us. There was already talk of previous private-school candidates fighting to get places from the grammar-school children. Ethne would learn to mix with children from all kinds of backgrounds. It was coeducational. And though I did not admit this to myself, it was fashionable. I was determined she should go there. Even Mike, who, as an ex–grammar-school boy, mumbled something about comprehensives not being the same, understood that.

My mother, despite actually being on the board of governors of that very comprehensive school, put up a much fiercer fight. Our arguments took place mostly over the Christmas holidays at Kettleside. It gave us a useful preoccupation. We took cold, windy walks which made me think of my childhood. Except that then, I had done without my mother.

Ethne and a girlfriend she had brought to stay ran ahead, following Araminta's youngest children towards the moors.

'Don't you see, darling'—my mother had allowed Nanny to wrap her in a huge cape of Araminta's, so that she looked an unac-

394

customedly bulky shape—'Ethne's so special, such an odd mixture of Mike's principles and sheer wilfulness; so clever, yet so often perversely keen not to use her brains, that she needs a special kind of attention.'

'Every grandmother thinks that her granddaughter is special.' I watched Ethne falling down with shrieks of glee into the springy heather. 'What she needs is to be made to feel ordinary.'

'But you can't make someone extraordinary feel ordinary. She'll just give up.'

'Do you know she's woken every night since she was a baby?' This was a fact that I usually tried to overlook, both because it made the nightly wrench more of an acceptable habit and because otherwise I might become worried.

'Exactly. She's hyperactive. She's still buzzing away in her sleep. What she needs is a small class in a small school where she feels totally secure and is right under the eye of the teacher. That way she'll be disciplined and happy.'

Looking back, it seems astonishing now that we talked about schools in almost entirely social terms; the education we barely considered. That was the way of the sixties and early seventies. Comprehensives were founded on these attitudes. The creators, my mother among them, were helping the underprivileged, as they said, but they were also reacting against the clever elite—not necessarily with jealousy. My mother, for example, always felt sorry for Augustus and his essential isolation.

I often thought about him myself. About his death, caused as it was by Ethne, a huge porpoise in a shallow pond. It had seemed the cliché of his life. My mother explained, 'It's a matter of scholarship. If you believe in scholarship, then you believe Augustus' life was fulfilled.'

'I believe in people.'

'Then you may say he was unfulfilled.' She paused and looked wistful. 'Though he had many friends. Look at the way he was flirting with Molly right up to the end.'

'He was a eunuch!' I cried out angrily.

My mother did not defend him. 'I always forget how young you are,' she said with resignation.

There was another sort of clever elite, separate from the Public School/Oxbridge axis, who also found it difficult to fit in easily with the world. Or so it seemed to my mother. This was the first wave of grammar-school boys that hit Oxbridge. Leonard had been isolated by his education as much as Augustus. 'But Mike's a product of a grammar school and perfectly well adjusted,' I would say defensively.

It was natural, I suppose, that politicians with a programme of Nationalisation should emphasize the importance of social aspects in education. It was just hard luck on Ethne that she was the right generation to suffer. I was as taken in by it all as anyone else. I was the swinging creator of 'Secrets'. When I went to parties with my handsome cousin over from Hollywood, I was quite a star.

I said on that cold Christmas Day, 'Ethne's different from the way we were as children. She's much more independent. She has so many friends I don't know half of them. She's much freer. She'll love a big school.'

'Friends are often a defence against insecurity.' My mother looked longingly at the four children, who had now started to climb the rocky outcrops above the bracken.

'And a very good defence, too.' I watched Ethne's friend pull her onto a ledge.

'It's foolish of me to interfere.' We had reached the bracken line, and my mother turned right so that we could continue walking along the grassy base of the mountains. She looked up again. 'It's strange seeing Ethne climb those mountains. When I was a child they were so far out of bounds, I hardly believed they were real. The most I dared was to run down the lawn between the rhododendron bushes.'

'I used to run down the driveway to school.'

'In my day Miss Tiptree had to come to the house. With her poor, stupid brother. I supppose it was wrong for someone so clever to devote her life to this little place.'

'If she'd been born half a century later she could have been head of a comprehensive school.'

'If I thought Ethne's teachers would be like Miss Tiptree, I would have no worries. Never mind, darling. I expect I'm just a terrible example of someone lacking the courage of my own convictions. We've made so many changes. I've made so many speeches—'

She was interrupted by a sudden scream. We both looked upwards nervously, but it was only Ethne sitting astride a rock shaped like a baby elephant and shouting to catch our attention. Above her I could see Araminta's children with their wild, shaggy hair climbing higher and higher.

'If only she didn't remind me of Eleanor,' murmured my mother. 'My mother hated these mountains, you know,' she said, speaking louder. 'That's why she ran away to Eureka. It was nothing to do with your father. She felt the mountain threatened her freedom. Poor Eleanor, she never found anything better after all.'

'I'm not so sure. She always seems to have a kind of crazy confidence.'

'A wasted life.'

'Quite happy.'

'Happy? What has happiness to do with it?'

'Everything! I want Ethne to be happy. And I certainly don't see the likeness between her and Eleanor. Look at her now. Does she seem threatened by the mountains?'

'Grannnieee! Mummeeee!' We watched her round bright face and waving hand.

'No,' said my mother, capitulating. She shouted and blew her a kiss. 'And now I must go in and write a speech about the continuing importance of free school milk and free school meals before Araminta puts me to picking sprouts. I sometimes think my whole career is founded on the need to avoid picking sprouts!'

'And mine to avoid cooking them. Do try and send Mike out. He really does need some fresh air.'

After that Christmas at Kettleside, I began a year of flying so high that I should have guessed it would end with a crash. 'Laugh before breakfast, cry before bedtime,' as Nanny used to say. She said it still, looking up from her copy of the *Tatler*. Nanny could probably have warned me about the way it would happen, too. For as a judgement on my sexual duplicity, I became pregnant, and I didn't know which man was the father.

At first I felt pure rage at my feminine organs, which had escaped what I believed was my efficient control, in those pre-pill days. As far as I knew I had never slipped up once, which was why I had no idea who was the father. After rage I felt humiliation. This was exaggerated by the circumstances in which I discovered the pregnancy. I was told by an American official refusing me a visa for California, where Eddie had persuaded me to make a business trip. My urine sample had shown I was pregnant.

'I can't be!' I screamed, but as I screamed I remembered the tenderness of my breasts and the slight sick sensation I'd been feeling for the last month or so. At least a month.

Then, at last, I began to think seriously. For the first time during my affair with Eddie I passed beyond my excited terror at the possibility of Mike's discovering it and considered how much I could hurt him, how much I was already hurting him. For even if he did not know I made love to Eddie, he knew that all my real energy and enthusiasm was reserved for activities outside the home. Even though I came back in the evening and we had supper together while I told him of my latest plans, he was not really part of it. Not even when he put up money to start the business. Eddie didn't offer that.

I assumed Mike's steady climb up the Civil Service ladder was giving him all the excitement he wanted, but maybe I was wrong. We sat at breakfast one warm September morning. Ethne was gobbling her cereal and Mike was gobbling his eggs. Normally I would have felt justified in feeling sick at the sight and saying so, but now I could say nothing. I was pregnant. It might not be Mike's.

Mike looked up at me questioningly. I realised I had been staring at him fixedly. 'Oh, God! I'm going to be sick!' I jumped up and raced to the lavatory. Mike came and held my hand. When I'd finished, he said, 'You're pregnant, aren't you?'

'Yes.' I burst into tears.

Then began the guilt. I had enjoyed two amoral years. Now I began to pay for them. Mike was gentle with me. I fought for the courage not to tell him about Eddie. It was extraordinary how the conception of the baby and the conception of guilt between them totally killed my passion for Eddie. One week I felt as if I began to live only when he was in the room, and the next I literally couldn't bear to be near him. His good looks, his confidence, his dangerous foreignness, which had all seemed infinitely desirable, now seemed vulgar and offensive.

Besides, he didn't even guess that I was pregnant. I took it as a personal insult, a sign of deep insensitivity, and a clear indication that he did not love me. He could not even love my body if he was not aware of the change in it.

I remember the last evening we spent together as lovers. We were in his flat. He had no taste of his own; everything looked as if it had been taken straight from a Harrods showroom, which indeed it had. I was working myself into a bitter fury against him. He was talking about an animated cartoon of 'Secrets' for the cinema.

'What you must never do,' he said in his drawling, confident voice, 'is stay in the same place.'

'I agree.'

'That way lies sterility.'

'Sterility?'

'Yeah.' Absentmindedly, he put out a hand. 'Do you know you've got the most sensational tits?'

'Eddie!' I jumped away furiously. 'Eddie! Can't you see? You stupid blind man! I'm pregnant! I'm going to have a baby!' I stood back for a moment watching his face—watching, I suppose, despite my mounting hatred, to see if there was any softening. But I saw only bewilderment. It gave me strength to lie.

'In case you care enough to wonder, it's not your baby. It's Mike's. My husband's. And in case you care enough to be interested in what I intend to do, I intend to stop seeing you from this moment because I've just realised that I don't love you and that you don't love me, and it's high time we both stopped using each other and grew up!'

It was easier to end our romance than to live with the end. I had a dreadful guilty feeling that now I had come out of my dream, everything would turn sour. Most of all I dreaded Mike's revealing that he too was having an affair. I deserved such retribution. The baby wasn't enough. Besides, once I had stopped seeing Eddie I began to come round to the baby, convincing myself that it must be Mike's. I began to believe it had been sent to give our marriage a new start. I began to cherish it growing inside me as I had with Ethne. In my lower moments I cheered myself with the idea that Eddie and Mike did not look very dissimilar.

In the middle of such personal turmoil, news from the outside world passed me by. I just about knew a General Election had been declared, but it was only when Mike began to talk excitedly about Labour's chances that I realised my mother could be restarting her career.

'She's nearly sixty,' I said to Mike doubtfully.

'That won't stop her if she wants it,' he said confidently.

'Does she?'

'Yes. For the moment, anyway.'

'It's a pity you're a Civil Servant,' I said. 'Or you could help her more.'

'If she's a Minister I can anyway.' Mike smiled with the intent look he wore only when talking about work. 'It's quite likely I'll be in her department. If old Winnie Beauchamp does her stuff.'

'How Machiavellian! Won't there be talk? Son-in-law and all that?'

'No one talks about the Civil Service. That's its strength. But don't say I said that to you, it wouldn't be looked on too favourably in some quarters.'

'I wouldn't dream of telling anybody.'

I lay back against the sofa, for at six months pregnant I already felt huge and exhausted. My life and friends were so far removed from his that there was no one I could possibly tell.

Mike and my mother had become very close over this election. It had made me realise that they both possessed the same strength of character arising from a basic unselfish belief in a course of duty. Neither of them had the amorphous sort of reverence for love and happiness that I did. Mike's love was always practical. Nettles and Ethne were perhaps the only people my mother had loved in a long life, and she had left Nettles for her work.

When I had told her about the new baby, she had sighed and said, 'Darling, don't let Ethne feel left out.'

'Oh, Mother!' I was irritated, for in my mind I had created of Ethne a free, independent spirit who needed the minimum of material support. 'I'm going to her school concert tomorrow. Greater attention has no mother.'

How odd it is, looking back, to see where and when one chooses to use one's main energy. Ethne had my concentrated energy for the first year of her life, but never again until it was too late to influence her. I was preparing to do the same for the new baby when at seven months all such thoughts became irrelevant.

I gave birth, prematurely, to twins. They dropped out of my womb like apples out of a damp paper bag. One weighed three pounds two ounces, the other two pounds fifteen ounces. They might have lived, but they didn't. With their weights added together, the total was still so small that I couldn't understand why I had seemed so big. 'It's the water,' the gynaecologist said, bringing faint echoes of Augustus' death. I said, 'It's my own fault.' He patted my hand sympathetically. 'It's a simple medical matter. Next time I can put a little stitch in the neck of the womb and then you'll have no trouble at all.'

'Even if it was twins?'

'Most probably. Though the odds against having twins again are very long. I gather from your husband that there're no immediately traceable twins in either of your families.'

'I don't know.'

'Rest now, my dear. You'll be amazed how quickly you'll recover.'

'I don't want any more.'

'No. No. I'll see you in the morning.'

It seems probable that the babies were Eddie's. Possibly there were twins on his mother's side of the family. But the matter of fatherhood now seemed insignificant beside the fact of their death. Besides, Mike naturally accepted my sorrow as if they were his children, and Eddie, so far as I knew, knew neither of their birth nor death. They were boys, identical twins, and although I never saw them, I gave them names—Peter and Paul, like the blackbirds who flew away. When a friend sympathised, 'Poor you. A miscarriage is so upsetting!' I cried fiercely, 'I did not have a miscarriage. I had two little boys. They lived for nearly twelve hours. Now I've had three children.'

When I came out of hospital and returned to our flat, I told Ethne she must include Peter and Paul in her prayers. She looked at me with her bright stare and said, 'I'm going through an atheist phase. I'll let you know when I'm out of it.' I did not feel strong enough to argue.

That night, lying in bed with Mike, I said, 'Do you think Ethne's all right?'

'How do you mean?'

'She seems so remote. Yet she has all those friends. I hardly ever see her. She puts white chalk on her lips. She says she doesn't believe in God.'

400

'I don't either.'

'No. But you're not a child. I wonder if I should get my mother to have a talk with her.'

'Your mother?' Mike sounded surprised.

'Why not?'

'The election's in two days.'

It struck me that I had got through the first tragedy of my life without my mother's help. I had not needed her, for I had clung to Mike. It seemed even more extraordinary that only a few months ago I had been risking his love for what had always been a trivial passion. Thinking it over, I was glad my mother had not been free to share even some of my suffering. She had borne enough already. She had no Mike. Let her shoulder public misfortunes.

'How's it going? Will she win?'

'She will, and probably Labour too. But not by much.'

Mike's estimation was correct. I lay in bed listening to the results coming in. Now, I suppose, we would have had a portable television, but then our set was securely pinioned in the living room. Instead we listened to a large, old-fashioned wireless. Clancy had come to keep me company. She was relieved, I think, that I was beginning to show an interest in outside events. She felt guilty that she had not wanted to enter into my suffering over the babies and also, I think, uneasy, if not actually guilty, over the whole Eddie affair. If she had not actually encouraged me, she had never discouraged me either.

'I'm sorry the reception's so bad.'

'Who would think we were the spearhead in the new generation of communicators? I've been waiting till you were better to tell you that the BBC want a whole new series. Fifteen-minute spots instead of those paltry five minutes.'

'You sound so professional.'

'There's not much else in my life.' I glanced at Clancy's face. She was still in her thirties, but the circles under her eyes, the greying patches in her bushy hair, and particularly her expression of 'I know the bad and I challenge the worse to follow' made her seem much older. I gave up any thoughts of denial and decided to change the subject instead.

'I should be up in Birmingham with my mother. I don't like her being alone after the elections.'

'She'll have her agent.'

'Then she drives back early in the morning. Tired. It makes me nervous.'

'You, nervous for your mother!'

'It's old age. Mine, not hers.'

'Listen. Isn't that the Birmingham results coming in now?'

401

We listened, but it was the wrong division. There was a swing to Labour. Large enough for victory. 'If she gets in now,' I said, 'she'll have been in Parliament for nearly twenty years. I should have let Ethne stay up. It might be her last go.'

Clancy sighed. 'I never could get very interested in politics. It's probably inherited from my mother. Poor Mother, she suffers terribly from arthritis.'

'The penance of a healthy country life. Oh, dear. We do sound depressed. Sssh. That really is her now ... Mrs Nettlefield, Labour Party, 18,027; Mr Higham-Potts, Conservative-Unionist, 13,582. She's done it! She's in again. And a much bigger majority. Now it's just a question of whether the telephone rings tomorrow.'

Not, I think, understanding this reference to the Prime Minister's summons, Clancy stood up and prepared to go. 'So don't forget this BBC series. I've had a few thoughts . . .'

'We'll speak tomorrow.' I was cold. She might have celebrated my mother's victory a little more. Yet after she was gone I regretted it. She thought my contribution to the world more important than my mother's. That was nice—if misguided. Perhaps it wasn't misguided. In many circles my name was better known than my mother's. I must not equate the loss of the twins with failure. At least Clancy was never hypocritical.

When Mike returned from an election party, I was asleep. He was excited and a little drunk. Almost immediately the phone rang. It was my mother. I lay back and heard them talk at each other. 'Good!' exclaimed Mike several times. 'What?' I nudged him. 'The PM's told her to stay by the phone tomorrow.' 'Good,' I echoed before falling back to sleep. My mother, the Minister, again.

Yet next day when I spoke to her on the telephone (she would not come over in case she missed the all-important call) I thought that my own success had come during the period when she was at least in partial eclipse. I wondered whether I would be threatened. It was strange that I should be in competition. In that way we were more like sisters. Perhaps it was because we had come to appreciate each other only when I was already grown up. She had never been much of a mother to me.

Tudor, on the other hand, who had seen no more of her as a child, behaved just like an ordinary son. With an extraordinary mother. He found her inexplicable. After he married his nice pretty wife, set up in business, and started having babies, he did not even disguise his essential conservatism.

'My mother is a remarkable woman,' he would say introducing her to his friends at his house, as if she were a cheetah he had just captured from the jungle. 'You must not believe everything she says even if our pen pushers from Fleet Street do.'

My mother did not seem to mind this treatment—I suppose she'd had to put up with odder treatment in the political arena—but it did not make them close.

She was close to Mike, with whom she had much in common, and to me. Another woman. Following my train of thought, I asked her that afternoon, 'How many women elected?' I knew she would have checked this, but I was surprised by the vehemence of her answer.

'Oh, what's the point of asking? When the number of candidates adopted dropped from thirty-six in 1959 to thirty-two. Same with the Conservatives. From twenty-eight to twenty-four. I sometimes wonder whether you don't need legislation to get women into Parliament.'

'I'm sorry I asked you.'

'I'm tired. I don't like sitting waiting to go to Number Ten. That's not true. Of course I'm incredibly excited. I've no idea what Ministry he wants me for, except that it'll have something to do with what's considered the women's end of things—Health, Pensions. As long as I can do some good.'

'But you've done so much.'

'Women are so obstinate. They vote against me. Can you believe that?'

'Shouldn't we get off the phone?' I suggested.

'Yes.' Her voice surged and grew stronger. 'How's Ethne? Tell her I'm coming to see her tomorrow.'

'At school. She's wearing a red rosette.'

'That is nice.' As my mother rang off I couldn't help thinking that if she, a Minister, preserved this amount of warmth for her granddaughter even on a day so triumphant for her politics, then it was hardly surprising that lesser women, more mortal women, never entered the political arena. Why should they when their own homes provided all the emotional cut and thrust they needed?

'The ambitious professional woman will always be a rare species,' I said to Mike when he came home from work.

'Your mother's got Pensions and National Insurance.'

'I expect she'll go to the Lords soon.'

'I hope not. Though there'll be another election in a year or two. I'm glad to see you taking an interest again.'

'I'm even writing. I've begun a series instead of the usual one-offs. I'm planning to weave it round a "clean up the environment" theme.'

'Mind you're not elected!'

'I'm certainly going to have the littlest creature campaigning for Nuclear Disarmament.'

Mike bent and kissed my cheek. 'What's that terrible noise?'

'Ethne et al. They're celebrating victory with two hours' solid of "A Hard Day's Night".'

'Do you like pop music?'

'I don't know. Ethne's in love with John Lennon. He's the clever one. Mike?'

'Yes.'

'I do love you.'

Chapter Sixteen

WOMEN'S FEATURES
Non-fiction heroines, women in history and women in the news, are the subject of this Wednesday's edition of *Isis*, the Oxford University Magazine.
The nineteen-year-old editor is better qualified than most of the ten undergraduate staff to deal with the topic, for she is a woman . . . 'I'm interested in women. Basically, I like them more than men. But I'm against a feminist like Simone de Beauvoir, who thinks that succeeding as a woman means being like a man.' She pulled at the hem of her bright pink skirt.
The Times. 17 October 1966

MONDAY WOMEN'S FEATURES
Rosemary Tonks is an attractive, vivacious blonde in her early thirties who has a principal claim to succeed the late Dame Edith Sitwell as England's leading woman poet.
'Poetry is a luxury,' insisted Rosemary Tonks just before leaving for Ischia to write a novel designed 'to make a lot of red hot money' . . .
She spoke with an intensity often bordering on active aggression. 'You can't turn your back on a whole way of life today. It is far more important for a poet like myself to read *Queen* and *Vogue* than the intellectual weeklies. You get much more of an idea of what is going on in the world from the glossies . . .
The Times. 16 October 1967

WHETHER you are a sophisticated nineteen or a young thirty-five, you can fulfil yourself in one of the most responsible roles in society—as one of London's policewomen. If you are five feet four or over, write to Chief Superintendent, Shirley Becke.
(Advertisement) *The Times.* 16 October 1967

When Ethne heard that my mother was to be made a Life Peeress, she went into her bedroom and slammed the door. The doorknob, which was loose, fell onto the floor. A placard of the Beatles stared defiantly back at me. 'The House of Lords is the best argument for euthanasia!' Whether it was the effect of the wood between us, or of her indignation, her voice sounded totally adult.

'Do control your daughter.' Mike chose that moment to come home from work.

The loud beat of 'With a Little Help from my Friends' boomed through our flat.

'She seems so old, so confident,' I appealed to Mike. 'When I was her age I had no opinions at all. None I dared voice, anyway. And certainly none on a grown-up's subject. I thought I was a child. An inferior being.'

'You wanted her to be free.'

'She despises my "Secrets", too.' I went to the kitchen and poured myself a glass of wine. 'She says they're revoltingly sentimental.'

'They're written for the younger child.' Mike took my glass of wine from me. I poured myself another.

'I used to think they appealed to all age groups.'

'You can't make a fortune and expect critical acclaim too.' Mike put his arms round me. 'How have the pop-up books worked?'

'Cheap. Nasty. What worries me is how Ethne will behave at my mother's Investiture.'

'Threaten her.'

'How? My mother is absolutely determined she should come. Lunch before, too. Ethne's quite capable of spoiling the whole thing. How can someone so clever be so perverse?'

'They teach her at school. It's called honesty. I expect she'll grow out of it.'

'Not in time for the Investiture.'

My mother was made a Life Peeress after the 1966 Election. She was sixty-one, and she said she no longer had the energy to carry on day-to-day responsibilities of a government which was in with a large enough majority to put through the policies it had been saving up for a decade and a half. Nor, after twenty years as a notably conscientious constituency MP, could she bear the thought of making that her whole life. 'I've been a back-bencher,' she said. 'I would rather join something new and concentrate on a few of my special interests.'

'You can hardly call the House of Lords new!' I said.

But she only laughed. 'It may be when I've finished with it. The Prime Minister's basically keen on reform. It just needs someone to chivvy him along a bit.'

So my mother was not retiring into the Lords. She did not allow us to suspect ill health. On the contrary, she was joining a new wave of socialists and women. At that time there were seventeen Peeresses, two of whom were to sponsor my mother's arrival into the Upper House. 'That should give them something to think about,' she said with satisfaction. We were standing in her flat while I tried on the red velvet and ermine which she would wear for the ceremony. I was reminded of my wedding day.

'Them in general, or them in particular?' I said. 'It sounded rather particular.'

'It was. My mother's father sat in the House of Lords. He was the first person to take me there. If he could have guessed how I would return, he would have died on the spot.'

'These robes are fine, although I still wish you'd bought some new. Your grandfather's dead now, I presume?'

'That would have been against my Socialist principles. Years and years ago. But someone equivalent has inherited the mantle. You'll see him; he has a walrus moustache and an eyeglass.'

'Extraordinary.' Although I was interested, I had too many worries about the lunch to concentrate on the past. I folded the robes away into their large cardboard box. Not only had Ethne insisted on wearing a Beatles T-shirt, but I had just discovered that Eddie had arrived from America the day before and was to be included in the party.

'After that lunch with my grandfather I went to the Serpentine, where I saw Nanny battling in adverse circumstances which were mainly due to my mother's selfishness. It gave me my first experience of social guilt. Have I told you about that before?'

'Yes.'

'On the day Augustus died. I remember. I'll tell you again. I went back to our house, the one that was bombed in the war, and cried on Flo's shoulder. She simply couldn't understand it. A young lady crying over her nanny. She put it down to lack of occupation. In one way she was right.'

'I'm glad Nanny's coming down for it, then,' I said, still not attending properly. 'Shouldn't we get started?'

We had a large table in the centre of the impressive Lords dining room. My mother sat at one end of the table; my brother Tudor, looking more at home than any of us, at the other. Beside him sat his boring wife and beside her their boring and perfectly behaved eldest son. Next to him sat Ethne, who had taken off her jacket to reveal her T-shirt better and whose cheeks were flushed with ex-hibitionism. Nanny, on her right, looking sweet and terrified under her invariable porkpie hat, patted her hand at intervals. This did not help matters. On Nanny's right, Araminta, dressed in some homemade garment resembling an armchair cover with fur trimmings, looked round with a dazed expression as if she couldn't quite remember why she was there. Perhaps she was in pain, for the arthritis in her hips was so bad now that she needed a stick. No one could persuade her to have an operation.

Winnie Beauchamp, on her right, was trying to make conversation, but even her efficient energy, her classical English face, which never seemed to change except for a few stage wrinkles, bent attentively towards her, could not cut through Araminta's smoke screen. Eventually she gave up and turned to Jack Logan, who was on her right and my mother's left. 'Won't you miss her?' I heard Winnie say. 'You're hoping to get the Abortion Bill through next year, aren't you?'

'It was the only thing I regretted.' My mother turned to one of her sponsors, a lady of formidable appearance, with a gentle expression. 'I've worked on it for years.'

'Then you'll see it through here,' said Lady Summerton, the sponsor. 'You'll find the bishops quite a handful.'

'You can count on Betty to see you're kept busy.' Jack drank his wine rather quickly, as if he wished this sort of ceremony could be passed through at speed. I felt from the glances that he cast round the table and, indeed, the dining room itself that he, at least, would support my mother in any reforms—the more drastic the better. He, of course, had begun as a Conservative. There is no one more fierce than the convert. Except, it seemed, my mother, the Catholic convert who worked so hard on the Abortion Bill.

Next to Lady Summerton sat Eddie and next to him, me. There was no way I could have avoided it. My mother's placements were always irrevocable. She assumed I would be delighted to see my cousin after so many years' absence. Two years' absence. On my right, and next to Mike, was my mother's agent from Birmingham, a man whom I had detested since I was a child for his imitation of my mother's early habit of calling me 'Little Violet'. He had always been self-righteously proprietorial about my mother. Beyond Mike sat Lady Mells, a nice, plump lady who owed her elevated rank to her husband's dying in the service of the Labour Party. She, I felt perversely, was much the most sympathetic woman at the table, and I wished I were sitting next to her.

'Who's missing?' said Eddie. 'We're odd numbers.'

'Our old friend Mrozek. He's joining us for coffee. At one point when Araminta got cold feet, it looked as if we might be thirteen. So we invited Nanny. Of course, that made Araminta come after all.'

'I love your Nanny.'

'Don't be sentimental.' Up to this moment we had spoken in warily neutral tones, not looking at each other's faces. But my sudden fierceness made us turn face to face. I immediately felt a sharp surge of relief followed by a lesser feeling of disappointment. I had been right. He was a stranger. He meant nothing to me. I did not even find his sunburnt good looks particularly attractive. His face was too flat, dead, heavy. Also, he looked old. I didn't feel he could understand half the things I said or thought. I turned away from him again. I wasn't even interested enough to wonder what he thought of me.

'Is that really your daughter?'

Then for a moment I did have a pang. For a moment I wanted to tell him about the twins who had died. But I knew my mother had told him the facts, and he had never even by a note or a card shown any sympathy. That sorrow had nothing to do with him. I smiled across at Ethne and was rewarded with a furious scowl. 'She's going through a farouche stage,' I explained.

'They all look like that in America. Dr Spock babies.' He indicated Tudor's son, who was neatly separating his segments of grapefruit. 'He would be sent off to a psychiatrist.'

'Is that progress?'

'Who knows? I see "Secrets" all over the place.'

'Yes. It seems to get more and more successful.' We were back to our previous stilted conversation.

The agent gripped my arm. 'I remember when your mother first came up to us. If we could have seen her now, sitting as easy as could be in the heart of the enemy, we would never have accepted her as a candidate!'

I smiled politely.

'Even now I don't know how she persuaded us. A woman. And from her background. At least, she had the sense to keep us well away from the WVS—WRVS as they are now. That would have finished us!' He laughed himself this time, and I smiled more honestly. I saw that what he was saying was true and spoke well of him. He had backed my mother against the odds, and she had come through. He was a sincere man. It was not his fault if I had blamed him for taking my mother from me. 'Of course, the Labour Party's not the same now. Even if we have come in with such a large majority.'

'Perhaps it's the times,' I suggested, 'not the Labour Party.'

'Greed,' said the agent, whose name I now allowed myself to remember was Bill Worth. 'I shan't hang on myself much longer. You can't help looking back.' He paused and looked around in a jolly way. 'Not that I expect to end up in a place like this.'

409

'I should hope not.' A fierce hiss came from across the table. Inadvertently he had caught Ethne's eye.

'Ssssh, darling.'

'Don't "darling" me!' She glared in turn at me; at Nanny, who was giving her best imitation of a Russian 'babushka'; and at her cousin, whose face expressed shocked disapproval.

'How old is she?' said Eddie, watching this performance with some admiration. She began to swing back on her chair, shaggy-haired faces mouthing across her chest.

'She's really quite shy,' I said feebly.

'Oh, to be young again!' said the nice Lady Mells to Mike. 'To feel so deeply!'

'Nice for her, perhaps.' Mike frowned furiously. Ethne tipped down her chair again and became relatively meek. My mother, it seemed, hadn't noticed. She was welcoming a man who had approached behind her—an old man now, but still in the game. Mrozek. She placed him between Araminta and Winnie. Araminta immediately became very animated. I wondered why. From where I was sitting I could not hear what she was saying, but Mrozek soon wore an unusual air of harassment. He reached across to the sugar bowl and popped a sugar lump into his mouth. When he felt threatened, he had an insatiable urge for sweet things. Of course. Clancy was Araminta's daughter. They were so dissimilar, and I thought of them now with such different associations, that I had almost forgotten their relationship. Was it possible Araminta was attacking Mrozek for ruining her daughter's life?

No one but Araminta, fresh from the mountains of Northumberland, could have conceived of such a thing. Mrozek was clearly far too sophisticated to receive such a naive reproof. Yet it did seem that way. Araminta's voice became more urgent, her pale face flushed, and Mrozek popped more and more sugar lumps into his mouth. I wondered why Winnie didn't intervene, but she sat listening with her usual expression of calm good sense. I just hoped Mrozek would not be cruel.

Not exactly by accident, I caught his eye. Immediately his face returned to its usual lines, and he smiled. Interrupting Araminta in mid-flow, he came round and, notwithstanding his age, crouched down beside me. 'Ah, darling Violet. The one that got away. Always the most desired. At least you will bring your first adult book to me?'

I looked across at Araminta. She seemed on the verge of tears. Winnie said something to her, and they both lifted their glasses of wine. They smiled at each other. It was a gesture of triumph.

'All my books are adult,' I said to Mrozek. 'What ever was Araminta saying to you?'

'Ah, my darling, surely you understand by now the usual role of a publisher? She wants me to publish a little book she has done, drawings and words.'

'A book. Oh. And will you?'

'Yes. Of course. For Clancy's sake. For your mother's. For yours. For Leonard's. For Leonard's especially.'

'Why?' I had never seen Mrozek look so nearly serious. But at my question he became evasive again.

'Another one who got away.'

I pressed him. 'Leonard didn't write, did he?'

'I could have founded my reputation on Leonard's writing. That's how I planned it. I read bits of his first book . . . bits of his second . . . bits, bits . . .'

'What do you mean?'

'He wouldn't finish anything. Or if he did, he burned it or lost it or got drunk and threw it overboard from a ship. He did that once. In Greece—near Greece. During the war. That one was about the Secret Service, so we probably couldn't have published it. I always thought I might get one when he retired—from his crazy life, I mean—but then he died. I expect it was a romantic idea, anyway. If he wasn't satisfied by anything he'd written by the time he was thirty, there was little chance he'd lower his standards afterwards.'

'Why didn't he like what he wrote?'

'Violet?' said Eddie, trying to draw my attention.

'We're talking about Clancy's father.'

'He was too clever. And had no roots he cared to reveal. He wasn't in touch with himself. You can't write if you won't be honest about yourself—however interesting you are about other people, about ways of the world, or however good technically. For the same reason, Leonard could never bear to be a proper husband to Araminta. For the same reason, he got drunk. For the same reason, he was a good secret agent.'

'So he was working for the Secret Service.'

'Oh yes. Of course. He drank whisky, not sold it.'

'But not for the same reason, he died.'

'No. That was just chance. Except that to die of a brain flurry at a wedding—your wedding, of course—is really quite what one might have expected from him.'

'He made people unhappy.'

'Not as unhappy as he made himself.'

'Violet!' Mike leaned across to stop us talking. There was going to be a speech. Tudor rose manfully. His wife gazed up with nervous blue eyes.

My record for not listening to speeches remained unbroken. But I

411

saw my mother smiling indulgently, and I was glad she was happy. Afterwards, Lady Mells and Lady Summerton took her away to be robed and have a practice run in the chamber.

We all went to find our places in the gallery. I took the opportunity to give Ethne's arm a spiteful pinch and tell her that if she didn't behave herself better I would send her to boarding school.

'There's a man staring at us,' she replied unrepentantly. We were standing in the huge marble hall just near the entrance to the debating chamber, and I couldn't resist glancing round. As usual, Ethne's diversion was quite justifiable. Standing a few yards behind me was a little, nearly hunchbacked old man. With bright eyes under black bushy eyebrows topped by a very un-English curly-brimmed hat, he looked like Bilbo Baggins. As I turned, he darted forward.

'Are you Mrs'—he hesitated—'Lady Nettlefield's daughter?'

'She's not Lady yet!' cried Ethne.

'Yes,' I replied curiously.

'Then I'm Blumberg,' he cried, sticking out his hand gleefully.

Ethne said, 'You're American, aren't you?'

I had never known a Blumberg in my life. His was not a face you would forget.

'That's right. It was you I recognised. Has anyone ever told you that you're the image of your great-grandmother?'

I had the clue. Vague recollections stirred.

'Am I really?' Ethne looked pleased and excited for the first time that day.

'I should know. I was married to her.'

'Of course, I've never seen her myself,' Ethne continued, uninterested in Blumberg's exact relationship. 'She lives on Eureka, the island. I've tried to persuade Mummy to let me go, but she always makes some excuse.'

'Eleanor was unfailingly original.' Blumberg sighed, though his eyes gleamed as gaily as ever. 'I can't say it wasn't a relief when she ran away from me. Her odd habits made it very difficult for me to practise . . .'

'Odd habits!' breathed Ethne excitedly.

'Drink.' I looked at the clock. 'I'm afraid, Mr Blumberg, we ought to be taking our seats. You see, my mother is being made a Peeress today.'

'But I know. I have a ticket. I gave up believing in coincidences long ago. Yet I guess it is odd. I picked this day for my visit to the fount of British aristocracy quite by chance. I wanted to see where Eleanor's eccentricity had been rooted. And what do I find but her daughter being made a Peeress in her own right and her granddaughter and great-granddaughter waiting to greet me.'

I thought this going a little far and could see Mike and Eddie wondering whether to get involved, but Ethne was quite carried away.

'That's extraordinary! It must be some astral link. You do believe in the stars, don't you? It's so much more satisfactory than coincidences. Where's your ticket? I just bet it's next to ours! Mummy, where are our tickets?'

'Daddy's got them,' I said with resignation.

So Blumberg became of our party too, which at least had the merit of keeping Ethne in high good spirits.

'The absurd thing is I'm still legally married to your great-grandmother,' I heard him whisper at one point. 'Such a protection against my patients. Which makes me, I presume, your great-grandfather.'

'Step great-grandfather,' I said—a little too firmly, for the Lord Chamberlain raised his eyes curiously. I flushed crossly. I wanted to concentrate on my mother, on her slim figure almost lost in the folds of heavy velvet, on the pale face set in solemn lines under the peculiar three-cornered hat. It was typical of Eleanor, I thought, to find such a ghost to represent her at the celebration. I remember what relief we had all felt when a letter had arrived from George explaining that they were too busy with wild-flower cultivation to come over.

I watched my mother and her two sponsors bob three times in front of the Lord Chamberlain. The ceremony would have been nearly the same when her grandfather was introduced, and yet the very fact of her sex made it part of a new era. Or did it? I looked round at the assembled Lords, half-searching for my unknown cousin, the earl. My mother had very obviously not pointed him out. Instead of finding him, I noticed the huge majority of old or old-fashioned faces that filled the chamber. Even a white moustache and an eyepiece were a distinguishing mark here.

The robed figures began to move out. The introduction was complete. Too late to cry out, 'Yes! There is an impediment!'

'I hope she's doing the right thing,' I whispered to Mike.

'We'd better go down and meet her.' Back we all trooped, along red corridors with panelled walls, back to the echoing marble. My mother's face glowed. She threw open her arms. 'Darlings! I'm so glad you all came! Could you see properly? I do hope so!'

I stifled my misgivings. One can't judge other people's needs. Blumberg appeared. When he was introduced to Lady Summerton, she clapped my mother on the shoulder in congratulation. 'I told you the Lords attracted all sorts!'

'Usually Boy Scouts and the Salvation Army!' cried Lady Mells heartily. They were like actors who had just finished a performance. My mother even kissed Blumberg's cheek, so that he disappeared for a moment under her cloak and plume.

Nanny, clinging to my side, wiped away her final tear. 'I'll have to retire now,' she said. 'Now I've seen the best!'

'Come along, Nanny darling.' Araminta, who had worn a look of inward splendour ever since her conversation with Mrozek, took Nanny's arm. 'We'll miss the train if we don't go now.'

Mike and Winnie and Mrozek and my brother's family left for their offices. Blumberg, showing such energetic determination that I understood why he had been too much even for Eleanor, whipped Ethne off to buy her a great-grandparently present in Fortnum and Mason—a shop she would have disdained in my company. Only Eddie and I were left to watch my mother resume her ordinary clothes and take her seat in the afternoon's debate.

For a moment I wondered whether it was wise to stay on alone with Eddie. I looked down at my mother. She had reached a more passionless state than I. I loved Mike.

'What's the debate?' Eddie slid nearer to me.

I found the slip of paper. 'Divorce. Oh, dear. Not a very good subject for my mother. Still, new members very seldom speak on the day of introduction.'

'I would have thought divorce would have been just your mother's kind of thing.'

I turned to him surprised. 'But you know she's a Catholic? She's had to adapt her humanist views. On divorce she's very Catholic. On abortion she seems able to take a more liberal view.'

'But does she believe in it all?'

'I don't know. We never talk quite as precisely as that. But I suppose she has basically decided the soul is more important than the body.'

'Strange for a politician. Particularly a Socialist politician.'

'Liberty, equality, fraternity. I suppose it's not an impossible position if you believe socialism is more than a charter to improve material comforts.'

'Does she believe that?'

'She used to. Possibly not anymore. She says the Labour Party has changed. But she suspects it might be her too. That's why she's left active politics.'

'But I thought ...' Eddie looked round at the chamber. Lord Gardner sat on his woolsack, Lord Longford, the Lord Privy Seal, whispered to Lord Shepherd. 'After all, there are socialists here; Catholics too. And work to be done. She looked so happy. She still does.'

I leaned over the rail of the gallery. I could just see my mother, almost directly below us, looking as composed as ever, with her neat black suit, legs discreetly crossed, face attentive. 'She looks tiny,' I said.

Suddenly I found he had taken my hand and put it to his lips. I turned to face him crossly. 'This is a public gallery.' Our eyes met as they had over lunch, but this time I felt a stirring of the past. 'We shouldn't be talking during a debate,' I said too weakly.

'Then let's talk somewhere else.'

Below us, the Bishop of Exeter had risen. 'To protect the lifelong character of the marriage vows from being utterly destroyed by the feasibility of divorce, it is essential that the final decision be that of the community and not of themselves.'

'I want to listen longer. You go.'

He stayed by my side silently now, and as the debate continued, I felt myself slipping into a curious trancelike state. Despite my determination this time to hear the words, I felt them slipping away from me. The Lord Chancellor rose. 'My Lords, I have the feeling—I may be quite wrong—that I am taking part today in what is, and will in future be recognised to be, an historic occasion.'

He spoke for a long time; his voice rose and fell in the soothing cadences of the actor he had once been. When the Lord Privy Seal took his place to interrupt the debate with a statement on Rhodesia, Eddie stood too. He took my arm. 'We'll get a cup of tea now. It's after four.'

I saw I had been too complacent in believing he had lost his power over me, for I found I was going with him passively. He kept his hand on my arm as we passed down the stairs.

'Will the debate last long?' I asked a little desperately to the black-coated usher.

'Hours, Miss.'

'And can I get back in?'

'We'll be glad to have you.'

I was protecting myself. I told myself it had been unreal to think I could put Eddie out of my life without ever talking about the twins. After we had talked I would return to the House of Lords and, when the debate finished, take my mother home for supper.

Eddie and I stood together on the wide pavement outside the Houses of Parliament. It was nearly dark, cold, and drizzling.

'We'll go to the Connaught for tea,' said Eddie.

'If we can get a taxi,' I said. 'Isn't there somewhere nearer?'

'I'm staying there.' Eddie looked at his watch. 'I've got a meeting there at five thirty.'

'Just time for tea, then,' I said gaily, although to my fury I was feeling definite disappointment. 'You must be doing well.'

'Yes. Ever since I stopped trying to set up things for myself and concentrated on other people it's been nothing but success.' He put out a hand and a taxi materialised in front of us.

'In other words, you're an agent.'

Eddie had a suite in the Connaught. He insisted on ordering tea up there, saying it was so much more comfortable. The sitting room was large, but overheated. I felt uncomfortably claustrophobic. I moved around examining his piles of scripts and neatly typed schedules of meetings. Burt Sneiderman at five thirty.

'Well, you were right about the sixties' being for the English,' I said in the brittle voice I seemed to have adopted.

Eddie had hardly spoken to me since we'd arrived, but he watched me wherever I went. I became more and more uncomfortable. I found I did not want to talk about the twins.

'I'd better go now.'

'Not yet.'

'Burt Sneiderman will be here soon. Don't you want to prepare your spiel?'

'He's preparing a spiel for me. I just have to listen.' He got up and came over to me. He put his arms round me. 'Violet. Look Violet darling, do you want to go to bed with me?'

'Now?' I cried ridiculously, turning round, scared. 'I mean, no. No. I don't want to.'

'Why did you come, then?'

'Because I wanted to talk to you.'

'Oh.' Eddie moved away slightly. 'Wouldn't it be easier to talk in bed?'

'Yes. But I don't want to.'

'Let's sit down, then. I can't talk to you roaming around like this.'

I came and sat beside him on the sofa. He had an expensive, new feel about him very far removed from London in wintertime.

'It wouldn't mean anything if I made love to you, because I don't love you any more.'

'I see that. I've got a girlfriend too. But it isn't an insurmountable problem, is it?' He leaned closer, 'Your tits aren't any smaller.'

I remembered when he'd first made that comment. At last I felt angry. 'Don't you know what I want to talk about?'

'Yes, I suppose. Your miscarriage.' Eddie's voice also sounded firmer. It suddenly struck me that he was going to be much less interested in me if I definitely refused to go to bed with him. Strangely enough, this gave me the strength to decide against it. I also decided not to talk to him after all. I stood up.

'It wasn't a miscarriage. I had two baby boys called Peter and Paul. But you're right. We can't talk without going to bed. We never could, though I didn't see it at the time. And since we're not going to bed, we can't talk. So I might as well leave you in peace. After all, we were never friends. Only lovers.'

416

'Only lovers. What an epitaph!' Eddie picked up my coat and helped me on with it. He looked just sorry enough not to be insulting. But he didn't look very sorry.

He took me to the lift. The doors opened as soon as we arrived. A man with a suntan like Eddie's and a camel-hair coat stepped out.

'Ed!'

'Burt!'

Burt turned to me with what I could think of only as lusting eyes.

'Mrs Oakley, my English cousin.'

'And to think I've been living in England for three years and not discovered one cousin. Some people have all the luck.'

I smiled at him. His assumption might be wrong, but his admiration, however unreal, was what I needed. My pride was soothed. My affair with Eddie felt a very long way past.

'We really are cousins, Mr Sneiderman.' I stepped into the lift. 'We spent the afternoon in the House of Lords listening to noble prelates talking about divorce.'

Back in my gallery seat, I found to my relief that I did not regret my decision over Eddie. I was not in love with him. It would have been perverted to go to bed with him in a way it hadn't been before. Baroness Summerskill was speaking. 'One reason why the proportion of undefended divorce cases is so high is that a married couple hold a mutually enjoyed, close spiritual and physical communion, and they cannot tolerate the thought of opening their wounds by relating their traumatic experiences before complete strangers in a court.' I began to listen. To my surprise, I realised that in this case she was not on the side of the so-called reformers. It was not as simple as that. 'I have done a lot in my life. I have won elections; I have come to your Lordships' House; I have helped to pass legislation; and I have had children. But the outstanding thing in my life, for which I am profoundly grateful, is that I married a really wonderful man.'

I looked to see how my mother was reacting. She was not there. 'We have to approach marriage in that way, and realise that marriage really is essential to every man and woman in order to have fulfilment,' Lady Summerskill continued. Presumably my mother would return. I was interested now and didn't want to leave.

Just before seven, I went out to look for my mother. I found her immediately in the marble hall. She still wore the look of exhilaration that had started with her introduction.

'Come and have a drink with us, Violet!' she cried over her shoulder as two noble lords swept her away. I followed.

'It's a fascinating debate,' I said when we were sitting down.

'Yes,' she agreed carelessly. 'Something sensible should come out of it.'

'Aren't you interested?'

'Of course, darling. You may have forgotten that I went through the whole "Let's pretend we're guilty" farce myself.'

'I thought that's why you'd be interested.'

'I am. I've worked for reform in my time.' But she turned away to her companions.

'I thought you might like to come home to supper?'

'Oh, darling! How kind! But the debate won't finish till at least nine. I might as well eat here. Besides, I've asked Molly. She couldn't get away for lunch. You go home, darling, and see that wonderful Blumberg hasn't kidnapped Ethne in recompense for Eleanor.'

I went home. I looked at Mike to see if he was a worthy substitute for hardheaded dynamism or illicit passion. He smiled at me warmly. That was nice. But was it enough?

'What are we having for supper?' he said.

'Pork chops.'

Ethne, who was lying on the floor with her homework, said, 'If we have pork chops once more I'll become a vegetarian.'

'Why not become a Jew instead?'

Mike laughed. It was also nice the way he always laughed at my jokes. Stepping over Ethne, I went to the kitchen. Mike followed me. He put his arms round my waist and kissed my cheek. 'Leave the unclean meat a moment and go and look on your desk.'

'Something good?'

'Very. It came while we were out at lunch.'

There was a telegram on my desk, informing me that the latest 'Secrets' had won a Children's Book Prize. 'How extraordinary!' I said. 'Who ever entered it?'

'I did.'

'You look as pleased as if you'd won it yourself!'

Ethne beat her heels in the room behind us. 'If we're going to have pork chops, let's get on with them. I'm starving!'

'After tea in the Ritz?' Mike crossed the room and nudged Ethne with his foot. She shook him off, but in a complacent, rather than an irritable, manner. Obviously Blumberg had been rather a success.

'He had Chinese tea and Gentleman's Relish, which he says is an aphrodisiac, and I had two strawberry milk shakes, three profiteroles, and two ice cream parfaits. He said he had never seen anyone eat so much and you must be starving me. I said you generally provided me with the basic necessities but stopped short at the luxuries that make life worth living. He laughed a lot and said I reminded him more and more of my great-grandmother. Mummy, how many times was Eleanor married? Incidentally, I am pleased about your award.'

This was a major breakthrough in communication. Perhaps Blumberg was a good influence, a good psychiatrist.

'Thank you, darling. I'm not exactly sure how often your great-grandmother married. As Mr Blumberg said, she was always original. He could probably tell you better than anyone. When does he go back to America?'

'In two days. He wants me to visit him. But I don't expect I will. Actually, I don't like being with him very much.'

'Oh?'

'He's so old.'

'That's not very grateful.'

'No. He bought me the new Beatles record, but only on condition I accepted some opera or other. By Verdi. He said I've got to listen to it once to every five times I play the Beatles.'

'That seems fair.'

Ethne got up and followed me into the kitchen. 'He's very odd. I don't know whether I like him or not.'

'Odd?'

'He doesn't treat me like you do.'

'Oh.'

'Like a child. He treats me like an equal.'

She sounded doubtful, as if this much-desired state were not so satisfying after all.

'Isn't that what you want?'

'Yes. It's just that . . .' She broke off and filled her mouth with a large chunk of cheese. When she had swallowed it, she seemed to have made up her mind about something. 'Mummy, I've been wondering whether I shouldn't go to boarding school.'

'What?' I was amazed. 'But your friends, all the things you do in London; your friends—'

'I know, I know.' She began kicking the table leg. 'It's just that you and Daddy and Granny . . .' She stopped again.

'Yes?'

'You're always watching me.' Her face had returned to its usual sullen lines.

'Watching you?' This was too much. 'But you have more freedom than any girl of your age! I never interfere. If you want to know about being watched, then try boarding school.'

'That's not exactly the point. I can't explain. I knew you wouldn't understand. I don't know why I bothered talking to you. Of course, I don't really want to go to boarding school.'

'Then. . . ?' But she was running to her bedroom. 'Ethne!'

Mike looked up. 'What's the matter with her now?'

'I don't know. She's suddenly talking about boarding school.'

'Send her.'

'She can't be serious.'

'Can't she? How's that supper getting along?'

'Nearly ready.'

'Actually, I'd rather you didn't send her. I'd miss her music and tantrums. She keeps me company when you're out wheeling and dealing.'

'Oh, I shan't send her. I don't believe in sending children away from home.'

Ethne's bedroom door opened slightly. She peered round the door. 'Where I'd really like to go,' she said in a quiet and reasonable tone, 'is Eureka. George Briggsworthy is there, as well as my great grand-mother. He could be my tutor. Granny had a tutor there when she was a girl, and look where she's got to.'

Her tone was so quiet and reasonable that I subdued my instinct towards irritable ridicule. 'Your grandmother was desperate to get off the island. This is 1966. Tutors went out fifty years ago!'

'All right. I just thought I'd mention it.' The door closed again, softly.

'What was that about?' called Mike.

'Ethne now says she wants to go and live on Eureka. Most peculiar.'

'It sounds no more peculiar than her usual ambitions.'

'The peculiar part is that when I discouraged the idea she accepted it immediately without a fight.'

'That's because she wasn't serious. No one could seriously want to live on a desolate island in the middle of nowhere. I don't even want to visit it.'

'No. Eleanor and George live there. Mrs Briggsworthy did.'

'Crazy!'

'Perhaps Ethne's entering a new, more malleable phase?'

'You never know.'

'No.'

'It would be a start if she lowered her hemline to cover her bottom.'

'Don't be irrelevant.'

'That's what parents are for.'

Chapter Seventeen

WOMEN OF THE WORLD UNITED—IN SONG,
LAUGHTER, WORK AND PROTEST
Lilia Filippova and Marietta Sepianants of the Soviet Women's Committee
(who went around wearing buttons saying 'Women Make Policy Not
Coffee') made a great impact . . .
    The conference also had its guiding stars in the form of the Yoko-
Lennons. Yoko's thesis was the 'evolutionary' argument currently fashion-
able . . . that as men had selected mates for centuries for their docility and
weakness, women should learn to select mates for kindness and sensi-
tivity . . .
The Times.   2 July 1973

MEN TEACHING GIRLS TOLD TO BEWARE CHIVALROUS INSTINCTS
'Girls are far tougher than you think and probably worse-behaved and you
would certainly be wise to forget any rosy view that they are likely to be a
civilising influence.
    'Do not be embarrassed into allowing girls greater latitude than you
would boys. Girls, in fact, have physiologically better bladder control than
boys, for instance . . .
Excerpt from classroom guide published by Assistant Master's Association.
The Times.   4 September 1973

WOMAN LIFEGUARD
Ann Jordan, aged 22, is to start a new job as lifeguard at Sandymouth, near
Bude, Cornwall . . . No men applied.
The Times.   16 July 1973

In 1973 I returned home from a promotional trip to Australia and New Zealand to discover that Ethne had run away from school. Since I hadn't been home, I wasn't clear whether she had run away from home too.

Mike, who'd been immersed in the furore over the Crossman Diaries, seemed equally unclear. Her bedroom was always in such a state of flux that there was no way of telling whether she had removed anything, even presuming she would have wanted to take anything if she had run away. I went to see the headmistress of her comprehensive school.

'It's not as if we pressured her to stay on for her 'A' levels.' Her tone and her large brown eyes were distinctly accusing.

'Nor did we,' I retaliated quickly. 'My husband and I never pressured her into anything.'

'There you are. She told a friend she couldn't bear the pressure.'

'It's ridiculous. She passed her 'O' levels easily.'

'And took that early 'A' level.' Our antagonism lessened. At least we were able to agree she was an intelligent child, well educated. Perhaps it was neither of our faults. Perhaps we should not look for blame. Perhaps it was in her nature.

'Are you sure she's run away?' As the headmistress looked up at me in surprise, I added, 'I mean right away?'

'She told her friends.' Her surprise had not lessened. I began to know what it felt like to be one of her pupils.

'I've been away myself.'

'Of course. But you knew about the boyfriend?'

Which boyfriend? Ethne had been going out with boys since she was thirteen. She had never been out of love since she first heard the Beatles. I tried to remember my impressions of her current boyfriend. As far as I could remember, he was more unprepossessing than usual.

'I just hope he hasn't swept her back to America.' The headmistress sighed. 'These girls think they're so grown up, but really they're no more mature than Juliet was.'

I digested this. The headmistress had had the advantage of interrogating Ethne's friends. I could see that either out of malice (jealousy of my success) or because she genuinely assumed I knew as much as she did, she was not planning to tell all she knew. I would have to interrogate her. This I was not willing to do.

The headmistress began to bundle some exercise books together on her desk. 'You'd better take these,' she said. 'We've no space to keep them here.'

I looked through the wide window at the endless concrete buildings beyond. 'No space.'

She stood up in a businesslike manner. 'They wouldn't be safe, anyway. She can bring them back if she returns. But girls seldom do.'

'Thank you.' I took the bundle. Several brightly coloured slogans and pictures were stuck onto them. Ethne's writing on the front was round and childish.

'If the police want to contact me, I'm here all the time.'

'The police!' My look of horror seemed to soften her, for she bent and produced a plastic carrier bag with a picture of Father Christmas on it.

'Pop them in here. I'll tell one of her friends to drop round anything else that turns up. Goodbye, Mrs Oakley. At least, it's good to know Ethne was on the pill. In my early teaching days one could be sure the girl was pregnant, which resulted in either an illegal abortion or a hasty, ill-omened marriage. In some ways these girls know how to look after themselves very well. In areas of sex and human relations they think our generation ridiculously naive, you know. And of course, that's the area that seems most important to them at the moment. Perhaps it *is* the area that's most important at any moment. Sometimes I wish we were brought up to be more selfish. Goodbye, Mrs Oakley. Let me know if there're any developments.'

The headmistress' words of comfort would have meant more if I had not been puzzling over her remark of being 'swept back to America.' I was sure she had no American boyfriend. All her friends that I knew came from her school.

I went back to the flat and telephoned my mother. Her voice was odd. She said she'd been feeling unwell and taken a rest, but now she was recovered. 'Do you know about this new boyfriend?' I asked firmly.

'I never did like Isabel,' she replied in this odd weak voice which made me more irritated than sympathetic. Everybody knew how strong she was. 'Or Isa, as she now calls herself. Is anyone going after Ethne?'

I saw she knew even more than the headmistress. 'What's Isabel to do with it?'

'Nothing, darling. It's her son. I'm afraid you've every right to be angry with me. I introduced them. He rang me up when he arrived from America, and I invited him along to the House of Lords for lunch. It seemed a good idea to get someone else in of his own age.'

'Ethne's only just seventeen.'

'They were such a beautiful couple. He's inherited Isabel's looks—that black hair, dark skin, and piercing blue eyes. And Ethne had got herself up in an incredible collection of bits and pieces. With that mass of streaky hair all down her back. I suppose they could hardly help falling in love with each other.'

423

'Mother!'

'Particularly in the House of Lords. All that panelling and languor.'

'I believe you encouraged them. I suppose you know Ethne's left school. Hasn't been there all week. And by the sound of it, I'd rather guess she's left home too.'

'Oh, darling.' My mother's voice became so weak I could hardly hear it. 'We'd better have a talk about it all.'

'What do you mean? Do you mean you know where they've gone?'

'I could guess. I've always said Ethne had a strong streak of my mother.'

'Eureka?'

'She was describing it to Ariel in very vivid, romantic terms. Poor Ariel has grown up in a very odd environment. I would guess the children of film stars have little sense of reality. Particularly the son of a film star as stupid as Isabel. Her father was pretty thick too, though we used to think it was shell shock.'

'Mother!'

'I'm sorry, darling. But I'm afraid he was the sort of boy to turn any girl's head.'

It was not difficult to discover after this that Ariel and Ethne had indeed gone to Eureka. My grandmother was still living there at the age of eighty-six with George Briggsworthy in attendance. In answer to my inquiry, I received a telegram saying 'Father O'Gorman not available for wedding service till winter gales abate.'

'That's some consolation, anyway,' I said to Mike. We had taken ourselves to a very expensive restaurant to talk the matter over. After our first bottle of wine, I began to feel relatively removed from the whole thing. In a year's time she would be outside my legal control anyway. It would be absurd to play the heavy-handed mother after all these years of studiously avoiding it.

Mike, on the other hand, seemed to be going in the reverse direction. He began to repeat at intervals, in an increasingly morose voice, 'But I trusted you. I trusted you to see she was all right.'

'What you mean is you left me to do the work.'

'I loved her. She knew that. I always made her feel loved. She knew I was always there. It's not in my nature to supervise.'

'Nor in mine.'

'A mother has to. It's part of the maternal instinct. A mother instinctively protects her child.'

'That's man's talk. In a minute you'll tell me the man goes hunting!'

'But I trusted you. I trusted you to see she was all right.'

I began to get angry. 'You're very good about loving and trusting.

But sometimes you have to take action. For example, if anyone does go to Eureka, I know quite well it won't be you. Will it?'
'I can't just throw up my work whenever I feel like it.'
'But I can?'
'Your work's more flexible.'
'It has to be, hasn't it?'
'For God's sake, don't start that Women's Lib crap. We came here to talk about our daughter, not about you. As far as I can see, you've done exactly what you wanted to do ever since you married me. I may be trusting and loving, but I'm not stupid or blind!'
He glared at me across the table. It was a righteous, accusing glare. I dropped my eyes suddenly. I realised without any possibility of doubt that he had known about my affair with Eddie all along. My old terror of discovery came rushing back, yet at the same time I sensed immediately that he did not want to expose my guilt. He had said so much only out of anger. He did not want to admit it further. He did not want to take it into account. He did not want it to become important.

Yet he knew. After the terror came a strange sort of relief that there was no secret between us anymore, and also the pity for what he had suffered, which I should have felt all those years ago. I thought that he must love me a lot. Although I respected his wish not to discuss it, I wanted to say something to show that he was right. My affair with Eddie was not important in our marriage.

Ostensibly we were arguing about Ethne. He was still angry. I put my hand across to him. He accepted it warily, as if waiting to decide its meaning. 'I suppose the point for us to decide is whether Ethne is honestly in love with this boy in a serious, long-term way, or whether she is suffering from the sort of infatuation which overcomes even the most sensible women, like measles or chicken pox, and leaves them quite unchanged.'

Mike understood. He kept my hand. 'No scars,' he said quietly.

I thought of the twins. I could not deny them. 'There is that risk.'

Mike looked down at my hand. 'I don't believe in telling people what to do.' He paused. 'On the other hand, Ethne is still a child.'

'I'll go and see her!' I needed to offer him something. I could hear my voice sounding light and eager. 'I'll go to Eureka as soon as possible. It's the only way to find out. I'll stay there a few days. The truth is I do feel guilty.' I could admit to this guilt if not the other.

Mike gave my hand back to me. 'You could even combine it with a little business in Dublin.'

That was not fair. I looked at him reproachfully, but his face was calm, without expression. My glad sense of relief lessened. I saw that Mike was not feeling the same warmth as I was. He had faced our

425

problems a long time ago and found his own way of solving them. He would accept any offering I made him in acknowledgement of his generosity, but he would not thank me for it.

'Let's just hope that George's winter gales are symbolic,' I said.

'The turbulent way to Christianity.'

'Exactly. I must say it's not the time of year I'd have chosen for my second visit to Paradise.'

Although I said this, I did not really consider the weather would be a serious factor in my chase after Ethne. The years had successfully dimmed my previous experience. Had I not just returned from a trip round the world with no worse problem than a headache due to the time change? Did I not take off for Europe or even America at less than twenty-four hours' notice? My mother's habit of talking about Eureka as if it were the far side of the moon had always seemed unconvincing, and I put it down to wishful thinking. If it was impossible to reach, she could not reach her mother, and her mother could not be reasonably persuaded to visit. In reality it was only a mile off the Irish coast, barely eight miles from Dublin. Planes flew to Dublin all the time.

I set off in this geographically practical spirit. Not at my instigation but at my mother's command, I was accompanied by Molly and her son, St John. He was a pilot employed by an Arab airline and only occasionally returned to England. I had seen him on few occasions since he had made a beautiful curly-headed page at my wedding. On the first, he had been going through such a fervent religious phase that even his Catholic boarding school, chosen by George for its strict observances, advised him to find other outside interests. On the second occasion, he had found other interests and left the school with several other boys under a mauve cloud. And on the third occasion, in his own bed-sitter in London, he talked to me with remarkable candour about his problems as a homosexual and the antidote he had discovered in training to be a pilot. 'No one suspects a pilot of being gay,' he had said with a mixture of sadness and self-mockery.

That was in 1965. Our discussion had arisen out of some clipping on the Homosexual Reform Debate in the House of Lords. We had been very serious, tentative. He had been defensive, apologetic. We had talked as if it were a problem that might go away if he only pulled himself together, showed half the strength of character of his mother, took cold baths, and avoided undesirable companions.

Times had changed since then. I met Molly and St John in Dublin airport. They were not difficult to pick out. A space had been left round them as if they were film stars. St John was very tall, and so deeply sunburnt that his face was several tones darker than his hair.

He was dressed throughout in layers of cream cashmere and suede, including an elegant satchel hanging from his shoulder. I approached warily. He looked like the sort of person who gave me an inferiority complex at parties in California. Molly, I thought, glancing at her, must feel it even more deeply. She was dressed up to resemble the Mother Superior of a forward-thinking convent. She wore an inches-deep grey cardigan and grey skirt, sensible shoes and stockings, and a heavy cross round her neck. Perhaps she was planning a last-ditch reconciliation with George. St John sighted me. He smiled and waved. Several observers turned to look for his mate and found me disappointing. I hurried forward.

'You are kind to come with me. I would have felt so heavy-handed.'

'Oh, darling!' Molly gave me a warm hug, and I felt her bristly grey hair brush across my cheek.

'And my godchild!' To my surprise, I was folded in a new embrace. Equally to my surprise, I realised that St John's sheer beauty was extremely attractive. I immediately stopped thinking of him as ridiculously gay—which was a good idea, since I was to become fond of him. 'I just hope we won't all freeze,' I said foolishly.

'We're much too interested to freeze.'

'St John's like a sheik who comes to London for the rain.' Molly smiled at her son proudly, and I saw that she too was enjoying his company. The Catholic ability to embrace deviants always impressed me.

'We'd better get to the boat before we miss the tide.'

Outside the airport, a high wind blew rain in our faces. It came from all quarters as if personally directed. St John donned a sort of plastic djellaba, which looked on him both elegant and efficient.

We found a taxi, whose driver seemed unaware of adverse weather conditions. He drove very slowly to the harbour, at intervals removing his glasses as if experimenting for the best vision. Only one windscreen wiper worked unless he put his hand out of the window and pushed. Every few miles his door swung slowly open. Each time he reacted with the same surprised indignation and banged it shut. We began to get hysterical. Molly giggled like a girl. The rain turned to hail and beat double time on our heads.

When we arrived at the harbour, our driver turned round to face us. 'You won't be taking the boat out in this weather.'

He was right. The waves broke against the harbour with a vicious slapping noise. The boat, despite its encasement of tyres, creaked protestingly as it was flung to the wall. Nearby a pile of cardboard boxes waiting, presumably, like us to be shipped to the island, were turning to sponge. The driver said, 'Shall I be waiting to take

427

you back?'

St John said meditatively, 'Of course, there's only one way to get across to the island today.'

'How?' I hurried back into the car, rubbed my misty window, and peered seawards. I wondered if that grey peak among the dashing black waves was Eureka or merely my imagination. I began to appreciate my mother's point of view.

'Small plane,' said St John, nonchalantly. 'Fly under the weather. Perfectly possible. If there's somewhere to land.'

'There is!' said Molly eagerly. 'I remember Vi telling me about it. An open space just like an airfield. Guests used to come that way after the war.'

'The First World War,' I said. 'The fields were like lawns then. And we haven't got a plane.'

I lacked faith. Apparently there is an international pilot Mafia which produces small planes on demand.

We took off from Dublin after a sustaining lunch of Guinness and sandwiches. The rain had stopped, and by some Irish miracle the sky had become almost completely clear. It was a winter blue sky, and below us the waves broke into crests of white foam, showing that the wind still blew strongly. Occasionally the little plane was pulled sideways from St John's hands, which seemed to give him pleasure rather than otherwise.

'This is real flying!' he shouted above the noise of the plane. 'You know you're not in a train. Watch for the island now.'

Suddenly it was below us. Very clearly visible, looking neat and small among the waves. 'There's the field,' I yelled. 'To the left!'

'I see it.' We slowed down and circled. Once round. Twice round. Some figures came out on the green patch in front of the castle. One flapped in the wind. I was sure that was Ethne, with her passion for hanging rags of clothes. The other was smaller. Not a man. Surely that couldn't be the ancient Eleanor out in this weather?

'Coming down.'

Before I could be frightened we were down, hitting with quite a thump, taxiing for not very far over bumpy tussocks and then stopping abruptly.

'I'd just severed my ties with this world,' said Molly. She let go of her cross, to which she'd been clinging.

'It didn't even turn me to prayer!' I congratulated St John. I felt a curious reluctance to get out of our snug little plane into the wild scene that awaited us. The field was some distance from the castle, and my shoes were not as sensible as Molly's. Besides, it was not certain what welcome awaited us.

We started to climb out. Two men came running towards us. They

428

stumbled in heavy boots over the thick grass. 'I believe one is George,' said Molly, who looked particularly composed. I clasped my head to tame my flying hair. 'One can't cut corners with children,' she added reflectively.

We began to walk after St John. 'I'm glad for him we live in a tolerant age,' said Molly. 'I only hope George sees it that way. They haven't met since he, as they call it, "came out". I would have liked him to marry, in one way, but then, I never made much of a success of it myself. As a matter of fact, you're the only person I know who has made much of a success of marriage.'

'I like to be secure. In a securely conventional setting.'

'Also, you picked an intelligent attractive, conventionally minded man.'

'Yes.' Mike's good points seemed very desirable and very remote at that moment. Ahead of us, St John, George, and Ariel were standing close together. They were all tall. Their yellow, white, and black hair fluttered in the wind like birds' crests. The blue sky was turning purple and red, and yellow streaks were rising from the horizon where the cool globe of sun had sunk. I remembered my mother's excitement when she has pointed out the island to me on our visit after the war. Above our heads a trail of sea gulls fled screaming to their nests. The noise of the sea rose as the wind began to drop slightly. I felt my spirits lifting at the sheer beauty of the scene. 'I don't think George will judge St John in quite the same way as if we were in London.'

Molly nodded. 'On the other hand, you'll have to find a pretty good story to retrieve Ethne.'

'She doesn't like cold,' I said, unconvincingly and unconvinced. I was no longer sure what she liked.

It was easy enough to appreciate Ariel. We shook hands. I immediately saw he had that relaxed manner of Californians which used to make me jealous and suspecting but was, I had lately established, as likely a cover for insecurity and passion as the Englishman's stiff upper lip. 'I guess I should say I'm sorry,' he said, looking closely into my face. I recognised this mannerism and his bright blue eyes from Isabel.

'There's no guess about it,' said George in an old-maidish fussy voice. 'You know you're sorry. You sat up all last night telling me so.'

I turned to George. Now that I was close to him, I saw how he had changed. The Briggsworthy inclination to fleshiness had left him, so that despite a bend to his back, as if he were a man used to heavy manual labour, he looked better than I remembered. In fact, his face weathered though it was by wind and rain rather than sun, his hair bleached by old age, and his lean height gave him a striking resemblance to St John. I thought how fine he'd look in a cassock.

'You weren't out here because of us,' said Molly. 'What were you doing?'

'Collecting flowers,' said George enthusiastically. He was directing most of his comments to me, as if he couldn't yet face direct communication with his wife and son.

'You'd never believe the varieties.' Ariel looked to me appealingly. I noticed now that there was a large pile of weeds a few yards behind them.

'It's quite a business.' George stared at the plane behind us. 'What a pity you didn't get to the harbour. There's a load of presentation boxes been waiting for days.' I remembered the piles of sodden cardboard on the quayside, but thought it wiser to say nothing.

As we walked towards the castle, which was still hidden from us by a grove of trees, George began to explain about the pleasures and the problems of the dried-flower business. I remembered how on our last visit he'd talked about trees. The problems, in a not surprising word, seemed to be 'rain'. 'At the moment we're doing it all by hand. But if the Hibernian shop put in the same order as last year, we'll have to have a proper harvest.'

I looked to see how Molly was reacting to this absurd scheme and was surprised to see her nodding happily. Ariel looked happy too, and St John had not lost his elation from flying the small plane. I began to see myself as the conformist killjoy, coming with the standards of The Big World to snuff out the vigour of experiment. This view was reinforced when Ariel said, 'We knew you would be interested because of "Secrets". All the best adventures take place in the underworld life of undergrowth. We thought you might get some wild ideas while you're here.'

'But you've only been here a week!' I burst out. What I meant was that his apparent total identification with the Island's cause— present cause—was nothing but a pose. Before he could answer, we had crossed through the dark fringe of trees and come out onto the dusky lawn in front of the castle. The two dancing figures had gone, but the door was open. I was surprised to see that the garden and hedges were reasonably well kept. My childhood memory had made them a wilderness. That had been nearly thirty years ago.

George ushered us genially through the oak door. Inside, it was still dark and there was no rise in temperature. He led us quickly through stone corridors until without warning we stepped into a blaze of light and warmth. We were in the great hall.

'I didn't know you had electricity,' I blinked stupidly.

'All mod cons!' exclaimed Ethne ironically. Ethne and Eleanor were curled up in armchairs either side of a dangerously large fire.

430

They wore identical expressions of nervous satisfaction. Their curling up was the prelude to a spring. This was odd in someone as old as Eleanor.

'Ha! Ha! Not forgotten your shotgun, I hope,' she said, and her strange mixture of accents, which I remembered so vividly, had become high-pitched and blurred with age.

'I am not interested in marriage,' I replied in a ridiculously defensive way.

'Ho! Ho! Ho!' cackled Eleanor in a witchlike scale. 'I thought you were the only one of us who was.'

'I just want to make sure Ethne is doing the right thing. She's in the middle of taking her 'A' levels. She's legally under her parents' care.'

'Do at least take your coat off,' said George.

'I'll make some tea. And the bread should be ready.' Ethne leaped out of her chair. I was impressed. I had never seen her help around the house before. I thought she might give me a kiss, but she didn't. Ariel watched admiringly as she smiled and skipped from the room. Again I was struck by her resemblance to Eleanor.

Ariel lifted my coat from my shoulders tenderly. 'I do love Ethne, Mrs Oakley. She's given my life meaning. Ethne and Eureka.'

'Oh.' I was not used to so much out in the open.

'I must say I could do with something to eat.' Molly placed herself firmly in front of the fire and rubbed her hands. 'There must be something in the air. You look remarkably well, Eleanor. And George too.' She turned to her husband and gave him an approving Reverend Mother's smile.

'The spirits on this island are healing,' said Ariel in a mystical tone of voice.

'Apparently Hollywood is very attuned to the spiritual world.' George patted his arm in a kindly patronage. 'It's restored my faith in the questing nature of the human animal. If someone as idiotic as Isabel and her ilk—sorry Ariel—feel it, then there is hope for everybody.'

'You have become mellow,' said Molly.

'Catholic.' George paused impressively. 'Catholic in the Way of the Lord.'

'Instead of the Way of Mrs Briggsworthy,' chirped Eleanor.

George seemed unmoved, and I noticed for the first time Eleanor's tankard of Guinness at her elbow. It mixed oddly with her fragility. Naturally, she saw my look. 'Ariel tells me this is called a chaser.' She sounded delighted at the idea. 'Such a useful boy to have round the house. And your lovely daughter too. I can't thank you enough.'

Ethne returned carrying a heavy tray loaded with slices of still steaming soda bread, strong tea, and fresh butter. St John, who seemed silenced by the company, tried to take it from her gallantly. 'We all have our tasks,' she refused him, darting a quick glance to see if I watched.

The bread looked and smelled delicious. I never ate bread, except one thin slice at breakfast. I would be the one to spoil the crazy but happy atmosphere of a child's tea party.

'But what are you going to live on? What are you going to do? Where will it all lead to?'

'Death,' replied George with sombre satisfaction.

'Well, I know that.' I sat up impatiently and found I had taken a large slice of bread. 'But I want to know how Ethne will fulfil her talents on this earth. That does come first.' I did not know George at all well, but his stance as prophet of right was beginning to irritate me. 'Ethne was in the middle of taking her 'A' levels. Both her headmistress and I had high hopes of her.'

Yet again this idea fell on stony ground. Even Molly could not bring herself to support these material values. Only St John looked slightly sympathetic.

'But I thought you knew all about it,' Ethne said. 'That's why I left the men to meet you.'

'About what?'

'The flowers. Next spring and summer. At this time of year there's not much to do, but next year . . .' She began to talk excitedly about seeding certain areas, pressing, hanging, displaying, pot pourri, sachets, bouquets . . . about the good luck of Ariel's having such a huge dollar allowance, which he planned to invest in the industry . . . how he had lots of 'cool' friends who would come over to help with the harvest, and some might settle so that they became a real community . . . and they would do up the farm cottages, which were absolutely falling down . . . and it would be all as beautiful as it was when Eleanor first came, except that it would be better because it would be real . . . the island would be working, too, instead of being just a plaything for the idle rich . . .

I looked at Eleanor, but she didn't seem hurt by this idea. If anything, she was smiling. Ethne continued, becoming even more impassioned. Ariel went to stand by her. I told myself this was a schoolgirl, an immature being, a minor who had seemed of minor consequence until a week ago. She was now describing George's role as farmer and manager, and he too seemed pleased at the prospect.

'. . . and it will all be wonderful and happy and productive and good!' Ethne had reached her peroration. The flames in the fireplace took over as the loudest noise in the room. I turned to Molly. Surely I could expect some support from her.

'Do you think this a serious proposition?'

'It's not a proposition. It's happening now!' Ethne shouted. Ariel took her hand.

He fixed his bright blue eyes on me. 'It's so rare, Mrs Oakley, that everything is as right for two people as it is for Ethne and me. I'd like to convince you of that.'

I decided he was using a Valium voice. Such calm could not be real. A wild idea that the dried-flower industry was really a cover for growing marijuana made me half-rise. But a look at those simple blue eyes, Ethne's guiltless happiness, and George's priestlike benediction made me sink back again. It was what they said it was. A dried-flower industry. Marijuana would have been more understandable.

'Call me Violet,' I said with bitter weakness.

'One of my favourite flowers.' Ariel eased towards me.

'Unfortunately it doesn't grow on the island,' said Ethne sharply.

St John who was sitting on a window seat half outside the circle of the room, leaned towards us. His deep voice was as calm as Ariel's, but in his case I found it soothing.

'If you are serious, you'll certainly need the service of a light aircraft. You can't rely on boats in this sort of climate.' For a moment I thought wildly he was going to offer his own services, but then I saw that what he had actually effected was a discussion on a totally different level from Ethne's wild dreams. They wanted to do it, but were they capable? Now came the practicalities. I need say nothing. They would condemn themselves out of their own mouths. I took another piece of bread.

St John, I felt certain, would find them out. The odd thing was, he didn't. Or perhaps it was odd of me to invest my bourgeois hopes in a homosexual Arab-airline pilot. He could have been on their side all along. I began to feel my grip on the situation slacken. But this time it was willingly. The exhaustion of the journey and the delightful heat of the fire, perhaps even Ethne's seductive bread combined to make me feel absurdly drowsy. The faces round me continued mouthing, but their words left no impression in the air. I felt relaxed and happy, with a holiday feeling I hadn't had for years. No one—no publisher or producer—expected anything from me. I was surrounded by people who hoped for nothing from me. As far as I was concerned, they wanted me to give up my responsibility. The idea began to seem desirable. The logs on the fire shifted downwards and sideways, revealing a rich bed of glowing peat. It was that which was giving out that delicious smell. I remembered it from my last visit. Why, I wondered idly, could one not have peat in London? I lay back in my chair. Let them get on with it.

And so they did. Even now, in my memory, that evening has a

433

dreamlike quality. After dinner and a keg or so of Guinness, George led off a party to the chapel on the hill. He made it seem the most natural thing in the world. The wind had dropped completely, and it was a quite clear starry night, much colder than before. When we reached the chapel, George became businesslike in the same way priests do on their home ground. He scurried round lighting candles and opening doors. Then he conducted some sort of service, which as far as I could make out was in thanksgiving for the good start of the flower business. I knelt with the others.

When we emerged, shaking with cold despite the Guinness, he took Molly and me to see his mother's grave. Next to it lay that of poor mad Henry. 'I don't blame you for his death anymore,' George said to Molly.

'Nor yourself, I should hope,' she replied tartly. But they were getting on well together, sharing perhaps their relief that St John had not turned out worse. I don't believe George had altogether summed him up. As St John crossed the wet grass ahead of them, I heard George whisper to Molly, 'He reminds me of one of those young deacons in Ghirlandaio's study for Christ. Would you say he was close to the Church?'

'Religious certainly,' said Molly with her usual conviction. 'Close to the Church, no.'

George sighed. 'That seems to be a very general comment on the young of today. Take this charming American Ethne's brought to us: I've never met anyone with a deeper sense of the spiritual significance of life, but with a greater horror of the organised Church. He says even our little chapel makes him feel threatened.'

'Don't worry.' Molly put a consoling arm through his. 'There're many roads to God. We mustn't be proud.'

'My own thought exactly,' said George. They caught up with us. 'Do you never feel the pull of a good Latin Mass, St John?'

We returned to find Eleanor being carried to her bedroom by Ariel. 'She's as brittle as a doll,' he said. Ethne held her feet tenderly.

'I can't think why.' Molly laughed her nice nun's laugh. 'Judging by tonight's performance she must be made of Guinness!'

'And soda bread,' said Ethne, who had not missed my appreciation of her cooking. I avoided her eyes. In the morning I would talk as a mother to her daughter. Tonight I just couldn't get the hang of the relationship. 'Good night, everybody.'

But the next morning, it was too late. After all, I had slept next door to the room where my daughter and her lover had shared a double bed. No doubt, if I'd cared to, I could have heard the springs bouncing.

Ethne felt confident. Like the devil, she took me up to the top of a tall hill and told me to look down. It was a cold, clear day, and the island spread in front of us, the green still brushed with frost like tinsel on a Christmas tree. I was not tempted. What she didn't know was that on the same tall hill I had sent Henry off to his death. It was a place of ill omen for me. I had woken up to find my holiday feeling of the night before had left me. On the other hand, my firm sense of parental responsibility had returned in a markedly diminished form.

'It's a beautiful view,' I said to Ethne, 'but that's not the point. What do you and Ariel mean to each other?'

'Oh, Mother. I thought you understood more.'

'There seem two points,' I began more energetically. 'The island is one, and Ariel—'

'Mother!' Ethne interrupted me impatiently. On this freezing day, she wore a kind of hempen shirt, jeans, and a long muffler which Eleanor had lent her. Her long hair splayed round her head in tangled cords, and her small nose was red. She looked lively and young. It made me feel old. If I had worn so little, I would have frozen into an ice beacon. 'Would it make you happier if I promised to go on studying for my 'A' levels?'

'Yes,' I said, looking beyond the island and beyond the encircling sea to the Irish mainland, which was, astonishingly, clearly visible. I had to admit it looked flat and dull. I tried to place the airport.

'That's easily done. I pinched all the textbooks. No one's interested in them at school. I happen to like the English literature syllabus.'

I realised she was serious. We began to walk down the back of the hill and discuss the idea. I found she knew far more about twentieth-century English literature than I did. Also, she cared more about it. As we talked, we began to like each other in a perfectly companionable way. We agreed that the bracken-covered slopes we were crossing reminded us of the moors at Kettleside and wondered why this did not worry Eleanor, who professed to hate Northumberland more than death itself, and particularly the bracken-fringed mountains. She had come to Eureka to escape just what we were enjoying.

'The answer, of course,' said Ethne, smiling, 'is that she never leaves the castle grounds.'

'She's old.'

'I'm sure she never did.'

'My mother used to describe being dragged up the hills to visit cottagers who lived round here. Eleanor was a very energetic woman.' I saw the look of curious disbelief on Ethne's face which the young reserve for the idea that the old were young. 'And then there's all that drink to consider now.'

Ethne understood that more easily. 'It really seems to suit her,' she said eagerly. 'I honestly believe she's quite happy. I told her about meeting Mr Blumberg at Granny's introduction, and do you know what she said?'

'Something unflattering.'

'She said that he was still after her and that he was the reason she'd lived on Eureka all these years. She said she couldn't stand men who were desperately in love with her. She was quite serious.'

'Perhaps she was right. Do you remember how Blumberg sighed over your resemblance to her?'

'But a wizened old creature like her . . . a funny old hobbit like him . . . and love . . .?' I realised by the sacred note that had entered her voice that she was thinking of her tall, blue-eyed lover. By now I found it quite natural to raise the subject of Ariel again. Now we had each other's trust. We talked about him for a long time, even to the point of her admitting he did have certain 'hang-ups' to do with Hollywood and being the son of a star. But her love would do what all the most expensive analysts had failed to do.

'I promise you,' she said earnestly, 'it will work out fine. Even if it doesn't last. In fact, there's only one problem . . .'

Glad that she felt confident enough to reveal her problems, I turned to face her. Our breaths mingled on the air.

'The pill. As you know, Ireland is a Catholic country, which makes it very hard—actually, impossible—for me to get fixed up. Would it be a terrible nuisance to send off a packet now and again? I'll tell you exactly what to get.'

Her innocent bluish-green eyes stared at me confidently. At the same time I sensed that if I would not act as medical postman, she would find someone else who would. Perhaps this was her way of bringing me into the intimacies of her life. I noticed a sprinkling of childish acne at the side of her nose. The sight was endearing. Perhaps I would include some Clearasil.

'Well?' she said in a fairly indifferent sort of voice. Nevertheless, she had given me a hold over her. 'You know we sleep together. I mean, you saw the bed we share last night. So there's no point in expressing outrage.'

'None at all.' I became brisk and sensible in what I hoped was a passable imitation of her headmistress. 'I don't want you to have a baby at your age. However, what I do say is this: No Contraception without Education.'

Ethne swung round—I thought angrily, but it turned out she was smiling. I suddenly found she had thrown her arms round me and was hugging me the way she used to as a baby. I had a sudden picture of her then, and it seemed far too long ago. I hugged her back.

'I knew you would understand,' she said in a muffled voice. 'I'm not really irresponsible or hard, but I can't risk losing Ariel. And it's not as if you'll be miserable to lose me.'

I wondered if that was a reproach. And if so, whether it was justified. I was not sure enough to argue. I looked over her head to the shoreline again, but a faint white mist was sweeping slowly across from the mainland, obscuring all behind it. 'We've had the best of the day,' I said. Cowardly, perhaps, but I still held on to her. There had been a moment when I chose my work rather than my daughter. I was glad, therefore, to hug her and glad to send contraceptive pills over the Irish Channel.

'Look!' cried Ethne, breaking away. George, Molly, St John, and Ariel appeared from the back of the island. Though quite near, they were silhouetted on a cliff edge. Their outlines were made ridiculous by sprouting bunches of greenery. Molly particularly, being short and relatively dumpy, looked like a moving bush. As their faces came out of silhouette I saw that Ariel had even poked some purplish flowers behind his ears. Unlike Molly, he looked beautiful. A thought struck me: 'Won't Isabel want her son back?'

Ethne shrugged. 'Ask him. She's just got married again. She likes him as an escort between marriages. She likes him because he's so good-looking, but she's not really interested.' She emphasised the word with a frown. 'He worships her, of course, which is why it's so wonderful he's escaped. He had hoped to find his father, you know, but he's dead.'

'I didn't know that.' I remembered Captain Hubert Creswell with a fondness for my childhood.

'He was pretty hopeless, from what I gather. After he gave up films, he kept failing in small businesses. He had an army pension from a war injury that kept him going.'

'He had lost an eye.'

'That couldn't have killed him. I think it was shrapnel in his stomach. He only did one great thing.'

'What?'

'Produce Ariel.'

Ariel and the others were upon us in all their green exuberance, so that I decided it would be inappropriate to mention my last meeting with Captain Creswell. Araminta's love life must seem infinitely remote to Ethne.

Sometimes it seemed to me that people spent most energy either tangling themselves into knots with each other or trying to get the knots untangled. What had my visit to Eureka achieved? I had not untangled Ethne from Ariel, but I had loosened the knot that bound

437

us together. Yet, remembering our talk on the hills, our hug, perhaps in one way I had strengthened it.

When Molly and St John and I had left the island, I asked Molly whether old age made human entanglements less of a problem. 'Less time-consuming'—she eyed me gravely—'but more important.'

'Odd,' I said tactlessly enough, 'when you're about to lose them.'

Molly didn't seem to mind. 'Humans are notoriously perverse. Your mother is finding herself jealous of Araminta for the first time in her life.'

I looked up, surprised. Araminta was dying. Slowly but surely dying. Having suffered for years from terrible arthritis without doing anything about it, she had suddenly been taken to Newcastle Hospital with some respiratory illness to do with high blood pressure. This was placing strain on her heart, so that although she had been allowed home from hospital, she was unlikely to lead an active life again. She did not seem an obvious subject for jealousy.

My mother and I had actually made the journey north to visit her. Over our British Rail dinner we talked gloomily about Kettleside. Tudor didn't want it; neither did I. But my mother hated the idea of selling it. It was where she had been happiest with my father. She was also worried about the fate of Nanny, now nearing her ninetieth year. Nanny could never exist outside a family. We had not solved that problem for after all, as I pointed out, there was always a chance Araminta might outlive her. She was twenty years younger.

'It's virginity,' my mother said dogmatically. 'Or more important, no children. When a woman uses her body like a man instead of as a receptacle for other humanity, she has a man's strength. She is not sapped.'

'That doesn't sound very Catholic.'

My mother looked defiant. It was an expression which always made it impossible to believe she was nearly seventy. 'I'm not a very good Catholic. At least, I find a constant battle between humanitarian values and spiritual. If I was a young woman now, I'd use birth control.'

'A lot of Catholic women do.'

She sighed. 'And yet it's so odious. I never used it myself. In common with most of my generation. We were romantic. We hoped. Or perhaps we were silly. If we were caught, we paid.'

'I paid.' Her expression, which had become impersonal, turned to me with surprise. 'I had to marry Mike.'

'So you did. Though I wouldn't have put it like that. You knew all about it then.'

'In a way.'

There was a pause before she continued, 'I've just been made

438

chairman of an International Catholic Commission to look into the needs of Birth Control in the Third World. Because we're Catholic, we call it the needs of the family. I start without knowing what I feel myself.'

'Perhaps you'll find out.'

'One must be optimisitc. At least I'll travel. Africa, South America, India. I've seen so little of the world. I'll be too old if I don't go soon.'

'Don't be silly.' I took all references by my mother to her increasing age as a shameful fishing for compliments. Since that hiccough of illness around the time of my wedding, and again about ten years ago, she had come to seem indestructible, thin and wiry, pared down for another twenty years of service to society. As she grew older she had become even more efficient and well organised. She ate only lean meat and vegetables. She no longer drank—not even wine. Letters were answered by return of post, telephone calls prompt and brief, punctuality daunting. I asked her once if she didn't ever feel the need to relax, to which she replied in a surprised tone, 'But I relaxed, did nothing, for the first thirty-five years of my life. I'm still trying to make up for that.'

On that train journey to the North I had wondered idly how her attitudes would fit in with India, Africa, or South America. But especially India.

And now here was Molly suggesting that she was jealous of Araminta. 'She's more jealous of Nanny,' I said.

'I admit she's not precisely jealous of Araminta herself. It's her family. Her children, her grandchildren. Her contact with so much warmth and love. Your mother suffers from being an individualist. You have quite a responsibility.'

I thought of Molly's words when we went together to my mother's flat to report on our visit to Eureka.

Even though she loved Ethne as much as she loved anyone, I could sense that she had allocated us an hour of her attention and no more, whatever the situation. I noticed when Molly and my mother met that they looked at each other with momentary sadness, as if still unused to the change of age. My mother's sadness was tinged with impatience, as if she thought Molly could have made more effort to control her humpy body and frizzing grey hair. Which, of course, she could. On Eureka she had taken quite a lot of trouble to keep her Reverend Mother outfit spruce. It was funny to see the two old friends still taking the trouble to irritate each other. We were five minutes late, and my mother looked at her watch in a gesture she tried to pretend was unconscious. Molly made a face at me. I smiled back.

Nevertheless, an hour of my mother's attention was always worth twenty-four hours of anybody else's. She questioned us closely about events on Eureka. Under her enthusiasm we found ourselves painting a picture that would not have disappointed Ethne herself. Everybody was well, happy, fulfilled. Ariel, though suffering from a compulsion to self-analysis, had Isabel's looks and Captain Creswell's simple affectionate nature. Eleanor would never leave the island again. George was eccentric but not mad, and St John had been the leavening influence without which our visit might have foundered into debilitating squabbles—although, of course, everything was so perfect and wonderful that that could not really have happened.... We said it, I suppose, because it was clearly what my mother wanted to hear, and yet as we spoke it seemed perfectly true. London did seem a grim, bitter, enclosed place after the light and freedom of Eureka.

'I am glad,' said my mother. 'It'll be a relief not to worry about Ethne. I'm afraid the news is not so good about Araminta. I couldn't persuade you and Mike to come up to Kettleside over Christmas? She may not last much beyond it. Tudor has promised.'

Molly gave me a meaningful look. I frowned back at her. I didn't believe my mother wanted to be like Araminta. Not that their relationship had ever been easy to understand. They disagreed about everything from Family Allowances to the correct time for cooking a cabbage. Nevertheless, Araminta had virtually brought up Tudor and me, and they had been closely associated for nearly fifty years.

'It was circumstances that drew Araminta and me together,' my mother said sadly, 'not any appreciation of the other's merits. But I've grown fond of her now. She was a fool though. Her foolishness drove even Leonard away, and he adored her.'

'She's an artist.' I came to her defence. 'If she'd been born thirty years later, or if there'd been no war, she'd have been as successful as Clancy.'

'No.' My mother was firm. 'She doesn't want it. Women have to want success very much or biology takes over. Even now. After all my years in politics I've come to this conclusion. If you want a fair representation of women in Parliament, you'll have to legislate for it. It's as simple as that.'

'But it's not. I didn't have to battle.'

'You're exceptional. Exceptionally lucky. Besides, you found yourself the perfect husband. So clever of you to have resisted the temptation of Eddie.'

As my mother grew older, she began to lose the inhibitions about personal affairs that had been one of her characteristics. For those of us whose attitudes remained unchanged, it could be disconcerting. I did not want to know how much she knew about my affair with Eddie. I didn't want Reverend Mother Molly to hear about it at all. I quickly returned the conversation to Araminta.

'Circumstances may have brought you together, but real affection holds you there. The only times you really disagree are when you come to Kettleside and pretend to be Araminta.'

My mother laughed. 'Since I never see her anywhere but Kettleside, that seems to cover our whole relationship.'

I suspect Araminta chose to die at Christmas. She always shone at seasonal events, with their natural party atmosphere. When Mike and I arrived with Clancy she was in bed, where she remained for the whole visit. The bed had been placed in the dark room which had been my grandfather's study and continued to be called by that name. It was a small room, and since there were always at least three or four people visiting, one had the impression of a court circling their queen. Clancy said, 'Poor Felix. He's ill too, but he only has Katynka.' I repeated, 'Poor Felix' with irony. But Clancy wouldn't rise. 'It's horrible being old. And dying. I shall go back to him on Boxing Day.

Araminta's whole family had come to stay, and for the first time I made an accurate count of children, husbands, grandchildren and great-grandchildren. The amazing total was thirty-two. Eight children, ranging in age from forty-six to twenty-seven. Six spouses, fifteen grandchildren, and three great-grandchildren. Apart from Clancy, they were all strangers to me. Even Leo, who was nearly my twin, and Henrietta, who had been my playmate, seemed like any other middle-aged farmer and middle-aged housewife. Since they could not all stay in the house, they had overflowed into a new motel on the road to Newcastle which had been built to cater for the summer tourist trade. They arrived in rotation for meals, but a grand Christmas Day lunch had been planned. Owing to the gap in ages, even the children had never been under the same roof all at once, so it would be a historic occasion. The husband of Clancy's twin, a pedantic man who was probably the main reason (Mrozek apart) why Clancy never married, had bought a battery of lights and a movie camera with which he planned to film the whole event. Araminta's bed was to be wheeled into the hall, where the feasting would take place.

My pleasure that Araminta was getting such a send-off was lessened by Mike's understandable horror at the whole event. Despite the rota system, there was a continual barrage of noise and activities, including hectic football games in the old kitchen. He tried to work in his room, but the cold drove him down. In the end, he and my mother escaped into long walks following the cart tracks that circled the bottom of the moors.

According to Mike, my mother had become obsessed by the question of Birth Control in an International Setting. 'I've never been too good on the individual,' she would say, 'and now I've got older, I find my wells of compassion are almost dry. But I can appreciate poverty and suffering by the thousand or million or hundred million with no trouble. And that's where I think I can do some good. Did you know almost half the population of the Third World is under fifteen years of age? And that's an out-of-date figure. It's probably over half now. What I want to discover is whether Aid can do it without birth control. What I need is the kind of personal vision someone like Barbara Ward has . . . I thought Catholicism would bring it to me . . . but it's not so easy.'

Mike reported her words. I wasn't surprised that she wanted to get out of this houseful of progeny, and I saved them up to explode Molly's theory for her. Was this the talk of a woman who longed for a heart like Araminta's—bursting with warmth and love? No. Here was a practical woman who was horrified by such human profligacy. No wonder she fled out for a nice unemotional conversation with Mike. Personally, I was too busy to talk to her or even to take walks.

However, between discovering I could bake a very good scone, I did occasionally slip in to pay homage to Araminta. Usually Nanny was there, sitting in the corner. Only her uncontrollable fingers, constantly playing invisible castanets, showed she was still alive.

'I pretend she's knitting,' Araminta whispered once when she saw where I was looking.

Although Araminta had never had the time to give me individual attention, I had benefited from her warmth as had her other children. Even in sickness she kept this quality. We didn't often talk, but once I mentioned the extraordinary and quite untypical trip to Venice, and she smiled. 'I've never been so miserable,' she whispered. 'I thought it might affect Leonard. How silly. It could have only made him think less of me. But in the end I never told him.' She smiled again. 'Poor Hubert.

On Boxing Day evening, her youngest daughter, Rosalind, who was unmarried and a nurse and had taken six months off work to nurse her mother, came to fetch me. We had passed through the climax of Christmas, and some of the clan were beginning to mutter about departure. Clancy had already left. Araminta, although obviously heavily drugged and very pale except when the effort of speech made her crimson for a second, had not seemed near death. If her eyes and her mind had wandered for part of the time, that could be easily attributed to nostalgia, and she had managed several perfectly comprehending smiles at the antics of the grandchildren. It was late when Rosalind called me. I had stayed up to read the papers in peace. She told me she thought her mother would not last the night and that she had something special to say to me. I was surprised. One small light by the bedside filled the study with tall shadows. As I came in, I saw myself slide blackly across the ceiling above Araminta's head. It looked too like an angel of death for comfort. I looked for Nanny, but she was not there. I had always thought this panelled room a stifling gloomy place filled with the ghosts of my grandfather's unhappy thoughts. I went firmly forward and sat close to Araminta. My shadow hunched and descended. Now the light circled only Araminta's white face. Her eyes were shut, as if she were already dead. Her face, which had never grown fat like her body, now looked as fragile as a sick child's. Rosalind had not followed me in. I would have to speak.

'It's Violet.'

The eyes half-opened. I immediately saw that Rosalind was right. The contact with the world which had been clearly visible the day before had now completely gone. I didn't think she could see me. I didn't expect her to speak. But gradually I sensed some sort of reaction to my presence. Her eyes were still open, and she was looking at me with what seemed to be surprise.

'Vi? Violet?' The words were mouthed, barely whispered.

'Yes. Rosalind said you wanted me.' My voice sounded unnaturally loud.

Her face moved upwards slightly in what I realised was an attempt to smile. I was glad she had enough drugs to be able to smile. Now she shifted slightly in her bed as if to wake herself up more. 'Your mother,' she said, in a fairly distinct whisper.

'Oh. You wanted my mother.'

'No difference . . . You thank her . . . thank her . . .' Her voice trailed away.

'But all she gave you was money.' I stopped, horrified at the inappropriate argumentative thought and my harsh voice.

Araminta lay still. Then she murmured, 'Money . . .' She stopped and then began again. 'Money is very important.' Once more came that attempt at a smile.

'It's only circumstance,' I found myself replying. Perhaps I was trying to shake her from the slipway to death. Perhaps I was echoing my mother's words. But this time she didn't answer. Her eyes closed. I sat waiting. Half an hour passed. She was breathing heavily but evenly. I began to have a dread that this regular beat of life would stop while I was alone with her. I wanted to go and fetch Rosalind. I had never seen anyone die. Unless one counted poor

Henry Briggsworthy. I removed that thought firmly from my mind. But then remembered Leonard's disappearance from my wedding and Augustus' crash into the shallow water. It seemed I had been party to many deaths. What I meant, I suppose, was that I had never been close to anyone who was expecting to die. My mother, I thought, whom Araminta had really wanted, would have been better in this situation. After her wartime experiences. I had been a child then, here in this house, looked after by this woman. I stared at her impassive face. I wondered how long her warmth would survive after her death.

I wanted her to speak again. Her last comment on life could not be 'Money is very important.' Not when her whole life had been based on a fine disregard for money. Surely no one whose last words were to be 'Money is very important' would have created so many children. She should have said, 'The creation of life is important.' I looked at her pale small mouth, willing it to speak.

Then I began to wonder if I'd got it wrong. Perhaps she'd said, 'Money isn't very important.' But I couldn't convince myself of that. At least she looked peaceful. It wasn't troubling her anymore. Did that 'Money is very important' mean she had always been jealous of my mother? Did it mean she hated her? Did it mean my mother had bought her? Was she, in a way, my mother's servant, allowed to indulge her feminine desire to have babies as long as she kept to her place? Kept the house—the home going. Like some poor cousin or aunt from the nineteenth century. I began to see Araminta's life as a tragedy. She had been placed by my mother, the feminist, in the traditional supportive role of the weaker sex. 'Money is very important.' Why would she not speak again and dispel those words?

After about two hours, Rosalind returned. She apologised for being away so long, and said she'd fallen asleep in a chair. She asked what Araminta had wanted to say.

'She really wanted my mother, Violet.'

'Oh.' Rosalind looked agitated. 'How stupid of me. I just never think of her as Violet.'

'Lady Nettlefield?'

'Yes. But she spoke to you?'

'Yes.' I was suddenly struck by the thought of what Araminta had actually wanted to say. She had wanted to thank my mother. I remembered her smile. Why should she be ironical at this time in her life? She *had* wanted to thank my mother. In all my obsessive analysis of her last words, I had forgotten her first. She was grateful for the help my mother had given her in allowing her to play her chosen role. I remembered the scene of yesterday with joy. The children, grandchildren, great-grandchildren. Araminta was dying at Christmas in the house she had lived in for forty years, surrounded by the love of friends and relations. She was even nursed by her own daughter. I smiled at Rosalind's strained face.

'She wanted to thank my mother,' I said. 'I'll tell her in the morning.'

'Yes,' said Rosalind, unsurprised. 'She couldn't have been herself without your mother.'

Chapter Eighteen

THELMA, LADY FURNESS, who in 1930 introduced Mrs Simpson to the Duke of Windsor, who was then Prince of Wales, collapsed and died in New York . . . Gay, elegant, and good company, she was one of the Prince's circle in which Americans were always prominent; he was reacting from his English background in which a certain deference was bound to be present and to inhibit the give and take of conversation . . . The Prince's American friends, among them Lady Furness, had a naturally free and easy manner which the Prince found highly attractive.
The Times.   31 January 1970

BESSIE BRADDOCK, former Labour MP for Liverpool Exchange, died in Rathbone Hospital, Liverpool . . . With her generous frame, rosy countenance and forthright North Country voice and manner, she was one of those MPs who always created a stir of interest in the public galleries.
The Times.   14 November 1970

MRS FLORENCE AMERY CI, widow of the Rt Hon L. S. Amery CH, has died at the age of 94. She had the gifts—beauty, capacity, charm, understanding and a natural friendliness—which made and kept friends wherever she went. Mrs Amery would, indeed, have been outstanding in any sphere, and if it had not been for her devotion to her husband and his career, she could, and no doubt would, have created and followed a career of her own.
The Times.   20 February 1975

My mother left for India two years after Araminta's death. It was her seventieth birthday. Nineteen seventy-five. I should have recognised the significance of three score years and ten. Although it was a freezing December morning, she was already dressed in her hot-weather outfit of a faded cotton dress which I remembered from years ago, flat-heeled sandals, and ankle socks. Over her arm she carried a large black plaited straw handbag stuffed with guidebooks, paper, and pens. She was planning to get India straight.

Perhaps because of her flat shoes and oversized handbag, she looked particularly tiny, frail, and old. There was, of course, no point in suggesting she should take care. This trip, which she was taking under the auspices of her Catholic World Committee on the Family, or in other words, on birth control, was the climax of three years' work and many more years of thought. She talked about India in a mystical voice of expectation which would have come more naturally from Ethne or Ariel (had they not been playing out their spiritual rebirth on Eureka) than from an ex-MP, and Life Peeress. It was this side of her which had, I suppose, become a convert to Catholicism.

'I would be happier,' I said, not for the first time, 'if there was another English member of your party.'

'They all speak English,' replied my mother, gazing out of my car window with bright, excited eyes. She had at least allowed me to drive her to the airport. Despite her recent trips to Africa and South America, she retained the older generation's nervous respect for air travel.

'That's not the point.'

Oh, darling. We have the British High Commission. Butlin's Holiday Camp, as I hear it's nicknamed.' She giggled like a child. 'And anyway, it's all too official. My fear is I'll see nothing of the real India. Of course, everything depends on Mrs Gandhi.' She went on to give her views of Mrs Gandhi's Emergency Act, which had been declared that year. She was torn between her desire to admire the woman and her horror of compulsory sterilisation programmes. Freedom of speech didn't worry her half as much—as no doubt it didn't the Indians either. For some reason, I felt reassured by the thought of a totalitarian regime. It sounded safer.

'The point is,' I said, 'not to forget your pills.' A look of sarcastic irritation passed over my mother's face which made me regret my words.

I had discovered my mother was a late-onset diabetic the day after Araminta's death. Rosalind, the nurse, had mentioned it casually, assuming I must already know. She warned me that my mother's attitude was extremely irresponsible, despite the resulting exhaustion and other more unpleasant effects. 'She won't admit she's human,' I

said with a certain amount of admiration. 'How long has she had it?'
'Seven or eight years,' said Rosalind with a nurse's look of disapproval at my tone. 'Perhaps more. She's not too bad. She doesn't need injections. But she must watch her diet and take her pills. That's why she's become so thin.' I remembered that period of exhaustion my mother had suffered some time ago.

Since this conversation I had schooled myself into a protective role. I had also told one or two other people to watch her. Yet if I ever approached her directly, as I felt bound to do on the way to the airport, she would respond with a worrying antagonism.

'Anyway,' I added, 'the sun should do you good.'

My mother gave me a look of contempt. 'I am not going to India to do myself good. Besides, I learned long ago that the will to do your body good is counterproductive. It's best to forget your body altogether.'

'Your body will like the sun whether you like it or not,' I said with feeble stubbornness, trying still to reassure myself.

'Never mind.' My mother softened and patted my hand. 'For your work you probably do need a comfortable body. *Mens sana in corpore sano*. Tough old birds like me don't need much to run around squawking.'

This image was a good one. I decided she could be right. I turned my mind to my other responsibility. 'I've insisted Ethne has her baby in a Dublin hospital.'

'She never will.' My mother smiled. It was a gleeful, conspiratorial smile that she never used in her thoughts about me. I had given up trying to understand why, hating Eureka and waste (and her mother), she gave every sign of approving of Ethne's extraordinary life there. It was particularly annoying because I felt certain she was the one person who could have influenced Ethne to return.

But now Ethne, despite my assiduous attentions with birth-control pills, was going to have a baby—an illegitimate baby, since her mystical union with Ariel excluded the possibility of a legal marriage. And my mother was going to India—to study the population problem.

I turned off the motorway to the airport and thought with relief about my own career. The problems of mother and daughter would seem even more insoluble if I was giving them my full attention. If I had been totally concerned, I could have arranged to accompany my mother to India or, alternatively, go to Ireland to be with Ethne during the birth. But neither of them really needed me, and certainly they did not want me. Instead, in a couple of days I was flying off to California, where I was to adapt my British television series for the American market.

My mother and I kissed in the airport. She had already discovered a companion, a nice fiftyish lady on her way to visit her brother who was a doctor in the British High Commission. Besides, Air India had sent a supremely polite representative in a sari to see she boarded the plane with no problems. One on either side, they walked her through the Customs. For a second, my image of secure protection turned to that of a prisoner between two gaolers. I shook it off as ridiculous and, as my mother turned round, waved a jaunty goodbye.

The planets appeared to be throwing my mother, my daughter, and me very far apart; yet there were links—Ariel would have called them astral—that held us together. When I arrived in Los Angeles, the first thing I noticed in the lobby of the Beverly Wilshire Hotel was stacks of newspapers headlined in vast black letters, STAR TAKES OVERDOSE. I didn't care about Hollywood's stars one way or the other, but like everybody else, I immediately bought a paper. My agent, who was with me looked over my shoulder. 'It's Isa!' he said in a surprised tone of voice. 'Now, that's one lady I would never have guessed would cut her life short. Not even now, when she's run out of success.'

Isa's near death and fight for life dominated the gossipy Hollywood papers during my whole stay there. No one can have been more interested in her continuance in this world than I. Although I was pretty certain that first, an attempted suicide would not move Ariel to abandon his spiritual wife and mother-to-be and that second, the news would never reach Eureka anyway, I did realise that in the event of her death he would be forced to return. I might not approve of Ariel, but I didn't want a fatherless as well as illegitimate grandchild.

Luckily, as the days passed and the pictures of Isa in her great roles of the past twenty years began to diminish, it became clear that she was as far from death as anyone else. The cynical even suggested that it was all a publicity stunt to restart her career. For as the trail of shiny-eyed, bow-lipped photographs came to an end, a new, up-to-date version appeared. A haggard, world-weary figure, 'European'—that is, sexy in the Jeanne Moreau, Simone Signoret manner. Within the week when her name was on everyone's lips and this new image was revealed, she had signed for a large role as neurotic, drunken mother of a new young boy star. A day after this news hit the headlines of *Variety* and *The Hollywood Reporter*—above a small piece about my own series—I met Isa in the lobby of the Beverly Hills Hotel.

I naturally recognised her, but was extremely surprised when I saw those huge blue eyes now encircled with suffering stare at me with recognition. She changed step, for she was on the way out and I was on the way in, causing her retinue to tangle up like the Red Queen's attendants. She came towards me with arms outstretched.

Still suspicious, I glanced over my shoulder. But although there were many watching Isa and many more fitted to receive her attentions than I, no one was preparing to welcome her.

I said, smiling, 'Isabel! How lovely!' She hesitated a moment, perhaps for greater effect or perhaps because my use of her full name surprised her. Her black hair was streaked with a strange nicotine grey which matched an expensive-looking silk poncho. In reality she looked nothing like as 'European' as her photographs. I thought how I'd once hero-worshipped her and now she had the hero worship of the world. I also wondered what she thought of me. She was on home ground.

'Sister!' She did not cry out as my untrained voice had to cross the space of people-filled air conditioning. She whispered. But at the word I felt a thrill go through all around her. Could I really be Isa's long-lost sister from England? She took my arm now, and I felt myself enveloped in the most delicious hot scent. 'We must talk. We'll find somewhere quiet. Are you staying here?'

'But Isa . . .' Anxious voices behind her. She had a press conference; she had an appointment with her new producer; a lunch date . . .

Isabel and I sat in the Polo Lounge drinking a wonderful cocktail made of peach juice and champagne.

'So Ariel is happy.' As this seemed more of an announcement than a question, I hastened to agree.

I described Eureka to her, painting it in the most glowing terms. I explained more about the cultivation of flowers than she already knew from a friend of Ariel's who had spent the summer there helping with the harvest. 'Beautiful,' I found myself saying often, 'beautiful.' I ended with a flourish, 'Of course, you know we'll be grandparents soon!'

This was a mistake. She hadn't known. 'Your daughter is having a baby?' The blue eyes narrowed in a way that would have seemed more effective if I hadn't seen it so often on the screen.

'You'll be a grandmother. Like Zsa Zsa Gabor.' I was bored with stepping lightly. To my horror, I saw huge teardrops forming at the side of her eyes. 'Aren't you pleased?' I said, deciding I had seen that move also. And then with a little more honesty, 'Actually, I wasn't very pleased when I heard.'

The tears swam round the saucer eyes without falling, making the blue pupils look young and glistening. 'I love Ariel,' she whispered piteously. 'If he had been here, I wouldn't have tried—tried to take my life.'

'I thought that was over your husband running off with that young girl,' I said cruelly. Nevertheless, the peaches and champagne were

451

beginning to have an effect. I really believed she did love Ariel. A little longer and I would fall completely under her spell.

'I did everything for him. I sent him to the most expensive psychiatrist in Beverly Hills.'

'He certainly knows how to talk about himself.'

'He had an obsession about England. There was nothing I could do about it. He felt he was English. He was determined. He wanted to find his father. His roots.'

'He hasn't been very successful, then.'

Isabel gave me a sharp look which I remembered from my childhood and not from her films. 'What do you mean?'

'Eureka is an Irish island.'

'I see.' Isabel allowed herself a smile. 'Perhaps he will become an Irish citizen.' For some reason, this seemed to please her. I realised one of the remarkable things about her voice was that it had retained all the accent of Britain in the forties.

'I was brought up in Egypt, you know. My mother was a princess, but my father was British. A British hero. He was killed out there. I came to England when I was twelve. Unfortunately, your mother never understood me.' Her gaze swept round the plush darkness of The Polo Lounge. 'America became my mother. When I am old I shall retire to Switzerland.'

Knowing the family story of Roly Royston, the shell-shocked major and the dark-skinned bride he had been too ashamed to bring home, I began by smiling cynically at the fairy story of her life. But as she thanked America and looked forward to a rich but stateless future, I felt sorry for her. My upbringing was as firm as the roots of an oak compared with the insecurities of her past. I leaned forward to her and touched her arm. She looked at me surprised. I was surprised at myself. I had not expected to make an appeal to her, particularly not on this subject.

'Leave Ariel,' I said. 'Don't try and bring him back. He and Ethne are trying to grow up together. They're working at it. Even if it does sound ridiculous.'

Isabel hesitated and then gave a loud, ringing laugh. Several heads turned towards us. I was so close I could see right down to the red flags quivering in her throat. 'The roles have become reversed. They're living off my allowance to Ariel, you know. I'm keeping them there. Unless one of my husbands forgets to pay alimony, there's a good chance I'll keep on doing it.' She gave another ringing laugh. This time I avoided a view of her throat. 'I don't want Ariel here. What is there for him here? Darling Violet, I don't need a son in my life, and I certainly don't need a grandson.'

'Granddaughter,' I replied automatically. But the audience was over. With an instinctive sense of timing, her courtiers surged back round her. She kissed both my cheeks with firm pressure and that delicious hot scent again, and then she was gone.

As I watched her go out through the door into a waiting limousine, I thought, with irritation, that I had not even mentioned my own reason for being in Hollywood. Nor had she asked. Was my work, after all, not as important as my daughter? I went back to the Polo Lounge and ordered another cocktail. It didn't taste as good without Isabel.

I stayed in California for six weeks, the same length of time my mother was due to stay in India. Since she had set out a few days before I had, she would be back a few days before me. It was also the time that Ethne was due to have the baby.

I was very busy, attending an endless series of script conferences, which left me exhausted and far more muddled about what I was supposed to be doing than before. Nevertheless, in the last week of my stay I began to find those worries superseded by a general sense of anxiety about my mother and my daughter. I kept seeing my mother as I had seen her last, the frail prisoner of two gaolers. I pictured her pathetic flat-heeled sandals and ridiculous ankle socks. Ethne I saw, as I had seen her two years before, dressed in nothing but a thin shirt and jeans against the icy blasts of Eureka.

I worried at night when I was alone. Eventually I confided in my agent, who was the nearest I had to a friend in Los Angeles. 'It's the atmosphere here,' he said sympathetically. 'Everybody's anxious. I'm sure there's nothing wrong whatsoever with your mother or your daughter.'

I knew what he meant. While I had been in Hollywood there had been two unexplained and particularly unpleasant murders among the Beverly Hills community, one of a man I had met. They were probably committed by heroin addicts looking for drugs, but rumours made the deaths more sinister. There had also been a bad fire, which had completely gutted three houses in the Hollywood Hills— one of which actually belonged to my agent, though he had rented it out to someone else.

The atmosphere encouraged anxieties. Nevertheless, I decided to conquer the time difference and Mike's disapproval of expensive telephone calls and ring him to see if there was any news. It was a Saturday, my breakfast time, his teatime. Bright sunshine for me, grey darkness for him.

'Oh,' he said. 'Nothing wrong?'

'That's what I rang to find out.'

'Here, you mean? I'm well. Ethne hasn't started her baby—at least, if she has I haven't heard of it—and I've just forwarded you a huge packet from your mother. It arrived by diplomatic bag. I think it's some kind of diary, but I haven't had time to read it. There was a note with it saying it was instead of a letter and would you hang on to it.'

'She must be well, then.'

'Oh, yes.' Mike sounded surprised at my relieved tone. 'Having a high old time. How about you? You sound as if you're letting the Company Town get to you.'

'I don't have you to talk to. Are you eating properly?'

'You didn't ring two thousand miles to ask me that. I love you, Violet.'

'Oh, darling. Let me know if anything happens.'

'Go and have a swim. Goodbye, darling.'

The package arrived the following Wednesday, the day before I was due to fly back. I opened it, thinking that by now my mother would be safely back in England. I read it in my hotel room in the Sunset Marquis. Outside, the skies were black, and rain as heavy as a monsoon poured down into the swimming pool below me. It had been raining like this for two days, and although everyone else complained that it was the wettest period for twenty years, for some reason it had caused my own spirits to rise.

The diary was written in my mother's bold rather childlike writing. It was very easy to read:

I'm so excited to be flying to India on my seventieth birthday. Not that I feel old myself, but I'm aware that many people feel they're nearing the end of the road at my age. Last night I had dinner with Winnie, who says she is looking forward to retirement, so that she can 'prepare for death.' She wants to 'contemplate', as if in that way she will face it better. She talked about it as if she was mugging for an exam. Perhaps that is right for her. She's a good person, so she may be more able to bear contemplating her life than I could. Personally, what good I've done is in my actions, not myself. My only preparation for death can be to carry on. So that's why I'm glad to be flying to India on my seventieth birthday.

I looked up. Why did this statement of intent to carry on make me fearful? Was it because my mother never usually talked about herself or the reasons for her behaviour? Why should she do it now? The note with the diary had said simply that she had found an obliging diplomat in Benares who was on his way to Delhi, who said he would send it to England. She thought it would be more interesting than a letter.

I read on. After the telephone rang a couple of times, I turned it off. It was a very full diary. The opening passage was not typical. Mostly it was a detailed description of places and events:

> The plane stopped at Kuwait, where a trail of young Indian engineers dressed in government-issue blue denims topped either by a safety helmet or a Sikh turban were returning for a holiday. I compared their passive excitement and pride with a British football team and found my own countrymen wanting. My British companion, Irene Golding, found their lack of proper footwear and their extreme humility pathetic and upsetting.
> We arrived at Delhi airport in a beautiful cool dawn. A deputation from the British High Commission, including the doctor brother of Irene Golding, had come to meet us. The engineers, who looked in their early twenties or younger, were met by their families, which often included as many as six children. I longed to talk to them, but instead I was marched off for a large English breakfast of cornflakes and boiled eggs, over which I was issued the usual warnings about drinking no unbottled water and eating no uncooked food.

I saw that my mother was irritated by what she considered British fussiness at a time when she wanted to grasp at India. I was certain that she had not mentioned her own dietary problems. I wished I had told Irene Golding she was a diabetic.

Afterwards they tried to make me sleep. But I forced them to take me to watch the sun rise over the Lodhi Tombs. Mrs Gandhi's 'new broom' has surrounded it by a spectacular park. My breath was taken away by the brilliant green parakeets, the great red monuments, the flowers like coloured stars fallen in the grass. The air was crystal as a Swiss mountaintop. I came prepared for dung and dust and found myself in Paradise!

The twelve-strong commission was still gathering from around the world, and for two days she did the sights in and around Delhi.

At Humayum's Tomb, I had my first view of a 'sacred' cow, pulling a lawn mower. At the Mutiny Memorial on the Delhi Ridge, I shared the shame of those Englishmen who inscribed on it 'City finally evacuated by the enemy.' At the National Museum, I admired the goddess' sinuous movements and globular bosom. Why does our goddess, the Virgin Mary, have such a lifeless image? I was taken to the Red Fort, which I hated, and to a *Son et Lumière* at the old Flagstaff House called 'Tryst with Destiny.' I do like hearing Anglo-Indian history from the other side. Nature here is splendid. I don't know which I love more—the Peepul Tree, where Buddha saw the light, or the Tamarind Tree with its sour orange-flavoured fruit. Yesterday I gave an interview to *The New Statesman*.

She had stuck the clipping into the diary, so I read it eagerly. There was no mention of the reason for her visit, only a celebration of all things Indian. I thought she sounded a little mad and wondered what the Indians thought. Perhaps they are used to eccentric English-women who wish only to see the best of their country.

Looking for the signs of ill health, I found a scribble at the end of one page: 'Managed three hours' sleep last night. Three times as much as usual. I read Indian history for hours. Who cares about sleep now? There'll be plenty of time later.'

On the fourth day she had her first meeting with the seven other members of her commission. Her exhilaration covered them with glory. 'I've never felt so pleased to be working with any group of people. Even the priest comes to our task with an open mind. The Indian representative is one of the most distinguished and civilised men I have ever met.'

After the meeting at which the itinerary was clarified, the Indian representative, K. C. Anand, from an important family of lawyers in Bombay, took them for a glimpse of the Delhi Polo Ground, followed by tea at the Gymkhana Club. Even this deference to bourgeois England charmed my mother by its humility.

Can you imagine, when they have such a culture of their own, choosing to keep Lady Willingdon's lawn and Lady Willingdon's bathing pool as status symbols? How subtly that puts the whole nonsense in its place. Yet how fierce they can be. Yesterday we saw the cemetery of the statues of the British Raj. They have been placed in a scrubby plot on the outskirts of Delhi near where Curzon's famous Coronation Durbar was held. Now only vultures linger round the broken trees, and poor George V and our grand viceroys stare dismally from their red plinths. They're for sale, I'm told. But who would want a chip off the old block when the whole of India awaits one?

At the end of her first week she travelled with her commission to Calcutta. My mother, who had never liked being one of the herd, had arranged via Irene Golding's doctor at the BHC to stay on her own in the Bengal Club. Again she assumed the English habits there to be a subtle parody of the original. On the lookout for mention of her diet,

I noted with some relief the typical menu she described of soup, fish, potatoes, peas, and gooseberry fool, washed down with Kingfisher beer out of silver goblets! She was clearly not going native in her diet, at least.

Oddly enough, she did not at this point describe in any great detail the rather different sights that she was now being taken to see. Perhaps she felt that poverty, overcrowding, and hunger were easy enough to imagine and the same throughout the world. They were visiting new community projects, talking to doctors involved in the sterilisation programme, and seeing all around them the spilling masses of a too great community. It was only after she and the priest, a Frenchman, had visited Mother Theresa that she began to set down her impressions. They had already been in Calcutta over a week.

I have never met such an impressive woman. Actually, she is sexless—a saint, to be sure. I saw even after talking to her for five minutes that she has managed to reconcile what has always seemed to me irreconcilable, the organisation of charity on a wide scale with the tiny personal acts of charity. This is because, as she says, 'It is God's work'—meaning, I believe, both that she does each act for God and that God, himself, is doing the act through her. It is selflessness. Yet, on the contrary, she has a very strong character. How odd! She reminded me of Father Wilson magnified a hundredfold.

I wanted to ask her so many things but knew I must not waste her time. She knew all about why I was in India, of course, and told me about a new organisation she has for sending Indian orphans to childless families abroad. She says there has never been such a demand for babies—owing to birth control, I suppose. I thought of darling Ethne and wondered if her baby had been born yet. I even told Mother Theresa that I was expecting my first great-grandchild, and she glowed in what I saw as a kind of blessing. To her every life is as precious as Christ's.

But she is not pleased with England. Apparently we are one of the few countries whose adoption societies aren't working with her. I felt quite ashamed, and said I would try and help. I thought Molly might know how to set about it. Then we said a prayer, surrounded by very young and pretty novices all smiling as gaily as if they were at a party. Actually, they had broken off from scrubbing floors. As we left I looked for a collection box, but Mother Theresa, seeing what I wanted, cupped her own scrubbed hands. I thrust in double what I had planned.

Coming out from that cool 'Mother House' filled with soft-spoken women, bare feet treading carefully on well-washed tiled floors, into the heat, glare, noise, dirt, squalor of a Calcutta street was (to use an Ethne phrase—I've been thinking of her a lot lately) 'mind-blowing'.

Seeing my expression, Pierre took my arm. 'Unfortunately, she's only one woman.'

I saw, despite the 'unfortunately', that he was not as impressed as I. 'But is that the point?' I asked. 'If her principles are right.'

'Wait till this evening. After we've been round some of the poor districts.'

'I've seen many districts. The facts are not what I need.'

'But that's what we're here for. To see the facts for ourselves. Later we decide what we think about it. Later we write a report.'

'You can never see all the facts, so what's the point?' I exclaimed, but more or less to myself because he was hailing a taxi, and he was, of course, quite right about the reason for our visit. I'm not here on a personal mission, whatever I may feel. On the other hand, how can one separate a personal view from a general view? And if one can, is it right that one can?

This afternoon as I looked at the poor little babies with balloon stomachs which Sunday newspapers have made as familiar a sight as an ashtray or a flowerpot, I still remembered Mother Theresa's loving eyes with a happy glow. I am sure that is the right road. And yet, is Mother Theresa, who works every day to make those stomachs healthy again, the only one who may say that? Can I, a selfish old lady who has lived all her life in comfort, allow countless millions to continue living in degradation? Or is it degradation? Is it even misery? Certainly it is poverty. As Pierre said, Mother Theresa is only one woman. Even a Christian can't believe she'll save the world.

Perhaps, too, as I get older I feel less horrified at the prospect of death. We all argue from the personal. I will die soon, so why shouldn't all these poor creatures? It's only sooner rather than later. And yet the babies . . . There was one little girl with a horrid sore on her mouth but the most enchanting lively eyes. I wish I did know about Ethne. I hope Violet has persuaded her to go into hospital.

The diary broke off here for several days, and the next entry was written in a much less bold, almost shaky hand.

So stupid. I managed to lock myself into my bathroom, and in my wild efforts to get out—it began to get uncomfortably hot and claustrophobic—I made a gash in my left hand. Nothing serious,

458

really. A nurse at the hospital was wonderfully efficient with anti-tetanus injection and special dressing. But it is infuriating to be less than my best just now. Really, it was quite absurd. A team of carpenters finally took the door off the hinges and found me sitting on the lavatory seat wrapped in a somewhat skimpy towel. I just hope the cut hurries up and heals. The climate here is so hot and sticky (despite being the most favoured time of year) that I fear it will take longer than in England.

Yesterday we saw the Governor of West Bengal and his beautiful wife. They were most helpful. They look on Mrs Gandhi's Emergency, which from England seems such an infringement of liberty, as an opportunity to create new freedoms to live in safety and do the work one is supposed to. Thank God I was not a politician in India. How petty it makes our problems seem! I even sometimes wonder why I made such efforts to become a Labour politician. Surely with my background I could have achieved more as a Conservative? Who knows, who cares . . .

So many dead I've left behind me. My father, Nettles, Leonard, Augustus, Araminta. Yet I hardly knew them—even my own husband. This morning I talked to the editor of *The New Statesman*. He says that journalistic support from England is what makes it possible for him to keep going, flying the flag of liberty in the face of Mrs Gandhi. Like Mother Theresa, he wanted my help in England. I felt like saying, 'I'm not interested in public liberty anymore. I'm not interested in public affairs at all. I'm a selfish old woman. I only care for what affects me personally. At this rather late stage I am trying to discover a personal morality.' But instead I agreed to do all I could.

Three more days followed in which she remained in Calcutta. On one she visited the poor tended by Mother Theresa; on another she saw a prison cell where forty children had ended up for lack of anywhere else to put them; and on her last day she was taken, as light relief, to see the largest banyan tree in the world. For some reason, she and her companions decided to walk through the park at whose centre the great tree grew. It was two o'clock on a hot afternoon. They had not stopped for lunch. When they arrived between its endless shady trunks, she fainted.

She became conscious to hear their Indian guide relating the story of how a student had hanged himself from the branch above their heads. Whether she was in an insulin coma I don't know, as she didn't even mention the word *diabetes* nor indeed explain how she recovered. But I immediately suspected that's what had happened. A minor coma perhaps curable by the glucose tablets she did at least

459

carry in her bag.

Since the diary continued for so many more pages, I even thought hopefully that this attack might have served the purpose of a much-needed warning.

At any rate, the next day she was off to a small town in Uttar Pradesh, where she had her first experience of overpopulation in the countryside, and from there to another town and another, till three days later they arrived in Benares. They had travelled by government jeep, until the last long hop south. She noted, 'It was a relief to leave the jeep, not just because of the physical discomfort (my beastly hand simply won't heal, and I'm afraid my tummy's a bit rocky), but because our arrival in many villages was a signal for an all-male exodus in case we were part of Mrs G's sterilisation programme.'

Their itinerary seemed to include a look at India's great sights as well as her least attractive, for Benares is Varanasi—the holy place on the River Ganges where pilgrims come from all over the world to say their prayers and, best of all, to say their last prayers. My mother wrote:

I saw a burning foot, this morning. It was on a funeral pile by the banks of the river. When it's burnt it will be tipped into the river. We got up at dawn and watched the holy bathers make their three dips by the light of the vast red globe rising out of a purplish mist. The rich have built themselves huge palaces on the banks of the river, but they are empty now. Only the crows and vultures fly in and out of the tower windows. Down in the river the unsophisticated, the poor, the sick, submerge themselves over and over again. On the 'ghats' holy men sit cross-legged under pale umbrellas. Behind them the streets wind up into the old city filled with temples and bazaars selling cheap necklaces and ornaments. I suspect Benares. I won't be sorry when we go on south.

My mother's entries were getting shorter. I was surprised that she should 'suspect' the validity of Benares, the holy centre of India. Probably her exhaustion made the inevitable commercialism of such a place irritating.

Still, I was glad, and would have said so, half jokingly and half seriously, if I had had anyone to talk to, that she was not thinking of dying in Benares.

There were about ten more pages of the diary. I skipped to the end and saw that if finished just before her departure for Kerala. I looked out of the window. The rain had stopped, and the sky was even showing some blue. It would be dark in another hour. I decided to rush out for some air and then come back to finish the diary.

Outside, the sun, despite its rainy sheen, was surprisingly warm. On impulse, I ran back for my bathing suit. Perhaps it was the thought of my mother fainting in the dust and heat of India, but a solitary swim in cool waters seemed irresistible. No one came near as I swam slowly up and down, my skin half numb in the rain-diluted water. I felt extraordinarily alone. Happily alone.

I hoped this was true also of my mother. It was the aspect of her journey that had most worried me before she set off, and now the diary confirmed my fears. I could sense from it, even from the very fact of her recording intimate thoughts, that she was on that knife-edge of loneliness when one becomes almost unbalanced. It can be exaggerated exhilaration, as at first it seemed to be in her case, or it can be depression. I feared now that the failings of her body to keep up with her mind would cast her from exhilaration to depression. The other alternative, that her mind refused to give in to her body, was too terrifying even to consider. That would be real madness. If only there had been someone there who knew her and could understand what was happening.

I jumped out of the water and, conscious of my own well-functioning body against a background of reddening sun and palm trees, returned hurriedly to my room. As if picking up my thoughts, the diary continued:

I have always enjoyed being on my own. On my own in company. Pierre talks with me about the place of charity, and although he lacks Father Wilson's warm heart, he is always sympathetic. Dear K.C. is endlessly considerate, so that the sun always shines in his eyes, never mine. The American representative, a Miss Murphy, makes me feel young with her assumption that I can scout any temple as quickly as she can. Perhaps she resents my age. Who knows? I don't believe they're very fond of disintegration in America. The funny thing is, only yesterday I discovered she's a nun. It gave me quite a start. She wasn't even interested to come with us to see Mother Theresa. Then there are an untypically quiet Italian committeeman from a good family, a voluble South American who leads off daily tirades against the Pope's Encyclical on birth control, and a self-possessed German businessman. He is the one who will actually write the report—I can see that already. He is so practical, listens to our warring consciences and talks about money. He was high on my list of favourites—I have always liked decided men—until yesterday, when he tried to persuade me not to go down south. As if I'd let a little tiredness cut this trip short!

From then on I looked for references to this sensible unnamed

German. But there were none. The pages were full of meetings with officials, visits to clinics, expostulations on the old men with their bicycle rickshaws. She was obviously keeping up with all the occupations of her commission, and there was no more mention of her health. At least, I reflected, Benares was a large town there would be an excellent Indian hospital nearby. I reached the last page.

We fly out tomorrow. A First Secretary who's been studying Hindi at the University here is taking this bulky collection of notes back to Delhi. He'll send it by bag to London. Already this journey is two-thirds over. I literally feel a different person from when I set out—not just physically! (I have to keep my hand in a sling now, although I pretend it doesn't hurt. Yesterday a beggar stuck the still unhealed stump of his arm through the window of our jeep, so what have I to complain of?) I'm particularly interested to go South because that, of course, is where the main settlement of Catholics is. I shall send this to Violet instead of a letter. I couldn't write a letter now. But read it, darling, and pass it on to Ethne. I think she might be interested. Really, she should be here instead of me! I have a feeling we're going to be so busy for our last fortnight that I may not be able to keep such a full diary again. At any rate, expect nothing till I return.

So the diary ended. The last two inches of paper were filled in with a picture of the Taj Mahal, with the comment: 'Have you ever noticed how the Taj resembles two bosoms and a pregnant stomach? A symbol for Mother India indeed! If Mother Gandhi was serious about her darling son's programme, she should make a Guy Fawkes of it all . . .'

I closed the book. It was an inconclusive document. The last date was nearly two weeks ago. Anything could have happened since she had made that lighthearted sketch. Obviously they were staying longer than originally planned. On the other hand, it would be absurd to be too worried, since bad news would travel quick enough even from a small village in southern India to a hotel in Hollywood.

Besides, I must not forget that my mother's tone was happy enough to be called rejoicing. She had never felt so alive. Tomorrow I would return to England. As my agent said, my anxieties were probably a product of my environment.

Nevertheless, when the following morning, just as I had finished packing, a telegram was brought up to my room, I sat down in a chair with shaking knees.

ETHNE DELIVERED SAFELY OF BABY BOY PROSPERO 9 LBS 3 OZ ON
EUREKA LOVE MIKE

I read it several times, flushing with happiness and relief. Although
my mother's diary had diverted my thoughts from Ethne, I had still
been aware of a basic anxiety.

I knew she would have it on Eureka! I told myself now in idiotic
joy and satisfaction. And an absolutely gigantic boy, too! That was a
surprise. I had been sure that she would carry on the train of women
that had started with Eleanor, continued with my mother, me (Tudor
was always Nettles' son), and Ethne. A boy—a huge boy called Prospero. It was unbelievable! Fantastic! Now I saw that it was time for a
boy to be firstborn. My excitement rose higher and higher. Oh, for
someone who would be interested in my boasting! Of course, Isabel.
The other grandmother. She would want to know.

I lifted up the phone and then stopped. Could I trust her not to
dampen my happiness? I looked at my watch. Besides, I should leave
for the airport. I decided to let the hotel send a telegram to Isabel.

At the airport, I wafted through Customs, wafted onto the plane.
The ten hours of confinement, which I usually passed with the help of
two hours' hard work followed by a sleeping pill, passed in a happy
daze. I even broke my usual transatlantic rules of no alcohol and
masses of water by drinking champagne to Prospero's health. Becoming expansive, I told a couple of air hostesses what I was celebrating and insisted they also drink champagne. My worries about
my mother evaporated. If I thought about her at all, it was with the
happy notion that if one anxiety had proved totally unfounded, so would
the other. My celebration was made greater by my preceding gloom.

The plane arrived at Heathrow around seven in the morning.
Although the champagne had done its work and I felt dehydrated as
well as tired and dirty, my spirits were still high. I did not expect Mike
to meet me and was surprised when I saw him waiting beyond Customs.

I was surprised also by his serious face. Had he not come to share
my happiness over the baby? He kissed me quickly and led me to a
darkish corner by the bar.

'The last thing I want is a drink . . .' I began. But he handed me a
copy of *The Times* he was carrying under his arm and pointed to a
paragraph on the front page.

LADY NETTLEFIELD DIES IN INDIA

'I didn't want you to see it on your own,' said Mike. 'I tried to
phone you in America, but you'd already left. I don't know much
more than that report. Nor does the British Consul, as far as I can
make out. It all happened in some godforsaken hole in the South. It

seems to have been very sudden. At least, the British Consul had received no messages about her illness before they were told of her death.'

I was not listening to Mike. The explanations could come later. 'I knew it,' I said. 'I knew it. I knew while I was reading her diary that she wouldn't come back. I knew it.'

'She was determined to go,' said Mike. 'No one could have stopped her.'

'No,' I tried to explain to Mike. 'She was obviously unwell, but happy. More than happy.' I gave up. He would have to read the diary for himself. Besides, I wanted to cry. 'Let's go home.'

It was several days before the details of my mother's death were known. I was told them by Irene Golding, who had just returned from Delhi. She also brought a case with my mother's belongings and a last note. She sat in the flat I'd had for twenty years with a look of bewilderment on her nice, kind face.

'I don't understand it,' she kept saying. 'Your mother was such a practical, sensible woman. Not at all the sort of woman who usually neglects her health, certainly not to the point she did. She never even told anyone she was diabetic! Not even my brother . . .'

I saw that if it had been any other woman than my mother, Irene would have condemned her behaviour as, at best, foolish and selfish and at worst, immoral.

'Tell me exactly what happened,' I said. Irene folded her hands in her wide lap and frowned.

'It was a combination of illnesses that actually killed her,' she said at last. 'Nothing bad enough to kill on their own, but in combination fatal.' She hesitated. 'That, plus her own attitude. You see, she was given a last chance for help, which she refused to take.'

'My mother wasn't suicidal!' I cried out suddenly, fearfully. .

'No. No,' said Irene, looking even more bewildered. 'When you read the note you'll see she didn't want to die. She had a quite positive reason for not taking the chance to help herself. At least, it obviously meant a lot to her. I can't understand it . . . But I expect my mind is simpler than hers.' She hesitated again. 'I'm sorry. I'm afraid my mind isn't very clear. I didn't sleep at all on the flight back. And I've been very worried about all this. It upset my brother so much, too. As a doctor. As the doctor to the British citizens in India. He can't understand either . . .'

'Why don't we have a cup of tea?' I said, feeling as muddled as she. Yet already I had grasped that my mother had not just faded away. Something had happened. I longed to look at her last note. Yet I wanted to know the preceding events and her state of mind before I read it.

After two cups of tea, Irene Golding settled down and told me as much as she knew. Apparently it had been obvious to all the other members of the commission during the trip down south that my mother was not well. However, such was her insistence that she was merely tired (like them all), had an upset tummy (like most of them), and a little scratch on her hand, that they took no steps to stop her continuing. Besides, their itinerary was subject to so many delays that they were already worried about missing several important areas and did not want to make a diversion to put her on an aeroplane unless it was unavoidable.

Thus they reached the southernmost tip of their travels, Trivandrum, with my mother still actively with them. The only real sign of her condition, as Irene told me rather reluctantly, was her need to pass water extremely frequently, which caused some delay to their progress. 'Someone should have known!' cried Irene indignantly.

No one did. However, when they arrived at the hotel where they were due to spend the last three days of their trip before flying back to Delhi, it was obvious my mother was feverish. The German, Herr Bonnheim, now tried to insist on taking her to a nurse, but she refused. He then made a second suggestion that she skip the last few days in Trivandrum, which were mostly filled with unnecessary meetings with officials, and fly straight back to Delhi.

This she agreed to consider. It now became a problem of finding a seat in the extremely full planes to the North. There was only one flight left that day. They all agreed it was essential she catch it. She had begun to talk slowly now, and she could no longer disguise the pain in her hand. Nevertheless, while they waited at the airport, she had enough energy to put up a strong defence of the woman as worker to the male chauvinist Father Dubois.

K. C. Anand set about finding a place for her on the plane. The plane was not just full, but overbooked. A large party of tourists from behind the Iron Curtain, shepherded by their fat and ugly party members, had already displaced all the less important ticket holders. The airport was filled with disappointed travellers, chewing betel nuts as they settled in to wait till morning. In fact, there was only one Indian still flying. Since India's friends from East Europe were clearly too valuable to upset, Mr Anand set about displacing his own countrywoman.

She was a young woman in a dark-blue sari, sitting alone and patiently in a corner. She had large, sad, dark eyes, which she kept fixed on the floor. Mr Anand approached the desk official. Soon he was in a fierce argument. It was very hot in the airport, and the punkahs whirring from the ceiling blew a hot wind, which lifted the two men's hair.

After half an hour, in which other officials were called in and glasses of warm beer exchanged (if not something else), K.C. returned triumphant. 'It's fixed, my dear lady. You will have a place. But please wait till the end.'

'Whose place?' said my mother, looking up.

'That's unimportant,' said Mr Anand, looking anxiously at the young girl.

'I know it's hers,' said my mother. 'I shan't take it unless she says I can.'

'No seat is anyone's in particular,' said K.C., really not understanding her point of view. Surely an elderly ill woman deserved a place before this young creature. Even considering the circumstances. Considering the circumstances, however, and my mother's determined if haggard face, he thought it best to keep them apart.

'We will have refreshing drinks now.'

'I am going to talk to the young lady,' said my mother. 'I'm bored with being a selfish old woman. She has as much right as I do. More, quite possibly. I shall ask her.'

My mother went over and introduced herself to the sari-clad girl. She spread her ringed hands and lifted her eyes tragically. My mother listened. When she had finished, my mother patted the girl's hands with her own good hand and returned to Mr Anand and Father Dubois.

'I will not go,' she said. 'That young woman is going to join her husband. He is in hospital after an engineering accident. Perhaps he is dying. Perhaps he will die tonight. Naturally, you will see that she must go before me.' She looked up and smiled. 'If you want to turf off one of those overfed party machines, that would be another matter.'

She was immovable. So were the tourists from behind the Iron Curtain. The officials, approached yet again, looked at my mother's flushed, determined face and decided she was not so ill after all. They left the airport again. As my mother passed the bench where the young girl still sat, she stood up and salaamed very low, holding her hands in the universal gesture of prayer. My mother smiled. 'A smile like that of a saint,' as Father Dubois, deeply emotional about the whole event, had described it to Irene Golding.

Back at the hotel, my mother retired to her room, saying she would not come down for dinner but would take a good rest before her flight the next morning. Nevertheless, a little later Herr Bonnheim sent some sandwiches up to her, which she took in and apparently ate, since they were not found. And later still, Miss Murphy, the American nun, looked in on her and she was already in bed, apparently asleep. At least, her breathing was heavy as a sleeping person's.

Before closing the door, Miss Murphy noticed a piece of white paper on her dressing table, but thought nothing of it. She also noticed that my mother had a rosary on her bedside table, which surprised her because she had not thought my mother would set much store by the Virgin Mary. This was the last thought anyone was to have about my mother as a living person, because the next morning she was dead.

As Irene with tears in her eyes came to this point, I took up the envelope she had given me and opened it. The note was written in letters so pathetically pale and wavering that I felt the tears start to roll out of my own eyes.

Darling Violet, I fear I'm not too well. In fact, although I've always felt death, like illness, was in our own hands, I have a strong feeling that I may be approaching it. Certainly I don't want it. I want to come back to you all and see Ethne's baby and be in the world a lot longer. I've always been a very worldly person, despite my efforts. On the other hand, I had a tremendous stroke of luck this afternoon. I was given the opportunity to do an unselfish act. It may not seem like that to others, but I expect you, having read my diaries, will understand. At that moment, in that hot, unbearably hot, airport, that girl's chance of seeing her husband before he died was the only thing that mattered. [She had underlined the last five words with an almost bold stroke.] So you see I had to let her go. At whatever the cost. It has given me such happiness. She was such a humble girl. Yet so dignified in her acceptance. I could never make Catholicism be for me what it is for Molly. Without Father Wilson's insistence on love I would never have entered the Church. Yet this one little act of charity has done it all for me. Oh, darling. Even Molly didn't want to die when she was ill in Spain. I don't want to die alone in this horrid little room, which smells, I suppose healthily, of disinfectant. But I have chosen to live most of my life alone, so I suppose it's only fitting. Besides, India has given me so much. If I'm not here in the morning, don't try to bring my poor old remains back to England. I wouldn't like the thought of all that bother, and I've never liked air conditioning. Tell someone to throw me in the Ganges if you like. It'll give the Japanese something to focus their zoom lenses on. Or if not, there's a very nice pseudo-Catholic cemetery we saw yesterday. It has a beautiful tamarind tree. It used to shock people how seldom I visited Nettles' grave. Love isn't to do with bodies. I think of you all with love—you, Ethne, her baby, Tudor, Molly, George, Mike, Nanny—even my mother! Goodbye, darling. Pray for me.

Irene Golding and I sat together sobbing. After a while, I got up

467

and found *The Times* obituary of my mother and passed it to Irene. I felt she should know something about the woman she was mourning. I was glad she was moved. It helped me. Soon Mike would be back, and I didn't want to be crying then, because I wanted him to understand that the apparently tragic circumstances of my mother's death had brought her happiness.

Irene's tears dried as she read the obituary. She was more intelligent than I had given her credit for. When she had finished she said thoughtfully, 'She was a very impressive woman. And yet how odd— she did nothing serious for the first half of her life.'

I stopped crying also. Even the memory of my mother was too abrasive for tears. 'In the modern jargon, she was "hung up on being a woman" for the first thirty-five years. Her big problem was reconciling her emotional life and her intellectual. Her intellectual side had taken over. That saddened her. She wanted to find her emotions again. But not the selfish emotions of a young girl. Something better. That's what she wanted to find in India.'

'And she did.'

I looked up at Irene. Focussing more on her, I saw that she was one of those ageless women of forty who have never been loved and therefore never found a positive appearance. 'You aren't married?'

'No. I wanted to be a doctor. Like my brother. But I couldn't pass the exams, so I became a nurse instead. I lived with my mother until she died last year. There was never time for men. I think I do begin to understand your mother a little.'

She stood up, gathering her old woman's bag and gloves from the table. 'I must go. But if you ever want to talk more—about events in India, I mean—please give me a ring.' She handed me a card. I glanced at it. She was matron of a very well-known private nursing home. So this unprepossessing creature had a world in which she was successful too.

'Thank you for coming. Thank you.'

After Irene Golding's departure, I sat down to wait for Mike and, while I waited, tried to compose a telegram to Ethne— 'Congratulations on Prospero. Granny dead.' The facts seemed too harsh. I thought how few of my mother's friends were left to tell about her death. Only Molly. She had mentioned Molly's will to live in her letter. And yet Molly said death was unimportant. I thought how odd it was that a total stranger should be the one to share with me my mother's way of death. I wondered whom Irene Golding reminded me of and realised it was Molly. Perhaps she was not such a stranger after all.

I began to wander round the flat, touching familiar objects, trying to put my mind out of gear till Mike returned. I thought fleetingly how lucky I was to have him.

I found I had been standing for some time with my elbow resting on a bookcase and my hand dangling in front of the books. My fingers were brushing the spine of a volume of Donne's poems. Remembering with a sudden flash of excitement how they had lightened the load of my seventeen-year-old *angst*, I took the book out eagerly. It seemed extraordinary that I had managed to live without them for twenty years.

I read crouched on the floor. At the back of my mind I heard Mike come into the flat. When I felt he was standing above me, I looked up smiling and read the lines which I had just reached:

> Seale then this bill of my Divorce to All,
> On whom those fainter beames of love did fall;
> Marry those loves, which in youth scattered bee
> On Fame, Wit, Hopes (false mistresses) to thee.
> Churches are best for Prayer, that have least light:
> To see God only, I goe out of sight:
> And to scape stormy days, I chuse
> An Everlasting night.

'I shall send that to Eureka,' I said. 'Mother would approve.'